To my children, James, Justin, Joshua and Jessica. I would s
lonely little girl wit

Thank you to Ashley Zuckerman, the man whose talent inspired within me something I thought was lost. I hope you continue to do great work and inspire others.

This book is a work of fiction. Names, characters, places, and incidents are products of the author's imagination. Any resemblance to actual events, or persons living or dead is coincidental.

Charlie
A love story

But not that kind of love story. This is a story about a guy, and a girl destined to be together but kept apart by their respective families. No, I am not talking about Romeo and Juliet. I hate Shakespeare. Okay, maybe hate is a strong word. But love is also a strong word. We have all heard the cliches. Love makes the world go round; all you need is love, love is blind, love will set you free, etc. We think of it as this beautiful thing that we all seek to achieve in life. Call it what you want, fate, true love, Kismet, romance; we all want it. Did you know that love can also be a weapon that cuts deeper than any knife? And when we think of love, we tend to think of it in terms of being between two people, as is the case of our two protagonists in this story. But not everyone has a clear definition of what love is. He did, but then again, he came from a wonderful loving family, whereas she, well, let's just say, did not. Still, their love was like nothing most people ever encounter. Their love was indeed the kind of love that was meant to be. I know it sounds almost hopefully romantic enough to make one want to barf. But I insist that this is not that kind of love story. So just what kind is it? Good question. I guess you will just have to keep reading to find out.

Chapter 1
And the Shit Begins

Alia Miller walked down the dark corridor with an uneasy sense of dread. With each step, she felt trapped in some kind of bad horror movie. The lights overhead were out, and the ones behind her flickered just dimly enough not to provide any real light. Ahead of her was only a soft glow reflecting off the wall. There was movement around her, but they were so quick and the lighting so dim they were nothing more than ghostly images, mere figments of her imagination. To add to the spooky atmosphere was the intense quiet of a place usually permeated by noise. She didn't like to be here during the daytime, let alone under these conditions.

Alia thought to herself, *the things I do for a few lousy bucks. And these conditions were not part of the job description. I sure as hell hope they catch the little shits responsible for this.*

As she walked, Alia ripped down the signs and banners that hung on the walls and picked up the ones that littered the floor. Not for the first time, she felt sorry for those whose actual job it was to clean up the messes like this day in and day out. This was why she always made a point of cleaning up her messes. Well, she tried to anyway. The life of a busy high school teen can sometimes put a kink in even the best of intentions. She had participated in enough of these events over her four years and done her fair share of damage. Now those days were behind her. Like it or not, she was officially an adult as of her birthday in February. And if her mother's life was any indication, it was all downhill from here.

No, I have a plan that will set me up for life unless I fail.

The keyword here, though, was fail. If that happened, then her mother's life may seem like a dream in comparison. For starters, if her mother, Trish, ever found out what Alia was planning to do, she may just kill her.

Well, at least then all my troubles would be over, right? she thought, knowing darn well death was not a solution. *My luck hell is real, and we both would end up there, where she would spend the rest of eternity tormenting me more than she ever did here.*

Besides, she had friends that would miss her. Okay, maybe not many friends but a few, and there was always Crystal. Crystal was the best of best friends ever, definitely a way better friend than Alia felt she deserved. Crystal's brother, George, would probably miss her as well since he often referred to her as his other kid sister. Then there was her
 other good friend Ethan. A few weeks earlier, Ethan had offered to take her to the prom when he found out she was three-wheeling it with Crystal and her date for the night. And see, this is where the not deserving to be the best friend thing comes into play. Alia had no clue who this boy was other than a student from their school. She felt totally blindsided when Crystal said she had been asked to the prom, having assumed they would go stag together long enough to say they did the senior prom thing. Then they'd go hang out in Ethan's basement till morning as they usually did for most of these stupid school functions. If Crystal had ever mentioned the boy or even that she was interested in someone, it must have gone on a one-way trip through one ear and out the other.

God, is it possible that my mother is right about me when it comes to at least this one thing? Am I so self-centered and selfish that I didn't even notice my own best friend had a crush? Or am I just so wrapped up in surviving my own day-to-day drama that I didn't make time to listen to my best of all best friends? Either way, she felt as she often did, like the worst friend ever.

Note to self, before prom, ask Crystal who the hell this guy is and why hadn't I heard about him before now. And most importantly, is this a thing or just a one-time-date thing? Because if it was a thing, it was her duty and obligation to pass on a little fair warning. Hurt my friend, and I will feed you your balls.

Okay, so back to the creepy corridor. Alia continued pulling down posters and banners as she moved thankfully closer and closer to the only sane and steady light that seemed to be in the whole building. And even that light wasn't quite right, but instead, a soft glow that reminded Alia of the Coleman lanterns she and her small group of friends would use when they went camping. Considering something wonky had happened to the electricity in the building, that's probably what they were.

The light was shining off the wall directly across from the main office, where hopefully the principal was giving those responsible for this chaos what was coming to them. She could faintly hear voices from that direction but was nowhere near enough to listen to what was being said. There was no shouting, though, which was a bit of a disappointment.

As big of a pain as it was for her to clean inside the school in the dark, Alia would bet that it wasn't much fun to be out at the game field cleaning up after hundreds of people as well. Those lights were on the fritz, too, not too long after the game ended. Alia only had a slim idea of how bad it was out there because when she arrived, the game was over, and Mrs. Branch was fussing at her for arriving so late for the cleanup. To be fair, though, Alia had just come from her after-school job at the library in town about a mile away and had to walk all the way here. Thanks to her mother, even at the age of eighteen, she still didn't have a driver's license. Not even a lousy learner's permit. Not that her mother would get her a car. Her father, Jonathan, was supposed to, but that is another story better left for later and not something she was too keen on thinking about anyway.

After about another half hour of stuffing trash into the thin, cheap bags Mrs. Branch gave her, Alia was almost to the front office and practically done. It's not that the hall was so long (although the longest in the school), but the mess was just that, well, messy. The school's soccer (*or was it baseball?*) team played its championship game earlier in the day. Students had spent the past week decorating the halls in anticipation of the celebration. Unfortunately, Alia's more carefree days of keeping up with things like school sports had ended that year. Between working several jobs, trying to keep her grades up, chores at home, and her future plans, she hadn't had a lot of time for fun that year.

At last, bathed in the light of not one but several Coleman lanterns, that creepy "stuck in a bad horror movie" feeling started to leave her. Instead, she was almost ready to go back to the absolute horror movie that was her life. From here in the front hall, Alia could see the familiar blue pickup truck that belonged to her mother's latest boyfriend Billy out in the parking lot. She could even make out his legs dangling over the downed tailgate as he lay in the back.

He better not have fallen asleep, she fumed. That man was hell to wake up. Amazing, he's managed to hold down a job.

With the last piece of trash picked up, bag tied, and left for the custodians to pick up, Alia walked into the soft glowing office. Mrs. Branch had told her to let someone in the office know when she was done instead of trying to hunt her down in the dark building.

Suddenly she felt very anxious and wanted nothing more than to get out of there. Anxiety wasn't a stranger to her. It was pretty much a constant state of being for her at home. School was its own source of anxiety, but feeling this right now at this moment was confusing to her. She wasn't in any trouble and hadn't been in some time, so she had no reason to be so anxious. However, because of her past incidents in numerous offices like this one, she got nervous every time going into one.

No one was at the front desk at this late hour, but more lights and voices were coming from Principal Edwards's office. Now she could make out some of what he was saying, and it did sound like he had caught someone responsible.

"But you boys swear to me you can fix this?"

"Yes, sir, but as we said, it's going to take a while. The program we used was corrupted or something. It wasn't supposed to happen like this, I swear. It was just a prank on the seniors. It should have never lasted this long." Billy Toomy, Alia was sure of it. Billy was a sophomore and part of the school's audiovisual club. She should know since she was in the club as well.

"No sir, Billy is wrong; it was less of a prank and more of a celebration, you know, of the win." And there was no mistaking that was Derick Willis. Derick had one of those distinct voices that were easy to recognize right away. He was another sophomore and AV club member too.

I will have to think of something really creative to get back at them for this one.   Thanks for making a shit job even shittier, guys. Now on top of everything, she was running late, and her mother's boyfriend Billy was probably passed out sleeping in the bed of his truck.

She walked up to the office door and confirmed that, indeed, Billy and Derick were sitting in the 'hot seat' of Principal Edwards's office. Mr. Edwards was sitting on the front edge of his desk and looking down at the boys. But they were not alone. Mr. Spear, the head custodian, was also there to the right of the desk, his arms crossed and glaring. They had made his shit job even shittier as well. Mr. Knox, the school's soccer coach(*so, it was a soccer game),* was to the left of the desk with his hands on his hips. To her surprise, though, were the three uniformed officers also crowded in the room. She knew all three of them, two only in passing, having seen them around town at various functions and one she knew rather well.

Deputy Sheriff Charles Harper leaned in on the doorway just inside the office, his thin, tall frame giving her just enough room to pop her head and half her body in. The Sheriff himself was not present; she also noted. Which may be why there was no yelling. Like a switch had been flipped, Alia felt a sense of peace and calm wash over her and take the anxiety away with it. From the corner of her eye, she could make out the Deputy looking down at her with a smile.

As much as she wanted to say hello to her old friend, she had enough sense to see this for the serious moment it was and got right to the point since everyone had noticed her entry.

"Uh, excuse me, everyone. Mrs. Branch said to check in with you before I left Mr. Edwards ."

He looked blank for a moment like he couldn't remember why on earth she would be there at such a late hour. Then it dawned on him. "Oh yes, I almost forgot we had some students still here. Thank you, Alia. I will let Mrs. Branch know. It's pretty late, is someone picking you up?" She looked up at the clock above his desk. *Shit.* It was later than she thought, already nearly eleven.

"Yes, sir, my ride is waiting for me outside."

"Very good, you have a good night. See you back in school on Monday."

With a small wave, Alia turned and locked eyes for the briefest of moments with Deputy Harper and felt her heart skip a beat as she looked into the green of them. She had forgotten just how beautiful and soulful his eyes were. Smiling to herself, Alia walked back out into the dimly lit hallway. As she did, she heard the Deputy say something to the others, then he called for her as he followed her out. Alia turned as she walked to acknowledge him, and as usual, when she saw him, she instantly smiled and then slowed down so he could catch up to her.

The Deputy stood about six feet, thin built, green eyes, and a mop of thick dark brown hair that always had a few stubborn locks falling over his forehead. She would be lying if she said he wasn't handsome, but then he had always been, even when they were kids. The Deputy was one of those fortunate few that never seemed to have gone through an awkward phase. Whereas Alia had always felt like nothing other than awkward all the time. Now at twenty-two, he was handsome as ever, especially in his uniform, which seemed like a natural fit for him, much like his father, just for different reasons. It was as if he was born to be a cop, Something Alia knew Charlie had wanted to be since they were little. And always when he was around, Alia felt instantly at ease like they were long-time best friends despite actually barely knowing each other.

"Hey, what are you doing here tonight?" he asked, falling in step beside her. Charlie knew Alia still attended school here but was surprised to have her pop into the office like that, this late at night. He had been in good spirits despite the long day from the moment he entered the building, and now Charlie had a feeling he knew why.

Alia was always such a tiny wisp of a girl at barely over five feet, especially compared to how long and tall he was. She held on to some of her baby weight, making her look less emaciated like some girls of her stature. Despite the foot difference in height, he never felt like he towered over her. Instead, it was as though she stood taller in his presence to meet him on more equal ground. Even now, as they walked side-by-side, he looked down at her but also not down 'on' her. She was growing into a beautiful young woman, and he felt his heart swell at the sight of her.

Had Alia known the way he felt at that moment, she might not have been so at ease. But then again, Charlie always seemed to have a calming effect on her. Even the creepy corridor with the flickering light way down at the end didn't bother her now. He just had that way about him, and it wasn't just her because others noticed it as well. She had spent so many years ignoring that her heart beat faster, her smile was more prominent, and her stomach flip flopped when he was around that she didn't even notice it anymore. Well, not much anyway.

"Just earning a few extra bucks helping to clean up this mess. What about you, Charlie? You're not going to bust those boys in there for a little school prank, are you? Or should I be calling you Deputy Harper now? " She smiled, knowing they both knew it was more than just a little prank.

"You know you can always call me Charlie," he said, giving her a smile and a slight bump with his arm. "No, we were already here dealing with the traffic when the lights went out. Right now, we're mostly trying to scare them a little. Principal Edwards doesn't plan to press any charges. You know how he is."

He was right; she did. Edwards wouldn't take any crap, but he was also fair. His students didn't have to fear him because they respected him. Alia herself respected the hell out of him, though she had to admit he still scared her a little.

They continued walking out the front doors, stopping on the sidewalk. Deputy Charles Harper looked over at the blue pickup in the school's front parking lot, one of only about four left there. He recognized it as one he had pulled over for speeding more times than he could count.

"Your ride, I take It?" he nodded at the truck.

Alia rolled her eyes and shook her head in embarrassment.

"So your mom is still working the late shift?"

"What else is new?" Working the late shift was her mother's way of being conveniently unavailable for Alia most of the week. Though the other way around wasn't much better.

"Want me to go over and put a little scare in him?"

If only he actually could. Billy swore he wasn't afraid of any cop, least of all Deputy Harper. "Sheriff" Harper, however, Alia knew he was terrified of…most people were. Still, she let him walk over to the truck with her even though Billy may tell Alia's mother she was hanging out with the 'pigs' again. They were about halfway there, talking about the power 'failure' when they heard it. Billy was badly singing some country song while laying in the back of his pickup…and he was drunk.

"Damn it, Billy. No!!" Alia sprinted the rest of the way to the truck, and the Deputy followed. Sure enough, they found Billy lying next to half a case of beer. The empty other half were around him in the truck bed. "Billy, what the hell are you doing?" She slapped him as hard as she could on his jean-clad thigh, and he sprung up at his waist like a shot.

"What…what, damn it, Alia…what the hell you go hit me for?" Billy said drunkenly and pulled his hand back like he would hit her. That was until his eyes focused a bit more, and he saw the Deputy standing beside her, giving him a look that made him change his mind. Billy let his hand fall back to his side. "Aw shit, if it isn't Little Deputy Dougie." he looked back at Alia. "You done messed up, didn't you kid?" he looked back at the Deputy. "You finally going to arrest this brat? Wah, she doo. Tell me, tell me wah wah she doo?"

"I didn't do anything, you idiot. The Deputy was escorting me out here because the power is out."

Billy looked around, his head swiveling in a way that should have been painful. "Is it...huh, I be damn...it is...did you do this, you little brat? You did, didn't you, trying to get out of work, huh?"

"No, of course, I didn't do this. How in the hell would I be able to turn all the lights off."

The Deputy watched the exchange and couldn't help but be amused. Alia had always been what his father called a little spitfire, and right now, she wasn't as mad as he had ever seen her get, but she was getting there. For some reason, he always found that a bit funny, well, to a point. If she got too mad, she had a habit of swinging.

"Yeah, you righ you too stoopid to do somein like that...too stoopid." Billy slurred.

Yep and there it is. The Deputy looked over at Alia just in time to see her face tighten and her fist as well. Knowing what was coming next, Charlie quickly got between the both of them, grabbing her fisted arm firm but gently as he could to not hurt her.

"Hey, hey there now, we can't have any of that. As much as I would love to see you kick this piece of shit's ass, you're eighteen now and know Billy is just enough of a prick to press charges." Charlie looked right in her blazing blue eyes as he spoke, calming her down in a way he knew only he could do. Her fist unclenched, and before she looked away, he could see the tears welling up in her eyes. He let her go, knowing she wouldn't want them to see her cry. Giving her time to get herself under control, he turned his attention to Billy, who was even now chugging a newly opened can of beer.

"Give me that," Charlie said, grabbing the beer and pouring out what was left on the ground.

"Hey...wah wah da hell man...das my beer. I earned that shit."

Alia spun back around, still pissed off but thankfully not crying. "Not yet, you haven't. You were not supposed to have even one until you got me back from Alexandria...Mom

10

said so," she shouted at him, shaking all over. "Damn it, I knew I should have waited till we got back. I told her you would do this. Damn it, Billy, you ruined everything." With that last word, she slammed her fist down on the side of the truck, then walked off a bit with hands on her hips. Yep, she was really pissed off.

"Hey, watch the truck, young lady…besides, it's no big dea…it was only half a case. I can still drive…I'm good."

Alia turned back to him, her head cocked to one side, looking at him as if he had lost his mind. "Dude, there is literally a cop right here," she said, pointing to the Deputy. "Even if you were sober enough to drive…which, let's be clear, you are far from, I doubt very much you would make it to the truck's cab before he had you in cuffs."

Billy looked at her like he was trying to understand just what she meant. Then he looked at the Deputy and started to laugh. "You, you mean deputy Dougie here...ha!" Billy laid back down in the bed of the truck, laughing and saying Dougie over and over. Ignoring him, the Deputy turned to Alia.

"Wait, what is this about Alexandria? That's at least an eight-hour drive away. What is he taking you there for?"

Billy rolling around now in the truck, laughed even harder.

"Shut up, Billy." Alia reached over the side of the truck like she was going to smack him again.

Deputy Harper grabbed her arm and pulled her to the side where they could talk better over Billy's incessant cackling. "Okay," said Charlie, his hands on her shoulders. "I want you to take a deep breath, that's right, good, let it out. Okay, now tell me what's going on. Why do you have to go to Alexandria?"

Exhaling again, she told him. "I have to be there by eight in the morning to take the SATS."

He stepped back from her for a minute, his brow furrowed. "Why didn't you take it here at school last year? Or even this year?." That's when Billy sat back up.

"It ain't like she goin to college anyway….you little girl are gonna work right next to your momma in that damn factory...now les go home." Billy waved her over with his arm so fast he lost balance and fell back in the truck bed with a thunk.

"For the last time, Billy shut the hell up!" Alia yelled at him again.

Charlie grabbed her gently again and pulled her further away from the truck.

"Ignore him." he looked her in the eyes as best he could in the darkness of the parking lot. "It's just the two of us out here. Tell me what happened."

Alia looked down at her feet, unable to face him. "You're mad at me. I can tell."

"No, I'm not mad."

"Disappointed then."

"Well, I don't know...maybe, I won't know for sure unless you tell me," he said teasingly.

Alia looked up, and he was smiling. The kind of smile all the girls were crazy about. All the girls. "I didn't take them last year because I figured I wasn't going to go to college anyway. My grades aren't horrible, but they are not scholarship worthy. And let's face it, it's not exactly like I could afford to go if I had wanted to."

He nodded, knowing she was right. Besides, he knew she had a plan, and it was one she wouldn't need college for.

"Then they started talking about the possibility of making at least community college free. The school counselor Mr. Freeman said I should take the SATs just in case, and I was going to. Then, of course, as my luck would have it, the day came to take the test, and I had the flu. My temp was already one-hundred-and-two when I left the house. By the time I got to the school, I was so out of it I didn't even know where I was. Mr. Edwards drove me back home, and I was sick in bed for two weeks. So I blew my last chance to take it here. They are having make-up tests in Alexandria, the last make-up tests for the whole state. I paid for it and everything, and now thanks to that drunken idiot, I'm screwed."

Alia walked away, and again he knew she was on the brink of tears. Charlie stood there thinking for a few minutes, came up with a stupid idea, but made up his mind to do it anyway. "Maybe not exactly," he said.

Alia turned back around to face him.

"Let me deal with Billy here and get him home, then I will take you to Alexandria. If we hurry, we should make it there in time to get you in for that test."

She looked at him like he had lost his mind because she thought he had.

Deputy Harper was using his shoulder radio to call to one of the officers that were still inside the school. "Charlie, I can't ask you to do this. It's at least an eight-hour drive, and you have probably been on shift all day. Not to mention the fact...."

Charlie cut her off right there. "You're not asking; I am telling you this is what we are going to do. Now, if you want to argue with me about it, we can do it on the way there because we don't have time for it right now. I don't know about you, but I need to eat something before we go, and some coffee wouldn't be a half-bad idea either."

He looked at her with those green eyes of his, and in them, she saw something that scared her. Before she could protest anymore, he waved over the officer he had called. Both of them went to the truck to deal with Billy, who was now drinking yet another beer.

Alia just looked at Charlie and shook her head. *What are you trying to do, Charlie, get the both of us killed?*

Chapter 2
On the Road

Alia watched as Deputy Harper and one of the other officers put Billy into the back of another patrol car. *My mother is going to kill me,* she thought. *First me, then*

Charlie. Another officer drove around with Deputy Harper's SUV patrol car then got into the patrol car Billy had been put in. Charlie waved her over, and they met at Billy's truck.

"Grab your things, let's go."

"You can't be serious." But she knew he was. This was Charlie being Charlie.

"Once again, you can argue with me on the way, but right now, we don't have the time." He opened the passenger door of the truck.

Shaking her head, she reached in and grabbed the duffle bag she had packed for the trip to Alexandria and her brown day bag she used instead of a purse. "You know you're going to get the both of us killed, right?" looking once more into those green eyes.

"Maybe, but you're taking that test first." he grinned.

`She knew arguing with him was going to be pointless. Tossing her bags in the back, Alia climbed into the front seat of his patrol car. She waited a few minutes as Charlie talked to the other officers one last time and handed them Billy's keys.

When Charlie got back in, he asked her to give him a minute as he fiddled with the dash computer. Done clocking out of work, he drove off.

Alia was silent for a few minutes and thinking things over, wanting to convey the importance of how dangerous what they were doing was, but also not really wanting to change his mind. *Face it. If he doesn't take you, how the hell else are you going to get all the way to Alexandria at this time of night?* "You're not arresting him, are you...no one read him his rights, so I'm assuming he isn't under arrest."

"Well, as stupid as this may be, I thought doing that may be suicide." he grinned at her. "They will take him back to the apartment, make sure he gets in, and wait outside for your mother to arrive. Hopefully, they will be able to assure her I didn't just kidnap you."

"Well, ya kinda did." she scoffed.

"So, do you want me to take you home instead? Because I'll do whatever you want. Right now, I would think the most important thing would be to get you to Alexandria in time to take that test." Charlie glanced over at her, then back at the road.

Alia covered her face and groaned. Of course, he was right, and under normal circumstances, a friend doing a favor for a friend would be no big deal. But her life was anything but normal. "No, no, of course not. Trish is going to blow her lid when they tell her you are taking me there. I mean, really Charlie, any cop on the force would be bad, but you? The only one worse than you is your father." Alia's mother hated cops, all of them. However, for some reason, one that Trish wouldn't tell Alia, she hated Sheriff Harper the most, and by that extension his son, the Deputy, as well. If her mother had any idea what she had been up to for the last few months, adult or not, Alia would be in for a world of hurt. Right now, things were going pretty good for her at home for a change, so she didn't want to ruin that. But this insane trip to Alexandria driven by this even more insane man may do just that.

"Gee, thanks." He said, but he was smiling with that grin of his, as he said it.

Alia reached over and smacked him playfully on the arm. "You know what I mean." she laughed. "Oh god, I was hoping I would at least graduate before I died."

"She's not going to kill you."

"HA!" she said, laughing out loud. "You need to get to know my mother better."

Charlie tried to keep a smile for her and not add to her anxiety, but it faltered when she said that. He knew plenty about her mother. Alia was, of course, the expert on all things Trish Miller, but Charlie knew enough himself. Thankfully she was looking out the window and didn't notice before he had a chance to recover.

"I have an idea. It won't make Trish like me any more than she already does, but it may at least make things easier for you."

"Oh boy, I can't wait to hear this one." she scoffed.

"Yeah, real funny, I'm serious. Personally, I don't care how pissed off she gets at me, you, on the other hand. Well, you have to live with her."

Yeah, ain't that the cold hard truth? "So enlighten me, what's your plan?"

"Simple, tell her that I was pissed for finding out you didn't take the tests when you should have and that I pretty much lectured you on the way up to Alexandria. Then you pretended to fall asleep in the back to shut me up. Also, tell her that I was going up to see some friends in Baltimore anyway, so I dropped you off." He glanced over at her to see her reaction. "Well, what do you think?"

At first, Alia just shook her head, thinking. One of the side effects of living with Trish was learning to lie. A liar, however, was usually able to spot someone else lying. It was a start, flimsy, but Alia was sure she could work on it. "Yeah, I think I can spin that. As long as I seem irritated enough, she'll hopefully buy it since she's not the sharpest pencil in the box. Maybe if I act like I am more pissed about you having the nerve to do me a favor, she will commiserate, and we can both hate you." And that was going to be a stretch since Alia was pretty sure she could never hate Charlie.

Besides Crystal and her family, Charlie was pretty much the nicest person in a town full of people who seemed to do nothing but look down on her. But then that was just how Charlie was. He was nice to everyone, and in a fight between two people, he was usually the one to settle both parties down. Alia never understood why he was nice to her, though, not when most people in her life either bullied her or ignored her outright.

"Only your mother could turn someone doing a favor into a reason to hate them more," said Charlie.

That sounded to Alia like maybe Charlie knew her mother better than she thought. "Well, you know if I knew why she hated your father so much, it could help me to understand her better and use it to my advantage." This time Alia was looking at him when his smile faltered at what she said. Instantly she wanted to take the words back, worried that she may have stepped over some imagined boundary.

Alia had known Charlie since they were kids, but up to this moment, they had never spent any real time alone together before. For as long as she had known Charlie, she really didn't know him at all. Alia looked away, not willing to see the look of hurt on his face and mad at herself for being the cause of it, even if she didn't understand why. "Sorry, sometimes I don't know when to keep my big mouth shut." From the corner of her eye, she could see him glancing at her. *Was he smiling again?* She couldn't tell and was too afraid to risk a more extended look to see for sure.

"Hey. Alia, listen to me, hey."

Alia risked a fast glance, and sure enough, he was smiling a little. As she looked at him again, Charlie took one of her hands in his and started rubbing the back of it with his thumb.

"You didn't say anything wrong. And I understand why you would want to know. The thing is, that isn't my story to tell. That's my father's story. When he's ready, he'll tell you." The truth was a bit more complicated than that, but a promise had been made, and it wasn't his place to break it.

Her hand in his was both calming and electrifying. No one before had ever had such an impact on her as he did. As always, Charlie had a way of making her feel not just more relaxed than she did around the vast majority of others but excited as well. Without knowing why Alia knew that she could never bear to cause any pain and grief to this boy. Yet there were times over the years when she looked at him; that's just what she saw in his eyes, and Alia had only herself to blame. It was fleeting, and, like this time, he recovered quickly, but she had seen it too many times to be mistaken about it. She squeezed his hand a little, her way of saying she was okay, and Charlie did the same for her before putting his hand back on the wheel.

"Speaking of your father, have you told him what you're doing yet?"

At this, he laughed. "No, I thought I would wait till we stopped to get food and then text him. Hopefully, he'll be asleep by then."

"Chicken shit," she said, and they both laughed.

Before jumping onto the five-o-one, headed for Alexandria, they made a pit stop at a Mcdonald's in the next county. Since it was so close to a major highway, it was the only twenty-four-hour McDonald's. Alia told Charlie what she wanted and then headed for the restrooms in the back of the restaurant. Alone in the bathroom, it hit her. Suddenly her chest tightened, her knees grew weak, her face broke out in an oily sweat, and her heart was racing. The full gravity of what she was doing hit her as the start of a full-blown anxiety attack. "No, not now," she whimpered. Trying to catch her breath, Alia closed her eyes and tried to remember the things her father taught her to calm herself down. Before she could imagine herself nestled in the comfort of a beautiful green forest, her mother's angry and yelling face flashed before her over and over. Trish yelled obscenities at Alia repeatedly with each flash of her tired and aged face.

    It had been a while since she had an attack this bad and was horribly out of practice in dealing with it. Head spinning, Alia could no longer hold herself up anymore and slid to the floor. Even the thought of her butt on the gross bathroom floor wasn't enough to stop the onslaught of her mother's angry face and words. She didn't know what to do. If anyone came in here and saw her like this, they would most likely call for help, and who else would they call for but the uniformed officer that right now was ordering their food. The thought of him coming in here and seeing her like this, a mess of herself on the dirty floor, sent more waves of anxiety crashing over her.

    Alia closed her eyes tight, and suddenly there he was, kneeling before her. Charlie's green eyes filled with concern, his hand reaching out for hers. Then somehow, she felt it. His hand was on hers, his long fingers soft, warm, and strong. It was just like back in his patrol car earlier that night when he held her hand for a moment to reassure her he was not upset with her.

    I'm here with you. Charlie said. *Here in the woods where nothing can hurt you, where she can't reach you.* Alia nodded, trying to take deep breaths as her father taught her many years ago. *The sun is shining through the canopy of trees overhead, birds are singing, and I am here, right here next to you.* His voice whispered to her. And he was. Not only could Alia feel his hand, but she could also smell his cologne and feel his presence. Just like that, she was there in the woods, and the sun was shining, as Charlie said. Best of all, he sat there next to her on a mossy log. Alia took a deep breath and could even smell the earth around them. *That's it*, he said. *Keep breathing, just like that.*

Little by little, her chest unclenched, a cool breeze evaporated the sweat on her face, and her heart returned to a normal rhythm. Charlie was there coaxing her the whole way. The feeling was so strong that Alia was shocked that he wasn't there in front of her when she opened her eyes back in the bathroom of the McDonald's. She was thankful to see that she was alone. After slowly getting up, she leaned on the sink counter, swearing, and just for a moment, Alia could still feel him.

"What the hell was that all about?" she said, looking in the mirror at her ashen face. The anxiety attack she understood. But calling on Charlie to dispel it, she did not. That is something Alia had never done before. She was always alone in those woods. Not even her father joined her, not even when Alia was desperate for him too. Unsure of how long she sat on the floor and not wanting Charlie to have to send someone in to get her (or worse, come in himself), Alia got to her feet. She splashed some water on her face, scrubbed her hands before using the toilet, and then scrubbed her hands again after. She then felt she looked closer to normal and was able to leave.

Out in the restaurant, Charlie was nowhere in sight. Feeling on the verge of panicking again, Alia saw a light flash outside. It was the headlights of his patrol car, and sure enough, she could see him behind the wheel slurping on a drink. Grabbing a few packets of salt and ketchup, she ran out to the car and got in. "Sorry, that took so long. I tried texting a friend but didn't get a response," she lied and immediately hated herself for it. "I'm sorry," she said, not looking at him. "That was a lie."

"Are you okay? You're looking a little pale there." While she had been in the bathroom, Charlie had been overcome with the feeling that Alia was upset. The sense of anxiety that came over him was unnerving, and he knew it was from her. As soon as he got the food, he came out to the car. Not sure that it would even do any good, Charlie reached out for her and imagined himself with her in a sunny forest. He knew the technique she used many times to calm her anxiety attacks. Charlie had no clue if it would work but tried anyway and could feel her calming down. Afterward, he was left a little shaken and then relieved when he saw her come out of the bathroom.

"I may have just had a little anxiety attack."

Reaching across to her, he cupped the side of her face with his hand. "Feeling better now?" he asked, concerned.

"Huh...oh yeah," she said, trying to brush the whole thing off.

Charlie rubbed her cheek with his thumb and then lowered his hand while offering a smile.

"I just need to eat. I haven't had anything since lunch." She reached into the bag he had next to him and pulled out her quarter pounder with cheese deluxe and her fries.

"Why in the hell haven't you eaten before now?" he chastised her as he pulled out onto the highway. He was a bit upset with her about it. He had known Alia for a long time and felt she never took care of herself as she should. He had hoped that was something she'd grown out of, but apparently not. "Let me guess. You went to work at the library right after school, then right back to school for the cleanup."

"Uh-huh," she mumbled around a mouthful of juicy burger and tomatoes. "No time," she said, swallowing. "We got a shipment of new books today. Those things don't come with all those stickers and checkout bar codes. Someone has to do all that by hand. I am that designated someone." She took another large bite, and her stomach growled. It was so good.

"Well, hell, you could have at least had a Snickers or something on the way back to school."

She looked at him with a mouthful of fries and rolled her eyes. "Okay, Charles, the last thing my fat ass needs is a damn Snickers bar. And don't think for a minute I don't see the irony of saying that while stuffing fries in my fat face."

Charlie gave her an irritated look. "Stop that."

"Stop what?"

"Putting yourself down like that."

"I'm not putting myself down anywhere. Truth is truth."

"Bullshit, you're not fat."

"I'm a little fat."

"No, you're not. That's your mother talking."

No, that was in the bathroom.

"Besides," he said. "We all could stand to lose some weight."

At that, she scoffed, looked at him as if to say 'yeah right,' and rolled her eyes again. "Okay Charles, I mean, come on, did you even have baby fat when you were a baby?" She didn't have to know Charlie most of his life to know he never had to struggle with a weight issue. He was just one of those fortunate types that had a great metabolism. He was always a thin, long boy, mostly all arms and legs. Although, she had noticed that he started to work out some around the time he got into high school, filling in what was once just a skinny frame.

"Okay, you can stop with that too."

"Now what?" knowing damn well what he meant

"Keep calling me Charles, and I'll start calling you, young lady," he said with an evil grin.

Okay, that shit isn't funny. He knows how much I hate being called that. No one was ever called a young lady when people were happy with them. "Call me young lady, and I will have to deck you," she said, giving him an evil grin right back.

"You would never." he laughed.

"Try me, Po-Po."

When she said that, his jaw dropped comically.

21

Alia had to hide the giggles at the look of him, behind her hand.

"Oh really, we're going there now?" He tried sounding stern, but she could see his smile at the corner of his mouth. "You do realize you're about to become one of us Po-Po's, right?"

Alia sighed heavily, choosing to look out the windshield at the road in front of them instead of at him. All the giggles were out of her system now.

Noticing her change of mood, he glanced over at her, concerned "That's still the plan, right? You're still going to the academy after graduation, right?" he asked, almost afraid to hear her answer. "You do still want to be a cop?" And not just any cop but one working right alongside him and his father in the Sheriff's office. That was the plan, or it was supposed to be. He worried that she may have been having cold feet. Or worse, that they were pushing her into doing something she didn't really want to do, therefore being no better than her controlling mother. Well, not them exactly, more like his father. From what Sheriff Harper had said, it had been her idea, for the most part anyway. Harper mentioned years ago he thought she would make a good cop but was still surprised when she came to him a couple of years ago saying she wanted to be one. Sheriff Harper told her he would help her if she was serious. The Sheriff's department would pay for her training and have a job ready for her when she graduated. The plan was a good one. It would get her out from under her mother's control to become her own person and not just the daughter of Trish Miller. Something she wasn't very proud of being.

"Yes, of course, that's still the plan." *As long as my mother doesn't kill me for first hopping into Deputy Harper's patrol car, that is.* "But one step at a time, Deputy. I haven't even graduated high school yet. Finals are in two weeks, and if I blow them, I still may not graduate." That right there was her biggest fear at the moment. Not only failing herself but letting everyone else down.

Charlie wanted nothing more than to pull the patrol car over and talk to her face-to-face until she had her head on straight. If they were not so pressed for time as it was, he would have. The problem with Alia was that she let her mother get inside of her head too much. At least, that's what her father used to say. Crystal's brother, George, confirmed this as well. Charlie realized it couldn't be easy being told constantly how stupid and worthless you were all the time. Still, he hoped that was something else she'd eventually grow out of. The fact that Alia was still letting Trish get into her head was even more reason for her to get away from the women before her spirit was utterly broken beyond repair. She needed to spend more time around people like him who believed in her and were willing to tell her so until it got through that stubborn head of hers.

But Alia wasn't supposed to be around him or anyone who would lift her up instead of breaking her down. There was Alia's best friend, Crystal, but Trish also hated her. Even at one point, she accused the two of them of having a lesbian affair. Trish felt people only wanted people for what they could get from them. Alia had nothing to give other than herself, so the two of them must be going at it with each other. Why else would anyone like Alia? Crystal was not just a friend but a fierce friend that had butted heads with Alia's mother on several occasions.

George often talked about his kid sister's best friend, and through him, Charlie had been able to keep up with what was going on with her, even if he couldn't always be around. That was something that had gotten harder to do as they got older. Charlie had been the one that introduced the two girls to each other back when he was a counselor at summer camp, the year both girls were thirteen. He had a feeling back then that they would be good friends, and he had been right. They had stayed the best of friends, despite Trish's attempts to rip them apart.

Not realizing he was about to step on dangerous territory, Charlie tried offering a helpful solution. "You know, if there's anything you're worried about having trouble with on the finals, I could help you out."

Of course, he could, she thought. He had gotten good grades like school was a cakewalk, whereas she had to struggle just to keep a low B average. That's not what ended up setting her on edge, though. It was so easy for him to offer when she had more to lose. Saying with as much sarcasm as she could muster, "Yeah, sure Charles, you can just come over to my place after school one day. My mom will bake us cookies and say motherly stuff like 'you kids behave now,' when we swear we are only going to my room to 'study'".

Charlie's hands tightened on the steering wheel as he stared out at the road ahead, his brow furrowed. The attitude from her actually pricked him this time.

Not only had Alia hurt him this time, but she had also intended to. She hated herself for actually wanting to hurt him. *It's just so easy for him. It's not fair. Nothing is ever easy for me, nothing.*

Charlie was hurt a bit, but she was right. He wanted to call her out on it, even be upset with her, but he knew if he did the way he was feeling right now, he would sound more like his father than the Charlie she knew. That would only make things worse. So he stewed for a bit as he drove down the dark highway, wondering which one of them would break the silence first. Knowing her as he did, Charlie figured it would have to be him, so he had to wait for the sting of her words to wear off. Thankfully that didn't take long. Charlie was usually a pretty laid-back person by nature. Some aspects of his job had worn off a bit of that shine over the past few years, but he was still pretty much the same. After sitting in silence for a few miles, He noticed she hadn't finished all her fries. That gave him an opening he hoped would turn this little spat of theirs around.

"You know those fries are going to taste like shit if you let them get too cold," he said, hoping she would see that he wasn't mad.

Alia looked at the fries but found that she had lost her appetite. She wanted to say something, anything. She wanted so much to get them back to that easy back and forth banter they had going before she ruined it, but Alia also didn't like to apologize. Instead, she thought Charlie should think a bit more about saying certain things to her before he actually said them. Or maybe she was just being a bitch like her mother and ruining things as usual. *This is why you don't have any friends,* said that all too familiar voice of her mother. Luckily for her, Charlie wasn't like most people. Neither was their relationship, no matter how hard she tried to deny it.

"Okay, so maybe sometimes I don't know when to keep my big mouth shut either," he glanced over at her. "But I also know you know what I meant, too."

"You also need to understand it's not that easy for me. I wish it was Charlie. I wish things could be like that, I really do, but I don't come from a family like yours," she said, with her arms crossed and still sulking.

"I know, and I know how hard she makes things for you. But you can't spend your whole life pushing people away. That's what she wants. She wants you to have nobody but her."

"That's it, though you don't even know the half of it. No one does, not even my father did, and he knew more than most. As bad as she allows people to see her, it's nothing compared to how she is when we are alone." The voice inside her told her to shut up, and she usually would have, but, as always, there was something about Charlie that made it so easy to talk to him. "When we're alone...it's a nightmare. She's a nightmare."

"Seriously?" he asked. Charlie always suspected that things at home were terrible for her. There was even a time when the evidence was obvious. But Alia had become adept at lying, like her mother, and would never admit to the truth.

"Seriously. And Trish has spent years drilling into me that what goes on at home stays at home, so if your next question is why I never said anything, don't bother. Not that it would have done me a damn bit of good."

He wanted to tell her she was wrong, that had they known, people would have stopped it. But would they? Would they have been able to? Charlie knew Alia's father could never pin anything on Trish that would stand up in court. If he couldn't then, what could anyone else do?

25

"Did you know that I change my grades on my report card before she sees them? And no, not to better grades but to worse? " Here it was. She could feel the onrush of emotional outpouring she was about to unleash on this poor man.

"No, I didn't."

"George found a program a few years ago. Thankfully she can't even tell the difference. For years though, I couldn't figure out what her deal was. If my grades were too good, she would be mad and start accusing me of all kinds of crazy stuff. I was trying to make her look bad, trying to be smarter than her, even accusing me of sleeping with a teacher...when I was ten. If I failed or they got really bad, she would get furious. It took me a while and quite a few beatings before I figured it out, but I finally did."

Charlie looked over at her as she sat there, her arms still crossed, glaring out the windshield at the night. There it was, the word that he had been afraid to hear. It was one thing to wonder if she suffered physical abuse but a whole other thing to know for sure. Charlie had seen the marks when they both were younger, bruises, welts, burns, but Alia either explained them away or refused to talk about them at all. Charlie clutched the wheel tighter, glad she was looking at the road and didn't notice. He didn't want her to think his anger was in any way directed at her. "What the hell...but that doesn't even make any sense Alia."

"Yeah, no shit, but it does in her warped messed-up mind. She dropped out of school in the tenth grade to have me. The idea that I may be more intelligent than her drives her mad. My dad always told me she was jealous of me, but I could never understand why. Most parents want their kids to be smarter and better, but not mine."

"I'm sorry, but that still doesn't make any sense."

"That's because you were raised by good people, Charlie. My mother has one goal in life as far as I am concerned. That's getting me to eighteen and graduating, hopefully without getting knocked up in the process, not that she is averse to that either. She has threatened for years to take away any baby I have before eighteen to raise as her own. Trish said she wouldn't want me to abuse it, not even realizing that in itself is abuse. Even if I had ever wanted to have sex with anyone, I would have been too terrified to do it. As of right now, she's almost reached her goal. Then she can gloat and shove it in the face of all the people that said she could never do it, that she could never raise a child on her own. After that, I don't think she gives a shit what happens to me one way or the other."

"If she needs you to graduate, then why get mad over good grades. You would think that would be a good thing."

"You would think. You don't need good grades to graduate, just passing ones. She can't stand the thought that I am better than her at something. I have to be just good enough to get her what she wants and no more. Same as why I was never allowed to play sports. It was never about money, like she said. She didn't want me to be good at something. Trish didn't want me getting any attention she couldn't get or be a part of. I missed out on so much growing up because of her. My one aunt wanted to teach me piano. My drama teacher wanted me to try out for school plays. But I wasn't allowed to do any of it.

And when my grades were awful, it was beatings and grounding until my grades came back up. When they were too good, she resorted more to mental abuse. She did and said everything she could to cut me down to size, to remind me that I wasn't and never would be smarter than her. She made sure I knew my place and stayed there, under her foot where she likes me. So as long as I kept a C average, things were fine, or at least about that anyway. When the time came that I couldn't keep the C average grades any longer without screwing up my life more than it already was, I changed them. And it wasn't just with school either.

God forbid I would ever try to help her with something when other people were around. We were at the bank this one time, and she was trying to balance her checkbook. The numbers weren't coming out right, and Trish couldn't figure out why. I looked over and noticed right away what she had done wrong. All I wanted to do was to help her, so I very discreetly tried to show her what she did wrong, and I do mean as discreetly as possible even though no one was near us. Well, she went nuclear. She started screaming about how I was trying to make her look stupid in front of everyone. How I was just some dumb kid that was barely passing school, and how dare I embarrass her in public like that." Alia stopped to take a shuddery breath. Realizing she just went on a rant, part of her wanted to melt into the seats.

All of this was really not a surprise to him. Charlie had seen her mother go off more than once, not just on Alia but others as well. "You forgot your place for a minute," he said.

"Exactly, and her outburst called more attention to us than if I had talked to her at full volume. Oh, and you can believe that it didn't end there. By the time we got home, she had done her usual trick of making a mountain out of a molehill. When she was done, I couldn't go outside for days."

Charlie looked over at her. She still stared out at the road, but her jaw was clenched, and she was shaking just a bit. He wanted more than ever to pull the patrol car over, reach out to her, and hold her in his arms. He wanted to do anything he could to take it all away, to take her away. Charlie didn't dare pull over because if he did, he knew he would never let her go. She had to do what she needed to do to set her plan in motion. For now, the best thing he could do for her would be to get her to that test on time.

"The only thing she cares about when it comes to my future, past the next month, is being able to control me as much as she possibly can. That's why I'm not even allowed to have a cell phone. Once again, not because we can't afford one like she says, because we can." Alia says this as she reaches into her jeans pocket and pulls out a smartphone. "Crystal's parents got me this for Christmas a few years ago. I looked it up, and it costs no more than a hundred dollars, and most likely, they paid less. I pay thirty dollars a month for it with a Walmart debit card they helped me get. My mom doesn't know I have either one of them. I hate to think what she would do if she did know.

And I'm sure you know I don't even have my learners let alone a driver's license. Once again, her excuse is money. According to her, her insurance rates would go up too much if she added me to her policy. What she didn't take into account is the fact that I could make more money if I had a car, even just some beat-up clunker."

"Yes, but you would also be able to get away from her more. You having a car or even just your license would mean she stood to lose some of the control she has over you. Keeps you from advancing too far as well."

"Exactly. Oh, and would you like to know what I got for my eighteenth birthday? A bill! She actually handed me a bill for what she figured I owed for my share of the household expenses."

"You're shitting me?" he almost laughed at the absurdity of it. Charlie's mom practically begged him to stay living at home when he had moved out. And up until he did, neither of his parents asked for so much as a dime from him.

"Not one bit. I pay Trish at least sixty dollars a week every week and buy my own meals and personal items unless she is feeling generous and cooks something. Oh, and I have also had to buy all my senior items. Yearbook, cap, gown, you name it. However, Trish did buy my graduation dress, and she is throwing me a graduation party. Or should I say she is throwing herself a party so she can strut around like a proud peacock in front of family and friends?"

He thought all of this would explain why she was at the high school late at night trying to make a few bucks, having just gotten off of work in town. When he saw her around town, she always seemed to be in a rush to go somewhere. He knew she babysat, dog sat/walked, and cleaned yards on Sundays when the library was closed. How she managed to have any time for schoolwork, he didn't know.

"Oh, and I have a perfect one for you—she does have a plan for me! Now, I know I said she didn't care much about what happened to me after I graduated, and I believe that, but she still concocted this crazy plan. And I think she knows damn well I will not go through with it. But that's okay too because if I don't, and I screw my life up, which she is banking on, she can say that she did what she could and blame it all on me. And the thing is, I didn't even find this out from her but her sister instead. So apparently, after I graduate, or soon after, I am joining the military."

That news almost made him slam on the breaks. "Oh really? She just decided this for you without even talking to you about it?"

"Not just decided, but told pretty much the whole family."

"I'll be damned if I am going to…I mean…even if the academy wasn't an option." Charlie was so mad at this point he couldn't even finish. What he wanted to tell her was that he wasn't going to let her do something so foolish, but he didn't want to make her think he was trying to control her. Not now, not while she was so upset over this. That could backfire on him and make her mad at him again.

"That's not all of it."

"There's more?"

"Yes, you see, I am going to be a good little soldier, do my four years, and save up most of my money which will be really easy because I will send it to her, and she will put it away for me."

At this, Charlie laughed. "Yeah, I'm sure she will."

"Then, once I am out, we will use my good credit to buy a pet store. The woman that kept a dead iguana in a tank for months and goes through countless pets because she grows bored with them wants to own a pet store. And despite it being my money, we will use it for buying this store. She will be the owner and the boss because, of course, I'm not smart enough to run it myself. And then we'll get a house and live together, where once again she will be the boss."

Charlie laughed. "No way can she possibly believe you would do this, or it would work if you did. Doesn't she realize enlisted people don't make that much money?"

"I honestly don't understand what her thinking is anymore. I even thought maybe her sister made it up since she and I have our own history, which I believe you are aware of," said Alia

Yes, he was actually, and her aunt was another piece of work along with that husband of hers.

"But sure enough, at Thanksgiving last year, that's all she seemed to be able to talk about. The whole time she acted like it was a plan we came up with together."

"I knew your mother was a piece of work but damn. I mean, what did you even say to her about it?" he said.

At the risk of looking like a coward in his eyes, she said, "Nothing…I mean, what could I say. If I denied it, she would say I was lying and blame me for ruining everyone's Thanksgiving. I got sick for Christmas a few years ago, and she still lords it over my head how I ruined that. And it's not like I can tell her or anyone else my plans, for that matter. She would do everything she could to screw it up for me. I know she would."

"Yeah, that doesn't surprise me. I'm sure you becoming a cop is not high on her list of good things. But what about your family? I would think someone would say something in your defense.", he said. Most of her family lived in another county since her grandmother had passed away, so Charlie didn't know them very well.

"You mean the same family members that haven't stood up for me all this time despite being pretty sure of the kinds of things she did to me. Besides, this was our plan, according to her. The only reason why her sister dared to say anything to me is out of her own guilt and because she knows how my mom is. I doubt that you know this, but my aunt is very sick. Even with her heart medications, she's not expected to last much longer. So she came to me one day and said she felt like she owed me one."

After what her son tried to do to Alia, she owed her more than just one, he thought. Yet another subject best not to think, let alone talk about right then.

"She told me what my mom said to her and said she wanted to clear her conscience in case she died."

They were both quiet for a while. As much as Charlie felt like he needed to hear all of this, he was glad she seemed to have gotten it out of her system. He didn't think he could bear to hear much more right now. As she talked, it was getting harder and harder to remind himself he was a cop—not just a cop, but a good cop—because, at the moment, he didn't want to be. Right now, if her mother was in front of him, Charlie would probably run her ass over...then back up and do it again.

That was a lot she had just revealed to him, and he let it all sink in as he drove. Just like most cops, Charlie wasn't immune to the horrors of the world. He had seen his fair share of child and spousal abuse cases. But for the life of him, he didn't think he would ever understand it and hoped he never would. How a person could hurt the people they were supposed to love the most, he just didn't get it. This, however, was worse. This was personal because it was her. A promise had been made a long time ago, and today Charlie realized it had never really been kept. He, himself, was partially to blame.

Charlie looked at her. She didn't look angry anymore but instead seemed very tired and defeated. He wasn't sure how much more of this life of hers she could handle and still be his special girl—how much more before things changed her to become someone he didn't recognize anymore.

"I'm sorry," she said.

He glanced over at her again. "For what?"

"I don't know. Honestly? I don't even know why I'm telling you all of this or why it's so easy to. I don't even talk to Crystal about most of this crap." Alia was upset with herself. She didn't want to hurt him, yet she knew she had at the very least bothered him. For some reason, she knew he needed to hear the truth, as much as she needed to let it out, but she hated herself for it. It's as if they both had been waiting for this very night to happen for years. And now that it did, she wasn't sure if it was right to have burdened him with her pain. It was just that, alone in this car together, it had been so easy, too easy to open up to him. She had at least enough sense to spare him the worst of it, but she couldn't explain why but she had the feeling he knew that as well. Maybe someday, she thought. For tonight, she couldn't bear to put him or herself through anymore.

"You're telling me because you needed to. You know deep down you could and that I wouldn't judge you for it. I don't see how you've managed to keep this all wrapped up inside you all these years as it is." He wasn't just talking about only what she said, but also all the ugly truths he knew she didn't say. "I know we haven't spent time like this together before, and we don't get to spend the time together I am sure we both want. But I promise you, Alia, if you ever need me, even if it's just someone to rant to, I'll be there."

Alia felt tears welling up in her eyes. He didn't have to say it. She had always known it. For years she tried denying the special connection she had felt to the boy sitting next to her. Denied it because it hurt too much, not too. And now, tonight, she had to face the absolute truth and be honest with herself. There was something exceptional about Charlie, and if she let him, he may one day reveal his truths to her as well.

"You know, Charlie, I think you have seen me at some of my worst moments. You've definitely witnessed my temper a time or two. Yet you don't avoid me like most people seem to, or worse, talk shit about me behind my back."

"You know, you just might be surprised by what some people are actually saying. It's not all as bad as you think," he said

Sitting up and composing herself a bit more, she said, "Well, it doesn't matter. I'm over that kind of shit for the most part, anyway. If there is anything I have learned in the past eighteen years, it's that most people talk shit about people behind their backs. And most of it is just that, nothing but shit."

He was happy to hear her say that, proud even. It showed how much she had grown and matured, and he told her so.

"Oh, hush."

"No, I'm serious. You have learned a great fundamental fact about life. That's pretty impressive at your age. But then you've always seemed very mature and thoughtful. Maybe it's all those books you seem to always have your nose in," he teased.

She laughed a little, and, just like that, all the tension in the air evaporated like magic. "Funny, my great-grandmother used to say I had an old soul. She said that's why the cats at her house liked me so much. I never understood what she meant by the old soul thing until I read about it in a book. Maybe that's why I seem so different from most people, well, at least my family anyway. I'll never understand why even amongst my own family, I've never felt like I belonged."

Because maybe you don't, he thought to himself. *Perhaps you belong somewhere else, to someone else.*

Thirsty from her rant, Alia reached for her drink in the center console, looking it over before taking a sip.

"Don't worry, it's not a cola."

"You remembered. Impressive." Even her own so-called family kept forgetting she couldn't drink colas anymore. There was something about them that had made a festering ulcer she had burst several years ago. The pain had been so bad that now even just the taste or smell would turn her stomach.

But Charlie had been there then, as he always seemed to be in those days, hanging out almost in the background, with a group of other kids she knew. They had all gone to see a movie, one she was able to go to because her father had slipped her a few bucks. Alia had gotten a large fountain drink that she drank while watching the movie. The pains in her stomach that were becoming all too familiar started while watching the movie. Still, she drank, not associating the pain at the time with what she was consuming.

After the movie, they were about to walk home to their own neighborhoods when the pain became worse. The hot summer day suddenly became unbearable. The pains became stabbing, made worse by walking. Charlie had already ridden his bike half a block away, but somehow he was still the first at her side when she collapsed to the ground. The burning, stabbing pain in her stomach grew worse, making her cry and curl up in a fetal position. Charlie was the oldest one there and immediately took charge. He had one boy flag down a car for help while the other kids helped him move her into the shade. From there, he wasn't sure what else to do. Charlie asked if anyone saw her get hurt or stung by a bee or something, but no one did. He tried asking her, but all she could do was cry out in pain while clutching her stomach. He had the others help him pull her hands away, and he lifted her shirt, careful not to go too far, but he couldn't see any kind of wound or even redness. So Charlie did the only thing he could, and that was holding her hand. She nearly crushed it in hers. He was amazed at how such a little girl could be so strong. He was becoming frantic when finally an adult showed up.

From that point, it was just chaos. More adults came over, all asking what was wrong, who was she, did any of them hurt her. Charlie never let go of her hand the whole time, no matter how much it started to hurt. He was relieved to hear the siren of a police car. Even more so when his father sprang out of the Sheriff's car. Not far behind him came the paramedics as well. His father told him to let go of her as they tended to her. He didn't want to. He didn't care if she crushed his hand. He didn't want to let go. Harper pulled them apart, and it wasn't until then that Charlie realized he had been crying. He reached out for her again, but his father pulled him back.

"Let them help her, Charlie, you did good, son, now let them do their job.", said Sheriff Harper. The paramedics loaded her on a stretcher and into the waiting ambulance. As they drove away with sirens blaring, Charlie sat there in his father's arms, much too old to cry like he was, but not caring.

So yeah, that was something Charlie wasn't about to easily forget. He begged his father to let him go to the hospital to see her, but he told Charlie he couldn't, and he knew why. So they both went home instead, where Charlie sat on the couch in his mother's arms and cried some more.

A few hours later, Charlie calmed down, his sore, swollen hand wrapped in ice.

They found out Alia had been taken into surgery to repair a perforated ulcer. Another call came in a little while later that she was out of surgery and recovering fine. A few days after that, Alia got to go home. Charlie later found out that she didn't remember much that day beyond walking out of the movie theater, least of all almost crushing his hand as he held hers. And that, he thought, was just fine with him. Charlie never forgot, including his parents telling him how the doctors said it was the colas that did it, and she should never have any ever again.

When Alia put the drink back in the holder, she noticed he had gotten a frappe. She loved McDonald's frappes. Picking it up, she shook it at him accusingly.

"You seriously didn't get me one...dude, that's cold. I'm hurt." she laughed. "Why didn't you get me one? I would have paid for it. I love these things."

"Because the last thing you need right now is caffeine. What you need is to get some sleep."

"And leave you driving all night by yourself? Uh uh, no way."

"Were you planning on staying up all night to keep Billy company?"

"Are you kidding me...he was going to make me drive at least halfway. I still can, by the way. A few sips of this, and I'll feel like I can run beside the truck the rest of the way." Alia didn't drink caffeine much, but it hit her like a bus when she did. It messed with her ADHD, but she felt like she could do anything.

"Absolutely not. You are not drinking that, and you sure as hell are not driving. Didn't you just tell me you don't even have your learners yet?" he said

"Yeah, so? My dad taught me how to drive years ago. He even used to let me pull the fire trucks out of the bay for wash day."

"And I happen to recall a story about you putting his van into a ditch in front of the fire hall." Charlie grinned at her.

"Okay, first of all, I was like five at the time, and second it was his fault. He gave it too much gas on the turn."

"Still not going to have an unlicensed driver drive my patrol car."

"Okay, but I can still have a few sips, right?"

"No."

"What?"

"You need to get some sleep. If you still want one in the morning and we have time, I will buy it myself. But right now, you need at least a few hours. I don't want you falling asleep in the middle of the exam."

Alia looked at him, pouting. Literally stuck her bottom lip out and pouted.

He wanted to be annoyed, but she looked too cute to be mad at. Charlie laughed. "You can have the cream on top if you want."

"It's half-melted," she said, tilting it so he could see.

"It's fine. There's even some chocolate still drizzled on top. Take it or leave it."

Lip still out, she popped the lid off and used the straw to scoop out what was left of the whipped topping.

"And I'm watching you, cream only."

"I'm watching you," she mocked him under her breath.

Happy that the casual banter between the two of them was back, he didn't even say anything when she snuck a few sips of the good stuff. Charlie wasn't even put off by the out-of-character spoiled brat routine of hers. He doubted very much she got away with that kind of thing at home, even at an age when it was expected. He loved that she felt safe and comfortable around him enough to be a little silly. That got him thinking again about her home life, something he didn't really want to do. It hurt his heart to think of her going through all that and worse, all alone. She was a good person. Charlie knew she had a big heart, and it wasn't right that her mother was allowed to crush it. At least when her dad had been alive, she had him to lean on from time to time.

That was another story as well. Because of her mother's promiscuity, he knew that Alia's father, Jonathan, had been a reluctant father at first, not even sure if the kid was his at all. But as she grew, you only had to look at the two of them to know that Alia was his kid. Even though her hair was lighter and her eyes a sparkling blue to his dark hair and brown eyes, the rest of her was all him. Thanks to his mother being a full-blooded Native American, Alia was fortunate to carry the genes that bronzed her skin in the sun. It gave her a honey-like tan even in the middle of winter. Alia had eventually won over her father's heart despite all the obstacles Trish tried putting in their way. Then at the tender age of thirteen, she lost him, and a piece of her went as well.

When she finished getting every speck of the cream (and a little frappe, too), Alia put the lid back on and handed it to him. "If you want me to sleep, then drink. I don't want to wake up to you flipping us over an embankment somewhere."

"I'm sure I'll be fine," he said, drinking it anyway because he knew he was going to need it. "I put a blanket and pillow in the back seat. You can crawl back there and sleep if you want or sleep up here. Either way, you need to at least try and get some rest."

"Yes, Deputy Harper."

"Don't start," he scolded with a smile.

Alia reached in the back and grabbed a small pillow in a white case and a gray microfiber blanket. The pillow was squishy, and the blanket soft and warm. "The offer still stands. If you need me to drive, just wake me up." Making sure the door was locked, she propped the pillow against it and draped the blanket over herself.

Charlie tugged on the blanket till it covered all her back and then said, "You'd probably be more comfortable in the back, you know."

"I'm good. I used to sleep like this all the time going out on late runs with my dad." And with that, she settled in, listening to the rhythm of the tires on the road.

Charlie glanced over at her now and again as he drove through the night. It had been many years since he saw her sleep. He thought to himself, *She still looks like an angel.*

Chapter 3
Alexandria

Alia slept until just after dawn when the sun came shining through the passenger window while she leaned against the door. She sat up, rubbing her stiff neck, then stretched out her arms and legs.

"Good morning, princess," said Charlie, which got him a mock angry look from Alia. "Okay, so that's a no on the princess," he laughed. "How do you feel? Get any good sleep?"

"Pretty good. I think I'm ready for this today. What time is it?"

"Six-thirty. We still have about an hour to go."

Damn, that's cutting it a bit close, she thought. "I could use a bathroom break. Maybe that frappe you promised as well."

"Hmm. I don't know. The deal was you only had the cream, and I'm pretty sure you had a bit more than that."

"Uh, no, the deal was that I get some rest, and I did. But four hours isn't going to get me going for long, so pony up, boy."

"Yes, ma'am," said Charlie grinning. "I didn't know you woke up so cranky," he joked.

"Don't get me a frappe, and I will show you cranky," she smiled back.

They got off the highway at the next exit and pulled up to another McDonald's. "You go do what you need to, and I'll get the frappe and a few breakfast sandwiches. Make it fast. We don't want you to be late," Charlie said as he got out of the car.

"If we run a little late, you could always just switch on the siren," Alia said, getting out as well.

"You would love that, wouldn't you?"

"Oh hell, yes," she laughed as they parted ways.

Alia went into the bathroom feeling a quickening of her heart. *Oh no, you don't. No time to freak out today. Cool your shit, Alia.* She thought of Charlie with her hand in his, took a deep breath, and relaxed as her heart settled.

After she used the bathroom and Charlie got their drinks, they were back in the car and on the road. They managed to make it to the school, offering the test with fifteen minutes to spare, no sirens needed. Charlie pulled up in the bus drop-off zone, where they saw other students being dropped off as well. Getting out, Alia reached in the back to get her bags.

Charlie had gotten out, too, and came to the passenger side. "Why are you getting all your stuff? I'm not going to snoop or anything if that's what you're worried about."

"Because I'm going to need it for the trip back home, of course." Alia stood there with her backpack flung on one shoulder and holding the other bag in one hand.

Charlie leaned his hand against the side of the patrol car, looking at her. "And just how did you think you were going to get back?"

"I guess I'll figure something out. I'm sure there are other kids here I could get a ride with at least part of the way. From there, I could call Crystal. If that won't work, there's always the bus or train." Alia looked at Charlie and smiled. "But I do want to thank you, Charlie, you've saved my skin on this. I'll owe you one," she started to walk off, but he grabbed her arm, pulling her back.

"Now, you really didn't think I was going to just drop you off and leave you here, did you?" He looked at her incredulously.

"Well yeah, Charlie I kinda did. We talked about this last night, and you even said you were dropping me off."

Charlie shook his head. "No, that's the story we're going to tell your mother so she won't flip out. I'm not just going to leave you here in a strange city all by yourself."

"Charlie, no, I can't let you do this. You have done more than enough already, and you're tired as hell. Don't tell me you're not. I can see it in your eyes. You're practically asleep on your feet." Charlie's eyes were red-rimmed, his eyelids half-closed, and she could see him sway on his feet a little as he stood there.

Charlie had to admit that he felt like garbage and wanted nothing more than to crawl into the back seat to sleep for a few hours.

"Not to mention it's not like we can just drive on back into town together."

"Yes, I know, I realize that. But I'm not going to just drive eight hours back home right now anyway. You're right. I need some sleep. I'll go find a nice shady spot in a park somewhere and get a few hours while you do your test. But I am sure as hell not leaving you here by yourself to maybe get a ride. I brought you here, so it's my responsibility to make sure you get back home." Not to mention that his mother and father both would have a fit if he left her here alone.

"No, it's not Charlie. I'm not a kid anymore, and I can take care of myself."

"Look, I know you can, but as I said, I can't leave until I get some sleep anyway. There is no point in me leaving without you. As for what we do when we get back to town, we can figure that out on the way there. Maybe Crystal can come to get you at that McDonald's we stopped at. I'm not leaving you here." His tired eyes pleaded with her.

Alia realized there was no way he would be able to drive a whole eight hours back right now, and she wouldn't want him to try. She felt he had done too much already, risked too much for the both of them.

"I'm not leaving without you, Alia. Beyond that, we will figure it out. Right now, I need you to go in there and focus on one thing only, and that's the test. Don't worry about me, about getting home, and sure as hell, don't worry about your mother. When you're done, I'll be here. If you still want to yell at me, then you can have at it."

"I don't want to yell at you, Charlie. And I know what you're saying makes perfect sense. It's just that you don't seem to be afraid of my mother, and I'm telling you, that's a mistake. She..."

"Is the last thing you need to be thinking about right now." he interrupted her. Charlie wrapped his arms around her, hugging her tight. Then he cupped her face in his hands. "This is about you right now, no one else but you," he whispered as he looked into her dazzling blue eyes. "Let the future us worry about everything else. Now go get in there and nail that test."

"Promise me you'll get some sleep?"

"Promise. Now go before you end up late after all." He brushed his lips against her forehead, sending a shiver through them both, and let her go.

Alia tossed her overnight duffle bag back into the patrol car's front seat. Walking towards the school, she turned around for a moment. "Thanks, Charlie. You're a pain in the ass but a very good friend."

"Yeah, well, you're a pain in the ass, too." he laughed.

She was about to walk into the school when he called for her.

"Hey, Alia."

She turned, acting annoyed.

"You got this, sweet girl, don't doubt that for a minute."

Alia smiled and waved, then went into the school feeling more confident than she had in a long time. That boy always had a way of making her feel better.

Charlie got back into his patrol car, starting to feel the hours of driving draining him. He parked in a shady spot at the end of a local recreation area parking lot a few blocks away. The spring day was cool, and a nice breeze came through the half-opened windows of the patrol car. Before he forgot, he sent off a text to his mom letting her know they both made it there safe. She sent her love back, telling him to get some sleep. Charlie then got the pillow Alia had used and stretched out on the back seat, half asleep before he even closed his eyes.

Several hours later that afternoon, the test was done. Alia walked out of the front doors she had gone in, talking to Casey, a young blond girl with whom she had gone to middle school. Alia had asked her if she thought her mother would mind her tagging along back south. It's not that Alia thought Charlie would lie to or abandon her, but it was never a bad idea to have a backup plan just in case. She hadn't had one to get up here, and if Charlie hadn't come to her rescue, she never would have made it here in time.

As the two walked out, she saw him right out front like he said he would be, leaning on his patrol car with his hands shoved in his pockets. Alia gave him a short wave that he returned, then turned to talk to the girl.

"That's your ride?" she asked. "Alia, I always knew you were a bit of a badass in school, but police escort for the SATs, what did you do?"

"Oh no, it's nothing like that. Charlie is just an old friend. My first ride flacked on me, so he offered to run me up. We didn't have time for him to get his truck or even change...so yeah."

"Hmm, he's kinda cute too, sure he's just a friend?"

Alia looked back at Charlie and remembered how she felt last night when he held her hand and again that morning when he hugged her. Then shaking her head, she dismissed that thought right away. Charlie was nice and all, but boys that looked like him...didn't go for girls that looked like her. No matter what he said, she had more than a few extra pounds, and her idea of fashion was things like the jeans and t-shirt she wore today. Her clothes were baggy and loose because tight clothes showed her fat rolls, and they made her feel like a slut because that's all her mother ever wore. Trish had even tried to get her to dress as she did, but Alia could never feel comfortable enough in her own body.

So, no, despite how friendly Charlie was to her and how she felt about him, the two of them? Well, that wasn't going to happen. *No matter how bad I want it.* A thought popped in her head, but she chose to ignore it. "I've known Charlie forever. If he really liked me, he certainly has never said anything. Not in that way, you know."

"Damn shame, something about you two just screams cute couple. Oh, he must be in a hurry to whisk you away, though; that's something," Casey said, gesturing in his direction.

Alia looked back and saw that he was waving for her to hurry up. He looked to be in a bad mood, as well. *But then, he always seems a little moody when he's not smiling.* She wondered what had changed and hoped to hell it didn't involve her mother.

"Yeah, I better go. We still have at least eight hours ahead of us. Nice seeing you again, Casey. Good luck with the test."

"You too, and stay out of trouble. I'd hate for your friend there to have to cuff you or anything," she laughed.

Waving goodbye, Alia laughed as well. Casey sure hadn't changed much. And it wasn't surprising that she had missed taking the test at her school because she was busy giving birth to her now three-month-old son. Alia ran up to the patrol car, where Charlie opened her door. "Something wrong?" she asked, getting in.

He shut the door. "Bit of bad news, good news situation."

With that, Alia felt all the blood rush from her face. She gripped the door feeling as though she was going to faint.

Charlie saw her go white and put his hand on hers. "Whoa, hey, no, don't pass out on me. It's not that this isn't about your mother if that is what you're thinking."

She let out a gust of air. "Then what is it?"

"There have been alerts going out on the phones and all over the police scanner. My father called, too. There is a huge line of nasty storms rolling across Virginia between here and home. State police are shutting down the highways. Truckers and travelers are pulling off the roads in droves. Hey, are you going to be okay? You're as white as a ghost."

"I'm fine. You just scared the crap out of me for a minute, Charlie."

"Sorry. I didn't think." He reached out and cupped her face as if he had to touch her to assure himself she was okay.

Once again, sparks shot through her, and she silently begged her teen hormones to give her a break.

"Anyway, we can't leave town," Charlie said, removing his hand. "I found a motel a few miles away that is holding us a room. But the manager is only doing it because I'm a cop, and he can't hold it forever. So we need to go." With that, he patted her hand and ran over to his side, and got in.

Alia took out her phone that she had, of course, turned off, turning the testing. As soon as she turned it back on, several alerts came up. Sure enough, the radar on the weather app showed a large swath of massive storms, including several tornado warnings just south of their area.

"I tried getting us two rooms, but the manager wouldn't go for it. I hope that's okay?" Charlie said, pulling out of the parking lot. "But I did get one with two beds."

Alia nodded and pretended she was busy with her phone. The truth was she just couldn't look at him right then. All she could focus on was that bit about two rooms. Her penchant for overthinking things was already working on her. *Of course, he wants two rooms. Who would want to share a room with you,* said that nasty little voice that hid inside her head. Then it dawned on her that she would have to call her mother. They were expecting her home sometime later this evening. Not only that, but she would have to come up with a plausible story as to where she was hunkering down for the night. If she didn't know better, she would think the universe was out to get the two of them killed.

"So, how'd the testing go?" Charlie asked and got no answer from her. "Alia, hey, are you sure you're okay?"

No, she wasn't. This whole trip was bad enough. Now she was going to spend the night in a motel with the son of her mother's least favorite person. Public enemy number one as far as Trish was concerned. Alia was already going to have to put up with some shit for letting him drive her here. If Trish ever found out where she would be tonight, she didn't even want to think about that. Still, she needed to be calm and rational about this. The last thing Alia wanted was to upset Charlie. She was sure he felt bad enough about his part in what Alia had to face when she got home. That was just how he was. She didn't want to make him feel worse. *If only he had just left me here.*

Charlie reached out and touched her shoulder, making Alia jump a little. She was lost in her head again, which he knew from experience was not a good place. "Hey, are you alright? Talk to me."

With a sigh, she turned to him and smiled. "Testing was fine. Actually better than fine. I was astonished how easy most of it was." *And now I am paying for it and pulling poor Charlie right down with me.*

"That's great, see I told you you could do it. You're far from stupid, Alia; you just need to work on your confidence some more." Something he was more than happy to help her with. Despite what she thought, Charlie only wanted two rooms for them because it was the right thing to do, as his mother had pointed out. Glancing over at her, he frowned. "If everything went so great, then what's wrong. I would think you would be ecstatic right now."

Alia slid down in her seat, covering her face with her hands. "I have to call my mother," she mumbled.

Shit, of course, she does.

"Uh, I hate this. One lie is one thing, but now I have to come up with another, and she's already going to suspect something is up." Alia sat back up and looked out the window nervously.

"But Trish can check the weather herself. I don't know about the trains but buses have already stopped going that way. Just tell her you won't have a ride out till morning. It's not like you're lying."

46

"Yeah, I know it sounds easy, but you have no clue what it's like having someone that doesn't trust you. Trish may not be very bright, but she's like a dog with a bone. If she thinks for one minute the two of us are shacked up for the night, she will keep badgering me till I screw something up. Trish knows how to get to me, Charlie. And maybe I'm wrong, things have been going pretty good the closer it gets to graduation, so maybe she won't suspect a thing. You can never tell with her. She's bipolar as hell. If she has been sitting at home all day stewing about me leaving town with you, then she will be waiting for a fight. And before you say it, no, I can't just not call because that would make things worse. That would just prove I have something to hide."

Now Charlie was feeling bad. Sometimes, it was so easy for him to forget that their lives were so different. Earlier his parents had called him. Even though he knew his father wasn't exactly thrilled about him leaving town with Alia, that wasn't even mentioned. Their only concern was that the two of them, not just him, but the both of them, would get someplace safe for the night. He wouldn't be surprised if her mother insisted she come home, storm or not.

"I'm sorry, Alia, this is all my fault. I should be the one to have to deal with this, not you."

"Damn it, Charlie, it's not your fault." Alia was getting aggravated, not with him but the situation as a whole. She would have to be careful, though. Charlie had a big heart, and the last thing she wanted was to hurt him again. "My mother being psycho isn't your fault, and the storm is just life's way of saying to hell with me. I should have known things were going too well. Seems like anytime anything good happens or things are easy, I end up paying for it in the long run. But I won't have you blaming yourself. You're a good person. You've just had the misfortune of tagging along with the queen of bad luck." she sighed.

"Queen, really?" he teased, desperate to make her feel better. "I mean princess maybe, but a queen. I don't know." He looked over and gave her that award-winning smile of his.

"Stop trying to make me laugh, Charlie; this is serious," she said, trying to hide her own smile. She couldn't help it. His smile, like his laugh, was infectious.

"Look at it like this. You're with me now, so surely some of my extraordinary good luck should rub off on you. In the meantime, how about we not make it a problem until it is? This morning you were worried about the test, and that went better than you expected. Maybe the call will go better as well."

"And if it doesn't?"

"Then we will deal with it together. Because the bottom line is we are in this together. I didn't leave you here, and I'm sure as hell not going to leave you to deal with her alone if it all goes to shit."

That is precisely what she was afraid of the most. It's one thing for her to be on the receiving end of her mother's crap and another for Charlie to be. No matter what his father had done to piss off her mother so bad, Charlie was a good man and didn't deserve her hatred. What Alia didn't know was that it wasn't just Charlie's father that Trish had hated so much, but the whole family, maybe Charlie the most.

"I don't deserve you for a friend Charlie, I really don't."

"Sure you do." *Some friend I have been. I knew she was hurting, had been for a very long time, and I just walked away.* " I just wish I had been a better friend to you all these years. But I promise you I am going to fix that. To hell with your mother." He smiled at her in a way that warmed her heart. If only it could also ease her mind.

A few minutes later, they pulled up to a motel on the side of the highway. It was far from new, but it was clean and looked like it had been cared for by the owners as best as it could over the years. All the rooms were on the ground floor and accessed from the outside. The parking lot was almost full, even this early in the afternoon. In the back, they could make out several tractor-trailer trucks parked behind it. Inside, the lobby was full of truckers, travelers, and businessmen, waiting in one of three lines to get a room or over in the little coffee area.

The two of them got into one line only to have the manager, a middle-aged man of Indian descent, motion them over to him.

"Excuse me, folks, please allow me to deal with this officer real quick," he said with a slight accent. To Charlie, he said, "Deputy Harper, I have your room key all ready for you. I just need to run your credit card, and you can go get settled in."

"Thank you, I really appreciate you holding the room for us."

"Of course, we are more than happy to help our law enforcement officers."

Charlie got out his credit card and was about to hand it over when Alia stopped him.

"Actually, Charlie, I should pay for that. You haven't let me pay for anything yet, so I can at least cover our room."

He just gave her a look that said hell no and handed his card to the manager.

She smacked him on his arm, but he laughed. "I tell you what. If you insist, you can pay for dinner." Charlie grabbed a pen to sign his receipt and then stopped. "Wait, there's been a mistake. When we talked on the phone, I said I needed a room with two beds."

"Yes, I know, but we have so many people having to get off the roads. Some of the truck drivers are staying four to a room. You only have two people. I can't give up two beds for only two people when so many people need rooms. Most hotels are full already. I'm sorry. Besides, it's a queen, a big bed, and plenty of room for the two of you."

Charlie looked over at Alia, who just shrugged, so she was no help.

"Why don't you want to share a bed with the pretty girl? I'm sure she won't bite," the manager said, nodding to Alia.

Charlie looked at her again, and this time she laughed.

"I make no such promises," she said, speaking without thinking. Looking away, she felt herself blush, but it had been worth it to see the shocked look on Charlie's face.

Shaking his head, Charlie went ahead and signed the receipt, took the room key, and thanked the manager again. Back outside, he said to her, "Well, you were no help in there."

"Oh, I'm sorry, I thought you didn't want my help. Besides, the manager was right. Look at this place. It's packed. One bed will be fine. Now let's go. I have a phone call to make. Faster it's over, the better." Still, getting back into the patrol car, she had mixed feelings. The idea he thought they needed separate rooms upset her. The thought of them sharing not just a room but also a bed made her nervous.

Charlie drove the patrol car closer to their actual room, and then the two of them went inside. Yes, indeed, there was a queen bed, but for the life of him, Charlie would swear it still looked small. It wasn't that he didn't want to share the bed with her. It's just that her age and his being a cop complicated matters. Having feelings for her was more of a hindrance to his sense of right and wrong than it was a help. Charlie resolved right then to sleep in the tub that night. These thoughts were quickly vanquished from his mind when he saw her on the edge of the bed. She was frowning at the phone. Charlie pulled over one of the two chairs sitting at a small round table by the window and sat down in it across from her. He then took her left hand in his.

She gave a little squeeze but didn't look away from the phone.

"Do you know what you're going to say?"

She had thought about it and had come up with the most plausible lie that she could think of, one that was mixed with a bit of truth. "If you had decided to go back home and ditch me after all, I was going to try and get a ride with Casey, that girl I came out of the school with. We knew each other from one of the dozens of middle schools I went to. Her Mom was there to drive her back. They live a couple of counties north of us, but I figured Crystal could get me from there."

He was hurt that she thought for a minute that he would ditch her. But given how people were in her life, he also kind of understood.

"I'll just tell her I'm with them in the motel." She sat there still, not picking up the phone.

Charlie could feel her elevated pulse through the touch of their hands, and as much as he wanted to believe her hand in his was the cause, he knew it wasn't. "I think this is going to have to be like a band-aid. You need to just do it fast and get it over with. Prolonging it is just going to make you more of a nervous wreck."

Alia nodded.

"Do you want me to stay with you, or would you feel better if I left?" *Please tell me to stay.*

She sat with her head lowered, not answering him, just thinking.

Charlie tried looking her in her eyes, but she quickly looked away and not before he saw the tears welling up there. He was about to take her into his arms when she spoke softly.

"Could you wait outside, please?"

"You sure?" Charlie rubbed her hand in both of his in an attempt to reassure her.

"No, I would rather have you here, but if she starts, I couldn't stand it if you heard her yelling at me over the phone." She spoke honestly, hoping he would understand.

Charlie was sure that was part of it, but he was more sure she didn't want him to see her cry if it came to that. He had seen her get yelled at plenty of times. Caught her very upset to the point of tears. Seen her in a rage more than once (that fiery temper of hers). What Charley had rarely seen was her actually crying. He knew she hated to cry in front of people. He didn't want to leave her to do this on her own, didn't think he should, but he knew it would hurt her too for him to see her like that. And in his state of mind, with lack of good sleep, Charlie could go into a rage of his own if he did.

"Only if you're sure. I said we would deal with this together."

"Yes, I'm sure, besides that was if this all blew up in our faces. I think without you here, I will be able to lie to Trish easier." *For some reason, as good a liar as I have become, it's so hard to lie to him. Lying in front of him won't be any easier, I'm sure.*

He gave her hand another little squeeze, even brushing it with his lips though she didn't seem to notice. "OK. I'll be right outside if you need me. If she gets too psycho, don't feel bad about hanging up on her ass," he tried for a smile. Charlie got up and walked to the door. "When you're done, there's a Pa Pa's pizza down the road. If you're any decent human being, you love Pa Pa's pizza." With that, he left, but not before he saw her smile just a little, and it lifted his heart.

Alone, Alia grabbed the phone's handset, took a deep breath, and dialed her mother's cell phone.

"Hello?"

"Mom, it's me." Alia held her breath, waiting for the explosion.

"Where in the hell are you?" There it is. "I came home last night to cops out in the parking lot…cops, Alia! Do you have any idea what went through my mind? You know better than to involve the cops in anything. And they were in the apartment too. And if that wasn't bad enough, they said you ran off with Harper's son. Have you lost your mind, Alia?"

"I didn't have any choice, Mom. Billy was drunk when I came out of the school, and the cops were right there."

"That's a lie, and you know it." Trish bellowed over the phone. "Billy said you brought that little shit deputy out with you."

"He escorted me from the school, there was a power failure, and all the lights were out. It was no big deal until we found Billy drunk in the back of his truck."

"No big deal? You're lucky he didn't get arrested. You and your little friend Charlie must think the two of you are really cute. I guess the two of you figured if you waited long enough, Billy would have drunk too much, and that boy could come to your rescue." This was precisely what Alia had been worried about. Her mother had all day to stew about this. She wasn't going to go down without a fight.

"No, Mom, Charlie had no idea I was there until I was about to leave. And Billy should have never started drinking in the first place; he knew we had a long drive ahead of us."

"Don't you try to blame Billy for your bullshit Alia. He didn't have to do you a favor in the first place. That test is just one big ass waste of time. He's had a hard enough day as it is. He was worried about his truck getting impounded, which, lucky for you, it did not. He worried all day about the cops coming back to lock him up. You are a damn lucky little girl. Now, where is that son of a bitch because I would like to give the little pervert a piece of my mind."

"Who…Charlie? He's gone, Mom. He dropped me off at the school this morning and left for Baltimore."

"Don't give me that bullshit, Alia. The two of you have always been sneaking off together behind my back."

"Mom, I haven't even seen Charlie in years. He was at the school last night directing traffic for the game."

"And you expect me to believe he just happened to be there to take you all the way to Alexandria. And what the hell were you thinking, Alia? He is a grown man, and you are still just a child. I don't give a damn if you are eighteen now. You have no idea how some men can be and how to defend yourself."

Alia gripped the phone tight. *I do so know how men can be, and you damn well know I do. And it was you that insisted I get Billy his damn case of beer before we even left town.* It was then that it hit her. Billy getting drunk and unable to drive her was the plan from the start. She may not have counted on the school lights going out and her job taking longer, but Alia had no doubt that her mother knew Billy would start drinking. She actually wouldn't put it past her mother to even have told him to do it. Trish knew damn well Alia wouldn't get in a car with someone who had been drinking. Being the daughter of a fireman, she had seen first hand the lousy end results of drinking and driving. Alia was suddenly furious. Gripping the phone even tighter, it was everything she could do to keep from bashing the headset on the wall next to her.

"If he put one finger on you, I swear I'll kill him."

Like you even give a damn. Alia wanted to scream at her mother, wanted to ask her where she was when her cousin had bound and gagged Alia when she was little? Where was she the nights Alia had to defend herself against her mother's drunken boyfriends she brought home from the bars? It would be one thing if Alia believed Trish gave one ounce of shit about her, but she didn't. Alia could even hear it in her voice. This was all about Sheriff Harper and whatever grudge she had against him. Had it been any other cop, she might get a little pissed but would never raise these kinds of accusations.

"Where are you, Alia, and don't you fucking lie to me."

Alia took a deep breath. "I'm at a motel. I can't come home tonight. The highways are shut down because of the storms."

"So the two of you are shacking up in a motel...."

"No, Mom, he isn't here. I told you he dropped me off and went to Baltimore. There's some girl up there he's spending the weekend with." Alia was at the point of being in a rage right now and wanting to go off on her mother, but that would make things go from bad to worse. She had to handle this, play it right, and calm her mother down. As much as what she was about to say would hurt like hell, she had no other choice but to throw Charlie under the bus. Fighting with her would only make her mother more suspicious. But the two of them united against a common enemy would surprisingly go a long way to getting her and Charlie off of the hot seat.

"That piece of shit dropped me off at the school hours ago, almost making me late too. He spent half the trip up here lecturing me about responsibilities and scolding me for not taking the test when I was supposed to last year.

Charlie acted like an ass and wouldn't even hardly let me get any sleep." *I sure as hell hope he can't hear any of this shit.* She didn't care if he understood or not. She felt worse than dog shit lying about him like this. "And he wanted to arrest Billy. I practically had to beg him to let the other cops just take him home. When he dropped me off, and I told him I didn't have a way to get back, he just told me I should have thought about that before I fucked up because he had shit to do, and he drove off. If I hadn't run into a friend from back home, I would have been stuck here on my own. And no, he didn't try anything. He was moaning over how he was going to spend the weekend with some woman he knew in Baltimore. That's the only reason he drove me here in the first place because it was on his way." Alia took a deep breath and held it, waiting to see if her mother bought any of that load of garbage.

Trish didn't say anything for a few minutes. "Well, you can't say I didn't warn you about them, Alia. Cops are bad enough as it is, but those Harpers think their shit doesn't stink. I actually thought you and Charlie used to be friends."

Alia let out the breath she was holding and practically collapsed on the bed, not even realizing she'd been standing to begin with. She was relieved, but you wouldn't haven't been able to tell that if you saw her. She shook all over and looked like she was about to be ill.

"No, not really. I mean, he hung out with some kids I rode bikes and shit with sometimes. I thought he was nice at one point, too." A little truth thrown in was always good. "But he never said two words to me in high school. I haven't even seen him at all in the last three years. Then last night, he showed up out of the blue bitching about Billy having a few beers and threatening to lock him up if he tried to drive me. I don't know what happened to him, but now that he's a cop, he's turned into a real dick." *I'm so sorry, I don't mean it, Charlie.*

"Yeah, well, the apple doesn't fall far from the tree. His father is a real piece of work too. You know I have tried to warn you about them."

Well, you sure are right about that. You're a lying sack of shit, and I guess so am I now, too.

"Your best bet is to just stay the hell away from all of them. That family is nothing but trouble."

The use of the word family caught her interest. Her mother never before said anything about Charlie's mom and really not even much about him other than to not play with him. She always made it out to be like it was Sheriff Harper that she had an issue with. She had called Charlie a pervert, as well. Alia wondered if there was anything to that or if she was just reading too much into it.

"Who are these people you say you're with...I don't remember any Casey."

That's funny because she remembers you telling her how she was a little tramp and would be pregnant before she was eighteen. That part ended up being true but still.

"I doubt you would. I only went to school with her for a few months in middle school." Alia left out the part where Casey lived just a few doors down in the same trailer park as they did. Since Alia wasn't allowed to have friends over to the house, she doubted Trish would remember Casey if she walked right up to her. At the moment, that didn't matter. Trish didn't really give a shit about her and wouldn't really care who she was staying with as long as it wasn't Deputy Harper. She had succeeded in taking the wind out of her mother's sails. Trish would never apologize for yelling at her or accusing her of things, but her tone and demeanor changed. That's all that mattered.

"We tried driving back, but the state police have the roads blocked. They even made the truck drivers turn back."

"Yeah, Billy has been watching the weather channel all day. It's not supposed to come down this far south, but it's already making a mess. Well, I have to go. Billy is going to want dinner soon, so I have to start cooking. I guess we'll see you when you get here tomorrow. And if I find out you're lying to me about that little shit and he's still there, you will have hell to pay when you get home. You listen to that girl's mother and don't be going out running around all night. See you tomorrow." And with that, her mother hung up. No goodbye, no sorry, no "I love you," nothing.

    Alia slammed the phone down with both relief and anger. She laid back on the bed for a bit, trying to will away the shakes and the loose jelly feeling in her legs. She honestly had doubts her mother was going to believe her lies. Trish had a way of getting the truth out of her. Perhaps it was because it was over the phone. After several cleansing breaths and more than a few cleansing tears, she was able to walk to the bathroom, where she washed her face off with cold water. Alia was still very pale but felt she could handle the next hard part, facing Charlie after all the horrible things she said about him.

    Please, please, let him not have heard anything I said.

    Outside Charlie leaned back on the front of his patrol car, waiting for Alia to come out. He hadn't heard a thing from inside and wasn't sure if that was a good or bad thing. Charlie wasn't sure how long he should give her before going back in to make sure she was alright. He had this nagging feeling that she wasn't, not really. Just as he was about to make up his mind, the door opened. Alia walked out into the sunlight, looking pale, tired, and sad. It broke his heart seeing her that way, and he damned himself for leaving her in there alone.

    Alia slowly walked up to him, not saying a word. When he offered his opened arms to her, she went to him and wrapped her arms around his waist, burying her head in his chest as he wrapped his arms around her. They stood there together like that for some time, just holding on to each other. Alia felt too ashamed to face him or even speak. In his arms, she felt so safe, but she hurt more after what she had done.

    Charlie held on to her, not wanting to ever let her go. He would have sworn he could feel her pain going through her and into him. He knew that holding her was what she needed from him the most for right now. After a while, he asked her, "Was she mad?"

Alia nodded, not letting go or daring to look up at him.

"Was it horrible?"

She shook her head.

"Did she believe you?"

She nodded again.

"She believed it when you said I left you here."

Alia nodded again.

He chuckled a little in relief. "Then why are you so upset? Sounds to me like we're good." he gave her a reassuring squeeze.

"I said horrible things, Charlie."

"To her?"

She shook her head. "No, I mean about you."

He laughed at that, and she smacked him on his back for it.

"Don't laugh, Charlie. I feel terrible."

"I'm sorry, you're right. I shouldn't laugh. Did you believe it, though?"

"Believe what."

"What you said, the horrible things about me, do you believe them?"

"No, of course not."

"And Is your mother going to come up here and kill the both of us or kill you when you get home?"

"No." *Though there was still a chance of things getting heated again when I get home.*

Charlie let go of her, pushed her arms down to her side, and made her look at him. Her usually sparkling blue eyes were a grayer hint of blue, like storm clouds. "Then that's all that matters. If saying horrible things about me is what it takes to keep you out of trouble with her, then that's what it takes. Your lies to her can't hurt me. She can't hurt me."

Don't be so sure about that.

"And I am tired of just standing by while she hurts you. If you're a queen, then just think of me as your knight in shining armor or rather deputy's uniform."

There he was smiling again. The one where she could never resist and have to smile in return. He knew she was hurting, so all he cared about was making her happy again. And Alia wanted the same for him. All of which meant no matter how much she hated herself right now, she needed to get her shit together and try to be happy. Or, at the very least, she needed to enjoy this time with him. Alia needed to forget about her problems for the time being and embrace whatever it was about Charlie that made her feel like she was loved by somebody. Even if it was only for one night. Even if he didn't share the feelings, she realized she had for him, and they would go back to ignoring each other when they returned to town. She was determined to shut off that overthinking brain of hers and live in the moment.

"So what is this I hear about there being a Pa Pa's Pizza nearby?"

"There you go, that's my sweet girl. Come on, I don't know about you, but I am starving." He kissed the top of her head, reluctantly let her go, and walked to the driver's side of the patrol car.

"Same here. We had a lunch break, but my nerves wouldn't let me eat. At this point, I think I can take on half of one of their super extra larges by myself."

"Let's go then. Just don't make fun of what I want on my half."

"Can't be any worse than my favorite, pepperoni and pineapples." They had both gotten in, and instead of starting the car, he stared at her. "I know, I know. It's an abomination, an affront to all pizza kind."

"That's exactly what I like on mine too. My father hates it. We fight over it every time we get a pizza."

"See, now I know you're just teasing me."

"I am dead serious. Only it also has to have extra cheese."

"Yes, exactly, and Pa Pa's is the only place that puts the cheese...."

"On top, so the toppings stay on," he finished for her.

"Hell, yes." She smiled over at him.

Alia's blue eyes were sparkling like sunlight on water. Charlie wanted to lean over and kiss her right then and would have had it not been for what his mother said to him on the phone earlier. Instead, Charlie started the patrol car, and they headed towards the best pizza place on the planet.

They were almost there when Alia turned to him. "Thank you again, Charlie."

"Will you stop beating yourself up for having to lie about me?"

"Yes." *I will try anyway.*

"You promise."

"I promise, Charlie."

"Good. Then I only have one rule for the rest of the night...well, two."

"Yeah, what's that?"

"First of all, we are going to have a good time. We are going to eat too much greasy and nasty pizza, drink too much soda, and then talk and laugh about stupid shit."

"I can agree to that. What else?"

"No talking about your mom. And it's nothing personal or about you. I just want tonight to be about us. I have known you for years, yet I barely know anything about you, things that I really would like to know. Like how in the world did we manage to go so long without knowing we both like the same pizza toppings?"

"Well, we've never really talked. Even when we got a chance to hang out as kids, it was always with a whole group of us. And even then, we barely talked, not about ourselves ."

"Exactly. Tonight we need to change that. Agreed?"

"Agreed." *I just hope you still like me afterward.*

Charlie pulled into a shopping complex where Pa Pa's Pizza was. Two doors down was a Dollar Tree. "The pizza will take about fifteen minutes or so. Why don't you go to the Dollar Tree and get us some drinks and snacks for later?"

"Sounds like a plan. I'll meet you back here in a bit." Alia felt some of that old familiar anxiety try to creep its way back in *as they parted. Not tonight, damn it…you got to keep your shit straight for Charlie…you owe him at least that much.* She pictured his smiling face and relaxed as the anxiety melted away.

Chapter 4
One Wild Night

Charlie and Alia went back to the motel with pizza, snacks, and drinks purchased. With the horrible events of the day done with, they were able to relax and enjoy the easy natural flow they'd always had between them. They sat at the small table talking about their love of pizza and why Pa Pa's was the best. Neither one bothered with turning on the flat-screen TV on the wall.

Charlie talked about how he and his father would get into it over their choice of pizza toppings. Alia spoke about her many nightly adventures with her father. Their favorite place to eat was the Hot Dog Hut, with the largest and tastiest hot dogs she ever had. Charlie noticed her eyes glistening a little while talking about him, but she had a big smile on her face as well. Soda's were drunk, pizza devoured, and their laughter made the events of the day seem trivial.

After a few slices of pizza, Charlie suggested a round or two of twenty questions to better familiarize themselves with each other.

"Okay," Alia said, "But, like, what kinds of questions?"

"Anything, I guess. What about something small, like your favorite color?"

"Wow, slow down, Charlie. I don't know if we are ready to bring the big guns out yet."

"Shut up," he said, tossing his used napkin at her. Tilting his head slightly to one side, he just looked at her and smiled.

There was something about the way he looked at her, a mischievous glint in his eye, that warned her the more challenging questions would eventually come.

"Okay then, um, crap," she said.

"Oh, I see. It's not so easy now, is it?"

"Well, no, it's just, I mean I love different colors for different reasons."

"I think you're just stalling."

"I'm not, okay? I guess if I had to pick..no, see If I tell you that you're going to take it the wrong way."

"Take it the wrong way? About a color? How?" he laughed.

"Because it's kinda girly."

At that, he busted out laughing. "Oh no, please don't tell me it's pink."

She just smiled and turned a little pink herself. "Yeah, yeah, get it all out of your system. But you're wrong, sort of."

"Please, do tell," he said, still laughing.

"No, I'm not telling you shit anymore." she joked.

"Aw, come on. Okay, okay, I'll behave. Tell me, please."

"I only like hot pink."

"You would." he smiled back at her.

"See! I knew you were going to be like that. I don't mean like paint my whole room that color or anything. But you know, as an accent. A nice shirt, maybe."

Charlie just kept smiling, not saying a word. Thinking about it, though, he remembered that she had a black bike with hot pink trim at one point.

"OK smart ass, what's yours then? I swear if you say camo, I'm gonna kick your ass."

"No, not camo. It's blue. Like the color blue of your eyes," he said, not taking his off of hers for even a second.

She looked back, her heart rate rising, trying to gauge if he was messing with her or flirting with her. There was nothing in his eyes less than pure honesty. Maybe a hint of something else? *He seriously needs to stop looking at me that way.*

"Okay," she said, breaking eye contact. "My turn." She thought for a second. "What about food, not just your favorite, like what is your guilty pleasure kind of thing?"

"I'm a guy. We don't have guilty pleasures when it comes to food. We just eat," he joked.

"Oh, I see, a thinly veiled sexist joke. Gee Charlie, I would have thought better of you than that. What would your mother say?"

"She would smack me upside the head and tell me to stop being a sexist jerk."

"You're lying. Your mother would never smack you, Charlie. I know your mother. I'm going to tell her you said that."

"Well, of course, you know I mean like in a loving way. Trust me, my mom doesn't take any crap from my father or me. And I was joking, of course. I just like messing with you sometimes."

Hearing that, her heart sank a little. *So that's all any of this is then.* "Well, don't think I would be opposed to slapping you upside the head either if you need it."

" Oh, I know. You've hit me like three times already in the past twenty fours hours."

"I have not," she said, pretending to be offended.

"You just hit me out in the parking lot not an hour ago," he said, smiling and piercing her with those green eyes of his.

"Oh damn, you're right," she laughed. "But those were like love taps, so they don't count."

"Oh, okay," he rolled his eyes but still smiled.

"Yeah, and now who is stalling?"

"Fine. I will eat just about anything. I don't think I have ever been very picky. So I don't know as far as guilty pleasures go, but I would have to say popcorn, with way too much butter and salt on it. And not that crap from the theater either. I like the real stuff."

"That's not much of an indulgence."

"No, I mean like way, way too much butter. When I go to see a movie, I prefer the drive-in so I can take a thermos with my own melted butter from home. I use at least two sticks for one of the large bags. Just pour it on a little at a time, so it all gets coated."

Alia wrinkled up her nose. "I'm sure your dates just love that. Nasty, greasy fingers and lips."

"Actually, I have never taken a date to the movies," Charlie said, looking down and away from her slightly. If he were to be completely honest, something he wasn't ready to be, he would tell her he had never had a date. He had even gone to his senior prom with just a few friends. Oh sure, he danced with a couple of girls, most of the ones he had been friends with for years. But even that didn't feel right. Charlie ended up leaving early, his heart filled with guilt, feeling as though he had cheated on the only girl he had ever loved.

"Why not?" Alia asked.

Charlie just shrugged. Changing the subject, he said, "I bet I can guess what yours is?"

"Go for it," she said, knowing what he was doing but not wanting to press him. *I know exactly what it's like not to want to reveal things about yourself. Let him have his secrets if he wants. I have my own, too.*

"It has to be ice cream."

She looked at him, shocked. "Well yeah, but how do you know?"

"I know because I swear it seemed like when we were kids that you could hear the ice cream truck from blocks away. You would run home or wherever you went and come back with a few quarters or a handful of change just as the truck came around the corner. And the look on your face when you didn't have any was..." he was going to say pitiful, but he was afraid that might hurt her feelings. "Well, it was sad. One of the first fights I saw you get in was with some boy that practically towered over you. You couldn't have been no more than five because that was not long before you moved out of the county." *And I only got to see you when you came to see your father, which wasn't anywhere near often enough.* "One minute, you were fine, walking off with your cone, and the next, you were on top of this kid and whaling on him."

"Yeah, I remember that the little bastard smacked the cone out of my hand. Then some idiot pulled me off of him just as I was getting some good licks in."

Charlie shook his head. "So I'm some idiot now, huh?" he feigned being upset.

"What?"

"I'm the one that pulled you off of him. And he wasn't little either. He wasn't as tall as me, but he was a big kid for his age. Which was at least two years more than you."

"I don't remember you being there. But then I don't remember much after he smacked the cone out of my hand."

"So I guess you don't remember taking a swing at me either. You were a little thing, but it was all I could do to keep a hold of you. One of your hands slipped free, and you swung at me."

"Charles Harper, you are making shit up."

"No, I'm not." he laughed. "And it doesn't surprise me you don't remember that. You were in a blind rage at that point—like a little Tasmanian devil. The boy was on the ground bleeding from his nose and mouth. You were screaming for me to let you go so you could beat the shit out of him more. I came close to doing it, too, just to see what you would do, but the kid got up and ran off."

"Yeah, and all the other kids started yelling at me, telling me to go home."

"That's because we knew he had run home to go get his parents. And we weren't yelling at you. It's just that you wouldn't listen to us. Those two little ragamuffins that lived next door to you grabbed you and took you home."

"Now that I remember. That was my best friend at the time, Jayne, and her brother, Tony. They hid me in their house for, I don't know how long. We thought for sure someone would be coming to tell my mom what I did. Their mom found me when she came to get them for dinner or

65

something. They told her what happened, and she cleaned me up then sent me home. My mom was so stoned she didn't even know I was gone. And I guess no one ever came to the house. Shit. Sorry. I know I wasn't supposed to talk about her."

"We're not," he said and left it at that, so she did too. "No one came because we never ratted you out. Some big ass pro-wrestling-looking guy came out with the kid, asking who beat him up. We all pretended like we didn't know you."

"Really?"

"Of course. No one knew who the hell that boy was. You know how kids are. Our loyalty was to you." He saw her eyes glisten again as she sat back in her chair.

Alia had no Idea that she ever had friends who were that loyal to her. "I hated moving out of that neighborhood. After that, I never really could make any friends, not friends like that anyway. We bounced around so much. You're the only one I think I ever saw again. My Dad's house wasn't that far from your house but pretty much on the other side of town compared to where I had lived. I don't even know why you were always on that side of town anyway. Hanging out with us poor kids."

"It wasn't that far. The same school district, so I had friends over that way. And I used to ride my bike through the woods, which made it faster to get there." *Not to mention I had a good reason to ride over there every time I got a chance,* thought Charlie.

"Um, so yes, Ice cream." she laughed in hopes of dispelling the depressing mood she was sliding into.

And that was pretty much how the afternoon turned into evening. Just two good long-time friends, finally getting a chance to really get to know each other. They laughed, joked, and teased with an ease that was unlike anything they had ever experienced with anyone else before. Even Alia wasn't second-guessing his real intentions as much as she would with most people.

Charlie had always been the type to get along with just about anyone, so he had a lot of friends. Most people found him to be friendly, pleasant, and fair. Just an all-around great guy. Even those who didn't call him their friend knew him well by reputation. And the girls. They had flocked to him, lured in by his charm and good looks. Alia, though, was the only one of his friends who held a place in his heart. Something few people knew about.

On the other hand, Alia had struggled all her life to have friends. She had always tried to be friendly and never hurt anyone who wasn't asking for it. But nothing about her life made it easy to make or keep good friends. Most of that was because she and her mother had moved around so much. She seemed to almost always be the new kid. Alia had done the math once and figured that they had moved an average of two point five times a year between the ages of five and fifteen. One year, she even attended three different schools. Alia would no sooner make a friend or two when they would up and move again. Bullies targeted kids like her, and it didn't help that she had a fast temper because of things at home.

Then there was her mother. Trish had a knack for making scenes in public places, including school, at Alia's expense. After a while, Alia had given up even trying to make friends. Then one night, her father walked into a burning building and never came out alive. Her heart had been shattered, and she fell into a deep depression. Things only got worse from there. She was angry all the time. She'd take the dumbest dares that, to be fair, should have killed her on more than one occasion. Her life was spiraling out of control. She even ended up in a cell at the Union County Sheriff's office courtesy of Charlie's father.

Bored with the what's your favorite this and that type of questions, Alia found an app on her phone that provided random questions for occasions like this. Charlie agreed to give it a whirl, so she went first.

"Oh, here's a good one. If you could do something to your body, what would it be and why? That's easy. I have always wanted to dye my hair."

"Why, what's wrong with your hair?" In his opinion, nothing.

"It's not that there's anything wrong with it. It's just I always wanted to have the balls to make it some wild ass color."

"Like hot Pink?" he smiled

"Yes, like hot pink." She smiled back.

"So why haven't you? Plenty of girls do it. I don't see where it would take a set of balls."

"Okay, first of all, well, we can't talk about that. Let's just say I am not cool enough to pull something like that off."

In other words, her mother said she couldn't pull it off. He thought.

"And yes, it does take balls. You have no idea how brutal girls can be about shit like that."

"Alia, you have never struck me as someone who gives a damn what other girls may say or think."

"Well, that hasn't always been true. No one wants to be alone and not have friends, so I don't know. When you're someone like me, rocking the boat isn't always a great idea unless you want to be friendless forever. Once I had Crystal, I stopped caring so much."

"Someone like me. You say that like you're inferior in some way. You know those pretty girls all the other girls want to be so much like? Most of them are a mess and not worth trying to impress, let alone emulate." For just a moment, he thought he saw a flash of something in her eyes like his words stung just a bit.

"See, I'm not one of the pretty girls, you agree."

"You're right. You're not. You're beautiful," Charlie said, looking her right in the eyes.

No way he means that not in the way I want him to. He's just trying to be nice, so cool your jets.

"Real beauty is both inside and out. You're not just pretty; you have an amazing heart to go along with it."

"Thank you, but we already established that we don't know each other very well."

He shook his head. "I know enough. I have seen you rescue turtles out of the road. Stand up for the smaller kids when they get picked on, and you have never met a cat or a dog you didn't love and didn't love you back. Besides, your eyes tell the truth when you're not pissed off, of course."

She smiled. Alia knew precisely what he was talking about because she saw the same thing in his eyes, especially when he looked at her. *But that can't be. Boys like Charlie don't fall for girls like me. We are friend-zoned. He only says nice things because he's nice.* That last bit was not her voice.

"What about you?" she asked.

"Oh, I have amazing eyes," he joked.

"I meant your answer to the question. Not that you're wrong." *Oh my god, why did I just say that? Why the hell is it so easy to blurt things out like that when it comes to him? I know I will look back on this conversation later and want to die, yet I can't seem to keep my mouth shut.*

"Oh that, um yeah, I would have to say a tattoo."

Well, that is a surprise. "A tattoo? Really?"

"What, don't you think I have the balls to pull it off?" he teased.

Oh, please don't say anything stupid about his balls. Alia laughed, covering her face with her hands before her big mouth could get her in trouble. After she felt she could control herself, she lowered her hands and asked him what kind of tattoo.

"I'm not telling you; you'll just laugh."

"I'm already laughing, Charlie. You might as well just give it up. Besides, that's the rules."

"What rules?"

"The rules I just made up. Come on; I promise not to laugh. I mean, as long as it's not like a mermaid or some shit like that."

"No," he scoffed. " If I got one, it would be exceptional, something small, but somewhere I could see it when I needed to."

"Okay, I have to know. You have me intrigued now."

He looked down at the table, finding himself uncommonly shy to tell her while looking at her. "I would like to put the name of the person I love the most, whoever that may end up being, right here." he pointed to the inside of his right wrist. "That way, whenever she isn't around, and I'm having a bad day, I can just look at it." *Just four small letters.*

"Alright, I'm not going to laugh. But no, Charlie. A big rule with tattoos is you never want to put someone's name permanently on your body. What if you would break up? Then you'd have some ex's name to be reminded of. The next person you fall for may not be too thrilled about that."

"I know what you're saying, but I respectfully disagree, in my case anyway."

"Really, Charlie? Look, I know a guy that has the names of like six different women on his arm. Five of them are marked out with an x because laser removal is expensive and painful."

He shook his head and laughed. "I'm not just going to put any girl's name there. I'm talking someone special—someone I know I will always want to be with." *Someone I already know I'll always want to be with. Just have to be sure she feels the same way.*

"You really think there is someone out there like that?" Alia asked, getting serious.

"I know they are," he said with confidence. "Don't you?"

Alia thought for a few minutes, not taking her eyes off him. "I would like to think there is, hell, all girls do. It's just that the world we live in is so screwed up and filled with people that seem to take pleasure in hurting others, even those they are supposed to love." *I should know, I could write a whole book about it.*

"Even more of a reason to find that special connection. My parents did it. They may butt heads from time to time, but there is no doubt how much they care about each other," said Charlie.

"But what if you don't ever find that person or you do, and they don't feel the same way back. People fall in love and get their hearts broken all the time." *And some people have the dumb luck of falling for someone too good for them. Some people are so desperate for love that they mistake kindness and a good heart for it, knowing damn well they are just going to wind up in tears. Oh, what the hell am*

I even doing here? I should have just missed the test. Instead, I am here, with him torturing myself with thoughts I shouldn't be thinking.

"Then that wouldn't be the one, now would it?"

"But see, that's what I mean. How do you know it's that special kind of love? How do you know you won't spend your whole life looking, only never to find them?"

"I think you know you have the right person when you can't bear the thought of living in the world without them. When you would be willing to lay your own life down for theirs. I also believe that maybe it just takes time and patience. Like if maybe the other person just isn't ready to admit that they are worthy of that kind of love yet," he said, smiling at her. *Lucky for me, I'm a patient man, though it's getting harder to be one.*

Yeah, maybe if it's something like that. Or perhaps that person is ready, but she's just afraid to be wrong and get her heartbroken. He needs to stop looking at me like that. If he doesn't mean me, then he needs to stop. Say something, stop looking into his eyes and say something, anything. Too much more, and I think I'll burst into tears right in front of him.

"I have to say your parents do seem to be crazy about each other. I would have never thought of Sheriff Harper being a romantic. Still, those two can barely keep their hands off each other sometimes. It makes it very hard to study."

"Yes, it does...wait..what?" he said, sitting up a bit. "I'm sorry, but when have you seen my parents acting like that?"

"When I come over on Wednesdays before dinner to study for the academy."

Charlie cocked his head and looked at her like she was a bug. "You go over to my parents' house every Wednesday?" *She has to be wrong. I go over there every Wednesday for family dinner. What did they do, hide her in a closet?*

71

"Yes, Charlie. Since shortly after I turned eighteen. I thought you knew. That's the same night you have dinner there. How could you not know?"

Yes, good question. Charlie sat back in his chair, honestly taken aback by this revelation. He would have said he and his parents didn't have any secrets. At least not major ones like this, which was a major one.

"It's only been for a few months. We even go to the gun range on Sundays sometimes."

"You're shitting me?"

"They didn't tell you?"

"No, I had no idea. I take that back. I did see you leave the range a few times when he was there, and he said he was giving you some pointers, not that you needed them." He had said that she was a crackerjack shot that barely missed a target. Any gun she held was like an extension of her hand. "I don't understand. Why didn't you just stay for dinner?"

"I have work at the library late on Wednesdays. Charlie, I swear, I thought for sure you knew. I mean, we all agreed not to say anything to anyone else about it because, well, you know what would happen if a certain someone found out."

We had an agreement, too, he thought. *But this was different. It isn't like them to keep things from me.*

"You're upset. Please don't be upset with them, Charlie. I'm sure the only reason they didn't say anything was to .."

"Protect you," he interrupted. "And I'm not upset. I'm just surprised, that's all."

"I was thinking it was more to protect you. I mean, you are their son."

Yes, but I'm not the only one that is special to them. "No, they were definitely protecting you. If my parents didn't want me to know, they must have had a good reason." *And that was to keep us apart.* "Even if it was only your feelings, they were worried about protecting. Maybe they thought you would be embarrassed if I found out you were getting help. I don't know. But you have no reason to be."

"You sure you're not upset?' Because you kinda look upset." *And it feels like he is upset too. How is that?*

"I'm fine. But had I known you were there, I may have gotten off work early once in a while." *Which is precisely the reason why they didn't say anything.* "We haven't gotten to see much of each other since I graduated high school." *And they both know how much I've missed her. Maybe I am a little upset.*

"I just think your Dad didn't want me to be distracted." *And he would have been one big distraction.* "Even your mom didn't come into the dining room much while we were working."

"It was the same way when he worked with me before I went to the academy. But I imagine he has a bit more patience with you than he did me."

"Then I feel sorry for you because the last thing your father is is patient." They both laughed. "Okay, next question. Oh, I like this one. If you could be in a movie, what kind of movie would it be?"

Charlie wasn't sure if he was ready to leave that conversation yet, but for her sake, he relented. *It may be time to have a very serious chat with the folks when I get back home.* "Horror movie, hands down," he said after a moment's hesitation.

"I say the same. I want to either be a zombie or the final girl."

"Final girls don't get to have any fun," he laughed.

"Yeah, but they also don't get stabbed or have their heads hacked off while straddling their boyfriend."

"Okay, but if you're going to be in a horror movie, all the fun is in being a victim. The bloodier, the better."

"Hmm. I was figuring you were more of the psycho killer type."

"Really? You think I would make a good killer?" *That can't be a good sign.*

"Yes, you know one of those surprising kinds of killers where everyone thinks you're the good guy. Then bam, out of nowhere, it's revealed you were the killer all along. You have the perfect look for it. Cute enough to play the victim, but just moody enough to pull off being psycho."

She said I'm cute, well that's something. "That's nice to know that's how you think about me." He laughed, referring more to being cute than a killer. "Next question, please."

"Okay," she laughed and pushed the random question button. "Oh, I don't know if I should answer this one."

"Well, you have to ask it first."

"Okay, but if I go off on a tirade, just kick me under the chair. What makes you really angry?"

"Smartass girls." He joked

"Funny I was about to say, smart ass guys."

"Don't make me angry," he teased.

"Answer the question, Deputy."

"Alright, well, that's pretty easy."

Looking at her, she could see his eyes shift just a little, and a bit of the fun went out of them.

"Seeing the people I love get hurt or be hurt."

He looked at her with those penetrating green eyes of his.

"How about you? Or should I just assume it's your, well, you know who and leave it at that?"

"I think that goes without saying. However, I was thinking what gets me mad is seeing kids get hurt. You know, abused, bullied, stuff like that. It's the only thing about being a cop that worries me."

"Really, how's that?"

"I worry that if I see something like that, I may lose it and hurt someone."

"Well, that's good to know. The thing is, you're not alone in that. And we try to have each other's backs on those kinds of cases. The procedure is that we never go alone on domestic violence cases."

"Yeah, your father told me that. He also told me how he almost beat a father to death after the guy had shaken his baby so hard her little neck broke."

"Yeah, that was a bad time. He almost lost his job over that one." *He almost lost his mind over it as well. It just had to be a little baby girl.* "Okay, we need a better question because that was just fucking depressing."

"Agreed, sorry. Let's see, okay, the next one. Oh, this is probably not much better. What would you change about yourself if you could? Okay, god, where do I start?"

"You start nowhere; there's nothing about you that needs changing. In fact," Charlie grabbed her phone. "No more stupid questions like that. The world is too full of people worried about every little flaw they have and what others think of them. Alright, here is a good one. What makes you laugh the most? Same as the other one. Smartass girls," he said, looking right at her.

"Haha, hilarious, smart ass boy."

"I don't think that counts, but I'll allow it. Oh, this one you're not getting out of answering. What would you do on a perfect date?"

"You're full of shit. It does not say that."

"Yes, it does. Stop trying to get out of answering the question."

"Let me see it then." She grabbed for the phone, but Charlie held it up out of her reach. His arms were so long he didn't even have to rise from the chair to be well too high for her. "See? I knew it. You're full of shit Deputy, so give me the phone back."

"No, sorry, you're not getting it until you answer the question."

"I will forcibly take it from you if I have to."

"You could try, but I'm taller than you, so…".

Alia was about to jump up from her chair when the air around them suddenly changed. They both got quiet, feeling the change of the pressure around them.

"Pressure just dropped," he said, "and fast."

"Charlie…your arms," Alia pointed. The long dark hair on Charlie's arms had stood up. It was right then that both their phones started screaming a blaring alert.

Charlie jumped up, grabbing Alia and pushing her toward the bathroom. "It's a tornado. Run Alia, get in the bathtub now, go, I'm right behind you," he yelled as they were suddenly surrounded by the sound of what resembled a freight train.

She did as he said, and already she could hear the roaring sound getting louder.

Charlie grabbed some pillows and blankets then ran into the bathroom after her. Thankfully, this motel didn't have any bathroom windows, making it safer than the main room. Still, the noise was bearing down on them and getting louder by the second. And was it his imagination, or was the building around them almost vibrating? "Hurry, get in the tub."

Alia got in, and Charlie sat right behind her.

"Cross your legs, and I'll wrap mine around you," he shouted over the noise. As they did that, he covered them both the best he could with blankets and pillows. Those would be the only thing between them and flying debris if the roof gave way. Charlie then wrapped his arms around her. "Hold on as tight as you can, Alia. Whatever happens, I promise you I won't let go."

Alia held onto Charlie's arms as the noise above them got deafeningly loud, and everything around them vibrated. She wanted to scream as the pressure, and the noise got worse. Now, there was no doubt that the walls around them were shaking. Above them, the roof sounded as though it would break apart at any moment.

They both sat there holding each other for dear life, both wondering if this was how they were going to die and angry at how unfair that was. Yet, in the middle of it all, as Alia reflected on it later, she had a feeling of being safe and protected as she had never felt before. Charlie's long arms wrapped around her chest were muscular and strong. He held her tight as she did him as under them the tub vibrated.

The walls around them seemed to shake as the pressure and noise continued to rise. Just when they thought the noise couldn't get any louder without rupturing their ears, it suddenly abated. Around them, the walls and ceiling rattled a few more times and then stopped. The only sound left was a pattering of hard rain and hail on the roof. Alia relaxed her grip a bit, but Charlie still held fast to her.

"Just give it a minute or two. Let's make sure it's over." He said in her ear.

Alia had no problem with that because right then, the last thing she wanted to do was to let go of him. She felt as though she were sinking into his arms as they sat there waiting. On her back, she could feel his heart racing as her's galloped as well.

They waited a few more minutes, and when the noise didn't return, Charlie loosened his grip on her. "I'm going to take a look, make sure there's nothing out there to worry about." He took a corner of the blanket off and looked out, but the room was pitch dark. "Lights are off, of course. Just a second." Letting go of her, Charlie pulled his phone out of his front pants pocket where he had shoved it. Giving it a little shake, a light came on, and he looked again.

The towel rack had fallen off the wall, the little soaps and shampoos on the counter were now in the sink, but that was the extent of the damage. Beyond that, Charlie couldn't tell. He had closed the door behind them when they ran in. "It looks good so far, I'm gonna get up and take a lookout in the main room, but I want you to stay here, okay?"

Alia nodded but as soon as he started to get up, she tightened her grip on the one arm she still had. Her heart was hammering in her chest. She just couldn't bring herself to let go of him just yet.

Charlie sat back down and wrapped his other arm around her again. "It's okay. We're okay, but there could be other people that need help. We need to check to make sure everyone is alright too. I'll only leave you for a minute to check past the door. Then I'm coming back to get you. Alright?"

Alia nodded and was able to let go of him this time. "Be careful, Charlie."

"Of course," he said and kissed the back of her head. Charlie threw everything off of them, then untangling his long legs from hers, he got out of the tub. He opened the bathroom door carefully, expecting the worst, but when he shined the light around, there wasn't much to see. A few of the pictures on the wall fell off, as did the tower of soda cans they had made on the dresser. From outside, he heard people talking and saw someone had a light or two. Before checking it out, though, he went back for Alia. "Come on, it's fine in our room. Let's go check on everyone else. Can you get up?"

"Yeah," she said, getting up on shaky legs. Charlie helped her over the tub's rim, and they both went out to the main room. "It's almost like nothing even happened."

Outside was a different story. There were downed limbs, branches, and leaves everywhere. The hail had stopped, and the rain was tapering off. People were starting to come out of their rooms, some with crying children, some tearful themselves. One of their next-door neighbors held a rag to his head which was bleeding. Charlie ran to the back of his patrol car, grabbing a first aid kit and some flashlights.

Just then, the hotel manager came around the corner from the office, asking people if they were okay. He saw Charlie, still in his uniform, and ran right over. "Thank goodness you are still here. Please help. I want to be sure everybody is okay."

"That's just what we were about to do." He tossed a first aid kit and flashlight to Alia. She had thankfully seemed to be over her initial shell shock and attended to their bleeding neighbor. "Here, Alia, get started on him. We are going to go see how everyone else is doing."

"Okay. Send anyone hurt over here," she said as she went back to tending to the man's cuts.

"You sure you can handle taking care of the hurt people? No offense, but you're kind of young," said the manager.

Charlie pulled the manager after him. "She's fine. She's a certified first aid responder, she's got this." Charlie winked at her and smiled, then went off with the manager to check on the others.

How did he know that? Popped into Alia's head? No longer worried that they both would die, Alia went right into mother hen mode. She started to patch up the residents of the hotel that had been hurt by window glass, falling objects and falls in a rush to get to safety. Thankfully no one was hurt very badly. Even the guy that had sat at his window hoping to see the tornado didn't have any cuts that would need stitches.

"It was right over us, man," the guy said, reeking of weed. "It didn't form all the way, or our asses would be in Kansas by now. That was wild-ass shit, though. I got it all on my phone too."

"Yeah, well, maybe next time you might want to stay away from the windows," Alia told him. "You might not get so lucky again," she said, making a point of pulling a sliver of glass out of his face right next to his eye.

Charlie was about to help clean some of the glass from broken windows when a fire truck, its lights and siren blaring, showed up. He and the manager went to talk to them, assuring them that there wasn't any real emergency here, and they could go off and help some others.

The fireman informed them that only one power line was down, and a crew was already working on it. The lights should be back on soon.

After she was done dealing with the wounded, Alia joined some of the others in cleaning up glass and debris from the rooms and walkways.

Charlie and the manager checked over the hotel as best they could. Other than a few windows blown out, the motel itself seemed to have fared pretty well.

"I will have to have a crew come in the morning to do a better check, but I think it's safe for everyone to stay for the night...once the power is back on." And as if he summoned it, the power came back on right then. With the parking lot lights on, they could see that only a few cars had minor damage.

Over the next couple of hours, Charlie helped cut wood and board up broken windows. Alia helped clean up the parking lot and attended to more cuts and bruises she missed the first go around. By the time they were done, they were both dirty and tired. Everyone went back to their rooms, and the manager thanked them both for their help.

"No charge for the room deputy. I will reverse the charges on your card in the morning."

"You don't have to do that," said Charlie, and Alia agreed.

"But I will; it's the least I can do. The two of you were a big help tonight, and we lucked out. Things could have been much worse." They all agreed to that, and the manager returned to his meager apartment above the office.

Charlie put his things back in his patrol car and got out his extra uniform for the morning. The one he had on was covered in dirt, sawdust, and sweat. He came back to Alia at their door, smiling at her. "You did great tonight. My father was right. You're going to make a great cop."

She smiled back a little but only nodded her head.

"Hey, you alright?"

Alia nodded again and tried to smile more, but she fought the shakes. Now that the excitement was done and over, the adrenaline was leaving her. She was suddenly exhausted.

Charlie took her into his arms again. "Feel free to lose your shit now. You earned it."

She sighed heavily, shaking her head, then pushed him back with one of her hands. "Hoo Boy, you need a shower, you reek." She laughed.

He laughed too. "Yeah, we both could use a good hot shower and a long night's sleep." He walked her inside, tossing his uniform on the bed

"You go first. I'll clean the room up a bit," said Alia.

"No, you go first. You look exhausted. Besides, I'm going to call my parents and let them know we are okay. They will hear about this and worry if I don't."

"Alright, I'll be fast." She grabbed her overnight bag and went into the bathroom, where she plopped down on the toilet seat and began to shake. Looking at the tub, with the pillows and blankets still in it, made her shiver more. Alia wanted to run back into the room and into Charlie's arms again, but she didn't dare.

In the main room, Charlie sat down in one of the chairs for a bit, taking a few deep breaths. He felt he had done a satisfactory job hiding his own shakes from her, and now he couldn't control them anymore. The more he thought about how close they came to...well, he didn't want to think about that. *If, after waiting all this time, I had lost her when we were so close to this mess being over, I would have hated myself for the rest of my miserable life.* Getting himself under control, Charlie called his parents.

After the call, Charlie sat in a chair with his head hanging, absolutely exhausted by the adventures of the past two days.

Alia came out scrubbed clean and wearing a Rick and Morty tee with a pair of pajama bottoms. He was still sitting like that, not noticing she was now in the room. Worried, she asked if he was okay.

Charlie looked up and offered her the best smile he could manage.
Still, she could see the look of profound exhaustion in his eyes.

"Huh? Oh, yeah. Nothing a shower and some sleep won't fix. He sat up and rubbed a hand across his face, noticing he needed a shave as well.

"Well, it's all yours now. Go get in. I'll clean up the mess in here."

"Thank you." Charlie, feeling the soreness from sleeping in his patrol car and the after-storm work, grabbed his overnight bag and shuffled into the bathroom.

Alia cleaned their pizza mess, tossed empty soda cans in the trash, organized their things, and remade the bed. They had lucked out in the storm with their window not breaking, but several of the picture frames that fell were cracked. She put these in the closet along with Charlie's spare uniform for the next day. Before closing the closet, she reached out, touching the front of his uniform shirt and feeling butterflies of excitement that she told herself had nothing to do with him. *I'm just really looking forward to the day when I have one of these of my own.*

Yeah, sure, that's what it is. Said a voice that sounded like her friend Crystal.

With the room all cleaned, Alia put the covers on the bed down, rearranged the pillows, and got into bed. She pulled the current novel she was working on out of her day bag and read as she usually did before sleeping. Not that she managed it very well. Already her eyes felt gummy and were trying to close on her. When Charlie came out of the bathroom smelling of soap and aftershave, she snuck a peak and then pretended to read. Although at that point, she could barely see the words.

Charlie had changed into a white t-shirt with a pair of grey sweatpants from his academy days. His dark brown hair was slicked back, and his face was freshly shaved. He was unable to stand waiting until morning. Glancing at Alia on the bed, he noticed she had left plenty of room for him. Sighing to himself, he made a show of slowly putting his things away, grabbing a cold soda from the mini-fridge, even looking out the window at the night beyond. At last, Charlie approached 'his' side of the bed.

"I dried the tub out after my shower, so I just need a couple of pillows and a blanket, and I'll be fine," he said sheepishly. He wanted to just lay down right there next to Alia. The bed looked so comfortable. But he had his own voice in his head, and right now, that voice belonged to his mother.

Alia lowered her book. "What the heck are you talking about, Charlie?"

"I'm going to sleep in the tub," he said, grabbing two pillows. "It's that or the floor, and I'm fairly sure the tub is much cleaner." On the phone, his mother had once again gently reminded him that she had raised him to be a good man. The lure of the soft, warm bed was making it hard for him to remember that. Alia wasn't making it any easier either.

"You most certainly are not Charlie, don't be ridiculous. You're exhausted. You said it yourself that you need a good night's sleep. Now get your ass in this bed, and don't give me that look either. It's a big bed, and we are both adults. I think we can manage for one night. Unless, of course, you're afraid to catch cooties from me."

The look he gave her now said she should not be ridiculous herself.

"Am I so gross you can't stand the thought of sharing a bed with me?" she continued.

"Stop...you know...you know it has nothing to do with that."

"So, you do think I'm gross," she said, the start of a smile at the corner of her lips. Alia didn't need to hear the phone call to know his mother must have said something to him. She figured she might have to guilt him into sleeping in the bed.

"What? No, of course not...look, I'm too tired to do this right now."

"Exactly. So get your ass in the bed, Charles," she said, feigning sternness. With that, Alia went back to 'reading' her book. She watched from the corner of her eye as he stood there, barely steady on his feet.

At last, he nodded. "Okay, but I swear I'll be nothing less than a complete gentleman," as he had promised his mother he would be.

She rolled her eyes and tried hard not to laugh at him. "Whatever you need to do to make yourself feel better, Charlie, just get some sleep."

He nodded again, then got into the bed, putting the pillows back under his head. "For the record," he yawned, "I don't think you're gross. Far from it. It's that very fact that complicates matters, to begin with." Charlie rolled onto his side, facing her.

Alia smiled. Charlie, being Charlie again. "Oh Charlie, I could be a top ten model. I'm pretty sure as tired as we are, you could manage to keep yourself from ravaging me in the night. I'm more worried about your snoring keeping me awake," she teased.

"Personally, I think the top ten models are overrated. I'd take a girl I can have a decent conversation and a few laughs with over one any day," he said.

Alia put the book away and lay down on her side as well, facing Charlie. Now that they were here face to face, she wondered if making him sleep in the bed was the best idea. It's funny how sometimes you can know a person for so long and not really see them. It's not that she was blind to the fact that he was a very handsome young man; everyone knew that. But looking at him now was like really seeing him for the first time.

Here was a man who, after a long shift at work, drove her eight hours out of his way and then napped in his patrol car. That held on to her, promising not to let her go as a tornado came down over them. A man who just now was willing to spend the night in a bathtub, not because he didn't like her, but because he did. And that was a truth she had to admit to herself despite the voice of her mother in the back of her head screaming horrible things. Because laying here and looking into his eyes, she could see it. Even as tired as he was, she could see within his eyes the truth.

Charlie saw the same reflected in her own. Only hers was mixed with sadness and pain. He wanted nothing more than to reach out to her, to do whatever he could to take away that pained, sad look in her eyes. If he could be the one to take it away and leave behind only that one other thing, nothing would make him happier. However, tonight was not the night. This place was not the place. And for right now, they both needed sleep more than anything else.

"You know you never answered the question," he said with a smile.

"That's because there isn't an answer. Where the date takes place doesn't matter, it's the who that's important."

"I couldn't agree more." With one last smile, Charlie reached up for the light switch over the bed, clicked it, and plunged them into darkness. Laying back down, Charlie continued to look her way. Though he couldn't see her, he could feel her. "Good night, Alia," he whispered while already half asleep.

"Good night, Charlie," she whispered back, half asleep as well. Alia smiled to herself, smelling the clean goodness of him only two feet away, and faded off into sleep.

Alia and the girls ran through chamber after chamber of the cave system, squeezing through crevices barely large enough to allow them through. He was coming behind them; this they knew. How far behind they were not sure. Adding to the terror was the certainty that they were not just lost but perhaps going in circles. There was no time to stop, not a moment to try and get their bearings. They could hear the man behind them—the one who killed the others.

He had an advantage on the fleeing girls—he knew these caves. Every twist, turn, and crevice was etched into the sick fuck's brain. And he was relentless in his pursuit. The man didn't tire, didn't feel the wounds on his flesh given to him by a few of his victims who managed to fight back. He had no desire to rest, need to drink, or time to think.

The girls fumbled and fell; he strode and stood tall. The girls ran into cave walls and scraped their feet on rocks; he avoided all obstacles and ran faster. They panicked, and he roared in sick pleasure.

The girls came upon a larger chamber, one better lit. And air, they could feel air coming from somewhere, enough that it gave them pause, and that's when Alia saw him. Laying on the ground under a long, vented natural shaft was the crumpled body of a man. The man had on a blue shirt and dark blue pants. No, the man was wearing a police uniform. She could even see the radio handle attached to his shoulder and a gun in the holster on his hip.

The girls noticed Alia had stopped, and they screamed for her to run, to get out of there. One of the girls ran to her, grabbed Alia's arm, and tried to pull her along. But Alia snatched her hand back because there was something familiar about the man lying on the ground. It was hard to make out his face from where she was as it was covered partially by his wet, dark brown hair. Alia, no longer worried about the killer chasing them, approached the body. She was a few feet away when to her horror, she realized who it was that lay there motionless, covered in blood.

"No," she said, her dry throat only able to produce a sound barely louder than a whisper.

The girls screamed. "He's coming; he's coming, Alia leave him, he's dead, the monster is coming," they begged. She couldn't move; all she could do was stand and stare. *No, this can't be...it can't be.* "Charlie!!" she started to scream. "Charlie...no, not, Charlie!"

"Charlie!" Alia woke in the motel room bed, her arm reaching out, frantic to find Charlie in the dark, feeling nothing but the gulf-size bed. "Charlie...Charlie!"
Charlie grabbed her outstretched arm and pulled her into him. "Alia...hey...it's okay, I'm here...I'm here, calm down. It's alright. I'm right here."
Alia pushed him back, having to see him for herself, not trusting her ears. In the blackness of the room, she could just make out his features. It was enough to know that it was not only him but he wasn't covered in blood. She embraced him again, breathing heavy sighs of relief. "Oh my god...my god, that was so horrible."
"Yeah, I kind of got that feeling." He held her in his arms as she tried getting her breath back. "There you go, take a couple of deep breaths. You're okay."
"No, not me," she panted. "I mean, I was being chased by some...thing I don't know. Charlie...it was you. You were dead, I mean, I think you were. I couldn't tell. You were covered in blood and just laying there so still," she took a few more deep breaths.
"You're shaking all over. That must have been one hell of a nightmare."
She backed away from him a bit again.
"It felt so real. I haven't had a dream like that...I don't know if I ever had one quite like that."
"Yeah, well, that doesn't surprise me after the day we had. Here, let me get you a drink." Charlie went to the mini-fridge and got out some water for her.
Alia thanked him and then drank half of it. "I feel like my heart is going to run out of my chest. It was just so damn real, Charlie. I mean, you were lying there. You even had your uniform on. You were covered in blood, and you were

not moving. This man, or thing, chased us, but I didn't care. I had to find out if you were okay, but I was afraid to as well."

"You said us? Was someone with you?"

"Yeah, two girls. I don't even know who they were. Damn it, I'm so sorry. The last thing you need right now is losing more sleep because of me."

"Well, I'm pretty sure a horrible nightmare wasn't on your bingo card for tonight." He brushed back the hair from her face.

"Still, I'm sorry. I reached out to you but couldn't find you. I think that messed me up more than the dream. I swear if you tell me you went to sleep in that tub, after all, I'm going to kick your ass."

He laughed. "No, I was right here. I felt your fingers on my back and jumped a little. I thought it was a bug or something until you yelled for me."

Alia looked at him, and they both laughed. Then she collapsed into his arms once again, feeling tired beyond tired.

Charlie noticed that she was still shaking a bit. He held on to her, and after a while, the shakes stopped, her breathing was back to normal, and she yawned deeply. "Okay, come on, let's lay back down and try this sleeping thing again. What do you say?" Once again, he kissed her on the top of her head.

"I say I don't know if I can. My heart still feels like it's running a race with itself. I'm still a little freaked out to tell you the truth," but she also knew that Charlie needed sleep for the long drive back home. And he wouldn't if she wouldn't. "Can I ask you a favor, Charlie? I know it's going to sound silly, especially from someone that is supposed to be a cop in a few months."

"A cadet in training, actually," he teased. "But sure, whatever you need."

"If you could… hold me…just until I fall asleep. I know it sounds stupid. It's just…I just need to know you're here. That you're okay." She felt foolish to even ask. However, she knew that if they went back to sleep on their own sides of the bed, she wouldn't be able to sleep with that empty gulf between them. She had lost him once tonight and couldn't bear to lose him again.

Charlie earlier in the night had been willing to sleep in a bathtub because he felt that was the right thing to do. He promised to be no less than a gentleman because that was what his mother always taught him to be. His father had taught him that a man does what he needs to do to protect the ones he loves when they need him. And right now, he knew she needed him.

"Of course," he said. "I'll be right here for as long as you need me."

"Just till I fall asleep. If I wake up from another nightmare, I'll go sleep in the tub myself, I promise," she joked.

"The hell you will," he said, as they both lay back down, her back to him, and his arms tucked around her. Alia took his hand in hers and placed them both close to her chest, holding on to him as he held on to her.

Charlie lay there, Alia in his arms, spooned around her, as her breathing became more and more shallow. When he was sure she was asleep, he kissed the top of her head and closed his eyes, soon joining her in slumber as they were joined in the embrace.

Chapter 5
Flashback time

In January, less than a month before her twelfth birthday, Alia's father, Johnathan Cross, was diagnosed with terminal brain cancer. He was given less than six months to live. He told no one.

On her twelfth birthday that year, Johnathan threw Alia the biggest birthday bash she ever had. It was held in the town of Bedford's fire hall, where he was a volunteer. They both had a great time, and it was the first birthday party Alia ever had that people other than family showed up. Her mother had been furious at Johnathan for upstaging her, but he and Alia felt it was worth it.

A month later, on a cold March day, Johnathan was one of several firefighters responding to an extensive apartment fire on the edge of Union county. John went in, showed the way out to several people, and was never seen alive again.

Alia was devastated. No matter how many people told her how he had died a hero, could it even begin to make her feel better. Johnathan was buried with full honors. Alia rode in a car with her grandmother behind her father's hearse as they drove past scores of fire trucks, police cars, and crowds of people. At the cemetery, she stood graveside between her grandmother and Uncle, looking lost and forlorn.

Sheriff Harper had been there was even a pallbearer since having become a really good friend of Johnathan's over the years. He watched Alia as she stood there, grief etched on her face. It wasn't until the three bells tolled that she buried her head in her Uncle's side and cried. He noticed, too, that her mother wasn't there at all.

Shortly after the funeral, they all found out about the cancer. Trish seemed to take great joy in telling her daughter her father was no hero, just a coward who didn't want to die a horrible and painful death. Alia's grief turned into rage.

Even moving back to Union county didn't do anything to make her feel better. If nothing else, it only made it worse. Although her mother's job was closer to that side of the state, Alia felt her mother had moved back, after her father's death, out of spite. This only added to her anger.

That first summer back in Union county, Alia got a reputation for being fast to fight and even quicker to take on a dare. It didn't matter what it was or how crazy, she would do it.

One hot early summer day, Alia rode bikes with a group of kids. Charlie was with them as well. The kids all rode to the top of a hill used for sledding in the winter. In the shade of an apartment building, they rested. They had been talking about crazy stunts and tricks on their bikes when one of the boys dared them all to ride down the sledding hill from where they stood. From there, the sharp slope of the hill couldn't be seen, only the very bottom, which was pretty far off. Starting at the wall, it would be a blind run-up and a steep decline to the bottom. No one wanted to do it, claiming not wanting to damage their bike, it was too hot, and even that it was stupid.

Before anyone could stop her, Alia jumped on her bike and peddled like mad toward the hill.

Charlie was the first to holler after her. "Alia, don't do it. Shit, slow down; you're going too fast."

That only spurred her to go even faster.

They all watched as she neared the edge of the hill, not slowing a bit. First Charlie, then a few others dropped their bikes and ran after her. Everyone wanted to see if she would make it, while Charlie still yelled for her to stop.

"Damn it, Alia, stop!"

But it was too late. Over the hill and out of sight, she went. Then suddenly, they saw her bike flung up into the air. They were still only halfway to the edge of the hill when the bike went flying.

Charlie felt his heart drop so fast that he tripped and fell. The others made it to the edge as he was getting up, then hooting and hollering over they went. A moment later, he heard one of the girls scream.

"Oh my God…she's bleeding. Her throat is cut open!"

Feeling like his world was crashing down around him, Charlie ran for the hill, over the edge, down the steep slope, and came to a sliding stop next to Alia. Amazingly, she was sitting up and laughing.

Alia looked at her hand, covered in something reddish and wet. "It's not blood," she laughed. "It's just clay and mud." Laughing the whole time, she wiped at her neck again and showed them her mud-covered hand.

"Are you hurt, are you hurt at all?" Charlie asked. Wiping more mud from her neck, he saw only minor scratches. He looked in her eyes and saw the most maniacal glee to match the mad smile on her face. Yet still, Charlie could see there was pain as well.

"I'm fine, I'm fine, that was awesome. I should try it again," Alia laughed.

"Absolutely not," Charlie scolded her.

"That was epic," said one of the boys.

Charlie wanted to punch that kid but focused on ensuring Alia was okay.

The kids all gathered around, clapping her on the back, saying how cool that was, asking what happened, a few even asking if she was alright. Behind them on the hill was a large, oval, worn spot created while kids were sledding the winter before. Water had collected in it as well, so it was muddy.

"By the time I saw the hole, it was too late to stop. I flew right over the handlebars, must have scraped my neck on the tire. That was fun."

Charlie looked at her like she had lost her mind. "Are you sure you're not hurt?"

Alia reached up with her clean hand and touched the top of her head. "I think I got a bump." She smiled at him.

Charlie felt her head, and she winced. Sure enough, she had a nice little goose egg bump on the top of her head where she must have hit the ground. He was going to look for more when one of the boys called out to her.

"Dude, your bike tire is trashed."

Before Charlie could stop her, Alia jumped up and slid down the rest of the hill to where her bike landed. The front tire and rim were indeed toast, bent beyond repair.

"No, no, no, no, damn it," she cursed.

Charlie joined her and took a look. "The rest of it seems fine, but you'll need a whole new tire."

Alia just sat down next to the bike, shaking her head. There was no way her mother would get her a new tire. The bike had been a gift from her father, and Trish hated him for it.

Charlie looked at her and saw tears welling up in her eyes. "Hey, the rest of you should just go to the park, like we planned. I'll catch up later."

"You're not coming, Charlie?" Asked the girl that had screamed.

"I'll be there. I'm just going to help Alia get her bike home." What he wanted was for them to leave in case those tears fell. He knew she didn't like to cry in front of people. If she did, she would just get mad, and her anger had a way of getting way out of control since her dad died.

The kids all said they would see them later, then trudged back up the hill to collect their bikes. One of the boys brought Charlie's bike to the hill's edge for him.

When they were alone, Charlie helped Alia to her feet, then picked up her bike and carried it back up the hill.

All her laughter and joy were now gone as she slowly walked up behind him.

"You think your mom will get you a new tire?" He asked, already pretty sure he knew the answer.

Alia just gave him a disgusted look. "She's liable to throw the whole bike away."

"Really? It's still pretty much new."

"I got it for my birthday in February. My dad got it for me." Alia turned away from Charlie. "She hated him for throwing me a huge birthday party. So yeah, she would throw it away if she knew it was busted," her voice wavered.

Charlie took his time to gather both bikes, giving her a chance to recover. When she turned back, he let her take the handlebars, helped her hop it on the back tire, and walked with her towards her apartment in the same complex.

They walked in silence for a few minutes, then she turned to him. "You know you shouldn't follow me home, Charlie. If my mom sees me hanging out with the sheriff's kid again, a busted bike will be the least of my trouble."

"I know. I won't go far enough for her to see us. I just want to make sure you're okay."

"I'm fine. My head hurts a little, but it's not so bad."

They walked for a while, then he looked at her. "Why did you do it?"

"Why not? It seemed like a cool idea, and I bet I would have made it too if it hadn't been for that hole."

"You could have gotten hurt. I mean very hurt."

"So," Alia said, shrugging her shoulders.

Charlie stopped and held out his hand to stop her. "So? What kind of stupid answer is that?" He hadn't meant his tone to sound so angry, but what she said scared him.

"The kind I have, Charles. What's it to you, anyway?" She walked a few more feet ahead of him.

"Well, maybe I don't want to see you get hurt."

"Well, maybe you should just back the fuck off, Charles." Alia stopped and turned to face him again. "No one asked you to hang around anyway. What are you like, sixteen now? Shouldn't you be driving around, taking your girlfriend out, or something instead of hanging around a bunch of kids?"

Charlie tried not to be hurt by what she was saying. He knew she was still upset over her father dying. He couldn't imagine how he would feel if something happened to his dad, but Charlie was pretty sure he would be mad at the whole world, just like she was. "I'm only fifteen. My birthday isn't until December. Besides, I don't know if you noticed, but all those guys were around my age. You were the youngest one there. Which is another thing. You should be with kids your own age. Those guys aren't so bad, but some of the older kids I have seen you hanging with since you've been back are bad news, Alia. They would be more than happy to get you into trouble and then bail."

"What are you, Charles, a cop like your daddy? Let's get this straight right now. I will do whatever and hang out with whoever the hell I want. I don't need your help; I can take care of myself. Now go away before you get me into trouble."

Charlie watched as Alia wheeled off with her bike, angry. "Alia, I'm sorry, don't be mad at me."

She turned around long enough to flip him off and then stormed away.

He should have been mad but couldn't help but laugh to himself. *Little spitfire.* He thought. Charlie stood there watching until she went around one of the buildings. Getting on his bike, he rode home, no longer feeling like hanging out with the others.

The following day, Alia was having a bowl of cereal on their beat-up living room couch, watching a beat-up old square TV, when she heard a knock on the door. She panicked then realized her mother was working the day shift, so she was at work and not asleep. Alia opened the door with the security chain in place, but no one was there. Instead, something was leaning against the door. Closing the door again, she took off the chain and opened it all the way. A brand new bike tire fell into the hallway. Alia picked it up, looking it over. Then she dropped it right back on the floor, ran out her door, down the stairs, and out the heavy wooden door to the building. Alia looked around, but no one was there. Even when she went to the end of the building, she saw no one.

    Back at the apartment, Alia picked up the tire again. There wasn't a note or anything, but she was sure it had been Charlie that left it there. No one else knew or even gave a shit enough. Luckily she had managed to put her bike up in her room without her mother noticing it was busted. So as much as she was tempted to take the tire back (maybe throw it at him for good measure), she didn't see any harm in keeping it.

    After Alia changed the tire out, she took the old one to the dumpster and shoved it as far down in as she could. Her mother never took the trash out, but she was being cautious just in case.

    Alia didn't leave the apartment complex with the bike for a few days, not wanting Charlie to see her riding it and gloat. But by the next week, she rode around town telling herself she wasn't looking for him. Alia found a few of the boys he hung with but not him. Since she couldn't very well ask anyone, she gave up and went home.

    After that, Alai didn't see Charlie much. She continued to hang around the older kids, the good and the bad but no Charlie. One night she hid in her closet, crying and hating herself. She had finally driven away everyone and anyone that ever cared about her. And her anger grew.

To say that year was bad wouldn't even begin to give it justice. Making a point of hanging around kids Charlie had warned her about, Alia found out time and time again just how right he was about them. They had no problem daring her to do things she wasn't ready for yet. Like jumping the very high ledge into the water quarry. That time she had almost drowned and was only saved because a young couple was picnicking on the rocks nearby. The guy jumped in, pulling her up and out just as she had reached the point of exhaustion. Alia knew she wouldn't have been able to come back up again on her own.

There were more bike tricks, stunts on skateboards, and fights than she could count. Hardly a day went by when she didn't come home bleeding and bruised. And despite working the day shift, her mother hardly seemed to notice. There was a new boyfriend she was spending her time with. The only time she even talked to Alia was to tell her about the boyfriend or criticize her.

The guy was one big pile of gross. He had long hair, a long shaggy beard, smoked weed all the time, and never seemed to bathe. To top it off, when her mother would pass out early, he tried to come visit her in her room as others had. On the third night he tried, Alia pulled a hunting knife on him she had managed to shoplift from the flea market in town. He didn't bother to try again after that.

By the time school started, he was gone, and her mother was crooning over some new guy she met at the bar. Now her mother was home even less, spending most of her time off work at the bar where the new guy played pool. Alia was left home alone most weekends and evenings except for Sunday nights. That she didn't mind at all. The only real downside was the endless TV dinners because her mother didn't trust her to cook alone yet. That lasted only a few weeks before Alia experimented with a few meals. She cut her fingers and burned herself a few times for her trouble. Not that she cared.

When school started, it was hell. She had no friends. Mostly because her response to their smiles was her middle finger. All her classes were boring, and she was failing most of them. When her mother got her first report card, Trish had forgotten the no marks rule. She beat Alia with a wooden spoon, so bad Trish had to call in sick for her for the rest of the school week.

She also marched Alia to each of their neighbors, telling them they were to call Trish if they saw her outside other than going to school. So Alia spent the winter inside, holed up in her room reading. And her anger grew.

By spring Alia's grades were up enough that she was allowed to be outside again. A new family had moved into the building with the two little kids. Tommy was seven, and his little sister Julie was five. The two of them latched onto Alia and adored her right away. She even made a few dollars watching them once in a while. It became clear to Alia that the parents were not parent of the year material any more than her own mother was. They always went to the gym for hours, leaving the two home and outside alone. So Alia made a point of keeping an eye on them even when she wasn't being paid to.

One day in early April, the two of them came to Alia, the little girl crying. The story they had to tell was horrifying. And once again, her anger grew. Two days later, with a cut to her lip and a few bruises forming, Alia sat in Sheriff Harper's office while he glared down at her, his arms crossed.

Alia sat up in the metal chair, her arms crossed as well, glaring back at him. "If you're going to arrest me, then do it. I'm not in the mood for a lecture today." In the past year, Alia had suffered through more than a few of his stern-faced lectures.

There was the time he caught her smoking weed behind the Walmart. There had been others there as well (those kids Charlie warned her about), but they had run off. Alia, the smallest, was also the slowest, so she got caught. If he had told her he was disappointed in her once, he had said it at least twenty times.

Then there was the time he picked her up for shoplifting. Only she hadn't taken anything. One of the others had shoved a pack of cigarettes down her shirt, and they got busted walking out. Alia was back in his office a few hours after being let go, this time for beating the hell out of the kid.

There were fights he had to pull her away from and even found her hanging out with a bunch of high school kids at a keg party. Each and every time Harper had read her the riot act, then had one of his officers drop her off at home as discreetly as possible. His only saving grace was that he had never told her mother about any of it.

But now she had done something he couldn't very well just look away from, and a teen boy lay in a hospital bed there in town.

Sheriff Atticus Harper (Harper to everyone since his high school football days) was a giant mountain of a man. He stood over six feet tall, had big meaty arms, a receding hairline, and a low brow that almost hid his eyes when he was angry. To Alia, it seemed like he was always angry.

"Fine," he said. "Okay fine." Harper got up, walked over to the small single cell in his office, once a part of the original Sheriff's building, and opened the door. "Get in," He growled at her.

Alia sat, arms still crossed, and if looks could kill, Harper would have been struggling on the floor.

"Get in!" He barked.

Alia jumped up, marched defiantly into the cell, and dropped herself forcefully on the cot. "Not even going to read me my rights?" She sneered up at him.

Harper pointed a finger at her, trying hard to control his temper. "Oh, I'll read you something alright, missy." He walked away, mumbling to himself. Back at his desk, he pretended to do paperwork, but he could see her glaring at him from the cell.

About an hour later, his wife Ellen arrived with a picnic basket with the most amazing smells. As large as Harper was, his wife was the opposite. She was petite, not much taller than Alia, with Charlie's green eyes and the kindest disposition of anyone Alia knew.

Ellen looked over and saw Alia in the cell, still with her arms crossed but now glaring at the wall. She put the

97

basket down on the desk. "Oh, Harper. You didn't have to put her in the cell, did you?"

He looked up at her scolding eyes, then dropped his. "She asked for it." He mumbled

Ellen stood across from him, her arms folded over her chest.

"What do you want me to do, Ellen? She put a kid in the Hospital, for Christ's sake."

"She would do it again too." Said Alia from the cell

"Pipe down in there, young lady. You're in enough trouble as it is; try to remember that." Barked Harper

"Try to remember I don't give a shit," Alia retorted.

"Okay, the both of you stop," said Ellen.

Alia mumbled under her breath.

"You too." She scolded Alia.

Alia looked away with tears in her eyes. For some reason, this woman, Charlie's mother scolding her, hurt.

"Honestly, Harper, she's just…". Ellen leaned in closer. "Can't you see you're just making things worse? She has the same kind of temper you do, and the two of you butting heads isn't going to fix this mess." Leaning closer, she whispered into his ear. "Remember the promise that we made, Harper." Ellen stepped back and talked at a normal volume. "Besides, as far as the boy goes, he's what, three, four years older than her and a whole foot or so taller? Maybe the question that needs to be asked is why she was fighting with him, to begin with."

In her cell, Alia nodded but still refused to look at them.

"It's what she does, Ellen. It's what she's been doing ever since…."

With her eyes, Elen warned him not to finish what he was saying.

"I have to do something, Ellen, or this won't be the last time she sees the inside of a cell. It's not like this is the first time she's been in trouble. I have had her in here more times than I can count this year, you know that." Harper got up and approached his wife. "Our promise is the reason why she is sitting in an unlocked cell instead of being booked and put into a real one downstairs. I'm hoping if I put a little scare in her, she'll tell me what is going on because so far she has refused." He said low enough that Alia wouldn't hear.

"But you're not scaring her, Harper; you're just pissing her off more. You know, as I do, she wasn't like this until after her father died. Right now, she needs that soft, tender side of you that very few people know exists. Before we lose her for good." Ellen looked at him pleadingly, tears in her eyes.

"Yeah, well, I'm pissed off too."

"Why?"

"Well, she's...she's...she's just so damn stubborn." He said loud enough for Alia's benefit.

"And she's not the only one. As I said, the two of you are a lot alike. Now I'm going to go, but you need to let her out to eat lunch. Then maybe when you both have calmed down enough, you can talk about this instead of yelling." Ellen walked over to the cell, where Alia stared at the wall like she was mad at it. It broke her heart seeing the girl so upset and knowing she couldn't do anything to help. "Alia dear, please try to eat something. I made Charlie's favorite; it's fried chicken. He said it always makes him feel better, so he hopes it'll make you feel better too."

At the mention of Charlie's name, the tears Alia had been holding back fell. She hadn't seen him in so long and didn't realize till then just how much she had missed him.

Ellen saw the girl's tears, and it hurt her heart so much she wanted to go to her. But as angry as she was, Ellen knew Alia would only resent her for it. Instead, she turned away and left.

After putting the food out for them, Harper opened the cell and motioned for Alia to come out.

Having wiped her tears away and smelling the chicken, Alia left the cell but scowled up at him. "I'm only eating because I am hungry, I'm still mad, and I refuse to talk to you."

"Suit yourself, kid. I don't really want to talk to you right now either."

Sitting as far away from him as she could manage, Alia opened up the Tupperware container. The most heavenly smell wafted out. There was chicken, rice, string beans, and even a dinner roll. Alia hadn't eaten food so good since the holidays. And Charlie was right; it did make her feel better.

When they were done with lunch, one of the Deputies came into the room and whispered to Harper. When he left, Harper sat back in his chair, looking at her.

Alia kept her eyes down, busying herself with peeling the label off a water bottle.

"When I picked you up, why didn't you tell me that boy Chase had touched a little five-year-old girl inappropriately?" That wasn't the extent of what he had done, but Harper wasn't about to go into details. He was sure she knew anyway.

Alia scoffed. "I'm no snitch." the kids she hung around made sure of that. Snitches get Stitches, they often said. Not that Alia was a stranger to keeping secrets. "Besides, it's not like anyone would believe me anyway. Chase is one of you. No one takes our side over that of those rich assholes, so I took care of it. I doubt he'll be touching any little kids again." *And it felt good.* Usually, hurting anyone, even those that deserved it, made her feel bad. But not this time. She could still feel the wooden bat in her hands and would gladly beat him again if he was in front of her.

"Chase Winter's one of us?" Harper laughed. "No, sorry dear, I am far from Chase Winter's rich."

"You know what I mean, everyone knows the rich get away with shit like this all the time. All daddy has to do is make a little 'donation' to the Sheriff's office. You get a few new patrol cars, and that little shit Chase gets off scot-free."

"Oh, so now you think I am a dirty cop?" He crossed his arms again.

Alia gave him a well yeah, look.

"Well, despite what bullshit Trish has filled your head with, I'm not. I run a clean department. And I don't care how much money Chase Winter's daddy has. It doesn't matter shit to me. The only thing I care about right now is the truth and you."

"No one gives a shit about me." Alia scoffed.

"You may want to rethink that while the taste of chicken is still in your mouth. Also, you may not know it, but your father and I were good friends." he saw her hands tighten on the water bottle and even felt her mood change.

"I don't want to…."

"I know you don't want to talk about him." She never did. Harper felt that was part of her problem. " And we won't. I'm just trying to tell you I'm not the enemy here." Harper came from around the desk, moved a chair right in front of her, and sat down. He took the water bottle, now half-crushed, out of her hands and held them. Feeling them tremble, he held them firm but gentle.

Alia couldn't help but be reminded again of Charlie, and it hurt her heart like real physical pain.

"If you had come to me with this, I would have believed you. Then it would be Chase in a cell and not you."

Alia shook her head no refusing to look anywhere other than her lap.

"Why not?"

"Because I know what they do to little girls to prove they have been raped. She didn't deserve to be a victim twice," Alia said, her head down and on the verge of tears again.

Harper put her hands down then leaned back in his chair, looking at her, his heartbreaking for her. Of course, she would know what that was like. And he too knew what it felt like to give out justice due, the old-fashioned way. "You know if you work on that temper of yours, you could make an excellent cop one day."

Alia laughed and shook her head. "Oh, you sure are one to lecture me about tempers."

Harper laughed, "Honey, this is after working on my temper." He got up and went to the door of his office. "I'll be back in a few minutes. We're not done here. Don't burn the place down or anything."

While he was gone, Alia looked at Harper's desk and saw a few picture frames. One of them was a recent picture of Charlie, a school photo. She picked it up to look at it closer. He was smiling, but unlike when she had seen him in person, his eyes were not smiling. They looked almost a little sad. That made her feel not only sad as well but drained the anger right out of her. Why she couldn't say. When Harper came back into the office, she still held the photo.

"That's from this year," he said. "Charlie's a sophomore now. If you and your mother don't run off again, you'll be a freshman in the same high school during his senior year."

Alia didn't say anything, just stared at the photo.

"I know you two used to play together a lot when you would come to see your father."

Alia nodded. "I haven't seen him for a while, though."

"Yeah, well, he doesn't exactly hang around the type of kids you have been with lately. Besides, he's been busy with school. He wants to be a cop too, so he's been working really hard."

"He'll make a good cop. He's always been good at keeping kids from fighting, always the voice of reason. Sometimes annoyingly." she thought back to their last conversation and her heartfelt sick.

Harper took the photo from her and put it back on his desk. With a finger, he tilted her chin up. He didn't fail to notice the tears in her eyes. *Poor kid looks like she lost her best friend.* "Chase Winters is right now being handcuffed to his hospital bed and being charged with lewd and lascivious acts against a minor. He will also be charged with assault of a minor because it seems that several witnesses recall him making the first punch. The little girl's parents have come forward to press charges; their son was a witness. Since you cleaned her up after, there won't be any rape kit. And she won't see the inside of a courtroom either. If the Winters have enough sense, neither will the little boy. As for you, there won't be any charges. The Winter's lawyers have advised them not to pursue any, and I won't either because that would make me a hypocrite." Sitting back down and

102

retaking her hands, Harper dug in deep for that gentleness his wife talked about earlier. "Alia, I know things have been hard for you, and I know this past year has been tough. Your father was a good man. He was a hero, and he was a good friend that I miss dearly every day. I can't even begin to imagine the hurt and pain you feel. Because he was my friend, I know these things you have been doing would've broken his heart."

Alia hung her head, tears dripping from her face. She wanted nothing more than to run out of there away from this man and the horrible truths she needed to hear. But she had been running since the day her father died, and she was exhausted. The thought of all the years Alia had ahead of her, years with her mother, drunk boyfriends, moving from place to place. Years without her father, not even Charlie to look forward to playing with anymore, was just unbearable. The only running Alia felt up to doing anymore was straight into rush hour traffic. The thought of living any longer with all the pain was more than she could stand.

"He wouldn't want you to live like this, Alia. He wouldn't want you to hurt so much."

"Then he should have stayed, but he didn't...." She looked up at him, her chin trembling and tears running from her eyes. "He walked into that place and never even said goodbye. He left me alone with her."

Harper looked at her and could see just how tired she was. *The poor kid won't be able to hold on much longer at this rate. One day the call I get about her won't have her end up in a jail cell; it'll have her end up in a coffin.* "He was going to die anyway, Alia, you know that. He wanted to go out his way."

"But we could have had more time together." she sobbed, "Even if it was just a little."

"No, sweetie, he would have been very sick. He didn't want you to have to see him that way. Johnathan wanted you to remember him as the hero you always looked up to. You have to let him go, Alia. You have to let go of the pain, or it's going to eat you from the inside out no different than his cancer would have eaten him. That's the last thing he would have ever wanted for you." *It's the last thing I want for you.*

"I'm just so tired." she sobbed, shaking.

Harper took her into his arms, something he hadn't done since she was so much smaller, and held her tight. "I know, baby girl, I know, but I promise you it will get better. There are people here that love you more than you may ever realize."

Eventually, Chase Winter's ended up going to prison after pleading guilty. His family, torn apart by what he did, moved far from Union county.

A week before school ended, Alia and her mom moved yet again into a shoddy trailer park closer to town. One morning, Alia was walking to the convenience store in front of the trailer park to get milk when a red pickup truck passed by. The driver, a much welcomed familiar face, waved as he went past. It was the first time in a long time she had seen Charlie, and even though she knew he didn't dare stop, it made her day. It brought a rare smile to her face that even her mother took notice of when she had returned home. Trish made some snarky comment about Alia getting out of the shitty emo mood she'd been in, but Alia didn't even notice.

On her last school day in the seventh grade, the guidance counselor called her into the office. Alia had been chosen to receive a scholarship to attend a summer camp in the mountains. There was even a small suitcase on wheels and some items she would need for camp provided. The counselor had been disappointed that Alia wasn't more excited. Other than the rare glimpses of Charlie about town, nothing much made her happy. Not even the thought of a summer spent in the trees and mountains she loved. Alia figured her mother would say no anyway, so she was surprised when Trish had agreed to let Alia go.

"That will give me more time to work on that stud Billy Margie introduced me to ." she had said, signing the permission papers. "You, kid, are a cock blocker. Nothing scares a good man off more than a moody ass brat hanging around."

Alia had to admit that getting away from her mother for a while did make her a little happy. However, the bus ride up there put her into a sour mood once again. Until then, she hadn't known that this summer camp was one of those well-off ones most of the rich kids in town went to, the kind that had tennis courts and horses. Not to mention loads of loud, vacuous rich girls that talked about nothing but their hair, make-up, and trips to Hawaii when camp was done.

Even her nice new suitcase wasn't enough to make her feel like she fit in. By the time the bus rolled into the camp, she was ready to go back home, even if it meant listening to her mother talk about Billy all summer. Then she stepped off the bus and walked smack into the most incredible smile and pair of green eyes she had seen in her life.

"Charlie? What are you doing here?" And like magic, all the anger was gone. Looking at him, she noticed he had gone through a pretty good growth spurt. Charlie had always been a skinny kid, but now his arms and legs were looking not just long but muscular as well. Alia felt her heart flip at the sight of him but tamped her feelings for him way down deep like she always had.

"I'm a counselor here this year," he said, beaming at her.

"And why is it you don't seem surprised to see me?" she asked.

"Well, part of my job as a counselor is to know who is here, especially the new kids. I thought maybe a familiar face might make you feel more at home, so I found out what bus you would be coming in on."

Alia thought back to their last conversation. Worse, she thought back to the past year and all the trouble she had managed to get into that he warned her about. "Charlie...I never got to say...I mean, what I said to you that day I wrecked my bike on the sledding hill."

"It's okay."

His eyes smiled, but she saw a hint of sadness in them too. *He's disappointed in me, I can tell. But he's too much of a nice guy to bring up all the bad shit.* "No, it's not. I felt terrible about that. And I know that it was you that got me the tire, even after what I said."

Charlie looked her right in the eyes and smiled. "Alia, it's okay. It really is. Just tell me one thing."

"What's that?"

"Did the chicken make you feel better?"

Alia laughed and rolled her eyes. "Yes, actually it did. Since my mother isn't around, I can say it was the best I have ever had."

"I knew it," he said, beaming even more. "Come on, I'll show you to registration, then I have to get with my group and get them settled in. Welcome to camp, Alia."

Two nights later, Alia was deep into the trees on the edge of the camp nestled into a hidey-hole she had found. She was trying her best to read a book by book light. For the most part, she was still steaming about what the girls in her cabin had said to her. Spoiled little rich brats that they were. Somehow they found out she was only there because of a scholarship and just thought that was hilarious.

"So just how poor are you?" they asked in their snotty little shits way they have of talking.

Alia had gotten so pissed off that she grabbed her book and surprised herself by not bashing the face of the nearest girl with it. Instead, she ran off into the woods and found this nice dark corner of it to hide in. She would demand to go home in the morning, even if she had to fake being sick.

Alia was still fuming about the girls when she heard the sound of twigs snapping as someone walked in the woods around her. *Oh great, they found me...how in the hell could they have possibly followed me?* But when the leaves of the overhanging willow tree parted, it was not the girls she saw but Charlie.

"There you are," he said. Uninvited, he came in and sat across from her. "Nice little spot you have here. I almost didn't find you."

"And how in the hell did you? Why were you even looking for that matter?"

"Well, because when we did cabin checks to make sure everyone was in for the night, you were gone. I told them I had an idea where you were. As for how…hmm, I guess my Spidey senses must have been tingling." he joked.

"No, really, how did you find me?"

"Honestly, I don't know. I figured you were in the woods. I think I could just sense your anger."

"My anger?"

"Yes, that thing coming off you right now in waves. So what happened? It's only been two days. You can't possibly hate this place that much already."

"It's not the place."

"A person then, not surprised. So who is it."

Alia shook her head

"I can't help if I don't know what's going on."

"You can't help anyway, Charlie."

"Why not?"

"Because the problem is I don't belong here. Even if those little skanks didn't find out I had a scholarship, it's obvious I'm not one of them. Why the hell would they put me in a cabin full of brainless blond rich brats? I have no idea. I also have no idea why someone thought sending me to this camp was a good idea. I just want to go home. A summer sweltering in a trailer park is still better than this crap."

"Are you done?" he asked, sounding a little irritated.

"Don't be a smart-ass, Charlie, please; I've had enough of that for one night."

"Okay, I apologize. Do you know what your problem is?"

"Of course, I'm wrong. I'm always wrong. You're going to tell me you know those girls and butter wouldn't melt in their mouths, right?"

"Wrong, your problem is your right. You don't belong with those girls. Even if you got here on your own, they wouldn't accept you."

"Gee, thanks, Charles. You're making me feel so much better, jerk." she smacked him on his knee.

"Now take that back." he grinned at her.

"Why did it hurt your feelings?"

"Yes, you did, now what do you say? "he smirked at her.

Alia crossed her arms and shook her head.

"Say you're sorry."

"I'm sorry…you're such a bitch, Charlie," she said, and they both laughed.

"Yeah, I may be a bitch, but at least I can always put a smile on your face. Now, if you are done being mean to me, I'll show you something. Something I am sure will keep you from wanting to wander alone in the woods to read."

"If you're talking about this place's sorry excuse for a library, too late, I have seen it, and it's pathetic."

"Pathetic? Really? And here I thought you liked books."

"I do. Good books. King, Koonts, Saul, Brown, but most of the books here on my reading level are romance novels, which hardly qualifies them as books, to begin with."

"Okay, no romance novels, duly noted. Alia hates romance."

"No, Alia hates cheesy, desperate, lonely women hooks up with a beefy hot guy on the beach fake ass shit. It's like porn only more unrealistic."

Charlie laughed at that, then pointed at her book. "Says the girl reading a book about ghosts and ghouls."

"Still more believable than that crap."

"Okay, okay, I give. It's not the library anyway."

"Then what is it?"

"I guess you're going to have to come with me and find out."

"I don't know if I'm in the mood."

"Come on, have I ever steered you wrong? Just come with me." Charlie got up and pulled Alia up as well, leading her out of the willow tree, out of the woods, and back into camp. They went to the far end of camp at the line of the woods again when he stopped in front of an older-looking bunkhouse. Inside was a warm, inviting glow as well as chatter and laughter.

"What's this?"

"This is the only unisex bunkhouse in the whole camp. It is also the oldest bunkhouse in the camp. A few years ago, it was supposed to be torn down, but a group of campers fixed it up using spare materials from when the new cabins were built and turned it into a clubhouse of sorts. Later they got permission to use it as their bunkhouse."

"So what makes you think these kids will be any different than the last mess I was left with."

"You'll see, I have a feeling you will fit right in with this group. Come on, the one girl is the sister of my best friend. Her name is Crystal; you're gonna love her."

Alia highly doubted that. She hated meeting new people. They always disappointed her. She'd much rather read. Books very rarely were a disappointment. Still, this was Charlie, and after the horrible way she had been acting lately, Alia figured she would at least humor him.

Charlie knocked on the door then let himself in.

"Hey, it's Charlie," said one boy. The kids were all sitting around a table with a bunch of stuff that looked like a giant board game, with books, note papers, miniature figurines, and dice with several sides. "And he brought a friend."

"Hi Charlie, Hi Friend." they all said in unison.

Alia looked at Charlie and rolled her eyes, but he noticed she had the start of a smile as well.

There were six kids in the room, four girls and two boys. The boy that first spoke had light brown hair and was so skinny he made Charlie look like he had a few extra pounds. The boy seemed to her to be all elbows and prominent bushy eyebrows.

Across from him, tossing popcorn in the air and catching it in her mouth, was a tall girl with long red hair and a freckled face. She wore a gay pride shirt and a rainbow bandana around her wrist.

Another boy was hiding behind an enormous book sat up on the table, but all she could make out of him was the top of his curly black hair and dark brown eyes. Next to him was a boy wearing wizard robes and glasses with blond hair, blue eyes, and his share of a few extra pounds.

Looking around the cabin, Alia noticed first all the books everywhere. The shelves were loaded with them, with even more stacked in piles on the floor. Even from where she was, she could make out several fantasy novels as well as Harry Potter and, to her joy Stephen King. All around the room, hanging from the ceiling and on what little space on the shelves not taken up by books, were dozens of art projects, posters, and collectibles from Harry Potter, Dr. Who, Lord of the Rings, and Marvel. It reminded Alia of her room at home. Only the artists were much better than she was.

Charlie walked over to a girl at the table with long dark curly hair and glasses perched on the end of her nose. She had a large crystal in a pendant around her neck and crystal charm bracelets on both wrists. She was also wearing a cloak that Alia was pretty sure was a Hufflepuff robe."Crystal, this is the girl I told you about before we got to camp. Her name is Alia."

"Hi Alia," they all said in unison again.

Alia couldn't help but giggle a little that time. "What are you guys playing?" she asked.

"It's D&D. Have you ever played?" said a short boy with short dark black hair.

"I Have heard of it, but no, I never played."

"Oh, then you have come to the right spot, fair maiden, come sit. I will entertain you with my skills." said the boy she later found out was named Ethan.

Alia sat as the boy explained that the kid hiding behind the book was the dungeon master, and on and on.

She was so enraptured by what they were doing she didn't notice Charlie messing with her arm until she felt

110

something cold and wet on it. He had gotten balls covered in pink calamine lotion and was dabbing it all over her arms.

"You're covered in mosquito bites," Charlie said by way of explanation. "Go on, pay attention, I've got this." he continued to dab on the lotion while she watched the group play their game.

About half an hour later, sure that Alia was good and settled in with her new friends, he whispered to her. "I'll have one of the female counselors get me your things, and I'll bring them back, okay?"

Alia nodded, smiling at him, then watched the game.

A bit while later, he was indeed back with her suitcase. The two girls, Crystal and Rachel, helped her get her things set up on her new bunk. The three of them were talking and laughing when she saw Charlie try to slip away. Alia ran and caught him outside before he got too far. Running up, she gave him a big hug.

He hugged her back and almost didn't let her go when she let him go.

"Thank you, Charlie. Once again, you've managed to save the day."

"Does this mean you're going to stay?"

"Yeah, I guess."

"Good, glad to hear it. I've kind of missed having you around." he started to walk off then turned back. "It's nice seeing you again. Even better seeing you smile again." With that, he went off to join the other camp counselors at a bonfire.

"Nice seeing you again as well, sweet boy," Alia said to herself. She watched as Charlie walked off into camp, then went back inside to her new friends.

Chapter 6
Home

Alia felt herself waking with an inner sense of warmth, peace, and protection that she had never felt before. Grasping the source of these new feelings, she clutched Charlie's arm, still draped over hers, tighter. Alia opened her eyes, blinking away the sleep and gunk. Looking down without moving, she saw his arm still holding on to hers, despite that it was now morning. At her back, she could feel the warmth of his body on hers. Alia breathed in the smell of soap and aftershave. Felt his shallow breath on her shoulder.

Alia closed her eyes again, just wanting to soak in the moment. The last thing she wanted was to wake him and end this. However, her body involuntarily snuggled down deeper into his embrace.

Charlie responded by giving Alia a slight squeeze. Neither one of them had any desire to break the embrace, so they lay there for a few moments longer.

After a bit and with great reluctance, Charlie let go of her hand but rubbed her arm affectionately. "Sorry, I was so tired I must have dozed off. How did you sleep?"

Alia stretched, rolled over onto her back, and sat up some. She knew that this moment should be awkward for the both of them but didn't feel that it was. Later, when she was home, and he was gone, she was sure she would reflect on this as well as the rest of the time and have a full-fledged panic attack. For now, all was right with the world. Well, maybe not all. Just the thought of having to leave soon put a sinking feeling in the pit of her stomach. She would need to make arrangements for Crystal to come to get her somewhere. There was no way she would risk Charlie driving her into town. And with that thought, she jumped up out of bed.

"Shit shit shit...I forgot about Crystal." She said, running to the dresser where she had left her phone plugged in to charge.

"What about Crystal," asked Charlie, stretching his long arms and legs.

"I never texted her last night to let her know we were okay after the storm." Alia checked the phone, and sure enough, there were several frantic texts from her best friend. Alia was so used to having her phone on silent she never thought to turn it on at the motel.

Crystal: Are you two okay?
Crystal: Hello?
Crystal: Dad said a line of strong storms went through your way. Please answer.
Crystal: Alia, come on, call me!!
Crystal: I bet your damn phone is on mute. Call me as soon as you get this!!

Alia texted back.

Alia: Sorry, yes, the phone was on mute. Charlie and I are fine. We had a near
 miss but no big deal

Crystal: no big deal? Do you realize it's almost eleven already? You got to get your ass back in town before your mother has a fit.

Alia turned to Charlie. "It's almost eleven already."
Charlie checked his watch, and sure enough, it was ten forty-eight. "Shit." He said, jumping up out of bed. "I've got to get you back to town. Ask Crystal if she can pick you up somewhere. I'm assuming you don't want the two of us to just stroll into town together." Charlie grabbed his uniform from the closet and his day bag from the floor.
"No, I went through that last night just for us to be killed by my mother."
"I'll be fast. Make arrangements to meet somewhere, and I'll pack our stuff while you get ready." With that, he ran into the bathroom and shut the door.
Alone, Alia called Crystal.
"My parents said they don't care if you're their kid or not; you're grounded." Crystal said, picking up the line.
Alia laughed. "If we both come out of this alive, I'll be more than happy for that to be my only punishment."

"Your mother is going to have a shit attack. Please tell me the two of you have more sense than to just come back to town together. George has been here all morning waiting for us to hear from you. He was about to have the both of us come up there looking for you."

"Well, you can tell George and everyone that I am fine. He should know that I am in good hands with Charlie." And strong arms, she could still feel them around her.

"Yeah, but then my dad saw the weather last night, and you wouldn't answer your texts, and George has a new phone and didn't get Charlie's number. It wasn't Charlie we were worried about. We know you're safe with him."

Safe…yes, very safe and warm in those long muscular arms. "Look, I'll fall on my knees and beg for forgiveness later. Right now, I need a favor. We need you to pick me up somewhere. Maybe that McDonald's just as you come off of the five-o-one."

"Yeah, sure, we can do that. Hold a sec.".

Alia could hear Crystal talking to someone.

George says that's no good. Too many chances of someone from town seeing Charlie drop you off. He says Midland has a small park with a fishing pond. Charlie knows where it is. They used to fish there sometimes in high school. Not many people go there."

As she said that, Charlie came out of the bathroom, his uniform on and tie hanging from his neck. "So, can she pick you up?"

"Yeah, George said Midland park may be a safer bet, though. Fewer people."

He nodded. "He's right about that. Good call. Tell Crystal we will let her know when we are about an hour out. But we need to hustle."

Alia did, adding, "I have to go. I still have to get dressed."

"Get dressed…? Alia…please tell me the two of you….?"

"We don't have time for this right now, Crystal. I'll call you later." And she hung up as her friend continued to protest. Alia went running into the bathroom and noticed

Charlie was laughing while putting his boots on. "What's so funny."

"Was just wondering how she reacted when you said you had to get dressed." He looked up at her, grinning.

Alia shook her head, smiling back at him. "Let's just say I am going to have some explaining to do on that car ride home." She ran into the bathroom, shutting the door behind her. Ten minutes later, she was out, brushed, dressed, and washed, throwing the last of her things in her overnight bag.

Charlie came into the room talking to someone on his cell phone. "Yes, yes, we got it all worked out. I know. Hey, I need to go; she's ready; we should hit the road. Yes, of course. I will. Call you this evening. Love you too, Mom." He hung up the phone and pocketed it. "That was fast. Most girls would have taken at least half an hour or more."

Alia just looked at him and shook her head. "When are you going to realize I'm not like most girls?" She said, checking under and around the bed for anything they didn't already grab.

"Oh, I know. Why do you think I like you so much?"

I actually have no idea. "I think we got it all. Ready?" She grabbed her bag and headed out the door.

"Oh, so we are just going to ignore that question, are we?" He teased, following her to the back of the patrol car.

"I assumed it was rhetorical." She said, tossing her overnight bag in the back.

Charlie stood there looking at her for a bit, and then it dawned on him. "I just realized something. You're not wearing makeup."

"Wow, gee. We spent a good part of yesterday and last night talking, and you're just now noticing that? Way to flatter a girl Charlie." Alia said with a grin and turned to walk away. He followed behind her then passed her to open her door. "Well, at least I can see your mother taught you how to be a gentleman."

"My father, actually. Though I would have figured you realized that after last night." Charlie shut the door behind her.

"About last night." She began, then realized she didn't know what to say. How do you thank a guy for something like that?

"Last night was no different than the rest of this weekend. I was simply helping a friend."

Alia's smile faltered a bit, but then she quickly recovered.

It was too late. Charlie still saw the hurt in her eyes that told him those may have been the wrong words to use. "A very, very good friend. Who, by the way, I think looks beautiful without any makeup." He gave her that boyish grin of his then walked around to the driver's side.

Alia found herself smiling as she watched the boy walk around and get in on his side.

"I checked out already so we can just hit the road. Are you up to eating anything, or do you want to wait a while?"

"I could eat. Actually, yeah, I didn't realize how hungry I was. But I guess that's what happens when you sleep half the day away."

"Well, as long as we get you home without causing any drama for you there, I won't regret it at all. That was the best night's sleep I had in a long time."

Same here and probably the best I will have for a very long time.

After getting some food, the two headed back toward Union county. The highway was pretty clear by that time of day, but they could see signs of the storms as they drove. There were trees down, some houses missing roofs, and leaves and pine needle debris everywhere. Once in a while, the road was taken down to only one lane as they crept along. They were about an hour out of Alexandria when Charlie noticed Alia hadn't said a word and just stared out of the patrol car's passenger window. He didn't have to look at her to tell him that she was in a sad mood. He was afraid that maybe it was his fault and was unsure how to fix it.

"Did I do or say something wrong?" He asked.

116

Alia jerked as though she had been lost in thought. "Hmm?"

"You're over there looking like you lost your best friend."

"Oh no, it's not you, it's just...."

"What? Worried about going home?"

"No, I mean yeah, that's there in the back of my mind too, but no. You wouldn't get it."

"Try me."

Alia sighed heavily. "It's the trees."

"The trees?"

"Yeah. I mean, look at them. So many trees are broken and bent. Now they're just going to lay there and die."

Charlie looked, and she was right. The trees had taken a big hit by the storm on both sides of the highway. In some sections, acres of trees were broken halfway up their trunks.

"And yes, I know there's a lot of damage to homes and stuff too, but those places will most likely be rebuilt. But the trees, no one will give a damn about a bunch of broken trees. And don't you dare laugh at me, Charles. I'm serious."

"I wouldn't even think of it. And you're right. It is sad."

"It's just that I love it all so much. I don't know; I could hike for hours and never get bored with it. When I was little, and my life went to shit, as you know it often did. I would go out to the woods and just run. Or find a huge beautiful tree to sit under and stay there for hours. Every time I thought about running away, I imagined what it would be like to live in the woods. So yes, it's sad to see so many destroyed."

"I agree. I guess I just take that kind of thing for granted. We have had a cabin up in the mountains in northern Union county since I was a kid. Sometimes we assume things like that are always going to be there waiting for us to come back. I think I would be heartbroken to go there one day and see this kind of damage."

Alia nodded, thinking it was pretty cool that he understood.

Charlie hadn't wanted to spend their last hours together, for who knew how long, with either of them moody or upset, so he suggested they listen to the radio. So they did. He put her in charge of finding something good and found out that she had a wide range of musical interests.

As they drove down the road, they listened to everything from Ed Sheran to Lil Nas X. Bon Jovi and Pat Benatar appeared on the classics channel. Aerosmith and AC/DC were found on the heavy metal station. To all of it, Alia sang along, and sometimes Charlie would join her. A new song would come on, and he would get a kick out of how she'd get excited and claim. "Oh, I love this one." Over and over. So music was something else she enjoyed, another thing he hadn't known about her.

The hours and the miles went by with them singing, laughing, and talking about what made one song just so great. Charlie was struck again by the ease in which doing things he was usually uncomfortable with were so easy with her. As much as he was sure he had had his air guitar moments when he was young, singing wasn't something he did in front of others. And Charlie had the feeling she was the same way. Then she revealed to him that she had been in choir for a few years after she had moved out of Union county. When he asked why she didn't continue, she gave him a look.

"The same reason I never got to do sports, drama, or any after-school activities."

"No need to say more," Charlie said, not wanting to ruin the good mood and vibes they had going on.

At one point, Alia got on the country music station, and a song came on he hadn't heard before, but she, of course, professed to love. It was called Strawberry Wine, and Alia sang in vocals that blew him away. For hours she had been singing along to many songs but nothing like the way she had sung that one. It wasn't just her voice but rather the way she sang with such passion that made the song so special. Years later, when he would look back on this time,

Charlie would come to realize that if at any point he had fallen for her completely, it was then. He was so blown away he had even slowed down driving without noticing.

"If you're gonna slow down, then let me drive." She said, once done with the song. Alia had noticed how he was looking at her and was hoping to get him off the subject of her singing. It's not that she knew she sang very well. It was just that the look on his face said she did. Everyone loves to be complimented, but it happened so rarely for her that she often didn't know how to react when it did happen. It made for very awkward situations, and Alia tried to avoid that between them.

Charlie laughed a little, knowing just what she was trying to do. "You're not driving. My father would have my head." He made a point of speeding back up. "And, if you think I'm not going to mention how amazing that was, then think again."

"Oh please, I can barely carry a tune in a bucket." According to her mother anyway.

"Well, then I guess I better get my ears checked when I get to town." He teased.

"Yes, you should," Alia said as she dialed around the stations to find another song. "Oh, I love this one," she said, cranking up Sweet Child Of Mine.

Charlie shook his head and laughed, knowing deep within his heart he was in big trouble here.

They were a few hours from town, getting a little bored, and turned off the music for a bit to just talk. It was nothing of fundamental importance, just how things were going in school, what she and Crystal got into on the weekends, and what she had to do before graduation. They both avoided mentioning her mother. Charlie told her about his experience as a cadet in the academy and little of what she would expect from her training once he got back to Union. They were coming into a long stretch of the highway with few towns and little traffic. Without warning, Charlie pulled the patrol car over to the shoulder of the road.

"Okay, slide over." He said, getting out of the car.
"What? You can't be serious?"

"Hurry before my good sense comes back, and I change my mind."

Alia took care of the center console and slipped into the driver's seat, grinning from ear to ear.

Charlie went around and got into the passenger side, noticing that she was adjusting her seat and mirrors without being told to do so. He had left the car running, so all she had to do was put it into drive and pull out. "Okay, before you pull out, there are a few rules. You stay at the speed limit, no lights or siren (that she pouted at), and the first time you swerve or mess up, you're done, okay?"

"Yes, sir, Deputy," Alia said, beaming. A few minutes later, she drove them down the highway staying at the posted fifty-five and doing a great job.

"Not too bad." He said. "Looks like you do know what you're doing."

"Told ya. Not much I am very good at, but driving, I feel, is definitely in the top three."

"Yeah, what's the other two?" Although as far as he was concerned, there were more than three. He had seen the way she had dealt with the people that had been hurt the night before. Everyone from kids to the elderly she took her time with and reassured them they would be okay. Then she organized groups to clean up sections of the parking lot and sidewalk areas. Alia not only had an excellent bedside manner but leadership qualities as well. Also, there was her singing and how she sounded like an angel when it came to certain songs. Charlie had a feeling that once she got out from under that woman she called a mother, Alia would discover many things she was very good at.

"Cooking for one. The advantage to being a single child left home a lot is that I had to learn to cook. Mostly I spent a lot of time in the kitchens of the older women in the family. My grandmother was a fried food lover, so I can make crispy chicken that is juicy and falls off the bone. My great-grandmother, well before Alzheimer's, kicked in. She was great at baking. It took me a while to make my dougies as good as hers, but I finally nailed it."

"What's a dougie?"

Alia looked at him, shocked.

"Eyes on the road there, Betty Crocker," said Charlie.

"I can't believe you have never had a dougie...wow, what a deprived childhood." She joked. "Okay, so I know you have had to have a funnel cake before, right?"

"Of course, can't go to the fireman's carnival or county fair and not get one, wouldn't be right."

"Exactly, well dougies are kind of like those but better, and we eat them for breakfast. And don't turn your nose up, I saw that. I said they are like that. The difference is in a few key ingredients, the fact that dougies are pulled and made flat before frying. You slather the things in butter and dust with powdered sugar when it's done. We also like to put sausage gravy over them sometimes instead of on biscuits. They are amazing, and my great-grandmother made the best. I promise one day I will make you some. You just have to promise afterward not to fall too madly in love with me." She laughed.

Too late, he thought but laughed and said. "Not sure that's a promise I can keep, but I'll try. That leaves the third one."

"Well, according to your father, I'm a crack shot. Maybe even better than you." She said coyly.

That got his attention. "That's what he told you? Because you know, at the risk of sounding like I am bragging, I am pretty good."

"I know he said that too. But he also said you have been handling guns and rifles since you were a kid. Unless you count duck hunt, I've never picked one up before until the first time he took me out to the range. He says I'm a natural." She shrugged her shoulders, not entirely convinced.

"Well, if he says it, then you are. My father can be pretty tough. He doesn't give compliments that are not deserved. It's good too. I'm glad to know you can handle a weapon and take care of yourself. It's not like we go on weekly shootouts with the residents in Union county or anything, but it's good to be able to hold your own just in case. As long as you can hold a gun with complete confidence in your ability to use it, that energy transfers to anyone you have to pull it on, and they'll cooperate."

"So as long as I look like a badass bitch when I pull my weapon, I most likely won't have to shoot anyone?" She grinned.

"Yeah, something like that." He laughed.

They were about another twenty minutes down the road when they came behind a white pickup. It had pulled out of a side road about a quarter of a mile in front of them.

Alia followed behind him and frowned. She checked her speed, and sure enough, the driver was going five under the limit. "What the hell is up with this guy?"

"What? He looks good to me. Did you see something?"

"Yeah, I saw the speed limit, which is fifty-five. He's barely doing fifty."

"Well yeah, and he's not going to go any faster either."

"Why the hell not? Don't tell me that piece of shit can't do five more miles an hour."

Charlie laughed at her. "Did you forget you were driving a patrol car?"

"Oh yeah." She said as it dawned on her. "But still, dude could at least do the limit."

"Some people won't chance it. You have two lanes. Just go around him."

Alia thought about this. "Or we could motivate the driver to move out of our way."

"No, I said no, siren."

"What about lights?"

"No."

Alia didn't say a thing, just drove behind the pickup, refusing to go around.

Still just as stubborn as ever I see. "Okay, you can hit the lights, but only for a second. He'll get the hint and move."

Alia did, with a huge smile of satisfaction, and sure enough, the pickup driver pulled right on over into the breakdown lane. Alia sped up past him, doused the lights, and continued at the speed limit.

"Happy now?" He asked her.

"Siren would have been more fun, but yea, I can live with that," Alia said, grinning.

Charlie couldn't help but smile back. He could tell already she was going to get him in a lot of trouble. *But I'll be damned if it won't be worth it.*

When they were an hour from the park Charlie would drop her off at, he got back behind the wheel again. "This never happened." He told her as they passed each other in front of the patrol car.

"Of course. Thank you, Charlie."

"Yeah, well, just remember my father finds out, and we are both toast."

"Oh, believe me, I have seen your father angry. This shit doesn't even go down in my diary." She joked. Back on the road, Alia called Crystal to let her know they were an hour out. After the call, she became quiet and just looked out the window. *Well, this was fun while it lasted. Wonder how many years before the next time we talk or even see each other. That is if my mother doesn't find out and kills both of us.*

Charlie was lost in his own thoughts as well. He knew there was a plan, and he knew that he had agreed to it, but it still didn't seem fair or right, for that matter. They hadn't done anything wrong. The two of them were caught up in the lies and bullshit of a madwoman. They had been held hostage for years. It wasn't right, and it was vital that it ended. He needed for it to end. Because Charlie knew now just what he was sending her home to and his heartfelt sick because of it.

The fact that she had said things were pretty good at the moment didn't make him feel any better either. Her mother had severe mental health issues that he had no doubts about. People like her tended to snap with no warning. And Alia would be her first target. Charlie couldn't help but feel like he was driving her closer and closer to a powder keg.

About fifteen miles from the park, Charlie knew he had to do something to lighten the mood. He had put himself in a funk, and even though she smiled at him as they drove that last hour, it was a smile that didn't quite reach her eyes.

"So, can you believe George is going to be a father? I mean, George, of all people? I didn't see him settling down so soon. He's still as much a practical joker as he was growing up."

"Yeah, he hasn't changed much. Just now that he works, he has more victims." Alia laughed.

"Do you remember what he did at our senior year homecoming game?"

"You mean when he convinced our football team that the other team stole our mascot? Oh, they were so pissed, but it was also the first time in years they won a homecoming game."

"Yeah, and guess who got stuck with the cat..".

"No, you didn't." She laughed so hard at that.

"We still wanted to go to the game, so I tossed the cat into my bedroom and told my mom to stay out till we got back. You know that damn thing shit all over my bed?"

"Oh my god, Charlie, that's hilarious. Why didn't you get a litter box?"

"Ask George. When he grabbed the cat from the school, he didn't stop long enough to get anything, just brought it over to my house. I had to hurry and clean the mess up before getting ready for the dance. And George was no help. My mother comes in because she hears me hollering at him, and I'm hollering at the cat. She goes and scoops the damn thing up like it's a baby, and it cuddles all up to her purring like it didn't do shit wrong."

"Shit wrong." Alia cackled with laughter.

"I've got George on my floor laughing so hard he's crying, my mother is mad at me for hollering at the damn cat, and my room smells like shit…literally. And I'm trying to be mad, but the whole situation was just insane. The only good thing was that my dad was at work and never found out."

"Yeah, George told us that night what happened. His clothes were covered in cat hair because he had to bring it back to school. I don't remember seeing you there, though."

"I was for a bit. I saw you there...and that meathead J.J."

"Oh God, don't even mention him. What the hell was I thinking?"

"I was surprised. I didn't even know the two of you were dating."

"We weren't. He was hanging out with some people we were hanging out with at the game. That was the first time we had ever even met. We had gone to concessions at halftime, and I was about freezing. All I had on was a t-shirt. He offered me his jacket, and I wore it the rest of the game."

"Aw, love at first sight." he teased to cover the feeling of jealousy he had.

"Oh no, hardly. I never really cared for him all that much. But the looks I got from the other girls. A freshman walking around wearing a seniors letter jacket? An unpopular freshman at that. Oh boy, I suddenly became one of those basic bitches. I didn't like him. I liked the idea of being a freshman dating a senior."

"Any senior would have worked, huh?"

"Well, I don't know, I guess. I mean J.J., he was nice enough to me and all, but it was pretty much about the jacket. He let me wear it a week before he asked for it back."

"So if I had asked you out instead of him, you would have gone with me?"

"Honestly, Charlie, I would have gone out with you regardless of the jacket or what people thought. You know, if I didn't think my mother would like, come and burn the whole school down just to keep us apart. At least you would have turned out to be nice and not a total shit bag like he did." Alia wasn't about to mention the things he had tried to do, the things she wasn't ready for at all, let alone wanting him to do to her.

"Yeah, but my girl got him back, didn't you? You know that video is still on YouTube. Got millions of hits too.

A few hundred from me alone watching it and laughing my ass off."

"So how is it you saw me there, but I didn't see you?"

"I didn't stay very long."

"Oh, you and your date were anxious to get to the after-party, were you?"

"No," he chuckled. "I didn't go with anyone."

"Well, damn it, Charlie, why didn't you come over. I would have danced with you if you had asked. Not like my mom would have found out."

"You seemed to be having a good time. Besides, I had to wash cat shit off my bed stuff, thanks to George."

I Would have had a better time with you there, Alia thought.

A few minutes later, they saw the sign for the park and pulled into the drive, following a winding dirt road down to a parking lot where Crystal and George waited. It was full-on dark by this time, so they had parked under one of the few working lights there. Charlie pulled the patrol car up next to them.

"Hey Charlie," yelled George from his place in the driver's seat of their mother's Buick."

"Hey, George. Thanks for coming to get Alia. Her mother had enough of a fit, I took her out of town as it was."

"What is that woman's hang up with you and your father anyway?"

"Remind me to tell you sometime. For now, we better get Alia home. The sooner, the better." Charlie went to help Alia get her things out of the back. He walked her to the back of the Buick, where he lifted the trunk, and she tossed her overnight bag in on top of a bunch of books.

So this is it. Thought Alia *Once again, it was good while it lasted.* "Thank you again, Charlie." She closed the lid of the trunk, but they both didn't bother to leave just yet. Alia felt her heart rate rise and her eyes become moist. The last thing she wanted to do was to say goodbye to him. "I don't know how to pay you back for this. If it wasn't for you, I never would have made it there in time for the test. Then last night...."

"How about you just try and stay out of trouble for the next few weeks so you can go to the academy, and we'll call it even."

"No guarantees, but I'll try." Alia started to turn to walk away.

Without even thinking, Charlie grabbed her arm, gently pulling her back. "You know I had a really great time this weekend. Besides the near-miss tornado, of course. I don't see why we can't see each other more. I mean, as long as we are careful and don't go skipping down the main street together, that is." Charlie looked her in the eyes, his heart thundering in his chest.

Alia's mouth talking faster than her brain could shut her up, she heard herself say. "Well, Deputy Charles Harper, if I didn't know better, I would swear you were asking me out," she said, being her typical smart-ass self. Any laughter went out of her when she saw the look on his face. *Is he being serious?*

"Maybe I am. You did say you would go out with me if I asked. So maybe I am asking." *And if you say no, I think I'll just die right here where I stand.*

Alia searched his eyes and knew this wasn't some kind of cruel trick or joke. Suddenly she was both excited and terrified. For the first time, being with him all weekend, she felt he was a little too close, his cologne a little too pleasing to her nose and his eyes, his gorgeous green eyes, looking too deep into her soul.

She hadn't said anything, so Charlie tried again, making his intentions perfectly clear this time. "Alia, would you like to go out with me sometime? I don't mean as just friends either." he smiled. Charlie had an overwhelming feeling that if he didn't stand up right now and make his intentions clear when she rode away, he would lose her forever. Four weeks suddenly felt like a lifetime. He had to do something now to hell with the consequences. Charlie moved closer still to her, reached down, and took one of her hands in his.

Alia wasn't sure what to say. Was yes enough? Hell yes? Super hell yes? And there was this annoying voice way off in the back of her mind screaming. It reminded her of when the wicked witch had gotten wet, only she couldn't make out what the voice was saying. That was probably due to the rushing sound of blood coursing through her veins at the moment.

At last, she found herself able to answer him. "Yes, Charlie, I'd like that very much." Right then, she knew that the smile on his face and the merriment in his eyes would be enough to sustain her through any shit storm in life. "Give me your phone," she said before she could lose her courage and call it all off, or worse, run into the woods.

Charlie gave it to her with a shaky hand.

As she talked, she typed her number into his phone. "Now there have to be rules with this, okay. You can't call me, text only. Remember, my mother doesn't know I have this phone. Most of the time, when I am home, it's turned off or at the very least on mute. So don't freak If I don't answer right away." Alia handed Charlie back his phone. "When you know what you want to do and when just let me know. Okay?"

"Okay." he nodded. "There is one thing I would like to do right now." Before he could lose his nerve, Charlie leaned down and kissed her gently on her lips once ever so softly, then again harder, more passionately. He held her face in his hands, kissing her more, enjoying the sweet taste of the strawberry balm on her lips.

Alia became lost in the kiss, leaned in closer, wrapped her one free arm around his back. Her head was spinning, her heart racing, and she wanted nothing more than to stay like this until the end of time. Nothing this long weekend, not even him holding her all night, prepared her for this moment. All she could think was, *I hope he likes strawberries.*

Charlie stopped kissing her and put his forehead on hers, taking a few shuddering deep breaths. "I have been wanting to do that for such a long time." he exhaled.

"Charlie? How long? Why didn't you say anything?"

"Most of my life." he said, "But it was well worth the wait. I was just doing what I thought I should to protect you. But the truth is that I failed. We all did."

"Charlie, you have never failed me." The mixed look of sadness and remorse in his eyes broke her heart. She could see that he was hurting and struggling with something.

"I have, though, but I won't do it anymore, I promise. I can't do it anymore." Charlie kissed her on her forehead and stepped back slightly. "We'll talk later. I promise that too. As much as I hate it, you have to go home now. "

Alia looked at Charlie and realized he had tears welling up in his eyes. Here this man in uniform, one of the bravest, kindest, gentlest men she knew, was tearing up at the thought of sending her home. Alia wished she hadn't told him how bad things could get. She didn't like to see the look of hurt in his eyes, as she could tell it was killing him to make her leave. Standing up on her toes, Alia kissed him this time.

Charlie took her in his arms, lifting her for a bit off her feet, then put her back down and whispered in her ear. "I've loved you since the first moment I laid eyes on you." and kissed Alia one last time. Then Charlie took her by the arm and walked her to the back door of the car, opened it, helped her inside, said a goodbye hardly above a whisper, and quickly strode away back to his patrol car. Charlie drove off, not able to look back at Alia even one last time, not because his tears fell and blurred his vision, but because he knew if he did, he'd never be able to let her go.

Chapter 7
WTH

George and Crystal, sitting in the front seat of the Buick, watched as Charlie drove off and out of the lakeside park. They both looked at each other a moment, then turned and looked in the back seat at Alia.

"What the hell!" they both said

"Dude, what the fuck was that all about?" Asked George.

"Did he really kiss you?" Asked Crystal.

"Oh, he definitely kissed her, and she kissed him back," said George.

"Have you lost your mind?" asked Crystal.

"Just what the hell happened this weekend?" asked George.

"Nothing happened, right, Alia?? You told me nothing happened," said Crystal.

"No, something happened," said George

"Something had to happen," said Crystal

"Okay, okay, okay, hush the both of you for a minute, damn. I'm still trying to process this shit myself." Alia sat there for a few minutes, head-spinning, trying to catch her breath.

It wasn't until she looked up that George and Crystal realized she was having a panic attack.

"Shit!" They both said in unison. The two of them got out of the car, opened the passenger door, and pulled Alia out gently. She took three steps forward, went down on her knees, and threw up what was left of the last meal she had, which thankfully wasn't much.

"George, get a bottle of water for her." Crystal went down to her knees next to Alia, who was now gasping for air, unable to fill her lungs as panic gripped them tighter. "Slow down, Alia, take deep breaths, slow deep breaths." Crystal rubbed her back much like she had done over the years with other attacks Alia had. "Slow deep breaths, Alia, try to relax."

George returned with a water bottle and opened it for them. Crystal took it and tipped it up to Alia's mouth to drink. She took two sips, then spit it out and took two more. Alia sat back on her butt in the dirt parking lot, breathing a bit better. She looked up at her friends, her head still spinning a bit. Crystal encouraged her to drink more water, so she did. Then Crystal and George both joined her in the dirt.

"He asked me out." She said by way of explanation.

"He did more than that," said George.

Crystal elbowed George in the ribs. "Hush George, give her a chance to recover a bit. Are you feeling better? Think you can explain some things to us now." Crystal talked in a gentle, soothing voice one often uses for children.

Alia nodded her head but drank another sip of water first. "I don't know what happened. I mean, I do. I was there, but hell. I was just so calm when he was here. I may have even been flirting with him. I mean the whole weekend…just no idea…no well, I mean there was last night…but then that was nothing really, well maybe not nothing I mean it meant the world to me…but still…I didn't think he meant anything by it, not really, we're just friends, right?" Alia was rambling and on the verge of another panic attack.

"Uh, I think Charlie broke her," said George. Crystal gave her brother a scathing look then turned her attention back to Alia. "Okay, Alia, slow down and take a deep breath."

Alia did.

"And another."

She did again.

"Okay, try your best to slow down and tell us what happened last night."

"It was after the storm. After we had gone to bed, I had this horrible nightmare, and when I reached out for him, I couldn't find him, which made it worse."

"Because he was in another bed, right?" asked George.

"No, there was only one, But it was a queen. He wanted to sleep in the tub, but I refused to let him." She went on to tell them about the dream and how she didn't think she could go back to sleep, so she asked him to hold her till she did.

"You did?" Asked Crystal. "You actually asked him to hold you? You?"

"I'm telling you, Crystal, I don't know what comes over me when he's around. I feel so comfortable with him like I can tell him anything. But still, I never thought. I mean, he said some nice things, but you both know Charlie, he's a nice guy. It's just how he is."

"Well, I thought I knew him," Said George.

"What's that supposed to mean?" Said Alia finding herself surprisingly defensive on his behalf.

"Well, I mean, it's just. To tell the truth, a lot of us thought he was gay."

Alia reached out and slapped him hard on the arm. "What the hell you mean he's gay."

"Well, obviously, he's not. I mean, that was one hot kiss even from where we were sitting."

"But you're his best friend, wouldn't you know for sure or not?"

"It's not like he said anything one way or the other, and I wasn't about to ask. You know how hard it is for some people to come out. I didn't want to make him feel like he had to. But Alia, I have known him since the sixth grade, and I have never seen him with a girl. Or even a guy, for that matter."

Alia looked at Crystal.

"He's got a point. I don't think I have ever seen him with or talking about a girl, other than you, that is."

"And it hasn't been for the lack of trying on their side either," said George. Some of the hottest girls in our class tried to go out with him, and nothing. He was always very polite and friendly as usual, but he turned them all down. So you know, we figured he was gay and just hadn't worked out how to tell others yet. He even went to the prom stag. He didn't stay very long either. He danced with a couple of girls but didn't look like he enjoyed it much. Come to think of it, he looked rather sick. Almost like he was angry with himself."

"His senior year homecoming dance, he said he was there, but I never saw him," said Alia.

"That's because he walked in and walked right back out. I had to chase him down in the parking lot, and when I caught up to him…well, he looked pissed."

"He was mad?"

"Yeah, said something about kicking JJ Cullen's ass."

"I was at the dance with J.J. He just told me a little bit ago about your prank with the mascot."

George laughed. "Yeah, that was epic. He hated that damn cat. Charlie helped me return the cat, and then we went to the gym for the dance. He walked in and then just turned around and stormed back out."

Alia felt like she was going to be sick again. "When he kissed me tonight, he said he had wanted to do it for a long time. And earlier, he said he saw me at the dance with J.J., But I don't understand, if Charlie has liked me all this time, then why didn't he say anything when I broke things off with J.J.?"

"Well, you were kinda scary. It would take a man with real balls to ask you out after what you did to J.J.." said George

Alia slapped him again. "Think, George. You can't tell me he never said anything to you about me. Ever?"

"No, I didn't say that. However, Charlie never said anything about wanting to go out with you. He just always asked how you were doing. He even asked me if I thought you and Crystal would make good friends. But he never said anything about liking you, not like that."

Alia looked at Crystal.

"I have to agree with him on this one. Charlie was always asking about you, though. But whenever I offered to invite you over while he was at our house, he said not to. I thought he was into you too for a while, but he never seemed to want to hang out when you were at our house."

"Okay," George said. "So all that happened last night was he held you till you fell asleep. You sure he didn't say anything else."

"Nothing, but there was a bit more to it than that."

"Ha, I knew it."

Crystal smacked him this time.

"Okay, you two, stop hitting me."

"So, What else happened?" asked Crystal.

"Nothing, it's just that he didn't hold me till I fell asleep. When we woke up in the morning, he was still holding me. And God help me, but it felt so good. I have never felt more safe and protected in my life. I felt like the world could have ended around us, and nothing would touch us."

"Well, I guess we don't have to ask how you feel about him." Said George, and he flinched.

Crystal looked into Alia's eyes. "And how do you feel about him? I mean, if I didn't know you, I would say throwing up after a kiss wasn't an excellent sign."

"That had nothing to do with him. That was just the panic attack. I had one in the bathroom of the Mcdonalds after he decided to drive me up there too."

"You know as well as I do your panic attack was because of him. What I want to know is, is what he did a good thing or do I need to, you know, have a little talk with him."

"No, no, no talk, it was a good thing. I just...I mean...it was just from out of nowhere...I think."

"You think?" asked Crystal.

"Well, I mean, we talked a lot, and he said some really nice things. But I don't know. Charlie has always been nice to me. He's nice to everyone."

"I wouldn't say everyone," said George. "Yeah, sure he's nice and all, and he's always been the one to stop a fight, but he doesn't like everyone any more than anyone likes everyone. In fact, and speaking of J.J., well, maybe I shouldn't say anything about that. Charlie is a cop now."

"Say what?" asked Alia.

"Well, you know how after the thing with J.J. in the cafeteria, when you roasted his ass for telling lies about what the two of you did together?"

"Yeah, I remember very well how he went around telling everyone how he fucked me because I begged him to. The little shit. Knowing damn well I never did anything more than kiss him, and even that sucked."

"Well, you know how he didn't show back up in school for last week before Christmas break, and we all thought it was just because he was embarrassed? It wasn't. He was in the hospital. Charlie beat the hell out of him."

Alia was stunned. She had never seen Charlie get into so much as a schoolyard brawl, let alone beat someone. She had only ever seen him angry a small handful of times.

"I was in bed asleep a few nights after your roasting when I heard a noise at my window. It was Charlie. He was holding his hands up like they were hurt, and he was crying, Alia. He kept telling me he fucked up, that he just meant to scare the little prick, but he couldn't stop. He wouldn't come into the house, so I took him to the garage, and Charlie showed me his hands. His knuckles were all scraped up and covered in blood. He told me he beat the shit out of J.J. Charlie was freaking out too, saying how he just fucked his life, he was never going to be a cop, his dad would be so mad at him. I ended up raiding dad's beer stash and making him drink a few real fast. Then he told me where he left J.J., and I sent a few of our buddies out to find him but didn't tell them what happened.

They found him and dropped J.J. off at the hospital, with some lame story that he got drunk and picked a fight with the wrong person. I cleaned Charlie's hands up, made him a pallet bed in the garage, and got him drunk enough to fall asleep. He was a mess, Alia. I've never seen him like that before or ever again. In the morning, he hung out at the house until his hangover wore off and then went home."

"And it never occurred to you that all that had something to do with Alia?" asked Crystal.

"Well, of course, it did. But hell, a few of us guys were talking about kicking his ass. Charlie just beat us to it and apparently got a little carried away."

"Okay, maybe I can buy Charlie getting in a fight, and maybe I can even buy that he did it for me. But how in the hell did we not hear about this? How did he not get into any trouble?"

"The little shit didn't say a damn thing about Charlie. J.J. told everyone he got jumped, but he didn't see anyone. End of story. Only Charlie told me everything, and J.J. knew who was beating him up and why. Charlie made sure of that."

"I'm still amazed J.J. didn't say anything."

"Well, Charlie has lots of friends. Maybe he was afraid he'd get his ass kicked again if he told the truth. I know Charlie was worried."

Alia shook her head. So much had happened in such a short time. Part of her was still riding high on that kiss, and another was terrified and worried for Charlie. Most of all, she was just confused by the whole thing. Why hadn't he said anything if he had loved her all this time? Was he that afraid of her mother? Or was it like he said that he was trying to protect her? She wanted so badly to talk to him. Needed to know that he was okay. After the way he left, the things she had just learned, Alia didn't know what to think.

"If you're not going to barf in the car, we need to get going." Said, George.

"George is right. The last thing we need on top of everything else is for your mom to start wondering if you ran off with Charlie after all. We can talk more about it on the way, but we should go."

"I think I'm good." She said, but as she got up, she became dizzy and almost sat down again.

"No, you're not good, which is why we need to talk. The last thing you need to do right now is to start overthinking everything like you always do." Crystal put her hands one to each side of Alia's head and looked her right in the eyes. "This is a good thing, Alia. And I won't let you spoil this for yourself. You have been crazy about Charlie since I've met you, probably longer. It's about time he stood up and took notice too."

"Wait, what? I never said anything to you about Charlie," said Alia.

"You didn't have to; you're my best friend. Now get your ass in the car before your mother tries to hunt down your boyfriend and cut his balls off."

They all piled back into the car and headed back on the half an hour trip to town. They were about halfway there, having been talking about the weekend in better detail when Alia got a message from Charlie.

Charlie: I'm sorry I left the way that I did. The last thing I ever want to do is hurt you. I hate sending you back there, back to her. If you need me, if shit gets bad, promise me you'll call me. If you can't talk, text 911, and I'll come to get you.
I swear it, Alia, I don't care what she'll do to me. I won't let her hurt you anymore.

Alia texted him back.

Alia: I promise. And don't worry about the way you left, I think I understand. I'm fine. I'll let you know when I get home.

Charlie: Please don't forget. I'm in front of my parents' house right now, getting ready to go in. I may not answer right away. I need to talk to them about something.

Alia: I won't forget.

Charlie: I meant what I said tonight. I know you may feel a little confused right now. I don't blame you if you are. But I meant what I said. I love you, Alia, I always have.

Alia: I love you too, Charlie. That's one thing I'm not confused about. Not anymore.

Chapter 8
Charlie's Confession

Charlie read that last message from Alia five more times before finally getting out of his patrol car. He had been so worried that after all these years, Alia would reject him. Reading her text made his heart soar, despite the task that lay before him.

It was a bit late for Charlie to drop by his parents, but this was something he felt he couldn't wait till morning to do. To his relief, his father's patrol car was not in the drive, which meant he must have run out on a call. Hopefully, that would give him some time to talk to his mom before his father returned. She would better know how to approach him with what Charlie needed to say. Either way, Charlie knew his father wasn't going to be overjoyed. There was going to be some yelling in his usually happy childhood home. But all Charlie had to do was think of the things Alia had told him. That would get him through this—that, her last message and the feel of her lips on his. Charlie took a deep breath at the door, read her previous message one more time, and went in.

"Harper, is that you? I hope you're not dragging anything into the house. I just cleaned." Charlie's mom Ellen walked to the end of the little hall in the kitchen where Charlie was in the mudroom.

"No, Mom, it's me. I know it's late, but I need to talk to you and dad about something." He took off his boots then turned back around to face her.

As soon as Ellen saw the face of her only and much-beloved son, she knew something had changed, and something was wrong. Maybe a little right too, but still wrong. "Oh, Charlie, what happened?"

He came to her and enveloped her more petite frame within his long arms. They were a hugging family, but it had been a very long time since her son had wanted to be held by her.

He's gotten so big. He's not my little boy anymore. He's not my little miracle baby.

Charlie broke the embrace and looked at her with tears in his eyes.

Nope, not my little boy anymore. He's a man now. Even as a tear fell from his eye, she knew. *He's not a boy anymore, and he's not just ours anymore either.* As soon as she had heard about him running out of town with Alia, Ellen worried about the two of them, even before they knew of the storms. She had reminded Charlie over the phone that he had been raised to be a gentleman. But he was also still just a boy.

"I think I might have messed things up," Charlie said, trying to contain his tears. He had been holding back this wall of grief he had felt since that first night. He tried to hold it all back for Alia's sake, but now the damn was bursting. He may be a man, but Charlie was a man that was hurting.

Ellen had been having a strange feeling even before she found out the two had run out of town in the middle of the night. Harper would be upset when the night was done; she was sure of it. But she was also confident there was no one to blame. You can only keep two strong forces away from each other for so long.

"Charlie, put your gun away, then come join me in the living room. Hurry, we need to talk before your father gets back." Ellen left him to do that while she went to the living room. She picked up a specific photo album off a shelf and leafed through a few pages. Hearing her son come into the room, she put it back and wiped away a tear of her own before turning back to him.

"Sit, Charlie. You're going to tell me what happened, and quickly. But first, I need you to tell me the truth." She didn't even have to ask what she already knew.

"I didn't do anything, Mom. We didn't do anything. I wanted to. I probably could have. But it wasn't right. You have always said if it didn't feel right, then don't, and I didn't." Charlie sat on the couch and his mother in her chair across from him.

"So nothing happened?"

"There was one thing, well two, actually."

"Oh, Charlie."

"No, mom, just listen. There was only one bed, and I offered to sleep in the tub as you told me. But she wouldn't have it. It was a big bed, and we were nowhere near each other. I was just so damn tired too." Up to this point, he was looking at his mother, but he found it harder to as he went on. It's not that he felt shame or regret. He was just afraid she would be disappointed in how he handled himself. "Then she had a nightmare. Alia asked me to hold her just until she fell asleep. Only I couldn't bring myself to let her go. In the morning, we woke up in each other's arms. But that was it, I swear. I wouldn't have even touched her if she hadn't asked."

"It's okay, Charlie, I believe you. And I don't for a minute believe you would ever hurt her." Ellen had insisted on raising her son to treat women the right way, and so had Harper. She was proud of him. However, she knew there was more to his story.

"Yeah, well, will dad believe me? If he finds out, we slept in the same bed, that's going to be bad enough."

"It's going to be okay, Charlie, your father loves you. He may indeed get angry and yell. Hell, he may even throw something, but he will eventually calm down and listen to reason. And it's not like the two of you are children anymore. That's something he's going to have to learn to deal with."

Charlie looked at her as if he had his doubts.

"But for now, tonight at least, when we talk to your father, we just skip all that stuff about only one bed and holding her all night. Okay?"

Charlie nodded vigorously.

"Now, seeing how I am your mother and I know you as well as I do, there's more, isn't there?"

"Yes," he lowered his head. " When I dropped her off tonight with her friends…I told her that I loved her…and I asked her out…."

"Oh God, Charlie, your father is going to go through the roof."

"I know, I know, I screwed up, I know. But you have to believe me, mom. I didn't plan it. It's not like that. Hell, I didn't even ask her out at first. I just said I wanted to spend more time with her. But I couldn't leave it at that. I had to be sure Alia understood how I felt. I don't know what it was, but I felt like if I didn't, if I let her get in that car and drive off not knowing how I felt, I may never see her again."

"Charlie, you live in the same town together. Of course, you'll see her again. And you only had to wait four more weeks."

Charlie shook his head. "No, I couldn't, I couldn't do it anymore. Not after what she told me, not after what I saw her go through. Mom, it's not like we thought, it's worse, it's way worse. How she isn't broken into a thousand pieces by now, after all, she has been through." Charlie stopped to take a deep breath feeling his emotions getting the better of him. His mother was right. He wasn't a child anymore. He needed to deal with this like the man he was. "You and dad made a promise...we all did. You promised to protect us, to protect the both of us. But you didn't, not really. The only one you protected was me. She has spent fifteen years all alone. And the worst part is, she didn't tell me everything, Mom. She held the worst of the stuff back. I know she did. I could see it in her eyes. We failed her Mom. And I don't care how mad dad gets, I for one, can't do it anymore. I won't."

Ellen went to her son, her little miracle baby that shouldn't even be alive, hugged him with all her might, and cried with him. She didn't have to question him or know what Alia said; she believed him. All these years, they professed to love them both and that they did, what they did, to protect them both. But Charlie was right; they failed her. They had failed Alia a long time ago.

By the time sheriff Harper arrived home, from the last-minute call he had gone on, Mother and son were sitting on the couch waiting for him. After they had a good talk, Ellen sent Charlie to clean up in the bathroom. She got them both a good strong shot of whiskey. Just enough to put a little liquid courage in Charlie. They decided to leave out the part about the hotel bed and that Charlie had kissed Alia when he professed his love for her.

"He doesn't need to know all the details, and it's not proper to kiss and tell anyway. Besides, I don't have time to pack up any of my good crystals, so we don't need to get him in a throwing mood." Charlie's father had never raised a hand to either one of them. But his temper was notorious, and he had a penchant for throwing things when he got mad enough.

While they waited, Charlie told his mom what Alia had told him. He held back as well after seeing how crushed his mother was becoming. Ellen even got up at one point and got another shot. To calm her nerves, she told him. The truth was she wanted to cry again but couldn't have his father coming home, finding them like that. Harper loved Alia too, and Ellen was afraid he might do something that would only make things worse for them all.

Harper came in, taking off his boots at the rack in the mudroom off the kitchen. "I saw Charlie's patrol car out front, so I guess they made it back okay, told you not to worry, Ellen." He called out to her from the kitchen. "That's a good boy we raised." Harper was putting his gun away when he noticed Charlie's in the safe. Looking out the back window, he saw Charlie's truck was still parked in the backyard. After such a long drive, he was surprised to know Charlie was still here. When he went into the living room, Charlie and Ellen were sitting on the couch, waiting.

Charlie couldn't bear to look at Harper. He just hoped his father remembered what he just said, that Charlie was a good man.

"Well, if this is an intervention, it's a lousy one. I can smell the whiskey from here."

Ellen got up, kissed Harper, and told him to sit, that she was going to get him a beer.

"Yeah, very lousy intervention." Harper looked over at Charlie, but the boy wouldn't meet his eyes.

Charlie continued looking into his lap and concentrating on taking deep breaths. He wasn't afraid of his father, wasn't even really afraid to be yelled at. However, he was apprehensive about disappointing him. They had made a promise, the most important one their family ever made, and Charlie broke it.

Harper is far from a stupid man. Sitting there in his favorite chair, looking at his son, making a point of not looking at his father, he had a feeling he knew what this was going to all be about. Part of him wanted to demand to know what was going on. But his immense love for his son and seeing that he was not just afraid, but hurting as well, was the only thing keeping him in his seat and his mouth shut. Ellen brought him his beer, and he made it a point to finish it all off in only a few gulps. Then he tossed it into the trash beside him because he was pretty sure he wasn't going to want to have anything in his hands.

Ellen sat down beside her son furthest from her husband. She wanted Harper to be sure and get a good look at Charlie and realize this wasn't easy for him. She cleared her throat. "Before we start, I just want to point out that Charlie is trying to do the right thing. He's not hiding anything; he came straight to us." Charlie looked up at his mother, and she gave him a reassuring smile.

"Um-hmm." Said Harper. "Okay, I will keep that in mind. And I guess I am correct in assuming this has to do with Alia and your little weekend together."

"Oh, Harper, don't say it like that. For goodness sake, you make it sound scandalous."

"Well, wasn't it? You go running off in the middle of the night, not just with any eighteen-year-old girl still in high school, but the daughter of the one person hell-bent on ruining your life for doing something just like that. For god's sake, son, did you...."

"No, sir!" Charlie looked up at last. "I didn't lay a hand on her, I swear it."

"And if I talked to her, would she say the same thing?" Harper didn't fail to notice the tears in Charlie's eyes.

Charlie nodded. "But I can't do this anymore. I can't sit back any longer and watch, knowing what I know now. Knowing that she thinks there's nobody in this world that loves her. I didn't touch her, but I did ask her out, and I plan on seeing her again...soon. I have too."

"Damn it, Charlie." Harper pounded the table in front of him with his rather large fist. "We made a deal. We had a plan. Hell boy, you only had to wait four more weeks. After all these years, you mean to tell me you can't keep your pecker in your pants for four more weeks."

Charlie jumped up from the couch and stomped over to their fireplace, unlit on this warm spring evening. He was furious. He wanted to yell at his father, wanted to tell him to shut up and that he had no clue what was going on. That all these years, Harper had no clue just how bad things were.

"Harper, now stop. This has nothing to do with that. Charlie hasn't had so much as a date. If that's all this was about, there are plenty of girls lined up to give him that. You know damn well our son isn't like that. If he says nothing happened, then nothing happened."

"Then why Ellen? Tell me why he would risk not only himself but her as well. We did this to protect them both."

At that, Charlie turned around, pointing an accusing finger at his father. The rage on his face was one like they had never seen before. And the pain in his eyes was evident, as were his tears. "WRONG, YOU NEVER PROTECTED HER. YOU TOLD YOURSELF YOU WERE SO THAT YOU WOULD FEEL BETTER SO THAT YOU COULD SLEEP AT NIGHT. THE ONLY ONE YOU EVER REALLY CARED ABOUT PROTECTING WAS ME! WELL, I DON'T NEED YOUR PROTECTION ANYMORE."

"Don't Charlie...don't you dare...you're not the only one that lost her....your not the only one that loves her. You are our son. We couldn't risk losing you too."

"NO, YOU HAVE NO IDEA. NO CLUE. THE THINGS THAT SHE TOLD ME...THE THINGS SHE DIDN'T HAVE TO TELL ME."

"REALLY CHARLIE....DO YOU THINK I DON'T KNOW? EVEN WHEN SHE WAS OUT OF THE COUNTY, I KNEW WHAT WAS GOING ON." Harper took a moment to calm himself, knowing that the both of them yelling wasn't going to solve anything. "Son, I promise you I never lost tabs on her. NO matter how many times her mother dragged her from one shit situation to another, I knew where she was. I had people watching out for her. You know we have people here that help us watch out for her. I know what kind of crap she has gone through. But I did my job as a father and a husband and kept as much of the ugliness as I could from the both of you."

"Then why didn't you help her? You claim to protect her, to love her, but it didn't stop anything from happening to her."

"Because son, as a cop, you know as well as I do that there is a big difference between knowing something and being able to prove it. And Trish had that little girl terrified to make so much as a peep about anything." Harper got up from his chair, confronting his son. " And I did stop some things. Myself, Johnathan, and a couple of guys from the fire hall made damn sure that sick bastard her mother married wouldn't lay another finger on Alia again. We couldn't protect her from everything, and that is something I will have to live with for the rest of my life. But I did what I felt like I could." Harper approached his son and whispered so Ellen couldn't hear. "Just like I know you did with that boy in high school."

Charlie's head shot up, and he looked his father right in the eyes.

"And I protected you. I may not be proud of some of the things I did, but I don't regret it." Harper walked off back to his chair.

"Neither do I. I love Alia. It's more than some invisible connection between us. This weekend was the first time in years, in ever really, that I got to spend any time with her. I know that I love her. And I didn't ask her out because I couldn't wait any longer. I did it for her. I did it because of the way she looked at me all weekend. I did it because I realized when we were holding on to each other in that bathtub, sure that we were about to die, my biggest regret was never telling her the truth. That I never told her how much I love her."

All three of them were quiet for a bit. Everyone thinking, everyone, trying to calm down. This was the most significant family fight they ever had, the only one they really ever had. It was a fight that had all the power to tear them apart if they let it.

"You wanted to wait four more weeks, and I was okay with that. But I no longer believe that's the right call. We can't just dump everything on Alia days before she joins the academy and hope she doesn't end up hating us. Going away like that will be hard enough without that on her mind as well. If it costs Alia her one chance at getting out from under Trish, she may never forgive us...I...I can't live with that."

"She's not going to hate us, son." Said Harper. "We have been through this."

"He has a point, Harper," said Ellen. "I mean, I was never thrilled with the idea of dumping it on her days before she leaves. Even if she understands and isn't mad at us, it's still a lot to take on. Not only on her own but under all the pressure of the academy as well. Besides, what's done is done. He can't very well go back or change his mind."

"Why not?" Harper growled, knowing damn well that she was right.

"Because I won't do it...I can't hurt Alia like that."

"Of course, you can't, Charlie. Harper, you know damn well he can't."

"Should have never asked her out in the first place. I knew the two of them running out of town was going to end up a mess. And the trouble he could have caused her with Trish still could. Hell Ellen, Charlie could have at least come to us first. We could have had a plan, a strategy of some kind."

"Oh yes, my dear, how very romantic, a plan for how he should tell her he loves her. Harper, like it or not, they are both adults now, and we need to trust that they will make the right decisions. You said it yourself; it's only four weeks. If they are careful." Ellen turned to Charlie, "And I mean very, very careful. I don't see why they can't pull this off."

"She has to know." Said Harper. "Not just some of it, all of it...All of it, Charlie. Are you ready for that? Because if she doesn't hear all of it from us first, Trish will be sure to tell her skewed version of things. We know she's not above lying to get what she wants."

"I'll help you, Charlie. I'll tell her the hard parts if you need me to."

"No, Charlie should have to tell her. If he can't, then he's not ready yet. They're not ready yet."

"Oh, Harper, you can't very well put him through that. It's hard enough for me to talk about it. We are a family. We have always done things together, and this is no exception. We had a plan, and we will stick to it. All that has changed is that the timing has been moved up. In the long run, I think that will end up being for the best. We should have told her all of this when she turned eighteen."

"You know why we didn't. The same reason why I'm still not happy with this. If she's mad at us, that's one thing. If the whole thing just freaks her out and she wants nothing more to do with us, that would be worse. But if Alia gets mad and tries to confront her mother about it, this whole mess could blow up in our faces."

"I'll handle her. I'll see to it that she doesn't do anything stupid," said Charlie.

"So we tell all of it. Then we let Alia choose what she wants to do next. Agreed, Charlie?"

"Agreed, yes, sir," said Charlie.

"Ellen?"

"Agreed. But we do this my way. I still remember what it was like to be a naive young girl and madly in love. Charlie, tomorrow you find a way to see her safely. Tell her before the two of you go on your first date we would like her over for dinner. Tuesday is the earliest day she doesn't have the library right after school. Assure her there's nothing wrong; we would just like to talk and work some things out. After dinner, we tell her everything." Ellen went up to her son, now taller and bigger than her, and wrapped her arms around him the best she could.

Harper joined them, his big meaty arms enough for them both. *And there's still a little room to spare,* he thought.

Chapter 9
Not So Happy Home

"And that's pretty much it." Said Alia as George pulled the Buick into a parking place in front of her apartment.

George turned off the car, and He and Crystal looked at Alia. She had just finished telling them everything that happened over the weekend.

"So he lays in bed snuggled up to you all night, doesn't try a thing, and you wonder why I thought he was gay?"

Crystal smacked him twice that time.

"Shit, Crystal, why twice?"

"Once for me and once for Alia," said Crystal.

"Why can't she hit me? You hit harder," whined George.

"Because George, she's distraught."

Alia giggled a little. "Okay, you two stop. So I mean, what the hell, right? What do you think?"

"Well, this is a good thing, isn't it?" asked Crystal.

"Yeah, it's great, Alia, right up to when your mother kills the both of you."

"George, stop; she doesn't need that negative shit right now. Alia, everything will be fine; you just need to believe that. When we gave you that cell phone, you thought for sure it was only a matter of time before you got caught."

"What makes you think I ever stopped. And I don't know, maybe I am worried over nothing, but after what Charles said tonight, I have to admit I am worried."

"Well, what could he have possibly said to freak you out more than that he loves you?"

"Something about protecting me."

"Charlie said he did what he thought he should to protect you but that he had failed," said George.

"Uh, you were listening?" asked Alia.

"Well yeah, you two were just at the back end of the Buick, not on Mars."

"What I think," said Crystal, " is that as usual, you are overreacting because that is your go-to panic mode."

"Okay, so what is he supposed to protect me from? I realize he's talking about my mother, but it's not like he has anything to do with how she treats me. He certainly can't do anything to stop her."

"Maybe somehow he thinks he is responsible." Said George. "I mean, he is a cop. It's his job to protect the people of his community."

"No, George, I don't think that's it. Alia is special to him. That's been obvious for years." Said Crystal.

"What are you talking about for years?" Alia was beginning to think that the only person that didn't know about Charlie…was her.

"The first time I met you, Charlie brought you to our cabin at camp. After introducing you, he sat there with us for a while, even putting calamine lotion on you. I always had the feeling like he stayed just to make sure you were okay. To make sure we would all be friends. And While he was there, he hardly ever took his eyes off you. To tell the truth, I always thought the two of you had been off, kissing in the woods somewhere before you showed up."

"Why?" Alia laughed.

"Because the two of you looked like George and the girl next door did when dad found him and her kissing in a closet."

"They looked terrified because I am pretty sure I was terrified," said George.

"No, I'm talking later, after dad gave you two his little speech. He let you walk her home; that's what I'm talking about. All out of breath, a little flush and grinning at each other like lovesick loons."

"I did not." Said Alia.

"Uh, yes, you did, the same way you looked tonight getting in the car."

"Yeah, right before you turned pale, then green," said George.

"So you thought the two of us were together all this time."

"No, of course not, But you have been in love this whole time. And for all, I know even longer."

I have loved you since the first time I laid eyes on you. Charlie had said. But when was that? Not in the apartments, but maybe when we moved to the little red house? That would have made me about four, five at the most. Okay, so perhaps he was exaggerating. Or maybe just being romantic.

"Okay, Charlie has liked me for a while; let's say I believe that. He still shouldn't feel like anything has been his fault."

"Well, you're just going to have to ask him," said Crystal.

Alia looked at her phone.

"No, not over the phone," said George. "You're an adult now, and as someone that is married, I can tell you shit like this needs to be done in person. I still don't know why but it does."

"So The next time I see him, I'll ask him. I can manage that, right?" She tried to sound convincing, but her stomach didn't agree. Shit, I have got to go. My mother is already going to be on the warpath as it is."

They helped her with her bag in the back, each hugged her and said goodbye.

"Text me in a bit, so I know she didn't kill you," said Crystal.

"Sure thing."

Crystal and George drove off, and Alia looked up at the building she lived in. It wasn't half bad of a place, much better than most places they had lived. The complex had been brand new when they moved in two years prior.

Despite being a weekend drunk, Billy was a champ at fixing things, so he had a decent job as a machine mechanic for a grocery chain. He worked exclusively out of their main warehouse building near the mall. Still, no matter how nice it was, even with her having her own bathroom and a huge closet, it, like so many before it, never felt like home.

Going upstairs and into her apartment felt like she was a late tenant at a hostel or Airbnb. Everyone else always seemed settled in and at home, and she was the intruder. This night was no different. As she shut the door, her mother called out from the living room, and their (or rather her mother's) miniature poodle Ebony ran up to her.

"That you, Alia? If it's a killer, come back later. I'm too tired today."

Alia walked down the short hall to the living room, trying her best not to look like she just got kissed by a guy that she's pretty sure she's been mooning over forever. Her mother was on the couch alone, not a good sign, but she also wasn't in her; I was waiting for you to come home so I could yell at you, position, either, which was a good sign.

Trish had Alia when she was sixteen, which made her only thirty-four. However, you would think she was much older to look at her. Years of heavy drinking, drug use, stress, and smoking aged her badly. Still, Trish acted like she was much prettier than she was, often lying about people saying she and Alia were sisters, not mother and daughter. Trish kept very thin, whereas Alia had struggled some with her weight. Trish made sure her hair stayed a radiant blond. No matter where she went, work, or play, Trish had a habit of wearing tight clothes to show off her ass and tits (what little of each she had) and what Alia thought of as gobs of makeup.

Part of the reason Alia didn't wear makeup and tended to wear looser-fitting clothes was because of her mother. It would be one thing for Trish just to dress as she did, but she was also very promiscuous and flirty. The last thing Alia ever wanted was for people to think she was like her mother.

"It's me, Mom, no killer today."

"Oh well. It's pretty late. Don't you have school in the morning?"

"Yes, roads were a mess heading back into town. Which is why I am going to take a quick shower and get in bed. Where's Billy? I ever so much wanted to thank him for all his help." She said sarcastically.

"He already went to bed, early call in, in the morning, one of their freezer systems crashed over the weekend. And you leave him alone anyway; he had a tough weekend after that shit you pulled."

Alia's jaw dropped. "He had a rough time?"

"Well, he woke up with a damn hangover first of all. Then he was worried about where you were."

Oh yeah, I am so sure he was.

"Then he spent the rest of yesterday wondering when Harper was going to come banging on the door to arrest him for getting drunk."

"I told you he didn't have to worry about that. The worst he did was drink in a drug-free zone."

"First of all, Alia, I told you never to trust a cop. Sure as hell don't trust one from that family. And the apple doesn't fall far from the tree. I told you that Harper has it out for me."

"Yeah, well, you have never told me why."

"Because Alia, he's a dirty cop, and I know it. They all are, but he's the worst. He knows I know, and he's always had it out for me because of it. You may not remember how many times he tried getting you to lie about me, but I do. You're my kid; if I think you need to be slapped around a little to pay attention, that's my business."

Alia did remember. And it wasn't several times; it was only twice. Both times Alia lied, just like she was told to, and said nothing happened. The bruises were from wrestling with her cousins. The burn marks were her fault; she's such a klutz. The knot on her head she got from playing under a table. Alia remembered too that over the years, her mother had gotten more clever and made marks that were harder to see. Trish pulled Alia's hair, pinched the inside of her arms, squeezed and pinched her toes almost to the point of breaking. And when Alia started to get bigger than her mother, Trish turned up the psychological abuse. But if anyone asked, things were fine.

"What goes on in the home stays in the home." Her mother always said, "Because if they put me in jail, I will get out…and god help your ass when I get home."

"Well, I need to get in the shower, it was a long ride back, and I feel grimy." She started to walk off, and her mother waved her back.

"You didn't say anything to that boy, did you."

"What, Boy?"

"Don't be a smart ass, Alia; you know what boy I mean, the Deputy. That's a long drive up there. Are you sure the two of you didn't have a nice long chat?"

"Mom, I told you already he was pissed off and being a dick. I got tired of him lecturing me from the front seat of the patrol car, so I laid down and pretended to sleep until I actually did. The last thing I wanted to do was talk to him anyway. What Billy did was embarrassing enough. Oh, and tell your boyfriend he owes me forty bucks for the beer."

"Oh, you're not getting that money. That's the least you owe him after scaring the shit out of him with the cops."

"What?!! Billy was the one sitting in the back of his pickup, drinking half a case of beer. That's not my fault that's on him."

"If you had stopped fooling around and got your job done sooner, he wouldn't have drank so much. And you're the one that came waltzing out of the school with your buddy, the Deputy."

"The lights were out at the school, call up and ask. It took me a bit longer to clean in the dark, and when I went to leave, the Deputy was there. The principal wanted to make sure I had a ride, so Charlie followed me out. You know what, forget it, just forget the money. Lesson learned. I'm going to bed."

"That's right young lady, you learn to be on time next time."

Shaking her head Alia went back down the hall to her room, making sure not to slam her door shut like she wanted to. Slammed doors in her mother's home got those doors taken off the hinges for a while. The last time that happened, one of Trish's creep boyfriends spied on her getting dressed. When Alia complained to her mother, she was told to stop lying, but if he was, then maybe, she would learn not to slam the door again. Alia had to give that much to her mother; she hadn't slammed a door ever again.

In the relative safety and comfort of her room, Alia locked her door, put down her bags, grabbed some nightclothes, and went into her bathroom and locked that door too. With the shower running, she pulled out her phone and texted Charlie.

Alia: Made it home. All is good. Getting a shower and going to bed. I hope you are too. Goodnight.

Alia waited a few minutes to see if he would respond, but he didn't. She felt herself go cold, and her heart quicken. *There's nothing wrong.* She told herself. *Charlie said he had to talk to his parents; he's not answering because he's busy, not because he regrets what he said.* Alia could feel another anxiety attack coming on and tried to fight it. Instead, that ugly voice rose from the back of her mind.

He doesn't love you…why the hell would he love an ugly thing like you.

She shook her head, trying to clear her mind and rid it of that all too familiar voice.

No one could ever love someone like you. So ugly. Don't bother with the makeup.
Makeup on you is like putting tits on a bull hog.

Alia tried to put herself in the woods, tried to block out the voice of her mother.

He won't text back. He's happy to be rid of you. Probably scrubbing your stench off of him.

Realizing she was too tired to fight it off, Alia cranked the shower water to cold and jumped in fully dressed. The water was painfully cold, but the voice ran from her mind screeching. Alone in her mind, at last, Alia slid down and sat in the tub under the shower. There she stayed until she could breathe again. After a while, she turned the water up warmer and quickly washed up and got out. Her phone was on the floor where she had dropped it. Alia admonished herself for leaving it out in the open(locked doors never meant shit in her family) when she noticed there was a message from Charlie.

Charlie: Alia, are you okay?

Alia: Yeah, I"m fine. I just got out of the shower.

Charlie: Sorry I didn't see your text till now. About to leave my parents' house.
Glad you're okay. I hope she didn't give you a hard time.

Alia smiled and felt like a giddy little school girl.

Alia: No hard time at all, well nothing I'm not used too

Charlie: Why does that not make me feel better?

Alia: It's okay. She just always has to get a word in. I took care of it. Pretty sure she bought it all.

Of course, she bought it; I would have been dead as soon as I came in the door if she hadn't

Alia: Did everything go alright on your end?

Charlie: Yes, nothing to worry about. You work in the library after school tomorrow, right?

Alia: Yeah.

Charlie: I might stop by to see you. I'll slip in the back, so don't worry. You should get to sleep, you've got classes in the morning.

Alia: You too. You've got to be exhausted. It was a crazy weekend.

Charlie: I will. Out in my truck, about to head home now. And yes, it was. But it ended pretty well. Right?

Alia: I think it ended very well.

Charlie: I like the strawberry, by the way

Alia: I'll have to make a note of that. Let me know you made it home, okay?

Charlie: I will, but you have to promise me you'll be in bed by then.

Alia: I promise. Now get home. I won't be able to sleep till I know you're there.

Alia hoped he didn't find that very cheesy. It was true. Ever since they got back, she had this creepy feeling slithering around in the back of her mind. She was worried for him but not sure why.

Charlie: On my way

Alia took a deep breath, then another. *I'm going to stop freaking out over everything and enjoy this.*
While it lasts, said the nasty in her head.
She pushed that last thought out and got into bed. Before turning off the lights, Alia texted Crystal, letting her also know all was good at home. Well, as good as it gets anyway. She waited for Charlie's text, reading over the ones he sent already (I'm just reading them, I'm not going to overanalyze them and overthink).
There wasn't a picture of him on his messages to her because she didn't have one. So Alia went to the web page for the local sheriff's department and was able to find a few pictures of him there. Picking out one where he was smiling just a little, she copied it to her phone and then added it to her messenger account under his name. It didn't occur to her that having his picture on her phone may be a bad idea. She was too tired and too much in love with the idea of him to worry. As she lay down, sure she would not be able to sleep, Alia started to drift off with her phone in her hand. She was almost under when she felt the phone vibrate.

Charlie: Made it home. Goodnight, sweet girl.

Alia glanced at the message, smiled, and fell into a decent sleep, but one not nearly as good as the one she spent in Charlie's arms.

Chapter 10
A poem and A kiss

Awaking to her alarm next to her bed, Alia found her phone still in her hand. Wide awake now, she snatched the phone under her blankets as if to hide it. No one was in the room, of course.

"That was stupid." She said out loud. *Got to get my shit together; if someone came in and saw the phone, it would be hell. Four weeks to go, I can do this; I just need to be smart and stop taking chances.* Alia was about to shove the phone in her backpack when she saw a familiar handsome face on the screen.

Charlie: Good morning. I'll see you after school. Hope you have a good day
Love you

Alia felt her heart swell as she reread the text.

Alia: Good morning to you too. Please stay safe. Love you more.

Alia looked over what she had sent, then shoved the phone in her backpack before she regretted sending it off. It felt strange to her, this whole being in love thing. One minute she felt so happy, the next terrified. The words she wrote didn't feel like enough. They felt like too much. All the confidence and relaxed, easy nature Alia had with Charlie all weekend was gone. Now she felt aloof, sad for no reason, terrified for plenty of reasons, and uncertain that she was doing the right thing. At times Alia even felt like she had imagined it all.

Several times during the school day, Alia had to check the messages on her phone to ensure they were still there. She walked around the school all day in a daze. Even Crystal couldn't seem to break her of the funk.

At lunch, Alia was a no-show. Crystal checked some of her usual spots around the school and finally found her sitting in a dark corner of the school auditorium. Crystal sat down with her, at first, not saying anything.

Alia put her head on the shoulder of her best friend doing her best not to cry.

"You're overthinking too much again."

"I know."

"So stop. You're the only girl I know to get the guy you've always wanted but turn out more depressed than before."

"I'm not depressed."

"Oh no? You have moped around all morning. You don't look like you're even here. And you keep checking your phone. Please don't end up being one of those girls that obsess over their boyfriend so much they lose it if he doesn't text a million times a day."

"It's not that. It's the opposite of that. I keep looking because I keep expecting them not to be there. None of this feels real. Not since Charlie left the parking lot. I had nightmare after nightmare last night. All of them that this was some kind of joke. Or I would see him again, and he'd act as if nothing happened. Hell, one, he acted like he never even knew me."

"That's because you're letting your mother into your head again. What did my father tell you? You have to imagine...."

"A door and shut her out, I know I know." Crystal's parents were both marriage and family counselors. They were always good about listening when Alia needed help or advice. It took her a while to trust them, but after she did and was able to open up more, they both helped her by showing her ways to deal with her inner demons. Like the place Alia built in her mind to go during anxiety attacks, these little tricks had made it easier to function over the past few years. Bit by bit, she was rebuilding her confidence and self-esteem. There was still a lot of work, but enough was done to encourage her to sign up for the academy. However, now she felt a bit of that resolve start to slip away.

"This isn't that, though. This is something different. I can't stop thinking about something he texted."

"Then stop looking at them until you see him again and can ask him about it. Let me see what he sent." Crystal took the phone from Alia and looked over the messages. "Cute pic of him, by the way. Where did you get it?"

"On the Sheriff's station's website. It was his academy photo. He just looked so happy in it."

"George said Charlie had always wanted to be a cop. Even dressed as one most Halloweens."

"I remember that," said Alia smiling.

"Well, maybe you are a little loony because I don't see anything bad here. A little corny maybe, but sweet."

"In the beginning, he said he needed to talk to his parents about something. It's got to be about us. I mean, what else would it be?"

"So? That's good; that means he's not trying to hide it from them. Two fewer people you have to hide all this from."

"Unless they talk him out of it. Convince him it's not such a good idea to date me after all."

"Why would they do that?"

Alia sighed heavily. "For the same reason why they didn't tell him about me coming over to study every week. Or the gun range, for that matter. Charlie said something about them protecting us, but it sounds to me like they have been trying to keep us apart. It's bad enough I can't for the life of me figure out what he sees in me in the first place. Now I am worried his parents; I don't know, won't approve of him going out with poor white trash."

"Now that is your mother talking."

"No, it's the truth. Just a few years ago, we lived in a trailer park, in some crappy trailer, barely able to make ends meet because she was spending most of our money on weed. And it's only a matter of time before we end up right back there again. She's already cheating on Billy with some asshole she met at the bar. When he finds out, we're gone."

"Actually, your mother will be gone because you will be out of there for good. Just four more weeks to go, Alia. Then it's no more the two of you; Trish will be on her own, as she needs to be."

"You mean as long as I don't fuck anything up, that is."

"Exactly, because you won't. Your problem is for the first time in a long time; hell ever, even your life is going in the right direction. Good things are happening, and it's about damn time because you deserve a break. Stop waiting for the other shoe to drop and chunk that thing. You keep looking for the bad, it's going to drive you crazy, and you won't be able to enjoy the good."

Alia smiled. "You're right. And I was doing so good all weekend. I honestly don't think I have ever been so happy as I was when he kissed me."

"Hold on to that. Hold on to that feeling. And when you see Charlie again, tell him how you feel."

"Uh, the last thing I want to do is go whining to him every time I feel like shit is too good to be true. I am going to wind up sounding ungrateful."

"Or you're going to find out there's nothing at all to worry about."

"So what about you? Who is this guy taking my best friend to the prom?"

"Just a boy." Crystal smiled.

"Are you dating him? And am I the worst friend ever for not knowing?"

"No, you are not. You've been busy this year. Between school and all your odd jobs, not to mention your real job, I know you haven't had as much time to just hang out. I get it."

"But the boy?"

"I like him. We have some classes together and some of the same activities. So I don't know, we'll see how prom goes and go from there."

"Uhg, prom. Are you sure you won't let me beg off? I mean, you have a date."

"Not a chance. It wouldn't be the same without my best bud there."

Above and around them, the school bell went off.

"Did you even eat anything?" asked Crystal.

"No, I went to the cafeteria, but my stomach turned, and I ran back out." Crystal reached into her brown paper lunch sack and tossed a sandwich to Alia, then helped her up.

"We need to get to class, at least try to eat that. I've got plenty of junk in here to keep me happy."

Alia and Crystal walked out of the auditorium and went separate ways in the hall. Crystal had a math class during this period, and Alia had one of her two language arts classes upstairs. She made it through the door just in time but still managed a look of disappointment from her teacher Mrs. Bell.

Now even though this was their senior year, and even though there were only two weeks left of full days and classes, Mrs. Bell was not one to let her students off easily. Every class of those two weeks was going to be spent doing work, right up to the last minute. While in most classes, they were allowed to goof off or just study for their finals, in Mrs. Bell's class, they were going over the latest book they were reading.

The book was ONE DAY IN THE LIFE OF IVAN DENISOVICH. Alia had loved the story and had read it three times already. Usually, she was eager to talk over aspects of the book with the class, but today she found herself staring out the window, lost in a fog. So much so that she didn't even notice class was over until Mrs. Bell, sat down in front of Alia, spoke.

"So, what's his name?" She asked. Mrs. Bell was, well in student terms, like a hundred years old. She sometimes joked she was here teaching so long that there wasn't even a school when she started. She was tall, rail-thin, and had a habit of reading to the class in such a spirited way that Alia felt sorry for her when they all snickered. Now the often stern, no-nonsense teacher she had all year was looking at Alia with a knowing smile on her face.

Realizing the class was over, and all the students were gone, Alia got up, but Mrs. Bell patted her back down. "I'm sorry, I must not have heard the bell."

"Of course, you didn't. You weren't here. I don't know where you were, but it certainly wasn't my class. No sense in being in a hurry now. I don't have a class this period, so we can chat."

"I'm sorry, Mrs. Bell, I'm just not feeling quite here today, I guess."

"I know. That's why I asked what his name was."

"What makes you think this is about a boy?"

"Because I was young once, back when the dinosaurs roamed." She laughed. "And I was a very bright and attentive student like you. And then one day I met this boy, and my head got lost in the clouds for a while. I remember feeling then, the way you look now."

"And how's that?"

"Ecstatic and terrified all at the same time." She smiled

Alia smiled back, then frowned. "Not sure if I should say. His name, I mean. I have a feeling it's all supposed to be some secret."

"A good secret or a bad secret?" she asked with concern.

"Good, I think. Let's just say my mother would disapprove."

"Hmm." Mrs. Bell said, thinking for a bit. "I think it's time for me to show you something. I was going to wait till the year was done, but I think you need to see this now." Mrs. Bell got up and walked over to some filing cabinets set up. "I have gotten in the habit over the years of keeping a few good works from a few good students I have had. I have several of yours as well." she pulled a file out, then a sheet from that. "This particular student I only have one thing collected from. It's a poem. He was a good enough student, did his work well, got good grades, and didn't make as much fun of me as the others. But a writer, he was not. That was until we did a section on poetry." She sat back down in front of Alia, still holding the paper where Alia couldn't see. "When this young man turned his assignment in, I knew it was special and pretty good too." Mrs. Bell put the paper down on the desk and slid it in front of Alia.

Alia looked and saw four paragraphs neatly typed. There was no title, only a name.

A poem by...Charles Nathaniel Harper.

Alia's heart gave a little jump at the sight of his name. She read the poem and discovered it was a love poem. An incredible love poem. "I don't understand; what does this have to do with me?"

"Look closer. Do you see the first word and the first letter of each paragraph? Tell me what you see."

Alia looked closer at the words and letters. She felt like her heart did a flip in her chest when she saw it. She looked again; sure, she had seen something wrong, but no. The first letter of the first word in each paragraph spelled out,

A L I A....ALIA

"Charles wrote that in his senior year. It was so good I asked him if I could keep a copy, knowing he would want the original back. I didn't make the name connection until you started taking my class this year. As soon as I saw the spelling of your name, the uniqueness of it, I knew I had seen it before and without even realizing it. Sure enough, when I pulled the file there, it was plain as day."

Alia could only stare at the poem in disbelief. Four years ago, well before the night at the motel, Charlie had written not just a poem but a love poem. Rereading it, she realized the verse was describing her.

"How, how do you know?"

"That your behavior change has anything to do with the young man that wrote that poem four years ago? Well, maybe that was a bit of speculation on my part. I like to think I channeled my inner Agatha Christie. Last Friday in my class, you were your normal attentive self. Then Friday night, I saw you and the now Deputy Sheriff Charles Harper drive off together. I also knew you needed to get to Alexandria to take the SATs and assumed he had taken you there himself. Now what I won't do is speculate on what happened while the two of you were out of town for two days, but I'm guessing the young man in question finally made his intentions clear. Clear enough, that is."

Alia nodded, still feeling stunned. She shouldn't be, though, she thought; *he told me, he kissed me. Why am I having such a hard time with this? I know damn well Charlie would never hurt me.* Then suddenly, a horrible revelation dawned on her. "Wait, if you know the two of us left town and were both gone for two days, then half the freaking town knows." Alia felt like she was going to faint. It wouldn't be long before word got to her mother if the town knew. She had to warn Charlie.

"Oh, I doubt that very much." She chuckled. "No, dear, I think your secret is safe for now. I only knew because I was here Friday night. And even then, I wasn't sure until I saw you today. You have the look of one love-sick young woman. Don't you worry, no one will hear a peep out of me. I would be the last person to want to ruin such a romance as this. As for knowing you two were both gone for two days, that I figured out from watching the news. They said that the highways and mountain passes were closed till morning between here and Alexandria."

Alia looked over the poem again. "This is, I mean, it's beautiful."

"Yes, it is, and I am so jealous of the two of you, happy too. So you take that, I have plenty of copies. And from now on, when you start to worry and feel overwhelmed by all of it, read the poem. Because I am telling you, the boy that wrote that was madly in love with the girl he wrote about. No doubt about that."

Looking at the poem again, Alia smiled.

When classes were over for the day, Alia got a ride with Crystal the mile into town to her afternoon job at the library. Before they left the lot, Alia handed the copy of the poem to her to read.

"You do realize this poem spells out your name, right?"

"Yes."

"Where did you get it from?"

"Mrs. Bell gave it to me today. She said Charlie wrote it four years ago. She kept a copy because it was pretty good."

"That's an understatement."

"She didn't make the connection it was about me until she had me in her class. And even then, she wasn't positive until she saw us leave out of here the other night."

"You don't think she'll say anything, do you? You know about the two of you?"

"No, I think we are pretty safe in that regard. We better go. I don't want to be late. The last thing my nerves need is Mrs. Stackhouse mad at me."

Crystal drove off from the school. "Oh, please. You are about the only young person, as she calls us that she likes. You wouldn't have the job if she didn't."

"She likes you too. She likes most people, well maybe tolerates is a better word." They both laughed.

"Nice to see you in a better mood. I'll be sure to tell Charles to write you poems whenever he makes you mad instead of getting flowers."

"It's crazy, though. I find myself having a hard time wrapping my head around this whole thing."

"Only one way to take care of that, and that's to talk to him." Crystal pulled her parents' Buick into a space in the parking lot behind the library. "Has he texted?"

"No, not since this morning. And yes, before you ask, I am trying not to freak out about it. He's working, and I was at school all day. So I am telling myself he just didn't want to bother me."

"Yeah, but are you listening?"

Alia grinned and shook her head. "Yeah, no, not really." She laughed, getting out of the car. "He may drop by later, so I'll let you know if we get to talk. Bye"

"Bye, and stop overthinking this. Charlie is a nice guy, be happy."

Alia waved goodbye and went in the back door to the public library. She wasn't late, and Mrs. Stackhouse wasn't mad, so she tried to keep herself busy. Still, Alia kept finding herself looking at the clock on the wall and checking her phone. Time was unusually creeping slowly by.

Alia loved her job so much that mostly her time here went pretty fast. She had always found solace and comfort deep in the stacks. As a kid, she would find the least used section to hide in a corner and read. Most of the time, the bullies she ran from would never follow her into a public library, and Alia would be safe. And other times, they boldly marched right in like they owned the place only to be scolded by the librarian. Of course, that was outside of Union county.

Here for a little over four years, this time around, the bullies had been lacking. There were always the mean girls that could cut with their words better than a knife, but they bothered her no more than they did anyone else. There were also a couple of boys she learned to avoid (and more than a few that knew to avoid her), but even they seemed to have lost interest as they got older. Still, from the moment Alia arrived, she made the library her sanctuary.

When Crystal was busy or gone during the summer (at the camp Alia only got to go to once), she spent hours of every day roaming the rooms and stacks reading with a frenzy. Eventually, she started to help put books away and directed people where they needed to go and recommend books. A few years ago, Mrs. Stackhouse offered her a job.

"For all the time you spend here, you should at least get paid for it." She had said sternly (she pretty much said everything sternly), "Besides, you know this place almost as well as I do."

Alia felt that was the best compliment she had ever gotten. Today though, the place felt more like a prison to her, as she served a stiff sentence of the slowest workday she'd ever had.

About an hour into the job, Alia was pulling the return cart behind her in the stacks when suddenly it stopped. She looked back to see Charlie, in uniform, holding on to the other end of it.

"There you are," he said, "I swear I think I have been here ten minutes trying to find you in this place." He grinned at her.

Alia's heart leaped for joy at the sight of him. All the doubts, fears, and worries she carried with her all day, washed away with just one look of those piercing green eyes. She looked around, but since they were deep in the non-fiction part of the stacks, no one was near. "Did anyone see you come in?"

"Only Mrs. Stackhouse, I came in through the back door."

"Well, she doesn't miss anything. Surprised she didn't fuss at you."

He laughed, "She did, for using the back way in. I told her I was here on official police business, and she just rolled her eyes and walked away."

"Official police business, really?"

"Yeah, this guy I know, he's a Sheriff's Deputy, he wanted me to give something to you."

Before she could even ask him what he was talking about, Charlie came to her, cupped the side of her face in his right hand, and kissed her.

Glad that she applied her strawberry lip balm every five minutes, Alia kissed him back.

"Ahem." Was suddenly heard from the end of the row of stacks.

They both jumped and turned to see Mrs. Stackhouse at the end, books in her arms, peering at them.

"Young lady, the non-fiction section of the library is not the appropriate place for that kind of business," Mrs. Stackhouse said, more stern than ever. Then she smiled and looked at them over her glasses. "The least you could do is take it over to the romance section." With that, she winked at them and walked away.

Alia stood there gaping. She thought for sure she was about to lose her job. *This whole thing just keeps getting weirder and weirder.* She turned back to Charlie, and they both laughed, then shushed each other and laughed some more. *Why was I so worried all day?* She thought. *Charlie is here, everything is fine, and I couldn't be much happier.*

Charlie kissed her a few more times, then, with a hug, let her go. "Been thinking about that all day." He smiled at her. "So everything is still cool at home?"

Other than having another anxiety attack then walking around like a brain-dead zombie all day, yeah, sure.

"Yeah. Avoidance is my best strategy right now. How about you? You said you had to talk to your parents about something. I assume that something was us."

"Yes, it was," he said, frowning slightly.

"Well, I see you're still in one piece, so it must not have been too bad."

"No, not too bad, there was some yelling, but we talked everything over. They want you to come to dinner tomorrow night. I promise there won't be any yelling if you do."

"But they want to talk to the both of us?" Her heart sank a little.
"Yes, but it's nothing bad; they're not upset, just concerned."

"Even your father?"

"Okay, honestly, he's a bit upset. I told you the thing between him and your mother was his story to tell. He's not exactly ready to tell it just yet, but he will." Her eyes had lost that sparkle they had when Alia first saw him behind her. Charlie took her in his arms again, kissed her forehead, and looked into her eyes. "Everything is going to be okay, I promise you. I don't want you worrying about this all night, okay? We are going to have a nice family dinner, all four of us, and then talk some things through."

"I don't understand, Charlie. Obviously, whatever happened between the two of them is sort of a big deal. And I can't help but worry. Harper and I haven't ever really seen eye to eye. I know he doesn't approve of me. Otherwise, why not tell me before now? You talk about protecting me but refuse to tell me why."

"I know, and I'm sorry. You're right; it is a big deal. It's the reason why we have to be so careful. But it's not your fault, and you're not in any trouble with my folks. They are crazy about you."

"They are?"

"Yes, they are. Even my dad. Why else would he work with you to get into the academy? If he were trying to keep us apart, he would have never offered to pay for your training and give you a job."

"I don't know. I mean, your mom is the sweetest, but your dad. Charlie, he locked me in a jail cell when I was only thirteen."

Charlie laughed.

"It's not funny. I thought I was going to jail. He was so mad. Your dad kinda scares me."

"Hmm, the story I heard was that you kinda needed to be scared. My mother described the two of you as two bulls locking horns."

"Okay, maybe I was a little angry."

"Little spitfire he used to call you. Said you had your mother's temper and bullheadedness."

"Well, he isn't winning any points with that description."

"Look at me. Have I ever lied to you? Have I ever hurt you?"

"No, Charlie, of course not," she said, looking into eyes that had nothing but love in them. *No, I'm the one that has hurt you time and time again, and I feel like a real shit for doing it.*

"Then, believe me, you have nothing to worry about." *I wish I could say the same for myself.* Charlie kissed her like the first time again made her promise to text him when she got home safe. Then Charlie left before he broke down and told her the whole story himself. *Not that I would be able to reveal it all.* He thought. Just thinking about it hurt his heart. *I just hope you still look at me like you do now after you know the truth.*

With Charlie gone, the books put back in the stacks, Alia returned to her seat at the front desk. Mrs. Stackhouse sat next to her checking out a few books for a woman. When the woman left, she glanced over at Alia.

"Was the deputy able to finish his official police business?"

Alia looked over and was surprised to see the Librarian smile. *She should smile more,* Alia thought. *She looks radiant when she does.*

"Yes, ma'am, sorry about that, it won't happen again."

Mrs. Stackhouse waved her hand at the girl and shook her head. "While I will admit I don't exactly want orgies going on in the stacks, I do understand that in some cases of love, a certain amount of discretion is needed. Charlie is a fine young man. I have known him and his family for a long time. And you young lady have grown to be a fine young woman yourself. I trust that, unlike others, the two of you are capable of making good choices and don't need to be scolded like a couple of children." She turned to look right at Alia, even taking her hand. "This, for the most part, is my place. And as long as it is, this is also a safe place. You understand?"

Alia nodded because, strangely, she did. Though why this woman was offering her most sacred place to them where they could meet without too many prying eyes, she didn't know.

Letting go of her hand, Mrs. Stackhouse opened a small drawer and took out a key. "I realize you won't be working here much longer, but while you do, I want you to have this. It's to the archives and storage in the basement. Just promise me to use it wisely."

Alia took the key, smiling. "I promise, and thank you."

"I was young and in love once too, my dear."

During the last hour of work, Alia felt fine. On the bus ride home, she felt okay. On the walk from the bus stop to her apartment, in the dark, alone, she started to feel not so okay anymore. This was a walk Alia had taken hundreds of times and had usually enjoyed the alone time before heading home to who knows what.

Trish was at work until late, but Billy would be home, and he was bad enough. At the very least, there would be a mess in the kitchen from him getting food. And no one seemed to care that Alia not only worked but paid rent as well. She still had to do the dishes, even Billy's. If he had a hard day at work, he often would leave a trail of his belongings around the small apartment, knowing Alia had to have the house cleaned before her mother got off work. And no, Billy wouldn't clean that up either. It was always that he had a hard day at work. Alia should be glad she's even still living here. Stop being such an ungrateful bitch.

But Alia's apprehension had nothing to do with Billy. The closer she got to the apartment, the more the joy she carried with her from being with Charlie that afternoon was sucked out of her. Now she wasn't sure if she would last four weeks like this. Part of her even wished for a second that Charlie had kept his big mouth shut and waited till she was out of the so-called home she lived in.

Alia quickly admonished herself for thinking that hoping she didn't jinx the whole relationship with that one thought. Besides, that would have sucked, too, because then she would be gone away to the academy for three months.

For the life of her, Alia couldn't see how this was going to work. She wanted more. More time, more talks, more hugs, and a shit ton more kisses. *OMG, his kisses are amazing.* She knew she should just be happy with what she had, but Alia couldn't help but feel like it was so unfair. Any other girl would be able to walk down Main Street hand in hand with him, but she couldn't because of her psycho mother.

"It's only for four weeks, only four more weeks." But was it really? Yes, she would hopefully be out of the apartment for good then, but what if that wasn't the end of it. What if whatever beef her mother had with Harper meant they could never truly be together? What could be so bad for it to go that far? And even if they could, there were the three months she had to be away at the academy to think about as well. Feeling the need to vent to someone, Alia ducked behind a tree and was about to call Crystal when she got a text.

Charlie: You make it home yet?

Alia: Almost. Walking back from the bus stop

Charlie: Any way you can come up with a reason to leave the apartment for a bit?

Alia: I have to take the dog for a walk after I get in, but I won't be able to be gone for long

Charlie: That's good enough. Meet me behind the maintenance building for the pool. I'll be there in fifteen minutes.

Alia: okay, see you soon.

    Alia's heart leaped with excitement, all the worries she had just had gone once again. She found herself practically skipping the rest of the way to the apartment. At the door, she took a few sobering breaths. *Can't be too happy when I go in. Billy is an idiot but not a blind idiot.* Alia went inside and was instantly greeted by Ebony. He jumped and danced all around her, yapping.
    "Quiet barks," she scolded, and he made barking motions with no sound. "Good dog, good boy."
    "He needs to go out; been whimpering at the door for twenty minutes." Yelled Billy from the living room.

Well, then why didn't you take him out, you lazy bastard? "I'll take him out in a second, gotta pee myself."

"Yeah, well, if he pisses on the floor, you're cleaning it."

He's never pissed in the house, not even as a puppy. But I would let him if I thought I could clean it up with your face. Alia ran into her bathroom, first tossing her backpack on her bed. She didn't need to pee just needed an excuse to check herself before seeing Charlie. Being mindful of the time, she brushed her teeth, then her hair applied more balm, and even spritzed a few sprays of the perfume Crystal got her for her birthday. *Oh Lord, help me, I've become one of those girls.*

Before going out, Alia flushed because once again, even Billy wasn't that stupid. Alia grabbed the leash by the door, clipped it on the collar, and ran out. Outside she went to the far end of her building, turned left, and followed the fence that went all the way down to the pool and tennis courts. After stopping twice for Ebony to pee, Alia cautiously walked into the dark behind the pool's maintenance shed. It occurred to her as she did that this would be the perfect opportunity for a killer to lure her out here alone. Suddenly there was a small light, and in its glow was Charlie. Alia ran to him and was enveloped in his arms, letting go of the breath she was holding.

"You alright? You didn't spook yourself coming out here, did you?"

"No, I just didn't realize how much I could use a hug until I saw you."

Charlie stood there for a bit, just hugging Alia, needing it as much as she did. Then he began to kiss her ear, her jaw, and at last those strawberry-tasting lips he had been yearning for.

Down at their feet, her little dog looked up at them like he was grinning.

Charlie picked Alia up (for someone that thought they had a fat ass, she wasn't heavy) and gently placed her on a stack of pallets. He then reached down and petted the dog making sure to get the good spot behind the ears a scratch. "Now you be good. I'm just going to borrow her for a few minutes."

Ebony sat back down, staring up at them both with his goofy grin.

Charlie gave his attention back to Alia, putting his hands on her hips kissing her again.

Alia put her arms around his neck. Her one hand found the back of his head, so she put her hands through his thick dark hair. *OMG, his hair was amazing too.* When they came up for air, she reluctantly let him go.

"I was headed home for the night when I realized I needed to see you again. Saying goodnight through a text just wasn't going to cut it for me." Alia had been on his mind all day. Both worried for her and wanting to hold her in his arms again. Their little liaison at the library earlier was unbelievable but only left him wanting more. Charlie had waited patiently for so long. Now he felt like he couldn't get enough of her.

"Is everything okay?"

"It is now." *I just want it to stay that way.* "I hate not being able to see you all day. I missed you." And he had, but not just that day. The years they had been apart had been some of the hardest of his life. It would have been torture had it not been for the academy and his job keeping him busy. If she had known how many times he patrolled through town just for a chance to have a glimpse at her, she would probably think he was some kind of creepy stalker. Now that he knew for sure that his love for her wasn't just some kind of fluke, he didn't want to waste any more time.

Alia laughed. "You know what I think? I think you wanted a goodnight kiss."

"You got me." He laughed. "Actually, I had this feeling that you may need a goodnight kiss."

"Funny, I was kinda thinking the same thing." This time she was the one that reached up for him and kissed, marveling over how brave she was when Charlie was around.

"Look, I know this isn't an ideal situation and far from romantic. But it doesn't have to be like this forever. Just give me some time to work some things out so we can spend more time together. If that's what you want." said Charlie.

"Of course it is; it's exactly what I want."

But will you still want it after you know the truth? Will you still love me then?

"You okay, Charlie, you kind of lost your smile there for a minute."

Damn, she caught that. I need to be more careful; I'm supposed to be here to ease her worries, not make them worse. "Yeah, I'm good, just tired. I didn't sleep much last night. Had some beautiful girl on my mind all night."

"Well, she better let you sleep tonight, or I'm gonna have to kick her ass."

"Don't say things like that; now I'm going to be thinking about your ass all night." He laughed. Charlie kissed her again and then again like he didn't want to let go. Picking her up, he helped her down from the pallets. One more kiss, then the last one on her forehead, and Charlie watched as she walked off.

Before fading off into the darkness, Alia called out. "Stop looking at my ass, Charlie."

"Never." He laughed

Alia felt like she was floating all the way home. Ebony even seemed to catch her mood and jumped around more than usual. Part of her wanted to run back to him, gushing like a schoolgirl. But she was an adult now and needed to act like one, which meant handling his departures with maturity. The last thing she wanted was to make things harder for Charlie.

Alia used to have the same issue with her father. She loved spending time with him so much that she would start to pout when it came time for her to go back to her mother. She even full out cried a few times. When Alia was younger, she didn't understand, but as she got older, she realized that not only was it spoiling the last bit of time they had together, but hurting him as well. When her father died, all those times returned to her, making Alia feel more miserable for wasting her time with him. That definitely could not happen with Charlie; she wouldn't make a mistake like that again.

Back at the apartment, Alia ate what she could of some cold chicken and pasta salad her mother had the rare decency of leaving for her. Then she cleaned the kitchen, picked up around the house (the bastard could've put his shoes on the rack, not in front of it), and retreated to her room. Alia had stashed her phone in her room after getting back, so she checked it as soon as she got in.

Charlie: When do you usually go to bed

Alia: Bed around ten and reading until eleven. Why?

He didn't answer right away, so she figured he may still be working. There was another text, this one from Crystal.

Crystal: Call me when you can, no rush, no worries

Alia went out to the living room, acting like she was getting something from the kitchen, but really she wanted to see what Billy was up to. The living room was empty, and the bedroom door closed, so he went to bed early. Back in her room, Alia and Normandy crawled all the way to the back of her closet. She had lined this part of the closet with soundproofing that they were throwing away at school. There was also a giant bean bag chair, battery-operated string lights, and one of her favorite soft blankets. The two of them settled in, and Alia called Crystal. She must have been waiting because she picked up the call on the first ring.

"Well, that was fast, eagerly anticipating my call?"

"After you moped around all day, of course, I was. You sound like you feel better. I take it you got to see him."

"Twice, actually." Alia recounted the evening's events to Crystal, even the part where she was upset walking home. They were the kind of best friends that rarely kept anything from each other (except the mysterious boy taking Crystal to the prom).

"See, I tried to tell you everything was going to be okay."

"Yeah, but I still get this sinking feeling in my gut when I think about tomorrow. I'm worried that when Harper tells me what's going on, I'm not going to like it."

"I've been thinking about that. I bet all that happened was that he arrested Trish one time and accidentally brushed her boob or something. I wouldn't be surprised if she threatened to scream rape if he bothered her again."

"I don't know, maybe, it feels like something bigger than that, though. Why would they feel the need to protect me from that? If that's all it is, then it's not that big of a deal."

"Maybe not to you but with Harper not only being a cop but county sheriff, an accusation like that could ruin him. Even if he was found not guilty."

"Okay, then why include Charlie? When I lived in the county when I was little, she used to have a fit if she thought I was hanging around with him." By fit, Alia meant Trish used to beat her.

"Let's not forget that your mother is a bit of a nutter. Also, I have heard her say stuff like the apple doesn't fall far from the tree. So maybe she's afraid Charlie would try to do something to you."

"Okay, all that makes sense except for the last part. I find it very hard to believe she's afraid of anyone doing anything to me when she brings drunk boyfriends home to her teenage daughter. Besides, I think she was just afraid I would say something to him he would run to his dad about."

"Once again, your mother is a nutter. Trying to figure out why she does things is just going to make you as crazy as her."

"Ha Ha, oh wait, I have a text."

Charlie: Just want to know when to tell my sweet girl goodnight.

"Let me guess, Charlie?"

"Yes, of course. You know when he came over tonight, I know it was dark where we were, but for a minute, I could have sworn I caught a look of worry in his eyes."

"You need to stop, just stop. See, this is what you do. You overthink things. You're looking for a problem where there isn't any. Charlie is crazy about you. Even George could see that."

"George also thought he was gay."

"And see, that is more proof of how much he likes you. He didn't even date anyone because he was crushing on you so hard."

"I just find that whole thing so hard to believe," said Alia.

"Why, because you're not good enough for him, not pretty enough, not skinny enough. Did it ever occur to you that those things don't matter to him?"

"Oh yes, I am so sure he loves me for my sparkling personality."

"Well, maybe if you weren't such a smart ass sometimes. But seriously, Alia, you are nowhere near as bad as you make yourself out to be. All that negativity is your mother talking, and we just established she's a nutter."

Alia laughed. "I know what you're trying to say, really I do. But if I'm so great, then where are all the boys lined up to go out with me?"

"There you go again. I believe that is one of Trish's motherisms you love so much. Did you forget you had a senior boyfriend in freshman year?"

"J.J. was a piece of crap. And we only dated a few weeks."

"Crap or not, still a boy that liked you."

"More likely saw a sad little fat girl he could trick into having sex with him. The fat ass perv."

"Okay, so then what about that boy from your martial arts class? The one you thought was so cute and nice because he wouldn't smoke around you? He wanted to ask you out but knew it would ruin your reputation if he did. So see he liked you. and there have been others as well, but all you seem interested in when it comes to boys is being friends with them."

"Can you blame me? Boys our age only think of one thing, and the last thing I ever wanted was to get pregnant. I am not bringing a baby into this shit family. You know she threatened to take it away from me if I did. No way I am putting another kid through her crap."

"I'm just saying it's not just Charlie; there have been others. You're a nice person Alia. If you weren't, I wouldn't be friends with you. I think Charlie is the lucky one here. You are, if nothing else, a very loyal friend. Pain in the ass but a good friend. If you're half as good a girlfriend as you are a friend, he'd still be lucky."

"Well, I guess I am a pretty good friend." She joked.

"And a smart ass, don't forget that." Crystal laughed.

The two talked for a bit longer before hanging up to get ready for bed. Alia got showered, brushed, and crawled into bed with a book. At precisely ten o'clock, she got a text from Charlie.

Charlie: What are you reading

Alia: If it bleeds, Stephen king. Perks of working at the library I know when all the good stuff is available.

Charlie: They don't scare you? Give you nightmares before bed?

Alia: If only. I find it very hard to be scared by books or movies anymore.
I have watched king since I was five and read king since I was ten after fishing Cujo out of a dumpster. Besides, real life is much scarier.

Charlie: Yeah, I see your point. Don't stay up too late. I'll see you tomorrow. Goodnight, I love you.

Alia: Goodnight. Love you more

About an hour later, Alia was about to put her book down and call it a night when her phone went off again.

Charlie: Go to sleep!!

Alia: Yes Deputy

Chapter 11
Things May Never Be the Same Again

Charlie: Good morning. Can't wait to see you tonight. Mom says dinner is at five thirty. Have a good day, I love you sweet girl.

Alia: Good morning. Be safe. See you tonight. Love you more sweet boy.

    Alia's day at school was a little bit better than the last. Still, she worried over how the night was going to go. She was just thankful that finals weren't this week since there was no way she'd be able to give them her full attention.
    The day dragged on, adding to her stress, so to combat that, Alia took out the poem Charlie had written and looked it over again and again. By the time the day was over, she had read it over a dozen times.
    Crystal gave her a lift home in the Buick, where Alia took a quick shower, and Crystal helped her pick out something nice to wear.

"You want me to do your makeup?"

"What makeup?"

"I brought some," said Crystal.

"No thanks, this is a family dinner, not a date. Besides, I think Charlie likes me without it as long as I keep using the strawberry balm." She laughed.

It was still a little early, but Billy was on his way home, so they left a note (going to Crystal's for dinner, be home late.). It's not that they gave a shit, but the first time she didn't, they would get pissed.

During the day, they can't exactly just drive up the driveway of the town Sheriff just in case someone sees Alia in the car. So they parked at Harkening Hill park, a small wooded park about a block from the house. Behind it, the woods went all the way to the sheriff's house and further. There were several paths, one of which went to the small lake at the end of their property.

Crystal wasn't allowed to drive alone at night yet (parental rules), so she had to leave Alia at the park even though it was early. "Text me when you need a ride back. George is staying over for dinner tonight so he can drive us."

"He didn't have to do that. I would have figured something out."

"Oh, don't feel bad for him, any excuse to eat at home. Margie is great and all but not a good cook."

They said their goodbyes, and Alia started on the trail to the lake. She tried taking her time but found that she got to the lake faster than usual. From the lake, Alia could see their entire backyard, complete with a new fire pit, and into the house. The lights were on, and someone was walking around the kitchen.

Every time Alia saw this house, she was overwhelmed with a warm, homey feeling. She didn't know how she could feel since she never had a place long enough to feel like home. But the glow of the lights was like a warm invitation. All the unease Alia had been feeling was fading away as it often did when she came here. The first time she had come up this very same path for her first lessons, Alia almost turned and ran back into the woods. But the glow from the windows on that cold February day pulled her in. And not one day since did she ever regret coming here, despite the past she had with Harper. For the first time in two days, Alia was looking forward to the dinner this evening.

Taking a deep breath, Alia climbed the small hill till she got to the stepping stones that led up to the house.

Before approaching the door, Ellen saw Alia out the window and waved. She opened the back door a few seconds later and let her in. "Come in, come in, brrr, it's chilly out there again tonight. I don't think spring has entirely kicked in yet." Ellen gave Alia a hug, as she always did. Although this one was a little longer than usual, perhaps. "You're a bit early. The boys won't be home for another half an hour at least. But if you're up for it, you can help me in the kitchen."

"Sure, I would love to." Alia took her shoes off at the door, and the two went into the kitchen where a baked chicken was cooking in the oven, and a few pots were on the stove with corn and potatoes in them. The smells were amazing.

Alia loved being here. Crystal's house was the only other place she ever felt this at home. Coming here once a week to study had become the highlight of her week since she turned eighteen. Even Harper, with his bigger-than-life persona and deep thunderous voice, seemed softer and kinder within these walls. Alia had a feeling that Ellen had a lot to do with that. The complete opposite of Harper, Ellen was a petite woman only a smidgen shorter than Alia and several inches shorter than both her boys, as she was fond of calling them. Her voice was soft and gentle, and her eyes green and kind like her son's.

Any anxiety Alia had about tonight wasn't evident at all in how she interacted with Ellen. The two of them set the table, put biscuits in the oven, and set the carrots and potatoes to cook on the stove. The way they worked so well together, anyone watching would think this was mother and daughter playing out a routine they had done hundreds of times before. However, Alia had never helped cook dinner before and was always gone before Charlie arrived home, and it was served.

Everything was almost done when they heard the doors of the patrol cars shut outside at the side of the house. A couple of minutes later, Charlie and Harper came in the side door and into the little mudroom that led into the kitchen.

"I smell food." Boomed Harper's big voice

. Alia heard some rustling around as he and Charlie took off their boots and coats. No shoes in this house, definitely no boots.

Harper poked his large head around the corner, made a strange face then called back to Charlie. "I think we got the wrong house, son. There's not one beautiful woman in the kitchen but two."

Alia felt herself flush. She and Ellen exchanged a look and rolled their eyes laughing.

Charlie came in behind his father and smiled when he saw Alia."Yeah, but the food smells delicious, so I think we should stay anyway." He clapped his father on the back and winked at Alia while walking to the sink to wash his hands.

"Harper went up behind his wife, grabbing her at the waist and kissing her neck."

"Harper, stop before you make me burn one of us," Ellen said as she was trying to lift the pot of potatoes off the stove.

He gave her one last smack on the cheek and joined his son at the sink.

Laughing at them both, Alia took the basket of hot biscuits she'd been holding out to the dining room table where the chicken and salad had already waited. Charlie came up behind her and gave her a kiss on the cheek after checking that his parents were not looking.

"You smell great," he whispered to her.

A few minutes later, they were all sitting at the dining room table, passing around bowls and plates of food. Harper was at his usual spot with his wife across from him. Charlie sat with his back to the big bay window facing the backyard and lake with Alia sitting across from him. Charlie had told her this was a family dinner, which was no joke. The four of them sat around eating, talking, and laughing like this was what they did every night.

Like when she was with Charlie, Alia felt so at ease it was almost dizzying. She also noticed how no one had said anything about her and Charlie's current situation. She was pretty sure the conversation was also steered away from anything to do with her mother or home life. And that was perfectly fine.

Alia much rather hear stories about how Charlie rescued a half-drowned kitten from the lake (said kitten now a big cat that curled around their feet as they ate). How Harper got sprayed by a skunk that had taken up residence under the house one year. How Ellen, despite being a fantastic cook now, had burned their first Thanksgiving turkey. All teasing was lighthearted and well-received even when Ellen scolded Harper for what she called un-table-like conversation.

Alia also got to see a side of Charlie she hadn't gotten to see much. They had laughed and joked back and forth plenty that night at the motel, but this was different. Here, the love he had for his parents was evident in the ease and way they talked to each other. It was nothing like she had experienced, not even with her father. Charlie laughed and smiled so much his eyes sparkled. Alia didn't think It was possible to love the man any more than she did, yet here she was, almost unable to take her eyes off of him.

They still sat for another ten minutes or so when the meal was over. Harper polished off the last story he was telling about how he and Ellen met, with Ellen, of course, correcting what he forgot about. With the story over, they all started to clean up, putting the dishes in the dishwasher, lids on leftovers, and into the fridge. It had gotten quiet then, and Alia could feel the mood shift. They all still smiled, Harper and Ellen giving each other knowing glances, even Charlie, but the sparkle was gone from his eyes.

Here it goes, she thought. Like it or not, Alia had a feeling the evening was about to get serious. As Charlie took her out to the living room to sit, she overheard Harper whisper to Ellen.

"It's time, Ellen."

Ellen nodded her head, and they put their arms around each other.

If it hadn't been for Charlie being right there with her, Alia might have run from the house. And he must have felt her anxiety because he held on to her and whispered in her ear.

"No matter what, just please remember that I love you." he kissed her on the forehead then held his to hers, closing his eyes. When his parents came into the room, he directed Alai to the couch then sat in the chair across from it, close to her but not beside her.

Harper sat in an oversized recliner that she could have picked out as his even before he sat in it. Ellen went over to a bookshelf in the corner and picked out a photo album. She walked over with it and joined Alia on the couch. Alia looked over at Charlie and saw that his smile was gone. It made her heart sad and worried her.

Whatever this is, whatever they are about to reveal to me, it's bad. Alia thought.

Ellen sat on the couch, holding the photo album tight to her chest like she was afraid to let out the secrets held within it.

Clearing his throat, Harper sat forward and began. A man that usually looked at her sternly, Harper's eyes held in them a soft kindness she had only seen from him once or twice before.

Alia took a deep breath bracing herself for what they were about to tell her.

"First, I just want to say, Alia, that we always had every intention of telling you everything. That was a promise we made ourselves a long time ago. We wanted to wait until you were at least eighteen, but also when you were done with school. So we were going to tell you all this in a few weeks."

Alia looked at Harper and realized she was seeing him in a new light as well. She had seen him angry, very,

very angry, seen him joking and laughing, and she thought this was the first time she had seen him sad. However, looking at him now, she had a flash of a memory of him graveside. It was the first time in a long time that she had remembered he had been there at her father's funeral.

"But seeing how Charlie jumped the gun a little by asking you out, we thought it was best you hear it now. We hope that by telling you this, you will understand how important it is going forward that the two of you be careful. And that you understand that while we may have kept some things from you, we only did it to protect you, the both of you."

Alia was already not liking the way this was going. The last time Harper talked to her this seriously, he threatened to lock her up for her own good if she didn't stop her reckless behavior. That was almost a year after her father had died. She looked over at Charlie, hoping his smiling face would help her overwhelming sense of unease, but he looked down at his feet, not meeting her eyes.

Ellen took one hand off the book and one of Alia's in hers and gave it a squeeze before letting go. She then put the photo album on the coffee table in front of them. "We want to show you something. We believe you may recognize it." Slowly she opened the album to a page marked with a paperclip. In the middle of the page was a single photo that Alia recognized right away.

She looked at it for a moment, sure her eyes were playing tricks on her. "I don't understand," she said barely over a whisper. "I know this picture. My mom has it or had it anyway. But how did you get it?" The picture was of a little boy about four with dark brown hair wearing a blue jumper. Next to him was a baby girl no more than a year old. The boy held her hand like he was helping her to walk. Alia suddenly felt hot tears in her eyes. The baby was her, and according to her mother, the little boy had been her foster brother.

Alia shook her head. Looking at the picture then at Charlie, there was no doubt in her mind who the little boy was. For the first time in years, tears fell from her eyes in front of others. She felt Ellen put a tissue in her hand but couldn't get her hand to move to use it. Looking once again over at Charlie, her vision blurred.

"I don't understand." she turned to Ellen, visibly shaking. "The little boy, it's Charlie, isn't it?"

Ellen nodded, tears in her own eyes as well.

"My mom told me he was my foster brother."

"But she never told you his name, I bet," said Harper.

Alia shook her head. "She just said he was...."

"Teaching you how to walk," Charlie spoke for the first time since sitting down. He tried looking at her but couldn't bring himself to do it. He knew she was crying and could hear it in her voice. He felt like his heart would shatter into pieces if he saw her like that right now. Charlie knew the picture would look familiar to her because they had talked about her having gone into foster care when she was a baby the night at the motel. It was only briefly mentioned because they were trying to avoid the topic of her mother. Alia had mentioned the picture and what her mother said about it. It had stunned him that she was aware of being in foster care at all, and Charlie somehow managed to hide that from her.

Lifting Alia's hand up, Ellen helped her wipe away some of the tears but more followed. "You're right," she said. "That's our Charlie, and of course, the baby girl is you." Ellen flipped through the photo album where there were more pictures. Some just of her but most of her and Charlie.

Years ago, Alia's mother had told her that she had to put Alia in foster care. Seemed to be proud of it. Said she had needed some time just to be a kid again herself. Trish had made it seem like her decision, but Alia's father had suggested otherwise. Johnathan had also said that he'd tell her the real story one day when she was old enough. He never made it that far.

"But how...and why...why.." didn't you say anything? She wanted to say but couldn't get it out. All she could do was look at Ellen and Harper, the couple that had once been her foster parents. And Charlie. She had just told him about that very picture. It was the only one left from her time in foster care.

Ellen turned to Harper. "I think you should tell this part." She then wrapped one of her arms around Alia, who was trying her best to control her tears.

Harper took a deep breath and sighed heavily. "We were at home in bed one night. It was late, well past midnight. A call had come into dispatch about a crying baby. Well, more like a screaming baby. The address they gave was a, well, it was a known crack-house. The officer on duty wanted to know if he should handle it, but I told him that both of us should go. Never know when things like this can go south, and I wasn't about to send one of my men there without backup. When we arrived, the door was practically open. A man and a woman were on a couch in the filthy living room, stone-cold, passed out. And sure enough, in a dirty playpen with about four German Shepherd puppies was a little baby girl. And she was screaming like she was mad at the whole world."

"My mom told me about this. She said my great Aunt came and got me."

"Yeah, well, I'm not surprised that woman fed you a load of horseshit," Harper said gruffly.

"Harper, please, this is hard enough," begged Ellen.

"I'm sorry," he took another deep breath and continued. "The two on the couch were useless. Whatever they took, it had them out good. And here I was looking down at this little baby, not even a year old yet. She had scratches from the puppies, wet diaper, and filthy from head to toe. We took the puppies out so they would stop clawing at her. She took one look at me and screamed even louder. I didn't know what to do. It was around three in the morning, social services offices were closed, and Charlie was about the only baby I'd ever touched in my life. So I called Ellen. She no sooner got there then she scooped that baby up and ran into the kitchen toting one of Charlie's old baby bags."

"When he told me over the phone what was going on, I ran up to the attic and grabbed a few of Charlie's old things. It was funny because Charlie had come into the bedroom saying the baby was crying right before Harper called. I just dismissed it as a dream at the time." she had turned back to Alia. The girl's tears had stopped falling, but they were still welling up in her eyes. "You were such a little thing. And Harper was right. You were screaming like you were mad at everyone. I cleaned you up, changed your diaper, and tried for the life of me to get you to stop crying. We had nowhere else to take you, so we took you home. And still, you cried the whole way. We had left Charlie at home in bed with a neighbor watching over him. He must have heard you crying from outside because he was coming into the living room rubbing his eyes when we walked in. Suddenly you stopped crying, I mean just like that. I swear the two of you looked at each other, and you both smiled at the same time. Charlie told us later that you were...."

"The most beautiful thing I had ever seen," Charlie said. He glanced at her quickly. "You looked like an angel. I couldn't explain it then, and I still can't now, but I was convinced they brought you home for me. That you were mine." A tear fell from his eyes, and Alia's heart ached for him.

"Yep, Charlie's Angel. That's what he always called you, his little angel. He was only four years old, but when I put you in his arms that morning, he held you like he knew what he was doing. Charlie went and sat in his father's chair and declared that baby angel was hungry. We had stopped at a store on the way home to get bottles, some more diapers, and baby formula. I fixed you a bottle, and Charlie insisted on feeding you himself."

Over in his chair, Alia saw Charlie smile a little. She wanted to go to him, to take him into her arms, but she could barely breathe, let alone move.

"After he fed you, I burped you and put you back in his arms where you fell asleep. The whole thing was the most astonishing thing I'd ever seen. And Charlie, he was beaming from ear to ear."

Alia dried her fresh tears. "So the two of you were able to keep me?"

"Well, there was a lot involved in that, but pretty much." Said Harper. "The thing was, at first, we had no idea who you were. By the time social services came to the house later that morning, the two from the crack-house were still out of it. The only reason why we were allowed to keep you at first was simply that we had already been approved to foster anyway."

"You see, Charlie was our miracle baby," said Ellen. We were not even supposed to have him. Despite some bumps along the way, I managed to carry him to full term. He came out just as healthy and beautiful as any baby ever was. But there wasn't going to be anymore, not from me anyway. After a few years, we decided we still had a lot of love to give, so we became foster parents. Then you came into our lives not a week after we got approved."

"It was like it was meant to be," said Harper. "So we got temporary custody while we tried to find out who you were. The two druggies woke up, but they weren't your parents after all. They could only give us your mother's first name. She had dropped you off there and was supposed to be back in a few hours. But she had been gone for days, and they didn't know where."

"She was out getting drugs." Said Alia. "She admitted that much to me. Said all I did was scream and cry, so she needed something to cope." Inside of her, Alia could feel a rage building. *All these years…the lies…so many lies.*

"Well, a couple of days later, one of your Aunts, a tall woman by the name of Barbara, came to the police station. She had heard on the news about a baby being found and thought It might be you. According to her, your mother had made a habit of dumping you off on various relatives and then disappearing for several days. They got fed up and wouldn't take you anymore. She said it had been about two weeks since anyone had seen the two of you."

"Two weeks. I can see maybe the mother, but two, two weeks without knowing where the baby was. I could never get over that," said Ellen. It was clear to Alia she still held a lot of anger about that.

"The judge wasn't too thrilled either. Even if she had wanted to take you, I don't think he would have let her. So we got to bring you back home and keep you for even longer."

"And poor Charlie, the babysitter said he was inconsolable since we left with you. The whole time you were with us, he didn't let you out of his sight. If you were hungry, he fed you. If you were tired, he'd put you to sleep. I never had to check your diaper. He would tell me when you needed a change. I may have been your foster mother, but you were Charlie's baby."

Again Charlie smiled and sighed heavily but would only spare them the quickest of glances.

"A few days later." Harper continued, "Your mother showed up at the station in hysterics. Said she left you with a sitter for a few hours. Hours she said. By this time, we had already had you over a week on top of the two; you had already been gone. Trish said when she got back, everyone was gone. I was so angry, but then, all I could see was this poor young kid, a mother at sixteen, strung out and scared out of her mind."

"So then there was another day in court. Only this time, We took Charlie with us," said Ellen. "The last time we didn't, and you screamed the whole time. So after that, the family court judge allowed it as long as he was on his best behavior, and he was. Didn't make a peep the entire time. Neither did you."

"Well, that's not altogether true, Ellen. You cried once, Alia. After the judge ruled against your mother, she was allowed to hold you to say goodbye. You cried then, but to be fair, she had been crying as well. The judge gave your mother a laundry list of things she needed to do to get you back. The biggest, of course, was getting clean. Meanwhile, we were awarded custody. We were officially your foster parents."

She lied to me about that as well. Told me the judge was granting her some time from me to give her a break. That story never made any damn sense to me. All the lies. All these years and all the damn lies. Thought Alia.

"But you gave me back." Alia suddenly realized why all this time, why this home and why Charlie was always so special to her. *But they gave me back, back to her...back to the hell.* Alia also understood why Charlie seemed a bit worried about tonight. As much as she was starting to love them all, now she was growing angry at them as well. The tears returned as she sat there and thought about how much of a loving family life and home this was and how they took that away from her.

"It wasn't quite as simple as that," said Harper. "Your mother was a mess, but that family of hers wasn't much better. We thought they came into court as support for her but instead, they were there to make sure she didn't get you back. And not because she was a bad parent but more because they were tired of being burdened by you both. The judge himself said he wasn't surprised she turned out the way she did when they hadn't bothered to report either one of you missing for nearly two weeks. Trish was still underage, so she was still your grandmother's responsibility, you as well. The judge felt bad for Trish, and against our better judgment, so did we."

"So we made a deal with your mother. We would allow her to come over and see you, but it had to be in our home, and she had to be sober," said Ellen

"That didn't work so well the first few times. But after that, she got cleaned up enough to see you twice a month. And that was more than most foster parents would do."

"Yet we did even more," said Ellen. Even knowing the sooner she got herself back on the track, the sooner we would have to give you back, we still helped. A child should be with their parents Alia. And at the time, your mother either didn't know or refused to say who your father was, so she was all you had. We did what we could for her. Twice a month, she would come to see you, and it looked like things were going pretty good, except, well, we had some issues with Charlie."

Charlie got up from the chair and went to the fireplace, keeping his back to them all. Alia wanted to go to him once more, but his mother pulled her attention back to her.

"As you can tell, Charlie was crazy about you. He taught you to walk, talk, even to read, believe it or not. We had the hardest time getting him to go to school, and he only would because we promised him you would still be there when he got back. But as much as he seemed to love you...."

"He hated your mother just as much."

"Now, Harper, I don't think hate is right. But it became obvious he had issues with her. At first, it was cute. Even Trish didn't seem to mind. He'd go up to her when she held you and tell her that you were his baby. That's Charlie's baby, Charlie's angel, he would say. And your mother would nod and say yes, it was Charlie's angel. After a while, he became a bit more insistent. He wasn't being nasty to her or anything, but you could tell it was starting to bother her. I think what really started to bug her was that he kept correcting her when she didn't do something right. Baby Alia didn't like the way she was being held. Baby Alia didn't like the song she was singing. You're not feeding Baby Alia, right. It was always something. And to be fair, you were always such a good baby, except for when your mother came over. You cried and fussed and didn't want to stay in her arms. You would sit there reaching out for Charlie. When she put you on the floor to play, even as you got older, you would ignore her and play with charlie. Anytime she held you, you would cry."

"Trish was pinching her, I saw it," Charlie said, still with his back to them.

"That's what he used to say, but we never saw anything. After a while, though, things were going downhill fast. Trish was getting more and more upset with Charlie. She would tell him that Alia was her baby and one day she was going to take her home. Charlie hated that. The next time Trish came over, Charlie actually hid you in his toy box. He was convinced she had come to take his baby away."

Harper nodded. "It got so bad that we ended up having to take Charlie to his grandparents' house while your mother was over here. He had begun yelling at her, tried hitting her, even bit her once when she wagged her finger at him."

Alia looked over at Charlie and could tell this whole thing was making him feel uncomfortable. Again she wanted to console him, but she wanted the end of this story as well, even though she was pretty sure that the worst was yet to come.

"Charlie kept telling us that Alia, that you didn't like your mother. That you, you wanted me as your mother." Ellen said with fresh tears in her eyes.

And I did too. I may not remember any of this or any of them, but I feel it in my heart. No wonder she feels so special to me.

"We tried explaining things to him, but it only made him cry. Still, we continued to help your mother get back on her feet. We got her into rehab, got her new clothes, made sure she saw a doctor. We were as much her parents as we were yours." said Ellen.

"Everyone tried to warn us that what we were doing was nice but not a great idea. But your mother was so grateful," said Harper.

"Trish would even help me around the house, and it seemed like she was trying. Even the whole thing with Charlie seemed not to bother her too much. She got better and better, got a job, got an apartment with a roommate that had two kids, both girls. It was all working out." Ellen looked over at Harper.

"Then we had a court date," said Harper.

Charlie abruptly moved from the fireplace over to a chair by the front door. He sat with his head down and his hands linked over his head.

Alia went to get up, feeling the need to wrap her arms around him, but his mother patted her back down again.

"The faster we get through this next part, the better, dear," she said low enough for Charlie not to hear.

So Alia sat back down, but she couldn't bring herself to take her eyes off of him. *It's almost like I can feel his pain. He's shaking. I can tell he's crying. I feel his grief like it's my own. This is it. This is the part where I have to leave him.*

"We didn't take Charlie with us this time," said Harper. "Mostly because your mother would be there. Besides, you were a little over three now and didn't really cry much like you used to."

"We knew…we knew when we left that day…." Ellen's tears flowed more, and she couldn't continue. She just looked over at her son and cried.

"Your mother had done everything she was supposed to do." Harper paused, willing the tears in his eyes to go away. "Still, the hardest thing I have ever done in my whole life was hand you over to her."

Alia looked over at Harper and saw that even his eyes filled with tears. She could see it. As he told the story, she could see his love for that little baby girl. For her. Seeing his and Ellen's pain, feeling Charlie's Alia wasn't mad at them anymore. She knew they had been given no choice.

"When we came home without you, well, it just about destroyed Charlie," said Harper. "For the first time in his life, I saw he had my temper. He screamed at us to go get you back and told us that Trish was going to hurt you. That she was going to hurt his angel. The more we tried to calm him down, the madder he got. He hit us, told us we were horrible for leaving you and liked to tear the house apart. He went on for hours. I was scared. I really was. I thought we would have to call a doctor to come to give him something to calm down. Then suddenly, he collapsed. Finally, too exhausted to fight anymore."

"I held him in my arms," said Ellen. "He tried to struggle free, but then he just laid there and cried. We both did. He just laid there crying and calling for you over and over. It broke my heart to see him like that. I sat with him in my arms for hours that night. He wouldn't sleep; he just cried. The next morning he got a framed picture of you, one of your baby blankets, and laid down on the couch. He wouldn't eat, would barely even drink anything, only got up to use the bathroom, then was back on the couch. He wouldn't talk to us either. Wouldn't even look at us."

"After a couple of days, we knew we had to do something," said Harper. So we thought maybe if he saw you. Saw that you were okay, that you were safe, it would make him feel better. So we called your mother and told her how upset he was and if we could bring Charlie over to see you. That maybe we could set up playdates once in a while like with the visitations we let her have."

It was then that they heard a door slam. Charlie had left the chair and gone outside onto the front porch. It was dark, but the porch light was on, and they could see him at one end of the porch leaning on the railing.

For the third time, Alia tried getting up.

"He'll be OK out there," said Ellen. "This part will be the hardest for him."

"We tell her all this," Harper continues. We plead with her for Charlie's sake. Ellen was on the extension in the kitchen, so we both heard what your mother said. At first, she just laughed. Not a joyous laugh either. Then she started saying the most horrible things about Charlie. Calling him a freak and a psychopath. Telling us we better lock him up."

Ellen nodded. "We couldn't believe it. You have to understand up until this point, your mother never said a harsh word in front of us. She was nothing but polite and grateful for all our help. Even at court, when she got you back, she cried and hugged us both, thanking us."

"And Trish didn't stop there. She warned us that we better keep Charlie away from you, or she would go back to court and tell the judge what kind of sicko he was. We tried to tell her Charlie was almost sick with grief, and she didn't care. She just went on and on about how he was disturbed. That it wasn't natural for him to like you so much. When we begged her, told her we did so much for her, we only asked this one thing she denied we ever did anything for her. She actually denied it. When I said I would talk to the judge myself if I had to, well that's when she threatened.." Harper paused, taking a deep breath. "That's when she threatened to tell the judge about Charlie molesting you."

Alia jumped, feeling like she had just gotten shot in the chest.

"No, Alia, don't you think it for a minute. Our boy never laid a hand on you. He wouldn't even be in the same room I was changing your diaper in." Ellen was full-on crying now. "He loved you. He would never do anything like that. I promise you, you have to believe me."

Harper came over to the couch and took his wife into his arms. "It's true, Alia. Had we thought, even for a minute, we would have put an end to it. And there was no way for your mother to know anything we didn't because we never left her alone with you. I always had a hard time fully trusting her. But the way she said it. It wasn't even like she was making it up; it was like she believed it. Told us she had seen it herself when there was no way in hell she could have. When I told her so, and she had no evidence, she said she would make some then. Trish said if she had to rip you apart, that she would. That she would hurt you to keep Charlie away from you." Harper shook as talking about it brought up his rage.

Ellen broke from her husband, gaining some control over her emotions. "We helped her get you back, and she repaid us by accusing Charlie of doing the most horrible things. The whole time she had lied to us, told us she did. Trish told us she had fooled us, that she was using us to get you back, and now that she did, we would never see you again. And if we tried to, she would tell everyone what Charlie did. Trish said she had convinced us that she was a good mother so she could convince the judge and anyone that listened. Even if it meant having to hurt you."

Alia felt herself shake all over. She had no doubts at all they were telling her the truth, no doubt that her mother said those horrible things. Trish wasn't brilliant, but she was one hell of a good liar. Alia had seen her lies at work for years even became an excellent liar herself.

Harper moved to sit on the coffee table in front of Alia."We couldn't let her do it, Alia. We always planned on being part of your life. We never meant to be so distant from you. But we had to protect you. We had to protect the both of you. We were so afraid she would say something," said Harper.

Ellen was drying her tears with one hand and holding one of her husband's with the other.

"And we still had Charlie to deal with," Harper continued. "He hadn't heard anything said over the phone. Didn't even know we called Trish. We held off telling him the worst of it as long as we could. But right then, we knew we had to do something to try and make him feel better. So one day, I borrowed a car from one of the officers at the station. We knew where the two of you were living because we were the ones that found the roommate. Trish didn't know that one of her neighbors was an old friend of Ellen's. She told us that your mother had a routine. Around the time the mail would come, she'd sit outside waiting for it smoking, and you were always out there with her.
We packed up Charlie, drove the car over to the complex, and parked far enough away she wouldn't see us and close enough where Charlie could see you."

"And there you were riding a busted up big wheel that was much too big for you. Up and down the sidewalk faster and faster," said Ellen. "Charlie sat there with us for almost an hour watching you. For the first time in days, he had a smile on his face. When the mail came, and the two of you went back inside, he crawled into my arms and cried. We were able to convince him that you would be okay. And that anytime he wanted to see you, we would bring him over. Charlie never really was the same after that. Always quieter than kids his age. But he would eat again and sleep and eventually went back to school."

"And we made a promise," said Harper. One as a family. That no matter where you went, we would find a way to keep tabs on you. That we would always be watching out for you. But for Charlie's sake, and yours, your mother could never know."

"Do you understand now? Do you see why we waited to tell you the truth? Even now, it's important that your mother never finds out about you and Charlie," said Ellen.

"She doesn't have to prove he did anything anymore to destroy his life. Now that he's a cop, an accusation like that would destroy the confidence the community and his fellow officers have in him. You may be eighteen now, but you're still in high school. So the perception is that despite your age, you're still a child. Which is why he was supposed to wait," said Harper. "We were going to tell you everything before you left for the academy.

It was then that it dawned on Alia. Charlie had been waiting for her all this time. That's why he never asked her out in high school. It was why he seemed to disappear once they both were teens. Why he wouldn't let Crystal invite her over when he was visiting George. As the two of them got older, she saw less and less of him. All this time, Alia felt things were so much easier for Charlie, but the truth was they were a whole lot harder.

Alia shook all over, once more. She could feel the rage like that of the bad year building inside her. Everything she had just heard was whirling in her head like a tornado. The lies, the years of being afraid, the abuse, and for what? It wasn't because Trish loved her. It was because she had to prove to everyone she could do it when they said she couldn't. Trish ripped Alia from a loving home and family and then tried to destroy them all for her own petty, selfish needs. Alia felt her breathing quicken, her hands turned into fists, her heart ached for the pain she knew Charlie was going through right now because she could feel it. Even from outside, she could feel him racked with grief and worry.

Suddenly Harper was in her face. A man for whom rage was a familiar vice, he recognized the signs of it in her. She was shaking all over like she was about to burst.

"Alia…Alia, look at me, sweetheart, please. I know what you're feeling right now, and believe me, it's only going to make things worse."

Tears streamed down her face, but she looked at him. "That bitch. She took away the only real family I ever had. She never loved me…she just used me. And

Charlie...," Alia choked, almost unable to say his name. "How could she...and she would have too I know she would have. She couldn't stand the fact that somebody loved me. She...she...hated me, but she couldn't let anyone else have me. Poor Charlie.."

"Ellen, get a shot of whiskey, hurry. Alia, I need you to calm down. I know you're angry, but you have to let it go. If you don't, if you try to confront her right now, she will destroy both of you. She'll destroy all of us."

"She's just a stupid, high school dropout that can barely read...she can't do shit."

Ellen came back with the shot of whiskey and gave it to Harper. "I don't know if this is such a good idea."

Harper took the shot, ignoring her. "Yes, she can, Alia. All she has to do is plant a seed of doubt. We may not see anything right away, but it will grow and grow and grow until one day Alia, one day someone is going to come along and hurt Charlie. Someone that thinks he is the monster she says he is. Do you want that, Alia? Do you want someone to take Charlie away from all of us?"

Slowly Alia started shaking her head.

Harper put the shot glass in her hand and told her to drink it. "All at once and do it fast."

Alia did, knowing just what to do, having seen her mother and her parade of drunken boyfriends do it hundreds of times. The liquid was white-hot as it ran down her throat to her stomach, where the burn spread out. She closed her eyes, trying to breathe.

"That's it, you have to let the anger go. Think about Charlie. Think about how much he loves you. You have each other now, and that's all that's important."

"Do we? Do we really? How long before she finds out? How long before Trish ruins this too?" Alia said, her rage still spiking.

Harper took Alia's hands, swallowing them in his larger ones. "We won't let that happen, Alia. That's why you have to let go of the rage inside of you. You can't let Trish find out. You can't be angry or confront her because she will take him away from you if you do."

Alia nodded her head, unable to talk, still trying to just breathe, feeling the first effects of the whiskey.

"You believe us, don't you?" asked Ellen. Charlie's biggest worry was always that you wouldn't believe us, that you would hate him, that you would believe he could.."

"No!" Alia said, at last, choking back the tears. "No…no….he could never…I would never…I believe you…."She burst into tears, the rage being replaced by grief she hadn't felt since her father died.

They both wrapped Alia into their arms and hugged her long and hard. Eventually, Ellen got up and got her wet washcloth from the downstairs bath.

Harper took it from Ellen and wiped Alia's face. "You're okay now. You've calmed down enough."

Alia was not just getting calmer but feeling a little lightheaded. She wasn't sure if it was the alcohol or the events of the evening. She nodded as best she could, feeling her head float.

"Okay, good, because I think Charlie needs you right now," said Harper. "I think he needs to know that you believe…."

"He could never…I know he couldn't. He held me all night…but he never…."

Harper looked at his wife questioningly.

"We'll talk about it later, now is not the time," she told him.

Harper nodded and continued to clean Alia's face off.

When Alia felt she was calm enough, she asked. "Do you think it's okay if I go see him now? I need to see him."

"Of course it is," said Harper.

Alia fell into their arms once again and hugged them tightly. Then she slowly got up on shaky legs and looked outside. Charlie was still on the porch, his head hung low. Taking a deep breath, Alia walked across the room and opened the door.

As soon as she did, Charlie turned around, his tear-filled eyes searching hers, fearing he would see a look of contempt in them. Instead, he found sadness, but most importantly, love.

Alia ran to him, and he picked her up in his arms.

"I'm so sorry...I'm so sorry for what she put you through." she cried. "I know you would never do anything to hurt me, Charlie. I have loved you forever, and I always will."

Filled with relief, Charlie held on to her and cried. His angel had finally come back home to him.

Later that evening, the four of them returned to the living room, this time with rounds of coffee for everyone.

Ellen gave Alia a blanket that she wrapped around Charlie's shoulders. He had been cold and shivering from standing out in the chilly evening for so long. For a while, they talked again about how they had promised to keep an eye on Alia as best they could. Harper had found out when Alia was about five that her father was one of the volunteer firefighters at the town's local fire department. He had actually known Johnathan in passing but became good friends with him after that.

"We were both sure that things at home were, well, complicated for you. He had, had his suspicions about just to what extent that was, but he could never get any good evidence or for you to admit to anything."

"She had gotten really good at hiding the marks or making marks that would look like a kid got them from being clumsy or playing. I remember she used to push me a lot, make me fall down to scrape myself up. As for not saying anything that was code in our house. Plus, she always told me no one would believe me anyway." Charlie and Alia sat together on the couch, his arm around her, her hand on his leg. Neither one of them liked talking about the abuse Alia had suffered as a child, so they drew strength from one another to get through it.

Harper sat in his chair again , and Ellen sat on the arm of the chair with her arm around him. Harper told them that after Alia and her mother moved out of Union county, he got John to insist on seeing Alia. That had been a bad year for her. They had moved to the city in the next county and into a three-story apartment home in the middle of a crack-infested area. She was often left alone when her mother went to parties even though she was only around six years of age. Worse was when the parties were at home. The abuse got terrible during that time because the only people who saw her were those at school. They were not lacking abused and neglected kids to deal with. It wasn't until Alia ended up having to be taken by ambulance from home one night to the hospital with a dangerously high fever that abuse was first mentioned.

Trish, having freaked out when they rushed her daughter to the hospital, had called her mother upset. They wouldn't let Trish in the room with her daughter, and she couldn't understand why. Her stepfather came to the hospital (her mother refused) demanding to know what was happening. Before he had left, though, he had called Johnathan. They had both arrived about the same time, and once Johnathan proved he was her father, they let him in to see her. Two officers were in her room along with a portly older woman from the department of children's services.

Alia had been brought in to control the high fever, but they found several bruises and marks once they examined her. The girl refused to say anything other than that she fell a lot because she was clumsy. They eventually released Alia to her mother. Not long after, Alia went to live with her grandparents for several months while her mother found a suitable place for them to stay outside of the city. The truth, though, was that they left the city to avoid having to answer to the alleged abuse.

After that, Alia got to see her father a couple times a month unless she was too bad and had to be grounded. That didn't take much to happen at all. But the good thing was that John lived close to the Sheriff, which meant for the first time in a long time Charlie could not only see Alia again but play with her as well.

"When you lived in the little red house, we had no idea at first that Charlie would ride his bike over to that side of town to play with you. When I found out, I admit I was furious," said Harper.

"But Charlie had been smart about it. He never went to your house, he always played with a group of kids, not you alone, and he kept an eye out for your mother to show up." Said Ellen. "Harper wanted to refuse him to see you again, but I wouldn't allow it."

"Later, when you would come to see your father, we made him follow the same rules, just in case. When your father passed, we were afraid we would lose track of you again. Any idea why your mother moved back to Union county?"

"The usual. She broke up with a boyfriend and needed somewhere to go. She still didn't have a car or license by then so getting to the factory on the edge of the county was easier from here. Up until then, her boyfriend had been taking her. I swore at the time Trish did it all for spite, though. I still think she did."

"Well, for whatever reason, I'm glad she did." Said Charlie. "Only after your dad died you kind of…well you kind of lost it there for a bit." He kissed the side of her head.

"Understandably so, of course." Said Harper.

Alia grinned at him. "You didn't seem to be too understanding when you put me in that jail cell."

"Oh, believe me, dear, that was him being understanding." Laughed Ellen.

"Besides, it worked. You straightened up after that."

Alia looked at Charlie and gave him a knowing grin.

"Or not." Said Harper, giving them both a stern look.

"There were a few issues at camp, but things calmed down after I introduced her to Crystal and her friends." Said Charlie.

"As for the camp. I am guessing the two of you had something to do with my scholarship?"

"We send a kid to camp each year. A lot of community members do it. that year we pulled a few strings to make sure you would get in."

"So Charlie, who was a counselor at the time, could keep an eye on me."

"Well, that and we thought getting away from your mother for a summer would do you some good. We didn't have any control over who they would bunk you with." Said Harper. Charlie had told them about that much, at least.

"You know, at the time, I was mad about being sent there. Mostly because I had a feeling it was because of you. I was even a little resentful of Charlie at first. I really did end up appreciating it, though, so thank you. After that, I didn't see much of Charlie again."

"Yes, well, you two were beyond the age where just hanging out in the neighborhood playing was an option." Said Ellen.

"And I had been friends with George for years, so I knew his little sister was into the same kind of things you were. I had a feeling the two of you would be best of friends. And No before you ask, she did not know we were trying to keep tabs on you."

"We did, however, talk to George and her parents." Said Harper. "We felt that it was best if Charlie backed off some, well maybe more than some."

"It's just that, it started to become obvious to us, well me mostly, that Charlie's feelings for you were not only growing but growing into something more than just good friends," said Ellen.

"That's my mother's subtle way of saying I was falling in love with you." Said Charlie, and he kissed her temple.

"And our worry was that that would lead to more complications. It's not that we made him stay away from you, Alia. It's just that we thought it best there be more distance between you both. Fewer temptations that way," explained Ellen.

"Also, Charlie needed to focus on his future. I tried to explain to him that if it was meant to be between the two of you, your lives would be much better with a good education and a good job." Said Harper. "And I still feel that way which is why we have been helping you get ready for the academy. Even if things didn't work out between the two of you, we wanted to help ensure you have a better future than you did." Patting his wife on the leg, Harper got up. "Okay...I am going to go out and build a fire, a nice big one.

I figure the two of you may want to be alone for a while before Crystal and George come to get you." Harper grabbed a coat and walked out.

"We have only been doing what we hoped was best for the both of you. I know it may not seem like it."

"He's not very happy about all of this, is he?" Asked Alia

"No, he isn't. He's worried for you both. For all of us, really. That's why it's essential for the two of you to be careful. And I'm not saying you can't see each other or even be seen together. We have a lot of friends in the county, some fully aware of just the type of person your mother is, Alia. But it's also a big county and one your mother grew up in, so she knows a lot of people as well. People that would love nothing more than go running to her if they thought something was going on between the two of you. People in her circle practically feed off the drama of others."

"Fortunately, I guess, I have developed a knack for keeping things from my mother," said Alia pulling out her cell phone. "She hasn't found out about the lessons going on for the past few months either. I don't think Charlie would even be on her radar right now if it wasn't for me."

"And don't you dare blame yourself for that one? Harper would have been really upset if you had missed that test again. Or worse, driven off with that drunken jackass behind the wheel. To be honest, he had a bit of a fit anyway, but we both agreed you two dealt with it the right way."

"Yeah, I can usually tell if my mother isn't buying my crap, and this time she seemed to. It just kills me. I have gotten so good at lying."

"Don't fret over it, dear. I have a feeling that's a skill you're going to need this month. Once you graduate and come back, things can change, but until then, I can't stress to the two of you more the importance of Trish not finding out. Not for now anyway."

A little bit later, Charlie and Alia sat alone on a cushioned bench in front of the fire pit. At first, neither one of them spoke. The silence between the two of them was comfortable and welcomed after the chaos of the evening.

Charlie held her in his arms, thankful to still have her. He had been so afraid she would believe Trish's accusations about him.

Alia relished the love, warmth, and security she had felt very little of her entire life. Closing her eyes, she let her other senses take in the moment. There was the feeling of Charlie's strong arms around her, the warmth of his chest on her back, the slight tickling of his breath on her neck. She was reminded of the night in the motel when they had to take cover in the bathtub only without the fear and intensity. Alia felt comfortable, secure and had no doubt that Charlie would never let her go no matter what storm they faced.

Alia could smell the sweetness of the burning wood, one of her favorite scents, mingling with Charlie's cologne and natural smell. There was also a hint of flowers blooming lingering in the cool night air. The fire crackled, crickets sang, and Charlie sighed. She was so wrapped up in the sensation of the moment that it took her a while to realize his sighs were not of contentment.

Alia didn't want to end this wonderful moment, but it was clear Charlie was still upset about something. Whether he wanted to or not, he needed to talk. She felt that one of the biggest problems in the world was that despite all the means of communication, people didn't talk to one another. Alia felt that many of the world's problems could be solved if everyone just sat down and talked it all over. It was something she had always wanted to do with her mother and wished she could still do with her father. The relationships she saw that lasted the most and seemed to thrive were ones where both sides learned to communicate. Knowing that Charlie would be reluctant to break the calm spell of the evening, Alia took it upon herself to do so.

Pulling back from him a little so she could see his face, she said, "I know something is still bothering you, Charlie, but before we start could you do just one thing for me?"

"Anything." He said with that smile she loved so much.

"Kiss me." She said, feeling her face flush for asking.

"I thought you said something for you." He said and did as she asked, once again like the first time, gentle at first then more intense, more exploring with his tongue and hers." He pulled back, looking at her inquiringly.

"When did you drink whiskey? There wasn't any in my coffee."

"Not the coffee. Your father gave me a shot earlier. I guess I was a bit upset." More like in a rage.

"I have to say I prefer the strawberry balm." He smiled and kissed her again. Charlie then put his forehead on hers and sighed heavily.

Alia kissed him once on the forehead and sat back from him again. "Whatever is bothering you, you need to talk about it."

"Even if talking doesn't do any good?"

"Talking always does good. Even if you don't like what you hear."

Charlie nodded. "Alright, maybe I was wrong to say it that way. what I meant was that it isn't going to change anything."

"No, maybe not, but at least it would help me understand what is going on in that head of yours. If something is bothering you, I need to know. I can't even begin to help unless I do."

He smiled, his eyes a bit sad but loving. "How is it that you know so much about these things?"

"I have seen my fair share of bad relationships. Everyone wants to talk, but no one ever wants to start. So start, Charlie."

Charlie nodded and took a deep breath. "Okay, but first, I want to thank you. You have no idea how afraid I was that you would hate me for all of this. That you might believe that I could…."

"Don't even say it, Charlie, please don't. I know you would never hurt me like that. You have always been nothing but kind and gentle to me, even when, even when I wasn't so nice to you. I know that I have hurt you." her bottom lip started to tremble, and Alia could feel the heat of tears coming back."

Not able to bear to see her cry anymore, Charlie cupped her face and kissed her.

"You're my sweet girl Alia. I know you never meant it, not really. Besides, I'm pretty tough. I can take a hit or two." He kissed her again then looked her in the eyes, her beautiful blue eyes that danced in the firelight. "I don't want you to go back home."

Alia had a feeling this was coming, but her tears were a shock even to her.

"Hey, no, please don't." Charlie cupped her face in his hands, using his thumbs to wipe away the tears. He kissed her forehead and the corners of her wet eyes. "Please, Alia, the last thing I want to do is make you more upset."

She shook her head and took a few deep breaths of her own. "I'm sorry I...." Alia closed her eyes, taking one more deep breath. "I know where you are going with this; Charlie and I can't, not yet."

"I'm not saying for you to come to stay with me. I would love nothing more than for that to happen, but I think we both would agree that's too dangerous right now. I thought maybe there is somewhere else you would stay for the next few weeks. I am sick with the idea of sending you back to her. I know you said things were pretty good right now, but...she's not right in the head, Alia, she can't be. I'm scared for you. I really am."

"I'm scared too, Charlie, but not of her. I'm scared of myself. I'm afraid of what might happen if the next time I see her, and I remember all the shit she said about you, and I lose it."

"Even more of a reason for you not to go back."

"It's more complicated than that."

"How?"

"Because she is still my mother. Ugh, Charlie, I know this sounds stupid, but I can't leave her like this...not yet."

"Alia, you don't owe her anything."

"This isn't about her. It's about me. I have to live the rest of my life with the choices I make. For me to have a clear conscience, I have to know I did all the right things. I have to leave things the right way as much as possible. Which means giving her her victory party. After that, the choice is up to her. If she wants to continue to be a miserable, hateful person, then that's on her. But if I leave, now I may regret it later. If nothing else, it's going to bother me. Not to mention how my family and other people would see it. I would end up being the ungrateful brat that couldn't give my mother one last victory."

"To hell with what other people may think. It's not like you will find many people that will feel sorry for her anyway."

"I can't, Charlie, I'm sorry. I have to be able to end it my way and walk away with my head held high, knowing I did the right thing. And there is you to consider as well. If I suddenly bail on her after leaving town with you, our story is going to fall apart. Trish may be stupid, but she's a paranoid kind of stupid. She would come after you and your family, Charlie and I won't let her do that."

Charlie nodded, knowing they couldn't risk Trish putting two and two together.

"It's not going to be easy. No matter how good she is trying to keep things at home right now, these next four weeks will be hell for me. I'm going to need you, Charlie. I am going to need your support and your strength to get through this."

Charlie pulled her onto his lap and into his arms. Alia was right, and he knew it, but he still hated it. He sat there for a long time, just holding on to her. Charlie kissed her hair, her cheeks, the corners of her mouth and held her some more. Part of him thought if he just held on to her, she wouldn't have to go. "Okay." He said at last. I don't like it, but I understand. And I will do whatever you need me to do to get through this. But you have to promise me, Alia, you have to promise that if it gets too hard, you'll go. That you will leave before it gets out of hand. The last thing I want is a call from dispatch saying…" he couldn't bring himself to finish the rest.

"I will, Charlie, I promise. But you have to promise to forgive me for ranting to you because it's going to happen." she laughed a bit. "If she gets on my nerves or I feel like I want to pop her one, I'm going to call you and bitch up a storm. Just ask Crystal she knows."

"You can call me and fuss at me anytime." he smiled and kissed her on the lips. "I'll be your punching bag for the next few weeks if that's what it takes."

Putting. hand on his chest, she joked. "I promise not to leave too many bruises."

"I think I can handle it if you did." They kissed long and hard and held each other, not wanting to ever let go. Neither one of them wanted the night to end, but Alia saw over Charlie's shoulder headlights from a familiar Buick coming down the driveway to the back of the house. Since it was dark, it was safe to pick her up at the house as it was unlikely anyone would see, and if they did, they would assume it was George coming to see Charlie as he often did.

Charlie held Alia tighter as if that alone would make her stay.

Alia held Charlie tighter, taking in every last breath of him that she could. When they let go, the tears in his eyes mirrored her own.

"I am going to text the hell out of you all the time." He said. "And yes, I am going to worry until you text back. If something goes wrong, I mean really wrong, don't call nine one one, you text me or call me first I'll get to you much faster."

Alia nodded and slid off his lap, having to bite her lip in order not to let the tears fall. The two of them slowly walked up to the back of the house, where Ellen and Harper were waiting on the back porch with her things. Ellen handed them to her and gave her a big hug.

"Don't forget, baby girl, you still have lessons tomorrow, and I insist you stay for family dinner night. I'll tell Mrs. Stackhouse myself, she'll understand"

"I'll be here," Alia promised.

Harper grabbed Alai and gave her a big hug as well, swallowing her in his big arms and chest. "I'm sure Charlie has already told you, but if you need anything...I mean anything, call us. Are you going to be okay? To see her, I mean?"

"With her work schedule, we don't see much of each other anyway. By the time the weekend comes around, I'll come up with some plan to avoid being home as much as possible."

"Well, if you feel it building up again, just leave Alia. Just walk away, even if you think it will make her mad, just get out of there until your head clears."

"I will, Thank you... both of you. Not just for tonight but for all of it. I'm never going to be able to repay you for everything you have done. And I'm sure I don't even know the half of it."

Ellen put a hand on Alia's face. "Having our little girl back is all the thanks we will ever need." She said with tears in her eyes. Ellen buried her head in her husband's arms, and they both went back into the house.

Charlie walked her over to the car, where he said a quick hello to Crystal and George. "Text me as soon as you get home. I'm staying here until you do. It's closer to you than my apartment. If there is any trouble at all."

"I'll be fine, Charlie...she's not even home."
He hugged her tight again for several minutes, not wanting to let her go. With one last long kiss, he put her in the car. As he stood there watching them drive away, Charlie wiped away another tear.

In the Buick, no one said anything at first. Alia took several deep breaths trying to keep back her own tears. She felt like she was leaving her family behind and going into the pits of hell. Still warm from his touch, her arms already longed to have Charlie in them again.

Crystal turned in her seat to talk to Alia but gave her a few more minutes. "So, how was the dinner?" she asked casually.

Alia looked up, and the absurdity of what Crystal asked actually made her laugh. "Dinner was good, actually."

"Oh good, because I thought maybe it didn't go so well. Perhaps it was what happened after dinner?"

Alia nodded. "Remember how I told you I was in foster care as a baby?"

Crystal nodded.

"Ellen and Harper were my foster parents."

George almost slammed on the brakes. "What?"

"Didn't you know George?"

"No…Charlie asked me years ago to keep an eye on you, but that was about it. He never said anything about being your foster brother. Just that you two had been friends, and you had a habit of getting yourself into trouble."

"Well, that was an understatement back then," said Alia

"So you had no idea they were your foster parents?" asked Crystal.

"None whatsoever. Trish said she didn't remember them. Trish said a lot of bullshit." Alia gave them a brief rundown of the events of the night and the conversation they all had. She left out the part where her mother accused Charlie of molesting her and just said she had threatened to say some nasty shit about them all. Alia trusted them, but she didn't want to put even the tiniest seed of doubt about Charlie in the minds of anyone, not even them. All she had to tell them was that if her mother found out about them, she would stop at nothing to ruin all of them.

"I don't understand why she would be so mad at them after they helped her," said George. "Are you sure there isn't more to this story?"

"I have no doubts at all that they told me everything, and all of it was true. My mother uses people. Not just her boyfriends either. She has burned so many bridges with family members it's a wonder they ever put up with her. Besides, she has a big issue with anyone that likes me. She broke up with a really great guy one time because he admitted to wanting to be my father. They wanted to still be a part of my life because I loved them, and she couldn't stand it."

"So now what?" said Crystal. "You can't just go home and pretend like nothing ever happened. I know you, Alia, she's going to do something to make you mad, and all this mess is gonna come out."

"It won't because it can't. At least not until I graduate from the academy. Once I can stand on my own two feet, then I don't care. By then, I won't be some kid in school anymore. I'll practically be a cop, so no one should think twice if the two of us are seen hanging out together or even dating. At least, I hope not. As for what I am going to do until I leave, I was hoping maybe we could figure something out."

"I'll talk to Mom and Dad, but I'm sure they will let you stay with us."

Alia shook her head and explained to them like she had Charlie about why she couldn't leave. "But maybe I can spend more time at your house than usual. During the week it isn't so bad. I have work, and I'm still going to do my lessons at their house and stay for dinner. She's not home then anyway. I pretty much just need a place to hang out on Saturdays. Most of my side jobs have already been canceled since I knew I would need time off for end-of-school-year stuff. Sunday night, I have no choice but to go home. Trish still has me on a ten o'clock curfew on school nights, eighteen or not."

"Don't worry, once I tell my parents what is going on, they will be more than happy to help find things for us 'to do. What about you and Charlie? He asked you out, are the two of you still going to do that, or is that on hold till this is all over."

Alia suddenly realized they never even talked about that. "I don't know. With everything, I never even thought to ask. Wouldn't have if I did. I do, however, have a place for us to go if he still wants to."

"Where's that?"

"Mrs. Stackhouse gave me a key to the archives in the basement. After she caught us kissing in the stacks." Seeing the alarm on Crystal's face, Alia continued. "I don't think we have to worry about her saying anything." They talked some more about the details of the night and soon arrived at Alias's mother's apartment.

Alia looked up at the apartment and thought, *this isn't my home. Never really was, and sure the hell isn't now. My home is where my real family is. Not all real families are blood.*

"You sure you want to go in," asked George. "Technically, you were having dinner at our house. We could always say that you fell asleep."

"That won't work," said Crystal. "It would be like that night that Charlene stayed over at Alia's house before asking permission. Her mother was pissed."

"Yeah, for now, it's better to just do things as normal as possible and well within the rules. If too many things about me change, she will start to wonder why and if she connects it to Charlie taking me to Alexandria, the whole mess could fall apart. I better get in. Charlie is waiting for me to text him." Alia got out, thanked them for the ride, and walked up the stairs to the apartment. It was almost ten late, so thankfully, Billy was already in bed. Alia grabbed the dog's leash and took him out. While he did his business, she texted
Charlie.

Alia: Made it home. Billy was asleep. Trish isn't home.

Charlie: That's good. Mom and Dad said goodnight. Go get ready for bed.
I am going to head home, will text you at 11. Are you going to be okay?

Alia: Honestly?

Charlie: Of course.

Alia: Yes and no. Right now, my head is still spinning.

Charlie: I know, I'm sorry.

Alia: But I'll be okay. I miss you already. All of you.

Charlie: We miss you too. I didn't forget about our date. I Will come up with something. I love you.

Alia: I love you more.

Charlie: More and more all the time, I hope.

Alia: Now you're catching on, sweet boy.

Charlie: Go get inside it's chilly out. I'll text you in a bit.

Alia: Okay, drive safe.

Alia hid the phone in her jacket pocket and took Ebony back inside. She showered, got ready for bed, and tried to read but couldn't concentrate on the words. Her mind kept going back to what was said tonight, the revelations made about her life.

For the first time in years, things were starting to make sense. Alia never really bonded with her mother because she had never really been raised by her mother. Even when she was a baby before she ended up in foster care, Alia knew she had spent more time with one family member or another than Trish. And she thought that maybe the reason why she never felt close to them other than her great grandmother was that they resented her for Trish's behavior. Alia knew that some of them, like her mother's brother-in-law, blamed her very existence on her mother's problems. Like it was Alia's fault she was born.

It would explain how she never felt like she belonged anywhere other than when she was at her father's house. She even hated moving out of Union county, although she knew when most people looked at her, they saw Trish. When they came back after her father died, Alia thought she would hate it because it would all remind her of him. And at first, she did. Maybe that was part of the reason why she was so angry all the time. But then Alia met Crystal, and through Crystal, she had friends for the first time in years. And Charlie, though not around as much, was still there once in a while in the background. His being around had always made her happy. She even now could admit to herself that she often looked for him both in school and in town.

There was something to that special connection Charlie talked about. Alia knew because she had felt it often. She just refused to think about it. But now that she did, Alia realized Charlie always had a knack for showing up when she needed him the most. He was there the day she stepped on the broken glass bottle at the playground. A shard went right into her foot. She had screamed so loud that Charlie had heard her from three blocks away as he rode his bike home. And even with all the kids in the playground, he had been the first one to get to her. He had been the one that pulled the shard out so gently she barely even felt it. Charlie had picked her up and put her in the car of one of her neighbors to take her back home, his t-shirt wrapped around her bleeding foot.

Charlie had been the one to grab her arm and pull her back when a board from Johnny Baxter's treehouse broke, almost sending her several feet off the side. He's the one that found her at her father's grave after beating up the boy that molested a little girl. At the time, Alia had been so upset she hadn't even realized it was him. Charlie also found her in the woods at camp in a place she was positive she was well hidden. And then, at the school, he was there again even before she knew she needed him.

There were other times when she was just down or upset after getting a relatively good thrashing from her mother. Charlie always seemed to be there to lift her up. All it took was one look at his smiling face and those amazing eyes of his to make her instantly feel better. Alia had spent years telling herself that he was just some boy when the truth was much stronger and more profound than that.

Right at eleven, as promised, Charlie texted her.

Charlie: Good night, my sweet girl. Try to get some sleep. I love you, always have.

Alia: Love you too, Charlie. Goodnight.

Chapter 12
Nightmares, Family dinner, and Allies

"Alia…oh my god Alia, what did you do?"

A voice, a very familiar voice, was shouting at her. Alia tried to look around, but her head felt like it was on a swivel, and the room spun. Red and blue flashing lights added to the funhouse effect of the room. *A room,* she thought. *But what room? Where am I?*

The person shouting at her grabbed Alia by her shoulders and began to shake. "Damn it, Alia, look at me…what have you done? Alia, please."

Again she tried to look at the face with the voice yelling at her. Not just any voice but Charlie. Why was Charlie yelling at her? Alia's head felt heavy and fell down almost to her lap. There were hands in her lap, her hands, but they wouldn't move when she told them to. *And why are they sticky…so sticky.*

A beam of a flashlight passed over Alia, lighting up her hands. They were red and sticky. She tried again to look around but was only rewarded with a flash of pain. However, she could tell there were others here, wherever here was. Alia could hear others running around, sounds of alarm, disgust, and distress. Flashlights danced around her; someone bumped her as they went by. Again the voice shook her; Charlie shook her.

"You have to talk to me, Alia; you have to tell me what happened. What did you do?"

"Bed," Alia mumbled her mouth, almost unable to form the words. Getting into bed was the last thing she remembered, and now she was here. Sitting somewhere, her hands covered in red sticky. A light flashed over Alia again, and this time she could see her pants were red and sticky as well. *What's going on? Why am I covered in red sticky? Why am I not in bed? Charlie, stop, please stop hurting me.*

Charlie smacked Alia's cheeks hard enough to bring tears to her eyes. That seemed to bring her around a bit more as her eyes widened.

Alia attempted to look again, and all around her was chaos. She was sitting on the apartment's living room floor, but she barely recognized it. There was glass and broken furniture everywhere. Worst of all, there was more of that red sticky stuff, lots more. And so much noise. Alarms were going off, people running around shouting, a dog barking, Ebony barking, and Charlie still screaming at her.

"Why did you do it, Alia?" He shouted, tears in his eyes, his voice cracking. "I told you to call me...why?"

Alia looked at him at last. "Charlie." She cried. "Charlie, what happened?" From behind, her muscular meaty arms grabbed her, hauling Alia up to her feet, but her legs were too shaky to support her.

"You killed them...you killed them all," Harper growled into her ear. "I tried to tell you she was broken, Charlie. We tried to warn you. Now it's too late."

"No!" she screamed. "No...No, I didn't do anything...Charlie please...please Charlie!"

Harper started to drag her down a long hall. "You killed them all, just wouldn't listen, would you? I knew you were nothing but trouble...I knew I should have locked you up when I had the chance."

Alia panicked as Harper dragged her down the long hall. "No, Charlie, please...Please help me." Alia reached out, but Charlie just stood there, not looking at her, his head hanging down.

"What did you do, Alia?" Was all he would say.

As she was dragged off, Alia saw in the chaos surrounding Charlie. There were several severed body parts and more of that sticky red..more blood everywhere.

"No, no...no, Charlie, please I didn't...please, charlie...Please...."

Alia struggled, but something held fast to her arms and her legs. She struggled more, feeling the bindings tighten, which only added to her panic. With a scream, she burst forth with all the strength she had, felt herself fall, and landed with a hard thud on the floor. Her breath momentarily lost, Alia struggled to get it back, fighting again to get on her hands and knees. At last, she could breathe again, and when she looked up, she realized she was in her bedroom, and it was morning.

Remembering the nightmare, Alia checked her arms and legs but found none of that sticky red from the dream on her. "What the Actual fuck." She said, leaning against her bed. Looking around her room, she could see that it was still early and only the faintest bit of light came through the window.

A few seconds later, her alarm went off, making her jump. "Fuck!" With her fist, Alia bashed the alarm until it stopped sounding. Her head and chest pounding, she sat there as the last remnants of her dream faded away. Once Alia felt like she could stand again, she got up and dug around on her bed for her phone, then panicked when she couldn't find it. She was on the verge of a panic attack when Alia heard it rattle against her headboard. It had fallen into the crevice between it and the bed. Snatching it up, she then ran into the only actual privacy she had, the bathroom. It was, of course, Charlie texting her.

Charlie: Good morning hope you slept better than I did.

Alia: Good morning. I Gotta get ready, leaving early taking the city bus to school.

Charlie: Is everything okay?

Alia: So far. Want to avoid running into her if I can. Love you, Charlie

Charlie: Love you more. Let me know you made it safe.

Alia: More and more all the time. Will do.

Alia silently scolded herself for not telling him about the nightmare. Still, she figured he didn't need to have that to worry about on top of not sleeping well. Alia wondered if he was having bad dreams or just afraid she would lose it. After the nightmare, she was worried. *That was a messed-up dream. And it felt so real yet so unreal at the same time.*

Since the best way to avoid making that lovely scene come true was to avoid her mother, Alia took a short shower (still felt the sticky all over). Getting dressed, she ran out the door a full hour earlier than usual. Being a high school student, Alia could ride the city bus or the school bus. The past few months were the first she had ever been able to ride the bus since her mother literally forbade her to. Back from work was okay for some reason, but to school was not okay until she turned eighteen. Just another one of Trish's controlling tactics.

At school, Alia texted Charlie then hung out in the library until everyone else arrived. The day should have been great. She had a new boyfriend, hell, a new family, there was dinner tonight, and of course, she would get to see Charlie in a place where they didn't have to hide their feelings. Alia found it increasingly frustrating not being able to tell anyone why she would suddenly smile for no reason and got caught staring off into space all dreamy-eyed in several classes.

Then there was the nightmare. Alia washed her hands every chance she got, still feeling that red sticky. At lunch, she barely touched her food, choosing to give most of it to Ethan. Her friends, of course, noticed something was off about her, but all she could do when they asked was look at Crystal. Crystal hated to lie, so she just shrugged her shoulders and refused to answer. To make matters worse, the day dragged on.

When the final bell finally rang, Alia beat Crystal out front at the buses. They said their goodbyes, with Alia promising to text how everything went. She then walked over to the city bus stop and got a ride to Harkening Hill park right down from the Sheriff's house. It was all Alia could do to keep from running through the woods as she started to feel better and better the closer she got. Upon reaching the lake down from the house, she texted Charlie.

Alia: At Mom and Dad's, I can't wait to see you tonight. Get your arms ready. Been needing a hug all day

Charlie: They are all yours. Dad left earlier. He should be there already.

Alia: Yeah, I see his patrol car from here.

Charlie: Well, go study. I'll see you in a couple of hours. Love you.

Alia: Love you more.

Charlie: More and more all the time, sweet girl.

After last night Alia was afraid that she would find returning here uncomfortable, at least at first. But seeing the house, she knew that wasn't going to be an issue. And It wasn't. Other than being greeted with warmer and longer hugs, everything was the same as it had been. Alia had always felt very welcomed into this home. She just hadn't known until last night it was because it had once been hers as well.

And Harper saw to it that the two of them got to work right away. "We only have a few more days left. The more we can cram in, the better prepared you will be when you get there."

"Well, don't cram too much; she looks tired enough as it is. You alright dear, have trouble sleeping?" Ellen asked, brushing hair back from Alia's face.

She told them about the nightmare even though she hadn't told Charlie yet.

"And maybe, for now, you shouldn't," said Harper. "He didn't seem to get much sleep himself last night. No need to give his mind something else to float around up there. Give him a few days to get used to things and get back to sleeping right."

"I agree." Said Alia. "I just hope he does. I don't like the idea of him worrying so much."

"Not much to do about that, I'm afraid." Said Ellen. "That's pretty much his nature. He worries about everyone else and thinks of himself last. Always has."

When Charlie pulled up the drive, Alia and Harper were just finishing up the day's lessons. Alia went out to the porch still in her stocking feet to greet him. As soon as he saw her, he smiled a smile that lit up his eyes.

"Hey there." He said. One look at her, and the weight of the day fell right off. No longer tired, Charlie ran up the steps and wrapped his arms around her. "I have needed this all day. I had the worst dreams last night." He kissed her once and hugged her again before they went inside, where Ellen and Harper were putting dinner on the table.

Like the night before dinner was spent laughing, telling stories, and eating loads of food. It was the first time all day that both Alia and Charlie felt like eating, and they made up for it with seconds of meatloaf, along with potatoes, gravy, and string beans.

"I don't know how many more of these dinners I'm going to be able to have before I start tipping the scales again." Said Alia. She had been working very hard the past year to shed a few pounds and keep them off, often missing out on some of her favorite foods."

"Oh, please." Said Ellen, "You and Charlie both could stand to gain a few pounds." She looked over at Alia "last time I went to his apartment, he had a thimble of milk, condiments, and some nasty old cheese. And it's not because he can't cook."

"I hate cooking for just one person," said Charlie.

"Well, it's a good thing that Alia is a good cook." She winked at Alia. "Between the two of us, we will fatten you up yet." They all laughed.

After dinner, Harper had them all gather in the living room.

Alia was a bit apprehensive after last night's revelations. *I mean, seriously, how much more do they think I can handle before I crack.* She thought, not knowing she could have saved her worries.

"Okay," said Harper. "I have one thing I need to do, then the two of you can go hang out at the fire pit or the lake for a while, I guess." Harper reached into his pants pocket and pulled something out without showing them. "After you two left last night, Ellen and I got to talking. Now, before I give you this…this isn't an endorsement to do anything".

Charlie was about to say something, but Harper stopped him.

"I know you two are adults, and you're going to do what you want. We just ask that whatever you decide to do, you be careful. You're both young; you have plenty of years ahead of you."

"What Harper is trying to say is now is the time to work on setting your futures up. There will be plenty of time for marriage and children if that is what you want."

Charlie and Alia looked at each other and smiled, blushing a little. They both felt like Ellen and Harper were jumping the gun a bit, but they knew it came from a place of love.

"Yeah, like she said. Have some time to just be kids yourselves. Anyway, we talked about how your options for spending some time alone were severely limited. I think that is a good thing, while Ellen, on the other hand, insists the two of you need your own space. Perhaps even a place that you could meet on weekends once Alia has earned free time from the academy." Harper walked over to where they sat on the couch and handed Charlie a small wooden hand-carved acorn with a few keys attached.

Charlie, of course, knew what they were and smiled. "These are the keys to the cabin up in the mountains." He said more for Alia's benefit than his father's. "You sure, dad?"

Harper looked over at Ellen. "Yes, I'm sure, we are sure" Or rather, Ellen had insisted he was sure. Remembering his own hormonal raging teens and twenties, Harper didn't think it wise to give them a place to act so unencumbered. The very last thing they needed was for Alia to get pregnant.

"You two need a place where you won't have to look over your shoulders just so you can see each other. We don't use it as much anymore. We have all the alone time we need right here. So it's yours for the summer." said Ellen.

"But come fall, I want my key back.." said Harper. "Some of the best hunting and fishing is on that land, and by then, I'll need to stock the freezer again."

Charlie got up and hugged his dad, thanking him. Then hugged his mom, thanked her more, knowing the idea had been hers. He whispered in her ear. "I promise no grandchildren until we all are ready."

"Don't wait too long." She whispered back, hugging him tightly.

Later Charlie and Alia strolled hand and hand along the lakefront, mindful of any others that may be around. The night was warmer, the promise of summer on the way, and the whisper of crickets were in the air.

"So, what did you whisper to your mother?" Alia asked, stopping to look up at him.

Charlie smiled. "I'm not telling you that, no sorry." he blushed.

"Keeping secrets from me already, Charles." She teased.

"I was just making her a promise."

"Well, as much as I appreciated it this past weekend, I hope it's not to be a complete gentleman again." She laughed. "That's cute for now, but."

"But what, you gonna ravage me?"

"Maybe," she said, blushing now herself.

"Promises, promises." Charlie took her in his arms and kissed her passionately. "Come with me." The two of them walked over to the boathouse and went in through a side door. Charlie lit one small light and then hoisted Alia up on a bench. Now they were face to face.

Alia looked into his eyes and shook her head.

"What?"

"You need to promise me you will get some sleep tonight."

"I'm fine," he said, trying to stifle a yawn as he said it.

"No, you're not Charlie. I can see it in your eyes. I love those eyes. I hate to see them so weary."

"Weary, huh," he chuckled.

"Stop teasing me; I'm serious."

"I'm not teasing. I honestly love the way you talk sometimes. A bit of that old soul comes out, and I love it. Seriously though, I'm alright. I was just worried last night, and when I did fall asleep, I had a horrible dream...what did you have one too?" Charlie had noticed a change in her eyes when he had said that.

"Woke up to one this morning, fell out of my bed. I wasn't going to say anything. I didn't want to worry you. More than you already do, that is."

"Want to tell me about it?"

"Not really. What about yours?"

"Yeah, no, not really. It'll get better. We have the cabin now, which by the way, you, my little lady of the forests and trees, you are going to love. It's cooler up there, even in the summer. There's a brook that runs behind it loaded with trout. Plenty of trails to hike along and barely anyone around. We have gone whole weekends up there without seeing anyone."

"Sounds perfect. I can't wait."

"Okay, this weekend then. We can meet here Friday after we get off work and drive up and stay all weekend if we want. The only thing you need to do is figure out what to tell Trish. Think you can do that?"

"Yeah, I may have a few friends in the know that would be willing to be accomplices in our devious plans."

"There you go with the words again. I have to warn you, oddly enough, that is a big turn-on for me."

"Duly noted." She said with a grin. They spent the last of their precious time together in each other's arms and locked at the lips.

Back home that night, feeling better about everything, Alia slept good but not great. As she always did, she heard her mother coming home because she had a bad habit of slamming the apartment door. Then she would always check in on Alia to ensure that she was in bed and asleep. Or, if there was an issue, Trish would burst into the room and drag Alia out of bed by her feet. It got to be so that the sound of a slammed door always made her heart race. That night was no exception. Although she had fallen asleep (after Charlie told her goodnight and sent his love), the slam of the door woke her up. Alia lay in bed, heart racing waiting for her door to burst open and her mother to come in all in a rage, having found out about her and Charlie. However, Trish only opened the door, as usual, then a few seconds later, it closed, and Alia was alone again.

For the most part, the next two days were pretty routine. Alia went to school, and after school, she worked a few hours at the public library. On Thursday evening, Charlie slipped once again through the back door. The two of them went down to the archives room alone, then they both had to get back to work. Back upstairs and at her desk Mrs. Stackhouse smiled at her.

"So I take it the deputy was here conducting official police business again?"

Alia blushed.

"How is it going between the two of you, now that all has been revealed?"

Alia looked at Mrs. Stackhouse questioningly.

"Yes, I know all about the Harper's telling you they were your foster parents when you were a baby. And it's about time too. I told them quite a while ago that you were ready to deal with it. But it was their choice to wait, so I respected it."

At first, all Alia could do was stare at the woman she had known for years as if she had never really seen her before. "I don't understand. How do you know about it?"

"I wasn't always a librarian. Sure I always loved books, but when I was younger, I wanted to help people. I went to college and became a social worker, a job I had for many years. Then, I was handed a case that made it clear it was time for me to change vocations."

"What happened?" Alia asked although she had a good idea of just what did.

"Your mother happened. As social workers, we have a few goals. The first of which is to ensure the safety of the children under our care. Another is to try and keep families together as much as possible. Unfortunately, sometimes the system doesn't work no matter how good a job we do. Despite my best efforts with your case, the system failed you. Your mother was a manipulative, angry, nasty person adept at wearing masks, so well very few people can tell. But little Charlie could tell, and he wasn't the only one."

"They said Charlie never seemed to care for my mother. He said she used to pinch me."

"Yes, unfortunately, we could never prove your mother ever did any such thing. In fact, she had the Harper's absolutely smitten with her despite how Charlie felt. But I saw past it all. I had dealt with enough cases over the years that I looked more for the bad in people than I ever did the good. I have a feeling you may understand that."

She did. Alia was so used to being stabbed in the back, abused, and abandoned that she expected it from people. It made her leery of forming new friendships and made it where she tended to butt heads with people, much like she had once done with Harper years before.

"And that is no way to deal with people if you ever want to have truly loving relationships. However, it proved to be an asset in your mother's case. While everyone else was beguiled by your mother's progress, I had my suspicions. She seemed more intent on getting through each step to gain back custody than she did on spending actual quality time with you. I saw her impatience with you where others saw a young inexperienced mother. Did you know when she was granted custody of you, the only thing other than the clothes you wore she allowed you to bring was a musical bear?"

"I still have that bear." Alia said, "It barely plays music anymore, it just sounds creepy as hell, but I still have it."

"Well, I have to say I am surprised she allowed you to keep it. She couldn't do much about it in the courtroom, and you were not about to let go of it. Once you were her's, Trish wanted nothing to do with the Harpers…well, I'm getting off on a tangent here. My point is I knew something wasn't right with your mother. Twice when she came up for review to get custody of you back, I spoke my mind and advised against it. I wasn't allowed a third time. Your mother convincingly made up some lies about me and was granted her request for a new social worker. Even then, I made my reservations known, but they gave you back to her in the end. When Ellen later told me what your mother said to them when they tried to get her to let Charlie see you, I knew then I couldn't do it anymore."

Alia looked at the librarian and wondered what other secrets people had kept from her all these years. "The Harpers were my foster parents, you were my social worker, who else is going to reveal a connection to my past? Is the whole town in on this?"

"No, not quite, Alia, but you may be surprised how many people you have on your side around here."

"Apparently not enough that Charlie and I don't have to sneak around just to see each other."

"Yes, well, it's a big county. Many people here consider this the south; therefore, they are still very old-fashioned and stuck in their ways. Sure, you are eighteen now and legally an adult. But you are also still a student. Some people may be able to gloss over the fact that Charlie is almost four years older than you, but not while you're still in high school. Perceptions are a funny thing. If your mother would start spouting off certain things about Charlie, it doesn't matter that they are not true; some would believe something was amiss. Unfortunately, a lot of those people still hold sway and power in our town."

"I know, Harper said as much. It was why they wanted to wait to tell me."

"Well, they wanted to wait because they knew how much Charlie had grown to care for you. Young lovers tend to be careless. Personally, I think it's very unfair. However, the two of you have waited this long, a few more months, just to make the old farts of this town feel better, shouldn't be too hard."

"Months." Alia sighed, realizing she was talking about spending her whole summer at the academy.

"I know it seems daunting. Right now, everything seems to be taking forever, and you probably want to rush right to the good parts. But a bit of advice. Do yourselves both a favor and take things slow. Enjoy your youth and your freedom while you have it. Realize that you are young, and the both of you have very long lives ahead of you. I have seen couples people thought would last forever burn out early because they jumped into marriage and family way too fast."

Alia laughed. "You and the Hoppers are all talking about marriage and kids, and we haven't even been on our first date yet."

"Look me in the eyes and tell me you haven't thought about it already." She said with a knowing smile. "Have you found yourself writing Mrs. Alia Harper over and over in your notebook during class?"

Alia blushed. "Maybe a page or two." She confessed more *like a hundred*.

"Nothing turns us into silly girls faster than love," said Mrs. Stackhouse with a grin.

"Is that why my mother does so much stupid stuff when she gets a new boyfriend?"

"Oh, honey, I would be surprised if your mother has ever known the first thing about love. I think for her, it's more like a game. One in which she gets excited over the prospect of what she can get out of or win."

"That actually makes a lot of sense. I mean, it doesn't, of course, but it does seem to fit her. You're right, though. It's hard to think of it in terms of having years ahead of us. I feel like we have missed so much time already as it is, but in reality, we didn't miss much, I guess."

"In ten years, you're going to look back on this time and wonder why you were so worked up over not being able to see each other every second of the day. Your best years are still ahead of you. The both of you need to focus on making a good life for yourselves, and the rest will fall into place."

Alia became quiet for a moment as she thought. "But what if they're not. What if we don't have ten years. I bet my father thought he had more time. What if this is all we have for now."

"We can't live our lives like there is no tomorrow. Live in the moment, sure. Suck every little bit of enjoyment you can get out of life. But do it with the hope there will not only be a tomorrow but many, many more tomorrows to come. You're a smart girl; I believe you will figure it out."

On the bus ride home that night, Alia had a lot to think about. All she wanted was to spend as much time as possible with Charlie. To be fair, though, between his work and her school, they were doing pretty good at seeing each other. Then there was this weekend. If her mother didn't have a reason to hate the Harper's, she probably wouldn't want her to know about Charlie anyway. Trish drove Alia crazy when she briefly dated J.J., and he thankfully never met her. She wouldn't want to subject Charlie to her mother's scrutiny.

When the bus dropped her off, Alia felt better about things. As long as they were careful, these next four weeks wouldn't be so bad. Her mother was in a good mood and treated her okay for a change. Then there were weekends at the cabin with Charlie to look forward to. Of course, those weekends could present their own challenges, but she was sure that Charlie wouldn't push her into doing anything she wasn't ready for.

Alia was about to head into the apartment complex when up ahead about two blocks, blue and red lights flashed once at the construction site of a new elementary school. Then in her pocket, she felt her phone vibrate briefly.

Charlie: Want to come say goodnight?

Again the lights flashed.

Alia: On my way.

Chapter 13
Cabin in the woods

The school day on Friday didn't seem to ever end for Alia. The night before, after saying goodnight to Charlie in the parking lot of the unfinished school, Alia had packed a bag for the weekend and put it with her school stuff. Then she wrote a brief note for her mother and left it on the fridge before bed. If Trish had any objections to her spending the weekend at Crystal's house to study for finals, she would let her know that night when she came in. Later after their goodnights over the phone and she had crawled into bed, Alia heard her mother coming home with the familiar slam of the apartment door.

Does she not care that people are asleep and have work in the morning. She wondered not for the first time.

After about thirty minutes of waiting, she was sure her mother wasn't going to storm into the room objecting to her weekend plans; Alia allowed herself to sleep. Sure enough, there was a reply on the note in the morning.

Sounds good. Billy and I have a soccer game on Saturday night.
Don't be too late on Sunday.
I'll have dinner for you if you get here early enough.

Hmm, dinner, she thought. Her mother was in a particularly happy mood. The new rule since turning eighteen was that Alia had to provide her own meals. She even invested in a mini-fridge after Billy's stupid ass ate her food several times. Once in a while, Trish would leave her some leftovers, but she never made dinners anymore. *I bet she has a new boyfriend. Would explain her good mood of late.* It wasn't unlike her mother to date another while she still had one on the hook.

After school, Alia worked at the library for a few hours. She tried to busy herself logging in a new shipment but kept finding herself making mistakes and not concentrating. She apologized to Mrs. Stackhouse and even offered to come into work on Saturday, but she wouldn't hear it.

"No, go on and enjoy your weekend. Just remember what I said, no rush, dear."

"Yes, ma'am." She said. Outback Crystal and George were waiting for her to take Alia to their house, where Charlie would come pick her up after work.

She and Crystal explained the plan to her parents, Albert and Rose. Although they were not usually ones to lie, they agreed to cover for Alia because they loathed Trish so much.

"You will be taking your books and getting some studying in, right?" Rose asked her.

"Yes, unfortunately, I don't have much choice. I didn't get anything done outside of school with everything going on this week. Luckily Charlie is pretty smart. I'm sure he will help."

"Good, spending the weekend studying is a good idea. Plenty of time for other things once you are done with school."

"Yeah, everybody keeps telling me that." she laughed.

Shortly after, Charlie showed up in his pickup truck, having stopped at his apartment long enough to shower and change. Alia grabbed her things, and the two were finally off on their own at last. Alia had expected to be nervous about the weekend once they were on their way to the mountains, but Charlie's presence once again set her at ease. There were butterflies in her stomach, but they were the good kind born of natural teen hormones.

"So I take it your mother was okay with you spending the whole weekend at Crystal's?"

"Yes, I told her we would be studying for our finals this week."

"And I see that you brought your books." Despite how long Charlie had waited to be with Alia, he wasn't disappointed, far from it. Although his nerves had calmed once she was around like they always did, he, too, had been feeling the jitters. Charlie wanted nothing more than to show Alia how he truly felt about her, but he also wasn't in any rush.

"Yes, I'm sorry, but I really should get some work done this weekend. I don't know what you had planned." she blushed a little.

"Honestly, I didn't, well, except that I am making you dinner tonight."

"Oh really, you can cook too?"

"Maybe not as good as my mother, but I can manage not to burn down the kitchen. As for the rest of the weekend, I'm just happy to be able to spend more time with you. I'll follow your lead. It's only our first date." he smiled at her.

Alia smiled as well, loving the sound of the word date for the first time in her life. They drove through the night, out of town, and into the mountains. The road turned to dirt, and the trees closed in right before they pulled up in front of a beautifully made log cabin. Alia had imagined something old and rustic, but what she saw was a place that was made to look rustic but had been very well kept. A light was on inside, which she could see through curtained windows.

"We have an older couple that acts as sort of caretakers for the place. They take care of a few other houses around here as well. I had them freshen up everything and get some groceries so we wouldn't have to make any stops before getting here. Fewer people see us, the better." They got out, and Charlie insisted on getting her bags, then they went inside, where he showed her around.

A standard living room with a massive fireplace and comfy-looking furniture was off the entrance. Off to the left, he showed her his parents' room and his side by side.

"We won't be staying in her because my room only has a single bed." He said. "Unless you're not comfortable with sleeping with me." Charlie grinned bashfully.

"I think I can fend you off if I need to." Alia smiled back.

Across from the living room was a guest suite with a full-size bed and its own bathroom. Here he dropped their things. "This is the guest room. I thought It would be better to give us more room. But that's all up to you." Charlie went up and gave her a hug then a kiss. "I'm in no rush to do anything. It's important that you don't feel rushed either. Like I said, I'll follow your lead."

"This room will be fine. For now, all I want is another hug and dinner; I am starving."

Charlie laughed, wrapped her in his arms again, added a kiss to her forehead, then headed off to the kitchen.

Alia looked around the room and was struck by how cozy it was. It was the same as the other rooms. You could tell there was a lot of love here, just like at their family home. While Charlie banged around in the kitchen, she put all her things away, finding empty drawers for her clothes. Done with that, she went out to the kitchen where Charlie was making spaghetti for dinner.

"Spaghetti, huh?"

"Not just any spaghetti, my dear, but my signature sauce spaghetti. I have been working on it for years, and I believe I have perfected it. May actually be the only thing I like better than Mom's."

"Ooh, I'm going to tell her you said that." she laughed. "Will I have time to take a quick shower? I feel gross from hauling books around at the library for hours."

"Sure, plenty of time, the sauce needs to simmer a bit." he bent over and pecked her on the cheek. "You don't feel gross to me, though." he winked at her.

"Smooth, Charlie." Alia laughed.

About half an hour later, Alia came out of the bathroom to delicious smells and a candle-lit dinner waiting for her. Seeing the table lit up so nicely with bowls of salad, spaghetti, and rolls, she felt inadequate wearing only jeans and a baby doll top. "Oh Charlie, this looks amazing. I feel like I should have dressed better."

He looked at her, puzzled. "Why you look great." He came up and kissed her on her cheek. "Smell great too." Taking one of her hands, Charlie led her over to the table and pulled out a chair for her. For the next half hour, they sat, ate, and talked.

Charlie wanted to do something nice since they couldn't very well go out to dinner and hoped this would make up for it. The candlelight bouncing off the shine in her eyes was all the confirmation he needed. Alia exclaimed several times over how good the sauce was and how much she loved the added touch of the candles.

After dinner, they joked around in the kitchen while cleaning, laughing, kissing, and touching as they went. Alia felt as if she were in a dream. Being with him was always pretty uncomplicated, but she had been nervous about being here with him alone. Especially with a single bed waiting for them at the end of the night. But aside from a slight blush here and there, over one comment or another, the evening was very comfortable and enjoyable for them both.

With the kitchen clean, they went to the living room where Charlie built a fire, and they sat on the couch in front of it. Both full and on the verge of sleepiness, they just sat for a while gazing into the blaze.

Alia felt like she was nestled inside a soft cocoon, safe from anything that could try to harm her. She wondered what was next as the fire died down and realized that Charlie had said he would follow her lead.

"It's getting late. I know you have to be tired. You don't look like you have slept much this week. So I am going to do us both a favor and get changed for bed." Alia got up, but he held on to her and pulled her back down to him, kissing her tenderly.

"I'll be in, in a bit," he said, letting her go. "Let me damp down the fire and lock the place up.

Alia nodded and went off to their room, where she changed into a two-piece pajama short set, the nicest night clothes she had. *I seriously need to do some shopping,* she thought. Sighing, she got into bed, snuggling into the warmth of the covers. A few minutes later, Alia heard Charlie come in, and he sat on the other side of the bed, facing away from her.

"Um, I usually only sleep in my boxers," he said shyly. "But if you would feel more comfortable, I could put on a t-shirt and sweats like I did at the motel." Charlie turned his head slightly to face her. He could see she was already half asleep, and he was fatigued as well. Alia had been right; he hadn't gotten very much sleep all week.

"I'm pretty sure we would both agree that what we need tonight is sleep. At this point, I don't think it matters what you wear. I hope you're not disappointed."

Charlie shook his head. "No, of course not. I'm happy to just be with you at all, Alia. I would much rather have you here than you be there with her."

"Come to bed then," she said with a yawn.

Charlie took off his jeans and flannel shirt then got under the covers next to her. Alia rolled over so he could spoon her from behind. Charlie held her close, drinking in the moment, gave her one kiss behind her ear, and before he knew it, they were both fast asleep.

The following day Alia woke to the sun shining through the windows, birds chirping outside, and Charlie, his arm still wrapped around her, snoring slightly. *How is this even possible? How am I even here...me?* She thought. Picking up her phone from the nightstand beside the bed, she saw that it was already eight in the morning. It had easily been the best night of sleep she had since the motel and since forever before that. Not wanting to wake him, Alia slowly slid out from under Charlie and got off the bed. She thought she had escaped without waking him when suddenly he grabbed her arm.

"Where do you think you're going?" He mumbled, still half asleep.

"Shit, Charlie, you about scared the hell out of me. Go back to sleep." Alia bent forward and kissed him on his forehead. "Get some more rest. I'll make breakfast."

Charlie nodded, let go of her arm, and fell back to sleep with a smile on his face. A little bit later, with a breakfast of bacon, eggs, fruit, and biscuits laid out on the table, he walked out still only wearing his boxers, scratching the stubble on his chin...and still smiling.

Alia turned around to see him standing there, his thick dark hair a mess, his eyes still sleepy but shining, and the rest of him. With a start, she realized this was the first time she'd seen him, well, almost undressed. *My long boy.* she thought. Charlie was not just tall; he was long as well. Long arms, long fingers, long legs, and long feet. Arms and legs were covered in long dark hair, more on his chest, and a thin dark line from his navel to below his boxers. Lean and muscular as well, Alia felt her breath quicken and her heart skip a beat. A tiny part of her regretted not making love to him the night before, but they had both been so tired.

"I could get used to this," Charlie said, sitting down. "An excellent night's sleep and a great breakfast are just what I needed. How did you sleep?"

"The best sleep in a very long time." She admitted sitting down herself.

"See, we are good for each other. I always knew we would be." He said, beaming at her while stuffing strips of bacon in his mouth.

"Thank you for last night, Charlie."

"What for this time?"

"Just for being you. For not expecting anything right away. I know it may not have been exactly what you wanted after all this time…."

"Stop right there," Charlie said, cutting her off. He took her by the hand. "Come here."

Alia let him pull her over to him and sat down on his lap. "The only thing I want, have wanted all these years, is for us to be together and you to be happy. There will be time for other things when you're ready. I love you. Nothing is going to change that."

This time Alia was the one to grab his face in her hands and kiss him, soft at first as he would then more passionately. "Love you too." She said, "I don't feel like myself when I am around you. I feel like a better version of myself. A more capable, confident version, and I like that."

"Alia, that person is who you are. You have just been made to hide it all these years. I want you to know that you don't have to hide anymore, you don't have to be scared, and you don't have to feel like anything less than the wonderful person I know you are. Spitfire temper and all." He laughed.

After breakfast, they took a walk down to the brook that ran in front of the cabin. It was a gorgeous spring day with only the hint of a chill in the air. They ended up walking a few miles in the woods, hand in hand, not another soul around. Back at the cabin, Charlie helped Alia set up her books on the patio table outside, where he quizzed her on some of her subjects.

Sure there was plenty of teasing, kissing, and hand-holding, as well as breaks for lunch and dinner, but the weekend ended up being pretty uneventful. Just the way they wanted it. There was a lot of flirting, teasing, and long moments in each other's arms, but the weekend was more for them to connect to each other on a personal level without the pressure of other expectations.

Sadly Sunday evening came much too fast for them both. Alia packed up her things in the bedroom while Charlie watched from the doorway. She kept reminding herself not to pout like a child because it would be unfair to him. When she looked over at Charlie, Alia realized she wasn't the one having an issue with her having to leave. He smiled at her as she packed, but she could see the sadness in his eyes at seeing her have to go. Alia started to second guess her hesitation about giving in to their desires, wondering if giving him more would have been enough to hold him over till next time.

Charlie watched from the doorway as Alia put the last of her things in her bags. He knew she was trying her best to stay in an upbeat mood, and he was as well, but he knew he was failing. Charlie wanted to stop her. He wanted to tell her to put it all back that she could just stay here where he could keep her safe. To hell with what her mother would say. But he had his parents to think of as well.

Alia sighed and sat heavily on the edge of the bed. "Maybe we should have…I don't know; made the weekend more special."

"No," Charli said, not moving from the door. "What we did was far more important."

"We could have done both." Alia offered with a smile.

Charlie smiled back and laughed a little. "I'm afraid if we had gotten started, we would have barely even come up for air and to eat. Besides, there will be other weekends."

"Well, mostly anyway. There's next weekend, then the weekend after that is Prom, which like an idiot, I said I would go to. The weekend after that is graduation, then the weekend after that the fun and awesome party my mother is having for herself, oops, I mean me…." *And now I am ranting and acting exactly like I said I wouldn't.* Alia hid her face in her hands in frustration.

Charlie went over, removed her hands, then, seeing the tears in her eyes, hugged her close.

"Damn it, Charlie, I'm so sorry. I promised myself I wasn't going to behave like this."

"Like what? Human?" He asked, caressing her hair.

"I just don't want to make this harder for you than it already is."

"Funny here I was trying not to make it hard on you and failing miserably."

"We haven't even talked about the big issue."

"I know, and call me a coward, but I'm not ready to talk about that yet. That's for future us to worry about."

Alia pulled back from him and looked at him. "How is it that we always seem to know what the other is thinking?" She smiled with a little laugh.

"I told you, sweet girl, we are meant to be together. And we will be, I firmly believe that. After all these years, all we have been through and will go through, we will be together and happy in the end. As for what we do on the weekends, we have just don't worry about it. Having you here with me where I can keep you safe is all I need for now." They kissed. Charlie helped her to her feet, grabbed her bags, and took her back to Crystal's house, where George and Crystal waited to bring her the rest of the way home. On the drive in the Buick, Alia thought over the weekend, making her smile and her heart dance. Charlie had done in one weekend what no one else had ever done for her. He made her truly happy. She should have known that it wouldn't last.

Chapter 14
Hell hath no fury

As soon as Alia walked into the apartment, she could feel the tension in the air. The lack of a particular poodle greeting her set off alarms as well. "Hey Ebony, where are you, boy?" She called out, trying to act nonchalant when in reality, she wanted to run to her room before the shit started.

"Billy had to take him out for a walk because you showed up so late."

After dropping her bags off in her hall, Alia reluctantly walked into the living room where her mother was waiting for her. She sat on the couch in what Alia referred to as her bitch mode. Leg crossed over leg, foot bouncing up and down, arms crossed with a cigarette in her hand, and looking like she wanted to start a fight.

"You're late." Trish scowled at her.

"It's not even nine yet," Alia said, honestly perplexed.

"I told you to be home in time for dinner," she sneered.

No, you didn't.

"You said you would have dinner if I came early enough. It's Okay; I already ate at Crystal's," Alia said in hopes of defusing the situation.

But Trish wasn't having it tonight. "Oh, it's okay, it's not you that made a nice dinner, so what the hell do you care. Your selfish Alia, all you care about is yourself."

Alia took a deep breath, trying to keep her mother from goading her into a fight. "Mom, we were studying, and the time got away from us. I have finals starting in the morning. I'm going to take a shower and go to bed."

As Alia turned and walked away, Trish grabbed something next to her and threw it. "Don't you fucking walk away from me." She screamed.

Alia barely heard it, she had seen movement out of the corner of her eye, and before she could react, something hard hit her in the face just below her right eye. Grabbing her cheek, Alia fell to the floor, hollering in pain.

"Oh, get the fuck up; it barely hit you."

Pulling her hand away from her throbbing face, Alia saw blood on it, a good bit of blood. Without even looking, she could feel the skin under her eye start to stretch and swell. If Billy hadn't chosen that moment to come in, Alia was later sure she may have lost all her senses and gone after her mother. Instead, Billy ran to her, seeing the blood running down her face.

"Shit." He yelled. "What the hell did you do?" He asked Alia.

"Oh, I threw an ashtray at her, and it barely hit her; it's not a big deal," Trish said from the living room. She couldn't see Alia on the floor in the hall behind the couch.

"I don't know." Billy said, "She's bleeding pretty bad, and it already looks like she's getting a shiner." He tried to look better at it, but Alia kept slapping his hand away.

"Leave me alone, leave me the fuck alone." She cried

Trish came from the other side of the couch and stopped short when she saw that her daughter was indeed bleeding bad.

"Don't just stand there," Said Billy, "Get a rag and some ice. Stop slapping me, Alia, let me look at it."

"Fuck you, Billy, fuck you both," Alia screamed as the whole one side of her face burned with red hot pain.

"Now watch your damn mouth." Her mother yelled from the kitchen. "It's still not that damn bad. It's your smart mouth that got you in this mess, to begin with."

My fault; you were mad because I didn't show up for dinner. That's no reason to smash my face in.

Trish came over to her with ice in a rag and tried to put it on Alia's face, but she flinched back from her.

Alia's mind was reeling. She wanted to beat the hell out of her mother right now. Preferably with the same ashtray. But her face hurt like it was screaming mad. *But fuck my pain, I can't let Charlie see me with a bruise on my face; he's liable to kill her. What the hell am I going to do…maybe it's not that bad, perhaps it just hurts like hell, but it's OK.* Alia looked down again at the blood on her hands and the blood pooling on her shirt and knew it was pretty bad.

Billy took the rag from Trish and was able to get Alia to let him put it on her. "There's a lot of blood. She may need stitches."

"Oh, for heaven's sake, she will not. She's just a hypochondriac. She'll be fine."

"I'm not fucking fine," raged Alia taking no mind to the things she was saying to her mother that would beat her for less. "Look at all the blood."

"Well, you would think by now you would learn to duck better. It's your fault anyway. I told you to be home for dinner."

Alia caught Billy, giving Trish a strange look. That's when she realized it didn't smell like anything had even been cooked that evening. *That fucking bitch didn't even make dinner. She's just pissed because she wanted me home early for some reason. That fucking psychotic bitch. She was lying in wait for me this whole time.* To add to the pain of her face, Alia now felt her heart burst out in panic. *Does she know? Is it possible that she knows?* Alia jumped up, pushed Billy out of the way, and headed to her bathroom.

"Yes, go clean it up, and you will see that it's not that bad." Her mother yelled after her.

But when Alia got into her bathroom, what she saw was not nothing. There was an inch-long gash along her right cheek just under the eye where the skin had split open on impact. Already the whole cheek was turning purple, and even her eye was red and swelling. Billy was picking her up off the bathroom floor before Alia had even realized that she had fainted.

"Come on, kid, sit up at least, don't pass out. If you pass out, I'll have to call nine-one-one, and you know that means the cops will come too. Your mother will shit if the cops come."

Instantly Alia was wide awake. "No, don't call them Billy, don't you dare, it's fine, I'm fine. It was just seeing all the blood, that's all."

"Good, good because it's both our asses later if the cops come and you know it. Course they may lock her up." Billy got closer to her and talked real low. "Maybe we should.

Fuck her, Alia; this is going too far. Fucking with you is one thing, but this is too much. Fuck her anyway. I know she's running around behind my back fuck her. Let's call the cops, and I'll back you up. I'll even lie and say I saw her do it."

Alia grabbed the front of Billy's shirt with her bloody hands and pulled his face up to hers. "You listen to me right now, don't you fucking dare call the cops. Do you hear me, Billy? Don't you fucking dare. Even if they lock her up, she will get out, then I'll have hell to pay. You can leave; I can't. I have to live with her, so don't you fucking dare do it."

"Okay, okay, calm down. I won't. I want to know how in the hell you intend to explain that shiner of yours when you go to school in the morning."

Alia didn't care about school. It was how she would explain it to Charlie that was the problem. "I did it walking the dog, you hear me. I'll think of something it's not like it's the first time I have shown up with something like this. I'll tell them I fell, I don't fucking know, but the cops can't know shit Billy, the Sheriff can't find out about this."

Billy looked at her and shook his head. "It's not the sheriff you're worried about, is it? It's your friend Deputy Dougie you don't want to find out, isn't it?"

"Shut up, Billy; you don't know what the fuck you're talking about."

"Bullshit, I may have been drinking that night, but I saw the way he was looking at you."

Alia grabbed him by the collar of his shirt again. "Damn it, Billy, if you don't shut the fuck up. You don't know shit; you didn't see shit." Alia was crying now. "Come on, man, I have never really been a total bitch to you. Don't fuck shit up for me. Keep your damn mouth shut, please."

"Hey, no-look, calm down. I'm not gonna say shit. I'm sober; you know I shoot straight when I'm sober." He was right about that. All of Billy's faults lay with the fact that he turned into a pure ass when he drank. Sober, he wasn't that bad of a guy. A bit of a dick at times, sure, but he had managed to keep an excellent job all these years. "But you have to let me clean this up for you so we can get some ice on it, or it's going to be really bad. I mean, it's already going to be shit, but maybe we can get the swelling to come down some."

Nodding, Alia let Billy clean up the blood to see just how bad it was. It took a lot for the bleeding to stop, but the gash itself didn't look so bad once it did. On the other hand, the bruising was getting worse by the minute and covered almost the whole one side of her face.

"Your mother should have been a pitcher. She must have wailed the hell out of that ashtray. I don't think it needs any stitches, though. Some of those butterfly bandages in my first aid kit should work. Keep ice on your cheek while I go get them."

"Billy, please, don't fucking say shit to her about Deputy Harper. Please," Alia begged.

"Don't worry, kid."

But she did, of course. Alia could hear Billy and her mother talking from the other room but not make out much of what was being said. Her mother was being a complete bitch that much she could tell and still blaming it all on Alia.

When Billy came back in, he had a first aid kit. "I didn't say shit, so don't ask." He said. "You know, I know your mother can be a bitch, but damn she's taking it far this weekend. She's been in a mood the whole time. Her team losing Saturday didn't help."

"Why what happened? Why was she in a mood?"

"I don't know, I came out Saturday morning, and she was on the phone and was pissed off ever since. Maybe that new guy of hers told her to go to hell, I don't know. The closer it got to you coming home, the more pissed she got, and when you didn't come home by seven, she was fit to be tied."

"She was mad at me about something?"

"No. Hell, I don't know. She gets pissed, she just likes taking it out on you. Though she was pretty pissed about you running off with Dougie last weekend. She done had him raping you and getting you pregnant with his demon spawn by the time you called Saturday. You know how she can get, how she blows things up. But don't worry, I didn't say shit about him making googly eyes at you that night. And

I won't either. Definitely won't now, sorry, kid, but after this, I think I may have to look into changing my living situation. She's fucking around on me anyway, I'm sure of it."

"Me too." Said Alia. "Thank you, Billy, I know I have given you a hard time sometimes, but I really appreciate you helping me," she said as tears from her good eye streamed down her face.

"No problem, kid. I never held it against you anyway. Half the fucking town knows how your mother is. It's no wonder you hate the men she messes with. Most of them are scummy anyway, present company excluded of course." He said with a chuckle.

Alia tried to smile, but it hurt like hell.

"Yeah, I wouldn't try to smile for a while if I were you. The split is sealing, so you shouldn't have too bad a scar, but if you keep opening it up, it's gonna be ugly. You can take a shower, but I wouldn't get your face wet without a rag, gonna hurt like a bitch if you do."

"Already hurts like a bitch," Alia moaned. *And boy would I love to hurt a bitch right now.*

"I'll go settle your mother down. Just stay in your room for the rest of the night. I'll take the dog out again if he needs to go."

When Billy left, leaving her some bandages, Alia locked the door after him, sat with her back against it, and cried. Not because her face hurt even though it did, but because she was afraid of what would happen when Charlie and Harper saw her. Unlocking the door, Alia reached into her hall and grabbed the bags she had tossed there. Shutting the door again, she locked it and leaned back against it. Fishing out her phone, she stole herself before turning it on. As she was afraid there would be, there were several texts from Charlie.

Charlie: Hey, did you make it home yet?
Charlie: Alia?
Charlie: I know I'm not supposed to panic, and your phone is probably off, but you should have been home

by now. I'm hoping you just forgot to text before taking a shower.
Charlie: Alia, is something wrong? I feel like something is wrong. Please text me right away.
Charlie: Alia, I called Crystal now we are both worried. Shit, Alia, I'm coming over there if you don't answer soon.
Charlie: Please be okay, Alia. I'm going to wait a bit longer, but if you don't text soon, I'm coming over.

The last text from him hadn't been, but five minutes ago, so she texted back before checking the ones from Crystal.

Alia: I'm so sorry. Trish was pissed I was home so late. We got into it when I got in.

Alia barely had the first text done when she could see he was responding.

Charlie: Are you okay? Just tell me you're alright.

Alia: I'm oka.

She lied, crying more as she did.

Charlie: Are you sure, Alia? I have a terrible feeling. It's strange. I keep getting this feeling like something is wrong. Are you sure you're okay?

Alia: I'm fine, Charlie. Please don't worry. I'm just agitated right now, that's all. I'm so sorry.

Charlie: You have nothing to be sorry about. Sorry, I texted so much. I know what you said when you gave me your number. It's just I had the most awful feeling.

Alia: Charlie, I'm alright, let me have time to shower, then text me, okay?

Charlie: Of course

Alia: Sorry I made you worry

Charlie: Don't it's okay, it's my fault. I've just been so worried about you.
I love you. Text you in a bit.

Alia: Love you more

Tears still spilling, her hurt cheek pounding and stinging in pain, Alia checked her texts from Crystal.

Crystal: Hey, are you okay? We dropped you off a while ago, and Charlie said you
haven't checked in. He's freaking out, Alia. I told him you might have forgotten. Text me when you get this

Alia: I told Charlie I was okay

Crystal: And are you Alia, are you okay?

Alia: You can't tell him, you can't tell Charlie, promise me

Crystal: Alia, what's wrong? You're scaring me, what's wrong? Charlie texted just now and said you got into it with your mother.

Alia: Promise me, Crystal.

Crystal: I promise, Alia, please tell me what's going on.

Alia dropped the ice rag for a minute to take a selfie with her phone.

Alia: You have to promise you won't freak out. You can't say shit to Charlie, not till I figure out what to do.

Crystal: I won't just tell me

    Alia sent the photo

Crysta: OMG, Alia, please tell me your mother didn't do that.

Alia: You promised Crystal you can't say shit to Charlie.

Crystal: You need to call the Sheriff. This is assault, Alia. She can't get away with this.

Alia: I can't. You have no idea what kind of temper Harper has. I can't say for sure he would do anything, but I can't take that chance. And if Charlie finds out, remember what George said he did to J.J.

Crystal: So you lied to him?

Alia: No, I just didn't tell him. I'm okay, it hurts like a bitch, but I'm okay.

Crystal: No, you're not Alia. George just saw the picture. He wants to come to get you.

Alia: No, that's only going to make things worse. I'm telling you I'm fine.

Crystal: Damn it, Alia, enough is enough, It's not safe there anymore. You can't hide this. Charlie will find out, and when he does, he will be pissed.

Alia: Which is precisely why I need time to deal with this. I have nowhere else to go.

Crystal: You can come here. My parents are in bed already but in the morning we
 can tell them what happened.

Alia: No, I'm telling you it's only going to make things worse. If I leave, Trish will say things about Charlie, horrible things. Things that could get him killed.

Crystal: She won't be able to if she's in jail, Alia.

Alia: She will get bailed out. Believe me, Crystal, I have thought about this kind of thing a lot. It was one thing when it was just me, but I won't put Charlie at risk.

Crystal: Alia, please. Go to your closet, walk the dog or something, but call me.

Alia: I can't. I have to get a shower. Charlie is going to text me back soon.

Crystal: Alia, you have to tell him.

Alia: I can't not now. Maybe in the morning, it won't look so bad.

Crystal: Are you kidding me? It's going to look way worse in the morning.

Alia: I have ice on it. The bruising and swelling should go down.

Crystal: George says it's not going to.

Alia: Maybe I can come over early, and we can put makeup on it

Crystal: Even if I had the foundation to match you, that would take a shit ton of it
And what are you going to do, keep hiding it from him? Charlie is going to find out Alia. Better now than later.

Alia: No, I'll wait till morning and see how bad it is, then I'll tell him I fell taking the dog out or something.

Crystal: He's not going to believe that. No one is. Shit, everyone will know who did this. It's not a secret what your mother is like.

Alia: Just give me time to figure something out. I have to get in the shower, he's going to be texting me soon.

Crystal: call the Sheriff

Alia: No

Crystal: Alia, please.

Alia: No, Crystal, you promised.

Crystal: I'll give you till morning.

Alia: I'll text you in the morning. I have to go.

Alia was barely out of the shower when her phone vibrated with a message.

Charlie: You ready for bed yet?

Alia: Getting in now. Love you, goodnight.

Charlie: I love you too. Alia, are you sure you're okay?

Alia: I'll be fine, Charlie, I'm upset about the fight, but I'll be okay.

> *Not a total lie, but I still feel like scum for saying it.*

Charlie: When you lay down, just pretend you're back at the cabin. I'll be there lying right behind you.

Alia: Okay, Charlie, I will. I love you.

Charlie: I love you more, sweet girl. Try and get some sleep.

Alia: More than you loved me yesterday?

Charlie: Of course, goodnight, sweet girl.

On the other side of town, Charlie sat looking at a picture of her on his phone. He had snapped a shot of her outside at the cabin. Her beautiful blue eyes sparkled, and she smiled back at him radiantly. Something was wrong, and he could feel it. There was something more than just a little fight going on he was sure of it. Sitting there in his small empty apartment, Charlie had never felt so alone before in his life. Already he missed her laugh, the way she rolled her eyes at him when he made a bad joke. The feel of her skin on his. None of that was as bad as the feeling he had that she was in some kind of trouble right now, and he was helpless to do anything about it. When he tried sleeping later, Charlie was plagued by nightmares, and he tossed and turned. Each dream ended with Alia lying lifeless and bloody in his arms. Something was wrong. He knew in his heart his girl was in some kind of trouble.

Even though Alia lay in bed and tried to pretend she was back in the cabin, sleep didn't come to her for hours. Instead, she lay there crying, terrified about how Charlie was going to react. She was scared for him, not of him. He would forgive her for lying, but he would never forgive himself that she was sure of. What she was afraid of most was what he may try to do to her mother. Like Charlie, Alia's dreams when she did sleep were nightmarish. Images of Charlie standing before her flashed in her mind, and he was covered in the red sticky.

Chapter 15
Aftermath

"Shit," Alia said, looking into the mirror in the morning. It was worse, much worse. The small gash itself looked like it had sealed up pretty well. However, the bruising was a deep purple that went down almost to her jawline and back as far as her temple. She also had a black eye, with the top lid looking purple and the bottom so swollen it made it hard for her to see out of it. No amount of makeup was going to even begin to hide it.

Alia texted Crystal, letting her know she was coming over that her face was worse, then got dressed. Not even bothering to eat, she grabbed her backpack and went to leave when she saw a note on her door.

If the eye is bad, stay home today. I'll call in when I wake up to excuse you.
Mom

Alia ripped the note off the door. Going into the kitchen, she jotted down a reply.

Can't I told you I have finals this week. Don't worry, I'll come up with a good enough lie to cover. Everyone knows how clumsy I am.

She may regret that last little bit later, but for now, Alia was pissed off. *Stay home…yeah, you would like that, wouldn't you?*

Leaving the apartment, Alia pulled the hood of her jacket up over her head and down low to cover her face as much as possible. Good thing for her teens walking around like that was pretty standard. She may get a few stares, but most people on the bus didn't look at anyone this early anyway. Alia walked out of the complex and to the bus stop, not passing anyone. Getting on the bus, the driver gave her a funny look.

"Caught a ball this weekend." She said by way of explanation.

"Ouch, that looks like it hurt like a bitch."

Nodding, Alia found a seat far from the four other people on the bus. Since Crystal's house was practically on the bus line, she only had to walk one more block from the stop to the house. Looking around, Alia made sure she didn't see any Sheriff vehicles, then walked as fast as she could till she got to Crystal's driveway.

When Alia got to the door, Crystal opened it, having been waiting for her. Behind her were not only her parents but George as well. The looks on their faces told her all she needed to know.

"I guess it looks pretty bad to you as well." She said. Crystal pulled her inside, and they all embraced her into one giant hug. When they broke, Crystal's mother looked at the bruising up close while her father went to get ice because more ice wouldn't hurt. Sitting on their couch with an ice pack to her face, Alia explained what went wrong the night before. No stranger to hearing the fights she and her mother had, they were still very alarmed that things had gotten to that point.

"So, what do you plan on doing about this?" Albert asked.

"There's not much I can do. For now, I need to get to school so we can start on our finals. After that, I need to figure out how to tell Charlie. I think he knows something is wrong even though I told him I was okay. He already has plenty of reasons to hate my mother. I'm worried what he might do when he finds out."

Albert thought for a minute. "I know the Harpers pretty well. I think your best bet would be to go there right after school. Tell Charlie's parents first, then see how they think you should approach him. I really don't think the boy will do anything stupid, though. He's never been anything less than professional."

Alia, Charlie, and George exchanged a quick look. "I hope you're right, but he didn't even want me to go home in the first place."

Later George drove the girls to school. Getting out of the car, Alia braced herself for the stares she was sure to get. She had told Crystal what she said to the bus driver, so that was the story they would go with for now.

"I'll be here right after school to get the both of you." Said George, then he drove off.

At school, there were a lot of stares and questions. Her friends Ethan, Rachael, Charlene and Laura, however, didn't believe the baseball to the face excuse. They had known where Alia had spent her weekend and who with, but luckily they were the only ones. Her teachers seemed very concerned, and even the principal paid her a visit at lunch. She didn't think he was buying the baseball story either. They made her go to the nurse to have it checked out, but there really wasn't anything to do about it.

Alia held her breath all day that somehow word wouldn't get to anyone in the
Sheriff's department, and eventually to Charlie. She was most concerned about the principal calling it in as abuse.

Charlie had texted her off and on during the day to see how her finals were coming and only asked once if she was sure she was okay. About an hour before school was out, they were done with day one of their finals and hanging out in the senior quad when Alia called Ellen. She told Ellen that she needed to talk to both her and Harper and that they shouldn't say anything to Charlie about meeting with her.

"Alia Honey, is everything okay?"

"Not really. I'm fine. It's better to talk to you about it face to face. Maybe even you before Harper gets home."

"Sure, I'll let him know. See you in a little while."

Where time at school usually crawled, this time it sped by, and soon George was back to pick up the girls. When they got close to the Harper's drive, Alia slid down into the car seat with her hood pulled up again. No sense in taking any chances. They both joined her in the house, not wanting to leave her to do this alone. She managed to keep her face covered at first when Ellen let them in, but when Alia got into the living room, she pulled it off then turned around.

"Oh my god." Said Ellen running to Alia, pulling the girl into her arms. Letting her go, Ellen tenderly put her hands on both sides of Alia's face. "Oh my god, my poor baby girl, what happened to you? Who did this, Alia?" She had tears in her eyes, and it didn't escape Alia, what Ellen had just called her. It made her heart ache, and she knew then that this was only the beginning. "Alia, Harper will be here any minute. You have to tell me who did this to you. It was your mother, wasn't it? Did she do this?"

Alia nodded. "She got mad and threw an ashtray at me." Alia started to tell her what had happened when they all heard Harper's patrol car pull up in the drive.

"Stay in here and let me deal with him for a few minutes." Ellen wiped her eyes and went to the kitchen, where Harper would come in through the mudroom.

Sitting on the couch, Alia started to feel a little sick. The three of them waited as Ellen spoke to Harper in the mudroom. There were some clanging noises, then Harper yelled.

"She did what?" They heard his footsteps pound as he came to the living room, not even having taken his boots off. When Harper saw Alia, he stopped.

Alia looked at him and saw both tears and anger well up in his eyes, making hers fall.

Harper went over to Alia and tilted her head so he could see the bruise better in the light. "She did this with an ashtray?"

Alia nodded. "A glass one. Little bigger than the ones they used to have at the bars."

"Did anyone see her do it?"

"No, Billy was out walking the dog. He came in right after, even helped me clean it up."

"And you didn't say anything to Charlie?"

"No, I just told him she was mad at me for being late, and that's why I hadn't texted him to let him know I made it home."

"He called me." Said Crystal. "Was freaking out because he hadn't heard from her. Kept saying he thought something was wrong."

"I didn't want to lie to him, but I was afraid of how he would react. The last thing I wanted was for him to come over there."

"Good, you did the right thing, Alia. That boy can have his father's temper. Sometimes I hate to say it. Mostly when it comes to you." Harper had not forgotten how Charlie yelled at and stood up to him last week. "You did the right thing coming to us like this too."

"I'm scared, Harper. He was so worried something like this would happen, and I told him it wouldn't."

"Don't worry, we are going to take care of this. We're going to get him over here, then Ellen is going to take you to the hospital to get looked at."

"No, no hospital Harper, you know we can't do that, they'll ask too many questions, they'll want to call my mother. I'm fine, really I am."

"Listen to me, we have to get you checked out and make sure you don't have any fractures or anything; Alia, it looks bad. We will just have to come up with some story, and no, they won't call your mother your eighteen now they won't call her unless you want them to."

"We have been telling everyone all day she got hit by a ball last night at a pick-up game." Said Crystal. "You think they will believe that too?"

"We will make sure that they do," said Ellen. "For now, you two kids should go get home."

"I should stay," said George, "I can help with Charlie."

"Thank you, George, but Ellen is right. I think the two of you shouldn't be here when Charlie shows up. I'm going to call in a few of my more trusted deputies to help make sure he doesn't go running off after Trish or anything."

After saying their goodbyes to Alia, Crystal and George left, and Harper started making calls. They waited for the three officers to arrive at the house before he called Charlie, who was at the Sheriff's office.

"Hey, Dad, what's up?"

"I'm at the house, Charlie. I would like you to come by real quick."

"Sure, but I was about to go see Alia at the library. Could it wait till after that?"

"No, Charlie, I'd really like you to come right now."

"Okay, I'll be there in a few minutes."

As they waited, Harper had two of his deputies stay inside, one at the back door and one at the front. "Whatever happens, Charlie is not to leave this house," he told the both of them. Outside he had a third deputy waiting in case Charlie tried to bolt that way. Harper hated taking such extreme measures, but this was all enough of a mess as it was without having Charlie go off half-cocked after Alia's mother.

In the living room waiting with Ellen, Alia got a text on her phone from Charlie saying he had to stop at the house and would be late to come to see her. She showed it to his mom.

"I guess Harper didn't tell him I was here."

"Probably just afraid that if he did, Charlie would know something was wrong. As you see, he's trying to control the situation the best we can. Charlie has grown into a wonderful young man. We are very proud of him, but sometimes he has his father's temper. It can burn quick and hot, not much unlike your own. Usually, it burns out quick too, but when it comes to you, well, he's always been a fierce protector, but more so when it comes to you."

"I'm starting to feel like this was a bad idea. Maybe I should have just tried to avoid him for a few days, blamed it on finals and everything."

Ellen shook her head. "No way that not only wouldn't have worked, it only would make things worse. After last night he would have been anxious to see you. If you tried avoiding him, he would have known something was up. Not to mention that eye is going to take more than a few days to heal."

"This is all my fault. If I had just kept my big damn mouth shut. I know how she is when she is in one of her moods."

"Alia, honey, in no way is any of this any of your fault. Your mother is a very sick person. Charlie told us some of the things she has put you through over the years. Nobody should ever treat a child like that, let alone a mother. If anything, it's our fault. Charlie tried to tell us something was wrong with that woman, and no one listened. Even one of the social workers your mother had on the case wasn't buying into her whole sweet kid routine."

"You're Talking about Mrs. Stackhouse, right? She told me she was one of my mother's caseworkers."

"Yes, she was. Unfortunately, we didn't listen to her. We were convinced your mother wanted nothing more than to be a good mother to you. That's what worries us about her. She can be so convincing, so conniving, especially when she was younger."

"It's because, in a way, she believes all the lies. She says them over and over until even she believes them. I have seen her do it time and time again. I guarantee she has some story going on in that head of hers to either make it my fault or some kind of freak accident."

Just then, they heard Charlie's patrol car pull up into the drive by the side of the house. Alia started to shake and broke out in a sweat. *This is going to be bad. This is going to be so bad. It's all my fault. If Charlie does anything stupid, it will be all my fault.*

Harper popped his head into the living room real fast. "The two of you just stay in here. Let me deal with him before he sees Alia's face." Harper got to the door of the mudroom as Charlie opened it.

"Hey, dad, uh, what's going on? If this is a surprise party or something, you do realize my birthday is still months away," he said jokingly. Seeing the look on his father's face, Charlie's smile faltered. "What's going on?"

In the mudroom was a large free-standing safe where the boys always put their guns when coming into the house for more than a few minutes. Harper stood in front of it with the door opened, his holster and gun already inside. "You know the routine, son, off with the holster and your boots, then we need to talk."

Charlie nodded, still looking at his father as if he could read his mind if he tried hard enough. Still, he took off his holster, placed it inside the safe then worked on his boots. As he did, Charlie noticed Deputy Tackard standing just outside the door. "Have I done something wrong?" he asked his father.

"No, son, but we need to talk."

Charlie followed Harper into the kitchen, where he could see Deputy Johnson standing in front of the back door. Charlie noticed the deputy still had on his holster and boots.

"Dad, what's going on here? Is mom okay?" Charlie had a sinking feeling in the pit of his stomach that something was very much wrong. He had another feeling as well.

"She's fine. She's waiting for us in the living room."

"I don't understand. If Mom is okay and I didn't do anything wrong, then what is this all about? Why is Alia here? I know she is. You have deputies standing guard like you expect trouble. What the hell is going on here?"

Harper looked his son right in the eyes. "I will tell you, but first, before we go to the other room, I need you to do something for me."

"Of course, anything."

"I need you to remember that you're a cop, Charlie. Not just any cop but a good cop. And the last thing you want to do is to screw that up, right son?"

Charlie nodded because that was all that he could do. The nagging feeling he had all day that something was wrong was starting to make sense. He could feel his heart begin to pound and his breath quicken.

"You're right. Alia is here. She's sitting in the living room with your mother."

Suddenly Charlie couldn't hear anything else his father was saying. His head started to spin, his heart felt tight in his chest, and although he wanted to run into the living room, he found himself unable to move.

"Charlie, are you listening?" Harper had grabbed his son by the shoulders forcing the boy to look at him because, for a moment there, he seemed to float away. "Listen to me, Charlie, before we go in there, let me tell you what happened."

"Happened?" Charlie asked, sounding like he was miles away. "Something happened to Alia?"

"Yes, but she's going to be fine," Harper explained to Charlie what Alia told them had happened the night before.

Hearing it, Charlie felt like the floor was coming out from under him. All his fears he had been having over the past week, hell, years were coming true. He knew something had been wrong last night, could feel it. *I should have gone there last night. No matter what she said, I should have been there.*

"How bad." he heard himself say.

"It looks worse than it is, Charlie, and your mother is going to take her to the hospital here in a little while to make sure."

Charlie shook his head, still looking towards the living room, still feeling miles away. "I want to see her." he started for the living room, but his father stopped him.

"Okay, we will, but remember what I said, it's not as bad as it looks. She's going to be fine. She even went to school all day. I know you're going to be upset, but you need to stay calm."

"Calm," Charlie said, the words sounding foreign to him as he nodded.

"Good, let's go." Harper walked into the dining room and towards the living room.

At first, Charlie just stood there unable to move, then like in a dream, he followed his father through the dining room and into the living room. At the door of the living room was yet another deputy, his name escaping Charlie's mind at the moment. All he could focus on was the considerable bruise on the face of the woman he loved more than life itself. *Yet she still looks like an angel. Was* the last thought he had before the red hot fury of rage swept over him.

They all saw it happen like a switch had been thrown. One minute Charlie stood before them, looking almost lost and confused, then the next his face slipped into a mask of rage. Alia had never seen him like this before. The smile that lit up his whole face and made his eyes seem to dance was gone. His amazing green eyes boiled with blind fury. She saw, too, before he turned as if to leave, that his hand went instinctively to where his gun would have been if he still had his holster on.

"Charlie, no!" she yelled after him.

Before Charlie could take so much as two steps, his father was right there in front of him. Harper was a good three inches taller than Charlie and had a bulk his son's thin frame would never achieve. He was pretty confident he could keep his son from leaving but looking at him now, Harper was glad he had called in the other deputies. The fury he saw in his son's eyes he'd only seen in one other, his own.

"Where are you going, son?"

"I'm just going to have a little talk with Trish." *Then I'm going to fucking kill her.* "Get the hell out of my way."

When Charlie tried going around Harper, he moved in front of his son again. "Charlie, son, I know what you're feeling right now, but you need to let it go. This rage your feeling right now is only going to cause more problems, and you don't want that."

"I don't care. I'm going to make sure she never lays a hand on my girl ever again." Charlie moved again to go around his father, and Harper stopped him again. "Get the hell out of my way." Charlie raged and pushed his father hard, but Harper stood his ground. Charlie shoved again with more force, and this time from the corner of his eye, Charlie could see Deputy Johnson leave his post and approach them. "Don't you fucking dare come near me," said Charlie in rage, pointing a finger at the deputy.

Harper grabbed the front of Charlie's shirt and backed him up a few steps.

"Now dammit boy, you listen to me, and you listen good. You need to calm your ass down. Even if you get past me, the Deputies won't let you leave."

"I'm not going to tell you again, Dad, get the hell out of my way. For years we stood by while that bitch hurt Alia time and time again…no more, I'm going to end this shit once and for all."

Sitting on the couch hearing this, not just the words but the sound of his rage, Alia trembled. This was just what she was afraid of and why she refused to tell him last night. She had never seen Charlie so angry before, and it was scaring the hell out of her. Alia wouldn't take her eyes off of them but allowed Ellen to pull her into her arms. *Please, Charlie, I can't lose you, not this way, not after all this time.*

"And then what, Charlie. What happens to Alia then. You go off and do something stupid and wind up in jail or, worse, dead. What do you think that will do to her. Who will protect her then?"

"But it's all my fault. I did this to her. If I had just waited as you said." Charlie started to shake as the fury he felt slowly bleed out, being replaced by guilt and shame. "I knew this would happen. It's all my fault."

"Charlie, remember what I said. It looks a lot worse than it is. Things like this always do at first. If you do something right now, you're just going to hurt her more than this ever could. You don't want to do that, do you, Charlie?"

Charlie shook his head. The fury was winding down. He looked back at Alia, tears in his eyes and tears in her eyes as well. They were pleading with him.

"Please, Charlie, I'm okay, really I am."

Slowly Charlie stumbled over to her, falling to his knees and burying his head in her lap. Ellen rubbed a hand over her son's back, feeling his grief, while Alia wrapped her arms around his head as best she could.

Harper motioned for the two deputies to leave, telling them to wait outside till he came out.

Charlie, his eyes red, looked up long enough to grab Alia and pull her down into his arms. "I'm so sorry. This is all my fault, my sweet girl."

"No, Charlie, she's sick. Billy said she was looking to pick a fight all weekend, and you know I'm her favorite punching bag. This had nothing to do with you."

"I should have protected you. I knew this would happen. I knew you shouldn't have gone back to her."

"There was nothing you could do, Charlie."

Charlie looked up at her, a bit of that fury still in his eyes. "It won't happen again," he said. "I won't let it. You can't go back, Alia." picking her up, she felt so small to him, so light. He gently placed her back on the couch and stayed kneeling before her.

"Charlie, we talked about this.."

"You owe her nothing Alia…not anymore…not after this."

"It was my own fault, Charlie. I know how she is. I should have never tried walking away from her when she was mad like that. I know better."

"That's her talking Alia. She's got you brainwashed into thinking everything is always your fault. It was the same way when we were kids. And what about next time? What if next time it's something larger, something heavier. Didn't you tell me she almost ran over one of her boyfriends? What if next time she gets mad, she's behind the wheel of a car or has a knife or a gun? You can't go back there, Alia. You said things were going good. Well, this doesn't look like things are going too fucking good to me."

With an ironic laugh, Alia said. "You would be surprised what qualifies as going good in my house."

"Harper, he has a point. We can't very well just send her back there," said Ellen.

"And I can't just not go back. Charlie, we have no idea what set her off other than that she was on the phone.

What if she found something out? What if she suspects something? I won't let her hurt you, not like that. I can't leave right now, not yet."

"Sure you can. Your mother doesn't even see you all week. She won't know you're not home if you manage to sneak out after Billy goes to bed."

Alia was shaking her head no. "Won't work, she checks in on me every night to make sure I'm in bed. And Billy doesn't always go to bed before she gets home. He may have helped me last night, but I don't trust him."

"Of course not." Said Harper, "Look, Charlie, I wish there was something that we could do, but without a witness, we can't even report this. Her mother will find a way to lie her way out of this, and then Alia really will be in more trouble. And you as well if she even begins to think we have something to do with it. It's like you said, it's just like when you two were kids."

"Right now, in her mind, what happened isn't a big deal and at the most my fault. She will play this off like nothing ever happened, like she always does when she messes up. But if I don't go home, it's just going to piss her off. Then she's going to look for someone to blame it on because there's no way she will believe I have the balls to leave her on my own. She's not smart, but she will put two and two together. She will come after you, Charlie, and I won't let her ruin your life."

"Alia is right, Charlie," said Harper. "Trish already knows I have tried to get Alia to confess to things going on at home. If she ups and leaves home, Trish is bound to suspect we have something to do with it."

Charlie sat at Alias' feet, his hands running through his hair, trying to make sense of all this mess. "We can't just let you go back either, Alia. Even If I staked out the apartment all night, there's no guarantee I would know anything was going on before it's too late."

"Charlie, Honestly, I don't think anything will happen. No matter how sick in the head she is, deep down, she knows she messed up."

"You said all of this already, yet here you are with the whole side of your face bruised up."

"I'm telling you, Charlie, please believe me. Trish is, if nothing else, rather predictable. She will be on her best behavior right now. I told you this graduation party is her victory, and she needs it. If not, she would have brought it up last night. She loves to dangle things in front of me then take them away. She can't use that against me."

Charlie shook his head more. "I can't, Alia. I have been worried sick as it is all week. The only decent sleep I got was at the cabin, and I know that goes the same for you. Do you really think you'll sleep well there after this?"

I have been through worse. She thought but didn't dare say out loud

"There has to be something we can do," said Charlie.

"I've been thinking about that," said Ellen. "A friend of mine had trouble last year with her teenage daughter. Typical stuff, sneaking out, hanging out with older boys, things like that. When she found out her daughter was also drinking and doing drugs, she put cameras in the house to watch her and make sure she didn't leave while she was at work. There was an app she got for her phone, and she could check in on her daughter anytime she wanted to. It even had a two-way speaker so they could talk. Maybe we could get one of those and put it in Alia's room. Then, Charlie, you could see her anytime you wanted and make sure she was alright."

Charlie looked up at Alia. "Would you even let us do that?" he asked. "It's a huge invasion of privacy."

"Would it make you feel better if I did? Because I have to go home, Charlie, there's no way around it, not without risking her finding out about us.."

"I still don't like it. I just don't think it's safe for you there. And if anything would happen outside your room, we wouldn't know." He looked at her, and his heart hurt to see the marks on her face. "If you're determined to go back home, then I want a camera there, a good one too with night vision if we can get it. We should have a code word too, something you can say if you think things are going sideways."

"That's a good idea." Said Harper. "But we need something for tonight. Where did this woman get her camera?

"At Walmart." Said Ellen. "That's why I suggested it. They are easy to come by and rather cheap too."

"We can get George and Crystal to pick one up. He'll know which one is good," said Alia. "Then I know a couple of tech boys that sorta owe me a favor that can install it for me."

"But first, you go to the hospital and get that looked at," said Charlie. "I know you said you're okay, but I want to be sure."

"Alright then, Ellen, you take Alia to the ER. Maybe one of the nurses you know there can get her seen right away. We don't have a whole lot of time. Trish gets out of the factory around eleven, and I assume home shortly after that. Charlie, you will stay here with me. You can call George and tell him what we are going to need, but I don't want you out of my site just yet."

"I'm not going to do anything, dad." *Though to be fair, given a chance…I don't know for sure.*

"And I'm not going to give you a chance too. I'll tell the deputies they can go back to work or whatever, but then you ladies need to get out of here." Harper walked off to the kitchen.

Ellen got up, helped her son to his feet, and hugged him. "Listen to your father, Charlie, please. I'll let you know how things go at the Hospital. Tell George and Crystal they will need to pick her up there. The fewer chances we take, the better."

Charlie nodded and hugged her back. She left to get her things from her room, and Charlie sat on the couch next to Alia. Cupping her face in his hands, he looked at her eye closer, his hands trembling. "Don't let me hurt you. I just want to see how bad it is."

"It's not that bad."

"That's bullshit, and you know it." He said a little spark of that anger showed in his eyes before they softened again.

Alia looked Charlie in his eyes and held them there. "You wouldn't really have killed her, would you, Charlie? It's not because I love her or anything. It's just, I don't see you doing something like that. It scares me to think you would."

Letting go of her face, Charlie pulled her into his arms. "I don't know, I'm sorry, but I don't. when I saw you…if she had been standing right here, I might have. I know I would have tried."

"Then she would have won, Charlie. Losing you would hurt me more than anything she could possibly do to me. It's what she would want if she knew about us. We can't let her win."

He cupped her face again, being careful not to hurt her. "Then we won't let her, I promise." He kissed her then laid his forehead to rest on hers.

Ellen walked back into the room, having waited so they could have at least this brief little time together. "We should go, Alia."

Charlie walked them both to the door at the side of the house. He gave his mother a hug and whispered in her ear. "Take care of my girl for me, Mom."

"Of course, I will." She whispered back.

Charlie hugged Alia again, giving her the briefest of kisses. When she tried to walk away from him, he couldn't let her go.

"I have to go, Charlie…you have to let me go…."

Charlie took her into his arms one last time. "I'm never going to let you go again. Not really. I'm right there with you, Alia. Just close your eyes, and I'll be there," he whispered. He then allowed his mother to pull her away from him. As he watched her go, his thoughts turned to poison. *I'll kill that bitch.*

In Ellen's car on the way to the hospital, Alia made two phone calls. One to George telling him what they would need and another to one of the two boys who made the lights go out. She would call back later and tell them where and when to meet her.

At the hospital, one of the nurses that Ellen knew was on staff and not only got them seen right away but hurried them to the back away from prying eyes. The nurse didn't know why the two didn't want to be seen together and didn't need to. Within an hour, Alia got a facial X-ray and even some mild pain meds.

When the doctor came in, Alia was surprised to find that he looked familiar. Turned out he had cared for her when she had poison ivy so bad it had gotten into her eyes. She had acquired it from a treehouse her father had built for her in the woods behind his house.

"I'm afraid to say as bad as your eyes were then this one is much worse now. How did you manage to do this one?" he asked.

"Foul ball at a pickup game last night." She said, trying to sound as honest as possible.

"Ouch, that hurt, I bet. Did you lose consciousness at any point?"

"No. It hurt like hell, and the cut bled a lot, but that's it. It didn't look as bad once the blood was cleaned up, so I just went home."

"I bet it shocked you when you saw it this morning. Your eye itself is fine, no retinal damage despite how bad it looks. Your cheekbone has a hairline fracture; however, it's a small one. You lucked out, kid, a bit further up, you may have caused a lot more damage to those pretty eyes of yours." The Doctor turned to Ellen. "So a baseball, huh?"

Ellen just shrugged, not saying a word.

"Well, whatever it was, it could have been a lot worse, so let's just be happy that it wasn't. I do have a few prescriptions I'd like to give her. I assume those should be in your name?"

"I would appreciate that, Dr. Kline."

Dr. Kline turned and winked at Alia. "I'll get those written up, and the nurse will bring them, then you two can get on out of here. Alia, just be sure to follow the directions on the scripts, and by the time Prom comes around, you should be healed enough that a little makeup will cover any bruising that's left. Goodnight, ladies."

When he left, Alia asked why the prescriptions would be in Ellen's name.

"Well, we can't very well have your mother find out about this. I'll pick the scripts up tonight and leave them at your school in the morning."

"But how did he know to do that?"

"Do you really think he believed the baseball story?"

"Not really, but then why bother telling him at all?"

"Have you ever heard of a thing called plausible deniability"

Alia nodded yes.

"So there you go. Legally if he is ever questioned about tonight, a baseball hit your eye. Most likely, nothing will come of it, but it's best to have bases covered just in case."

"You know I am starting to find out there are a lot of strange things going on in this town. People seem to know a whole lot more about my…situation than I ever thought did."

"Yes, they do, and you may be surprised how many of them are on your side, Alia. You were born right here in this hospital. As far as everyone is concerned, no matter how many times you have moved, this place is your home. And at home, we take care of our own. I know it feels like you have been alone your whole life, especially since your father died. But the truth is, Alia, a lot of people have made a point to be a part of your life just so they could help you along."

"You mean like Mrs. Stackhouse?"

"Exactly. When you return from the academy, you will see things will change. People will be more willing to accept your and Charlie's relationship. Your mother will have no power over you anymore, and she won't have any power over us either."

"I have been thinking about that. Can't Trish still just say all those horrible things about Charlie anyway?"

"She can, and she probably will. She could say it now, and most people in this town wouldn't believe her. It's the ones that would, that we worry about. Some of them carry a lot of sway in our town, and they can be old-fashioned old farts. Others are sad and angry people like her that are always looking for a fight. Right now, they all see you still as a child. But you would be surprised how people will see you differently once you come back, three months older, loads smarter, and in uniform.

I swore when Charlie came back, it was like he had grown into a man overnight. Even for us, he was different. So even though a few of the really old, old farts may frown on it, they won't care as much as they do now. And the ones rooting for you both will go a long and act like they knew nothing the whole time. 'Well, well well, what a surprise, Alia and Charlie, what a cute couple,' they will say. Granted, you may want to take things slowly at first, but I think you two will figure it out."

As they left the hospital, Crystal and George were waiting out in the parking lot in the old Buick. Ellen gave her a big and long hug. "You be careful tonight. I know you already know this, but just do whatever she expects of you and try to stay out of her and Billy's way. Wednesday, you're still coming to our place because we are not going to let her take even the smallest of wins away from us, are we?"

"No, we won't." Alia realized that her conversation with Charlie wasn't as private as she had thought.

"Before you know it, the weekend will be here, and the two of you can get away for a while. Don't forget to get your meds in the morning. I'll leave them with principal Edwards." Ellen gave Alia one final hug and let her go.

At the apartment complex, the three of them met up with the two boys from school. George showed them all the cameras he got. It indeed had night vision and a speaker as well. "When I leave here, I will go show Charlie and them how to get the app to work. How are you going to smuggle these two into your room?"

"By telling Billy, they came over to get some papers and stuff for finals for school."

"It shouldn't take very long to set this up. We should be in and out pretty fast." Said Derick Willis.

And they were. Billy had no objections to the two boys going in her room, he even asked her if her eye was feeling any better, but one look at it, he knew it didn't.

"Hell, Alia, it's worse than it was last night. Your mother is going to shit when she sees it."

Then she's not going to see it.

In her room, the boys found a great spot for the camera in a vent in the corner. It was an excellent battery-powered model that even came with rechargeables that only needed to be plugged in with a USB to charge. They showed her how and even advised her not to move the camera once they had it in a good spot but to just take out the power pack. Once they had it all set up, Alia Called Charlie to see if they had their end ready.

"I have it set up on my tablet for now, but I'll put it on my phone later too. Give us a sec…okay, yes there we go, there's my beautiful girl." Alia handed the phone to the boys to be talked through any adjustments while putting the vent cover back on. Once they had it perfect, they had to test the sound.

"I can hear all of you just fine." Said Charlie. "Can you hear me?" He asked through the camera speaker.

"Yes, we do," said Alia.

"But Charlie, you may only want to use it as an emergency. the vent is on the far side of the room, but the shaft may still carry your voice out into the other rooms."

Alia showed Billy and Derrick out and thanked them for helping. Back in her room, she looked up at the vent and smiled. Her phone vibrated a moment later.

Charlie: I'm still not happy with this, but at least I can see you, and you look exhausted.

"Can you hear me?" She asked, being quiet enough not to be heard over the TV in the living room.

Charlie: Yes

"I'm going to take a shower. I'll be right back." Alia grabbed her pajamas and went into the bathroom, being sure to shut the door. It was nearly nine by the time she got out, and she was indeed exhausted. The events of the day weighed on her like a lead coat.

Charlie: Mom wants to know if you have eaten yet.

"I forgot all about it. Not even hungry, really, mostly tired. Shit, I have to take the dog out. Give me a few minutes." Alia went out in the living room and saw that Ebony was asleep on the couch lying next to Billy.

"No need to take him out. I heard you in the shower and took him for you. And don't worry, I won't tell your mom about the boys.'

"Why are you being so nice to me?"

"You know your mom gives you a lot of shit, but you're not a bad kid. Pain in the ass, maybe, but I was worse at your age. And last night. Well, what she did was wrong. But talking to me at lunch today like it never happened, that's worse."

"Can I give you some advice?'

"Sure, kid."

"After my graduation party next month, leave. Pack your shit and run as fast as you can, as far away from her as you can. I have a feeling that by next fall, shit is going to hit the fan around here, and unless you want to be covered in said shit, you should go." She started back to her room then stopped. "Oh, and you need to pay more attention to where your money is going. She's about to flip you. Which means she's most likely squirreling away some money for when she does. It's her typical MO."

Billy nodded. "Pretty much have the idea she's replaced me. The lease runs out in October. I don't know what the two of you plan to do, but I'm not renewing it. I know the two of you may not be able to afford staying here without me, and I'm sorry. The whole psycho chick thing was fun at first, but I'm getting too old for all this drama shit."

"Well, don't worry about me. Do what you need to cover your own ass; I'll cover mine just fine." Alia was about to return to her room when she stopped. She didn't want to have Charlie on his mind again, but there was something that had been bugging her. With Billy feeling so nice and generous, it may be the only time to ask without consequences. "I have a question."

"Sure, kid, what is it?"

"Why do you call Deputy Harper Deputy Dougie? I asked him that night, but even he didn't know."

Billy started to laugh. "Oh shit yeah, I guess that show was a bit before your time. Damn, I was hoping the shit would get the reference." Seeing the look of impatience on Alia's face, he stopped fooling around. "Okay, there was this show a few years ago, well maybe more than a few. I used to watch it as a kid. This kid was a doctor in a hospital. He couldn't have been no more than a teen. Funny show. Anyway, the kid's name was Dougie. Deputy Harper is so young he reminds me of the kid, so I just thought that was some funny shit."

Alia shook her head. She should have known it was something stupid. "Goodnight, Billy."

"Goodnight, kid. Hey, and thanks for the warning about your mom."

"You keep your mouth shut about Charlie, and I'll consider it even."

Billy made a point of zipping his fingers over his lips and then laughed.

Back in her room, Alia found a few more messages on her phone.

Charlie: Mom says to eat. I didn't hear you leave. Did you walk the dog?

"Billy walked Ebony already. Remind me later to tell you why he calls you Dougie. For now, I'm hitting the bed before I hit the floor." Alia walked over to her bed and fell into it more than climbed in. "As for eating, tell Mom I said I am sorry, but I'm too tired. I love you, Charlie, but it's been a long twenty-four hours. I think I can sleep knowing you're watching me. But don't stay up too late."

Charlie: I'm staying here tonight. I don't think dad trusts me yet. I want to be closer to you anyway. Go ahead and get some sleep. I love you, Alia.

Alia turned out the light and waved. "Can you still see me?"

Charlie: You're green, but yes, I see you.

"Goodnight Charlie, I'll be fine, go get some rest. And please, just stay at your parents…don't do anything crazy."

Charlie: I won't, goodnight my sweet angel.

Alia was asleep before the message was even sent. Charlie stayed in his old room at his parents' house where he put his tablet he was watching her on, on his desk and sat down. That is where he sat all night, watching as she slept. When her mother came to check in on her later that night, Charlie could see her at the door. He pointed his finger shaped like a gun at her and pretended to pull the trigger.

Chapter 16
The Weekend

As dawn broke, Charlie sat at his desk, nearly half asleep. He watched as Alia rolled over a few times then smacked her alarm clock silent. She stretched, yawned, and must have suddenly remembered the camera because she looked at it real fast then covered her head with a pillow. That must have hurt because the pillow went flying, and she sat up. He knew she wasn't amused, but Charlie couldn't help but laugh.

Sitting up, Alia looked at the camera and shook her head. "You're awake, aren't you?" A few seconds later, her phone vibrated from where she stashed it between her mattresses.

Charlie: Yes. Good morning beautiful, how is the eye feeling?

Alia tentatively touched the bruise with her fingers and winced. "Still very tender. When do you go to work?"

Charlie: I'm not. Dad is making me take a couple of personal days.

"Why is everything OK?"

Charlie: He's worried I may run into your mother. I'm still furious. To tell the truth, I am afraid I may run into your mother.

Or at the very least over her, again and again. Got to get a grip on my anger. Look at the way she's looking up at me. Can't hurt her like that. I won't.

"Well, thanks for being honest with me. She's not worth you getting all worked up over, Charlie. And she's definitely not worth getting in trouble over."

Charlie: But you are worth it. I just wish you felt like you could have been honest with me as well.

Alia sighed. She knew this was coming. "Charlie, I'm sorry, but I don't regret not saying anything to you that night. I honestly thought it wouldn't look as bad as it did the next day. And I knew if I said something, you would have rushed over here, and that would have just ruined everything. Talk to your mom about this. She said some things to me last night that made a lot of sense."

Charlie: I know you were just trying to protect me, but I'm scared for you, Alia. I have to know that when you say your okay, you really are

"I know Charlie, and I hated to have to lie to you even just a little. This shit is just so screwed up. But it's a two-way thing here. I have to know if I'm honest with you, you won't let your anger get the best of you," Alia sighed, not sure if she should say what she wanted to. What she felt like she needed to. " As long as we are being totally honest, I have to say, Charlie, you scared me yesterday. I have never seen you so angry like that before." Still sitting on her bed, Alia looked up at the camera, hoping Charlie wasn't upset with her.

Charlie: I know, and I'm sorry. The last thing I ever want to do is make you afraid of me.

Alia shook her head. "I'm not Charlie. I know you're a good man. It's more that I am afraid for you than of you. Don't forget I'm practically an expert at anger. I know how hard it is to control, but you're going to have to learn how to. It's only a few more weeks. And we have the weekends. You're just going to have to trust me that if I say I'm okay, it's because I either am or I have shit under control. There's always our safe word, which I promise I will use if I need to. Well, I better go. I need to get ready for school. I have more exams again today.."

Charlie: Good luck today, and don't worry about me. Just try not to think about all this mess. I love you

"I love you too, Charlie. I'll let you know when I get to school. After that, you need to get some rest."

Charlie: Will do.

Charlie watched as Alia grabbed some clothes and went into her bathroom, shutting the door. He was glad she had been honest with him, but it still hurt to think of her as being afraid of him. And despite what she said, he knew she was. Even in his rage, Charlie had seen the look in Alia's eyes. And that was something that must never happen again.

Alia had been afraid that the trouble of the week would cause her to have problems taking the exams, but once she got started, she pushed it out of her mind and went to work. Alia's only trouble was having to wipe gently at her swollen eye off and on all day. By the end of the day, she felt pretty confident that she did rather well, putting her in a much better mood.

What made for an even better mood was Charlie surprising her at work. The two snuck down to the archives under the guise that he needed some research papers for a case.

As soon as they got into the room, Charlie grabbed her and hugged her like he hadn't seen her in a long time. Once again, he kissed her slowly and gingerly, then tasting her strawberry balm, he dove in. When they came up for air, not only was Charlie smiling, but he was laughing a bit too.

"Sorry, I might have gotten a bit carried away there," he said with that grin of his she loved.

"Well, to be fair, we did have to make up for yesterday."

"Yes, yes indeed we did."

Looking at him now, Alia could see that he was exhausted even though he was smiling.

"Have you slept?"

Charlie lowered his eyes when he answered. "I got a bit on the couch after talking to my mom this morning. You were right about what she said. It did make a lot of sense. Which is why I owe you an apology."

"Charlie, you don't …."

"Yes, I do. This whole shit situation is my fault. Or my doing rather if that makes you feel better. So it's on me to man up and take care of things, so you don't have to."

Alia looked at him with alarm.

"No, no, I don't mean to do anything, quite the opposite, really. I just mean I will do my best to make things easier for you and be there for you. And I'm going to be more understanding that things on your end are complicated. Whatever you think is best to deal with your mother, I'm here to support you one hundred percent, even if I don't like it."

Grabbing his face, Alia kissed Charlie long and hard. "Thank you, Charlie, that means a lot to me. And I don't like it either, but that part of things is almost over. Now, if you don't go home and get some sleep, I'm going to kick your ass."

"Well, I don't have much of an ass, so good luck with that."

"Boy, I will find whatever no having ass you have and kick it, so don't you tempt me."

They both laughed.

"Love you, my sweet girl."

"Love you, my sweet boy."

Being ever so gentle, Charlie kissed the very top of her right eye, about the only place on that side of her face that wasn't bruised. He hated to see her hurt like this, but he forced himself so she wouldn't have her feelings hurt. "I better go; my father is waiting out in the parking lot."

"What? He's been waiting this whole time?"

"Yeah, well, he insisted. I kind of hate they are treating me like a child right now, but I get it. When it comes to you, I guess I tend to get a bit emotional." he said with a smile. "But I don't want you to have to worry about me on top of everything else. I'll be fine."

"You'll be fine when you get some sleep," Alia gently scolded.

"Okay, okay, I will." he laughed. "I see why you and my mother get along so well."

"Don't make us have to gang up on you."

"I won't." Charlie held her tight and kissed her one last time, and left.

Later that evening, when walking home from the bus stop, Alia hopped to see lights flash up at the school but didn't. It made her feel lonely, but at least that may have meant Charlie was home getting some rest. When she reached the apartment, there was a small red cooler in front of the door with a bow attached to it. Curious, Alia looked inside and found a note with her name on top of Tupperware containers full of food.

Alia,
Mom says to eat, no excuses tonight. You can return the Tupperware and cooler when you come to dinner tomorrow night.

Crystal ;)

Only Alia knew this didn't come from Crystal, of course. She may have been the one to drop it off, but the containers were the same ones Ellen used, and she was to have dinner at the Harper's the next night. Family dinner.

Inside, Alia fought to put her things in her room, with Ebony jumping all around, happy to have her home. She pointed a finger at the camera to say, give me a minute and left to get the dog's leash. Noticing the apartment was quiet, Alia checked the living room but didn't see Billy. Later she would find out he was held up at work with an emergency maintenance issue. Shrugging, Alia took the dog out, pulling out her phone to text Charlie once she was clear from the apartment.

Alia: I'm home in case you didn't see

Charlie: I saw. I see you also got our care package.

Alia: Yes, I did. Tell mom I said thank you.

Charlie: She said she hopes you enjoy it. We had dinner early so she could send it over.

Back in the apartment, Alia double-checked to make sure she was alone and even locked the front door. That way, whenever someone did come in, she could hear them fumble with the door. Back in her room, she told Charlie she was alone so they could talk. He chatted with her while he sat outside on the back porch, and Alia ate dinner of pot roast, carrots, potatoes, roll, and even apple pie for dessert. The food was terrific and did about as much to raise her spirits as talking to Charlie did. Just when she thought things were not that bad, Alia heard a noise from the hallway. Putting her finger to her lips, she listened through the door. Ebony started going crazy, so she let him out, and he bounded down the hall after Billy.

"Hey kid, how's the face?"

"Better," she said and tucked back into her room. "Billy is home now, so."

Charlie: Understood.

"I need to get in the shower anyway." She blew a kiss at the camera and went to her bathroom.

Wednesday was a repeat of Tuesday at school. More tests only this time Alia was even more confident that she did well being able to sleep so much better the night before. After school, Crystal dropped her off at Harkening Hill park, and she had to keep herself from running all the way down to the lake and the Harper's backyard.

Walking into the house that day was like coming home. Harper was in the dining room setting out the lessons she was to work on for the day, and Ellen was putting away groceries in the kitchen. The only one absent was Charlie, so Alia figured he must have gone home. She was about to settle down to work when Ellen came over and whispered in her ear.

"Charlie is up in his room resting. I'll distract Harper so you can sneak on up for a minute." She then walked over to her husband, still in uniform from work. "How is my handsome Sheriff tonight?" She started to croon, giving him a big hug around his neck and turning him away from Alia.

Smiling at them both, Alia slipped out of the room and up the stairs. Charlie's door was open just enough for her to see him on his bed. His eyes were closed, his mess of dark brown hair rumpled, and his chin and jawline had a shadow of growth. At first, he seemed to be sleeping peacefully, but when Alia looked closer, she could see his face move in ticks, and every once in a while, Charlie would jerk his whole body just a little.

Knowing he hadn't gotten much sleep all week, Alia let him be and returned back downstairs, where Harper tried to give her a scolding look that didn't work for once. By the time lessons were over, dinner was almost done.

"Alia, honey, why don't you go on up and wake Charlie for dinner," said Ellen from the kitchen.

"Sure," she said and went back up. Alia had to turn a light on in the hall to see Charlie in his room. By the mess of his bed from just a bit ago, she could tell his sleep hadn't been very restful. However, now he was pretty still. Not really wanting to wake him, Alia walked in quietly and gently kissed Charlie on his forehead. Figuring he should just sleep, she turned to walk away when he grabbed her arm and pulled her into his bed.

"Just where do you think you're going?" he pulled her closer and kissed her. "Been missing you."

"I came up earlier, but you were asleep. Dinner is ready."

"Yes, family dinner night. And in two more days, I will have you all to myself again. I know every day just brings us one day closer to you leaving, but I can't wait for this week to be over." Charlie kissed her cheek ever so gently.

Dinner was excellent as usual. Afterward, she and Charlie helped clean up then the two of them walked down to the lake. Later Crystal and George picked her up, taking her back home.

Again Charlie spent most of the night watching as Alia slept, and he noticed something. When he heard the door slam indicating her mother was home, he saw Alia jerk in her sleep. Her eyes fluttered open for a moment, then closed just before her bedroom door was opened. When the door closed again, Charlie saw her let out a big sigh as if she had been holding her breath. He hadn't noticed this the night before, but then he had been exhausted as well. Having actually gotten some sleep, Charlie was paying closer attention. He wasn't sure, but his thought was (and the fleeting feeling he got) that Alia had been scared. *Something to watch out for*, he thought.

There was a tap at his closed door.

"Come in."

Harper opened the door and walked into the room, not surprised at all to see his son sitting at his desk watching Alia. He had been doing it for the past two nights non-stop. "How is she doing?"

"Seems to be good. Trish just came home."

"So that means you're going to be hitting the sack as well, right? No sleep, no work, that was our deal."

"Got it. I was just waiting for her mother to get home. I'll take a shower in a minute."

"Good because your mother is worried about you. She did say the two of you had a pretty good talk this morning, one that seemed to make you feel a little better."

"I still hate all of this. I still want her out of that house, but I get it. I do have a question, though."

"What's that?"

Charlie looked up at his father. "How is it that you have been so cool about all of this? I mean, don't get me wrong, I know you care about Alia as much as Mom and I do, but I really thought you would be kicking my ass on the regular until this whole mess was over."

"Oh, I thought about it," Harper said with a laugh. " And planned on doing just that. But you're not the only one that had a talk with your mother. Last week when this whole mess, as you put it, got started, we talked, I mean long into the night. She told me to put the both of us in your places and imagine how we would feel. I know you kids hate to hear all the gushy stuff. But I love and have loved your mother like nothing I have ever experienced before her. I never even really understood what that meant until I met her, and I thought I had been in love several times. I know how I would feel if she was ever in danger or hurt. That's also why I kept you close to home these past two days.

    Now I don't claim to understand why the two of you have had such a strong connection from such a young age as when we first brought her home. Still, I understand connecting with someone on that deep level. Just took your mother and me longer to find each other, I guess. More importantly, I know how you feel when it comes to protecting her. And how dangerous that feeling can be. You're a good man, son, and Alia is a wonderful girl, but she's also your Achilles heel, just like your mother is mine. The only difference is your girl is in actual danger, so you have to be very careful in how you react to the danger, or the shit might blow up in your face. So as much as I would like to put a foot up your ass for jumping the gun on all of this, right now, I think you having my support is more important." Harper walked to the door. "Now get your shower and get some sleep before your mother kicks my ass."

    "I will, and thanks, Dad. For everything." Charlie looked in on Alia once more, then showered and slid into bed after moving the tablet over to his nightstand. There Charlie fell asleep watching over his angel.

    Thursday, Charlie went back to work after sleeping most of the night. Alia returned to school for more exams and the library for work afterward. The two kept in touch during the day, both wanting it to end so Friday night they could be together once more.

    This may be the weekend, Alia thought. The idea alone sent tendrils of excitement throughout her body.

    Alia was on her way home from the bus stop when up at the school, red and blue lights flashed. Her heart jumped, and she had to keep herself from running the three blocks. When Alia was just feet from the car, she noticed two heads inside and stopped. She was about to back up, ready to run, when both the driver and passenger doors opened. Harper got out of the driver's side and Charlie the passenger.

"It's okay, Alia, it's us," Charlie said

Alia ran into his arms then smacked him on the chest. "You two scared the crap out of me for a minute." She hugged him again, burying her face in his chest. "Nice to see you back in uniform, though."

"Yeah, I thought you might want to see the boy." Said Harper smiling at them. "Sorry, we scared you. We also had a delivery to make." He reached into the back and pulled out a cooler.

"Keep this up, and I'm going to be big as a whale before I leave for cadet training." Alia laughed, taking the cooler and putting it down at her feet.

"Well, Ellen can't exactly help herself. Besides, we know you have been busy with work and the exams. She didn't want to hear about you skipping meals again."

"Tell her I said thank you. I think if I have to eat Trish's baked chicken too many more times, I will scream."

"I thought you said she was a good cook," said Charlie.

"Yeah, then I had your mother's chicken." They all laughed. Alia got a few more hugs in and even a kiss while Harper got back into the patrol car. Alia then walked home, not feeling so lonely as she usually did.

After walking the dog and eating, waving at Charlie when he texted her he was at his parents' house, Alia sat at her desk and wrote a note to leave for Trish. When she put it on the fridge in the kitchen, Billy was there.

"Your mom left food for the past two days. She says you haven't eaten it."

"Oh, yea, Crystal's mom has been sending me home with food. She knows I've been trying to spend most of my downtime studying." *And since when does she leave me food anymore? She may actually feel guilty over this whole thing.*

Billy walked over and looked at the note she had left.

Mom
Hanging out with Crystal all weekend will be home in time for dinner on Sunday.

"Good luck with that one kid."
"What do you mean?" Alia asked.
"She told me today we are all hanging out here this weekend...including you."
Suddenly Alia didn't feel so steady on her feet. "Why?"
"She said something about cleaning the place up. Personally, I think she doesn't want you parading around town with that shiner."
"She should have thought about that before she chunked the ashtray at my head."
"Um no, according to her, she tossed it to you, you missed, and it hit your face, but only after you hit it with your hand making it hit you harder."
Alia stood in the kitchen, her mouth hung open. "What the fuck? Is that supposed to even make any sense?"
"That's what she's telling everyone."
"Like who?"
"People at work and family, you know, in case anyone sees you. Or like she says, you go posting it on Facebook or something to get sympathy."
"Okay, first of all, Facebook is for you old farts. We use Instagram now. Second, I barely even do that, thanks to her. She followed me on Facebook and contradicted most of what I said there and then called me pathetic for lying."
"Just telling ya what she said. I mean, keep the note up. Maybe she changed her mind."
"Tell her I'll come home early Friday and clean the whole house, even her bathroom."
"I'll tell her, but like I said, this is about damage control. She is convinced you're telling everyone that will listen to what happened."

"I haven't. We have been telling everyone I got hit by a ball at a pickup game Sunday night."

"Oh, that's a good one. She should have gone with that one."

"That woman is fucking unbelievable."

"Now, now don't get your tits all in a tizzy. Like I said, she may change her mind."

"Yeah, fat chance of that happening." Alia stormed off to her room, where she smacked a box off the top of her TV in anger, forgetting for a moment about the camera. Almost immediately, her phone went off on her desk.

Charlie: What's wrong?

"Shit," Alia said and tried to calm down. She thought about lying to him, but after their talk about being honest with each other, she couldn't bring herself to do it. "Billy just told me Trish wants us all home this weekend. Some bullshit about cleaning the apartment. He thinks she just doesn't want more people in town seeing my face." Alia also told him what Trish said about how her face got that way. Done with her rant, she waited for him to text, but none came right away. *I bet he is pissed. He just got his head wrapped around this whole thing. Now she's gone and made things bad again.* It was a good ten minutes before he finally sent her a text.

Charlie: I know you're pissed I am too. I don't know what to say, Alia. Sorry but right now, I'm just really pissed off.

"I know Charlie. I'm so sorry."

Charlie: Don't you dare apologize for her.

"Maybe she will change her mind. I left the note on the fridge. If nothing else, we will know by morning." Alia turned away from the camera, afraid she wouldn't be able to hold back her tears.

Charlie: Alia, this is Harper. Do you don't think she suspects anything? Talk to the camera. I'm in Charlie's room.

Alia wiped her eyes and turned around, shaking her head. "No, I think Billy is right. She's hidden me before when I had an 'accident'. She couldn't do anything about school because of finals."

Charlie: Look, it's getting late. Go ahead and get ready for bed. Charlie and I need to talk.

Alia nodded, having a feeling that meant he had to calm Charlie down again. "Is he there? Can he hear me?"

Charlie: We all are, dear.

Alia didn't have to ask to know that it was Ellen. *If they are both in his room, he must really be upset. Damnit, Trish, why did you have to go fuck it all up again?* "I love you, Charlie. I love you all," she said, working hard to fight back the tears.

Charlie: We love you too, kiddo

Harper watched on the tablet as Alia got her things ready and went into her bathroom to take a shower. He turned to his son, who was sitting next to his mother on his bed. Ellen had his hand wrapped in a hand towel, and Harper could see blood was still coming up through it as Charlie's hand bled. The mirror on the back of his closet door was shattered. Pieces of it littered the carpet.

Harper knelt before Charlie and unwrapped the towel, trying to see how bad it was. He had to cover it up right away as blood began to drip, adding to the stain already on the floor. "He's going to need stitches, no doubt about that."

Ellen brushed Charlie's hair back from his forehead. "Charlie, you need to let your father take you to the hospital."

Looking over at the tablet, he shook his head. "I'll watch her, Charlie, and I'll have this mess cleaned up for when you get back too."

Charlie looked over at his mother then laid his head on her shoulder. "I'm sorry, Mom, I'm sorry if I scared you. I'm fine…I'll be fine, I was just."

"A tad bit pissed off, there for a minute?"

He laughed a little. "Yeah, something like that. It's just…after this week, we really needed this weekend. I needed her out of that apartment for a while."

"I know, dear, but remember what we talked about. You need to be strong for her. She needs you, Charlie. This weekend is going to be the hardest for her. You have us."

"So let's get you stitched up and back to her." Said Harper. "Good thing one of the perks of the job is getting to the front of the line. And this did happen on the job, right, son?"

Charlie nodded.

Harper took his son to get several stitches in the back of his hand while Ellen cleaned up and watched Alia.

When she came out of the bathroom, Alia looked up at the camera and gave it a little wave, and tried for a smile.

The camera quality was pretty good, enough so that Ellen could see just how tired the poor girl was. Not sleepy, tired, but the kind of tired one gets from being stressed for so long.

"Hang in there, my baby girl. This will all be over soon."

When Charlie returned, he hugged his mother and apologized again. "That was really stupid of me."

"Remind me one day to tell you the story about how your father did pretty much the same thing." She whispered in his ear. "As for our girl, she is in bed reading. I'm pretty sure she would like to hear from you."

"I don't even know what to say to her," Charlie said, looking at his bandaged hand.

"The truth, that you did something stupid, but you're fine now. You are fine now, right Charlie?"

"Hand hurts like hell, but yes, I'm fine."

"Let that pain be a reminder to think next time before doing something stupid." Said Harper. He gave his son a hug, and then he and Ellen left the room. Charlie closed the door and gave himself a moment before texting Alia.

Charlie: Hey, it's me this time.

"Hey yourself," Alia said, looking up from the bed. "Are you okay, Charlie?"

Charlie: No. I was stupid tonight, punched my wall mirror. Got a few stitches but nothing broken. Other than the mirror, of course.

"Charlie...," Alia stopped, not able to think of what to say.

Charlie: I know this is a far cry from making things easy on you. I'm sorry, I just.

"Felt like punching something? I'm sure you saw what I did. You're not the only one with a temper."

Charlie: Yeah, only you're smart enough to go after something that won't bite back.

"This time. When you come to see me at the library tomorrow, I will show you the scars on my hand from when I put it through a plate glass window, on purpose. You are coming to see me, right?"

Charlie: Of course I am. Don't worry about the weekend thing. The last thing I want is for you to get upset and have her hurt you again. So whatever Trish says, just agree to it. We will have other weekends, I promise you.

"I will, no matter how much I would rather chunk something at her head for a change."

Charlie: Very funny, now go to sleep, I promise not to stay up all night, but I will at least until she gets home.

"Well, prepare yourself for her yelling at me because she just might. Don't break any more mirrors. We don't need the bad luck."

Charlie: Goodnight, Alia. I love you.

"Love you too, Charlie." Alia put away her book, turned off the light, and then pretended to sleep to make Charlie feel better. There was no use in actually trying since she was sure Trish would wake her when she came in.

And like clockwork, the door slammed, then her bedroom door opened briefly. Alia hoped Charlie didn't think it was over because she knew it wasn't. Sure enough, a few minutes later, Trish opened the door again and turned on the lights. Before she could even shield her eyes, Trish started in on Alia.

"Absolutely not, no friends this weekend. I know you think you are grown now, but as long as you are living under my roof, you will do as you're told. You have been gone two weekends in a row and will be gone all of next weekend for the prom, I am sure. Not that I know why you even bother to go if no one will go with you. Hell, the way you look now, I'm sure Crystal's date isn't going to want you to tag along. That's if I even believe you she has one. I still think you two are going together, and you just don't have the balls to tell me you're a dyke."

"Mom, it's fine. I just figured you had games and stuff to do with Billy anyway. I didn't think you would care."

"Well, Alia, next time, how about asking instead." Then flipping on a dime, Trish sounded softer. " I tell you what, I know you're upset you fucked up your face. So how about we get some pizzas Saturday night and sit and watch horror movies like we used to do?"

For Alia, her mother changing on a dime like that didn't even faze her anymore. Still, she wondered what

Charlie was thinking if he was indeed watching this. *And he is, I know it, I can feel him.*

"You know it would be nice if you could spend some time with your mother before running off for the whole summer. I did pay for your dresses, and throwing you a graduation party it's the least you can do."

"Okay, that sounds great. Can I go back to bed now? I still have exams in the morning."

"I forgot about that. How are you doing? Don't fuck up and not graduate. I'm not going to support you for another year just because you fucked off all year."

Yeah, but you would if for nothing else just so you can throw it in my face later.
"I'm not breaking any records, but I'll pass." *With my three-point-five-grade point average, you know nothing about your damn Skippy I will pass.*

"Okay," and with that, she turned off the lights and slammed the door. No goodnight, nothing.

Alia looked up at the camera and shook her head. *Keep your cool, Charlie.* The phone in her mattress vibrated, and Alia risked taking it out, hiding under the covers with it.

Charlie: Wow, does she always change moods like that?

Alia: Constantly, I'm used to it.

Charlie: That actually made my head spin. You realize she's bipolar, right?

Alia: Yeah, no shit.

Charlie: I didn't think she was still harping on that thing about you, Crystal

Alia: Oh, she won't stop that until the day she dies. My mother is never wrong. Are you going to be okay?

Charlie: Yeah. Still not sure what I just saw.

Alia: You have been away for a while, Charlie. This is her in a halfway decent mood.

Charlie: Yeah, I see she hasn't changed. Try and get some sleep, sweet girl, don't let her get to you.

Alia: You either.

Looking at her on the tablet, Charlie thought, *No promises.*

Friday at school was the last day of testing and only half a day. Alia told Crystal about the weekend being ruined. She spent the rest of that morning just sort of being quiet and trying not to think about things. When testing was done, the seniors were told they could take off if they wanted to. Having anticipated that Crystal took Alia to their favorite restaurant for lunch to try and cheer her up, but it didn't work.

They went to Harkening Hill park, where they sat and talked about things other than how crappy the weekend would be. When Crystal mentioned the prom, Alia made a face of disgust.

"What, why the look?"

"I'm having second thoughts about this whole prom thing. Between going stag and my face, I feel pathetic at this point."

"Tell me how you really feel."

Alia rolled her eyes at Crystal's catchphrase.

"I think you don't want to go because you would rather spend time with Charlie, which I understand, but you promised me you would. Your face will be fine by then, and if you're really desperate for a date, there's still time."

"Hell no on the date thing. Before, Charlie was one thing but now, shit that would be even more pathetic. As for being with Charlie, I already know he and his dad will be working that night trying to keep us, stupid kids, from killing ourselves. I'll go. I'll just be miserable the whole time." she laughed.

"Well, good thing miserable looks so good on you. I think you will be surprised, though, and end up having a good time."

"Yes, you, me, your date and my misery…great company." They both laughed.

At work in the library later that day, Mrs. Stackhouse told her that someone needed help in the archives. So in her own mind, at the moment, Alia didn't even think about Charlie being there until she saw him. He looked tired again, and she knew he hadn't gotten much sleep, but then neither did she. Alia was about to give Charlie a big hug when she noticed the bandages on his hand. She had almost forgotten he broke a mirror.

"How's the hand?" She gingerly took it in her own and kissed it lightly.

"Itches. How's the face?"

"Itches and is turning the most awesome shades as you can see."

Charlie took her into his arms. "Still beautiful," he whispered in her ear. They spent most of the next half an hour kissing and exploring a bit with their hands. Charlie wanted to not only drink up every bit of Alia he could get but breathe into her what she would need to get through the weekend as well.

"I know this sucks, but we have all of next week, family dinner night, meetings here, and anything else I can squeeze in once my father lets me off my leash."

"Don't tell me Harper is still following you around."

"He would have relented by now, but the fist through the mirror set me back. Don't tell him I said this, but I like riding along with him again. It's like the months after I came back from the academy."

"Wait, he's not out in the parking lot waiting for you again, is he?"

Charlie gave her that boyish grin of his and shrugged. "Maybe."

"Charles Harper, we have been down here almost an hour already. Get your butt back to work. Your father is going to have your head for making him wait this long."

Charlie laughed, "It's all good. He told me to take my time. I'm not going to be able to see you tonight, though. He thinks it would be too much of a risk seeing how the factory sometimes shuts down early on Fridays."

"He's right. The school thing is great, but it is a risk. I'm going to miss the hell out of you this weekend."

"I'll miss you too. I'm picking up some extra shifts this weekend, but I will be keeping an eye on things on my phone. I want you to promise me something. Right now, I know you are beyond mad at her, but I need you to play it cool this weekend. I mean, red carpet academy awards cool. Do what she says, tone down the snarkiness, just whatever you need to do to not piss her off."

"I'm not snarky," Alia protested.

Charlie laughed and shook his head, knowing damn well she knew she was snarky.

"Of course, I will behave. It will take every ounce of will I have, but I will do it for you. Don't worry so much about me, Charlie. I know this all seems crazy to you but remember, I have lived with this for years. Hell, I might even enjoy the weekend. She got a little shitty last night, but I don't think she can help herself to not insult me at this point. Right now, I am convinced she will try and defuse the situation."

"I certainly hope so. But again, if it gets bad, leave. Say the code word if you can, and then just leave, go to the school or something." Charlie kissed her bruised cheek tenderly. "If she hurts you again, Alia...."

"I know Charlie, it'll be alright." She kissed him again then told him to get going. Upstairs at the front desk, Mrs. Stackhouse gave her a little wink.

"Going to be a long weekend, isn't it?"
Alia shook her head. "You don't know the half of it." They looked at each other and couldn't help but laugh a little. Because sometimes you have to laugh at life, or you'll go insane screaming.

Charlie was waiting for Alia when she got home. Her at the apartment, and he still at his parents' house. She blew him a kiss when she got in, a tiny gesture that made his heart soar. *Boy, do I have a surprise for you, my sweet girl.* He thought.

They talked via text and the camera for a bit until he caught her dozing off in a chair. Charlie told her to go get in bed, and she did. He stayed awake, watching as she slept until Trish came in to check on her, then a bit after to be sure. Once Charlie was confident things were done for the night, he went to bed as well. That night, like most of the time he tried sleeping that week, he had nightmares about slamming doors and Alia's head exploding on impact. He may not be shocked to know she was having pretty much the same ones.

With the Rolling stones blaring in the background Alia and her mother did clean the apartment Saturday morning. Billy managed to make himself scarce most of the day, of course. When they were done, Alia showered then ate leftovers from yet another dinner Ellen had sent over Friday night. In the living room, Trish was getting caught up on all the soap operas she had missed during the week. Alia couldn't stand watching them.

I could be with Charlie right now. This is being done out of spite.

Charlie had checked in on her in between calls he had all day. Saturdays could get busy, and the later it got, the worse it would get. But they hadn't even really talked much, which bummed her out a little.

When Alia took Ebony for a walk just before evening, she walked into the little copse of trees behind the apartment complex and sat under a large oak. Breathing in the smell of the woods around her was like meditating. Afterward, Alia felt she could better handle an evening of sitting with Trish pretending she didn't know all about the horrible things she said about charlie. And to be clear, she was still furious, not about the injury to her face as much as her saying those awful things.

Alia found that she had a hard time looking at Trish all day. She had even imagined pushing Trish's head into the bucket of soapy water she used to mop with. But now, coming out of the woods, Alia felt she was ready for the night.

As Trish had promised, they ordered pizza. Ebony went crazy running around, knowing when they picked up the phone it was for that. Then they watched the Fear Street trilogy because Trish hadn't seen it yet. Thankfully they were outstanding movies that Alia really enjoyed, so it took her mind off how badly she was missing Charlie. Well, a little anyway. The Sheriff reminded her of him a lot.

With the movies done around midnight, Alia returned to her room, blew Charlie a kiss, and went to bed. She waited to be sure her mother would be in her own room for the night before pulling out her phone. As Alia expected, her good night messages awaited her. That was enough to send her to bed with a smile.

The next day, Alia was put back into a foul mood again. She went shopping with Trish to get groceries, then, when they got back home, was told to stay in her room because she wanted to spend time with Billy.

What the fuck!!! And Trish must have seen something on her face (besides the considerable bruise she put there) because she started in on Alia again.

"Oh, for heaven's sake, Alia, it won't kill you to stay away from your lesbo lover for one more day. I'm sure you'll be stuck up each other's ass all next weekend."

Without arguing, like she promised Charlie, Alia went back to her room, trying to keep herself from kicking the shit out of something in case he was watching. With no other way to let off steam, Alia lay on her bed with headphones blasting hard rock and metal music as loud as her ears could take it. She didn't dare to take out her phone, not even in the closet with them being up and about during the day.

Trish suddenly wanting to spend time with Billy made her wonder if the call she got last week was about the man she was sleeping around with. Which meant she was trying to get back into Billy's good graces. And that meant he could no longer be trusted. That made Alia worry almost to a state of panic. If he spilled about what he said he saw the night Charlie took her to Alexandria, they would all be screwed.

Alia had grabbed a book to pretend like she was reading in case someone came in and was now gripping the book like she wanted to rip it in two. Under her bed, she could feel her phone vibrating but didn't dare chance a look at it. Instead, she looked at the camera, still mad as hell, and motioned for Charlie to keep quiet. After a while, the phone stayed silent.

When Alia went in to shower later, she checked her messages. Most were from a few of her friends, just wondering if she survived the weekend. The one from Charlie put a smile on her face.

Charlie: Just one more sleep, my sweet girl, and you'll be back in my arms again.
You can do this

I can. We won't let that bitch win.

Chapter 17
Prom

With finals over, most elective classes done for the year and other courses winding down the last week of school for seniors was fairly relaxed. Yearbooks came out on Monday, so most of that day was spent with kids running around getting each other to sign them. With no afternoon classes she needed to attend, Alia was allowed to leave.

Alia had already planned on getting extra hours at the library, which meant Charlie could come by early and see her. His hug alone filled her up with what she needed to last the long week. His smile made her heart sing. They made plans for the rest of the week, including seeing her at the school each night. Family dinner on Wednesday and at least a few hours up at the cabin on Sunday.

Alia's eye was also better, although her cheek changed ugly colors. Charlie's hand barely bothered him, and the horrible week they had was fading into the past.

As planned, Charlie met after work on Monday, at work Tuesday, after work again on Tuesday. Wednesday, She and Crystal hung out at the park watching some senior boys they knew play basketball. When Alia arrived at the Harper's house for her lessons, Ellen was the only one there. She had gotten Alia's study materials out on the table.

"Harper said they were busy with a little bust today, so they may be late. You are to continue where you left off last week and if you have any trouble to ask me."

"Alright. Though I have to be honest. Between this and school, I am about sick of studying."

Ellen smiled and motioned for her to sit at the table. "So how about a little girl talk for a bit? At least until I need to start cooking, then you can study some."

"Thank you." Alia laughed.

"I actually wanted to talk to you about the prom. Charlie said you were going."

Alia rolled her eyes. "Yeah, Crystal wouldn't let me back out of it. I get to play the role of the third wheel to her and her date. Yay me."

"What about a dress? Did Trish get you one?"

"Surprisingly, yes. She was getting me a graduation dress and got a deal on one for the prom. It's actually kinda nice. I still don't want to go. If it wasn't for Charlie having to work that night, I would just bail and go to the cabin with him."

"Well, I'm glad she was able to get you something, but if there is anything you need you just let me know. And no, you shouldn't miss out on your prom. Don't roll your eyes. If you do, you will regret it. Date or not, it's an important end-of-school event. I think you will be surprised and end up having a great time. If nothing else, it's one last get-together with your friends before you leave for three months."

Alia sighed heavily.

"Another sore subject, I take it," Ellen said with a smile.

"Yeah, just a bit. Charlie and I refuse to even talk about it yet. He says that is for future us to worry about."

Ellen laughed. "Oh my goodness, Harper used to say that all the time. It's funny he picked that up. Maybe if the two of you did talk about it, you would realize that it's not as bleak as it seems. As long as your class doesn't mess anything up, you will be free to leave on the weekends after the first two weeks. Academy is only two hours away from the cabin in the mountains."

"Really?"

"Yep. Charlie was at the cabin most weekends, but once in a while, he came home. I know it's barely two days, but it sure beats three whole months apart."

Alia and Ellen talked for a while longer until Ellen started dinner. Alia figured she should have something to show Harper when he got in, so she also began to work.

When dinner was close to being done, they heard Charlie and Harper coming in the side door to the mudroom. Both of them were laughing, joking, and generally making a racket. They could hear the boys putting their guns in the safe and taking their boots off, then the both of them came into the kitchen still laughing and talking.

Charlie was on the dryer side of being soaked through, his socks leaving wet splotches on the floor as he walked. The both of them were a mess of dirt, leaves, drying mud, and scratches to their faces and arms. And both were grinning like they just had the best day ever.

"Oh my word, what did you two get into today?" said Ellen. "Charlie, why are you wet?"

"You should have seen it, Ellen. You would have been proud." beamed Harper.

Charlie came up to Alia and gave her a peck on her good cheek.

"Yea, why are you wet?" she asked, touching his damp uniform shirt.

Charlie blushed a little, just smiling.

"It was great, Alia. Your boy here took down a tweaker who thought he would get away by crossing Broken creek. Charlie runs up this pile of boulders right before the falls, leaps into the air, and lands right on the guy."

"Charlie, it's a wonder you didn't get hurt," said Ellen laughing as well.

Even Alia was smiling, it was hard not to join in with them despite her concern for Charlie. She looked over Charlie and noticed his elbows were scraped and bleeding as well as a few spots on his good hand. Alia tried scolding him, but all he would do was look at her with those fantastic eyes of his dancing with light. "I see you enjoyed yourself."

"Oh yes indeed." he kissed her again, on the lips, just a little, paying no mind to his parents in the room.

Not that it mattered, Harper had Ellen in a big bear hug and was kissing her all over, despite her protests that he was covered in dirt and mud.

"Stop it now. The both of you get upstairs and get cleaned up. Dinner is almost done."

"Yes, ma'am," Charlie said, winking at Alia.

"And take those sopping wet socks off before you go on my Carpet, Charles Nathaniel Harper," fussed Ellen trying to push her husband out of the kitchen.

When they left, Alia looked over at Ellen. "What was that all about?" she chuckled.

"You better get used to that sometimes those two like their job a little too much. And it's usually days they come home looking like that."

At dinner, Harper told of how they had busted a meth house, one they had raided before. "And I tell Charlie, I hope you're ready to run, boy, because these guys, they always run." Sure enough, two ran out the back, and the chase was on. Harper ended up having to wrestle the guy he went after, getting dirty from head to toe in the process. Other officers came for that guy letting Harper run towards the creek where Charlie and the other guy headed. "I just got there when Charlie took his leap off the boulders."

Charlie was still beaming while Ellen and Alia just shook their heads, smiling.

"I admit I was surprised when Charlie came up out of the water with the guy already cuffed. I don't know how you did it, boy, but you did good."

Charlie just shrugged, smiling at Alia bashfully.

Alia found it hard to take her eyes off of him. His hair was a wet, tumbled mess, and his eyes, those green eyes of his, just sparkled when he looked at her. The bashful way he smiled and would look away as his father praised him delighted her. Alia could see in him the boy she had missed so much.

After dinner, Charlie and Alia spent some time alone out on the back porch. She fussed over his cuts and scrapes while he assured her he not only felt fine but great.

"Yeah, well, don't be surprised if you wake up sore in the morning. Right now, you're still riding the adrenaline rush."

"Oh, it's the adrenaline, is it?"

"What else would have you acting like a little boy in a candy store?"

"I don't know, maybe just being here with my sweet girl, having a dreadful week finally past us. I'm just feeling better about things, I guess. And speaking of things getting better, are you looking forward to the prom?"

Alia rolled her eyes. "Ugh, you and your mother both with bringing that nightmare up."

"What? I thought the prom was like the highlight of a girl's high school years?"

"Yeah, for ones with boyfriends or a date maybe. It would figure that I have a boyfriend I can't go with. My best bet was a pity date from Ethan. I mean, really, I don't know what is worse, that or going stag. And I'm not even doing that right; I'm third-wheeling with someone I think Crystal may even like. Not only makes me look like shit, but it also makes me feel like one for busting in on their thing."

"Now stop, you know damn well Crystal doesn't have a problem with you going with her."

"That and the fact that she wouldn't say if she did, doesn't make it any better."

"Well, I think you're going to get there, hear a song or two that you just love," he said, teasing her. "and end up having a really good time. Just go in there ready to live the moment."

"You're one to talk. Just how much fun did you have at your prom? Because a little birdie told me you left early."

"Remind me to kick George's ass later. Okay, yea, I just couldn't bring myself to get into the moment. And your right going stag was a bad idea. Hell going at all was a bad idea. There was this girl I wanted to ask but never had the balls to go through with it?"

"Why not?"

Charlie looking at her and smiling gave Alia a light kiss on the lips. "Because I was afraid once I held her in my arms again, I would never want to let her go. And I was right." Charlie held her closer, kissed her longer, and told Alia that he loved her in ways words couldn't.

"You know you're really not making much of a case for me to go. If I hadn't promised Crystal I would beg off, I really would. I know you'll be working that night, but I think I would rather stay at the cabin alone than go."

"But you won't, will you? Try to get out of it? Because I really would hate for you to miss it. I don't want you to have any regrets later. I certainly don't want you to not go because of me."

"No. As I said, I promised. Crystal's mom is picking us up early from school Friday to shop for last-minute stuff. Then Saturday we have hair and nails. I can't believe I let her talk me into doing that because just saying it makes me feel like a basic white chick." she laughed.

"Well, maybe you'll get to go to Starbucks too if you're lucky," Charlie said, teasing her again.

"Once again, not helping Charlie."

"So you got a nice dress and everything?"

"It's okay, I guess. It did feel kinda nice trying it on. I don't get to dress up much."

"Well, somebody better take lots of pictures of my girl in a dress because I can't remember the last time I ever saw you in one."

"You probably never have. I used to be in a summer dress faze there for a bit, but Trish gave me so much shit over it I stopped. I think she thought I was trying to flirt with one of her boyfriends."

"Well fuck her. You're going to the prom, you're going to look amazing, and despite everything, you're going to have a great time. I insist."

"If it'll make you feel better, I'll try."

"That's my girl."

They sat on the porch until the time came to part ways once again, and Alia went home.

Friday night, after their shopping was done, Alia stayed at Crystal's house, where they had dinner. If she couldn't be with what she considered her real family, this family was a very close second.

The talk centered around preparations the next day for the prom, where they would go afterward, and when they were expected home. Alia hadn't even expected to see Charlie at all Friday night, but shortly after dark, there was a knock at the door, and there he was.

"I couldn't bear not to see you, even if it's only for a little bit," he said, taking her out of the house to the driveway where his patrol car was parked.

Alia looked in the car. No one else was with him.

"All on my own, been for a few days now. I'm good. No more smashing mirrors. And the stitches come out tomorrow." Charlie said, showing her his hand.

Alia took it and gingerly kissed the knuckles.

"The bruising below your eye is almost all gone."

"Good, maybe the both of us can stay out of trouble for a little while."

"No promises." they both said together and laughed. Standing in front of his patrol car, Charlie and Alia spent some time together before Harper came on the radio.

"Okay, Romeo, break time is over. Get back at it, son."

"Copy that," he said into his radio and gave her a last hug and kiss. "Oh, one more thing, I was wondering if you could help us. A little cop work before you actually become one."

"Sure, I would love to. What do you need?"

"Intel. A lowdown on where the big after-prom parties are going to be."

"Oh, so you want me to be a nark," Alia said with a hand on her hip.

"No, no, just trying to make our jobs easier and maybe save a life or two. We had no deaths on my prom night, and it would be nice if the same could be said for yours. I promise we are not out to harass a bunch of kids. We just would like to know where to head off any trouble." he said earnestly.

Alia thought for a bit.

"Come on, Alia, we're just trying to save some lives."

"Dave Zimmer's house. That's going to be the big one."

Charlie ran back to her, giving her another kiss. "Thank you, I'm sure that will help."

"Charlie," she yelled as he ran back to the car. "Go easy on Dave. He's a good kid. We used to hang out in the eighth grade together. His parents are loaded and never home. That kind of thing puts a kid like him in a hard spot. But he's still a good kid."

"I'll keep that in mind."

"And you be careful, no crazy shit tomorrow night, I mean it Charles, your mine Sunday, and I'd like to have you unbroken." As he drove out, Charlie waved at her with a smile.

"Oh, he is so not listening to me." she chuckled to herself.

Saturday was crazy. Everyone had a job to help the girls get ready for the prom that night. George was there early to set up a nice area in the yard for taking photos. Albert made sure everyone ate, and Rose drove them to get their hair and nails done.

Alia felt silly letting people make so much of a fuss over her when she was just going stag, but Crystal and her mom insisted she get the works done just like all the girls would. Her own mother only contributed by leaving a note for her Friday morning saying it was okay for her to stay out until curfew Sunday night. But Alia figured she should be grateful for that much, at least.

Alia had gotten a slight trim to her shoulder-length hair only to get the split ends, then the ends were curled. Her nails were fake since her own were always kept trimmed. Even her toes were painted since they would show with the shoes she had.

Alia had to admit that she was starting to have some fun and even began to feel pretty.

Back at Crystal's, it was getting close to the time for Crystal's date to come to pick them up, so the girls put on their dresses and got busy doing makeup. This was one part neither she nor Crystal was very good or knowledgeable at, so Rose had called a cousin in the family that is a beautician to come do it. When it was over, and Alia looked in the mirror, she was surprised at how well it turned out. The girl had done a great job making her look as natural as possible while highlighting her naturally high cheekbones and hiding the last of the bruising.

Crystal and Alia were in Crystal's room as Crystal got the last of her makeup done when they heard a knock at the front door.

"Your date is a little early," said Alia. However, when George came into the room, he told Alia someone was there to see her.

Right away, her heart started to race. "Please tell me it's not my mother."

"Okay, it's not your mother."

"George!"

307

"It's not. Go look."

Alia put on the low heels she was to wear for the night and went out to the front door that George had shut. "Kinda rude shutting them up outside," said Alia trying to give George a scathing look. His shocked expression made her laugh instead. When she opened the door, Charlie was standing on the porch wearing a tux and smiling the mischievous smile of his she had grown to love so much. Alia just stood there on the verge of tears, not believing her eyes.

When Charlie saw her in the doorway in her red sleeveless dress and heels, he was so blown away he forgot for a minute what he was going to say. For several seconds he forgot to breathe. His beautiful little angel had grown into a gorgeous woman, and right then, Charlie knew he would never love another.

"I uh, was wondering if maybe you would let me take you to the prom," he said, having recovered, just barely. Charlie handed her a rose with a hand that was shaking.

Unable to speak, Alia nodded as a tear fell down her cheek. She stepped forward, but her legs were shaking so bad she could barely move properly. In an instant, Charlie was there taking her into his arms.

Behind her, Crystal's mother took pictures of the two of them as the whole family had gathered in the living room to watch.

"This is why I insisted on waterproof makeup," said Crystal.

George passed a box of tissues to Crystal, who gave a few to Alia to dry her eyes.

Every time Alia tried looking up at Charlie, more fell. So she just hung on to him with one hand and dabbed at her eyes with a tissue in the other.

Albert closed the door with the two of them outside to give the kids some privacy.

"You told me you were working." was all Alia could think to say.

"I was supposed to, but you would be surprised how persuasive my mother can be. She insisted Dad let me off for the night."

"But what about Trish? What if she finds out?" her tears were dry, and the shakes were ebbing away, having as usual been comforted just by Charlie being there.

"If anyone asks, my mom asked me to take you when she found out you didn't have a date. But she didn't," he said. "I told her weeks ago I wanted to take you. She is the one that came up with the idea, though, and talked Dad into it. We really don't think anyone at schools will care one way or another. We will just have to control ourselves and pretend like we are just friends. Though I have to say that is going to be hard with you in that dress." Charlie kissed her then looked at her again. "You look incredible. I mean, you're beautiful anyway but, wow, Alia."

"Stop," she said, blushing.

"No way, never. I am going to push every bad thought you ever had about yourself out of your head and fill it with how amazing I think you are, and I won't ever stop."

"You look really nice too. I love the bow tie," Alia said, giving it a little tug.

"Bow ties are cool," he said.

"Did you just quote Dr. Who?"

Blushing, Charlie nodded.

"Hmm, I didn't know you were so geeky. I kinda like that."

Looking around to make sure they were alone, Charlie kissed her. Then when she was able to walk, they went back inside.

Crystal's date arrived shortly after, and they all went to the backyard, where George had set up a nice archway area for them to take pictures. They started with Crystal and her date, Crystal alone, Crystal and her parents then finished up with one of Crystal and Alia. Then it was Alia and Charlie's turn and one with Alia alone for her mother. The hope was that she would never find out about her and Charlie. So they would eventually send the pictures of just

Alia to Trish and photos of the two of them to Alia and Charlie's parents.

With the pictures done, Charlie helped Alia get into his truck, apologizing for not getting a limo. He had wanted to, but his mother said that may seem like too much if they wanted the story to be believed. "We are also advised not to kiss, not to dance too close, and not look like we are crazy about each other." he laughed. But they both knew that was going to be impossible.

Driving around town to the Holiday Inn where the prom was, wasn't so bad with Alia concealed inside Charlie's truck. When they got to the parking lot, she started to panic a little. There were so many people there she had doubts they would keep this whole thing under wraps. *Whatever happens, just don't have her come here and embarrass the hell out of me, not tonight.* Alia begged whatever power in the universe that seemed to have fun torturing her.

When Charlie came to get her out of the truck, he felt her apprehension.

"Are you going to be alright?"

Alia nodded, not convincing herself or him.

"Hey, look at me. Take a deep breath."

"Charlie, what if she comes here? What if she finds out? I'm not so sure this is such a great idea." All Alia could think about was the horrible things Trish had accused him of, getting out.

"Listen, don't, don't do that to yourself. Don't even start to think about her. Come on now, take a deep breath."

Alia took a deep breath and let it out slowly.

"Now we are going to go in there, and for the next few hours, we are not going to think about Trish at all. My prom sucked because I couldn't be there with you, so this is our prom, our night. And we are going to have a great night, right?"

"Right," she said, trying not to be too aware of all the people around them, some even looking their way.

"Now, most of these kids are going to be too wrapped up in their own little lives tonight to even care about us. We do this for a few hours, then buzz by the after-party, and then it's off to the cabin. Sound good?"

"Sounds great," Alia said. Though now, she wished they could skip the first two parts and just rush off to the cabin.

Charlie took her by the hand and led Alia into the hotel, following everyone else to the prom room. The D.J. was playing the music loud, the lights turned low, and Alia's fellow classmates were having a great time already.

Alia found herself leaning on Charlie more and more as they walked. The noise, lights, and glances she saw looking her way increased her anxiety. It all felt so overwhelming that she felt herself start to shake.

Noticing, Charlie put his arm around her waist and pulled her closer to him. "You good?" he asked, whispering in her ear to be heard.

Alia couldn't understand why she was feeling the way she was. Usually, her fears and anxiety went away with Charlie at her side. It wasn't until she looked up at him that she realized it wasn't anxiety she was feeling, but instead a joy so strong it was unfamiliar and overwhelming. Turning to Charlie, Alia nodded as she ran her one hand up into the back of his hair, and her other she placed it on the side of his face. "How can I ever express to you how so very happy you have made me tonight, Charlie? Once again, you have managed to come to my rescue when I needed you the most." Then right there in front of everyone, not caring who saw Alai kissed her boy.

Charlie held Alia tight to him, his heart pounding, the feel of her hand in his hair driving him insane. When she stopped, he could see, even in the bad lighting, Alia was blushing. Her smile was radiant, and her blue eyes sparkled with unshed tears. *I would walk through hell and back if it meant I could make her look this happy every day of her life.* "I can see it," Charlie said. "That look in your eyes tells me all I need to know, sweet girl. I'm not so sure I'm the one doing the rescuing this time." The two were getting lost in each other's eyes when Crystal walked up to them.

"There you two are. Oh, I'm sorry, am I interrupting something?" she asked with a knowing grin.

Blushing more, Alia smiled and looked away.

Charlie took her by the hand and turned to Crystal. "No, we were just taking a moment to take it all in," said Charlie looking bashful.

"Well, come on, we found a table; everyone is there waiting for us," Crystal said and took Alia's other arm to show them to the table.

At the table waited Crystal's date Thomas, Ethan with his date, and their friends Raya, Lara, Joel, Carina, and Amy with their dates. Crystal had prepared them for Alia coming to the dance with Charlie, but the looks on their faces said they were still shocked to actually see it.

All the girls told each other how great they looked as they oohed and aahed over each other's dresses, hair, and makeup. Alia had been able to go to a few dances at school, but still, most of this was all new to her. She wasn't really a lot into the whole girly thing but had to admit that it was kind of fun since she was with her friends. Being around them also made her feel more comfortable. Alia hadn't failed to notice all the stares in their direction as she and Charlie walked hand and hand to the table.

Sitting down at the table till everyone decided what they were going to do, Alia glanced around, trying to make it look like she wasn't looking at people, but just around in general. As with the walk-up, she was getting a few looks her way. Most just glanced once and moved on, but a few did double-takes. There were a couple of snickers from the mean girls, but the looks they were getting seemed to be of approval for the most part. Not that Alia needed or wanted anyone's approval, she merely hoped no one would be petty enough to get word back to her mother.

About an hour later, after some punch and several songs on the dance floor, Alia stopped worrying about the looks and Trish. Despite what they had been told, she and Charlie clung to one another during every slow song. She lay her head on his chest as he held her close and danced her around.

A look into her eyes led to his lips on hers time and time again. At several points in the night, Charlie wanted to just whisk her away to some private corner to truly show her how much he loved her. Instead, he whispered in her ear how beautiful she was over and over.

After hours of bouncing between dancing, mingling, and having punch, Alia and Charlie took a break at the table, where they joined Crystal and Thomas.

"Looks like you two have been having a great time," Alia said to them.

"Us?, well yes, but I think you and Charlie are putting us to shame."

"What do you mean?"

"I mean, it's getting hard to explain to people it's a pity date when the two of you can't keep your hands off of each other. Everyone is shipping the hell out of the two of you. Even some of the teachers have taken notice."

"You think I should tell Charlie we need to cool it?"

"No way, it's all good vibes. A few snarky girls are talking shit, but they always do, so who cares. Most are buying the story. They just think the two of you should date."

At this, Alia laughed. "Well, just maybe we will then."

"I actually heard a couple of guys say if they had known you were so hot, they would have brought you themselves," said Crystal's date Thomas. "One dude said it right in front of his date, and she smacked the shit out of him."

"You're full of crap."

"No, I swear." Thomas laughed.

"They have even been asking if we all want to go to the after-party at Dave's house," said Crystal.

Charlie leaned over, laughing. "Yeah, that's a no-go. My father is going to have that place staked out tonight. Doubt very much of anything is going to go on there."

Crystal and Alia laughed. They had both known Dave in the eighth grade and seen his descent into the arms of the popular, rich kids. Like some of the kids Alia used to hang out with, most of those kids were using him. His mostly parent-free house was like a light beacon to moths.

During the night, there had been a few dedications and special dances. They were talking about heading to Ethan's when the D.J. came over the speaker.

"Okay, kids, we have a special dedication song, going out to Lotus."

Alia turned to Charlie, who had taken that time to stand up and offer his hand out to her. Lotus was their safe word, and since he couldn't use her real name, Charlie had used that one. Alia took his hand in stunned silence, allowing him to lead her onto the dance floor. Charlie took Alia in his arms heedless of those around them and danced with the girl of his dreams, locking his eyes with hers. The world around them disappeared with only the music and the lights to keep them company. The song was more than just a song. It was words he felt in his heart and he sang to her as they danced. Once again Charlie was finding it so easy to do things with her he never imagined he would ever have been able to.

Alia was hearing the song in a new way for the first time, realizing how much it mirrored their own lives. Alia smiled and danced as Charlie whirled her around, not taking her eyes away from his.

"So beautiful," Charlie sang with tears in his eyes. He closed them and kissed her, tender at first, then harder, his tongue exploring her. As the song ended he held her close. "I love you, Alia. I always will."

"And I'll always love you, Charlie, nothing, and no one will ever destroy that." They kissed again as the music changed and more people joined the dance floor.

Not much longer after their dance Ethan said it was time to head to his house. They gathered their things, said goodbyes to friends, invited others to Ethan's, and headed out the door.

Charlie helped Alia into his truck once again, stopping to kiss her before closing the door.

While Charlie drove down the road, Alia had her hand on his leg and couldn't take her eyes off of him. "You know we don't have to go to Ethan's. I'm sure you don't want to spend the whole night hanging around a bunch of kids." she rubbed his leg, causing him to swerve just a little.

"Oh shit Alia, I promised the little dude we wouldn't bail, that we would at least show up. We don't have to stay too long. Crystal explained to him the cabin was about an hour's drive out. And if you keep doing that to my leg, we won't even make it as far as his house, let alone there."

Alia laughed and removed her hand. "Is that better?"

"Hell no, but at least I can drive," he joked.

They managed to make it to Ethan's in one piece then joined her friends in Ethan's basement. Now, this isn't the cool kids' house. Ethan's parents were always home. They stayed up on the second floor as long as everything was okay, and the kids stayed in the basement. There was even a bathroom, so no one had to leave the basement for that either. It was furnished with a wet bar (alcohol locked up), giant T.V., pool table, speakers in the walls, and living room furniture. Alia and her friends had spent a good part of their high school years hanging out in Ethan's basement on weekends, after plays, sporting events, and birthday parties. Alia's eighteenth had been celebrated there as well.

Usually, there was just a small group of them, the primary friend group no more than ten at the most. Tonight the place was almost packed with kids. Plenty of refreshments were around, and pizza was delivered soon after they arrived. It wasn't THE party, but it was the only one Alia would ever want to go to.

Alia and Charlie staked out a claim on one of the couches sitting there in each other's arms, stealing a kiss here and there, laughing and talking with each other and those at the party. They stayed there for two hours. Some kids left, some more returned. A few had even come from Dave's, where they were bummed out to find the police parked out front. Most were just making the circuit from house to house, looking for free food and booze. When they realized there was no booze, most moved on. After the two hours, it was down to only about twenty kids, most of whom were friends of one form or another.

Again there was talk about how Alia and Charlie made an adorable couple and should date. Alia's friends were having fun playing along. When asked, Charlie looked at her with that mischievous smile of his and said they may have to talk about that. Alia just laughed and rolled her eyes.

The night had gone very well, so not wanting to push it, she suggested that it was time to go, and Charlie agreed. Saying goodbye to her good friends, Alia and Charlie tried to sneak out quietly up the stairs. However, they were spotted and the hoots and hollers of horny teens thinking someone was getting lucky tonight followed them up the stairs.

Once they were upstairs alone, Alia turned to Charle. "I'm sorry about that. I told you we should have bailed. High school kids are not actually the most mature." She tried playing it off but had her own hopes for how the evening was going to end.

Charlie took her into his arms. "Can't blame them or you. Besides, they're not wrong, are they?" he asked hopefully.

Alia's heart flipped, her stomach fluttered, and she kissed him. "No, I don't think they are." she said, feeling red and hot again.

"Then we better get going because this isn't where I planned for this night to end, but first." One hand in her hair, the other on the small of her back, Charlie kissed her for several minutes. "There, that should last me till we get to the cabin," he said, giving her that grin again.

On the drive, Alia held Charlie's hand until he got to the winding part of the road that he needed both to steer. It was the wee hours of the morning when they got to the cabin, but neither of them was close to being tired.

When they arrived, Charlie asked her to wait on the porch as he took her bags inside. Coming back out, he took her into his arms. "I was thinking, and I realize it's late, but, I thought maybe now that we are here, we could take things a little slow. We only get a first time once, and I just want to be sure we both enjoy every moment of it." Taking Alia by the hand, Charlie led her over to the front porch swing. Sitting down, he had her sit next to him with her legs up on his lap. "Is this okay?" he asked. "That we just make this night last as long as possible?"

"Of course, my sweet boy." *It's as if he read my mind.* Thought Alia, who had become increasingly nervous the long drive up.

"Are you sure you're ready for this?" Charlie asked.

Alia nodded, afraid if she tried to speak, she wouldn't be able to.

Charlie kissed her sweet lips with a smile, using his hand entwined in her hair to pull her closer to him. For about half an hour, they sat on the porch swing, caressing, kissing, and arousing each other only to break apart for a moment, then start again.

Charlie discovered how ticklish she was and where. Her giggles and protests only added fuel to his fire. The feel of her fingers combing through his hair sent chills through him. He couldn't get enough of the taste of her lips and mouth even long after the strawberry balm wore off. Her dress was silky smooth under his hand, her breast reacting to his touch even through it.

With her legs on his lap, Charlie was able to rub his hand up and down her one thigh, slipping ever so slightly under her dress, just enough to elicit a response from her and retreat back down again.

Alia would inhale sharply with a smile, then exhale a little at a time as her heart thundered in her chest. Wanting to feel the muscles of his arms in her hands, she coaxed Charlie into taking his jacket off. After, when he wrapped his arms around her, she relished in the strong muscular feel of them.

Feeling ready, Charlie removed Alia's legs from his lap, got up, and helped her up as well. Slowly they made their way inside, stopping every couple of steps to kiss and caress one another.

Inside after closing the door, Charlie took her in his arms and leaned her up against it. There he kissed her deeply, their tongues exploring, their hands caressing. He then led her into the bedroom, where he looked deeply into her eyes, grinned then literally swept her off her feet and into his arms. Charlie kissed and caressed her more as he lay her down on the bed. When he stopped for a moment to take off his shoes, Alia tried reaching for the bedside lamp, and he stopped her.

"No, keep them on. I want to see you, all of you," he whispered, drawing his hand on hers, down her arm to the front of her dress. He then slipped it behind her back and slowly unzipped her dress. Charlie then slid the dress off of her, revealing matching bra, panties, and the body he had longed for.

As much as she talked about being fat, Charlie thought she looked incredible. He took off her heels then returned to the bed and to her. He danced his hands and his lips over her belly and the curves of her bra sending shivers through her. As he kissed her, he fumbled with her bra in the back, both of them laughing a little over his increased frustration in trying to get it off. At last, it came free, revealing her breasts to him for the first time. Charlie tasted them both as Alia ran her hands through his thick black hair.

As they kissed, she helped him off with his shirt, then his pants. Their first skin-to-skin contact sent bolts of electricity through them both. For a while, they lay there kissing and caressing, exploring each other's bodies. Taking Alia's face in his hands, Charlie again professed his love for her. Then reaching over, he turned out the light.

The late morning sunshine eventually woke them up. Alia had lain on Charlie's chest most of the night with his arm wrapped around her. They ducked under the sheets without saying a word and made love again. They had gone at it for hours in the night, Immediately falling into a cadence and rhythm that took most lovers months, even years to accomplish. There was no pain, no shyness, no embarrassment, and no worries, only two bodies and minds working as one. It was evident that their connection to each other ran very deep. And it made it all the more painful when the time came for them to go and once again be apart.

Alia felt like she wanted to cry but didn't for his sake.

Charlie felt his emotions shift to that old familiar anger. He squashed it for her sake. However, they both knew what the other was feeling. Their bond had grown stronger than ever before.

Even though Trish had said she could stay out till curfew, Charlie was in a hurry to get her home before it got too late to avoid a repeat of the ashtray incident. They busied themselves cleaning up the cabin but constantly found themselves in each other's arms. And eventually, they found themselves in bed again. When it was finally late enough, they left reluctantly, promising that this wouldn't be their last weekend.

Back at Crystal's, they kissed goodbye so long Crystal thought she would have to turn the hose on them. Then Alia found herself in front of her apartment door. This time, there wasn't any cooler with dinner, which made her sad. Looking at the door, she couldn't bring herself to go in. Alia felt like this life, this nightmare wasn't her real life. Beyond this door were all the things in life that hurt her and made her feel less.

It's just two more weeks, just two more weeks, and you're out of here. Only that wasn't much consolation taking into fact that then she would be away from her real family for weeks, and only with Charlie on weekends. Alia realized that this was about more than just him, that she would miss them all terribly.

Crystal's family, with their Harry Potter references, game nights, and George that always treated her like a little sister. Not to mention the best of all best friends in the world that put up with Alia when she was still acting out a bit. A friend who also got Alia through the eighth grade so they could move on to high school together. Her mother and father that welcomed her into their home like they had known her forever, not caring about the rumors about her and her mother.

Her friends, something she honestly never thought she would have because the kids she hung out with, the delinquents, were never her friends. Ethan, who had offered to take her to the prom despite crushing on another girl.

Raya who was always good for a laugh. Carina, whose own life was a bit of a wreck, that loved to read the stories and poems Alia wrote. And others that had stuck by her over the years, despite how most of them were terrified of her mother.

The Harper's, her one true family because family is not always blood. Family is people that choose to love you and are willing to risk it all to show you. Harper who never gave up on her even when he had more than enough reasons to. Ellen who plucked a tiny screaming baby from a playpen and loved her like her own. And Charlie. Somehow, somewhere, something had blessed her with Charlie. A boy that loved her so much he had waited all those years for her. And now they were bonded in a way neither one of them had ever shared with another, and if the world was just, never would. Standing there, Alia could still feel his hands on her, his lips, his muscles, his gentle touch but firm touch. She could still smell him on the white t-shirt of his she had put on before they left.

If I wasn't such a coward, I would just grab my things and leave. Just go and never look back.

Unfortunately, Alia knew she wouldn't. She had made a promise to the only member of her family she gave a damn about, her great grandmother. Years ago and before her father had died, Alia, having just been beaten by her mother for stealing a few quarters to buy a book, was ready to call it quits and tell someone about her mother's abuse. But her great grandmother made her promise not to and to try and do right by her mother.

"No matter what she has done, she is still your mother. Has she made mistakes? Yes, plenty. Has she done right by you? No. But she gave you life, and if that alone is the only thing that keeps your promise to me, then that will be enough. Because you were put in the world for a reason, Alia, and one day you're going to know what the reason is."

My reason is Charlie," she thought, standing at the door, not wanting to go in. *And if the price that I have to pay to spend a lifetime with him is beyond that door, then it's one worth paying. All of it, all the years of pain and being afraid, has been worth it.*

Taking a deep breath, breathing in his scent from the t-shirt she was wearing, Alia opened the door and walked inside.

Chapter 18
Graduation

The final week before graduation left Alia feeling like time was going too fast and too slow simultaneously. School was basically over for her and her classmates. They busied themselves cleaning out lockers, taking home papers, school projects, and putting another senior class away in boxes. There weren't any classes, so they were allowed to go for the day once they were done helping teachers and staff.

Having only two weeks left at her job Alia spent extra hours making extra money. She would start receiving a salary as soon as the academy started and the Sheriff's department paid for her training. Still, there were other things she would need and a future to think about.

Her intentions were not to move in with Charlie, at least not right away. Alia had made arrangements to rent a small apartment over a garage. It was close to town and close to the Harpers and would give her the freedom and independence she craved. Harper also felt that their relationship would go over a lot smoother if the two had their own places, and it looked like they got involved only after she graduated from the academy. Only a few people in town knew the truth.

Alia's classmates were disappointed to find out. She and Charlie would not be dating. Despite how many times she was told the two of them looked great together, or they really seemed to like each other, Alia would just tell them they had no plans to date further at the moment. She hated saying that only because it felt like a betrayal to her, especially after what they did. But Alia also understood that discretion was the best thing for now.

The truth was that they still met every day at the library and Wednesday for family dinner. Most nights, Charlie would be there at the ever-growing school construction site. He found a place he could park the patrol car no one would see, and they had made love in the backseat on those nights. They could not take their time and enjoy it as much as at the cabin, but the passion of that night was still there. Afterward, Alia would walk home, smelling of him, smiling, and Charlie would drive home smelling of her and smiling.

The camera stayed up in Alia's room just to be safe. When she knew he was watching alone in his apartment, she would tease him with a peak or two. It drove him crazy, and he loved it.

Friday night, the day before her graduation, She and Charlie met at the school since they wouldn't be able to head out to the cabin until after the graduation. After their lovemaking, Charlie held her in his arms.

"I'll be at your graduation," he said, telling her for the first time. "In an official capacity, of course," he said as she started to protest. "It's all hands on deck to deal with traffic and parking. I'm going to try my best to sneak in. I want to see you cross that stage. In fact, I'm not supposed to tell you this, but Mom and Dad will be there too. She's going to act as one of the ushers. We talked about it and agreed that we wanted to be there to support you."

"Charlie, that is so wonderful. Your mom, I swear she's the best."

"Yeah, just try to remember you hate all of us," he laughed. "Trish is going to it, right?"

"Yes, she is, unfortunately. I think she will behave, though. Once again, more her victory than mine. A couple of relatives are coming, including her sister if she is feeling well."

"Is it the one that told you about the military thing?"

"That's the one. Oh, and I didn't tell you this because we have been doing too good, you know, staying out of trouble. But Trish had a recruiter come by the house the other day. I wasn't home, but he left me a neat little army bag and some goodies." Alia said sarcastically.

"Unfucking believable. So she's still harping on that?"

"Yep, Billy said she said that she doesn't want me to become an old maid and not get me married off because of working in a library."

"Jokes on her, girls that read just so happens to turn me on."

Alia laughed. "The way that we have been going at it, I don't think there is much that doesn't turn you on, Charlie." she joked.

"Just for that, you are in trouble, little lady." Charlie tickled her till she cried for mercy, laughing so hard.

The following day when she woke, Alia was once again worried about facing Trish. When she had come home Sunday night, ahead of curfew but still after dinner, Alia was nervous, Trish would read her face and know what she did. Or worse, smell it on her since they didn't have time to shower after their last little romp at the cabin.

Alia was saved by the fact that Trish and Billy had been fighting all weekend. Feeling the tension as soon as she got in the living room, Alia excused herself, saying she had to use the bathroom. What she did was turn on the camera in the vent in case things went wrong. Plus, Charlie was waiting for her to turn it on. She had managed to get it on just in time as her mother barged into her room.

Trish spent the next two hours in Alia's room ranting about Billy. You see, now that she was mad at Billy, Trish had reverted to her us against the world role with Alia. So she sat on the floor of Alia's room like she was some teen girl visiting and talking about boys while Alia put away the things she had packed up for the weekend. At one point, Alia rolled her eyes at the camera when her mother wasn't looking. Though she secretly hoped Charlie wasn't watching (knowing damn well he was).

No such luck. Charlie watched the whole thing paying very particular attention to the things Trish said. This person she was now was new to him. He listened as Trish actually complimented Alia, saying how pretty she looked that night, that she looked like she was glowing. Trish even asked about the prom, even though Charlie could tell she wasn't interested at all in hearing it.

It's like a game she is playing. Trish lets Alia talk just enough to pander to her and justify occupying the rest of the conversation. Alia knows and plays right along. Only Alia feigns sincerity much better than Trish does, and Trish is utterly unaware that it's just an act. Charlie only knows because he can feel her even from where he is.

By the end of Trish's ranting, there was no doubt in his mind that Trish was profoundly mentally disturbed. And congratulations to Alia for playing along so well. She seemed to know what to say and when to say it to keep her mother happy. Most of it was Trish complaining about how Billy had cashed his check before coming home that Friday. He always brought it home to deposit to her bank over Trish's phone. But this time, he just gave her what she needed for groceries and stuff in cash.

While he listened, Charlie took the time to clean his service revolver like he did every week regardless of use. When he was done, he leveled it several times at the screen, pointed it at Trish, and imagined the deep satisfaction he would get from pulling the trigger. It's not that Charlie wanted her dead or to kill her; he just wanted her gone. Still, it was a dark side of him that admittedly scared him.

Charlie was so glad that Alia played along with her mother feeding into her ego and psychosis. If she was hurt again by that woman, he wasn't sure if he'd be able to control that dark side of him. Not when it came to Alia. Charlie Realized this part of him was not healthy, especially if the two of them were going to be working together. She was bound to end up having a bad night or two. So Charlie would spend the summer, while she was gone, working on that by seeing a behavioral therapist.

The whole deal would be done outside of Union county and paid for by him. The last thing he wanted was to cause Alia any more pain than she already had to endure in life. Though Charlie knew he would always be a fierce protector of hers, those quick bursts of red hot fury he felt needed to be stopped. It was the right thing to do, the adult thing to do.

Concerned Trish would know something, Alia did her best to avoid her until she and Billy took her to school for graduation. That was easier said than done. Trish kept fussing over Alia, wanting to do her hair and makeup. Which Alia knew would make her look like a clown, or worse, look like a whore like Trish did. So she did her best to procrastinate. Alia took time to shower and shave her legs (Charlie loved to rub his hands over her calves) and claimed to be hungry or needing to use the toilet. At one point, Billy came to her room when Trish was busy and handed her a letter that came in the mail the day before. It was from her school.

"I thought maybe you would want to see this first. I assume it's your grades. It's addressed to you anyway, but you know how your mother is."

When he left, Alia opened the letter, and sure enough, it was her final grades. Good thing Billy was feeling generous because with everything going on, Alia forgot to get with George and change her grades. What was on the paper was very inconsistent with what Trish had seen. Not only were all her grades for the year there but so was an honor roll certificate and her final exam grades. To Alia's surprise, her new grade point average was now at three-point-seven, up from the three-point-three she held so far that year. She was no valedictorian, but she was proud of herself just the same. To top it off, Alia managed to leave the house without having her mother do her makeup.

Alia was living high because of her grades the whole way to school. She couldn't wait to show Charlie, Mom, and Dad. Then they got to the school, and Charlie was directing traffic into the parking lot.

"Oh look, there's the sheriff's little fagot son," said Trish in the driver's seat. "I should do the world a favor and run his ass over."

Alia became suddenly alarmed because Trish saying that was no joke. She had stopped Trish from running over one of her own ex-boyfriends simply because he wouldn't return her DVD player. Had Alia not grabbed the wheel and yelled, Trish would have done it too.

Thankfully Trish just kept driving, following the cars in front of her. As they drove past him, Alia and Charlie locked eyes for the briefest second before his attention went to the vehicle behind theirs, as if he didn't see her. She knew that was a good thing, but still, it hurt a little. It was enough to ground her, allowing for the anxiety of the day to creep in.

After parking, Trish and Billy went one way while Alia went to the staging area. She was so relieved to be away from them and just hoped Ellen could avoid running into the two.

The graduation was to be held in the auditorium, with extra seating in the gym to be viewed on televisions. The staging area was the cafeteria around the corner from the auditorium. There Alia met with Crystal, who knew right away something was wrong.

"So is Trish giving you shit again?"

"No, she just made a snarky comment about running over Charlie, you know typical Trish shit." she chuckled insanely. "I mean, I know she wouldn't do it here, but damn, if she knew, she sure would. I thought knowing why Trish didn't like him would make me feel better, but no, it actually makes me feel worse." *Am I ranting like a loon? I sound like I'm ranting like a loon.*

"Well, we are not going to focus on that, are we, Alia? We are going to focus on getting up on stage and back off without passing out."

Alia shook her head. Crystal's voice sounded like it was coming from far away despite being right in front of Alia. The anxiety was building up with every second. Suddenly Alia felt her knees go all loose and shaky. She didn't know how much longer she could stand up.

"No, Alia, you're not doing this right now. It's not like I can get Charlie in here, your going to have to do this on your own."

"I'm good, I'm okay," Alia said, trying to breathe.

"You don't look so good, Alia. You look really pale," said Ethan, coming to her side.

"Not helping Ethan," said Crystal.

Their friend Raya saw what was going on and came over just as Alia started to go down. She ran to Alia's side, getting down on the floor with her. "Breath Alia, deep breaths, just breath. Is the nurse here today," she asked those friends of theirs starting to gather around.

"I don't know," said Ethan, "But I saw an ambulance outside. Maybe we should get them."

Suddenly a woman pushed her way through the kids and got on her knees right in front of Alia.

"Alia, honey, look at me. Come on, dear, you need to breathe."

Alia looked up, barely hearing the familiar voice that sounded like it was coming through a tunnel, and saw Charlie's mom. "Mom?" she said, just barely above a whisper.

"Yes, my baby girl, look at me. I need you to breathe. Deep breaths in and out, okay?" Ellen cupped Alia's head and whispered in her ear. "We are here with you, Alia, Me, Charlie, and Harper; we are all here for you. You're going to be alright. Just breathe."

Alia concentrated on breathing, and in a few minutes, the sounds all around her came back. Ellen helped her to her feet, brushing off her white graduation dress.

"Are you going to be good now?"

"Yes, I'm sorry. Trish, we saw, she saw him." Alia could breathe but talking was another thing.

"It's alright, never you mind what horrible things, I'm sure she said. This is your day, sweetie, not hers." Once again, Ellen whispered in Alia's ear. "Charlie sends his love."

Alia hugged Ellen, her real mother, and thanked her.

"We will be there, all three of us, you probably won't see us, but we will be there. We are all so proud of you," she whispered again. "Now I've got to go." Ellen left Alia in the good hands of her friends and returned to the auditorium.

Feeling much better, Alia put on her cap and gown and then got in line. Surrounded by her friends and classmates, she walked into the auditorium. The room was packed with people, so much so it was hard to make out anyone. Alia managed to find Crystal's parents only because George caught her attention from his aisle seat on the way down.

One by one, Alia and her fellow classmates received their diplomas. Alia hadn't expected more than perfunctory applause when it was her turn. Instead, she was greeted with a bit more. And in that way of connecting that she and Charlie had, as Alia posed for pics, her eyes went to the far back left corner of the auditorium and right to him. As promised, all three of them were there, trying to blend in, in the shadows. She smiled at them and walked back to her seat despite wanting to run out to them. Charlie tipped her a wink and smiled in the way that lit up his face.

Once everyone was done, the valedictorians made their speeches. A few teachers did as well, then Principal Edwards got up for one last time, holding in his hand a red folder. Alia, whose attention had been on Charlie the whole time, now had her attention on him because she knew what a red folder was.

"Before we leave," he began. "I have one last thing to do. Last week we had our awards ceremony. However, there is one special award left to give, and it's one that I do so rarely that I like to do it on graduation day instead." Holding up the red folder, Mr. Edwards said. "Now, most of you, except the teachers, of course, don't know the significance of a red folder."

Oh, I do, and it's not good.

"A red folder is a folder that is used in the public school system for students that, let's say, have had some behavioral challenges. It is supposed to be used as an indicator to a new student's principal he may have difficulties with. It is meant as a warning, an alert to keep special close attention to the student. I understand the need for these things, but personally, I hate them. Some schools, unfortunately, use them as a way of ostracizing students, to lay blame on them before there needs to be. To watch over them or make life for the student harder. I, however, do not. Because a red folder may tell me a student has a problem, it tells me very little about the student themselves.

So every time I get one of these, I make a point of getting to know the student behind it and doing what I can to lead that student in the right direction. At the risk of tooting my own horn, I have a pretty good track record of making these red folders disappear, and I'm very proud of each and every one of those students.

Four years ago, I got a red folder of a student right here, right now on this stage, doing something that I was told was most likely impossible. Some students usually only have a red folder for a year or two before coming to me here. This particular student has had one…well for quite some time, let's just say that." A slight chuckle from the audience. "And it was thick too." Bigger laughs. " Most principals would see a folder like that and write that student off, wait for them to make one mistake, and get rid of them. I took it as a challenge, and let me tell you, the first time I sat down with this student, I knew I had my hands full.

I saw a kid that was tough, stubborn, hard-headed, smart-mouthed, foul-mouthed, and angry at the whole world. But I also saw a kid that was smart, kind, strong, scared, but most of all determined. Determined to beat the odds and just tough, stubborn, and hard-headed enough to do it. And I have to say of all the kids I have graduated from the red folder club, I haven't been prouder of one more. This student defied the odds and accomplished more than either of us thought possible. I firmly believe this student will leave here and go on to achieve so much more and make not just myself but all of us in our community proud."

Alia felt her heart speed up as she listened to what was said. She had a very thick red folder. She had a red folder for a very long time. And she remembered day one of her high school career, sitting in front of Principal Edwards, staring him down like they were already sworn enemies. *But surely he doesn't mean me.* Alia looked around at her class, wondering who else would fit the bill. There was the boy from her martial arts class she used to take. He drank, smoked, shoplifted, and dated all the hot loose girls in school. She doubted he had changed much in four years. She was surprised he graduated at all.

"So it is with great honor that I present this award, the Principal's Award for Excellence and Outstanding Improvement, to a very much deserving young lady…Alia Miller."

As the auditorium erupted into applause, Alia just sat there stunned and unable to move. Sadly her first thought was that Trish must be furious. It took Crystal, Carina, and Raya pulling Alia to her feet to get her going, where she stumbled more than walked to the principal in a daze. Around her, her fellow students stood and applauded, and as she reached him, the audience rose as well.

What is going on? This can't be for me…there must be some kind of mistake.

Alia looked on at the standing and clapping audience, unable to believe what she saw. When she looked up in the back left corner, cheering and clapping, the loudest were Charlie, Mom, and Harper. *I think they forgot they are supposed to be incognito.*

Principal Edwards put his arm around Alia and handed her a plaque that she managed to take with her shaking hands. He then applauded her with the rest of them for a moment before hugging her and sending her back to the open arms of her classmates. They patted her on Alia's back as she stumbled back to her seat, her friends hugging her before letting her sit down, feeling on the verge of fainting. Alia looked at the plaque in her hands, not believing it was real.

I've never gotten an award before.

After that, the principal announced their graduating class, and hats were tossed, and they filed out once more into the cafeteria. The whole thing barely registered to Alia, she felt like she was in a dream. In the cafeteria, Alia found a chair to sit in, her legs no longer held her, and she stared at the plaque. She was slightly aware of people congratulating her, teachers coming up and telling her how proud they were of her, and her friends taking turns to look at the plaque as well. The kids around Alia bled off as they went outside to catch up to their parents. Pictures were being taken, relatives hugging students and friends hugging each other. They were thankful this part of their lives was over and sad for the same reason.

Forgetting about Trish and the family that showed up, Alia continued to sit there until it was only her and a few friends left who were reluctant to leave her just yet. Principal Edwards came over, congratulating Alia again then telling her to go with him, that someone wanted to see her before she went out to see her family. Alia followed him through the cafeteria to an office in the back. Inside, her family, her real family, waited for her.

Alia ran to them, and they all embraced her. First Charlie on one side, Ellen on the other, and Harper on the outside with his big meaty arms around them all, and like he had thought, she filled in the little room that was left perfectly.

Alia was crying, and when they let go, Charlie held her in his arms.

"I'm so proud of you, my sweet girl," he said

"We all are," said Ellen. "When the principal told us you were getting a special honor, we had to come. We wanted to anyway but were afraid to risk it. We knew we couldn't pass up seeing this."

"You deserve it, Alia. You've come a long way from the kid I thought I was going to have to lock in a jail cell. I'm so proud of you." Hopper said, taking her from Charlie's arms to give her one of his big crushing bear hugs."

Then Ellen took her in her arms. "My baby girl, I am so very proud of you. I'm glad Charlie caved. We wouldn't be here if he hadn't." she cried.

They hugged some more then dried their eyes. "We have to go. The boys need to start getting traffic moving, and I...I just need to go cry some more," said Ellen. "But we will see you later at Crystal's. We have all been invited to her graduation party, so get ready to be hugged and cried on some more. You better get out of here before Trish tries to come to find you."

"Okay, thank you all for coming. I'll see you in a little while."

Before she ran out, Charlie gave her a few tissues and a kiss on the forehead.

Alia dried her eyes and tried to compose herself on the way outside. There were people everywhere, but her group was easy to spot as they hung off to one side alone. Along with Trish was Trish's sister in a wheelchair, her husband, Her great Aunt Barbara (the one that didn't want her as a baby), and two other great aunts and uncles. She hated to share her joy with these imposters but had no choice, so she ran over, trying to pretend like her excitement was all for them.

Trish surprised Alia by hugging her, but then she was showing off the most considerable achievement she ever had or ever would have. They all hugged her, but there were no tears like with her real family, and the hugs were stiff, not soft and warm. Everyone said they were proud of her award, though she saw a glint of anger in Trish's eyes when she said it.

"What took you so long to come out," Trish asked. Was there a hint of suspicion in that question?

"I had to take some photos with the principal for the award," Alia thought up on the spot, once again noting how easy it was for her to lie.

"Yeah, I was stunned by that. I mean, the whole red folder story was bullshit, of course, but still, whatever makes him happy. Sad to think no one else deserved the award. I mean, surely your fellow classmates had a better person to get it than a C average student. And that speech, what on earth could possibly happen to make this shit hole town proud of one of us."

And there it was, folks. Trish had an uncanny ability to knock Alia down to size and take the wind out of her sails. Here she had been not only happy but proud of all the hard work she had done over the past four years, yet Trish couldn't let Alia have that one moment unspoiled. With her old anger boiling inside her, she wanted to take the plaque and smack Trish upside the head with it.

I'm not one of you, and if I have anything to do with it, I never will be.

Trish may have taken a chunk of her happiness away, but Alia had filled that hole with the kind of anger that made her more determined than ever to succeed with her plans.

I have a letter in my pocket that is proof I'm not the dummy you always said I was and a plaque that shows anyone can change, even a useless nothing like me.

Alia's great Uncle Walter came to her rescue. "Well, the award has nothing to do with grades, really. It's more about all-around improvement, and it's only for red folder students. The red folders are real. I've seen them. And you, kiddo, I am very proud of you. I will see you at your graduation party next week." He said his goodbyes so did the others, leaving her with Billy and Trish.

"Yeah, well, don't get all too high on that horse of yours, Alia. High school means nothing in the real world. You still don't have much of a future without college. You need to take time this week to go talk to that recruiter. If you insist on the Army, fine, but if you don't do something, you're going to find yourself flipping burgers."

"She can always work with you at the factory." Piped in Billy. He then slyly gave Alia a wink knowing Trish couldn't see.

Trish rolled her eyes. "Oh please, as lazy as she is, she wouldn't last a day."

Alia wasn't about to argue the fact that she had a job, even if the academy hadn't been an option. It was all pointless. Trish was never wrong, so she just agreed and said she would see if she had the time.

"There's no rush for now. I have the summer camp job first."

"Yeah, well, plans can change. I think you are wasting your time with that summer camp thing, but you won't listen to me, you never do. I have a feeling that basic training in the summer would be much better than in the winter. Just saying. Speaking of plans, I guess you will be off to Crystal's. You know it's people like her having their graduation parties today that ruined it for us. We had to wait till next week, or no one was able to come."

"Uh yeah, well, she starts her internship in a week anyway, so they had to get it out of the way. But yea, I'll be either there or at one of my other friends' places."

"Oh Alia, what other friends?" she scoffed. "It's not like they are breaking down the door every day to come see you."

At that, Billy started to drag Trish away. "Come on, the kid is done, let's go get some drinks, this whole school mess just depresses me, and there are too many cops around here."

"Okay. Alia, don't forget curfew at ten Sunday. And don't give me that look. I don't care if you are grown and graduated or that school is over. You still have a curfew as long as you're living under my roof."

Which won't be much longer.

Crystal and a few of their friends had come up behind Alia at that point.

"Damn." said Raya, "She is on a tear again."

"This is her being nice," said Crystal, and they all laughed.

With things winding down, Alia, Crystal, George, and their parents piled into the Buick to head to their house. On the way out, they passed Charlie again, and this time he waved at them all, giving Alia a wink.

"See you all when I'm done," he said as he waved them through.

Alia blew him a kiss and laughed when she saw him blush. *My sweet boy.*

The graduation party at Crystal's was lovely, full of family, love, and laughter, as was the case in their home. Ellen was the first of the Harper's to arrive. She sat with Alia talking about the award and excitement over everything. The boys showed up a bit later, having safely gotten everyone out of the school. When they all were there, Alia showed them her grades. Harper gave her yet another of his big crushing hugs and told her how proud he was of her. Ellen hugged her and cried. Charlie told her it didn't surprise him at all and gave her a peck on the cheek, being sure no one would see. There were amongst friends here, but it was best to not push things.

Before long after everyone had their fill of good food and cake, Alia hugged Crystal goodbye, and she and Charlie headed for the cabin. On the ride up, Charlie apologized for his reaction to seeing her come to the school. He just thought it was best to pretend like he didn't see her.

"You know I can't look at you without smiling at least a little," he said. Then you would smile and…."

"And the shit would hit the fan if she saw."

"Exactly. So are you ready for this last week, at home, I mean?"

"That's not my home Charlie. Never was. I feel more at home at your house than I do anywhere except for Crystal's…and the cabin, which is strange since I've never been there before."

"Sure you have. We took you up there all the time. You loved it, used to play in the creek trying to catch toadies, as you called them. And I taught you how to fish."

"No, now wait, I thought Trish and my Uncle taught me how to fish."

"Nope, you caught your first fish right there at the cabin. You were about two at the time."

More lies. Is my whole life one big lie or what? "I wish I could remember. It sucks I can't remember any of it. I remember the apartment we lived in after she got me back, but that's about as far back as I can."

"It's not about what you remember, Alia. It's about how you feel. And I know you feel like we are family. That's what is important."

"You're right, of course."

"Back to what I was saying, though, have you packed any?"

"As much as I can without it being obvious. George is coming over Monday and getting what I have in the closet and some of my clothes. I'll have to pack most of it once she leaves for my Aunt's Saturday morning to get the party ready. I'm surprised she is letting Crystal drive me over and not making me come set up. It's not like it's a surprise or anything."

"Any neighbors we have to worry about? I don't want you to be moving out stuff, and she gets a call."

"I don't think so. Even if there is someone, I don't think she would leave the party. I would just have to come up with something to calm her down, but I don't think we have to worry about that."

"Good, okay, almost there, so no more talking about that."

"I don't need to talk about what I want to do," she said coyly, dancing her fingers along his leg.

"I don't know, some talking is okay." he smiled.

At the cabin, Alia called dibs on the shower. She had barely gotten wet when Charlie joined her as she had hoped he would. Once again, their connection was more substantial than it had ever been before. They took turns cleaning each other, taking their time, enjoying the moment right up until the water ran cold. Laughing and kissing, they towel dried each other off, then ran for the warmth of the bed covers, where they spent the rest of the night making love.

Chapter 19
It's my party

Monday morning, it didn't feel right to Alia to not be getting up and going to school. It didn't feel like it usually did during a typical summer vacation, either. Today she woke up knowing that part of her life was over. Alia had mixed feelings about it.

Alia sat up in bed, looking around the room that would no longer be hers by the end of the week. Most of her things were still unpacked, so it wouldn't look like she was leaving for anything more than a summer away. Saturday morning, after her mother left to go to her Aunt's, Crystal and George were coming to pack up the rest of what she would be keeping. Her whole life, other than a few things she would need and what she had to leave behind so Trish wouldn't suspect anything, was to be taken to Crystal's house and stored there until Alia returned.

Sitting in bed, Alia was hit with a disturbing range of emotions. She was happy to finally be moving out from under Trish's control. She was looking forward to a life framed by her choices, good or bad. There was worry mixed in there, of course. Worry that Trish would somehow find out and try to stop her. Worry that Alia would do something to mess it all up. She was scared of Trish's reaction if she found out but realized that she was even more scared of what Charlie would do if Trish hurt her again.

The one that surprised Alia most of all was that she was sad. Sad mostly of what could have been. Eighteen years is a long time. Alia herself had grown in ways she would have never thought possible. In only four years, she had become someone she could be proud of, and in three months, if all went well, she would have grown even more. So why was it then that someone like Trish could change so little.

Still, just a child herself when Trish had Alia, there was plenty of room to grow and mature. Yet she seemed stuck. Sure she had a job, paid the bills, and did a somewhat decent job of keeping a roof over their heads. Yet emotionally, Trish was still that nasty, angry girl that treated good people like the Harper's like dirt while bending over backward to please the bad ones. Although things got better from time to time, Trish never abandoned her abusive ways, only modified them to better suit different situations.

Even Saturday, after seeing her only child accomplish something many told her would never happen, Trish had to use words that cut. It was like she couldn't genuinely be happy for Alia no matter what. Now sitting here on her bed, Alia wanted nothing more than to be gone from this place, yet tears spilled down her cheeks.

This is it; it's over. Any chance she ever had to be a decent mother to me ends when I walk out of here Saturday, even if she doesn't realize it yet. There is no way she will ever want to speak to me once she finds out I am a cop. I really don't want to talk to her anymore anyway, so why the hell am I sitting here crying?

Alia glanced up at the camera, knowing that Charlie wasn't watching at the moment. Since the first night they made love, she had always sensed when he was watching and when he wasn't. He was working the early shift so they could spend at least some of what time they had left together.

Alia herself actually needed to get ready to go to work but still couldn't bring herself to get out of bed. Inside she felt as though her mind was waging war with itself. One side wanted to be happy to soon be free. The other was sad that things were ending while so many issues were unresolved. Alia felt like she needed to talk to someone she trusted who could give her advice on how she was supposed to deal with this conflict inside of her.

I want my mother, And not the one in the other room either.

As if the thought conjured her, Alia could hear the woman that stole her from her loving family in the kitchen. A few minutes later, she smelled coffee brewing. Getting up, Alia went to her bathroom, washed her face, and put a few drops in her eyes to hide the redness from crying. She then got ready for work, hoping to escape before her mother started any shit.

Once dressed, Alia went out to get Ebony for his morning walk and realized she had one more thing to be sad about. She was going to miss the little dog. Ebony belonged to her mother, but Alia was the one that took care of him most of the time. Pets were another thing Trish was oddly controlling over. She insisted all the pets were hers, even one's gotten specifically for Alia. Like the rabbit she had years ago (which died when she and her mother had to leave their house for a week because her then-boyfriend had gotten into a drunken rage). And Goldie, the dog they had before moving back to Union County, which her mother insisted they couldn't afford to keep.

Yet when it came to cleaning up after them, that was always Alia's job. Just like it had often become her job to get rid of them once her mother had grown tired. Ebony was the only pet they had ever kept for so long.

I would take you with me if I could dogo.

In the kitchen, Ebony was under Trish's feet trying to get her attention, but Trish was not much for anyone until her morning coffee, not even that cute fluff. As soon as he saw Alia, he bounded over to her and jumped into her arms.

"You ready to go outside, boy." Barking, he jumped down, ran down the hall, and grabbed at the leash nailed next to the door.

"Wait before you go. What are your plans for this week?"

Getting the fuck out of here

"I start a little late today, but I have work at the library all week. dinner at Crystal's on Wednesday, and I have a bit of shopping to do before I head to camp on Monday."

"I still don't understand why you have to be there so early. The rest of the kids won't be out of school for at least two more weeks."

"I told you they need people to clean up. The place has been empty all winter, so there is plenty of work to do. And I could use the money."

"Yes, and speaking of which, how will I get my money? You may not be here, but I'm not storing your shit for free. I'm still going to need something."

Of course, that is all you fucking care about. It's always what you can get out of people, even your own kid. "I'm getting a cell phone. The way they pay us is on a debit card that has an app, so I can always just send you the money." *Not that you should be getting a damn dime.*

"What do you need a cell phone for? You have managed this long without one."

That's what you think. "I'll need one for work. Everything is done on smartphones now, you know that. If it wasn't for the tablet the school provided, I would have needed one."

"Well, I don't care as long as I don't have to pay for it and you still pay your bills. Also, as long as you're under my roof, I will have your number and your phone code to get it open."

"Why the phone code?'

"Because Alia, adult or not, I am still responsible for you."

Uh no, you're not that's what being an adult is all about.

"That and I don't trust you."

Well, at least that is the truth.

"You have poor taste in people and bad judgment. I'm not going to have your stupid shit cause me problems."

"Okay, fine, I'll let you know when I get it. I better take Ebony out before his bladder bursts." Outside, at last, walking the dog Alia no longer felt sad about leaving.

For once, Trish's shit has put me into a better mood.

The rest of the week, Alia did her best to avoid Trish. After Trish had gone to work Monday, George and Crystal picked her up from the library and took her to the apartment. There they got out as many boxes and things Trish wouldn't notice missing when she checked in on her at night as they could. Then it was back to work. Charlie still came to see her and went by the school on Monday and Tuesday night.

Wednesday, early before going to work, Alia went to the Harper's house. Charlie and Harper gave her several tests and asked questions, some trick questions, on all the things she had learned over the past few months. Alia ended up doing a great job, and Harper felt confident the little leg up would put her on equal footing with the rest of the class.

"You have to understand that in a lot of cases at that academy, your classmates come from police families, so they will be familiar with the material before they even get there. So now you should know as much as they do, with that and how well you shoot I have no doubt you'll do good," said Harper

Alia thanked them all and went to work for the day before returning later for dinner. Coming up from the lake, Alia noticed that both patrol cars were in the drive behind the house. She was the last to arrive. Had she come from the front, the surprise graduation party they threw for her would have been ruined when she saw all the cars.

When Alia walked in, they all jumped out in surprise. Along with the Harper's were Crystal and her family, her close friends, Mrs. Stackhouse, Principal Edwards, and even a few officers she knew.

That evening sitting on the couch next to Charlie, their hands intertwined, Crystal next to her, her friends and family around her, Alia felt a little homesick. She leaned in on Charlie, and he put his arm around her knowing just how she was feeling. All this time, she had been so focused on missing Charlie she didn't realize just how much she was going to miss all of them as well.

Thursday, Alia was invited back for one last family dinner. That night it was just the four of them and Ellen's fantastic food. During the meal, they all laughed and talked, avoiding the subject of Alia going away for the time being. After dinner, they sat in the living room talking about anything other than how this was their last night as a family for a while.

Alia and Charlie would eventually get together on weekends at the cabin, but coming into town would be too much of a risk. It had to seem like Alia really was away at the camp. Harper and Ellen did have plans to come up for the Fourth of July for a few hours during the day, but then towards dark, the boys would have to come back to town to work. They would have their fourth on the third so they could all be together.

Friday was Alia's last day working at the library, and she found that to be almost the most challenging part so far. This particular library held nearly as many memories for her as it did books. When she was little, this was the first library outside of a school she had ever been to. Right away, she fell in love with everything about the place, from the thousands of books right down to the smell.

When Alia had come to see her dad, the library was a sanctuary from bullies and a safe place for her to stay when her father had a fire call. When she moved back to Union county, the library was like home to her and where Alia would often go when things at home got terrible, or she just needed to hide from the world. Eventually, it ended up being her first job. Later she would find out her boss was also once a social worker that had fought on her behalf but lost. And for the past month, it had been one of the very few places Alia and Charlie could get together. It wasn't going to ever be her last day walking through those doors, but like with many things, it would be different when she did.

Saying goodbye to Mrs. Stackhouse was like saying goodbye to someone that was more than a boss or a friend. It was like saying goodbye to family. Only a good family, not the people she'd grown up with. Before they parted, Mrs. Stackhouse gifted Alia with something that she would always treasure far beyond what it was worth. She knew that the first Stephen King book Alia ever read was a copy of Cujo Alia had fished out of a dumpster when she was about ten. Mrs. Stackhouse had found her another copy, only this one was a first edition signed by King himself. Looking at it, tears came to her eyes. She grabbed Mrs. Stackhouse, hugging her for all her worth, and thanked her profusely.

"You must promise to write to me while you're at the academy. No calls, you know I like things more the old-fashioned way." She smiled that radiant smile of hers and hugged Alia. "You, my dear, are like a granddaughter to me, if you don't mind me saying."

"Not at all. I take that as a compliment." Her own grandparents were gone; the last one, her father's mother, passed a year prior in Florida with her Uncle, who had moved there shortly after her father died. Though pleasant enough to her, that side of the family never reached out to her either. This kind but stern woman was the closest thing she ever had to a grandmother for a long time.

With summer in the air, that Friday was very busy. So Alia walked home from the bus stop alone, no Charlie to go see at the school. After taking Ebony out for a walk, Alia lay in her bed, holding onto the little furball and crying. It was her last night in the room she'd had longer than any other room she had ever had before. As much as a large part of her was happy, there was still a part that was a little heartbroken.

Saturday morning Alia woke up anxious. If anything was going to go wrong, today would be the day. Of course, if Trish did any real snooping once Alia left, she would realize Alia took an awful lot of stuff not needed at a summer camp. Like her father's fire helmet. The pictures of him and others she had made copies of so those could stay as well as her collection of horror movie posters. There were some things she would have to leave behind forever because they were too easily missed. Like the dream-catcher Crystal had gotten her a few years ago when she had been plagued by nightmares. As well as her collectibles from sports teams, amusement parks, and special trips. Those things actively displayed on her walls and shelves would be missed by her, but they would also be missed by Trish if she came into the room.

Alia also had to leave most of her books behind though she was taking her most valuable ones to store at Crystal's. She took pics with her phone of some things, others could be easily replaced later. Most likely, once Trish found out Alia was gone for good, she would toss everything out. The thought of her tossing out books upset Alia, but the risk was too significant to try and save them. The idea that Trish may not even be mad never occurred to her. She knew Trish would be pissed. It would have been one thing for her to leave. But for her to become a cop? That would just be a slap in the face. Then when she found out about Charlie…shit would really hit the fan.

Until Trish woke up and left, Alia had to busy herself looking like it was just any typical Saturday. That meant taking Ebony for his morning walk, feeding him and herself, and taking a shower. Around ten, Trish was awake as well as Billy, and so far, she seemed to be in a pretty good mood. Still, Alia did her best to avoid her, claiming to have to pack her bags, so she could hide out in her room. At noon Trish and Billy left. When Alia was sure they were gone for good, she texted Crystal.

About twenty minutes later, Crystal and George knocked on the door. Charlie had wanted to come and help, but she talked him out of it just in case Trish did have her being watched. The two of them helped her pack the last of her things that she felt she couldn't live without. Then one last time, Alia walked Ebony, who seemed to know something was up. The poor thing clung to her and whimpered the whole time.

Back inside, Alia loved on the dog for a while then let him go with tears in her eyes. Crystal gave her a big hug telling her it was all going to be worth it in the end. Before leaving, the last thing they did was take the security camera out of the vent.

When they arrived at Crystal's to unload, Charlie was there. Alia went right to him, where he wrapped his arms around her and let her have a good cry. "I should have stolen the damn dog." She said, "Would serve her right."

With all the things she wasn't taking to the academy packed up in storage, Alia went to say goodbye to two people that were also like parents to her. They gifted her with a stationary set and made her promise to write them despite being able to call and text.

"Writing is different. It gives you time to reflect on the day and really appreciate what is going on around you," Albert said. Being as they were catholic, they did a blessing of protection for her as well. Alia didn't ever have the heart to tell them she was atheist and, despite not believing, took the gesture for what it was, their way of telling her they loved her.

Back outside, they left her and Charlie alone for a bit. Alia would be coming back to him tonight for one final weekend at the cabin, but for now, she needed to lean on him for strength to get through the rest of the day. At the end of the Buick where they had their first kiss, Charlie held her tight, whispering in her ear.

"Just one last thing, Alia, that's all you need to do and more than she deserves. You've got this. Remember, you owe her nothing. This is all about you, don't let her forget that." Charlie kissed like the first time, then once on the forehead, and let her go despite how much he wanted to make her call it off. With final waves, she, Crystal, and George headed out of town and out of Union county to her Aunt's house.

About forty-five minutes later, they arrived. Alia was surprised at how many cars there were parked not only in the driveway but the road leading to it and the apartment complex behind it. That's where Alia told Crystal to park, and they got out. Alia hung by the car. With Charlie not there, she felt the anxiety growing in her as they had driven closer. She didn't think anything would happen today since it was her mother's victory day, but Alia had a feeling that since she woke up, things would not go smoothly.

"Take a deep breath, and let's go do this thing," said Crystal. "Sooner done sooner, you can get back to Charlie. And look, our friends are here." She said, pointing to the front of the house where Raya, Ethan, Lara, Joel, and

Carina were standing around, most likely avoiding her mother until Alia got there. Still, she wouldn't move.

"So what's going on? Are we just going to stay out here in the parking lot all day?"

Alia looked around at all the cars. "This is a circus. And I'm the clown, only not funny."

"Maybe it won't be so bad. You did say you got along with some of them right."

"Yes, I get along with them. But I don't know them. I used to be close to a few of them, but that was before we moved back to Union county. Most of them I only see on holidays now. I've tried calling, interacting online, the usual, but these people never have time for me. I'm just the kid that used to be dumped on their doorstep all the time. Never once have any of them ever made any real effort to make me feel like family. Here I am wasting my time with a bunch of people that under normal circumstances won't give me the time of day when my real family wants to be with me and can't." Alia ranted and wiped a tear from her eye. *Seems all I ever do anymore is cry.*

Crystal took her best friend into her arms and gave her a big long hug. "I don't think you're a clown." she offered a smile. "You said it yourself, though, that you have to end this all the right way. If not, you could have stayed at my place these past few weeks and been done with her. You didn't put yourself through all of that to walk away now. It's good there are a lot of them here. More witnesses to see that you are letting your mother have her party. You end this the right way and if they don't want to have anything to do with you, then fuck them. Because it's a two-way street, Alia. You don't have to beg anyone to be a part of your life. There's plenty of us that want to be and wouldn't make you beg. Now let's join our friends, and you walk into that backyard with the biggest grin you can muster. Think of Charlie if you have to. In a few hours, your part will be done and what they do from there is up to them."

"Have I ever said how much I love that you are so much smarter than me?" Alia grinned.

"And you are so much stronger than me…so let's go prove it." The three of them joined the other kids, and they all walked in together.

It's like I brought my own army, Alia thought with a laugh.

The back of her Aunt's yard was full of people. Aunts, uncles, great aunts and uncles, cousins, even some non-blood family that was like family (to her mother, not her). Seeing them all made Alia homesick for her real family. Not one of these people gave a shit about her enough when she was a baby to foster her. They didn't lift a finger to help her mother get her back either. All those days and nights Alia had spent in fear, not one of them tried to help or even console her. Just looking at them all drinking, eating, and acting so happy made her sick. Alia stopped before anyone noticed the group arrived, feeling the urge to flee.

"You need to put a smile on your face and act like you're happy, or you're going to blow this whole thing." Said George. "Think about Charlie. Hell, think about wringing Trish's neck if you have to but smile."

The thought of that actually did make her smile. Taking a deep breath, Alia plastered the best smile she could manage and joined the party.

The party went pretty much as Alia had imagined it. Her impostor family greeted her with open arms, but their hugs felt stiff and forced. Trish, already working her way through a case of beer, bragged nonstop about how everyone said she would never graduate now here she was. By the skin of her teeth, maybe (of course, she couldn't help getting a barb in), but she did it. And if you listened to how she put it, it was all because of her, even though Trish never once helped Alia do schoolwork.

Alia was congratulated on not only graduating but also the award she got. The party was decorated with her school colors and many graduation things she knew for a fact her mother got at the dollar tree. The giant full-size sheet cake was very nice, though, and professionally done. On a table was a small pile of gifts and many cards.

The party started off slow. Alia and her friends sat to one side, joined by a few cousins around the same age. When it was time to cut the cake, Alia did so, trying real hard to not imagine plunging it into Trish, who at that point had drunk herself into her flirty whore stage where she thought she and Alia were best friends. That meant Trish was hanging all on her with an arm on Alia's shoulder while she cut the cake.

After that, Alia got to sit back down and open the gifts and cards. There were a few cute things like a bear, sunblock, a book on plants. What she found amusing was the framed photo of the last family reunion they had the year before. Alia wasn't even in the picture. In fact, there was never a family reunion group photo with her in it. At first, that had just been an accident. Alia had wandered off to read or play in the woods. But the last few, she had avoided the photoshoot on purpose, not wanting to be part of the whole fake ass mess.

The cards she got were all the basic corny graduation congratulations. It was what was inside them that she was hoping for, and that was the cash. Trish's sister had gotten her a savings bond that would be worth one hundred dollars…in five years. Alia, usually grateful for any gift, had to work hard not to roll her eyes at that. It didn't help that her uncle went on and on about how if she saved it, the money would be a pleasant surprise….in five years.

After that, some of her friends left (telling her they left things for her in Crystal's car that were police related), and Alia sat with some of her older relatives talking. They all had questions for her, but her Uncle Walter monopolized most of the conversation.

"So Alia, now what are your plans? Taking the summer off or getting right into it."

Oh, boy, was she tempted to tell them all the truth. Especially since Walter was one of the few members of her family, she kinda liked. But of course, Trish was right there, and so were too many people that would snitch.

"I have a job this summer as a camp counselor at a summer camp I went to once as a kid."

"She got a scholarship that year. I certainly didn't pay for her to screw off all summer. After all the trouble she had gotten into that year, she's lucky I let her go." Said Trish like she was proud.

Ignoring her, Uncle Walter continued. "When does that start?"

"Monday. Some of us are going early to clean up the place and get it ready for the kids to show up in a few weeks."

"That sounds good. It should be fun. What about after?"

"I still have my job at the library, only now I'll be full time. I may take some college courses online as well."

"But no more free rides from me." Said Trish. "Starting when she gets back, she pays her third of the bills. That is unless she does what I told her to do, and if she's smart, she will."

"Oh yes." Said Walter. "The military thing. That's nice and all, but if you can work and go to college, I would think that would be the best option." He said, giving Alia a wink.

Alia could see Trish becoming visibly upset. "You surprise me, Walter. Since you're a vet, I would think you would encourage her to do the smart thing and join the navy or the army. They can send her to college too, you know."

"Yes, they can. After four years of sacrificing both her mind and body, she can. If she's not dead from a war, some idiot has gotten us into. I believe Alia is smart enough to know what is right for her. Of course, you could give her a break and let her stay with you for free so she can afford to take more college courses at one time."

Alia felt like slapping her forehead with her hand. The last thing she needed was Walter starting shit for her.

"No, no, absolutely not. Her free ride is over. If she wants to waste her time trying to do college, fine, but she's going to pay her own way. She needs to learn how to support herself. I certainly won't be doing it."

From then on, the conversation turned to lighter topics like stories from her childhood that were comical, if not a bit on the sad side under the circumstances. About an hour later, her Uncle asked her to walk him out to his car as he was leaving. Once they were alone, he gave her a hug.

"Okay, kiddo, now tell me what you're really doing this summer. And don't give me that bullshit story about no camp either. Your mother may see past it, but she's never seen much past her own damn self. I know bullshit when I hear it," Walter said lightheartedly.

Alia turned to him, not sure how to proceed.

"Come on, I saw the look on your face, hell I saw the look in your eyes. You have had a look about you all day like you're playing along and want to be here about as much as the rest of them do. You're a smart kid Alia. To hell with what your mother says. If you don't have a real plan, I will be sorely disappointed."

"I have a plan, but it's complicated, not really something I can talk about, not without maybe causing issues for people I care about."

"I wonder," Walter said, looking like he was pondering something. "Is it possible that you already know? You do, don't you?" He said more to himself than to her. "First, let me tell you a little story. Years ago, when I married into this family, I didn't know what I was getting into. Hell, my wife didn't know. She was young and naive. Slowly I started to realize that there were some deep down fundamental issues at the core and heart of this family. The closet racism, sexism, and homophobia that can penetrate all families were the least of those issues but still enough to make me second guess being a part of it. By the time I learned that there were deeper and darker issues, the pedophilia, missing wives, and other things too dark to mention, it was too late for me to do anything other than be a part of it."

"What did you do?"

"I cheated on my wife when she was pregnant. I was young and stupid, and she wasn't fulfilling my needs at the time. It was a mistake I instantly regretted and never did again. The girl got pregnant. I went to some of the older men in the family asking for advice. What I got was help. Help I didn't really want. Not like that anyway. Let's just say the situation was dealt with, and my wife was none the wiser. But that gave them the dirt on me they needed to trap me. That trap ended eight months ago when my wife died. I have plans too. My bags are packed, and my house is sold. They think I'm going into a retirement home to rest easy. They don't know that I am getting as far away from them as my old ass can get.

My point is that you are the only reason I have stuck around these past several months. For all the years I stood by, knowing the hell that your mother was putting you through, I felt the least I could do was tell you the truth before I went. And maybe offer a little help. But you already know, don't you?"

"I don't know what you're talking about."

"I think you do, I think you know all about the Harper's, and I think it's them you're protecting. It's no secret the people your mother hates more than her own family are the ones that were your foster parents."

Alia stood there, looking at this man, her great Uncle wondering if he indeed was an ally. To be fair, he had treated her better than the rest of them did. Her being dumped off at his house never seemed to be a burden to him or his wife. She always thought it was because their own kids had run off years before leaving them alone. Now she wondered if there were other reasons as well.

"Your mother, of course, spins a different story than the truth. To hear her say it, they were more than ready to be rid of you. But that was just another of her lies we let her have. Those people loved you like you were their own. They were only doing the right thing by helping your mother get on her feet, and in the end, Trish turned on them as soon as she got what she wanted. Now I don't know what she had on them or if it was even real, but you can guarantee even if it wasn't, she would have convinced people it was. That's what she does. Everyone in this family has dirt on one another. She's the only one that has actually gone outside of the family with it. I'm sure you have heard stories about your cousin Ray?"

"Of course, he went to prison for rape."

"For raping your mother, to be exact, only that wasn't necessarily the truth. Your mother, well, she was very active at a young age."

"You mean slutty."

"Well, that's a vulgar term, but not inaccurate. Granted, he was eighteen and should have known better, and no, I'm not excusing what he did. I'm just saying he wasn't her first and far from her last. And it wasn't just the one time like she said. There wasn't a problem until he got a girlfriend, his own age he fell in love with and dropped Trish. Your mother went straight to the police, and she knew what she was doing. She knew the family took care of this kind of thing in house."

"Yeah, like they did with Bobby? She tried going to the cops then too."

"No, what she did was take you to the hospital and put you through something she didn't have to just to prove a point. She knew damn well he never got that far. Trish used that as leverage to force their hands into giving her what she wanted. And what happened to him...well, it wasn't the family that set him right...not this one anyway."

Alia was about to ask him who it was then? Someone, several someone's, had beaten the man to a pulp. Then thinking she may even know, she decided she didn't want him to confirm it after all. Some things are best left alone.

"My point, though, is that your mother will stop at nothing to win. Even ruining a good family isn't above her. And you, of all people, understand just what she is capable of. So I am hoping that before I leave, you realize that you need to get as far away from her and this family as you can before they trap you as well. If you have a plan, I can help. I can't do much, but I have to do something."

Alia thought about this hoping she wasn't kicking a wasp nest. "I leave Monday morning for the Police academy. I have a job at the Sheriff's office in Union county waiting for me when I return. And yes, they told me everything."

"More importantly, you believed them?"

"Of course, as you said, I know what she is capable of."

"You know once she finds out, hell once the family finds out, your own your own."

"No, I'm not. I have my real family and friends to look out for me," Alia said, realizing the truth for herself the first time.

"Glad to hear it," Walter smiled. Out of his pocket, her Uncle pulled an envelope. "This is your real graduation gift."

Alia opened it and saw a check for five thousand dollars. "Uh, uncle Walter, I think you wrote this check out wrong."

"I most certainly did not. I may be old, but I'm not foolish. I don't know what all you have planned, but this should help get you started your new life. Use it if you need to. Save it if you can. Because once word gets out what you have done, well, you were never really a part of this family anyway. You always belonged to someone else." With that, Walter got into his car. "Good luck, kid. I have my new phone number in there. I expect to hear how you're doing."

Alia waved as he drove away. *My life just gets stranger and stranger, I swear.*

Not long after that, Alia was more than ready to go feeling like she had spent a fair amount of time watching her mother strut around like a peacock. Her Aunt had been taken inside to rest, so out of pure courtesy, Alia went in to thank her for hosting the party. Trish was in the living room when she came out of the bedroom.

"So, I guess you're going?" She said,
It was apparent that Trish had had more than her fair share of the alcohol that had gone around the party and was now past the point where she was nice. Alia wanted to bolt from the house but stood her ground because this would be the last of it.

"Yeah, I have something to do tonight. George and Crystal want to get home before it gets dark as well. It's a long drive."

"Oh, don't give me that shit, Alia. You think I don't know you by now, you think after all these years I can't read you like a book?"

I'd like to see you try to read a book.

"You have been in one of your shit moods all day. I spent, hell, lots of money to get this party for you, your family has spent...they gave you gifts...and the money. Oh, by the way...give me the money."

"What are you talking about?"

"I'm talking about the fact that you are not going to leave me high and dry. I think you think you are just going to walk out of here and not pay me for a few weeks. I got news for you, chickie; it ain't gonna be that way."

"Mom, we talked about this. I told you I would pay you to store my stuff."

"Yes, you will, and your first two weeks install,...payment is due now. So eighty bucks, fork it over."

Shaking her head, Alia reached into her pocket and fished out the money. Alia didn't want to give it to her but had promised Charlie she would keep her cool. The last thing they needed was a fight just days before going to the academy. Handing the money over to Trish.

"And don't try to screw me out on the rest of the money, or your shit will be out on the curb, including your precious crap from your daddy," Trish said with a sneer.

"I won't," Alia said and tried to leave.

"So just what is it you're in such a big hurry for? Huh, what are you really up to?"

Alia turned back around, and Trish was giving her a strange knowing look.

"I told you I'm going to Crystal's. We are probably going to someone's house to hang out for the night."

Trish walked closer to her. "Who are you really going to see, Alia? Who is it you're not telling me about? Is it whoever is texting you over Crystal's phone?"

All day Charlie had sent heart emojis and general words of encouragement to her via Crystal's phone since Alia couldn't very well just pop out her own. She didn't even want Trish to think she'd gotten her new one yet. Alia assumed Trish hadn't even noticed. She never seemed to notice Alia any other time.

"Whoever it is sure did put a smile on your face."

"It was just memes. Funny stupid memes."

"Memes my ass. I know the sound of a text alert when I hear it, Alia. Just how stupid do you think I am?"

Oh, that was the million-dollar question now, wasn't it? That was one that Trish was very fond of asking, and Alia wanted to answer so bad it almost made her sweat not to. She had always wanted to have the balls to tell her mother just how stupid she was, and now would be a perfect time. Only she couldn't. If Trish hurt her again, Charlie may do something he would never be able to come back from. She could never put him in a position like that.

"One of our other friends was sending us memes through messages, so yes, in that regard, you are right."

"Then I guess she wouldn't have an issue showing me."

Alia laughed and shook her head. "Look, you're drunk, you don't know what you're talking about, and Crystal, sure as shit, is not going to show you her phone. I'm going now, I'll get a phone and call you in the morning, and we can talk then if you want." As Alia tried to walk away, Trish came up behind her, pulling her by the back of her shirt, essentially choking her a bit. Alia spun around, and Trish was right there in her face.

"Don't lie to me. I'm not stupid. I know all about you hanging around the gun range with that piece of shit, Sheriff."

"Seriously?" Alia said, trying to stay calm. She hadn't been to the range for over a month. "You need to go lay down somewhere you're drunk, and you have no idea what the hell you are saying."

"I do so know. Last week, I got a phone call from someone who saw you at the range last month talking to the Sheriff. Funny how that was right before you ran off with that faggot son of his. You know he's a faggot, right Alia? I always knew he was a little freak. People say they have never seen him with a girl."

"We're not talking about Charlie. We are talking about Harper," Alia said, hoping her mother was drunk enough to divert the conversation to a slightly better topic.

"Yeah, I know you have been hanging around him. You have been lying to me too. I knew you were. I knew something was up. Tell me, Alia...have you fucked him yet?"

Alia wasn't totally shocked by Trish's accusation, but she still felt her face burn red hot. "I'm leaving, you're drunk, and I refuse to talk to you when you're like this. I'll call you in the morning."

"Oh, what's the matter? You can't deal with the truth."

"No, I can't deal with you when you're like this. Nothing I say is going to be good enough for you anyway."

"So you admit it."

"That I was talking to the Sheriff, yeah sure, so fucking what? Did whoever call you tell you I was at the range collecting brass to turn in to make money for my senior projects? Huh? Of course, they didn't." That was actually true, as she did collect the brass after shooting to make some money.

"Typical Alia, you have an answer for everything. Still doesn't explain why you were talking to him."

"He talked to me. He wanted to make sure I was staying out of trouble, I guess, I don't fucking know. You're just being paranoid. You have had too much to drink, and when you do, everyone's out to get you. I'm not out to get you. I'm just going to spend some time with my friends before I don't see them all summer."

"Fine, then get the hell out of here." Alia went to walk away. "But Alia...if I find out you have said anything to anyone, it will be your ass when you get back. You're still living in my house, you will stay the hell away from that pig and his faggot son. You have no clue what kind of people you're messing with."

Oh, I have a pretty good idea.

Alia walked away shaking so much that she didn't even bother to say goodbye to anyone else. She just marched angrily out to the back yard then down the drive to the front. In the Buick, on the way back to her real life, she told George and Crystal what Trish had said after she had a chance to calm down.

"That would explain why she was so pissed that week she took a shot at my face. Billy said she had gotten a phone call."

"Who do you think ratted you out?"

"Could have been any of her crackhead friends. Not someone real close to her, or she would have found out about it sooner. I didn't go to the range after the week they told me about being my foster parents. Harper felt it may be too risky. Besides, Charlie and I were trying to spend as much time together as we could."

"It doesn't matter." Said Crystal. "It's done, Alia. You're free from her."

"Am I really? Best case scenario I graduate from the academy, she's still here in town. We are bound to run into each other. Hell with the way Billy speeds, I'm sure of it."

"But you won't be alone. Harper said the first three months, you are still in training and will never be left alone."

"Great, it'll be like my childhood all over again when she flips the fuck out."

"Only in this case, she will end up in cuffs. She's not going to start shit with you, and even if she does, you have the entire Sheriff's department that's got your back. Your free, Alia...even if you don't graduate from the academy. I doubt Charlie would have you go crawling back to her. It's over."

"Yeah, I know." *Then why is it I don't feel like it is?*

Getting into Charlie's awaiting arms when they got to the Harper's house was what Alia needed more than anything. The anxiety and tension she felt all day instantly melted away. Suddenly she was exhausted and just wanted the whole day to be over.

"How did it go?" He asked

Alia began to sob in his arms. Charlie held her tighter. "It's over, Alia. You don't have to deal with her or any of them ever again if you don't want to. At least not without me by your side."

"Can we go…can we just get out of here?" she asked, looking up at him.

"Yeah, sure, of course. I think Mom and Dad would like to say goodbye first, though. You up for that at least?"

Alia nodded, then as she let go of Charlie, she noticed something odd about his left wrist. Taking his hand in hers, she turned it over. Charlie's wrist was wrapped in plastic wrap, the same kind used for leftovers. Under it, there was a very small patch of his skin that was red around four little letters tattooed there.

"Charlie…you really did it?" Looking down again, Alia couldn't believe she was seeing her name on the inside of his wrist where it would always be.

"Told you I wanted to. I figured now would be a good time. You know, so when I got to missing you, I could just look at it."

"Does it hurt?"

"Not now. It did a little when it was being done, but as you can see, it's small, so I didn't have to suffer long." Charlie smiled down at her. "Still think I shouldn't have done it?"

Alia laughed. "No. Of course not. It's beautiful, Charlie. But if you think for one minute I'm going to dye my hair hot pink, think again." she joked, and they both laughed.

"You'll always be a part of me, no matter what, sweet girl. Now you have to stay mine forever." Charlie kissed her on the cheek.

"Promise?" Alia asked, looking earnestly into those green eyes of his.

"Of course," said Charlie looking back deeply into her blue eyes.

Smiling and holding back more tears, Alia turned to Crystal. "He tattooed my name on his wrist," she said.

"I see that. Now come on one last hug, and I'll let you two get out of here." Crystal took Alia into her arms, hugging her for what seemed like forever. "Don't let her get to you too much, Alia. Remember to shut that door."

"I will."

"And do good too, although I have to admit the idea of you running around town with a gun scares the crap out of me." She joked.

They hugged again, then she hugged George, and they left. Putting his arm around her, Charlie led Alia into the house where his parents had been waiting to say their goodbyes.

Alia was surprised to see that Ellen had been crying. Her eyes were dry now, but they were still red. Going to her, Alia allowed herself to be enveloped in the arms of the woman she would spend the rest of her life calling Mom.

"I'm going to miss you so much, my baby girl." Taking Alia's face in her hands, she looked the girl in the eyes with her own eyes welling with tears. "Don't let any of those guys in class push you around. Remember, you're a tough girl Alia. You've taken on people much bigger than you your whole life. And never forget that we are so proud of you no matter what happens." They hugged again so long that Harper had to peel them apart to get his own hug in.

Alia felt so small in the arms of this monster of a man but ever so safe and secure. No one could ever replace her father, but this man was a very close second.

"Just remember everything I taught you and do your best. You're a crack shot that in itself will help you out. And if you have any trouble with anything don't hesitate to call. Ellen is right, we're very proud of you, and we know you're going to do great." the three of them hugged again, then the four of them when Harper pulled his son in as well.

"Oh, one more thing." Said Ellen reaching for a small gift warped package on the table next to them. She handed it to Alia. "We thought you might like to take this with you."

Alia unwrapped the gift to find a framed photo of the picture they showed her weeks ago of Charlie teaching her how to walk. Her eyes filled with tears.

"It's only a copy, so don't worry about losing it. We thought it might serve as an inspiration, a reminder of how far you have come. That as well as we will always be with you...."

"Helping to teach me how to walk," Alia finished, tears spilling from her eyes. She hugged them all again. Then with a look, she begged Charlie to get her out of there, or she would never be able to leave. The mantra Alia was telling herself that it was only three months was failing her as her heart felt on the verge of breaking for going away so soon after finding them again.

Out in his truck Charlie didn't say a word, just let her cry it out in the front seat as he drove out of the drive and out of town. Even after they got to the mountains and winding roads to the cabin, neither one of them said a thing. Alia was afraid if she spoke, nothing but tears could come out, and Charlie knew she needed time to just sit there and breathe.

When they got to the cabin, Charlie told her to go get a shower while he got her things inside. When Alia was done, he had two shots of whiskey on the bedside table. "Here, take one. It'll help you sleep. I know today was hard on you. Whatever you need from me, Alia, I'll do it."

She swallowed the whiskey down with a shiver. "Could you just hold me…like you did that first night?"

"Of course," he said. "Go on, lay down. I'm going to lock up and be back in a minute."

Taking off her robe and handing it to him, Alia slipped beneath the bed sheets they first made love in.

Charlie came back, undressed down to his boxers, and joined her, cradling her in his arms like their first night. Taking a deep breath, he breathed in the sweet clean scent of her and smiled.

Alia grasped Charlie's arm, being careful of the tattoo, tucked it under her chin, and felt secure like only he could make her feel. He hugged her, and she could feel the muscles in his arms flex, his breath on her neck, the warmth of his chest on her back. For the first time all day, she felt safe.

In the morning, when they woke, they made love in the rays of the sun coming through the window. Charlie had her stay in bed while he made her breakfast of pancakes, fresh fruit, and hot tea that he brought to her. They sat and talked about things that had nothing to do with her leaving or Trish. After cleaning up, they walked in the woods holding hands, talking, and laughing. For lunch, they got some trout on the very same deck Charlie had taught her how to fish years before. They walked in the woods again in the afternoon, played a few chess games on the back porch, and sat on the front porch swing in each other's arms. Through it all, there were no tears, no worries about the months that lay ahead of them, and no talk of what happened at the party.

That evening before making dinner, Alia got a bag from the bedroom. Inside was one thing she was afraid to leave in storage and knew she couldn't take with her as much as she wanted to. Sitting on the couch next to Charlie, she held the bag in her hands.

"There's something I need you to do for me."

"Of course, anything you need."

"I have something I was wondering if I could leave here for safekeeping. I'm afraid if Trish found it, she would toss it out." Reaching into the bag, Alia pulled out a teddy bear that was both blue and light blue. "My father told me it had been the only thing I had been allowed to take with me from foster care when I went to stay with Trish."

With a smile, Charlie took the bear from her. "I can't believe you still have this."

"Yeah, it's a bit beat up, though. I used to take it everywhere with me and slept with it all the time. It's kinda gross at this point, but I still love it."

"Of all the things, though," he said, shaking his head.

"So you remember it?"

"Remember? Alia, this used to be my bear when I was a baby. That first day you came to live with us, I gave it to you. You didn't have anything, not even a blanket. You carried it around everywhere. I used to wind the crank to play the lullaby for you when you went to sleep." Charlie turned the bear over and grabbed for the crank.

"No, don't do that," Alia said, taking his hand. "It barely plays, and when it does, it sounds like it's trying to come alive and eat people."

"That's a shame. You loved that lullaby. Of course, you can keep it here."

Taking the bear back from him, Alia hugged it. "I can't believe I have had this all this time and didn't know it had been yours. Charlie, you have no idea how many nights I would lay in bed holding on to this thing for dear life and listening to it until it just wouldn't go anymore. I often felt like it was the only friend I had." With the bear in her hand, tears in her eyes, she hugged Charlie around the neck. "You never left me, sweet boy. You were always there with me. If only I had known."

"And I always will be sweet girl. Even when we are miles away, you will always be on my mind." Charlie kissed her and held her in his arms.

For dinner, they worked together on making a pot of spaghetti with meat sauce, rolls, and salad. They ate by candlelight, flirting and engaging one another until the sexual tension reached its zenith, and Charlie chased her into the bedroom. Late into the night, they made love slowly, teasing and exploring each other's bodies. On their last morning, they awoke in each other's arms.

Charlie could feel her grief and admired how strong she was being for his sake. For his part, he tried his best to smile for her as they hurried to shower and dress for the day. He busied himself cleaning up while Alia packed the last of her items into her bags and her bags out into the jeep.

When Alia came back in, Charlie was standing at the sink, having finished with the dishes, just hanging his head low. Alia went to him, wrapping her arms around his thin waist from behind, laying her head on his back. Charlie grabbed her arms with one of his but didn't try to turn around. She knew he didn't want her to see the tears in his eyes.

"Please don't do this to me, Charlie. I'm barely hanging on as it is."

"I'm sorry," he said, nodding but still just standing there.

"It's just for a few weeks. It's not forever. I'll come back."

"I know." he barely spoke above a whisper.

"We can see each other every night. We can face-time every evening if you want." This time Charlie only nodded. Alia could feel the pain coming off him, washing over her and threatening to drown her out as well. "I love you, Charlie. I'll come back to you, I promise."

Charlie spun around on her, picked her up in his arms, and buried his head in her neck where she could feel the warmth of his hot wet tears.

The damn Alia was holding back burst as well, and the two stood there holding each other as tight as they could. When he finally let her go, Charlie wiped both their tears, then kissed her again like the first time, her lips tasting of strawberry balm.

Chapter 20
Academy

Charlie and Alia pulled up to the academy center parking lot. Around them, other cadets were also being dropped off, saying last goodbyes to their girlfriends, parents, and siblings. Some came alone in their own cars, most of them living close enough that they could go home each evening when the probationary period was over.

"They are going to be the ones that ride everyone else the hardest. They'll want to get out of the barracks as soon as possible and go back home to their families." Charlie warned. "But you worry about you. Don't let them intimidate you. Even the ones from cop families are just as wet behind the ears as you are."

"Well, I'm from a cop family too, so they better watch out," she joked, trying to lift his spirits. Charlie was taking this whole thing a lot harder than she was, but Alia understood why. For her, this was an exciting new phase of her life she had been looking forward to for some time. As much as she would miss him and everyone else, she was also eager to get started. Alia had always loved to learn new things, even when she wasn't good at understanding them.

Charlie, however, was just losing his girl. Albeit temporarily, but that was little consolation. He had finally been able to share his love for her after all these years, and here she was having to leave him again. He came close last night several times to getting down on one knee and begging her to stay, that he would take care of her. However, he knew this was something she wanted and needed to do. Alia would say yes. He knew she would. Later, she may resent him for not allowing her to stand on her own two feet. Or worse, she wouldn't resent him, and he would feel like he took this away from her just to make him happy.

Charlie got all her bags out for her, kissed her one last time, then leaned against his truck, arms crossed as she walked away. Cadets had to go in alone from there.

At one point, Alia stopped and looked back at him. "Come on, Charlie, I could use one last smile. It's going to be a long few weeks."

He hadn't even realized he was frowning until she said that. Lifting his hand in a wave, he gave her his best and laughed when she blew a kiss at him. As she went into the building, Charlie looked down at his wrist and smiled.

Alia had been well prepared for what to expect on her first day, but still, the rush to get everyone organized took her a bit to get used to. As she promised, Alia kept her mouth shut, listened, and did as she was told as fast as she could. At their first lunch, she met with a few of the other cadets. Then it was back to getting their gear, meeting instructors, learning the rules, and settling into their rooms.

Harper told Alia that she was fortunate to be training in the facility that she was. Not only was it the same one that he and Charlie had graduated from, but they took their training a bit different than most academies. The rooms were more like college dorms with two cadets to a room. Military-style marching was substituted for running since they held fitness as a top priority. The instructors were strict and demanded respect but were not allowed to yell or belittle cadets. Punishments, when needed, were in the form of running or push-ups. Boots and uniforms were required to be maintained; however, they were less strict about it because they wanted the cadets to spend their time studying rather than polishing boots.

There were twenty-five cadets when the week started, three they lost once they realized this was not for them, and one got kicked out after trying to start a fight with his roommate.

Alia's roommate was a twenty-year-old female with short crop cut hair that came from a non-policing family. She had grown up on a farm and was stocky and muscular. She and Alia struck a deal right away. Maggie would help her with the physical fitness part of the training, while Alia would help her with academics. They had hit it off right away where other cadets had issues with their roommates with everything from snoring to being a slob.

The first week of early to bed and early to rise, coupled with running every day and classes, made it go by faster than she thought possible. Phones were banished during the day, so when Alia got back to her room at the end of the day, Charlie had left her several text messages. As promised, she face-timed him every night, even if only for a few minutes since she and Maggie had to study.

Maggie, herself, didn't have a boyfriend, so she face-timed with her parents. Most of their off time the first week was spent catching Maggie up and an hour each night at the gym. The first few days, Alia had been so sore in the morning that she didn't think she would be able to get out of bed, let alone run. Maggie was right there the whole way, encouraging her and pushing her to keep going.

Their first Saturday morning had arrived. Since they were still on probation, they spent most of the day doing physical fitness exercises. However, in formation that morning, Alia was told to go to the main office and speak to one of the training officers. Everyone gave her funny looks as she ran off, thinking she was in trouble. At the office Instructor, Brendon was waiting for her.

"Yes, sir, instructor Brendan, I was told you wanted to see me." Brendan was a large man with a hard, angular but not unhand-some face. His stern looks and large size were all he needed to put fear in the hearts of any of his cadets. He was a man that demanded respect but gave it in return. Alia liked him. He was tough but fair, yet standing there in his office, she couldn't help but fear him a little as well.

"Yes, cadet Miller. I had a nice long chat with your future boss, Sheriff Harper, we are pretty good friends, in fact, and he told me that you have never been able to get a driver's license."

"Yes, sir, that's correct."

"Well, you happen to be the only cadet we have at the academy right now that doesn't have one."

With that one sentence, Alia felt her familiar enemy anxiety creeping up on her.

This is it. Not even here a whole week, and I'm getting the boot, and that fucking bitch is to blame. Brendan must have seen something in her face because he started waving a hand at her.

"Relax, we don't kick people out for that. Usually, we would tell you to take care of it once you go back to town when your probation period is over. However, it is my understanding that isn't possible. Apparently, your whole stay here has a clandestine element to it."

"Yes, sir. I have a relative that works at the DMV in my town." It was only a cousin and not even one she was very familiar with. However, it was one that would run to Trish in a heartbeat.

"And you don't want certain people to find out what you're doing until you've been successful, yes I know. And lucky for you, I happen to owe Harper a favor. So I need you to go back to your barracks, put on your uniform and meet me back here in twenty minutes. You and I are going to rectify this situation, and no one else needs to know."

"Yes, sir," she said and ran off, both excited and nervous.

A few hours later, Alia and Brendan walked out of the local DMV with her holding a new driver's license. In the car on the way back, she kept looking at it and frowning.

"What's wrong? Picture turn out really bad?"

"No sir, it's just...well, I mean, is this really a real license?'

"Of course it is. I know those new ID ones look a little strange, don't they?"

"No, sir, it's not that, it's just that...well, I didn't take any tests or anything. I mean, there was the eye test, of course, but I thought I would have to take a driver's test or something."

Brendan laughed. "No kid, you show up to a DMV in a police uniform needing a license, they are not going to worry about any tests. Besides, according to Harper, you know how to drive."

"Well, yes, sir, I do...wonder how he knows that, though." she laughed a little to herself.

"There will be some driver's training while you're here anyway, pursuit training, so anything you may have issues with, we can clean up then."

"Thank you, sir. You didn't have to take time out of your day to do this. I really do appreciate it."

"Your funny kid," said Brendan

"How's that, sir?"

"Harper also told me you have a bit of a temper and attitude. I'm just not seeing it."

"Yes, sir, well I really want this, I need it. And no one has pissed me off yet, so there's still time."

Brendan laughed. "Yes, there is."

Sunday was a free day, but no one was allowed to go home yet. Those that participated went to church at a small chapel on the campus. Alia and Maggie spent most of the time studying and working out when they were not on face-time calls.

Charlie had wanted to know how she felt about everything after her first whole week, but he didn't even need to bother. The smile she had wasn't just for him that he was man enough to admit. She had a glow about her, and already he could see her growing into the fine woman she would become.

The following two weeks were much of the same as the first. Running in the morning, breakfast then classes, then lunch then more classes, the evening ending with dinner. Then it was back to the barracks to study and work out. Saturdays it was all-day physical training which included hand-to-hand combat training. It was there that Brendan finally got to see some of that temper of hers.

On their last Saturday on probation, the cadets were all suited up in pads and had a go at each other with some of the combat techniques they had learned. Alia and a male cadet had shown the most skill, so they were paired. Alia knew it was a mistake right away. Jones was a meathead. He was a big burly guy who thought his large muscles were all he needed to take down a perp. He lacked the skills and finesse that Alia did, who had learned to use her small frame to her advantage. When she took down Jones faster and easier than he thought fair, he tripped her on the way back to the mat for round two. Forgetting where she was, Alia sprang back up and shoved Jones as hard as she could.

"What the hell was that all about?" she yelled as some of her schoolyard brawling days came back to her.

Jones put his hands up in a defensive position like he had done nothing wrong. Brendan told them both to break it up and get back on the mat. In round two, Jones made a dirty move that resulted in him backhanding Alia in the face busting her bottom lip. Before anyone could intervene, Alia managed to trip Jones with one leg while pushing him down with her hand to his chest so fast he landed on his back on the mat with a smack that shook his head. She then put her boot on his throat, blocking off his airway. Before Jones could turn a pleasing shade of purple, Brendan grabbed Alia by the waist and pulled her off of him. She hadn't heard his orders to step away until then. Brendan let Alia go, and she stood there mad as hell, lip bleeding so bad it dripped into a puddle on the floor. Jones tried professing he did nothing wrong, but the whole class saw the move as well as Brendan. Jones was made to run laps, lots of laps the rest of the course. Brendan hollered at Alia, telling her to go to the infirmary because she was bleeding all over his gym.

Later at dinner, Jones made a point of coming up to where Alia sat and whispered loudly in her ear. "You may think you're tough little girl, but crooks don't play by the rules, better get used to it, or you won't last very long."

Looking up at him and grinning, Alia said. "You put your hands on me like that again, and your dick won't last very long." The cadets around her snickered at Jones. Even Brendan had to hide a chuckle over at his table.

That night while waiting to face-time with Charlie, Harper rang her instead. As soon as she saw the call, Alia knew she was in trouble. Sure enough, when the video came on, he didn't look happy at all. Harper's brow was so furrowed she could barely see his eyes.

Maggie took one look, chuckled, and walked away, pretending to mind her own business.

"I hear there was a little trouble today. From the look of your lip, I'd say I was right."

"Just some guy whose ego got in his way, I took care of it."

"It's not that you took care of it that's the problem, Alia. It's how you took care of it. Putting him on his ass is one thing, the foot to the neck...that's going too far, that's your temper getting the best of you. Remember what I said to you years ago about how I run a clean unit? Well, I meant that. Family or not, that kind of thing won't be tolerated in my office. Do I make myself perfectly clear?"

"Yes, sir." Alia's face felt flush but worse, she was ashamed of herself for disappointing him.

"Being a woman, there are going to be people that will try to get under your skin. You can't let them do that. Don't tolerate anyone pushing you around but do it the right way. You do things the right way. We'll always have your back."

"Yes, sir, I'm sorry it won't happen again."

"Good." Harper visibly softened, and she could see his eyes again. "We miss you, kiddo. We'll see you soon, just hang in there. Ellen sends her love."

Wish she would send me some of her fried chicken instead.

"Oh, and you might want to try and fix that a little before Charlie sees it."

With Maggie's help, Allia tried, but the busted lip was still too noticeable. Alia saw Charlie prickle as soon as he saw it on call later that night. She assured him she was fine, but his eyes spoke volumes.

"Don't worry," said Maggie, "She put the prick in his place. Plus, we got her back."

"Yes, I heard what happened. I know dad has already talked to you, so I won't lecture you…this time," he said with a smile. "Besides, I'm not exactly one to talk about tempers, I guess. Try and keep her out of trouble, Maggie. I don't want to have to have a talk with this prick."

"I'll try, but I'm on the, he deserved what he got, side," Maggie laughed.

"Well, no provoking him, you know what I mean, Alia. You tend to talk first and think later."

"I thought I wasn't going to get a lecture?" she smiled.

"I'm just saying, I've seen you bait people into fighting you before, remember?"

"See, I knew you had a badass streak in you," said Maggie.

"Yeah, you gotta watch her, Maggie. She comes off all meek and mild, but she's a spitfire when riled up."

"No, no, no more of that. That was when I was angry all the time. I've got you now. I'm not angry anymore. You make me the happiest I have ever been."

Maggie made a gagging motion then laughed. "Tell that to Jones the next time you make him turn purple."

Later after the call was over and they were getting ready for bed, Maggie kept looking at Alia and grinning.

"What?" asked Alia.

"You just surprise me. Here I thought I was toughing up this wet behind the ears kid, but you're pretty tough already."

"No way, PT here would kill me if it wasn't for you. All the studying we did, and Harper didn't think once about taking me to the gym or for a run."

"No, I'm not talking about physical strength. If I went through some of the shit you have told me about as a kid, I'd be mental. My parents are incredible. They didn't want me to be a cop necessarily, but they have always supported me. I can't imagine going through this if they didn't. You can't even tell yours you're doing this."

"Yea, but I have Charlie, and his folks are pretty much mine anyway."

"But have you thought about what you're going to do when you get back home, and your mother finds out you lied to her this whole time?"

"I'm going to do my job. If she chooses to act a fool, which I'm sure she will, that's on her. I've done nothing wrong other than lying to her. I'm even paying her each week despite having moved out. The ball is going to be in her court. I'm not afraid of her anymore."

"Good, I'm glad to hear it."

Now, if only I could rid my head of her voice, things would be perfect.

The rest of the week went off without a hitch, only just very slow. By Friday morning, they were told they were off their probationary period. By six pm Friday, they were free until eight pm Sunday night.

Alia texted Charlie telling him they were off probation. Friday evening, once they were released from classes for the day, Alia and Maggie went straight to their barracks, where Alia packed a bag for the weekend.

"What about you, are you going to go home?" she asked Maggie.

"No, the farm is too far away to make it worth the trip. For the fourth, I will but not every weekend."

"So, what are you going to do?"

"Study," she said with a laugh. "I need it. Even with as much as we crammed, I didn't score as well as you did on our last tests. I may go to town to see a movie too, check out the local wildlife at a bar."

"Yeah, well, just behave. After a weekend of Charlie cooking for me, I'm going to need to work out like crazy when I get back."

"Don't tell me the boy can cook too?"

"Not as good as his mother but close."

"And no brother's either, huh?"

"Sorry, no," she said, stuffing the last of her things into a duffle bag.

"Please at least tell me the sex is bad." she joked.

Alia didn't say anything, just smiled and blushed deep red.

Maggie threw a pillow at her. "You suck." she laughed. "Back home, all there is to choose from is the southern fried farm boys that I grew up with. So what are you two doing all weekend? And yes, I want the deets."

Alia threw the pillow back, "Well, you're not getting the deets," She laughed. "All I know is we are going to the cabin his parents have in the mountains. I can't be seen around town. Kinda sucks. I miss my friends and his parents. It would be nice to go out and do something."

"Oh, poor you, a whole weekend in bed having sex with an amazing and good-looking guy, however, will you recover," Maggie said sarcastically.

"I know, I know, I really shouldn't complain. And I'm not really. But I will be glad when this whole thing is over, and we can be together somewhere other than the cabin."

"So, are you two planning on moving in together?"

"No, I have a place waiting for me when I get back. I think we will take things slow, you know, let people get used to seeing us together. Besides, I'm looking forward to having my own place, even if it's just for a little while."

"I would have thought with the way you two are with each other you would get married soon after graduation."

"What do you mean?"

"Come on, Alia, it's so obvious the two of you are madly in love. I mean, usually, this kind of thing is a one-way street. One person always seems to love the other person more. But the two of you, well, I never believed in soul mates before, but then I met you and Charlie. The way he looks at you, even just on face-time, it's like he's seeing the most wonderful person ever. My parents get like that at times, but they have been with each other forever."

"I know what you mean, his parents are like that too. The only thing I have to compare it to is my mother's disastrous relationships with men."

"You mean Charlie is your first?"

"We are both each other's first. He couldn't bring himself to date, anyone. Told me he felt like he was cheating. I had a boyfriend for half a sec my freshman year, but it always felt wrong somehow. Mostly I went out with him because he was a senior."

"Well, If I ever have a relationship half as good as the two of you do, I will be delighted."

"What are you talking about? Maggie, you are gorgeous. I'm sure you have guys lined up at home wanting to take you out."

"Yes, I do." she bragged. "But where Charlie looks at you adoringly, most guys only look at me lustfully. And for some reason, being pretty means you're also loose. Or they want you to be."

"Oh, trust me, some men don't care what you look like just as long as you are loose. Trish has had plenty of men, and she is in no way pretty." They both laughed. Maggie had seen a picture of Trish and agreed.

At ten of six, they both went to the last formation. Brendan drilled them all on the importance of staying out of trouble (looking right at Alia) and being sure to return for formation no later than eight pm Sunday. Anyone late that still had a pulse would be out of the program.

Once dismissed, Maggie walked with Alia to the parking lot, where some got into their own cars, and others joined family. Charlie was standing in uniform in front of his patrol car, leaning on it, waiting for her. When she saw him, she had to keep herself from running. A few feet away, she couldn't stand it any longer, dropped her bag, and ran into his arms, where he picked her up and swung her around. Putting her back down, Charlie gave her a quick kiss then licked his lips.

"Damn, I missed that strawberry balm." Holding on to her one hand, he grabbed her bag with the other and put it on the patrol car's hood. He then turned to Maggie. "Hi, Maggie. Nice to get to meet you in person this time."

Maggie gave him a hug saying hello. "Nice to meet you as well, Charlie. Now you take good care of my girl here and make sure you bring her back in time. I need her help to pass these tests."

"No worries, I know the drill. Brendan was my instructor as well. When he says eight, he really means be here by seven-forty-five."

Maggie and Alia hugged goodbye while Charlie put her bags in the car. They were just about to pull out when Maggie waved to them, pointed to Jones, and pointed at her lip.

Charlie looked at the guy, fully understanding she was pointing out the one that had hit Alia.

"Charlie, just forget about it. He's not worth it." Alia could see him gripping the steering wheel tight.

Charlie closed his eyes. When he opened them back up, he looked at her and smiled. "I'm good. Let's go get some dinner." However, on the way out of the parking lot, Charlie stared Jones down.

On their way back to the cabin, the two stopped to have a nice steak dinner while Alia filled him in on everything that she hadn't been able to tell him during the week. On the drive back, about an hour from the cabin, Charlie looked over, and Alia was asleep, much like she had slept in his patrol car that first night. Watching her, he became aware of just how far they had come since then. At the cabin, he opened the front door, then came back to the car, lifted her out, and carried her inside.

"Charlie, What are you doing?" Alia asked before he got her inside.

"You just go back to sleep, sweet girl." Inside, he laid her on the bed, removed her shoes, and spread a blanket over her. As he went to walk out, she reached out for him, her eyes still closed.

"Charlie."

"I'll be right back." After bringing in her bags and locking up, Charlie stripped to his boxers and joined her in bed. With her more petite frame nestled into his larger one, he was able to get his first decent night's sleep in three weeks.

The following weekend was the fourth of July on a Saturday. That gave them their only four-day weekend for the entire training. Mom and Harper surprised her by bringing Crystal up to the cabin on Sunday when the boys were off. They all had a great family time together and even went into the nearest town on the other side of the mountain to see the fireworks. Charlie and Alia sat on a blanket together, almost in their own little world.

As the weeks went on, they got into a routine. During the week, Alia and Maggie worked hard, achieving more together than they would have alone. Face-time was a nightly ritual for them both. On Fridays, Charlie would pick Alia up, go out to dinner, then the two-hour trip to the cabin. There they would spend the weekend in each other's arms as much as possible, as well as fishing and walking in the woods.

There was a TV in the cabin, but the only time it came on was when it rained and most of the time not even then. There were weekends where storms cut the power out, and they would make love by candlelight and cook their meals out on the porch.

The dread and longing they had experienced from the onset got better to deal with and manage as time went on. They got used to being apart, even if they still didn't care for it, and made up for the time when they were together. The only downfall to graduation was that Maggie had become a great second best friend to Alia.

In the last week of their training, they had multiple tests to ensure they learned what they needed. Being the smallest and youngest in the class, Alia had been worried about the physical part of the tests. However, with Maggie's help, she gained pounds in muscle and even had a nice set of abs. The little fat girl she had once been was no longer in residence.

In the physical portion of the testing, Alia ended up third in her class behind Jones and Maggie. In defense, she had ended up first with Jones and Maggie right behind her. However, the second and third place cadets were an impressive distance behind her when it came to the firing range portion. Brendan even suggested that she come back for the five-day sniper course they offered once she is settled in Union county. In academics, Alia came in second behind Jones with another cadet, then Maggie fourth in class. By the end of the week, they all had something to be proud of.

Their last week on Saturday was graduation. Getting ready that morning in their room, Alia was more nervous than she was at her high school graduation. Not only was Charlie, Mom, and Harper coming, but so were Crystal, George, and her parents. Maggie's parents and grandparents were coming as well, and even she had the jitters. Before they were to head out, there was a knock on their door. When Alia opened it, Jones was standing there.

"Maggie, could you give Alia and me a moment alone?"

Maggie looked at Alia, who nodded a yes. On her way out, she warned Jones not to lay a finger on her, or she would have the whole academy in there on his ass. When they were alone, Jones began.

"I want to apologize for my behavior." He said. "I was an asshole to you those first few weeks, and that was uncalled for."

Alia gave the man the once over, but she could tell he was being sincere. "Yeah, what the hell was up with that anyway? Why single me out?"

"Because I could tell from the start that you were my toughest competition. It's one thing to get blown away by anyone on the range or in class, but to get your ass handed to you by a girl in PT, well where I come from, I would get reamed for that," Jones said humbly.

"So, what changed your mind?"

"You did, Alia. See, I hate to lose, especially if I lose because I failed myself. But to lose because someone else is just better than me because they have great skills, well that doesn't sting as much."

"Still has to suck to get your ass kicked by a girl," Alia said with a smile, secretly loving his groveling.

He laughed. "Yes, it still does. However, I have a feeling you have been defending yourself your whole life. Skills like that, and that temper, are usually earned. I am a pretty big dude, always have been. I haven't had to fight hardly a day in my life. Being bested by the best doesn't suck nearly as much."

"You really feel that way?"

"Yes, I do. And I'm sorry I let my own temper get the best of me. I still stand by what I said, though. Criminals don't follow the rules. Keep your eyes sharp, and no matter what anyone tells you, don't lose that temper, not all of it. It just might be what gets you out of a jam one day." Jones turned to leave then stopped at the door. "Oh, and if you could get that boyfriend of yours to stop looking at me like he wants to see my head on a pike, I'd appreciate it."

"I'll see what I can do. I'm not the only one with a temper," she said.

"Yeah, I got that feeling too. Skinny little fucker would probably take my head off. Congratulations, cadet, you have earned it and my respect." Jones left, and Maggie came right back in.

"Well, that was a shocker," said Maggie, in awe.

"What did you do listen in to the whole thing?"

"Of course I did. I told Charlie we had your back, and I meant it. Wasn't about to leave you all alone with that meathead."

An hour later, they stood on the stage of the Training schools Auditorium. Charlie and the rest of her extended family sat together in the audience. She, along with her fellow cadets, received their certificates and badges. Alia was awarded the top shot award for stellar marksmanship, the most improved physical training, and best defensive cadet awards. Maggie got honors with Jones for physical training while Jones took the top academic award for the class.

After the ceremony was over, Alia and the other top cadets took some photos for the academy. She then met up with her family and friends in the reception room in the cafeteria. They all took turns giving her big hugs and congratulating her. Charlie gave her a bouquet of carnations, her favorite flowers.

Maggie introduced her parents to Alia then gave her a big hug goodbye. "I hate to leave so fast, but we have a very long drive ahead of us. I want to thank you, Alia. You made this thing not only a hell of a lot easier but a lot more fun." They said their final goodbyes, with promises to call and write.

Before leaving, Brendan came over and talked with them. "You all should be very proud of her. Never once did I feel like she gave us less than a hundred percent."

"We are," said Harper. "But then we were before anyway."

Before going home, everyone met for dinner in town. They all had a great time laughing and talking. When they were done, they all split ways. Crystal and George went with their parents, Ellen and Harper headed home while Charlie and Alia headed for the cabin for what was to be their last summer weekend. The camp was supposed to wrap up that weekend. Her mother didn't expect her home until later in the week since Alia said she would stay over to close up the park. Monday morning, with the help of Charlie and her friends, Alia was to move into the small garage apartment she had made arrangements to rent in town.

Academy done, Alia's field training started in a week, and soon Trish would realize she was not only not coming back home but was a cop as well. On the ride to the cabin, Alia thought about what that might mean and fell quiet.

"What's wrong? What are you worried about?" asked Charlie.

"Just thinking about what happens now. Honestly, Charlie, up to about halfway through the academy, I never thought I would get this far. Now here I am, and I realize I may not have thought this through all the way."

"Are you having regrets about becoming a cop?"

"No, not at all. If anything else, the training made me want to be one even more. Thanks to Harper helping me, it's the first time I ever tried something that I felt like I was good at. What I didn't think about too much was how Trish is going to react to all of this."

"You don't have to be afraid of her anymore, Alia. It's not just us that has your back now. You have the whole Sheriffs' department as well."

"It's not that I'm afraid she's going to hurt me or anything. It's just with her you never know what she is going to do. And I'm still worried about what she might try and say about you."

"I'm not worried about that. You shouldn't be either."

"Well, we should be."

"What is she going to do, hmm, try to bring up something that she swears happened years ago but she never reported? Try to say those things are happening now? Let her. I don't think you see it or realize it, Alia, but you have changed these last three months. You're stronger. You look older. You carry yourself with a confidence I have never seen in you before. You have grown, sweet girl. No one will believe that I or anyone else is making you do anything you don't want to do. Let her talk. We always knew she would. We did what we did to lessen the damage she would have.

The only thing we have to do is remember to keep our cool, the both of us."

"How has that been going?"

"It's been going good. As you saw, I didn't rearrange Jones' face." he laughed. "Seriously though, I get angry when people hurt you, Alia, because I have had to sit back for years and watch the world hurt you and couldn't do anything about it. I don't have to do that anymore. We both don't have to do that. And you're strong now, stronger than you ever have been. So as far as your mother goes, I'm not worried about her. She will do what she will do, and as long as we keep our cool, we have nothing to worry about. I got your back. Always will." he smiled over at her, the grin that drove her wild.

"You really think I've gotten strong?"

"And even more beautiful. That reminds me, I need to send Maggie a thank you card for making my hot girlfriend even hotter."

"Okay, stop, now you're just teasing."

"No, I'm not. Misses, my fat ass don't need a snickers bar. Remember you told me that that first night? Well, I'm pretty sure you're safe to eat all the Snickers you want now. Just wait, I'll show you."

And he did. When they made love that night, Charlie pointed out how toned and muscular her body had become, including her once fat ass, that he never thought was terrible, to begin with. With every touch and kiss, her confidence soared. Charlie always had a way of making her feel better. Now he showed her how to make herself feel better. Her new sense of self-worth made their lovemaking hotter and more intense than ever.

Chapter 21
Letter from Dad

Sunday, Charlie and Alia slept in. They lay in bed enjoying the company of one another before having to face reality and the start of a busy week. The Harpers had a small graduation party at their house for Alia that afternoon. The time had come for all of them to stop hiding Alia away like she was some kind of dirty secret. The plan was for the two of them to drive right into town and home like it was the most normal thing ever because it was.

The idea made Alia very nervous. She knew no matter what, her mother would soon find out everything. The new Alia was ready to face it head-on, but the scared little kid inside of her sat in a corner, trembling. It was hard for her to reconcile the two sides.

Knowing how she felt, Charlie allowed her to procrastinate as long as possible. He kept her in bed, spoiling her with breakfast and massages. He told her countless times how beautiful she was. When the time finally came for them to get ready, he had brought her nerves down a bit.

Still in his truck on the way into town, Alia felt her heart rate increase, and she kept looking out to see if she could spot Trish anywhere. Hopefully, the woman stayed home or close to home and wouldn't spoil the day with her presence.

After the winding road part, Charlie held her hand all the way to his parent's house. He made a point of looking over at her with the grin he knew she loved the most until she smiled back.

"It's going to be okay," he said. "You're not alone anymore, Alia. And it will be nice not having to hide anymore."

She nodded, knowing he was right. Of course, he was. Still, the longer she could go without dealing with Trish, the better.

When they pulled into the Harper's drive, the sight of so many cars put her back on alert again. Alia tried pulling her hand from Charlie's, but he held fast to her.

"Relax, Alia, we don't have to go in until you're ready."

"Why are there so many cars?" she asked, not taking her eyes off the driveway. There were more than a dozen cars, not including ones belonging to the Harper's, even a few cop cars from the Sheriff's department.

"I told you, Alia, you're not alone anymore. This isn't just your party for graduating from the academy. It's a celebration of your freedom. We have nothing and no reason to hide."

Alia looked at him with his beautiful smile and striking green eyes filled with so much love and compassion she felt her heart skip a beat.

I can do this. With *him at my side, I can do anything.*

Alia leaned forward and kissed her boy, much like he often kissed her. "I love you, sweet boy."

"Love you too, sweet girl. Are you ready?"

She nodded, and with another quick kiss, they got out and walked to the back of the yard hand in hand. Alia still felt nervous and shy, but those feelings quickly faded as she was enveloped in the arms of friends and family.

With the Harpers were Crystal and her family, several of her friends from school, Mrs. Stackhouse, and even Principal Edwards. And the handful of officers from the Sheriff's station that she knew. They all greeted her like she was family. Not one person mentioned the two of them showing up together like they did, though she was sure it would be all over town the next day. That's just how things were.

The party was very casual with plenty of food and drinks. Charlie even slipped Alia a small shot of whiskey at one point.

Alia told stories about her time in the academy to those that asked. A few people gave her gifts, some silly, some sentimental. For the most part, she and Charlie sat on a lounger together with his arm around her shoulders. She eventually got to the point where she didn't want to bolt. However, Alia looked around from time to time, expecting to see Trish come raging into the party.

Charlie noticed and did his best to keep her engaged.

Towards evening before the party could wind down and people started to leave, Harper pulled Charlie aside. The two talked with their heads close together, and in hushed tones, Alia couldn't hear.

"What are those two up to?" she asked Ellen.

Ellen only smiled and feigned ignorance.

"Mom, what's going on?"

"You'll see. Let the boys have their fun."

Charlie came over and gave Alia a kiss on her forehead (putting another shock into her). "I'll be right back. There's something Dad, and I have to do."

Alia grabbed his hand, and a sudden panic rose up in her.

Charlie squeezed her hand and kissed it. "I'll be right back. This will only take a few minutes." he winked at her, and she let go of his hand, the panic thankfully receding. While they were gone, Alia continued to talk to Crystal and her friends.

A few minutes later, Ellen got a call. "Okay, I'll bring her out." she hung up the call then motioned for Alia and Crystal. "Come on, you two, it's time."

Crystal almost squealed when she got up, pulling Alia to her feet.

"Okay, really, what's going on," asked Alia.

"Just come on, it's a surprise." giggled Crystal. "Oh, and you're going to need this." Crystal handed Alia one of those small plastic-wrapped packages of tissues.

Ellen and Crystal took Alia by her hands and led her to the side of the house where Harper and Charlie waited. Alia's friends and even a few others followed them out, most not knowing what was happening. Charlie and Harper smiled, but she caught a hint of sadness in Harper's eyes as well.

"Alia, there's one last gift we need to give you," Harper said. "As I have told you before, your father and I were good friends. Before that day, the day of the fire, he wrote me a letter that he left with his lawyer. In it, Johnathan explained that he was sick and wouldn't be around for when you grew up. He asked me to keep watching over you, which of course, he didn't have to ask. Jonathan also left a will and something in a trust for you. He asked that when the time was right that we get it for you, and we couldn't think of a better time than now ."

"You're telling me my dad left me something after all?"

"Of course he did," said Charlie. "He just couldn't very well leave anything Trish could get her hands on. Nothing would be left for when you were ready to be on your own." Turning Alia around, Charlie put a hand over her eyes. "It's out front, now we'll lead you there but keep your eyes closed." With his one hand on her eyes and another on her shoulder, he led her into the front yard. "OK, are you ready?" Charlie asked when they stopped.

Alia nodded though her heart was racing, and she shook some. When Charlie took his hand off her eyes, what stood before her brought tears to them instantly. A brand new black with hot pink trim, Jeep Wrangler, was sitting in the driveway with a comically massive bow on the hood. Seeing it and understanding that this was a gift from her long-deceased father, Alia suddenly felt weak in the knees, and Charlie had to shore her up.

"Your father wanted you to have something he knew would be important to you and your future," said Harper. "He couldn't give you the freedom from Trish he wanted to when he was alive. He hoped this would help one day. He left the money in an account, and Charlie went and picked it out last week."

Alia buried her head in Charlie's chest, crying. She felt so overwhelmed at the moment. It took her several minutes of Charlie holding her before she could manage to stop crying long enough to even look at it again.

"I hope you like the colors," he said when she finally did.

Alia nodded, shaking. Not only was it a gift from her father, but the boy she loved the most in the world got to pick it out. Nothing could ever be more perfect than that. Harper handed her the keys, the keychain she noticed had been her father's. He made it out of an old diecast toy fire truck and carried it around for years. That started the tears back up again, and Harper took her into his arms.

"He would have been so proud of you, Alia. I wish he could have seen the beautiful women you have grown into." Ellen and Charlie joined in on the hug, and for a few minutes, they all shed a few tears together.

"Go on and crank her up," Harper told her when they let go and dried their tears.

Legs still a little wobbly and a few tears still running down her cheeks, Alia approached the Jeep. Charlie opened the driver-side door for her, and she got inside. The interior was done in hot pink trim as well, she noticed. As Alia started the jeep, she would have sworn that she felt her father right there beside her for a moment or two. She could even smell the burning smoke of his gear. Charlie got in the passenger seat, and Crystal and a couple of her friends got in the back.

"We will wrap up the party for you kids. Go have some fun, just be careful," said Ellen. She and Harper waved to them as Alia drove out of the driveway.

Alia drove them around town, out into the countryside, and up into the mountains for about two hours. Not once the whole time did she worry about seeing Trish or even think of her. Instead, she found herself tossing between emotions. One minute Alia would be sad thinking about her father, worse realizing that time had come when she thought about him less and less. The next, she would be exhilarated at the feeling of freedom and having the vehicle under her control.

I can go anywhere. I can do anything. She thought. Then she would look over at Charlie and see how he was looking at her and know that she didn't want to be anywhere but right here, right now. So Alia drove on over the mountains and onto dirt roads to get a feel for it. Even driving back to town, dusk on its way, made her happy.

When they pulled into the driveway at the Harper's, most of the cars that had been there were gone. The food had all been moved inside and the tables and chairs put away.

They all went inside to eat again and talked about where they went on the drive. Then she and Charlie left again so Alia could take Crystal home. That, too, had brought tears to her eyes. The very act of taking Crystal home was like the perfect topper for the day.

Once again, Charlie and Alia returned to the Harper's house, only this time they stayed in the jeep for a while to be alone before going back in to get ready for bed. Alia was staying there that night, then in the morning, Charlie would help her move her things into her new place before heading to work.

Charlie opened the glove box and pulled out a letter. "I thought we should save this until after you were done driving. It's from your dad."

Alia looked at Charlie, hesitated for a moment, then took the letter with a shaky hand. On the front, in her father's neat handwriting, was her name. She carefully opened the envelope and pulled out the paper. It was written on her father's old company stationery. Just the sight of the familiar logo brought tears to her eyes again.

"Do you want me to leave you alone to read it?" asked Charlie.

"Don't you dare," said Alia with a smile. "I have a feeling I'm going to need a shoulder to cry on." Taking a deep breath, Alia read the letter to herself.

My dearest Alia,
         Baby girl, I am so sorry for the pain I know I will cause you. It's not my intention to cause you any more grief than you have already had in your short young life. I can't bear for you to see me slowly slip away right in front of your eyes. I have instructed my good friend Sherriff Harper to

give this letter to you once you are grown and able to understand why I am leaving the way I am. I am hoping that you will understand and be able to forgive me.

    I know I wasn't the best father in the world and not there the times when you needed me the most. But I assure you I never for a moment stopped loving you. When I think of all the things I will miss out on, it tears my heart apart. I won't be there to see you graduate, drive your first car, or walk down the aisle. I won't get to see you grow into the incredible person I know you're capable of, and that hurts worse than the cancer.

    As I write this, I am parked in the shade of a giant willow where you can't see me. You're at the park playing kickball with a group of kids, and you're giving those boys hell. No sitting on the sidelines being a cheerleader for my daughter, that's for damn sure. And you're not letting any of those boys give you any shit either. Well, that is except for one. Even from here, I can tell Charlie is special to you. That boy has stolen your heart even at your young age, and I hope as you read this, he hasn't given it back or broke it. I don't think I have to worry about him breaking it, though. I just hope he's tough enough to handle the fire you have always have had inside you. And I hope that flame is never extinguished.

    I know things are complicated, and I know my death may prove to make things even harder, but I hope you have come to realize that my love for you didn't die when I did. And I hope you allow the special people in your life, like the Harper's, inside those walls you have built up around you. Despite what your mother has drilled into you all these years, you are loved. I hope you like the gift. I trust Harper to pick something special. Use it well, even if it means turning your back on everything you have known. If that's what it takes for you to be happy, then you do it. All I ask is that when you think of me, you try not to be too pissed off and understand I am only doing what I think is best.
Love,
Your Father
Jonathan Cross

Wiping her face with more tissues, Alia handed the letter to Charlie, letting him read it. Still sitting in the driver's seat, Alia sat back and sighed, shaking her head.

These past several months have been so revealing to her. Seeing life through the lens of Trish and her influence was like looking into a dark pit of despair. Now Alia could see things in the light and knew she never wanted to go back to looking into that pit again.

I just may have to turn my back on some things, no matter how hard that may be. Well, some people anyway.

"What's up, sweet girl?" Charlie asked, taking one of her hands in his. He had put the letter back in the envelope and in the glove box of the jeep where it would remain for years.

"Just all these feelings. I feel a freedom like I have never felt before. My father knew the perfect thing to leave me. Here I thought he only spent time with me out of a sense of obligation. But it turns out he knew me better at twelve than I ever imagined."

"I remember your dad. He was crazy about you, Alia. He wanted to take you away from your mother, but she would never give permission for him to do a blood test to prove you were his to the court. If he didn't show you how much he loved you all the time, it was probably because he knew it would only make it harder for you to go home. I remember a few times you actually hid from him when it was time for you to go so you could stay for another night."

"Yeah, and all that did was make my mother mad at the both of us. Then she wouldn't allow me to come over for a while. I think I eventually got it through my head and stopped."

"He loved you, Alia. Never doubt that for a minute."

"I know, and the horrible thing is that after he died, I hated him for the longest time." Here came the tears again.

"You were mad because he left when he still had some time. That's understandable."

"No, Charlie, I was mad...because he didn't take me with him," Alia confessed. It was a truth she kept even from herself.

Charlie looked up at her, startled by the revelation. He gripped her hand tighter when he saw a single tear slide down her cheek.

"That whole time, after we moved back and I was acting out, taking dares, getting into fights...it wasn't because I missed him as much as it was because I didn't want to go on anymore. I was so tired, Charlie. At twelve, I was tired as if I had lived to be very old. The thought of another twelve years or more of the shit life I had just seemed too daunting. I didn't have the courage to end it myself as he did. I figured if I pissed enough people off, one of them would do it for me. Then I lost you too. After that day with the bike, you were never around anymore. And after what I said, I only had myself to blame."

"Alia, no, what you said had nothing to do with it. I thought by leaving the bike tire, you would see that. I wanted to leave a note, but I was afraid your mother would find it first. I mean, you were right about me being older and having other things to do. I wasn't around that summer because I was a camp counselor that year, just like the year after when you came there. When I got back, my parents just thought it better to concentrate on building my future and back off a little. Mom could see how I felt about you. Then we had Crystal and George to help us keep up with you. You never lost me, Alia. I just wanted to be sure that when we were ready, I was somebody you would want to be with, that you would be proud of." Charlie reached over and wiped away a tear, and gave her a kiss on the cheek.

"How could I ever be anything but proud of you Charlie? You were almost as much of a hero to me as a kid as my dad was."

"Yeah, well, maybe things like the middle finger that day threw me a little." he joked.

Alia laughed. "I was a little pissed at you that day. No, that's not fair, it wasn't you. I was just mad because you called me out. I knew wanting to die was stupid; I just couldn't bear to keep going."

"So what did it? What made you change your mind? My dad thinks it was when he threatened to lock you up."

"That had some to do with it. Not him locking me up, though. We had a good talk that day. For once, he talked to me instead of lecturing and actually got through. We have your mother to thank for that, I'm pretty sure. But even after that, I couldn't get over that feeling of being tired all the time. Now, of course, I would realize it was depression. Actually, in a way, I have you to thank for that as well."

"How's that?"

"Because if you hadn't introduced me to Crystal, I don't know how much longer I would have been able to hold on. Crystal stayed my friend despite Trish, which was a first. And like you, I felt like I could talk to her about anything. By then, though, my carelessness was a way of life, I guess. I didn't pick as many fights as before, but I still did some stupid stuff. Then there was the day the semi almost creamed me."

Charlie had been sitting back and relaxing like she was. Now he sat up and turned in his seat to face her.

Alia, however, kept looking out the window as she talked. "We were going to the store one day, walking there from her house. It was a pretty nice warm spring day. I wasn't even really upset much about anything. We had walked across one parking lot and needed to get across the road. Instead of going down to the crosswalk, I just stepped out into the street didn't even look. I never did. I'm pretty sure I've done it dozens of times, mostly without even thinking.

I was picking myself up off the ground before I even realized how close I came to getting nailed, the sound of the semi's horn still blasting as it skidded down the road. Crystal had managed to catch me by the back of my jacket just in time. When Crystal gets mad, she doesn't say much, she gets real quiet, but she let me have it that day. Told me if I insisted on killing myself, fine, just don't expect her to stand around and watch me do it. The look in her eyes, the look of hurt that I knew I had caused. It was like I was back on the day of the bike wreck again. I had hurt you that day. I know I did because I felt it, even with as mad as I was. I have been hurt many times by many people, but I haven't hurt too many people in that way before. And I didn't want to do it ever again. Not to her, not to you or anyone else I loved.

It wasn't something that happened overnight, but I was trying. For the first time since my father died, I was actually trying to live. Shit was still hard, Trish was still a bitch, and school was not the most fun place for me. But it got better. And when it was terrible Crystal, and George and her parents were always there for me. And so was Harper…though I have to admit it took me a long time to be anything other than pissed at him." she laughed, still not looking at Charlie.

Charlie wanted right then to go back to Crystal's and give her the biggest hug. She had saved his girl for him, and all this time, he never knew.

It should have been me there. I knew how bad she was hurting, but I walked away, telling myself it was the best thing I could do for her. If she had died because I wasn't there, I would have never forgiven myself. I'll never walk away from her again.

Charlie grabbed Alia around the waist pulled her over the center console and into his lap, where he just held her tight. "Promise me if you ever get tired like that again, you'll let me know so I can carry you."

"I do, I promise."

Charlie never said a word more about it and never had to; neither did she. She could feel both his pain and relief, and he could feel hers. When they were done embracing, they kissed. When they were done kissing, they joined the rest of the family in the living room for a few late-night snacks and drinks. Later that night, the two of them shared his single bed as she slept at home once more for the first time in a very long time.

Monday morning, the two woke up in bed to the smells of breakfast cooking downstairs.

"Have I told Mom how amazing she is in a while," Alia asked with a smile.

"I think she hears it every time you call her Mom," said Charlie.

Downstairs they joined Ellen and Harper for breakfast of eggs, pancakes, and sausage. It was a nice change from the stuff they got at the academy. Alia felt like she made a pig of herself and still didn't eat half as much as Charlie.

"Charlie, how do you stay so thin eating like that?" she laughed.

"Easy, the boy doesn't eat unless he is here," said Ellen.

"That's not true, Mom."

"Charlie, I have been in your apartment and seen your fridge. TV dinners and Pizza is not real food." she scolded.

During breakfast, Harper told Alia that when she was ready, he would need her to pick up her uniform before starting work the following Monday. That then brought them around to the topic of Trish, and just when she thought Trish would find out, Alia wasn't coming home.

"I wasn't due in until this afternoon. So either when Billy notices I'm not back yet or when she checks in on me tonight. She most likely will expect me to be awake and waiting up for her."

"What do you think she will do after that?" asked Ellen.

Alia put her utensils down and sighed heavily. "I'm guessing she will call me. She has my number now and has had it since shortly after I left."

Now it was Harper's turn to put down his utensils and sigh. "I thought we had decided not to do that, that you would talk to her from the phones there if you needed to."

"Any calls from phones there says that it's a call from a phone there. I would have had to use someone else's cell phone, and with some of the shit, she can say I wasn't about to do that. Besides, she insisted on having a number she could reach me by."

"You did the right thing then." Harper thought for a moment, then made his mind up. "So until she does try to contact you, I want you to stay here at night with us. I don't think you should be alone until we know how she is going to react to all of this."

"I agree," said Charlie.

"Now wait, I understand what you're trying to do, but I don't exactly want an audience when she calls. And if she thinks I am here, she just can't be trusted."

"Which is exactly why you need to be here. She doesn't need to know that you are, not that I care. Personally, I would like to see her try and do something stupid. We already know she will try and make life miserable for all of us anyway. What Trish doesn't realize is that all her bullshit isn't going to work this time." said Harper

"I'm going to be with you, Alia. I swear I won't say anything, but I won't make you do it alone. I have seen how even a phone call with her makes you feel," said Charlie

Alia shook her head. "This is between Trish and me. I really don't want to drag you all into her crap. I can deal with her." *I think.*

Ellen came over to Alia kneeling beside her. "Sweetheart, your family. And we have been in this thing with Trish from the beginning. You're not dragging us anywhere. We did our best to protect you as much as we could from a distance, but now it's time to stand with you. I know you're embarrassed by her and the things she says but believe me, there's nothing she can say to us that is any worse than what she already has said."

"Ellen's right Alia, we are in this no matter what. Besides, it would be good to witness the things that she says. Your whole life, it's been her word against yours, well not anymore."

Ellen got up and gave Alia a kiss on her temple. "Okay, no more of this for now. We will deal with her when it's time. Right now, you two kids need to get Alia's stuff moved into the apartment. And when Charlie goes to work, you and I are going shopping. This is a good day, and we are going to make it good if nothing else but to spite that woman." Ellen then sat down to finish her breakfast.

Alia looked over at Charlie and grinned.

"Mother has spoken." he laughed.

When they were done with breakfast, Harper went to work, and Ellen hurried the kids out of the house, not allowing them to help clean up. Since her two-door jeep didn't have much room, She and Charlie used his truck to go over to Crystal's and get her things. Alia kinda felt like she was shoving their whole relationship down people's throats awfully early. Still, he assured her it wasn't that big of a deal.

When they arrived, Mrs. Porter, her new landlady, was waiting out on the front porch having tea which she insisted they stop and join her in having. Mrs. Porter had been a nine-one-one dispatcher until she had retired a few years earlier. Since then, she had rented out the space above her garage that once had been a home office for her husband before he had passed almost fifteen years earlier. Most of her renters were temporary, most affiliated with the Sheriff's department in one capacity or another.

Her last tenant had been a young man that had moved in over the summer while waiting for his permanent place with the forestry department. The young man had just moved out two weeks prior, which gave her plenty of time to freshen up the place for Alia.

Mrs. Porter didn't know much about Alia other than what Harper had filled her in on and dispatch reports over the years (including Alia's bad one where her name came up often). Basically, Alia needed a place to stay to be on her own for a while after leaving a very controlling mother. The two of them had met a few times to get the details of the move settled but never really talked. So they sat there indulging her as Mrs. Porter asked Alia about the academy and her life in general.

Alia had warmed up to the women almost right away. She was intelligent and funny with a surprisingly girlish laugh. In her late seventies, the woman had virtually wrinkle-free skin that she would contribute to drinking water and having a rather dull life if asked. She was about the same height as Alia and thinner. Mrs. Potter kept giving the two of them knowing looks with a, I know something you're not telling me, grin. Not that she had come right out and asked either. Not directly anyway.

"So am I right in assuming I will see a good bit of this handsome young man hanging around," she asked Alia with that knowing grin again.

Alia laughed, seeing Charlie turn a bright shade of pink. "Yes, mam, I would say that's a safe bet."

"Well, as we discussed before, as long as they behave, I have no issues with you having guests. But I draw the line at wild parties."

"That's fine with me. I'm not exactly the wild party type anyway. I'm going to be pretty busy once my training starts next week."

"Yes, you will. Harper runs a tight ship. Charlie can tell you, I'm sure. I'm guessing he didn't give you much of a break when you first started, did he."

"No, ma'am, he did not. To be honest, I'm positive he was a lot harder."

"And it worked. I've heard nothing but good things about you, Charlie. But then I always knew you were a good kid." She turned to Alia. "I've heard some things about you as well, young lady, but I've been assured you've gotten your misspent youth out of your system," she said with a warm smile.

"Yes, ma'am, been out of my system for some time now."

"Good, nothing wrong with raising a little hell when one is young as long as one knows when it's time to stop. Well, I have kept the two of you long enough. I better let you get things inside. If you need anything, let me know, I'm home most of the time unless I'm at bingo." Mrs. Porter handed Alia the keys to her new home. "Go on, shoo, I'll put all of this away."

It didn't take them long to put Alia's things in the apartment since she had surprisingly little other than books. Ellen was right, they would have a lot of shopping to do. The apartment came unfurnished. There was a small living room with an adjacent smaller kitchen. Off from that was the bedroom and a small bath. Alia had access to a washer and dryer in the garage, a hose outside, and some storage in the apartment. It was small, but it was clean, warm, and most importantly, all hers. For now, that was all that she needed.

There was no point in unpacking since there wasn't any place to put anything. Charlie had gone down to double-check they got everything. When he came back, he held the only thing left, a medium-sized rectangular box that she didn't recognize.

"This was all that was left," he said with a smile that told her he was up to something.

"Funny, I don't believe that's mine, though."

"Hmm, you sure, it's got your name on it." Charlie handed it to her, and she could see that it did indeed have her name on it.

"Charlie, what is this?"

"I think you should open it up and find out."

Carefully Alia opened the flaps on the box, then she reached in and pulled out a stuffed bear. But not just any stuffed bear, it was the same one she had left at the cabin before heading for the academy. Only now it was cleaned so well it almost looked brand new. The only real indication that it was the same bear was the little melted spot about the size of a dime on one of its paws. Trish had gotten it with her cigarette. The bear had taken one for the team.

"Oh Charlie, my sweet boy, you got it restored."

"So, do you like it?"

"I love it, of course, I love it, Charlie, it's wonderful, you are amazing."

"That's not it. Here let me show you." Taking the bear from her, Charlie turned the crank in the back, and Brahms' Lullaby began to play. He then handed the bear back to Alia.

Totally amazed and with tears in her eyes, Alia listened as the tune played out, feeling a peace and calm, she only got in the arms of her boy. When the music was done, she got up on her toes and kissed him. "This has got to be the sweetest thing anyone has ever done for me, Charlie. Thank you so much."

"I thought you may like to have him around and keep you company when I can't be here." Charlie took her into his arms and kissed her back. "I love you, Alia. I'm so happy to have you back." *Please don't ever leave me again.*

Stepping back from him, Alia looked at the room, her new first apartment. "It's not much, is it?"

"Well, not yet, no. When I first moved into my place, all I had was a futon. I slept on the mattress on the floor for days trying to put the damn thing together. Mom tried to help set the place up for me, but of course, I was hard-headed and wanted to do it all myself. That meant I lived out of boxes for months before I finally broke down and realized I needed furniture." he laughed. "So do yourself a favor. If mom wants to help you shop, let her. Cooking is her best skill, followed closely by shopping."

"Oh yeah, she is so going to kick your ass for that one." Alia laughed, her arms around his waist.

"No, don't you dare tell her I said that."

"Sorry, I'm family now, no secrets." she teased.

Putting his hand on the side of her face, Charlie looked her deep into her eyes. "Yes, you are, aren't you, my sweet girl. I know for now you need to be on your own in a way. But I do plan on making it official one day. If you'll have me, that is."

"There's nothing else I want more." They kissed again, and Charlie lifted her up, spinning her around laughing. At that moment, they both felt like nothing could break them. They had no idea how hard something was going to try.

Back at the house, Charlie rushed to get ready for work. Once he was gone, Ellen and Alia went out to lunch in town to discuss all Alia would need and want for the apartment. As they sat outside a little cafe just blocks down from the Sheriff's station, Ellen could tell Alia was on edge. At first, she just sat and enjoyed her drink, watching as Alia kept looking around like she was on high alert.

"You are going to make yourself into a nervous wreck before the week is out at this rate," Ellen said at last.

"Hmm, oh, I'm sorry, I don't think I was here for a minute, was I?"

"No, you were not. Honestly, Alia, you need to relax. Not doing that ulcer of your any favors worrying so much."

"I know it's just that…well, she has an uncanny knack of showing up when I'm doing something wrong. Like she hones in on me."

"But you're not doing anything wrong."

Alia laughed. "I'm consorting with the enemy. And out in public for all to see no less."

"Would you be more comfortable if we went inside?"

Alia shook her head. "And miss out on such a pretty day?" she smiled. "No, it's just something I'm going to have to get used to."

Ellen reached across the table and took her hand. "I'm going to remind you again that you're not alone. Your family, we are in this together, and together we will deal with her. Then when it's done, it's done. She can try all she wants, but she can't hurt us. She can't hurt you, not anymore."

Alia agreed but still had her doubts. Just because Trish couldn't hurt them didn't mean she would go down without a fight.

After lunch, their first stop was a second-hand furniture shop where they got a comfy couch and a cute table and chair set. They got her a brand new bed at the mattress store to go with the headboard they also found at the furniture store. All of that wouldn't be delivered until the next day. Then they spent hours in Walmart getting everything from dishrags to a small flat-screen TV.

Still, the whole time, Alia looked around like her mother would pop out at her any second. Her only other concern was the amount of money she was spending. It wasn't like she didn't have a good bit after spending pretty much nothing the three months at the academy as much as she just wasn't used to having money to spend like that.

When they had literally three carts full, the next chore was fitting it all in Alia's jeep. The only real issue was the TV, and for that, they ended up having to call for backup. By the time Charlie arrived in his patrol car, the two were almost hysterical from laughing so hard trying to cram everything in the jeep.

Charlie took one look at all the stuff they had shoved into the small Jeep and shook his head. "Don't you think you two got enough? Looks like you bought out half the store."

"Oh Charlie, she's not even done yet," said his mother. "Good thing I remembered we had the jeep."

As Charlie came to get the TV from where they sat it down, Alia leaned into him and whispered. "Help me, Charlie, your mother is insane. Pt didn't wear me out this much." she laughed.

"Tried to warn you." He smiled back at her.

Charlie followed them to the apartment long enough to drop off the TV, gave Alia a kiss, and went back to work. Alia and Ellen had to take several trips up the flight of stairs for all the bags and things.

Ellen was helping to put some things away when she looked in Alia's closet. "Alia dear, is this all of your clothes?"

"Pretty much. I left a few things in the closet at the other place in case Trish would look in there. Oh, and I have some jeans and shorts in that box down there. No Dresser yet."

"Remind me about that tomorrow, I forgot. And please don't be offended, but you seriously need a new wardrobe." Alia looked at her old and outdated clothes in her closet, consisting mainly of t-shirts and two pairs of slacks that would probably fall off her now.

"Oh, believe me, non taken, I agree. Honestly, I don't even think half the jeans will fit me anymore. To tell you the truth, I really don't understand what it is your son sees in me." Alia laughed.

"He sees plenty, but there is no harm in having a few nice things to wear as well. No problem, we can take care of that too."

399

"Yay, more shopping," said Alia sarcastically, and they both laughed.

"Okay, I get it. I ran you ragged today. I tell you what, why don't we stop for now? I need to get home to cook dinner anyway. You can relax a bit while I do that."

Alia drove Ellen home, where she ended up helping to cook dinner only because she enjoyed it so much. Working in the kitchen with Trish had always been a combative situation with the two of them. No matter how hard Alia tried to please her, it was never good enough. Even when Trish messed meals up, she found a way to blame it on her. Hell, she did it when Alia wasn't even around. With Ellen, it wasn't even a chore. They listened to the radio singing and dancing around the kitchen despite how tired she had been earlier.

When the boys got home, they had yet another nice family meal. Charlie had to go back to work for a few hours after dinner, so Alia retired to the living room to read. Only she barely cracked the book open. Instead, she sat listening to Ellen and Harper clean the kitchen, which they forbade her to help with.

Growing up, the places where she and Trish lived seemed to always be filled with anger and arguing. This night amongst the clatter of dishes, there was more laughter and music coming from the kitchen. Then it would get quiet for a moment or two, and Ellen would either fuss at Harper to get back to work, or she would giggle. Listening to them, Alia hoped that things would one day be like that with her and Charlie in their own place.

When they were done, she stayed in the living room as they sort of watched TV. Ellen crocheted something with yarn in pretty fall colors while Harper halfway read the paper while glancing at the TV from time to time. And not once did Alia feel like she was intruding as she often had visiting even her own family member's homes.

A little after nine, Charlie came home stinking of smoke that smelled like burnt toast and grease and his hair all a mess. There had been a small kitchen fire at a house he had responded to for screaming coming from it. Turns out the screaming was a young new housewife that had burnt her new husband's dinner and a good part of her hand.

Charlie had gone into the kitchen and put the fire out while her husband took his wife outside to wait on the medics. She was later taken to the hospital.

By the time Charlie was out of the shower, they both were tired from the long day.

At eleven, everyone was ready for bed. As tired as Alia was, though, she couldn't bring herself to go to sleep. She kept making excuses or reading another chapter (or the same one over and over since she couldn't focus on reading anything), till finally, Charlie called her out.

"You can't stay up all night waiting for the phone to ring, Alia."

"I know, but it also seems pointless to go to sleep only to have her wake us up." But as she looked at Charlie, she could tell he was drained. "Look, why don't I go read downstairs and wait till around midnight. If she hasn't called by then, I'll come back up."

Charlie shook his head. "Give me your phone a minute."

Alia handed it over.

"OK, good, see your phone has this feature on it where you can personalize a busy message for certain phone numbers. Is this her actual number on the phone?" Alia nodded. "Great, now when she calls, if she calls tonight, she is going to get a message telling her to call you in the morning."

"Charlie, we all agreed to deal with this."

"And we will, but on our time. You can't let her keep dictating your life, Alia. And I sure as hell won't let her control mine. I'm tired, you're tired. Mom and Dad are already in bed. Let her leave whatever message she wants, but we will leave it to be dealt with in the morning." Charlie put the phone down and, taking her by the arm, pulled Alia into bed. She slipped under the covers with him, spooning up against him. As was usually the case once she was in his arms, it was like all the cares of the world were gone. Before she even realized it, Alia was fast asleep.

Chapter 22
Trish

In the morning, Alia woke early. Doing her best not to wake up Charlie, she checked her phone. There were several calls from Trish and several texts as well. Even three calls from another number that she assumed was Billy's. Trish's idea of being clever. Alia checked Charlie and saw that he was still asleep, so she tried to sneak out of the bedroom.

"Where are you going?" He woke up with a start. Charlie saw her phone in her hand and shook his head. "Nope, nope, come on now, we said we were going to do this together." he sat up in the bed, wiping a hand over his face and stubbly chin. "Come here, let's see."

Sitting down next to him, Alia showed him the calls and messages.

"Wow, that's a lot."

"Which means she is good and pissed off."

"Good." Said Charlie. "Fuck her. She can get pissed all she wants." he ran his hand through his thick dark hair and over his face. "Well, let's get it over with."

Alia hesitated, and he took her other hand. Sighing, she took a deep breath and clicked on the first voicemail.

"Alia, where the hell are you? Billy said, you never came home like you were supposed to. It is almost midnight, and you're not home. I don't care how grown you think you are now when you say you're going to be home you better be here."

"Well, that wasn't so bad."
"She's just getting started, Charlie, I'm sure."
The next message proved her right.

"Damn it, Alia, where the fuck are you? You need to answer my damn calls. No, I'm not going to wait till morning. I am your mother, and I demand to know where you are. As long as you still live under my roof, you will follow my rules, young lady."

And worse on the next.

"I just looked in your room good for the first time all summer. Where the hell is half of your shit? Stop playing games with me, Alia, and pick up the damn phone. Don't make me have to drive around town banging on doors looking for you."

And worse still

"Goddamn, it Alia, where the fuck are you? I know you didn't take all your shit with you to summer camp. What the hell are you up to? I knew something was going on. I knew it all summer. You better pick up the damn phone or so help you the next time I see you...."

And at last.

You damn site better call me first thing in the goddamn morning, or I will put the rest of your shit outside and burn it. You think you're so smart and so clever, your not Alia, you were always a stupid piece of shit like your father, and you always will be.

By the time they got to the last message, Alia had her legs drawn up to her chest, and her face buried. Charlie put his arms around her then pulled her into his. "You okay."
"I'm fine, just embarrassed. You see why I didn't want you all to hear that. And that's not even that bad."
There was a knock at the door, Charlie told them to come in, and Harper poked his head in. "I heard yelling. Am I to assume Trish left some messages last night?"
"Yeah, and a few texts as well," said Charlie.

403

"Okay, let's all wake up a bit, then meet downstairs in fifteen minutes. I want to hear those messages. Then we will figure out what to do next."

Twenty minutes later, they all were sitting in the living room, having heard the messages and read the texts that were along the same lines.

Ellen sat shaking her head, quiet but obviously distressed by what she heard.

Harper was pacing and got angrier the more they listened. "I have half a mind to go over there and get the rest of your stuff."

"Nothing I left there is worth it, Harper. Nothing that can't be replaced."

"It isn't right the way she talks to you," said Ellen.

"It's only going to get worse. When she finds out I'm a cop...she's either going to really blow her top or worse...not say a thing."

"How is that worse?" asked Ellen.

"I have a feeling that means she's going to do something instead." Said Harper.

"Exactly," said Alia.

"Look at this point, I don't give a shit what she says or tries to do. I want it done," said Charlie. "It's time we get on with our lives. Alia, I know she's your mother, and a part of you still cares about her, but she has a choice. She can accept what you have done and just maybe still be a part of your life, or she can have nothing to do with any of us again." Charles was sitting on the couch next to Alia. "Alia, whatever you want to do, you know I will support you."

"We all will." Said Harper.

Looking into Charlie's eyes, Alia took a deep breath and nodded. "Okay, let's get it done then before I lose my nerve." Picking up her phone from the coffee table, Alia was dismayed to see her hands were shaking. While she dialed her mother's number with one, she grasped Charlie's hands with the other. Alia then put the phone on speaker, and Harper put a recorder in front of Alia. The phone barely rang when the line was picked up.

"About fucking time you called me....I have been up all night. Alia, where the hell are you...and don't keep giving me that bullshit about some fucking camp."

"I'm here in town. I have been since Sunday." Alia's voice shook, and she gripped Charlie's hands tighter.

Ellen moved over to the empty spot on the couch and put her arm around Alia.

"What the hell, Alia? You could have fucking said something. Why is most of your stuff gone? When are you coming home? What the hell is going on with you?"

"I'm not...I mean...I'm not coming back to the apartment," Said Alia feeling better with the two at her side.

"Where the hell do you think you're going to stay, don't even fucking tell me your staying at Crystal's and mooching off of them now. How long do you think they will put up with your shit before they kick you out on the street? Then I guess you'll think you can just come crawling back here, don't ya?"

"I'm not staying at Crystal's. I have my own place here in town. You can do whatever you want with what I left. I have everything I need."

"Don't give me that shit, Alia. If I didn't know better, I would think you were shacking up with somebody, but who the fuck would want you to so much as suck their dick, let alone fuck them."

Charlie rose and began to say something, but Alia shook her head and let go of his hands to put a finger to her lips. She knew this was only going to get worse, and as embarrassing it was going to be, she also wanted it done. And recorded. If Charlie spoke up now, all it would do is shut her up. They would still have to deal with her eventually.

"Of course, I guess even you could find someone pathetic enough. Some men will fuck anything, I guess."

You should know

"I guess you think you're grown now. I guess you think that means you don't have to pay me anymore. I got news for you, little girl. You're not shit, nothing but a pathetic little spoiled brat. That money better keep coming to me, or when you fuck up as you always do and lose whatever shithole you say your living in, my door will be closed to you. And I will make sure everyone in this town knows just the kind of person you really are."

Taking a deep breath, Alia was now past being upset but instead on the verge of getting very angry. It wasn't even the things her mother was saying because this is what she had heard day in and day out for years and way worse. She was saying such nasty things in front of the people she cared about. Not that Trish knew, of course.

"Look, there's not going to be any more money. And you don't have to worry about me coming crawling back to you. I have a new life now, a new home, and a new job. The only thing you need to think about is whether you're going to be a part of my new life or not."

Half-crazed laughter came out over the phone. "Oh, listen to you, little Miss, I am grown. You don't know shit, Alia. You barely graduated high school. You won't survive a week without me. And what new job? Just what the hell have you been doing all summer, Alia? I'm not buying that summer camp bullshit. This whole thing was planned. You left out of here with all your shit that matters to you. All your dead daddy's garbage he left you instead of any money. All your good books are gone, even your winter clothes. You planned this shit which means you lied about where you were all summer. Have the balls to tell me the truth, at least."

At this point, Alia was shaking with rage. She was so focused on the phone in hand and trying to resist the urge to chunk it across the room that she had completely blocked out everything and everyone else. It was as if Trish was there in front of her, smoking a cigarette, her hands going through her hair, spit foaming on her lips like a mad dog. Grabbing hold of some strength deep inside her, Alia told Trish the truth.

"Your right…it was all planned, and I have been lying to you. I've been lying to you for months. Even before I knew the truth. Before I knew all the lies, you fed me my whole life. I have been planning for years on getting the hell away from you."

"You fucking little...." Trish started, but Alia cut her off.

"No, you're going to shut up for once and listen to me, or I will hang up the phone, and we will be done forever." Amazingly it was silent on the other end. Alia had to make sure the call was still ongoing. "No, I didn't go to the summer camp, I spent the summer training at the police academy instead, and I graduated with Honors. Harper is giving me a job at the Sheriff's department here in town. I'm a cop now, well cadet in training for the first few months. I've got my own apartment and even my own car. Most importantly, I have a new family now. One that doesn't treat me like shit."

Once again, silence, then hysterical laughter. "You a fucking cop? No, Alia, I'm not falling for that bullshit. There's no fucking way the academy would even take you, let alone you make it through. Unless, of course, you sucked dick your way through like that little bitch Charlie did."

This time Harper had to make sure Ellen was the one that stayed quiet. He was recording this whole thing and didn't want Trish to know anyone else was listening in. At least not yet. Trish was digging herself a considerable hole with every word she said, and if she knew they were there, she might stop.

Alia didn't register any of this. Her hand holding fast to the phone was white from the grip. Her face was hardened and determined even though she shook all over.

"And what fucking family Alia? I'm your only family, you have burned so many bridges with the rest of them none of them would ever want you."

I burned bridges. That's a riot coming from you.

"The same family that wanted me when you didn't. The ones that rescued me from the crack-house you left me in so you could go fuck and do drugs." Alia spit that last part out with venom. "I know the truth for once. I know all about my time in foster care and how you manipulated your way to getting me back."

For a minute, there was no response. Alia once again had to check to be sure the call was still ongoing.

"I should have fucking known that son of a bitch Harper had something to do with this. What lies have they filled you with, Alia? I told you, you can't trust them. They tried their best to tell stories about me, even had that little shit of theirs lie and say I was hurting you. Whatever they said, Alia, it's not true. I worked my ass off to get you back. The Harpers wanted you because that week little bitch Ellen couldn't have children anymore. Hell, she's probably a victim, too, for all I know. Harper probably raped her, and that's why she can't have kids anymore. It's all lies, Alia. Come home, and we will talk all about it. Come home, and I'll tell you once and for all just the type of person Atticus Harper really is."

Alia was barely aware of Ellen leaving her side as she ran into the arms of her husband in tears.

Here it goes, this is where she tries to make a last-ditch effort to win me back over by telling me how everyone else is the liar, and she is the only one that ever told me the truth.

"Oh, poor stupid gullible Alia...I told you, you won't' make it without me. You can't tell the difference between bullshit and the truth to save your life. What did they tell you, huh? About how horrible of a mother I was? About how I abused you? You know I never laid a hand on you, Alia."

What the actual fuck??!!

"But you know who did? That little fucking bastard of theirs. Oh, he just couldn't keep his hands off of you. Harper, too for all I know. And when I found out and threatened to tell, they said they would take you away forever. They said they were going to kidnap you, Alia. I even had to change social workers. They had her stupid ass so brainwashed. And I should have known. I should have stopped you from leaving this summer. I told you I knew you had been hanging around that pervert and his fucked up spawn. How long has it been going on, Alia, huh? How long has he been diddling you hu? Or is it both of them? Does Charlie like his daddy's sloppy seconds? Does he Alia?"

Alia was trembling so hard now she could barely keep her grip on the phone. Tears and sweat streamed

408

down her face as she shoved the phone at Charlie, no longer able to bear hearing any more of it.

"I'm done, I'm done." she cried. "I can't take her shit anymore; I won't take it anymore. I'm done with her. Someone shut her up, just shut her the hell up." Alia buried her face in her hands, trembling with rage.

Trish continued to scream obscenities over the phone, asking who the hell she was talking to, demanding them to leave the two of them alone.

Harper took the phone from Charlie and covered the mouthpiece as best as possible with his big hands. "Charlie, get her Two shots of whiskey and make sure she drinks them both. Ellen get her a few wet rags and try to calm her down. I'm going to give this bitch a much needed piece of my mind."

Harper went out the backdoor with the phone, turning off his recorder as he went while the others attended to Alia.

"Now listen here, you fucking bitch. This ends here. Alia is back with us now, and if I so much as catch you on the same street as her, I will lock your ass up. I will forget that I have been a good cop for over twenty years and do everything in my power to make sure you never see the light of day again."

"Don't you fucking threaten me, you piece of shit. You give me my daughter back, or I will make sure the whole town knows about your little pervert of a son. I will ruin all of you."

"Good luck with that lady because no one is gonna believe you. Charlie is a good man and a damn good cop. No one in this town will believe the lies of a little tramp like you anymore. Especially not once they hear the conversation I just recorded you having with your daughter."

"How stupid do you think I am, Harper? You may have her brainwashed, but I'm much smarter than some stupid little kid. I'm much smarter than when you two tried to steal Alia away from me."

409

As proof, Harper played back a part of what she had said to Alia over the phone. The silence on the other end was all he needed to know.

"The sad part is I think you believe some of the shit you say. I think you are so far gone that you're buying your own crap."

"Yes, I'm crazy, Harper, you may want to remember that. It would be a shame if something happened...."

"Like what, huh? You have nothing to hurt my family with anymore, you lying bitch. And if I was you, I would think twice about so much as looking at Alia the wrong way. She's not the same scared kid that she used to be, Trish. She's strong now. And if Charlie and I have anything to do with it, we will keep making her stronger. You are done, women. Try your best, I dare you, but you are done. Leave Alia alone. She just said she wants nothing more to do with you, so don't be stupid and just leave her alone."

"I am her mother, Harper, and not you or anyone else can stop me from seeing her."

"She can, Trish. She's a member of my force now and therefore under the protection of all my men. If she doesn't want to see you, then you better stay the hell away from her. You don't want her anyway, you just can't stand to see the kid happy. And that is just pathetic. You, Trish, are pathetic."

Harper ended the call resisting the urge to slam the phone to the ground. Instead, he shoved it into the pocket of his robe even as it started to ring. Back in the living room, Alia was in Charlie's arms, crying in rage. Ellen and Charlie both had tears on their faces, and it enraged him. He poured himself a shot of whiskey then brought another one over to Charlie.

"Give her another one, son. Make her take it if you have to."

"Dad, she already had two. She doesn't drink, a third is liable to put her out."

"Exactly the point. She needs a break, son. She needs something to bring that rage down before it drowns her."

Charlie gave Alia the shot, which she took without argument and went back into his arms. Slowly her rage ebbed out of her, and the shakes got less and less.

Ellen dried her tears and kissed both her kids on the head, then went into the arms of Harper, needing a bit of solace herself. "What are we going to do, Harper?"

"Nothing, we have the recording. The ball is in her court now. We just keep a close eye on the two of them. Other than that, we do the one thing that will hurt her most of all. We get back to being a wonderful loving family."

Looking over at Alia now half-asleep in Charlie's arms, Ellen wondered if that was even going to be possible.

Harper had gone off to do a few things, including informing all of his staff to keep an eye out for Trish and let him know if she was hanging around or causing any problems. He then spoke with Alia's landlord, being sure not to alarm her. Then he got a few things he needed at the hardware store. Shortly before lunch, Harper returned to the house. Alia was out cold, laying on top of Charlie, who had stretched out on the couch to let her sleep, his long legs dangling over the side.

"I'm going to need your help with something, son," he told Charlie

"Sure, just give me a minute. I'd like to let her sleep if I can." Charlie stroked Alia's hair and kissed the top of her head. As soon as he tried to slip out from under her, she woke with a start and grabbed onto him instantly awake.

"Hey, hey, it's okay, Alia." Charlie felt her terror, and then he felt it slide away as she eased her grip on him.

"Sorry, I don't know why but I thought you were falling."

"Yeah, well, the three shots of Whiskey may have something to do with that." he smiled up at her. "How are you feeling?"

"Like I could use a nice long hot shower. Ugh, Charlie, I'm practically sticking to you. How can you stand to have me on top of you? I feel like I'm burning up."

"Also the whiskey. It's not that bad, just a little damp. Besides, there's nothing I love more than holding you in my arms. I do need to get up, though. Dad needs me for something, and I should get ready for work soon. I don't want to have to stay working all night, not after this morning."

With the reminder of the morning's event, Alia frowned, shaking her head. Trish's voice, which she had gotten so good at ignoring most of the summer, was back screaming louder than ever.

"Hey, It's going to be okay. The hard part is over now," said Charlie.

"No, it isn't, Charlie. Trish is not going to go down without a fight. Believe me when I say she's just warming up."

"And neither are we. I will do everything I can to protect you from her, Alia."

"That's what worries me, Charlie." her eyes welled with tears.

Charlie smiled the smile he knew she loved and kissed her forehead. "I don't plan on letting her hurt me either, don't worry about that."

"You better not Charles Harper." Alia smiled back at him.

"Why don't you go on up and get that shower? I need to go see what dad wants. We have new lives now, Alia. It's time we get to them. Let Trish do what she will." Peeling herself off of Charlie, Alia went to shower, and Charlie joined his father and mother in the kitchen.

"How is she doing?" asked Ellen

"Little wobbly going up the stairs, but I think she's going to be okay. She's taking a shower right now, that will help. Mostly I think she's worried about us."

"Well, I'm worried about her. I don't think Trish will come after us, not directly anyway," said Ellen. "But she's never going to see Alia as anything other than a scared little girl. Now I realize she has grown a lot in the past three months, but that woman is crazy. She may not be able to see it, especially if she doesn't allow herself to see it."

"Which is why we are going to set up some security for her at the apartment," said Harper. "Nothing too big, of course, but if someone tried to get into her place, at least it would let us know." Said Harper. "We need to turn our system back on for a while as well. I don't think she will come at us either, but we have it, so it would be foolish not to use it. So that's why I'm going to need your help with Charlie. Mrs. Porter has agreed to allow us to set up a few cameras and a control panel, so we will get that done before heading into work. I would feel a lot better about her being there today with it set up."

"Okay, I'll take Alia out for some lunch and fresh air when she is done with her shower," said Ellen. "That should give the two of you enough time to have it all set up and show her how it works."

They made arrangements to meet at the apartment at around one in the afternoon then the boys left.

Ellen waited for Alia, happy to see when she came downstairs that she looked much better than she had that morning.

"So, how are you feeling?"

"Little lightheaded still. I think you're going to have to drive today."

"Good. Do you think you're up for some lunch? I was thinking about the same cafe as yesterday. In fact, you will come to realize that is my go-to place. When I was younger, and Harper and I were dating, I used to go there just so I could catch a glimpse of him driving around in his patrol car. Pretty sure I single-handedly kept that place in business," she said with a laugh.

"That sounds good. In fact, you know what, that sounds great. I've had to hide and sneak around long enough. We all have. Personally, I'm tired of it. I'm done with letting her intimidate and control me. If I can't get over her and her shit, how will I ever be a decent cop? Then all this hard work, training, and being away from Charlie will have been for nothing. Maybe I've gotten away with doing that to myself all these years, but I won't do it to Charlie or you and Harper either, for that matter. All of you have been too good to me to give up and let her win." Alia took a deep, cleansing breath and smiled. "I think I'm ready to get on with my life."

Ellen grabbed Alia in a big warm hug. "I am so happy to hear you say that. I'm so proud of you, baby girl. And don't ever forget you're not in this alone. In fact, right now, the boys are setting up a little security system at your new place just in case. Just something to make sure no one tries to mess with anything. We have one as well. We just haven't used it in forever."

"Well, maybe you should. Not so much when Harper is here but for when he's not. She won't try anything with him, I don't think, but she may see you as an easy target."

"Already taken care of. Now let's get lunch. We are supposed to meet up with the boys in an hour."

At lunch, Alia still couldn't help but look around in case Trish drove by. When Ellen used the bathroom, Alia pulled out her phone, checking her text messages. Most of them were from Trish and extremely vulgar, but at least she had stopped trying to call. Alia took screenshots of it all like Harper had told her to in case they would ever need it but refused to rise to the bait and answer.

A few texts were from Crystal. Trish had called there several times looking for Alia, accusing them of hiding her because there was no way she believed that Alia had a job and her own place. She sent a few texts back, and they made plans to meet up at her house later to talk and hang out.

Once she was able to relax a little, lunch was excellent. Times with Ellen ended up being like what Alia always imagined hanging out with a mother should be. They gossiped, laughed, and talked about shopping they would do later on. No criticizing the way Alia talked, or ate, or her hair, or scolding her. It was such a pleasant relief from the life she had spent with Trish.

After lunch, they went to the apartment, where the boys finished installing the security system. There was a camera outside to film the driveway, one at the door and staircase and one in the central part of the apartment she could turn on at night. The control box was just inside the door, and Charlie showed her how to use it and the code. There was also had an app he downloaded onto her phone to get alerts while she was away, control the system and even raise an alarm.

"Now, all of this may be going to extremes, but I'll feel a lot better about you being here alone with it." Said Harper. "And later, you and I are going to do a little shopping of our own. I want you to have your own handgun, separate from the service piece you will be getting next week. You don't have to carry it with you, but you should at least have one. Even without issues with your mother, just being on the force can put you on the radar of some nasty people."

"He's right, and a lot of them think a woman cop is a jab at their manhood or something," said Charlie.

The boys said their goodbyes needing to get back to work. Before they left, Harper looked at the phone messages shaking his head. "You may want to consider blocking her number, but for now, let's see what all she says. If she starts making threats, I want to know right away.

With the boys gone, Ellen and Alia busied themselves, setting up the things they got the day before for the apartment. The security system announcing someone had arrived at the foot of her stairs outside liked to scare them both. They went to the door in time to see a delivery man about to knock.

"Well, at least we know it works," Alia said.
Soon after the mattress guy left, another truck showed up with the couch, kitchen table, and chairs. The place was starting to look like something finally. Once they left, Ellen called for a break.

"I think we should do something that always puts me in a good mood."

"Yay, more shopping." Alia joked.

"Yes, but this time, clothes shopping."

Alia laughed because Ellen looked so thrilled at the prospect when for her clothes shopping was always a complete horror show.

"Let me guess, you hate clothes shopping?"

"Look, if you say let's go book shopping, I will beat you downstairs, but clothes…ugh."

"I have to say you're the first young woman I have ever met that didn't like to go clothes shopping. We are going to fix that, come on."

To Alia's surprise, she did just that. This was another experience that had been ruined by Trish. First of all, they never had money. At least not for Alia (plenty to do drugs and drink with), so she was always regulated to shopping discount stores and clearance racks. That didn't leave many options. Couple that with the fact that Alia always felt she was fat (and constantly told by her mother that she was) and wanted to hide behind loose-fitting clothes. When Alia had remarked she didn't know what Charlie saw in her, she wasn't joking.

Her experience with Ellen that day was unlike any other. Not only did she not once remark about Alia being fat (which, to be fair, any baby fat she had disappeared since training), but she took her to nice places like Old Navy and Target. For someone that grew up on Walmart and Kmart rejects, that was the clothing equivalent of fine dining.

However, it wasn't just Ellen that made the whole experience a lot of fun. Once Alia started trying things on, she began to realize she was in much better shape than she had given herself credit. Charlie had noticed and pointed out her sleek new lines and curves, but it really hit home when she put her first few pairs of skinny jeans on.

To help make things even better, Ellen had a knack for knowing what would look good, what would match what, and what Alia should under no circumstances ever wear. Ellen also considered Alia's style, which is something Trish never did.

Between the two stores, they had a whole new wardrobe for her, including bras, panties, socks, and shoes. When Alia got home putting everything away was a bit overwhelming.

It was getting late by the time they were done, and they both were tired. "I have a great idea," said Ellen. "Why don't we have the boys meet up with us somewhere in town for dinner? I'll run home and get ready, then come back and pick you up. That way, we can show off some of your new duds."

"You think Harper will be okay with going out to eat from work?"

"Of course, he will. We do it all the time since Charlie moved out. Besides, I like it when he goes out with his uniform on, something hot about that man in a uniform I don't know what it is."

Alia smiled, feeling the same way about Charlie but not about to say that to his mother, that's for sure. "Okay, if you think the boys will be alright with it, then great. Uh, can I ask one thing, though?"

"Yes, of course."

"I know this is going to sound dumb considering what we did today, but…what do you think I should wear? I mean, I don't know. If you haven't figured it out, I'm not exactly hip to fashion of any type. Could you help me pick out something nice?"

Ellen faced Alia, tears welling up in her eyes.

"I'm sorry, did I say something wrong?"

Ellen hugged Alia, the tears falling. "No, baby girl, you said all the right things. You have no idea how long I have wanted a daughter to go shopping with. Oh, when you were with us as a baby, I got you the cutest dresses and outfits. Funny though, you always wanted to wear what Charlie was wearing when you got old enough to speak your mind. And that wasn't very old. You've made my day, hell, my entire year. I would be more than happy to find you something, and I know just the thing." Ellen went into Alia's closet and picked out a black skirt (one of a few she talked Alia into getting) and a purple silky long sleeve shirt. To it, she added a matching bra and panties set and a pair of low heel dress shoes she also insisted Alia get a few pairs of. Ellen then headed out, needing to go home to shower and dress.

That left Alia alone in her first apartment for the first time ever. Shutting the door and setting the alarm, she felt her old familiar friend anxiety build up in her. Alia looked around the small apartment that was still a mess of boxes and packing materials from the things they had bought. It was lonely and so very quiet. Way too quiet. She was used to at least having the sound of a TV in another room, noises from people upstairs, or the soft sounds of Charlie snoring. Okay, maybe not so soft. The quiet, which she usually loved in the library or out in the woods, felt heavy to her now.

Before getting into the shower, Alia turned on the radio to a local station, not even minding hearing people talking between the music. She was about to get in when another text came to her phone. Alia glanced at it and saw it was from Billy's phone. Assuming her mother was now using his phone to try to harass her, she looked at the text anyway.

Billy: Hey kid, it's Billy. It's really me. I'm out walking the dog. I'm going to call.
Please pick up. Your mother has done lost it. Please pick up when I call.

Sure enough, a few seconds later, her phone rang. Taking a deep breath, expecting it to still be a trick, Alia answered.

"Hello?"

"Jesus Christ, kid, are you okay? Your mother is going off the deep end, I mean more than usual. She keeps going on and on about the Sheriff kidnapping and brainwashing you, that his son is raping you and all this other shit. I don't know whether to believe her or not. Do you know she didn't go to work today? She never misses work. Shit, kid, what the hell did you do? Really are you okay?"

"Billy, calm down. I'm fine. No one kidnapped me. They sure as hell haven't hurt me."

"Then what the hell is she going on about? Why didn't you come home? She keeps calling people in the family, telling them all this crazy ass shit. And are you a cop now? Shit kid, you know how your mother is. I don't know what to believe."

Alia explained to him how she had been planning to join the academy and move out for almost a year. She then gave him a cliff notes version about the Harper's being her foster parents once upon a time. She also assured him that no one was hurting her or holding her against her will.

"I've got my own place and even my own car now. I'm free from her, Billy, and that's what is pissing her off."

"Pissing her off...that is putting it extremely mild. She has the place torn apart. Your room is a wreck. She's busted or torn apart anything you left behind. One minute she is mad as hell at you the next, she is talking like you're some kind of victim. I told her to go to the cops, and she's all like, you idiot, the cops are the ones that stole her away from me. You need to talk to her, Alia, try and calm her down or something."

"We tried that already, and she went off on me. I told you, Billy, I warned you about her when you first got involved with her. I told you to run and to never look back, but you wouldn't listen to me."

"Shit, kid, I thought you were just some jealous brat. I mean, sure, after a while, I got the idea she was a nut, but...you know the sex was good. But shit, now she's not even putting out anymore."

"Leave her, Billy. The apartment lease ends in October, right? Tell them you're leaving and just go. Listen to me this time. As bad as she has been, you haven't seen anything yet. This is just the start. She will blow this whole thing out of proportion as best as she can, and she will take out anyone that stands against her. I mean, you're kinda an asshole, but I still don't think you deserve to put up with this shit."

"Already been working on that, Kid. I got some money stashed that she doesn't know about, and my shit is almost packed. I was doing like you said and trying to wait till after summer. But if shit is cool with you, I'm out of here soon."

"My shit is cool, Billy. I couldn't be any happier than I am right now. Well, I mean, if I didn't have a psychopath for a mother, I could be happier, I guess. I have a family for the first time in my life and the most amazing boyfriend, a girl, could ever ask for. Nothing she says about any of them is true, not a word."

"I should be getting back, she's gonna be pissed if I'm gone too long, and she has no one to vent to. Little warning, she's trying to find out where you are, so don't be surprised if she pays you a little visit. Hey, shit, are you really a cop now? I mean, I don't approve, you know that, but damn Alia, I never thought you had it in you."

"Yes, well, a cadet in training for the next few months. And don't worry about her coming to see me. We have that covered."

"Yeah, no shit, you a cop now..huh. Look, kid, I know I was a complete asshole to you most of the time, but....you know I'm really proud of you, kid. Not the whole pig thing, of course, but you know...getting your shit straight and getting out of here. Fuck that. I'm proud of you for that, too. It takes real balls to stand up and take the chance to do something you want to do. Just try not to give me too hard of a time when you pull me over, okay. Cop or no cop, my ass still gonna drive like a freak."

Alia surprised herself with her eyes filling with tears. "Thanks, Billy, in some fucked up way coming from you, that means a lot to me."

"Take care, kid, and watch your back."

"You too, Billy." Alia ended the call having no way of knowing that Billy would come up missing in two months and never be heard from again.

When Ellen picked her up that evening, Alia didn't mention the phone call. She didn't plan on saying it at dinner either. For just that night, she wanted to forget about that woman and focus on getting on with her life. Dinner out with the family was a great way to do that. When the two of them got to the restaurant where they would meet the boys and parked, Alia realized she was nervous and not because of recent events. Instead, she had jitters and butterflies like she was about to go out on a first date. Technically, it was their first in public, not counting the prom.

Even Ellen noticed. Alia fussed with her hair and clothes before getting out. "You look fine," said Ellen as they got out.

"Thank you, I'm just not used to the whole skirt and heals thing."

Like putting tits on a bull hog, her mother's voice chimed up inside her head, causing her to wince.

"You look great. Nothing wrong with showing off those fabulous legs of yours once in a while."

Alia blushed, "Why does that sound strange coming from the mother of my boyfriend." she laughed.

"Okay then, if It'll make you feel better, think of it as coming from your mother. Well, maybe not your mother, but you know what I mean."

"Yes, I do, and thanks, Mom, thank you for all of it today, not just imparting your fashion wisdom onto the fashionably hopeless."

"Oh, dear child, you are far from hopeless. You're young, yet you still have plenty of time to learn a few things. I was like you at your age. Bookishly smart, clueless about boys. Then I met Harper. Suddenly I wanted to be beautiful and flawless like all the other girls just so he would notice me. But guess what? He already had. In fact, the whole reason I noticed him was that he would try and show off in front of me. She stopped walking and faced Alia. "One thing I have learned about relationships all these years is how little what you look like on the outside really matters. If you're ugly on the inside, it's never going to work. That goes for both men and women. A person can be lovely on the outside, but eventually, that ugliness on the inside eats away at that outside as well. Just look at Trish. She was a pretty young thing when she first came to us. That didn't last very long."

And Ellen was right. Alia remembered seeing pictures of her mother when she was younger, and she had been pretty. But Alia's memory of her mother going back as far as she could remember was always of someone that looked dragged down and worn. Drugs had some to do with that. But she never got into anything more than speed and not even that for long. She drank a lot too but so did a lot of young girls. The hate, though. Her hatred for everyone and everything was worse than the booze and drugs combined.

Arm in arm, the two women, kept walking around the block to the front of the restaurant where Harper and Charlie stood waiting for them.

When Charlie saw Alia, he felt his heart skip a beat, smiling he mouthed the word Wow at her and smiled even more.

Once again, Alia felt herself blush.

The dinner was terrific. They ate, talked, and laughed. Alia took notice of a few people glancing their way and wondered to herself what they were thinking. She even noticed a few bowed heads and whispering. Most likely trying to figure out who their Deputy Sheriff was out having dinner with, she doubted anyone here would have known her. She would have been surprised who all did.

After dinner, the boys walked them back to Ellen's car. Charlie held Alia back from his parents just enough so they wouldn't hear him. "Do me a favor and don't take that outfit off until I get off work tonight. I mean, if it's okay that I come over."

"Of course it's okay. I really don't want to spend my first night there alone. I'm surprised your father hasn't demanded that I stay at their place again tonight."

"If it wasn't for the security system, he may have. I told him I planned on staying if you wanted me to. I don't think we really have anything much to worry about, but I would feel better if you would let me stay over for at least the next few nights."

"Well, we may have more to worry about than you think," Alia told him about the conversation she had with Billy. "Don't tell your mom, not yet anyway. She's been enjoying mother and daughter time. I don't want her to have to worry anymore than she already does."

"I won't, but I'm telling Dad when we get back to work. Are you sure you're going to be okay till I get off work? You can always go stay with Mom, and I'll come to get you."

"No, Crystal plans on coming over when I get back. She hasn't seen the place yet, just shoot me a text when you're about to get off, and I'll shoo her out the door."

"Great, sounds like a plan. But any trouble, I mean anything I want you to call me." He leaned in closer to whisper. "And please do not take that skirt off." he grinned at her.

Back at the apartment, Ellen told her pretty much the same thing about calling if she needed anything, then began fussing around the apartment.

Alia laughed at her. "You can go, Mom, Crystal will be here soon, and she will stay until Charlie gets here."

"I know. I just hate the thought of leaving you here. You know if you feel uncomfortable staying here, you and Charlie are more than welcome to stay at our place another night."

"I'll keep that in mind."

Ellen looked over at the beautiful young woman before her. At the restaurant, Charlie hadn't been able to take his eyes off of her. "But you won't, and it's alright, I understand. I know Charlie is eager to have his girl all to himself." she smiled.

No sooner than she left, Crystal pulled up in the Buick. Having gotten enough miles under her, her parents were letting her drive alone more often, even after dark. So she was more than happy to hang around until it was time for Charlie to get off work.
Alia filled her in on everything going on, including the call from Billy.

"Yeah, I didn't want to say anything, but she's been calling our house like crazy all day. She got into it with my father, trying to convince him that you were kidnapped and brainwashed by the police. After that, she got it in her head we were not on her side. She cussed him out a lot then didn't bother to call again."

"She's done, lost it."

"Are you worried she's going to try and do something?"

"Oh, I'm sure she will. Billy said she didn't go to work today, so I'm surprised she hasn't done something already. The thing is, though, other than running her mouth, I don't know what she thinks she can do."

"So what about you, Charlie and the Harper's, what are you all going to do? You said Harper had her recorded."

"Not much for now. What she said over the phone was nasty. No one wants to have that come out unless we don't have a choice. It's just being used to keep her from doing anything too stupid. Hopefully anyway. You know, I knew this whole thing would be a shit show, but part of me was just hoping Trish would accept it and move on. I mean, according to her, I've been a burden to her my whole life. The only reason she works at the plant was because of me. You would think she'd see this as finally getting her freedom."

"My father was talking to me about this earlier, and he says it has nothing to do with that. This is about control. It's like those awful stories you hear about girls finding this great guy, then suddenly she's not allowed to talk to anybody or go anywhere, and he comes off all like he's just afraid she will cheat on him. All those years ago, you cheated on your mother with another family. And now she's lost you to them. She only wants you around because you're the only thing in her life she ever had any control over. Losing you to become a cop was one thing. Losing you to them was just an added insult."

"Well, what the hell did she think was going to happen?"

"That you would believe her version of events over theirs, of course."

"Trish actually had the nerve to say she never laid a hand on me. Sometimes I wonder how much of what she says is a blatant lie and how much she believes to actually be true."

"If that's the case, you may have more to worry about than you thought. If she is just angry because she lost control of you, that's one thing. But if she's nut-so enough to believe what she's saying, she could prove to be dangerous. And not just to you."

"Believe me, that's one thing I've been worried about the most. This is why Harper put in the security unit. He's going to take me to get my own gun as well. The thing is, though, no matter how mad or crazy she is, I don't see her doing much beyond harassing me. I think once she gets it into her head that she can't hurt me anymore, she'll just give up, and if we are lucky, go away."

Alia should have known that she was never that lucky, and nothing was ever that easy.

Later Alia got a text message from Charlie saying he would be there in about ten minutes. Crystal was set to leave then stopped.

"First night in the apartment, and you're wearing a skirt?"

"Your point?"

Crystal sighed. "You know, if you watched something other than a horror movie once in a while, you might know something about setting a romantic scene." Crystal went around the apartment dimming lights, putting a scarf over the one lamp on the floor in the bedroom, and putting the radio on to a jazzy easy listening station. "You can thank me later," she said, hurrying out the door. "Oh, and put the heels back on and be sitting all casual like on the couch when he comes in, don't greet him at the door. Looks too desperate."

"Get the hell out of here, Crystal." Alia laughed. However, after taking one last look in the bathroom mirror, she did indeed put the heels on and sit on the couch pretending to leaf through a magazine.

I feel silly, she thought. *It's not like we haven't been going at it like rabbits every chance we have gotten.*

However, she also knew that Charlie was every bit as much of a romantic as she was. There had been candlelight dinners, breakfast in bed, and walks in the woods under the moonlight, even at the cabin. It had never been just about the actual act of having sex for them. The build-up to it was always just as significant. Sitting there, Alia still felt silly and nervous. When she heard his boots on the stairs, the butterflies started their old familiar dance. Then his face appeared at the window of the door, and she was once more instantly set at ease.

Letting himself in with his own key, Charlie smiled over at her, taking notice of the lights and music. Alia looked back up at him with those diamond blue eyes of hers and smiled as well. And just like that, the weariness he had felt since after dinner was gone. Not saying a word, Charlie locked the door, made sure the alarm was on and the living room camera was off. Then he took off his boots. Coming over to the couch, he sat sideways as she did in front of her. Alia had tossed the magazine she was reading (like hell she was in that lighting), so he was able to get right next to her.

"Hi Charlie," she said, her eyes sparkling even in the low light.

"Hi, my sweet girl." with his right hand, Charlie traced his fingers up one of her legs. They were soft, smooth, and taut in all the right places. The skirt, which already ended well above her knees, was even higher now with her sitting down. He wondered not for the first time if she had any idea how much she drove him crazy.

Charlie's hand continued to move up over her knee to the line where the skirt ended. He knew what she wanted, what she needed, and he planned on stretching it out as long as he could, in no hurry to get anywhere beyond the here and now. As his fingers breached the line of her skirt to the skin beyond, Alia reached out, grabbed his tie, and pulled him to her. They kissed, teasing each other while the heat built up between them. His left hand went to her long brown hair, while his right hand went higher under the skirt and flirted with the lacy hem of her underwear.

They went no further than the couch for a while, and no further than two young people would allow themselves to if they had parents just in the next room. Charlie ran his lips over the contours of her neck and jawline, his right hand out from under her skirt exploring under her silky blouse instead. He was pleasantly startled when he felt the lace of the new bra she wore. When he rubbed his thumb over her nipple, he knew she was as well.

With his tie already tossed aside, Alia unbuttoned his uniform shirt. Pausing for a moment, Charlie threw it aside as well and was going back in to kiss her when she shook her head and began lifting his undershirt up over his head. As he kissed her one hand in her hair, one feeling her nipples through her bra, she rubbed her hands over his muscly back and chest driving him insane. When her hands got down to his waistband, taking off his belt, Charlie couldn't take it anymore.

Getting up, he lifted her into his arms and carried her into the bedroom and onto the bed. Before she was barely down, he had her heels off, taking time to caress her muscular calves and kissing them ever so lightly. He then left his pants on the floor and joined her in bed, where he took his time removing her undergarments, kissing and teasing her as he did.

Their love-making that night was slow as well, taking their time to enjoy every little nuance of it. As good as it had been for them before, they both felt this night had been even more special than even their first night. It was as if the start of their relationship was that night with her out on her own, ready to begin their new lives together.

The next evening the four of them were together again at the Harper's home for family dinner night. Alia and Ellen spent the day together again, getting the last of the things she would need for now for the apartment. They were talking about that and the boys' workday when a call came first to Harper's cell then to the house phone immediately after but only rang twice. That was code for an urgent call from the station.

Excusing himself, Harper took his cell into the living room. A couple of minutes later, he came back. "Come on, Charlie, we need to get to the station right now."

"What's going on?" asked Ellen.

Harper glanced over at Alia, wondering if he should even say anything. "It's Trish. She's at the station and giving them a bunch of shit."

Charlie and Harper went to the mudroom to put their gun holsters back on, Alia followed.

"I'm coming too," said Alia

"No, you're not." both Charlie and Harper said at the same time.

"The hell I'm not. This is my fight. I'm not going to back down from her."

Harper went to her and put his hand on her shoulders. "And if she confronts you, then don't dare back down. But right now, she's in my office going after my people. You're not officially part of the force yet. You going in there is just going to cause more problems. We are going to handle this mess the right way. Ellen make sure she stays here. The last thing we need right now is to worry about you." Harper left her and continued to get ready.

Ellen put her hands reassuringly on Alia's shoulders. "He's right, dear. Let the boys deal with this for tonight at least."

Charlie ran over to her and gave her a quick kiss on the forehead. "Please just stay here. We'll be right back. I love you."

"Just be careful with her, Charlie. She's going to try and goad you into a fight, don't let her."

Charlie winked at her as they ran out the door.

When Charlie and Harper walked into the station a few minutes later, Trish stood at the front desk, still yelling at Deputy Rusty, who was on desk duty that night. She heard them come in and whirled around to face them.

"Well, if it isn't the Sheriff and the little shit Deputy. Where is my daughter Harper! I demand you to tell me where she is."

Harper had hoped the woman was drunk or drugged, but she looked utterly sober. The steely red hot look in her eyes gave him an idea of just how pissed off she was, but there was a spark of insanity in there as well.

"Damn it, Trish, you can't just come here and harass my deputies. Your daughter left of her own free will."

"Like hell she did. How long, Harper? How long have the two of you been turning her against me?"

"The only one that has done that is you," said Charlie.

"Shut up, you little pervert. Yeah, I know what you have been doing with my little girl, you sick fuck." Trish turned to Harper. "I want to press charges. If you don't tell me where my daughter is, then I want to press charges against him for molesting her."

Charlie started to say something, but his father held him back. "Trish, Alia is eighteen years old. She is free to go where she wants and do what she wants. I know that's hard for you to come to grips with, but you're going to have to face it."

"I'm not going to face shit, Harper. No eighteen-year-old girl just leaves home without saying anything. Not a girl like Alia. The two of us have never kept secrets from each other before. Suddenly, I find out she's been hanging around the two of you, and then she just ups and leaves me. And you expect me to believe she did it of her own free will? That's bullshit, and you know it. Eighteen or not, she's still just a child, a very naive child at that. Now damn it, I want to see her, I want to talk to her."

"You did that already. We were both there and heard what you said to Alia. She doesn't want to talk to you. Now you have two choices, you either go home or spend the night downstairs."

"I bet you were there. I bet you were right there coaching her along with what to say. There's no way you're going to convince me she is doing all this willingly unless I get to talk to her face to face. And I'm not going anywhere until I see her. If you try to lock me up, I'll sue your ass for police brutality." she seethed.

Harper looked over at Charlie, who he was surprised to find had been quiet so far. Even more of a surprise was the half-smile on his face. "What are you thinking, Charlie?"

"I say we give her what she wants. But then this ends here tonight. After you talk to her, that's it. Once she tells you to go fuck off, you leave us the hell alone."

"And if she wants to come home with me, will you let her?"

Charlie laughed a laugh with no humor in it. "I'll do better than that. If she wants to go home with you, I won't try to see her ever again."

Trish smiled like she had won already. "So you little shit, you admit you have been seeing her. Did you hear that…" Trish turned, but the Deputy behind the counter had made himself scarce.

"Damnit, Trish, knock your crap off. If you want to see her, that will be up to Alia, but I'll be damned if I am going to stand here and allow you to insult my son like that."

"Fine. You'll see Charles Harper, and when you do, I'm going to make sure you stick to your word this time."

"Alright then," said Harper, "We will bring her in, and you can talk to her, but it gets done here. We can use the interrogation room." *so I can film it.* "And Charlie and I will be in there too."

"No way we are in there alone, or it's no deal. Besides, I don't want this little pervert anywhere near her."

"What the hell did I just say, Trish."

"It's okay, dad. She can insult me all she wants. I will get the last laugh tonight you can be sure of that." said Charlie with a grin that sent chills through Trish. Charlie advanced a foot, but Harper held him back with one arm.

"Fine. If Alia is okay with it, the two of you can talk alone. Just give us some time to get her over here. But I'm warning you, Trish, when she tells you she doesn't want to come home with you, you will leave quietly or so help me I will lock your ass up."

Trish walked away smiling to herself, convinced that no such thing was going to happen.

Harper turned to Charlie. "Call your mother and tell her to bring Alia over here and to come in the back way. Enough of a spectacle has been made over this as it is."

"You really think Trish is going to go quietly?"

"No, not at all, and I know you don't like the idea of leaving the two of them alone, but we will be watching from the next room. And, of course, we will be recording it. If she doesn't get her way, I wouldn't put it past Trish to bring us up on assault charges. I'll give Alia a signal to give us if she thinks things are going to get out of hand, as well."

"I'm not worried. Alia can take care of herself now. If I was, I wouldn't have allowed it in the first place. I actually think this will be good for her. She needs to see she has the power to stand up to Trish. And I want to see the look on Trish's face when she sees how Alia looks now." Charlie left to go call his mother.

Harper looked over at Trish, now sitting in the front waiting area, as she mumbled to herself. *This isn't going to end pretty.*

About ten minutes later, Trish was in the interrogation room waiting. Charlie met Alia and his mother at the back door of the Sheriff's office while Harper was setting up to record their talk. Charlie explained to them what was going to happen and the safe word Alia could use if she needed it.

"Now, if you're not up to this, I'll call it off. We don't want to force you into dealing with her if you're not ready yet." Charlie looked at Alia and brushed a strand of hair back from her face. Looking close and knowing what he was looking for, Charlie could see a faint scar on Alia's cheek from when the bitch threw an ashtray at her four months earlier. There were a few others as well that happened when she was a young child. Seeing them made him wonder if this had been a mistake. His argument about Trish not being able to hurt Alia may not be as accurate as he hoped. Her scars were proof that Trish had done just that in the not-so-distant past.

"I'm ready, Charlie. You're right. It's time we finish this. She's not going to like what I have to say, and I don't care at this point. And don't worry, nothing she says is going to get me to go home with her."

"That is one thing I was never worried about. Try not to let her hurt you, though, she puts one more scar on that beautiful face of yours, and I'm going to lose it."

"Just be adamant with her, Alia," said Ellen. "Stand your ground and let her know enough is enough."

The three of them walked to the room together.

"Now you see that mirror there, it's just like in the movies, that's a one-way mirror, and we will be on the other side. Everything is being recorded just in case we need it for later, so you might want to mind what you say. Don't let her goad you into a fight. And don't let her upset you either." Charlie kissed Alia on her forehead and put his to hers. "I love you," he whispered. "You've got this."

Alia gave the two of them time to get into the other room, then, taking a deep breath, opened the door and walked into the interrogation room. The first thing Alia noticed was that Trish looked older and more tired than ever. Her face sagged, her wrinkles were more prominent, and her hair was an unusual mess. A woman that usually never went out without her hair done and makeup on, Alia was surprised to see her in such a state.

She's actually losing it with me gone, she thought. But when she looked into Trish's eyes, she could see the dark steely hatred and anger there Alia had come to know so well over the years. She warned herself not to be fooled. Underneath it all, her mother was pissed off, sitting there coiled like a snake and ready to strike.

When Trish looked up and saw Alia, she had to hide her shock. Always a little on the chunky side, the girl before her was now all lean and muscular looking. She wore shorts showing the muscles in her thighs and calves. The short-sleeved blouse Alia had on showed her arms were muscular as well. But what set Trish on edge was the look in her eyes. They no longer were the eyes of a scared little girl. Instead, they looked back at Trish hard and cold.

For a minute or two, they just stared at each other. Alia stood only a foot in from the door with her arms crossed.

At last, Trish spoke up. "Now that we are alone, how about you tell me what is really going on? The truth this time, Alia.

Alia shook her head. "You were already told the truth. You just don't want to believe it."

"Of course, I'm not going to believe that bullshit. I am your mother, Alia. I can tell when you are lying. There is no way your lazy fat ass made it through the police academy. I don't care what the Harper's said to you or what bullshit they tried blowing up your ass, but we are alone now. You can tell me what is really going on. I know that Charlie has taken advantage of you he as much as admitted it. I don't know where they have been hiding you all summer or what kind of crazy brainwashing they have done on you, but it's over now. Cut the shit, and let's go home before you get me good and pissed off, and you don't have a home to come back to."

Alia laughed. "You don't get it, do you? Once again, you've bought into your own delusion. There's been no threats, no brainwashing, and no rape. For god's sake, listen to yourself. The only one telling lies here is you."

"What lies? I've never lied to you, Alia. I may have had to tell you some cold hard truths, but I never lied to you."

"Never? Are you sure about that? What about all the times you lied to me about Dad not wanting to see me on the weekends? Did you think I would never ask him? Or all the times you told me he didn't love me? Oh, I bet it would shock the hell out of you to know that he left money for me to get a car, wouldn't it?"

Trish's brow furrowed.

"Yeah, that's just what I thought. And what about all the times you lied to me about not having enough money for me to play sports or get my license? Oh, but there was plenty of money for you to go to the bars and smoke dope. How about how you lied about not knowing who my foster parents were?"

Trish got up on her feet but remained where she stood. "I lied to you about that to protect you. That's why I told you to stay away from them, Alia. Charlie, that little bastard couldn't keep his damn hands off of you. And for all I know, Harper was diddling you as well. No wonder you cried all the time. And Harper said if I told anyone, he would have me locked up, and I'd never see you again. I did it all for you, Alia."

Alia looked at Trish and smiled. She had to give it to her this time, it was her best performance yet. She even managed to squeeze out a drop or two as well. Shaking her head, Alia started clapping. "Bravo. Splendid performance Trish."

Ooh, she flinched at me using her real name. That stung.

"And the tears are a nice touch but don't forget you told me years ago about that little trick. How all you had to do sometimes was squeeze out a crocodile tear or two to get your way."

Trish sat down, the tears in her eyes replaced by scorn.

"You lied to me all the time about everything, and the sad part is you always thought I was stupid enough to believe you."

"You are stupid, Alia. If not, you wouldn't have barely passed high school. It's why it's been so easy for them to manipulate you. They are mad at me because I took you away from them, so they are using you to get back at me. Why can't you see that?"

"I don't know maybe it's because I'm not as stupid as you think. Maybe it's because I figured out a long time ago that if I made it look like I was, just stupid enough, mind you, that you would get off my back. You never saw my real grades in high school. You only saw what I allowed you to see." Alia walked closer, put her palms down on the edge of the table, and looked down at her mother. "You see, after years of being manipulated and lied to by you, I learned a few tricks. With the help of a friend, I changed my grades to make them meet your approval. Just like I lied to you about where I was this summer and what I have been doing for months before graduation. I have had a cell phone for two years, and you never had a clue. I never really bought into your bullshit, but I have been lying to you for years, and you had no clue. And it was easy because I learned from the best. So you see, Trish, I know the Harper's are telling me the truth because, after a lifetime of you and your bullshit, I know the difference."

Trish's face turned more twisted and angry. "And I know you, Alia. I can read you like a book. Your week, naive, nothing but a scared little girl with no clue about how the real world works. You're going to find out, though. When they get tired of you and your shit and they toss you aside, you will see. When Charlie gets board fucking the easy, fat, ugly girl and leaves you for some hot bitch you will see.

You'll want to come crawling back home crying with your tail between your legs like the bitch that you are, but when you do, it'll be too late. If you don't walk out of here with me right now, I'm done with you, little girl. And don't try to go crying to the rest of the family either because they are already done with you. They wouldn't even help get you back, just like last time. They don't care; I'm the only one that cares about you, Alia, so you better wise up right now."

Walking back towards the door, Alia shook her head. Turning back around, she faced Trish with a smile that Trish didn't care for one bit. "You're pathetic. And sad. You know I don't hate you anymore. I feel sorry for you. The only one that is crawling on their hands and knees is you. You come here demanding to see me, disturbing our family dinner, to say what? I better come back now or else? Back to the lies, the abuse, to being controlled by you and forced to beg for even the smallest bit of affection from you? That may have worked on the old me, but I've grown a lot this year. I'm stronger than I ever was and the happiest I have ever been in my life. I have my own apartment, my own car, not just a job but a career I can be proud of. And best of all, I have a family and the most amazing boyfriend anyone could ever ask for that loves me, faults and all. And in case you haven't noticed, I am far from a fat and ugly little girl anymore. Tell me, why the hell would I give all that up? You need me. You have always needed me because with me under your foot, you could at least say you were taller than someone. So to answer your question, no, I won't go back home with you, ever."Alia turned to walk out the door stealing herself in case her mother chunked something at her.

"Don't you walk away from me! Dammit, Alia, I am warning you I will destroy everything and everyone you love if you walk out that door. I won't stop until I ruin Charlie, and he will only have you to blame for it. I know things. You have no idea the things I know and what I'm capable of."

Alia turned around to face her mother one last time. "Bring it," she said and walked out the door and into the arms of the man she loves.

"I'm so proud of you," Charlie said, hugging her tight. In the interrogation room, they could hear banging and clattering of the metal furniture in there being thrown around.

"I don't think she's taking it very well." At that moment, they heard glass shatter as the chair smashed the two-way mirror. Officers from the other room came running in, as did Harper and Ellen.

In Charlie's arms and standing in the hallway, Alia watched as Harper and the deputies went in to restrain Trish. Harper then hauled her out of the room in cuffs, Trish threatening to press charges against him the whole time.

When they got out in the hall, Trish saw Alia in Charlie's arms, and the look of rage on her face was almost comical.

"Get your damn hands off of her, you fucking little bastard. I will take her away from you and destroy you in the process," she screamed.

Charlie just held her tighter, and Alia wrapped her arms around him.

"I'm warning you, Charlie, after I'm done with you, she won't want anything to do with you…she's mine, Charlie…she's mine."

Harper handed Trish off to the Deputies and told them to take her down to the cells. The whole way, she screamed at them all.

"You all go home. I'll deal with this here. Go on, Charlie, get your mother and Alia home. I'll be there shortly."

Charlie took Alia and his mother out the back to where Ellen's car was parked. His mother drove them back to the house, where they cleaned up from dinner and waited for word from Harper. About an hour later, he showed back up at the house with a bandage on his arm.

"The bitch cut me," he said. "She had a piece of the mirror glass stashed on her when we took her out of the interrogation room. Only five stitches, it's not so bad. Alia honey, I'm sorry, but we had to admit her into the hospital's psych unit. She's on a mandatory seventy-two-hour hold at the very least."

Alia gave Harper a big hug. "It's okay. I know you only did what you had to. Besides, it might do her some good. I doubt it, but one could hope anyway."

"Well, the good thing is we won't have to worry about her for a few days. I told her we filmed her in the interrogation room, so other than running her mouth, I doubt she will try to do anything. You kids go home, it's been a long day. And Alia, I know Charlie has already said it, but I'm very proud of the way you handled yourself in there today. Your father would have been too. He had always hoped you would stand up to her one day." he gave the girl one last hug then shooed the kids out the door.

When he and Ellen were alone, she asked if he really thought it was over.

"Hell Ellen, as long as that woman is alive, it's never going to be over. Mark my words. This isn't the last showdown with her. If she's smart, she'll get out of Union county and go back to her family. If not, well, let's just hope she leaves the kids alone for a while. But I have a feeling we are going to hear a whole lot of ugly from her."

A whole lot of ugly was right. Trish was released that Saturday. The performance for Alia was nothing compared to the one she put on to get off the psych hold. Even Alia would have been impressed. Harper wasn't going to press any charges as long as she left the kids alone.

That didn't stop her from saying every nasty little thing she could think of about the Harper's, more specifically about Charlie. And as Harper expected, most people didn't give two shakes of a rat's ass about what she had to say. Some even had the nerve to laugh in her face seeing how Charlie had affected their lives positively in one way or another. Only those in her circle that already had a beef with the local Sheriff's department believed anything.

On Monday, Alia began her Cadet training in the Sheriff's office. The local paper did an article, introducing her to the town and surrounding county.

Trish saw the piece and tore her copy to shreds with a butcher knife. She then made a point of going around town and collecting as many copies as she could for a bit of art project she had in mind. Trish had plenty of time on her hands since, as of Monday morning, around the same time Alia was being sworn in as a cadet in training, she got a call from the factory. They fired her for not showing up to work all week. After fifteen years, she was unemployed.

A few days later, the people of town woke up to the front page of that paper literally plastered all over town accusing Deputy Harper of raping the young women on its cover. Everyone knew who did it, but Trish had managed to avoid any cameras or being seen. Harper had his men go around tearing all of them down before the kids could see them.

Still, a few had managed to escape their notice, and Alia and Charlie saw one anyway. Charlie was furious, and Alia was embarrassed. Still, they could do nothing unless they could prove it was Trish doing it.

For weeks Trish tried getting people to believe that Charlie had been with Alia well before she turned eighteen. The problem was that no one in town could ever recall seeing them together before fall. Even the kids that had seen the two of them at the prom didn't say anything. Realizing after a few weeks that what she was saying about Charlie was pretty much falling on deaf ears, Trish changed tactics and started in on her daughter.

Now at this, the response she got was different. Alia was a virtual unknown to a large part of the county. And since it was her mother saying these things about her, people were apt to believe it. The more people would listen, the more Trish would spin her tales. Some even became worried about her working for the Sheriff's department and voiced that opinion to the Sheriff himself.

Harper did his best to set the story straight, letting people know that there were some issues between Alia and her mother. Alia had graduated from the academy with honors and was doing a fine job with the rest of her training. Still, the rumors persisted, and both Alia and Charlie noticed how some people would look at the two of them, mostly her, with disdain.

Free for the first time to show their affections for one another, they instead held back out in public, waiting for the rumors to die off. Trish had branded Alia a slut that had fucked and sucked her way through the academy and now working her way through the Sheriff's department. She also told anyone that would listen that Alia left her owing a lot of money for rent and other bills she had refused to pay. Alia was also supposedly a thief, a liar, a drug addict, alcoholic, lesbian and racist. Not very many people believed it, and most did note that Trish herself had been accused of several of these things. Still, the rumors didn't stop.

The family talked about the topic from time to time but refused to make it a big part of their lives, believing that eventually, like all rumors, these too would die off. Then after what happened at the end of November, just after Thanksgiving, put a stop to the whole mess. The county, more specifically the town, had other concerns on their minds. Most prominent were the fates of two small children.

Chapter 23
Missing

By the time Thanksgiving had arrived, it had been almost three months since the confrontation at the Sheriff's office with Alia and Trish. During that time, the Harpers did their best at damage control. For her part, Alia had to be an even better cadet than she would have usually been. They made a point of having her at the forefront of any community activity to show the good person she was and officer she would be.

There were a few dirty looks and even a lewd comment directed towards her here and there. Still, Alia handled it with the utmost professionalism. Hitting the punching bag at the department's gym after a hard day helped a lot.

As a cadet, Alia rode with at least one other officer at all times. This allowed her to endear herself to those she would be working with and learn different techniques and tactics. Even the officers that had not already known her soon grew very fond of her. Alia was bright but lacked the ego and cockiness of some cadets. She was good with children, patient with the elderly and mentally challenged, brave when called for, and loyal. Alia was kind, funny, aloof at times, and pulled her weight, never asking for help unless she absolutely needed it. The fact that she baked some of the most incredible tasting cookies and brownies didn't hurt either.

The best thing was that they all approved of Alia and Charlie's relationship. Their bond never got in the way during duty hours, and aside from a smile here and there, most wouldn't even have known had Trish not made a point of telling the whole county.

Trish would make a visible appearance from time to time. She showed up in Alia's driveway several times, mostly at night. When Charlie went out to confront her (most of the time only in his boxers, to Alia's delight), Trish would just walk off like she had every right to be there.

"Just visiting my daughter." she would sneer at Charlie. "You certainly don't leave her alone much, do you, Charlie."

"No, I sure don't," he said sternly. "Just leave before I arrest you for trespassing." From then on, Alia either stayed at his place if he had to work late, or he would be at her place.

Once she showed up in the Harper's driveway. Harper wasn't as nice as Charlie. He cuffed Trish and took her in to be booked. After that, Trish avoided the Harper's home.

Trish and Alia didn't cross paths much, and she was never alone when they did. Trish would run her mouth only to have one of the Deputies come out in her defense. When Charlie was involved, Trish always ended up in cuffs and at the station for a few hours. He and Harper both lost their sense of humor with Trish right away.

Trish ended up moving out of the apartment she had shared with Alia and into Cooper's Town trailer park just down the road from the factory she worked at. That put her miles further out of town, making life a tad easier for them. Alia knew shit was getting very bad for Trish with her moving into that particular trailer park. A cesspool of drugs, criminals, and prostitutes, it was the one place the two of them never wanted to end up.

Trish would often remark. "As long as we stay out of Cooper's Town, we haven't completely hit rock bottom."

One day Deputy Tackard came into the Sheriff's office and went right to Alia with a broad grin on his face. "Just gave your mother a ticket for speeding, only she wasn't driving that nice new little ford anymore. Now she's driving some beat-up old clunker."

"I heard she's working at Lucky's Bar," said Deputy Johnson from his desk. "Got to be pretty low to work in that shit hole."

"Okay, guys," said Alia. "I know where you're getting at. But I'm not one to gloat or relish in someone's failures, not even hers. Besides, she has a friend that works at the bar, which used to be her favorite hangout place when I was a kid. Doesn't surprise me at all that's where she's working. " *Good to know though, always good to know where she is at.*

"You only say that because you're a good person, Alia." grinned Tackard. "Me, on the other hand, I am an asshole. Just ask my girlfriend," he joked. "And I will be more than happy to celebrate her misfortune for you."

"Same here," said Johnson.

Tackard went over and high-fived Johnson, then came back and clapped Alia on the back. "Don't worry about her kid. We got your back."

"Damn straight," said Johnson.

"Thanks, guys, just don't be too hard on her. Her life is a shit show right now. That's punishment enough."

Tackard shook his head as he walked to the back to change and clock out for the day. "After all the shit she said about Charlie, you sure are good at turning the other cheek. You are too good, Cadet Miller, much too good for someone like her."

With him gone, both she and Johnson went back to their paperwork. Alia couldn't get what they had said out of her mind, though. *She really has hit rock bottom. That just means she has less to lose. And that leaves me as the one with everything to lose. Not so sure I'm happy about that.*

Life began to settle into a routine of work, home, and Wednesday night family dinners. Charlie and Alia spent most of their time outside work together, either alone or with their friends. When they hung out with Alia's friends, it was at her place and Charlie's place when it was his friends. They would go on hiking trips on the Appalachian trail on their days off, spend a night or two at the cabin, or just lay around at home reading. Their lives were happy and comfortable. The few times they had to deal with Trish becoming less and less of a problem. Still, she hung over them like a dark cloud.

In early November, Alia was staffing the front desk of the Sheriff's office when an older woman in her sixties came in. She recognized the woman right away as Meredith Wise, Billy's mother. She seemed genuinely pleased to see Alia behind the desk and in uniform.

"Don't you look nice in your uniform Alia? Or should I call you Deputy Miller?"

"Not Deputy quite yet, Mrs. Wise. It's Cadet Miller for now."

"Well, it just so happens you are the very person I wanted to see."

"Yes? How's that?"

"Have you seen my Billy? I have looked just about everywhere for him, and I can't find him," she asked, sounding concerned.

"No, I'm sorry I haven't seen him since before summer. I talked to him a few times after I got back, but that was months ago. That's pretty unusual for him, he usually checks in with you regularly. I'm assuming you tried calling him, of course."

"Several times, but my calls go right to his voicemail."

"You sure he's not just out on a bender somewhere?"

"He only gets bad like that when he's upset about something, and ever since he left your mother last month, I haven't seen him happier in ages."

"So he did leave her? "

"Yes, the lease ran out at the end of the month, but he moved in with me around the fifteenth of October. Said he couldn't stand being in that apartment with her since she lost her job. I'm sorry to have to tell you this, dear, but your mother lost her mind when you didn't come home."

"Believe me, I know. How long has it been since you have seen Billy?"

"Been a week now, at least. At first, I thought he must have found himself a new girl and would be back in a few days. When he didn't return, I tried calling."

"Have you tried to get in touch with Trish? Maybe he went back to her and just didn't want to tell you?"

"Yes, I did. She's living in a crappy little trailer park on the edge of town. That nasty one, Cooper's Town, I think it's called."

"Yes, I'm aware."

"She swears she hasn't seen him since he left the apartment. But I'll believe anything that woman says when pigs fly."

Not able to help herself, Alia chuckled a little.

"And all those nasty things she has been saying about you and Deputy Harper. She should be ashamed. Billy told me none of that mess was true, and even if he didn't, I wouldn't believe it. Awful women. Sorry dear, I know she is your mother, but that woman. I never did like Billy going out with her."

"No need to apologize. I think I better call the Sheriff in to talk to you about this. A week is a long time even for Billy."

"That boy has his faults, Alia, but he would never go this long without contacting me. And he couldn't have planned on going too far. His car is still in the driveway."

The more she was hearing, the more Alia didn't like the sound of all of this. Sure it's likely Billy was enjoying his newfound freedom and off drunk somewhere, but she found that hard to believe.

When Harper came in, he let Alia sit in on his talk with Billy's mother, mainly because Alia knew her and for training. After getting all her information, including a number for his work, Harper sent her home, assuring her they would call if they heard from him.

"What do you think of all of this?" Harper asked Alia.

Alia shook her head. "Some things are not adding up. Billy is a flake and can't drive the speed limit to save his life, but for him to just up and disappear like that is unusual."

"Did he ever do anything like that while he was living with Trish?"

"Long weekend bender's, and stayed drunk the entire time he was on vacation, but nothing this long."

"What's the next step you think we should take?" he asked to see how good her head was in the game.

"Personally, I would call his work, see if he took some vacation time or if he's shown up or not. One thing Billy was always serious about was his job. I can see him blowing off his mother if he was shacked up with someone and drunk as hell, but not his job."

"Very good, that was my thoughts as well. Let me ask you this, though, do you think Trish may be involved?"

Alia sighed heavily, wondering when he would get around asking that. "I thought about that too. Honestly, I want to say no, but...."

"But what? Did she say anything to you before you left?"

"Not about him directly, I mean, she's always going on about cutting this one, and that one's dick off if they piss her off, but she's been all bark and no bite. She let that husband of hers beat the crap out of her all the time."

"There's more, isn't there? I can tell when you're holding back, Alia. This isn't the time to do it."

"It's just that, well, she's threatened to kill me more times than I can count. But there have been a few times she actually tried."

Harper walked away for a second and came back rubbing his face much like Charlie did when he was frustrated. "Damn it, Alia, why didn't you ever say anything? That's exactly the kind of thing we could have used to get you away from her, to put her away."

"Because she had me convinced no one would believe me, least of all you." Alia felt like Harper still didn't understand just how under her mother's control Alia was. It had taken everything she had to walk out of the woman's life and may not have had it not been for Charlie.

"How did she not succeed?"

"What?"

"What made her stop before she killed you?"

"A couple of times, her boyfriends pulled her off of me. One time I blacked out and came too with her doing some half-assed CPR."

"Alia, honey, I had no idea. Charlie said he thought there was more you weren't telling him, but I would have never imagined it would be that bad."

That's not even the worst of it.

"It's over, Harper. What's done is done. My point, though, is that when she is mad enough, I think she's capable of anything."

"Is it possible she's that mad at Billy?"

"On top of losing both me and her job, hell yes. He was the only one working and paying bills, then he moved out early. This wasn't just some guy leaving her. He left her with nothing more than what she may have saved in the bank. And if she has moved into Cooper's Town and lost her car, then she's broke. She always said as long as we stayed out of there, we were still doing good."

"Meredith gave us his work contacts, go ahead and call them. Let them know you're calling from the Sheriff's station about a missing person's report. Just don't tell them you're a cadet. If you have to lie, I'll cover you."

"Yes, sir, I'll get right on it. Oh, and please don't tell Charlie what I told you. Things have been going good. I don't want to upset him."

"Sure thing, kiddo, but you might want to think about telling him one day."

Alia nodded and went to her desk to make the call.

After only ten minutes on the phone, Alia found out that Billy hadn't shown up in a week and certainly didn't take any vacation time off. They had thought about reporting him missing as well and just didn't get around to it.

Alia reported this to Harper, and an official missing person's case was opened. In the following weeks, they questioned several people about his last known whereabouts. Alia was allowed to sit in on all the questioning. That included when he brought Trish in.

After avoiding them for several days, Charlie and Harper found Trish coming out of a bar early one evening. She was trying to get into her car when it was more than obvious she had too much to drink. Harper told her he wouldn't bust her if she just came in and answered some questions.

When Harper walked into the interrogation room, followed by Alia, a mask of rage came over Trish's face.

"What the hell is she doing here?"

Harper looked at Alia and, giving her a wink that Trish couldn't see, turned back to Trish. "Cadet Miller is in training. This is part of her training."

"I know what this is, Harper. You're trying to shove the fact that you won in my face. Well, it's not over yet now, is it?"

"Oh, it's over," Said Alia, finding it easy to look Trish in the face for perhaps the first time in her life.

"Okay, both of you, stop. Miller, I will remind you that you are here to observe and learn, nothing else."

Alia nodded her head. "Yes, sir."

"And Trish, this isn't about that at all. Not everything is about you."

"Then what am I in here for? If you're going to arrest me again, just do it."

"We need to ask you some questions about your boyfriend, Billy."

Alia had been paying very close attention to the faces and reactions of everyone they interrogated. Trish was no exception. At the mention of Billy's name, a dark cloud came over Trish's face, no more than a sec then was gone.

For the next hour, Harper asked Trish many of the same things he had asked others concerning Billy's disappearance. No matter how many times or ways she was asked, Trish stuck to the same story of not having seen him since the last time he was at the apartment moving out his things.

Alia stood behind Harper, her arms crossed, and stared down at Trish the entire time.

Trish starred right back, but it became apparent that having Alia there unnerved her. As much as she tried keeping her attention on Harper, it was drawn towards her daughter standing before her almost defiantly. Oh, how she wanted to wipe that smug look off her face. Would have, too, if Harper had been foolish enough to leave them alone. She didn't care how grown Alia thought she was. Trish felt she could still take her own.

When they were done, Trish was surprised they were letting her leave. On the way out of the room, she looked her daughter up and down and sneered at her. "It's far from over, little girl."

Alia stood her ground and not only wouldn't drop her eyes like usual, but she had the nerve to grin back at her. "For your sake, it better be." And she made a point of placing one hand down on the top of her holstered firearm.

I will wipe that look off your face one of these days, so help me. Trish thought.

When she was gone, Alia let out a big gust of air. She and Charlie had been working on dealing with her mother, and she was surprised how well she did.

So was Harper. At first, he wasn't so sure Alia would be able to keep her cool, but the kid impressed him more and more all the time. She was growing up. "So, what do you think?"

"Oh, she was lying. Not sure what all about, but I'm positive she has seen him since he left the apartment anyway. So now what?"

"I want to hear what you think," said Harper.

Alia thought for a bit. "I think she's acting suspicious, however without a body or witness, we really don't have much to go on. This isn't small-town cop stuff. If we want to get to the bottom of this, we need help. But once again we have a problem. Billy is a known drunk with a penchant for speeding tickets and even a DUI. State boys most likely won't take this seriously unless we can find more evidence."

Agreeing with what she had to say, Harper left the case open, but there was absolutely no evidence of foul play of any kind. Billy was just gone. His cell was off, he didn't use any of his credit or bank cards, and no one had seen him since he left his mother's house for a walk one night. The only other thing they could come up with was that he had been drinking and may have been on his way to a bar to drink some more.

Harper got a handful of deputies to search the area Billy may have walked in, but nothing was found. The investigation was left open in hopes of running across more information or if a body showed up, but it had stalled.

Thanksgiving day was always a significant event in the Harper household, with that year being no exception. If anything, it was made all the more special having Alia back a part of their family once more. Days before, Ellen started cooking with Alia there to help when she could. They baked pies, cookies, cakes, and all kinds of tasty treats ahead of the big day. The hard part was keeping the boys from eating it all.

Both sets of Charlie's grandparents were still alive and flew in from Florida to join the feast. They had been kept up on the situation with Alia and were thrilled to see her again. They shared stories and photos of them with Alia as a toddler. Once again, Alia felt so very fortunate to have a real family.

Ellen's sister Nicci and her only remaining-at-home daughter came too. Her husband usually came with them but they were in the middle of a nasty separation. Beth was only ten years old, the youngest of three siblings, and Charlie was her favorite cousin. She was a little jealous at first of the girl that stole Charlie's heart. But after a pre-Thanksgiving night of playing games where the two girls ganged up on Charlie, the jealousy vanished. Beth ended up falling in love with Alia, who she came to think of as a big sister.

The actual event was much like it is in most households. Alia helped Ellen make breakfast for everyone, and they watched the parade from New York on TV. Later they all sat down for dinner, enjoying the substantial meal. Afterward, some sat in the living room watching football while others helped clean up.

Alia and Charlie went for a walk down to the lake with Beth tagging along behind them. She ran up and playfully threw handfuls of leaves at the couple till she goaded Charlie into chasing her. Watching him with her, Alia was getting a good idea of the kind of father Charlie was going to be. Beth squealed as Charlie lifted her up and tossed her into a pile of Harper's raked leaves. He then dove into them himself and Chased Beth around in the heap with him on all fours. Alia couldn't tell which one of them was having more fun.

At no time did Alia miss her own family. Not the uncle that always looked down on her. Not trying to avoid her pedophile cousin. Not her aunts that constantly asked when she would start acting her age, and most certainly not Trish. Alia really thought she would feel a bit homesick, but she hadn't. Instead, for the first time in her life, she felt at home, even with all the people there she didn't know. Charlie's family had accepted her as one of their own, no questions asked. Well, except for the one about when the two of them were going to make it official. Thankfully Ellen had come to their rescue.

"They are still young. They have all the time in the world to worry about that."

Alia agreed. She wanted to be a mother someday, but she wanted to be a good mother. Which meant she needed more time to grow up and get over the demons of her own childhood first. She knew as well there was only one thing that could ever take Charlie away from her, and thoughts of that nature were just best left unthought. So they were indeed in no rush.

The next day Alia was at the Sheriff's office front desk again when shortly before noon, a frantic phone call came in. Two children visiting family in the county for Thanksgiving had gone missing. The cabin that the family had been staying at was on the edge of the vast Jefferson forest National wilderness. They believed the two kids had gone looking for waterfalls the family was supposed to go see that day. But when they checked the falls, the kids could not be found.

Alia put in a call to the forestry department's Ranger station right away. He told her to get as many officers and volunteers as possible and meet at the cabin. Time was an issue, and they needed to act fast if they were going to find the kids before dark.

About an hour later, Alia joined Harper, Charlie, and ten of the officers they had on staff. Five were left to deal with things in town, and five were out of town for the holiday. They had with them about another twenty volunteers. The Rangers had half a dozen of their own guys and another fifteen volunteers.

As they gathered, the father of the two children spoke to them all. He told them how the night before, they had all been talking about going on a hike today to look at the waterfalls. Everyone had been very excited and looking forward to it. Only this morning, the adults had slept in. When they woke around half past nine, they realized the two youngest, Joey five, and Sasha almost seven, were missing.

They went to the falls right away to look for the kids, but they were not there. They know that they followed the trail leading to the river from the cabin because a pop-tart wrapper was found on the path. From there, they didn't know for sure. The kids had taken their boots but no coats.

As Alia listened with the others, she noticed a group of three teens hanging off to the side. As the father talked, they talked low to each other, shaking their heads.

The father described what the kids were wearing and other things. Alia slipped away from the group and approached the teens. She hoped they would talk to her since she was closer to their age.

"Hey there, I'm…Miller. I couldn't help but notice you all over here shaking your heads. Is there something the father is saying you disagree with?"

"Damn straight there is, but Chuck is a stubborn bastard, and he won't listen to us." said a boy of about fifteen with long black hair in his face and giving off skater vibes to Alia.

"Give him a break Spencer. He's just upset that his kids are lost." said a girl of about the same age.

"So am I. It may even be our fault they are missing, which is why he should at least listen to us."

"Whoa, wait, why would you think this is your fault," asked Alia.

Spencer just hung his head.

"Because my lame brain brother here told the little ones about these caves he wanted to go see instead of the waterfalls," said the girl. "He was hoping they would pitch a fit about the caves so we would hike there instead. Waterfalls are pretty lame."

The others all nodded in agreement.

"It's my fault. I hyped it all up, and now no one will listen to us. We didn't find them at the waterfalls because they went to the caves instead. I know they did."

"There was proof the kids followed the trail to the river, so why would they go to the caves from there."

"The caves are faster to find if you follow the river the other way instead of trying to take the trails there. The trail goes out of the way about a mile or so. There's a little stream that joins the river about two miles up. The stream comes from a spring inside the caves. I told them that's how to get there. It was stupid of me, I know, but I never thought they would go alone, I swear."

"So the caves are only a few miles away. Any idea why they wouldn't have just come back?"

"Because the cave system is like a giant labyrinth," said the girl. We went there a few years ago, but our parents were with us and we still almost got lost. You're a cop, they'll listen to you, tell them about the caves. If they go off in the wrong direction looking for our cousins, there is no way they will find them before it gets dark."

"It's going to drop below freezing tonight," said Spencer. "They'll die out there, and it's all my fault."

"I'll see what I can do. Maybe they will let a few of us go check out the caves to be sure."

"Thank you." said the girl. "Spencer didn't mean for this to happen."

Alia rejoined the group that was now surrounding a map on the side of the cabin outlying the forest. Ranger Dickson was the head of the forestry department. He told them how they would break into groups, making a line from the river as far up the cabin as they could, heading north towards the waterfalls and beyond.

When there was a break in his instructions, Alia excused herself. "Is it possible the kids were nowhere near the waterfalls in the first place? I just talked to the older kids, and they said there are some caves just a few miles south along the river."

Before she could even finish, Dickson was shaking his head. "The parents insist the kids were looking forward to the waterfalls."

"Yes, I realize that, but that was before they were told about the caves. I think it would be a good idea to send at least a few of us there to see if they went that way."

"Look, miss...who are you anyway."

Alia felt her face flush. "Cadet Miller, county Sheriff's department." Alia was aware of all eyes on her, including that of Charlie and Harper. She didn't dare look at them, afraid to see the same look on their faces as was on the face of Ranger Dickson.

"Well, Cadet Miller," he said with an attitude. "When you have a few years of actual police work under your belt, you will better understand the severity of situations like this. We have till nightfall to find these kids, and we don't have the resources to send people running all over the forest. We can't even get the canines here till morning. So if you don't mind, how about you let the adults run the show. Now, where was I...."

Dickson said more, but Alia could barely hear him over the rush of red hot blood that seemed to fill up her ears. She felt a hand on her back and knew it was Charlie but still couldn't bear to look at him. Just his touch, though, was enough to bring her anger down to a simmering level.

Later, when they were going down the main trail to the river to get to their spot in the search, Charlie bumped into her as a way of getting her attention. He could still feel the hot fury she was in. "Don't let him get to ya, Alia. He's an ass for the way he said it, but he's right. We should have twice as many people out here as we do and the dogs. The holiday is messing with us being able to get volunteers."

"So you think I'm wrong too?"

"Not entirely. I think you think you're right. And in a way, you are. But the trail to the caves is up past the house. Those kids went down to the river at least."

"Yes, and suddenly from there, the trail runs cold? We are talking about two little kids. They would have left some clue behind that they went to the falls if they actually went that way."

"And they may have. Those people up there are city folks. They don't know how to track. I bet when we get down to the river, we will see all kinds of evidence they overlooked."

Ranger Dickson, Harper, and the kids' father took the trail by the river as their grid. Alia and Charlie had the next grid up within eyesight of them on the trail and more forest people the next grid from there. When the line was ready, they all headed north alone on their grid, looking for the kids or clues to where they went. The waterfalls were only a mile away, so in no time, they made it there and were starting the search beyond.

So far, there were none of the clues they were hoping for. After another mile passed the waterfall with not so much as a footprint belonging to the kids, Alia wasn't the only one wondering if they went the wrong way after all.

Looking around her, Alia suddenly stopped.

"Come on, we should keep up with the line," said Charlie.

"For what, Charlie? Sorry Deputy Harper." It was sometimes hard for Alia to remember that she was supposed to call Charlie by his work name while on duty. "Those kids are not out here. They never went to the waterfalls."

"Rick must have seen enough to make him think he is still on the right track. He knows these woods better than we do. I doubt he would keep making us go the wrong way for nothing."

Unless he is letting his ego get in the way. She thought.

"People walk that trail to the falls and beyond all the time. Who's to say he isn't following someone else. I don't know Charlie. I just feel like this is the wrong way. If I was those kids, I would have wanted to see the caves. We have been at this for hours. We got what two hours left at most?"

"What are you saying?"

"I'm saying one of us should double back and check out those caves."

"Miller."

"No, just listen to me. I should go. I'm a pretty fast runner, I grew up playing in the woods, and I can get there in no time. You do the grid if they notice me gone tell them I felt sick." Alia started to walk off.

"Alia, damn it, I don't want you to wander off on your own. We don't need to have to go look for you too."

"You can't go, someone needs to stay on this grid. Besides, if I go and don't find them, then no big deal. The worst is Harper will yell at me and keep me a cadet longer. I won't get lost, Deputy. I'm better in the woods than most people."

"Fine, but take this." he tossed her his radio. "I hope for your sake you're right about this."

"I hope for theirs I am too." With that, she bounded off into the woods back the way they came.

Charlie looked around, could barely make out the people, both grids next to his up ahead of him. With one last look in the direction Alia went, he shook his head and continued on the grid. He couldn't help to feel apprehensive about those caves for some reason.

Alia ran as fast as she could back towards the trail they started on. After a mile, she had to stop to strip off the coat she wore and shove it into the backpack she had with her. There was some water in there her throat cried out for, but she wanted to save it if the kids needed it. The closer she got, the more she was sure she was going the right way.

At last, Alia came out of the forest and onto the trail they had initially come down from the cabin on. Luckily there wasn't anyone around. Heading down the path, she turned at the river and continued to run the next two miles.

Alia was going so fast that she almost passed by the little creek that fed into the river. Even with most of the leaves gone from the trees, she couldn't make out any caves from there but was sure she had the right spot. The little creek was barely a trickle as it ran through the forest, but it was large enough to follow up. Alia started up having to go around thickets and downed trees. This part of the forest was at an incline going up a mountainside. That slowed her down a little, just enough to notice there wasn't going to be much daylight left. Already temps were starting to drop. When the sun was gone, they would plummet.

Alia saw the rocky outcroppings and then the caves the kids talked about. Sure enough, there was a trail coming down the mountainside from the north that would lead her back on a roundabout route to the cabin. If the kids were not in the caves, it was possible they would be along that trail.

As soon as Alia walked to the cave entrance, she saw two sets of small footprints in the sandy soil. Concerned more about the dropping temps and forgetting about the radio, she plunged into the darkness of the caves.

Inside was not only dark but cold and damp as well. Water droplets fell from the ceiling and ran down the cave walls. Stopping to put on her coat, Alia also got out a flashlight. On the ground in front of her were more tracks. " Hello, Joey, Sasha, are you here?" She listened but heard nothing.

Following the footprints further into the cave, Alia could see several offshoots of the original path. Here and there, the footprints overlapped as if the kids had gone down one way then doubled back. Still, she went forward, keeping tabs on the prints and panicking for a moment when they disappeared on the rocky ground. Alia had followed them for a while when both pairs split off in two directions. The one she could tell they doubled back on most likely found a dead end, so she took the other.

At one point, Alia entered a cavern. A round open space about the size of a large room. There were several offshoots from there, so Alia stopped to make a marker out of rocks leading the right way out. Looking around to see which way to go, she suddenly felt that this place seemed oddly familiar. The hairs on the back of her neck stood up as she remembered the dream she had in the motel. Alia hadn't thought about that in months. Yet here she was in a cave system much like that in the dream. Over by the one wall, there was even a small platform and a very light shaft of light coming from above.

Stunned, Alia walked over to the platform and looked up. A long shaft that went up to the surface was above her, barely visible through the vines, leaves, and other debris. Coming through it, the glow of the sun's last light faded behind the mountains. A blast of chilly air hit her face, turning her instantly cold. However, it wasn't the air that gave her the chills. The resemblance to the nightmare Alia had was so uncanny she expected to see Charlie's body laying there when she looked back down. Another blast of chilly air sent her into a different kind of panic. She knew she had to find these kids soon before hypothermia kicked in.

Once again, Alia tried calling out for the kids but got no response. Looking on the ground, two pairs of small footprints had run around the cavern then down one of the offshoots. Making sure first that it was the only one they went down, Alia continued to follow, calling for the kids every few minutes as she went.

Every time she called out for the kids, Alia would stop to listen. At last, she heard, very faintly above, the sound of water dripping a tiny voice. It was so small and quiet she couldn't tell if it was a boy or a girl. Going in the direction she thought she heard it, Alia called again.

"Joey, Sasha…can you hear me? Shout real loud if you can hear me." From the direction she went, Alia could hear the voice again.

"Help, we're lost." came a voice, still very faint. Such relief washed over her that Alia felt a little faint at first.

"I'm on my way, don't move, stay right where you are."

"Hurry…the flashlight…it's going out."

Alia hurried along the passage toward the sounds. "Hey Sasha, sweetie, I need you to keep talking so I can find you. How about you and your brother sing me a song," she yelled.

At first, there was nothing, then faintly she heard the girl again. "What song?"

Alia doubled back, taking another offshoot and marking the ground with rocks for the way out. "Well, it's after Thanksgiving, so how about a Christmas song. How about Jingle Bells."

This time the girl's voice was even clearer. "Jingle Bells is really a song about thanksgiving."

Alia had to laugh at that. *Smart girl.*

"You're absolutely right, Sasha, it is. Could you still sing it for me anyway?"

The girl's tiny voice started to sing from somewhere in the cave system. A moment later, her brother joined her.

"Good job, keep it up, kids; I'm coming." Taking a few twists and turns, then doubling back a few times, the singing got louder and louder. It seemed to take forever, but at last, Alia could see the faint glow of a flashlight. Turning a corner, there the two of them were.

The little girl ran into Alia's arms, crying, making her tear up as well. "We were so scared, I thought I could find the way out, but I got so confused." The little girl stepped back and looked at Alia. "Hey, you're a police lady."

Alia went down on one knee. "Yes, I am. I work for the Sheriff's department. A lot of people have been looking for the two of you."

Joey, his face a mess of dirt, came up to her looking shy and worried. "Are mommy and daddy mad at us?" he asked.

The look on his face, his little lip pouting out, liked to break her heart. Alia took the boy into her arms, noticing as she did how cold he was. "No, not even for a minute. They just want to find the two of you. Here let me get a good look at you, are you hurt anywhere?"

The children told her they were not. Besides being covered in dirt and mud and being very cold, they looked ok to her.

"You're about half frozen, though," she said, taking them into her arms and trying to rub some warmth into them. Alia then remembered the radio, but there was nothing but static back when she tried to call out.

"Did you break it?" asked Joey. "My Daddy can fix it if you did."

"No, honey, I'm sure it's just because we are so far into the cave. Which means the two of you are going to have to be brave for a little bit longer and follow the clues I left to get out of here." Alia thought if she made it into a game, it would make the journey back less scary for them. "But first, I'm going to put my coat on the two of you. You'll have to share, so it's going to be like a three-legged race only with your arms." Alia put the little girl's arm into one sleeve and the boy's arm into another, then had them wrap their other arms around each other. As small-built as Alia was, they still looked lost inside the coat. Only the girl's arm was long enough to barely make it out of the other end of the sleeve, so she gave her the good flashlight then zipped up the coat. "There is that warmer now?"

They both nodded.

"Can we go now? It stinks in here." Said Sasha.

Alia didn't have to take a sniff to understand what the little girl was talking about. She, too, smelled a powerful, wrong sort of odor. It was a fleshy smell of decay, most likely a large animal that wandered in and got lost.

"Now you're going to have to be very careful and walk in front of me. When we get to a place where another path crosses, there will be a clue on the ground to tell us which way to go. You have to go slow. There are lots of holes and big rocks in the ground ready to trip you up. If one of you goes down, both of you will, so we are going to take our time. The two of you ready?"

They nodded and slowly started down the passage Alia had come in from. She walked behind them using the dim flashlight they had enough sense to bring with them. Right away, she knew the way back out would be rough without her coat. Under it, all she wore was her uniform shirt and a t-shirt under that. She hadn't bothered with a thermal shirt that morning, knowing she was going to be working in the nice heated office all day. When they got the call about the missing kids, Alia hadn't bothered to get anything warmer out of her locker either.

Harper is going to have my ass for this. Liable to end up sick and miss a few days of work.

They barely got started back, and she was shivering. To make matters worse, between the dripping water and brushing against the walls, Alia was becoming wetter and wetter. When they got to the cavern that resembled her nightmare, Alia shivered so bad she almost dropped the radio trying to get it to work. Standing under the shaft, she tried to make a call out. On the other end, she could just barely hear a voice, but the static and crackling of the radio was too loud for her to make it out. So instead, Alia clicked the PTT button three times rapidly, a distress code to anyone that could hear it. It wouldn't let them know where she was, but she figured Charlie told them where she went by now. She did it two more times before putting it away and hurried the kids along, her teeth chattering.

When they reached the entrance to the cave, Alia was very wet and so cold she was no longer shivering. She was also more tired than she had ever been. Despite having on her jacket, the kids were shivering now and even a little wet from their walk out. Alia had to decide whether to make a fire first or call for help. And for some reason, she couldn't think right and was unsure what to do.

"Okay, I need you two to sit here and don't move. We need a fire, so I'm going to go get some wood." stumbling on her feet, Alia walked out of the cave and into the night that was much colder than even the damp cave. Collecting the wood, she had to remind herself several times what she was doing and where she was. Part of her knew this was a bad thing, but the word for that bad thing escaped her mind at the moment. With hands half numb from the cold, Alia collected enough kindling and small sticks to get the fire going. Panic set in as she forgot where she was supposed to take the wood for a moment.

Charlie, I need you. Where are you, Charlie?

Like a puff of air, Alia's mind cleared enough, and she remembered the children in the cave. Stumbling back up the hill, she dropped everything in front of the cave and set about starting the fire. In no time, she had a horrible half-falling apart teepee of wood, but the fire below it was catching. Alia had enough going on that she made the fire close to the wall and entrance of the cave so the heat would reflect, though, at the time, she didn't know that. At this point, she was working more on instinct.

Back in the cave, the two kids were half asleep but doing better than she was, still mostly warm snuggled inside her coat. Outside of the cave, the two shivered a bit before she set them before the fire.

"How's that? Nice and warm." Only it came out so slurred the kids couldn't even understand. Still, they nodded.

Alia wanted to warm herself by the fire as well, but the little bit of wood she had collected wasn't going to last them long. So back off into the woods, she brought load after load of wood and added it to the flaming pile. It was everything she could do to just stay awake. Several times Alia caught herself staring into the fire in a dreamlike state. She gave herself a mental kick and headed back out, gathering more and more wood. At one point, Charlie was there helping her to stack wood in her arms. She pleaded with him to give her his coat, but he only smiled.

Meanwhile, Charlie, Harper, Ranger Dickson, and a few other rangers and officers hurried down the long trail for the caves. They had been given rides back to the cabin when they called off the search for the night. As soon as Harper saw Alia was missing, he knew where she had gone without even asking Charlie.

"Damn it, boy, why did you let her leave."

"Because what if she's right? We haven't found shit out here but some muddy prints that could belong to anyone."

Harper tried getting her on the radio with no luck.

Charlie knew Harper was more concerned about Alia than mad, so he didn't say anything about what he felt just before sunset. A small wave of panic had come over him, but it was quick. He knew it was Alia and hoped it just meant that she had been spooked by something and wasn't really in trouble.

On the way back to the cabin to regroup, Charlie and Harper were riding in a fire bus belonging to the forestry department when all the radios started making crackling noises all at once. Someone was trying to get through, but only a word or two could be heard. None of them understood.

"It's Alia, got to be." Said Charlie.

Harper picked up his radio. "Cadet miller is that you…can you read me…Alia!" nothing from the other end, only static. "If she's in the caves, she won't be able to reach us until she gets out."

"If she can get out, " said Ranger Dickson. "Those caves have more twists and turns than a backcountry road. This is what I was afraid would happen. On top of telling these people we didn't find their kids, now we have a cadet missing and possibly hurt."

"She's not hurt. I would know if she was," said Charlie. And right then, all the radios squelched three times rapidly and repeated two more times."

"You were saying?" said Dickson.

"I'll have to agree with the Deputy on this one. Alia is young, but she's been playing in the woods her whole life. If he says she's not hurt, at least not bad, I believe him. She's no dummy either. I think she found those kids. If she were alone, she'd just go back to the cabin, not call out for help."

"So I guess you expect us to waste more time on a wild goose chase looking for this kid?"

Getting irritated, Harper turned to Dickson. "Look, that kid is like a daughter to me. If she messed this up, I'll be the first one there to put my boot up her ass, and she knows it. I'm telling you, she found those kids, and we better get to her and them before they freeze to death out there."

"Fine, but not a word of this to the parents. I'm not going to get their hopes up over the actions of some wet behind the ears cadet lost in the woods."

At the cabin, the volunteers were let go for the night and told to check in at first light unless they heard news otherwise. Out of earshot of the parents, Harper told those of the Forest Department and his own men that it was possible Alia was at the caves and found the kids. Those who could go on were being asked to grab stretchers and medical supplies but discreetly.

Shortly after, a group consisting primarily of guys from the Sheriff's department led Harper, Charlie, and Ranger Dickson up the hill then down the trail that led to the caves. The other way would have been faster, but they may have missed the stream where they needed to go back up the mountain in the dark.

The closer they got, the more anxious Charlie started to get. As tired and cold as he was, it was everything he could do to keep from running down the trail.

Harper could see how agitated he was and pulled him down the trail further from the others. "What's with you, Charlie? You look like you're about to sprint away from us at any moment."

"It's Alia...I think...I don't know, but something's wrong. And I'm so damn cold, but I'm not cold at the same time. I think she's the cold one, frigid cold. We have to hurry, be damned if I don't feel like she's fading away."

Charlie had talked before of this connection he had with Alia. Like how when they were kids, he could always manage to find her no matter where in the county she was. As a baby, Alia would instantly calm down from any fit when Charlie was around. But since she had come back to them, it was as though the connection was more substantial. There were other things, small things, like Charlie, who seemed to know when she needed chocolate ice cream and a heating pad last month when Alia was cramping really bad. And flowers on days where the rumors had gotten to her before he had even talked to her. It put anything he and Ellen had after years of marriage to shame. So if he said she was in trouble, Harper believed him.

"Let's step it up now, boys," he called back to the others. "It's getting awfully cold for her and those kids to be out here."

Ranger Dickson gave Harper a look, but the deputies went faster.

They all smelled the campfire long before they could see it but didn't get their hopes up right away that it was them or even in the woods. Sure enough, as they got closer, they could see the glow of a rather nice-sized fire near some rocky outcroppings.

That was when Charlie did start to sprint, as well as some of the other deputies. He came around the side of the outcropping so fast the kids sitting before the fire were startled.

"Hey hey, it's ok we've been looking for you two."

The others came around, and shouts of joy went up into the night.

"I'll be damned," said Ranger Dickson, shaking his head in disbelief.

Charlie looked around but didn't see Alia. What he saw next to the fire was a large pile of wood and sticks, almost enough to get them through the whole night if needed. "Where is the woman that found you?" He asked the girl kneeling down in front of her.

"She went down there to get more wood. I told her we had enough, but she just kept bringing more. She's been gone a while this time. And she talks funny now."

Leaving the kids, Charlie ran down the hill calling for Alia, Harper right behind him. He hadn't gone far before he almost ran into her as she stumbled slowly back up the hill with a bundle of sticks in her arms.

Knocking the sticks out of her arms, Charlie pulled her into him. Alia was so cold and her clothes so wet it was almost as if he was holding a block of ice. Wasting no time, he picked her up and ran up the hill to the fire.

When they saw her, the others brought over blankets and helped Charlie bundle her up. Harper called on the radio for an ambulance to be ready for them when they got her back. One of the Rangers brought over the fold-able field stretcher he had carried like a backpack.

As they worked, Alia weekly fought them, mumbling incoherently about firewood.

Charlie tried talking to her, telling her she didn't need anymore but didn't think he was getting through to her in her hypothermic state.

Everyone there knew the urgency of the situation and how important it was to get her medical care before her organs started shutting down. In no time, they had her bundled, strapped in the stretcher, and six of them, including Charlie, ran back down the trail to the cabin carrying it. A few more went with them ahead of the others to relieve those carrying Alia when they got tired. Charlie wouldn't give up carrying her no matter how much they told him he needed a break.

The kids were bundled up as well and carried back down the trail. One of the rangers stayed behind scooping water from the spring-fed stream to put out the fire.

To Charlie, the run back carrying Alia felt like a lifetime. One hand holding the stretcher and one a flashlight, he didn't even dare look at her out of fear of tripping. He kept urging the other men on faster and faster. He pushed them on even faster when he saw the cabin's lights.

With the ambulance having been called and sitting in the drive, all the family members were outside waiting anxiously. When they saw the stretcher and the speed at which the men were running, their hearts clenched tight, but as they ran past, they were relieved to see it wasn't one of their kids.

One of the Deputies running behind them stopped and informed them that the kids had been found, and despite being cold and hungry, they were fine and on their way out.

Everyone was so happy and relieved, Spencer almost as much as the kid's parents.

"Who was in the stretcher then." The girl that had been with Spencer asked. When the others heard her, they, too, wanted to know.

"That was Cadet Miller from our Sheriff's department. She's the one that found the kids and kept them warm till we got there. She had the kids bundled up in her coat and even made them a fire. Unfortunately, she's suffering a bad case of hypothermia right now."

The children's mother looked over at the ambulance to see paramedics inside frantically working on the young woman. When the ambulance showed up, she had thought it had been for the kids. But instead, it was for the person she may very well owe the lives of her children to. Her relief of their well-being was replaced now with sorrow.

"Is she going to be ok?" she managed to ask, her voice hitching.

"Hard to say. She's in pretty bad shape. The only time I saw anyone worse was when we pulled a guy out of the lake last January." They all watched as the ambulance, siren blaring, raced out of the driveway.

Several hours later, Charlie, Harper, and Ellen sat at Alia's bedside at the hospital. Her temperature had fallen dangerously low. Because of that, her heart, lungs, and kidneys were not working at full capacity. They had hooked her up to a hemodialysis machine to warm and recirculate her blood and a mask administering humidified oxygen when first admitted. Alia lay unconscious, having passed out on the way out of the woods.

The doctors believed that the only thing that kept her from going into organ failure was whatever drove her to keep going up and down the hill to get firewood. With the temps below freezing and the few clothes she had on wet from the cave, they may have lost her if she had stopped for even a moment. The fingers on her hands were a bit frost-nipped, but they would heal in a few days with no scarring.

Word had already gotten around the hospital what Alia had done to not only find but save the children from freezing. Nurses and Doctors peeked in on them from time to time, wanting to see the hero everyone was talking about.

The news was getting around town as well. Already the room was filling up with Flowers, gifts, and get-well cards. Frankie and her family came by with flowers and a Teddy bear with a police uniform.

Ellen kept herself busy arranging things to look nice, so Alia could see them all when she woke up. The more that was brought in, the more she would get teary-eyed.

Harper had to run out once in a while to deal with the local media that was frantic to know how this young cadet managed to find the missing children and how she was doing. He told them what he knew and that they would have to wait until she could tell the story herself since they still didn't know many of the details. In the meantime, he asked for people to send their positive thoughts and prayers since she wasn't in the clear just yet.

Charlie, once allowed to see Alia, wouldn't leave her side. He held the one hand free of IVs and just looked at her with his head laying on his arm. The nurses had cleaned the dirt and soot from her face, but she was scratched all over from tromping through the woods in the dark. He thought she looked much like the day when his parents brought her home, her face a mess of scratches from the puppies. She looked like an angel to him then, and she looked like one now.

Ellen and Harper tried getting Charlie to come home with them as the evening turned late, but he refused. So they took shifts staying with him while the other went home to shower and sleep. At their home, the family members that stayed for the weekend asked after Alia and Charlie. Beth was adamant that she be taken to the hospital, and they promised to do so in the morning.

When Alia woke, it wasn't the cards, balloons, and flowers she saw, but Charlie, his head still resting on his arms, sleeping. She slipped her hand out of his and ran her slightly sore fingers through his thick dark brown hair.

Charlie woke with her smiling down at him, her blue eyes shimmering, sending a wave of emotion through him. Getting up, he kissed her on her forehead then rested his on hers. Sitting back down, he smiled at her shaking his head. "You know you gave us one hell of a scare, right?" he whispered, mindful of his father sleeping in a chair in the room with them.

"Nah...I'm not giving up that easily," she said, removing the mask of warm air for a moment. They had taken her off the blood machine in the night once her temperature had come up but kept her on the warm air and fluids.

Charlie was so thankful that he nearly cried. Instead, he pointed out all the stuff in the room, distracting her while he wiped his eyes. "You're the town hero," he said.

"So the kids are okay?"

"Thanks to you. Paramedics checked them out at the cabin, but they were fine other than being dirty and hungry. Had you not gone when you did.... I'm sorry I doubted you, Alia."

"I was afraid I might have dreamt it all. Things started to get a little weird after we got out of the cave. I couldn't seem to keep my thoughts inside my head."

"That would be the Hypothermia." Said Harper stretching in the chair. "Why the hell you didn't just sit in front of the fire I have no idea." He got up, went over to the bed, and gave Alia a kiss on her forehead. "How are you feeling, kiddo?"

"Half thawed out," she said with a smile.

"You need to get your strength up. I'll go tell them you're awake so they can get you some food. We are holding a press conference this afternoon as long as your doctor says it's ok."

"Press conference what for?"

"Didn't Charlie tell you? You're the town hero. Everyone wants to know the story about the young police cadet that defied procedure and brought two kids home alive. They all want to know what happened in that cave."

"It was nothing really."

"Nothing, hmm? From what I heard, you got the two of them to sing Jingle Bells so you could find them. And something about leaving certain clues to show the way out."

"Old Boy scout trick. Rocks in the shape of arrows to show where to go. It was no big deal, really. They even walked out on their own."

"No big deal?" Harper crossed his arms. "Alia, you almost died trying to keep those kids warm. You refused to give up on the idea they were there in the first place. Modesty aside, it was a pretty big deal, especially to the parents of those kids. It would be a whole different kind of morning had you not done what you did. I don't think you're going to have to worry so much about all those rumors anymore, either. Now I'm going to go get someone to get you some food before Ellen comes here and chews me out for not doing it."

"He's right Alia," Charlie said when his father left. "Even if we had checked the caves after we got back from our search, it would have been too late to save those kids. Dickson wouldn't have looked anyway. He had the search called for the night before we got your distress signal. I think he only went with us in hopes of rubbing it in our faces when we found you and not them too."

"I didn't do it to be a hero."

"Of course not. You did it because you're a good person and a good cop. Something my father saw in you a long time ago."

"You look tired. You've been here all night, haven't you? Don't give me that grin either."

Charlie kissed her hand and tried to get her off the subject of him when to his relief, Ellen came into the room. In her arms were more flowers and gifts, all of which she tossed onto a table as soon as she saw Alia was awake.

"Oh, my baby girl, I'm so happy to see those pretty blue eyes of yours again." She gave Alia the best, long hug she could, being careful of the IVs in her arm. "Have you eaten yet? I bet you are starved. I wanted to bring some food, but Harper said I better wait to see what the doctor said first." Leaning forward, she whispered in Alia's ear. "I did bring a few of those cinnamon rolls of mine you love so much. Oh, and take a look at this." Ellen went to the table and pulled a newspaper out of her bag. "You made the front page. Only our local paper, of course, but still."

Ellen gave Alia the paper, and there she was on the front page. The picture was the same from her swearing-in day as a cadet, only the front page heading read.

County Sheriff's Department Cadet Rescues Two Lost Children

"The article isn't very big. It's mostly about how the kids got lost. I will say it doesn't make Ranger Dickson look very good. But that's ok. He was always a bit of a pampas ass anyway." said Ellen.

"Mother." Charlie scolded.

"Well, it's true, Charlie, and I heard what he said to her. The egg all over his face is his own fault. I'd like to see Trish plaster this all over town. I have half a mind to send her a copy."

"You would be too late." Said Harper entering the room with a tray of food. "I sent one off to her first thing this morning, special delivery via Deputy Hawks. Next to us, he hated her the most. She pissed in his patrol car once. Texted Trish a picture of it as well. Funny, not one of their asses in her family has yet to call to see if Alia is ok."

Harper and Ellen helped put a table up for Alia and her food tray on it.

Starving, Alia opened it to find only broth, juice, and jello. She made a face of disgust, and Charlie laughed at her.

"Liquids only until your urine output is better." Said Harper. "Doctor's orders. They need to run a fresh batch of blood work here in a bit, make sure nothing is wrong and your kidneys are functioning right again. After that, you should be able to eat some real food."

"Meanwhile, starving is always fun," said Alia.

"Well, maybe next time you'll stop to think before running off like that. Hell, Alia, you didn't even have the proper gear to be out there as it was."

"Harper, I know you're upset, but maybe right now is not the time to fuss at her," said Ellen.

"Well, she's just going to have to deal with it because later I may not be mad enough. You should have never gone out on the search and rescue without your thermals, at least. You could have changed before you got there."

"I know, and you're right, but it was my understanding we were under a time crunch. And I didn't want to waste time going back up to the cabin either and having to explain to anyone what I was doing. I don't know if they could have held out much longer. If they had lost consciousness, I would have never found them."

Harper pulled a chair up next to Alia's bed opposite the side Charlie still sat on. Careful of the IV in the back of her hand, he took hers in his much larger one. "Alia, I'm not trying to discount the good thing you did at all. I am more proud of you now than I have ever been. But you have people that love and care about you. Hell, after this, you're going to have a whole lot more. We just want you to be more careful. We would hate to have gone through everything we have just to lose you."

Alia nodded, unable to speak. She knew she had gone through most of her life with reckless abandon. She also knew things were different now. Other than her father, never before had she ever felt so loved and accepted by the people in her life than right now. Most notably the ones in this very room. For her entire life, Alia had felt that if she was just gone, no one would really care. Now, coming so close to what she had wished for so many times growing up, she realized it was no longer just about her. The thought of causing that kind of pain to the people she loved the most hurt more than any pain she had ever suffered. It would prove to be both a blessing and a curse.

The doctors wouldn't let Alia do much of anything, not even use the bathroom on her own until the lab results came back. When at last she was cleared, they still insisted she stay for at least one more night. They removed her catheter, which was a tremendous relief, and cleared her to go downstairs later to have the press conference.

When they came with the wheelchair to take her down, Alia thought the conference would be someone from the local paper, maybe the local news station. The room where they had it, though, was packed with reporters and news crews from all over the state. Even a few from out of state. A long table had been set up where she and the others would sit. There with her were her three doctors to her left, to her right Harper, Charlie, and the parents of the two children. Alia noticed an absence of anyone from the forestry department.

Before being wheeled up to the table, Alia had met with the parents in a private room. The mother was crying before she had even gotten in there, and the father looked on the verge of tears. They kept calling her a hero and said they hoped she wouldn't get into any trouble for going against orders. They hugged her and insisted on giving her gifts of flowers and chocolates. She asked how they were doing, and the parents said the kids were fine and that Sasha said she wanted to be a lady officer as well one day. That got Alia to tear up as well.

At the conference, the doctors first explained severe hypothermia in detail. Then they briefly described the condition she had been in when she arrived and that now her core temperature was back to normal. All lab results were better, but she would remain in the hospital for at least one more night. There were a few questions for them, but not many.

Next, Harper explained the case of the two missing children giving details most already knew. He talked about the search but neglected to say how they had found very little evidence. Ranger Dickson would have to own up to his end of things eventually. Harper then told them how following a hunch after talking to the other children, Cadet Miller had taken it upon herself to search the caves. When the press asked why didn't more people go, Harper said that the Ranger from the forestry department was in charge of the search. And that Cadet Miller had gone off on her own.

When it was her turn to talk, the reporters all wanted questions asked first, but Harper put an end to that right away, threatening them with no story at all if they persisted. He had stood up in complete papa bear role, and his large frame and fierce personality were enough to put even the most seasoned reporter in their place.

With her turn, Alia told the story of how she gave the search team the slip (not wanting to put Charlie in the hot seat for letting her go) and how she went about finding them deep within the caves.

From there, Harper explained how they had found the kids safe and warm by the fire, then located Cadet Miller just down the hill collecting more wood. It was evident that she was severely hypothermic by then, so they rushed her out. Harper managed to tell it all, his voice barely cracking.

The reporters had a frenzy of questions, but the doctors insisted they keep it at only a few because Alia needed to get her rest. She answered them as best she could, looking to Harper for help when she couldn't.

Next up were the parents. How the kids went out on their own was already told, so they just kept going on about how they owed Cadet Miller the lives of their children. That without her, indeed, they both would have been lost forever. At the end, the mother cried, and Alia fought to keep back her own tears.

By the time she got wheeled back up to her room, Alia was exhausted. Allowed to eat real food, at last, she scarfed down the two rolls Ellen had brought her, then begged for a cheesesteak sub from her favorite place in town. While Harper went to get it, she had fallen asleep but woke a little later with a start.

Alia had been back in the cave. The cavern of her other nightmare, to be exact. She found the children again, only this time she hadn't gotten to them in time. On the same stony platform she had found Charlie in her other dream, the children lay in each other's arms. Falling to her knees in front of them, she tried to wake them up, but their bodies were cold and stiff.

When Alia woke from the nightmare, tears already streaming down her face, Charlie, still having not left her side, sat on the edge of the bed and pulled her into His loving arms. He rocked her as she cried, assuring her again and again that the kids were okay, it had just been a bad dream.

Once she was calmed down, Ellen got her a wet dishcloth to wash her face off. They asked about the dream, but she didn't want to relive it, so they didn't press her. After a while, they got her to eat the sub that Harper had brought and a few treats others had given her.

Later that evening feeling full and tired again, Alia insisted that Charlie go home and get some decent sleep. Harper had to practically drag him out of the room, promising to bring him back later to do a shift staying with her.

Ellen took over the first shift that night and helped Alia shower and clean up because she still felt dirty from the cave. After a few more treats at Ellen's urging, she had laid back to rest but was afraid to sleep. The image of the children lying dead in each other's arms kept playing over and over in her mind haunting her. Around midnight the night nurse gave Alia a sedative after declaring she needed to get some rest or would have to stay in the hospital longer. Thankfully the rest of her night was dreamless.

The next day Alia was discharged from the hospital and given orders to be on bed rest for several days. Charlie promised he would make sure she behaved after giving the doctor one of her, yeah right, looks.

There were still some reporters outside, much to her surprise. Ellen insisted Alia stay at their place so Ellen could care for her while Charlie worked. And since there was no arguing with her, that's where she went. Even there, they kept getting cards and flowers for the town hero. It was all a bit much she felt and owed the Harper's for keeping her grounded.

A week later, it all started up again when Alia received an award for her work in rescuing the children on the steps of City Hall from Mayor Judd Hopkins. She was also promoted to Deputy a few weeks earlier than she was supposed to be. Once again, Alia was on the front page of the local paper the next day. Once again, Harper made a point of sending a copy to Trish.

Things changed after that. No more did Alia have to put up with nasty looks and comments from some people. At first, most of them wanted to shake her hand when they saw her, even give her a hug. As time went on, it was mostly just smiles and greeting her by name, which was a marked improvement over the months prior. Most people in town now regarded her as a hero and figured her mother's rambling was just that of a bitter woman who had her own mess of troubles.

For the first time in their relationship, Charlie and Alia felt free to share their affection for one another out in public. They made sure to stay professional while in uniform, but they dated openly. And the town embraced their romance, as they now embraced her.

Trish tried once again to disparage Alia to those that would listen, but the problem was that no one wanted to any longer.

Harper, who had been keeping tabs on Trish since he didn't trust her to leave the kids alone, came to work one day telling them that she had moved, little camper trailer and all. Neighbors said she was moving to her sister's who was falling further and further ill. But Harper knew the truth. He knew Trish could no longer stand to live in the same town where her daughter was now a beloved hero.

Chapter 24
And time moves on

Time, as it has a habit of doing, moves on, and so did the lives of our young hero and those around her.

Christmas that year was one of the happiest Alia ever had. The Harper's were very big in giving to and working with charitable groups in and around Union County.

Ellen was a volunteer for several groups, including Toys for Tots, Salvation Army, the local soup kitchen, and the Angel tree program. While Alia still had some time off recovering, Ellen recruited her to help. The two of them had a great time together, to the point Alia was almost sad to go back to work.

The Sheriff's department also had their hand in ringing bells for the kettle and collecting toys for toys-for-tots. Alia's favorite was the bike drive. As a kid, a bike meant she had freedom she otherwise wouldn't have had. Seeing the looks on the faces of the kids was just what she needed to put her in a good Holiday mood.

The week before Christmas was when they did volunteer work as a family. They worked the soup kitchen several nights, donated toys, and rang bells for the red kettle again. Every year the Harpers chose both a boy and a girl from the angel tree, and this year she and Charlie did the same.

None of her other family members reached out to Alia, no cards, invites, or Christmas greetings. It was as if she didn't just leave her mother but had also left them. However, one did come from Uncle Walter, who left the family the night of her graduation. He was living in California and couldn't be happier.

The family stayed together in the Harper's home on Christmas eve. It was a night of hot chocolate and holiday movies, with Christmas music playing softly in the background. It was tradition for them on Christmas eve to open one gift each. Charlie gave Alia a beautiful cubic zirconia and amethyst bracelet that she adored.

Later, when Alia went missing, Charlie found her outside on the back porch with a blanket wrapped around her. Grabbing one for himself, he went out to join her. Together they looked up into the night sky for a few minutes. "So, just what is it we are looking at?" asked Charlie.

"Not at, for. On Christmas eve, my great-grandmother would get us kids together outside, and we would look for a red dot. She said it was Rudolph guiding Santa's sleigh."

Charlie laughed a little. "You know it was probably just Mars, right?"

Alia smacked Charlie on the arm. "I know, still it was fun. I kept doing it even after I got too old." Alia leaned in closer to Charlie, and he put his arm around her.

"You miss them, don't you."

Alia shook her head with a sigh.

"You know it's ok if you do. You won't hurt our feelings."

"It's not that. I mean, I do miss them, but my memories of Christmas with them are all skewed. It was seen through the eyes of a child that still believed that magic and miracles could happen. I look back on it now, and I can see the truth. The scorn, the false love, the dirty looks. Hell, even then, I knew I didn't get as many gifts or as good of ones as the other kids did. But at the time, I was so grateful to get anything I never realized the real truth behind it all. I don't miss them any more than I miss Trish. I miss what could have been, what should have been. And I miss my great-grandmother. She was about the only one that never seemed unhappy to see me. Even when I ate all the strawberries in her berry patch." Alia smiled at the memory.

Charlie held her tighter. "You don't have to worry about that kind of stuff anymore. And when we have kids of our own, we can bring them out here on freezing Christmas Eve nights and let them believe in the magic for as long as they want."

Alia wrapped both her arms around her thin boy. "Merry Christmas, Charlie."

"Merry Christmas, sweet girl." The two stood out a little longer, then joined Ellen and Harper inside for some much-needed hot chocolate.

The following week they all rang in the New Year out at the lake with fireworks. For the first time in a long time, maybe even ever, Alia looked forward to what the year may bring.

And life moves on.

Early in the new year, weeks before Alia's birthday, her great Aunt Barbara called to say Trish's sister passed away. Her condition had taken a nosedive shortly after Thanksgiving, and she had been put in the hospital. It was no surprise to Alia that this was the first she heard of it. Only a few relatives had bothered to reach out to her when they learned of her rescuing the kids.

Alia didn't want to go to the funeral knowing Trish would be there, and worse, grieving over a woman Alia herself heard her threaten her with death several times. However, both Ellen and Harper talked her into it. Like how she left her mother, they felt she had to handle this the right way to avoid regrets later. With Charlie at her side, Alia agreed to go. For her sake, she put aside any anger she had at her Aunt for all the years she stood by as her mother rained down abuse upon her.

Alia's biological family was rather large. Once those who had left the state came back, the church was very crowded. There was family in from Texas that had fled to a more republican and, in their opinion, god-fearing state. There were Trish's sisters from Florida and their families, cousins from New York, South Carolina, and Tennessee, and a smattering of cousins Alia knew very little about.

Alia had wanted to sit in the back, out of sight of her mother, but when the usher found out who she was, he said their spot was upfront right behind the husband and siblings. Charlie felt her anxiety heat up even before she gripped his hand so tight it hurt.

As they walked down the aisle, he whispered in her ear. "I'm right here, sweet girl. No one is going to hurt you while I'm with you."

Still, she put her arm around Charlie, getting as close as she could and still walk. Alia knew he was right. He may not have the bulk that his father did, but Charlie was just as tall and strong despite his lanky frame. And as sweet and kind his eyes could be when he smiled, he had a stern look that even hardened criminals would back down from. This was good because the look Trish gave her daughter when she sat in the pew behind her could have struck her dead if she had not backed down under Charlie's glare. With that one look, he made it clear to her that under no circumstances was she to say even one cross word to Alia in his presence.

Some of the others gave Alia an odd look like they were surprised to see her there even though they shouldn't have been. She felt like telling them that she was still family after all, but they were not worth her anger on this day. Others greeted her and Charlie warmly, even if some of that warmth was fake. Once realizing who Charlie was, a few had a hard time hiding their dislike. Alia had to admit that Charlie took it all like a champ. He made it clear in his posture and tone that he didn't give a shit what they thought of him as long as they left Alia alone. And so they did much to her surprise.

During the ceremony, which was thankfully brief, Alia stared at the back of her mother's head like she was trying to bore a hole through the woman's brain. To be so close to her after all the vile things she had said about not only her but Charlie was like sitting next to a pile of shit and trying to pretend like you couldn't smell the stench. When it was over, Alia couldn't wait to get out and get a breath of fresh air, so much so Charlie felt like he had to keep her from running.

When she finally did get a few gulps of fresh cold air, Charlie took her into his arms. "It's almost over. You're doing great."

"Yeah, real great, spent the whole time trying to mentally will brain cancer on that bitch."

"Well, that was better than what I was wishing on her." he smiled down at her.

"I couldn't have done this without you."

"I wouldn't have let you." he smiled at her. "But I have to admit, I am about one look of death away from punching one of these assholes in the face. A few are doing a relatively good job at hiding their disgust, but others are just blatant as hell about it."

"Welcome to the family, Charlie."

"Fuck that. We are your family now. These people have had their shot and haven't done shit. Not one of them called to make sure you were okay or to congratulate you. We wouldn't even be here if Mom and Dad hadn't thought it was the right thing to do. I won't make that mistake again. You hear me? You don't have to do this shit anymore if you don't want to."

"I know Charlie. But I'm glad we came. If nothing else, I am seeing that there really isn't anything I am leaving behind. I never belonged here or with them."

Charlie pulled her into him and hugged Alia tight. Over her shoulder, he could see a nasty look here and there as people milled around waiting for the casket to be brought out. Charlie gave everyone who looked the stink eye right back, almost daring them to say anything.

After the casket had been brought out and put into the hearse, She and Charlie joined the line of cars to the cemetery. The two of them were able to hang back some from the others, but Alia kept Trish in her line of sight anyway. That meant that Trish was able to glare back at her as well. Whenever she did, Charlie, with his arm around her protectively the whole time, made a point of kissing the side of her head then smirking back at the hateful woman. She wasn't the only one giving Alia dirty looks. Alia's uncle also glared over at her a few times.

"What's his deal?" Charlie asked.

"Oh, He's never liked me. Blamed me for ruining my mother's life. Thinks it's my fault his son is a perv. Even after he was caught molesting one of our other cousins. I have news for him, his son is a sick little bastard. Anything my mother accused you of, you can guarantee she got the idea from the things he's done."

Charlie looked at the man sitting next to the uncle. Even at his mother's funeral, he had a look on his face like some kind of a pompous ass. And no tears he noticed. Charlie knew he would have been inconsolable if it had been his own mother going into the ground. People say you can't tell a pedophile by looking at them, but it had been Charlie's experience that once he knew one, it didn't come as much of a surprise. This was one of those types of men. It would not surprise the both of them when later he would serve time in prison for molesting another little girl.

Looking around at her family as the service went on, Charlie made a few mental notes. It was hard to judge people when they were dressed up and grieving, but his years as a cop had already helped him see beyond the masks some people wore. The fake tears, awkward hugs, and smiles that didn't reach the eyes were clues. A way too young to be a drinking boy with a flask in his back pocket. The girl that couldn't keep her hands off her boyfriend's ass. The man checking out the women in skirts. Kids picking noses, making obscene gestures, or just wandering off and playing around the tombstones said more.

Graveside services done, everyone got back in their cars to join back up at the fire hall the husband had been a volunteer at for the reception. Despite telling a few that they would be there, Charlie had no intention of making Alia go. As Trish got into a car, she glared over at the two of them one last time. Charlie made a point of hugging Alia and glaring right back at her. He saw her mouth the words bastard and refrained himself from flipping her off.

All the way back to Union county Alia seemed to hold her breath. She let it out when they crossed the county line and slumped in her seat. "So, how did you like my family?" she asked with a laugh.

"They're not your family Alia, not anymore, not if you don't want them to be."

"They never really were. My real family rescued me from a crack house, those people left me to die in. I don't care to see any of them ever again."

"Then you won't have to," said Charlie, taking her hand and kissing it.

Only, she did.

In March of that year, Charlie and Alia got their first place together. They were very rarely apart anyway, so spending money on two places seemed pointless. The two found a nice inexpensive apartment in town close to work and the Harper's. It was a small one-bedroom, so anything they didn't use or had room for they stored in his old room at his parents' house. For a housewarming gift of sorts, Charlie came home one day with a small kitten barely weaned from its mother. One of the other officers had found it and brought it to the station. Alia immediately fell in love with The little all-white ball of fluff.

In April, Aunt Barbara called again and said her uncle had suddenly passed. When Alia asked how all they knew was that he fell asleep and never woke up. They were saying he died of a broken heart. Alia didn't buy that. You have to have a heart first. And for a man that had been cheating on his wife her entire sickness, his peaceful death was too easy. When asked if she would come to the funeral, Alia said no. Unlike his wife, she didn't feel she owed him anything. Her Aunt Barbera tried to appeal to her sense of family honor, but Alia just laughed and ended the call.

A couple of weeks later, Harper pulled Alia aside one night at family dinner. His contacts in the other county had been helping him keep tabs on Trish since she had moved there. They called him today to confirm that the cousin had kicked her out shortly after the funeral for his father. After that, they lost her whereabouts. No one had seen her here in town either. Trish had virtually disappeared.

And still, life moves on.

In May of the same year, Charlie was promoted to sergeant. Alia got to pin on his new rank at the ceremony herself. She couldn't get over how cute he was standing on the steps of city hall, bashful and red-faced.

Life became what life does. Days came and went. There were times when things were slow with work, which for cops was always a good thing. There were times when it wasn't so slow, and one or even both of them came home, wet, dirty, bloody, or even hurt. Charlie still got angry whenever something happened to Alia, but he learned to put his anger out in the gym.

The kitten grew into a sizable spoiled cat that loved to lay with them on lazy days at home in bed reading. Their love grew, not just for each other but for friends and family as well. They lived a happy life in their small apartment, hiked mountains on days off, hung out with friends, learned new things, and met new people. Much as anyone does in life. And they were happy, through the good times and the bad.

Time moved on, with yet another Thanksgiving (this one a lot less adventurous), another charitable Christmas, and yet another New Year that Alia looked forward to.

Their love grew.
And life moved on.

Alia was on call with Deputy Tackard, just driving around on a very slow late evening in April. A call came through the radio that there had been a disturbance at the high school in town. Someone was asking for Deputy Miller specifically.

"What do you think that's all about?" asked Tackard.

"Don't know. I still know some of the kids there. Maybe one of them thinks I can get them out of whatever trouble they have managed to get into." They drove to the school that only had a few lights on in the front office.

"I'll just wait here," said her partner. "Whatever the kid did, don't let them completely off the hook. Kick that ass if you have to.

Alia walked inside the school, and with most of it dark, she was reminded of the night she and Charlie had reconnected. She was amazed to realize that had been two years ago. So much had happened in that time. Alia had a life that two years ago she thought was only something of dreams. A life her younger, lonely self would have envied.

Walking down the hall to the principal's office, Alia took a moment to reflect on the past two years. The chance encounter here at the school with Charlie, their crazy night in the motel where she was sure they would die. His parents telling her the truth about her past. The long four weeks till she graduated. Charlie surprising her by taking her to the prom. The first time they made love up at the cabin. Three long months at the academy. Coming home, finally getting her freedom, and finding her place in her community surrounded by people who loved her. Alia had come a long way; they had come a long way, from the night she walked down these same halls feeling almost entirely alone in the world.

  Like that night when she walked into the main office, two Colman lanterns lit up the room. Alia found that odd and wondered if the little trick with the lights had happened again. Those two boys were seniors that year. Perhaps they hadn't learned the first time. Smiling to herself, Alia followed the only other light there was, and that was yet more lanterns in the principal's office.

  When she opened the door, Charlie sat there on the edge of the desk, in uniform despite having gone off his shift hours ago. Like that night, her first thought was, "What are you doing here?"

  Charlie smiled at her, his eyes sparkling in the light. "Two years ago tonight, you walked in that very door and back into my life again," he said. Alia could see that Charlie was nervous. She found it both endearing and cute. It was rare for him to be nervous at all, let alone around her. He was always so confident and sure of himself without any of the cockiness most guys had. "That weekend, getting to know you, spending time with you for the first time in years, good quality time, I fell in love with you. I swore to myself that I would never let you walk out of my life again." taking a small box out of his pocket Charlie, tears in his eyes, got down on one knee before her. He opened the box to reveal an exquisite diamond engagement ring. "Alia Miller, I have loved you since the first moment I laid eyes on you, and I have grown to love you more than I ever thought imaginable. There is nothing I want more in this world than to be with you forever. Will you honor me by becoming my wife?"

  Alia shook all over. Tears fell from her eyes that she fiercely wiped away because she wanted to see this moment, to take in this man with his beautiful green eyes and smile that lit up her heart, even on the darkest of days. She didn't say anything at first, only out of fear that if she did, the moment would be fractured, and she would be back to being that lost, lonely little girl again.

And Charlie, knowing in the way he had of knowing her, waited patiently like he had all those years they were growing up. He, too, wanted to take in the moment, to stretch it out for a million years just so he could kneel there, looking up into those incredible blue eyes of hers that shimmered like the stars. The eyes of an angel.

At last, Alia nodded. "Yes…yes…and yes again, my sweet boy."

Getting up, Charlie once again took her into his arms. Wiping tears from her face, he kissed her like the first time.

The whoops of several police cars came as flashing red and blue lights flooded the room from outside. While she had walked in, all of their fellow officers and friends had lined up outside in the parking lot.

Harper and Ellen walked in from the other room, having been close enough to hear yet not be seen. Ellen, of course in tears as she embraced the girl that would once again be her daughter, officially this time. Even Harper seemed a little misty-eyed as he took her small frame into his bigger one. For a while, the little family hugged, kissed, cried, and laughed. Their love was like an unbreakable bond. One that was on the verge of being tested in ways they never imagined.

Word of the engagement got around fast, not just in the town but the county as well (and surprisingly, beyond too). The couple was congratulated on the streets for weeks.

Ellen posted about their engagement in the paper, including a picture of that night with them in front of all the squad cars.

Harper was upset he didn't have a copy to send off to Trish. However, he got over that when the following week at family dinner, Alia asked if Harper would be the one to walk her down the aisle.

"You're the closest thing I ever had to father other than my dad, and I would think he'd want you to be the one to give me away."

That time Harper let them see him shed a few tears as he came around the table and picked Alia up in a hug.

Other than announcing Crystal would be her maid of honor and George his best man, the couple didn't immediately make any plans. The only thing they knew for sure was that the wedding day would be on the same day as their engagement, because why mess with a good thing.

After that, it was back to their lives, their jobs, their fat lazy cat, Wednesday night family dinners, and the love that had gotten them to where they were.

Chapter 25
The Return

"Your mother is here."

Alia had just arrived back at the station ready to be done with the day when Charlie, looking upset, met her at the back entrance. "What did you just say?"

"Trish is here. She's out front in the lobby."

Instantly Alia's blood ran cold, the hall lights seemed to dim a little, and she was slightly aware of Charlie putting out his hands to hold her up.

"Whoa, hey, you going to be okay?" Her face was white, and she trembled slightly as she rocked on her feet. The fact that after all this time, that woman could still have this kind of effect on her angered Charlie. Escorting her out of the hall, he had Alia sit in a chair in one of the empty rooms.

"I'm okay." she insisted. "Why is she here? What the hell does she want?"

Charlie knelt before her, trying to decide how to proceed. He wanted to tell her he would get rid of the women and tell her to stay out of their lives. But that wasn't his choice to make, to be fair. And the woman that waited out in the lobby was not the same Trish they had known. At least he didn't think she was.

"Look, Alia, I don't know what her angle is, but, I mean, it's weird."

"What's weird."

"Her. She's dressed up nicely. She hasn't raised her voice or insulted anyone. Shit, she even looked happy to see me. She started apologizing, saying she was a different person now."

Alia laughed, "Ha, where have I heard that shit before."

"She says she wants to talk to you. To apologize and explain things."

"Well, I don't want to talk to her. I told her I was done, Charlie, and I meant it."

"Then you don't have to." Charlie got up to leave and tell Trish.

"Charlie, wait." Over the initial shock, Alia got up, ready to face her demon. "I have to do this. It's not your place to tell her I'll do it."

"To hell with what my place is. Alia, you turned white as a ghost as soon as I told you she was here. She still has that effect on you, and I won't let her put you through that again."

If only you knew. Alia thought. *If only you realized that she never left me. She's been here this whole time, a voice in the back of my mind haunting me. Every failure, she is there. Every doubt, every time I screw up, she is there to tell me I'll never be good enough. When I can't decide what to wear, it's because she tells me how fat and ugly I am. When I'm leery of making new friends, it's because she is there telling me no one wants to be my friend, not really. When I wake up some mornings convinced this will be the day you decide you no longer love me ... .it's because she never left. And she never will if I don't face her. But I don't dare tell you that...because even now she is there.*

"I have to be the one to do this. If you do it, she'll know she still gets to me. Worse I'll know."

Charlie nodded and gave her a hug, willing his strength into her.

"Come with me, though. If she starts her shit, you may be the only one that can keep me from kicking her ass."

Charlie smiled. "Or I might be the one encouraging you to do it."

"Oh no, you have to be the one to keep your cool this time. I'm serious, Charlie. She may be here to try to provoke me to do something. We can't let her do that."

"Alright, but you're doing it next time." he gave her a kiss, and they walked out to the Lobby.

The woman in the lobby was barely recognizable to Alia. Charlie was right. She was dressed up, wearing a long dress, a blue blouse, and holding a blue purse on her lap like a clutch. What struck Alia most of all was the large golden cross Trish wore on a chain around her neck. The only time they had ever gone to church was on Christmas eve.

But that wasn't all. Trish looked better as well. Healthier, happier, just looked like a whole new person, despite putting on several pounds. So much so Alia would have looked skinny at her heaviest compared to Trish now. And she sat there waiting, not pacing, no leg bouncing up and down and no yelling. When she saw Alia, a big smile broke out on her face, one that even matched her eyes. Still, Alia couldn't help but feel like she was a fly about to be trapped in a spider's web.

To the officer staffing the front desk, Charlie said to get lost for a bit, and so with a shrug, Rusty grabbed his coffee mug and left. Charlie sat behind the desk, wanting to give them some space but still right there to intervene if needed. And boy, he wanted her to give him a reason. Charlie could feel that old familiar anger he had worked so hard to control build up in him again. As always, Alia was his Achilles heel.

With the desk officer gone, they were alone in the lobby. Alia walked out from the front counter, confronting her mother with a frown and folded arms.

"Yes, well, I guess I shouldn't be surprised you're not happy to see me." Trish shifted uncomfortably.

Alia liked the idea that she was making this woman uncomfortable. "Well, considering that the last time I saw you, you glared at me like you wished me dead."

"To be fair, we both did our share of glaring that day. Besides, that's the past. I'm a different person now."

Alia scoffed and rolled her eyes. For once, it didn't make Trish mad. It didn't even seem to make her flinch.

"I know you've heard that all before."

"And this is where you're going to tell me that this time it's different. Let me guess, you found Jesus, and he has taught you the error of your ways."

Over at the desk watching, Charlie thought Trish's eyes turned cold for a second. Sitting up, he looked again and saw only calm passiveness.

"I deserve that," said Trish. "I knew coming here and facing you again wouldn't be easy, and it shouldn't be. I was a horrible mother to you, Alia, and I wouldn't blame you for throwing me right out the door and never seeing me again. But I am asking, begging you to please just come talk to me, let me apologize at least."

Alia looked over at Charlie, and he shook his head."

"And Charlie, that goes for you too. Just give me one last chance to try and set things right. That's all I ask. If the two of you never want to see me again after that, then fine."

"When?"

"I was hoping today. Now. The officer at the front desk said the two of you were getting off work. I thought maybe we could have an early dinner somewhere here in town."

Alia looked at Charlie again, and he gave her a look that said it was up to her.

"No dinner," Alia said. "We can have drinks at the little cafe up the road, outside, not inside. You say your peace, then we are done. And you're going to have to give us time, so say about an hour."

"Yes, that all works for me. Thank you, Alia. Thank you too, Charlie, I promise you won't regret it." Trish got up and left the station.

Alia looked after the women, genuinely bewildered by what she had just seen. *If this is some kind of trick, she's doing a damn good job.* She turned to Charlie and could see he wasn't thrilled with her decision. "I know what you're going to say, so just don't," Alia said, sounding harsher than intended. "I know this has got to be some trick of hers or some act which is why I picked the time and place."

"You really want to be seen out in public with her? In the middle of town of all places? After all the shit she pulled?"

"Yes, actually I do. Let people see. Let everyone know that I gave her a chance to say her piece despite everything."

Charlie went up to Alia and discreetly took one of her hands. "Sweetheart, you have given her more chances than any person deserves."

"I know that. And I know my mother. Whatever act she is trying to put on, she won't be able to keep it up for long. Especially if we don't fall for her crap and let her know it. Just because I am willing to give her a chance doesn't mean I will be nice about it. She'll act an ass, and we'll have every right to tell her to go fuck off for good." *Again.*
"I hope you're right, Alia, something about this whole thing doesn't feel right to me."

"Not to me either. I'm not going to lie, my anxiety hasn't been this bad since the raid on that meth house."

"Hey, don't even start thinking about that. You're going to need a clear head when we talk to her. We both will."

Alia knew that whole thing with her getting shot had been hard on Charlie. It was a superficial wound, and she was fine in a few days. But the blood and her screams of pain haunted him. Sometimes at night, he would wake up from a nightmare calling out for her.

They clocked out for the day and drove home long enough to shower and dress. Alia made a point of remembering to put on her engagement ring. She didn't wear it at work for fear of losing it or it becoming damaged, so Trish didn't get a chance to see it yet. Alia hoped its sight would send her mother into a fury, losing the mask she was wearing.

When they walked around to the front of the Cafe from the back parking lot, Trish was already there waiting, drinking coffee. Seeing the two of them hand in hand, she smiled like it was the best thing she had ever witnessed.

"You know I was really hoping you two kids would still be together," said Trish as they sat down. "I was worried, once I saw the error of my ways, that the things I said and did would have torn the two of you apart. I'm so glad it didn't, one less thing I have to atone for then, I guess."

"So that's what this is all about? You as usual." Alia said, trying to sound as sharp as possible.

"Well, no, not entirely. I mean, this is for me as much as it's for the both of you. But yes, I have a lot to atone for."

"So, what's his name?" Alia gave her mother a knowing look

Backing down a little, Trish conceded. "It's Jacob, but it's not what you think. We are just friends."

Once again, Alia rolled her eyes. Under the table, Charlie squeezed the hand he held.

Trish went on to tell them about how after her sister then brother in law died and their son kicked her out of the house, she had hit rock bottom. She had lost everything, including her car, and spent all her time drinking at the bars. Then one night, trying to walk back to her sleazebag motel so drunk she couldn't walk, Jacob had taken her into his church, where he let her sleep till morning.

"And the first thing we did the next morning was go to an AA meeting. After that, we talked. For hours. I told him about getting pregnant at sixteen, raising you on my own, and how you had turned your back on me."

Alia started to say something, but Trish stopped her.

"I know now that's not what happened; just let me finish."

Alia nodded, allowing her mother to continue.

"So anyway, Jacob saw through it all. It was like he's known me for years the way he saw through my bullshit. And so I told him the truth, about you, about foster care, and how I treated the both of you. All the horrible things I said about Charlie. All the lies. Not at first, of course, but eventually. Then he didn't just tell me I was wrong, he told me why. Oh, how I hated him for it."

Trish paused as the waiter brought her and Charlie their drinks, both just sodas, since a nice stiff drink may have sent the wrong message. Neither wanted to look weak before her.

The waiter, Toby, asked after Ellen, and Alia said she was doing fine, then he left.

"You and Ellen must come here a lot."

"Yes, it's Moms' favorite place," Alia said.

Once again, Charlie caught it. Almost like a shadow crossed over Trish's eyes.
Alia hadn't seen it. Looking into her mother's eyes wasn't ever easy for her to do.

It was then that Trish noticed the ring on Alia's finger.

"Oh my goodness." she practically shrieked with delight. "The two of you are engaged."

"Yes," said Charlie, talking for the first time since they sat down. "I asked her to be my wife on the second anniversary of the night we reconnected." There it was again, a faint shadow across the eyes. Trish tried looking perplexed, but Charlie had caught it before she did.

"Charlie is talking about the night Billy was supposed to take me to Alexandria for my SATs."

Be damned if he didn't see it again. Alia was right. This act of hers wasn't going to last. Charlie wanted to say something and call her out on it, but he was curious about where this all was going.

"Oh yes, I always had a feeling there was more to that whole trip than you were willing to talk about. My fault, of course. You should have never had to hide that from me. The whole thing with Billy was my fault anyway. I knew he would drink those beers, I didn't tell him to, but I was hoping he would."

So she admits to sabotaging my chances to do the test.

Under the table, Alia was the one gripping Charlie's hand now and not gently.

"Speaking of Billy, have you seen him lately? How is he doing?"

Again with the shadow over the eyes. Charlie wondered if what he was seeing was really there. He and Alia looked at each other for a moment.

"He disappeared last November. You know that Trish, we questioned you about it," said Charlie.

"Well, I knew he was off on a bender somewhere, but I figured he came back."

"No, he never did, the case is still open, but there's no evidence, no witnesses, and no Billy."

"I'm sorry to hear that," Trish said sincerely.

"Okay, Look, this is all great and all, but just what is it you're here for?" said Alia, clearly getting agitated.

"I come to make amends. Alia, I'm sorry for the shit job I did as your mother. And Charlie, I'm sorry for all those things I accused you of, all the lies I told about you. But Alia, I've changed. I know that will be hard for you to accept, but I have. I just want to be a part of your life…."

Before she could even finish, Alia was firmly shaking her head. "No, absolutely not, it's not going to happen. You can pretend to be someone else all you want, but it doesn't change what you did to me. The hell you put me through. I still have the fucking scars, real scars. Ones I see in the mirror every day." Alia lashed out.

Charlie could see one now, the one Alia got on her cheek from when Trish threw a glass ashtray at her two years ago. It was tiny and went unnoticed by most, but he knew it was there.

"I know, don't you think I know all that? Once I got cleaned up and came to terms with what I did, it has haunted me. Not a night goes by that I don't have nightmares about the things I did to you. The things I allowed to happen to you."

Good, that makes two of us.

"I don't expect you to forgive me or even trust me again. I just ask you to give me a chance. I have changed, Alia, I swear. I'm a born-again Christian. I've gone through therapy. I've worked on me so I can be some idea of a mother to you. And you're getting married, I don't want to miss out on that. I've missed out on so much already, all those years wasted." Trish looked up at them both earnestly with tears in her eyes.

However, it wasn't the first time Alia saw Trish shed fake tears. She even used to tell Alia that squirting out a few eye drops would get most people to do anything you wanted. Alia thought for sure her mother would have cracked by now. "I don't know. Our lives are going pretty well right now. I don't know if I'm ready for all the drama again."

"No drama. There will be no drama. I promise you. Maybe we could meet once a week, like this, just the two of us and talk. We could reconnect again like you and Charlie did. They weren't all bad times, Alia. We had some good times too."

Oh, they were mostly bad, though. And when they weren't, I was in a constant state of high alert, wondering when the shit would hit the fan again.

Alia looked over at Trish for a moment. Once again, Alia didn't believe the act would hold up for long. As much as she wanted to tell Trish to fuck off, Alia had to admit she also wanted to see where this would go. Not to mention it may be possible for her to work out some of her demons by placating this woman and giving her rope to hang herself with.

"No phone calls. No, coming over to our apartment. No last-minute arrangements. And if you know what's good for you, you'll stay away from the Sheriff's office because if Harper sees you, he's liable to run you out of town. We meet here once a week, a time and day we decide when we meet. If you don't show up or have to cancel, there won't be any makeup days. I'm going to need time. We are going to need time before we even begin to believe you have changed."

Trish agreed to that and more. They made arrangements to meet the following week. Trish tried giving Alia a hug before leaving, but she put a hand up, backing the woman off. "There won't be any of that either."

Trish thanked them both again then left to wherever she was going.

Calling back the waiter, the two stayed to have dinner there. Charlie looked over at Alia, but she was staring off into space down the road off in the direction Trish walked off.

"What are you thinking?" he asked. He was getting from her a mixed bag of emotions, the largest of which was a wave of simmering anger.

Alia looked over at Charlie and tried a smile, but she knew it wouldn't match her eyes. "I don't know. If this is some kind of ploy of hers, it's a new one."

"Well, I don't like it. Not a bit of it. I still don't like the effect she has on you. Game or not, she upsets you."

"And don't you think it's about time I got over that? Let's say she isn't running some kind of con. I'm never going to trust her again regardless. I'm never going to let her get close enough to hurt me like that again. But maybe this will be a good thing. Maybe it will help me work out the last of that nagging voice in the back of my mind."

Charlie knew she was talking about the one that kept her doubting herself even with all the words of love and encouragement he gave her. Alia didn't know he knew. But then she didn't know she talked in her sleep, and at night was when her demons came out to play.

"Hey, you know whatever you do, I will support you. But I have a real bad feeling about this whole mess. I don't like the idea of the two of you meeting alone, even if it's out in public."

"I know, so do I," she said, taking Charlie's hand across the table. "Good thing I have my sweet boy by my side." she smiled. This time, it matched her eyes.

Charlie smiled back and kissed her hand. "And I always will be," he said.

At family dinner night that week, they told Mom and Harper about Trish. Harper slammed his mug of beer down so hard some of it sloshed back up at him. Ellen mostly shook her head, saying she didn't like it but understood that Alia wanted to give her a chance.

Harper didn't understand at all. He was furious they met with her and even more so that Alia planned on having lunch with her the following week. He said he wasn't mad at Alia, but that did little to make her feel better.

On the drive home, Alia was quiet and not her usual happy laughing self after one of their Wednesday night dinners. Like she had a bad habit of doing, she over-thought the whole night. Alia kept seeing Harper slam down his drink and glared at her. It's not like she didn't see it from time to time, but that was in his boss mode at work. At family dinner, Harper was in dad mode, and Alia didn't care for getting that look then. Yet there it was playing in her mind over and over.

"He wasn't mad at you, Alia. He was just mad at the situation," Charlie told her, sensing her discourse. Later that night, Charlie watched her get ready for bed. He loved watching her do her nightly routine. Brushing her teeth, cleaning her face, applying lotion that he loved the smell of. Tonight she wore her summer pajamas that consisted of shorts and a half tee. The shorts hung on her hips in a way that once in a while, Charlie caught a glimpse of the scare from when she got shot. The sight of which could strangely anger him and turn him on all at once.

Only tonight, it just upset him. Unlike Trish, the man that caused that was locked up for good and never would have the chance to hurt her ever again. That vile woman wasn't even here, and she was ruining what was usually their favorite night.

Alia continued to putter around the bathroom, cleaning what was already clean, holding off going to bed as long as she could.

Watching her, Charlie knew she was in for a restless night. "Stop, Alia, just come to bed."

She did but with none of the enthusiasm of regular nights. Laying in bed at night became one of their favorite things to do. For about an hour, they would read or, even better, just talk, holding one another, letting their hands explore the curves and lines they had come to be so familiar with. Some nights they would make love, others they would just fall asleep in each other's arms.

Putting aside the book Charlie had been pretending to read, he laid down and took Alia into his arms, her face cradled on his chest. "He's just worried about you, sweet girl. We all are."

"Which is why I need to do this. I'm not trying to upset anyone, Charlie. I just want her gone and gone for good. If, after meeting a few times, I have proven to myself that, I don't know, that she doesn't scare me anymore, I guess, then I'll tell her to have a nice life and walk away. If I don't and I'm haunted by her the rest of my life, It'll be my fault this time." Alia looked up at him. "I want children one day, Charlie. And when we do, I want to be able to give them my all. I want to be a good mother. I don't want to continue this cycle of abuse that you and I both know darn well happens all the time."

Looking down at her, Charlie smiled and kissed her head. "Sweetheart, you have nothing to worry about. Demons or not, you're going to be a fantastic mother. Your heart will win out no matter what you do because, deep down, you are a good person. We are both going to be great parents. Our kids are going to be so loved. They will grow up in a home where they have two parents that are so in love with each other that we are going to be a constant embarrassment to them." he laughed. Charlie's eyes smiled, and it was so infectious Alia couldn't help but smile back. He kissed her then rolled her over onto her back. "You know it's funny you should mention having kids," he said, feeling the elastic waist of her shorts.

On her leg, Alia could feel something else through his boxers.

"We do not need to be having kids now." she giggled, reaching down into his boxers despite what she said.

Feeling the warm caress of her hand, Charlie sighed heavily with a slight moan. "No, maybe not, but no harm in practicing." Hiking up her shirt, he took one of her breasts into his mouth.

Charlie had hoped their lovemaking would have been enough to wear her out. However, Alia still tossed and turned all night, even resisting being held by him till the early morning when they both got a few hours' rest.

Chapter 26
Wolf in Sheep's Clothing

The following week Alia was the one first to the Cafe, and she hoped Trish would pull one of her typical moments and not show up. However, before her raspberry tea arrived, Alia saw her walking down the street.

Once again, the woman who most of the time looked at Alia with annoyance or distaste had nothing but a smile for her. She made it like she wanted to hug, but Alia stubbornly stayed put.

"Yeah, I guess maybe it's a bit too soon for all that."

"You would guess right," Alia said in a mood.

"You're in a mood today. What's wrong? I know this can't be easy for you, but I was hoping you would at least meet me halfway. And where is Charlie? I was hoping he would join us."

Alia hadn't wanted Charlie to come. She wanted to observe Trish without the distraction of him being around. Alia thought Trish may slip easier or reveal what she really wanted without an audience. One of the things that used to drive Alia crazy was how normal and nice Trish could be in front of people sometimes. Some people thought Alia was a brat and her mother the victim simply because she was good at acting like a good mother when needed.

"He wanted to be here, but it's not easy for the both of us to get off of work at the same time, not even for lunch." That was not true, at least for meal breaks. They often got off and went to eat together, sometimes with Harper as well. Days off were different since no one wanted it to look like Alia and Charlie were given preferential treatment.

Alia leaned in on the table as if meeting her halfway was meant literally. "All right, why don't we cut the bullshit, what's the con?" For once, Alia looked her mother dead in the eyes. It was actually something she and Charlie had worked on all week with an old photo Alia had.

"Look her in the eyes, Alia. It not only takes away her power, but if she's lying, you'll see it there first."

Charlie had told her about the shadow he saw in her eye that first day but admitted he didn't know if it was a trick of the light or even his imagination. He wanted so bad to hate Trish that he was afraid he may have been manifesting what he saw.

And now, looking into her eyes, Alia saw it too. It was almost like a slight hardening or coldness in the eyes, but it was gone again in a split second.

Trish looked away, fiddled with her purse, even made like she was wiping at tears at the corner of her eye. "I deserve that I do. And I don't blame you either, Alia. Jacob told me this was not going to be easy. I really thought it would be. I really hoped maybe you would have missed me, even if just a little. Even if just because I'm your mother."

Alia flinched at the word feeling a stab in her heart at this woman calling herself that. Her real mother, who had sat with her at this very table so very many times, was a thousand times more than this impostor ever would be.

"Kind of hard to miss something you never really were in the first place," Alia said unwaveringly.

The waiter, Toby, came with Alia's tea and a complimentary blueberry muffin fresh from the oven, her favorite. He took Trish's order then left again, stopping to give Alia's shoulder a reassuring pat.

"Well, I see you're still pretty popular here, still the town hero," she said with none of the disparaging attitude Alia would have expected.

"Kinda helped that you left town and stopped trying to smear my name all over the place. Not to mention Charlie's."

"Left with my tail between my legs, you mean," she said with a little laugh. "You see, I can laugh about it now. I'm hoping one day the both of us will be able to together."

"You still haven't told me what con you're trying to pull."

Toby returned with Trish's soda, asked if they needed anything else, and left when they said no.

"I know it will take a while to accept, but this is me now. I did a lot of reflecting and a lot of soul searching and realized that Jacob was right. What I did to you, everything I did to you, was horrible. I have no one to blame for my actions but myself." Trish went on and on about how she became aware of her actions, recognized she had a problem and worked to better herself. And yes, she had her new connection to God to thank for it. That nothing about religion made any sense to her until Jacob explained it to her. He got her clean, off the booze and drugs, counseled her, and set her to atone for her sins.

"I want to be sure you understand something about Charlie," Trish said.

At that, Alia noticeably bristled.

"No, nothing bad. The opposite, really. When you were in foster care, I admit I was jealous of him. The two of you, it was like there was something special between you. Something you and I never had despite you being my own flesh and blood. I resented him for it. Oh God, Alia, the way that boy used to look at you. The way he looks at you now. I saw it last week; well, in between the times he was looking at me like he wanted to take my head off. It was as if the sun rose and fell on you. And he could always get you to smile and laugh. If I raised enough of a fuss, I thought they would keep him out of our visits, and we could bond better. They did, but you and I, it never did work out. So I began to resent you. It was a horrible thing to do and one I'm not proud of."

"So all that shit you said about him, accusing him, the things you accused him of doing to me, that was just because you were jealous?"

Trish nodded.

Holding on to her tea glass Alia felt the rage rise in her and had to grip the glass tight to keep from flinging it into that bitch of a face. She, of course, knew all the time Charlie never laid a finger on her. Still to hear Trish confess and for such a shallow reason as jealousy sparked the flame inside her. That also meant that Trish was well aware of her actions the whole time. "And you tried again just a couple of years ago when I left you. Knowing that as a cop, an allegation like that could get him at the very least fired. Worse shot by some psycho."

"Okay, now I'm not going to make any excuses for what I did because Jacob says that's what led me to mess this up with people in the first place. But to be fair, Alia, he's a lot older than you. I knew you had been sneaking around behind my back, so I thought for sure the two of you must have had a thing going for a while."

"Bullshit." Alia slammed her fist on the small iron table hard enough to rattle their glasses, spill their drinks, and alert those nearby. Trying hard to tamp down the fury, Alia leaned in again and talked as low as possible. "Charlie isn't a lot older than me, he's a few years older first of all. Second, I would've had to sneak around if you hadn't been such a psycho about everything." There it was, the shadow again. Alia locked on Trish's eyes and kept going, determined she was going to rip the mask this woman was wearing off her face for all to see right there. "I was never with Charlie until that night he took me to Alexandria. I had been going over to Harper's to study for the Academy once a week and to the range a few Sundays when I wasn't working. In fact, Charlie didn't even know about it. It wasn't until that night we had to stay in Alexandria because of the tornadoes that he even knew." There it was again, longer this time. Alia felt she was on the right track at last. "Yes, I was with him that night, we even shared a bed, and he was a perfect gentleman. So see Trish." she said, emphasizing the T. "You haven't changed. Your still blaming others for the way you are."

Trish broke eye contact and looked down at her lap. "Okay, I admit I still have a lot to work on. It's just that, it's not like our history with men has been all that great."

"You mean your history."

"We have both had our fair share of being burned, and you know what I mean."

"But Charlie isn't like that. Something you would have realized had you just taken the time to get to know him. You're the one that poisoned your opinion of him."

Trish looked back up. "And I'm sorry, Alia, I really am. Look, I don't want to fight. If you say Charlie is a good man, then I'll believe you."

"He is. Charlie has always been there for me when he could be. He surprised me by taking me to prom. He ran me out of the forest on a stretcher when I almost froze to death looking for those kids, and he has never so much raised a hand or voice to me in anger. And he's a good cop too, which these days seems to be hard to come by."

"I'm happy for you, Alia, I really am. I'm sorry I missed out on so much of your life. I had no Idea he took you to prom. That's something I should have been there for, and I'll regret that for the rest of my life."

Alia sat there looking at Trish. The anguish on her face seemed genuine. The fact that she conceded said a lot. Maybe she had changed. Perhaps this time, things were different. Still, like Charlie said, there had been those shadows in her eyes. Could it be she, too, had imagined them too? "I could send you some pictures, you know, of prom and my Academy graduation if you want them."

Trish's face lit up. "Really? You would do that for me. Oh, I bet the two of you looked so good together. He really did grow into being a handsome young man. I'll give him that."

Alia nodded, but her mother complimenting Charlie seemed to put her more on edge than her negative comments. Alia looked at her phone, noticing that Charlie had texted her several times, asking if she was okay. Before she could run a short text back, she heard the whoop of his patrol car as he pulled up to the curb at the Cafe.

"Shit, I'm late getting back. I've got to get work." Alia lied. One look at Charlie, and she knew he wanted her to end it.

Trish turned around to see Charlie waiting for her in his patrol car and offered him a smile and a wave. He only stared at her. "It's going to take him some time to come around, isn't it?" she asked, looking back at Alia.

"It's going to take us both some time. I'm willing to share a few photos, not my life just yet. I'll meet you back here same time next week if you want. We have a tab here, so feel free to get some lunch." Grabbing her things, Alia got into the car with Charlie.

Trish watched as he put a hand on her face and asked if she was okay. Even with Alia saying yes, Charlie still scowled at Trish as he drove off. Trish knew that Charlie would be the biggest obstacle to getting back into her daughter's life.

All of that week, Charlie paid close attention to Alia. Her mood was a bit shorter than usual but other than that, she seemed to escape the lunch with her mother pretty well. She had, of course, told him everything she had said even when she lost her temper. That, of course, he knew, which is why he texted her. After that, he made her promise to answer the texts right away because despite being out in public, he didn't trust that woman.

A couple weeks went by, and with it, a couple lunches with Trish. Alia didn't exactly look forward to them, but she started to dread them less and less. Her sleep returned to her standard version, and her temperament evened out.

Even Charlie relaxed, not feeling like he had to be on high alert so much when Alia was with Trish.

That's not to say that all the meetings went smoothly. When Trish said she was living on Jacob's compound with the other strays he had saved, Alia accused him of being a cult leader. That accusation set Trish on edge even with all the other touchy subjects they had broached.

Trish denied that she was in a cult, almost to the point of getting angry about it. When Alia called her out, she just apologized, saying that after all Jacob had done for her, it bothered Trish to hear Alia accuse him of such things. Understanding how that felt, Alia dropped the subject. She was just happy in the end that Trish wasn't in the county with them.

Fourth of July week, Alia told Trish they would have to postpone their lunch for the following week. She explained that the fourth was one of their busiest holidays, and with the weather being so perfect that week, it would be rough and busy.

The week after, Trish was at the Cafe first for once but only because Alia had been late. They all had been dragging after the busier than usual fourth they had. Alia's usual decaf raspberry iced tea was already waiting for her when she arrived, Trish having ordered for them. After getting Toby to fix her, a sandwich, Alia apologized for being late and explained how they all were running a little ragged.

First, there was traffic as the tourists all seemed to flock to the town simultaneously. That led to a few bumper-to-bumper accidents and one bad one involving a minivan full of kids and a pickup truck driven by some redneck already drunk at eleven in the morning. Thanks to seatbelts and airbags, the kids all came out with only minor injuries, and their moms in the front seats had moderate cases of whiplash. Still, that had taken the wind out of their sales as none of them liked calls that had hurt kids involved.

"And it didn't end there," she said. There had been more nuisance calls than usual, people parking illegally, fireworks in mailboxes, drunken fistfights at family bar-b-ques. They busted a drag race out by Parson's farm one night. Then to top it off, in the middle of the town, fireworks, a massive house fire, claimed the lives of several animals.

Then when everyone left, it was traffic jams and accidents all over again. By the time they got to spend one day off at the cabin on Tuesday, She Charlie and Harper spent most of the time sleeping in hammocks out by the river. They all had to deal with the usual summer stuff and a pile of paperwork from the fourth the rest of the week. So even a week later, they all were still tired.

"So you'll have to excuse me, but I'm going to actually eat lunch on my lunch break since we ran out the door without breakfast."

"Well, at least you can't say it's a boring life," Trish said.

"Just in the summer anyway. Once that's over, it goes back to being pretty much a sleepy little town."

"That's not what I heard. I heard you got shot last year."

Alia nodded. "Yeah, we were serving a warrant on a meth house that wasn't in town though but out in the country. The house was supposed to have been cleared. I was upstairs doing another sweep looking for drugs and guns when this guy popped out from behind a fake panel in the wall. I lucked out that he was a lousy shot and only got me in the hip, no major damage."

"And where was Charlie?"

It wasn't the way Trish asked but just the question that bristled Alia. She stopped eating her sandwich and stared at Trish. "Downstairs doing his job. We don't exactly work hand in hand all day long."

"I didn't mean anything by it. I was just wondering if he had been there or not. It must have been pretty traumatic for him to see you get shot."

"Yeah, well, he stopped the guy. Tased him as he came down the stairs. Which, by the way, is the procedure, despite what you see on TV or the news. We don't always shoot first and ask questions later."

"Don't be offended, Alia. It's not what I intended."

"Well, you're not exactly a champion for the police."

"I keep telling you, Alia, I have changed. I would have thought you saw that by now. You can rest easy, Alia, I'm not here for a fight."

"I agree you seem to be trying. And I'm really trying to wrap my head around that. But you can't just expect me to forget eighteen years of crap just because...." Alia paused like someone had turned a switch off, then not thirty seconds later turned it back on. "you've found god or got righteous with Jesus." she said like she hadn't missed a beat.

"Alia, are you okay?"

"Yeah, sure. Why wouldn't I be?"

"I don't know. It was like you switched off for a minute."

"Oh yeah, I guess I'm still tired as hell." They talked some more, made plans to meet again the next week, and Alia returned to work.

During a routine traffic stop later that day, Alia had been in the process of giving out a ticket when suddenly her partner for the day Deputy Cole was in her face."

"Miller...Miller, wake up."

Alia jerked. "Shit Cole I'm awake what the hell." She looked around and realized she was standing on the side of the road, just her and Cole. "Where did the car go?"

"You mean the one you gave a ticket to like five minutes ago. It left Miller, you gave them the ticket, and they left. You've just been standing here staring off into space since they drove off."

Alia shook her head and wiped a hand over her face. "Shit, I think I did something like that at lunch today too."

"If you're that damn tired, you could have just said something. I know you girl cops think you have to act so tough or be taken advantage of, but I would think by now you'd know I wasn't a sexist pig. Uh, no pun intended."

Alia laughed anyway on the way back to the patrol car. "Honestly, I didn't think I was that off."

"Well, there's such a thing called micro naps. It's the brain's way of shutting down when the body is too damn stubborn to lay down. Either way, you're done for the day. I'm taking you back to the station."

"I'll be fine. I can do my last couple of hours."

"The hell you will, something happens to you I'm not having Sergeant Harper pissed off at me. Sorry kid, as your senior, it's my call."

Back at the station Cole told Sheriff Harper what happened, and he agreed she was done for the day.

"Go home, take a nice hot bath and a nap. Nothing wrong with admitting you need a break from time to time." Since Alia was the type to work herself almost worn, he had no doubt that she genuinely needed some rest.

Before leaving, Alia texted Charlie, who was still out working. He told her the same thing his father had and said he would be off soon and meet her there. They could both have a nap then go get some dinner.

At their apartment, Alia did as she was told and ran a bath as hot as she could stand it, added some bubbles for fun, and slipped in. Sitting back in the tub, she was glad that she had listened. The warmth of the water and the silky feel of the bubble solution relaxed and comforted her.

The next thing Alia knew, Charlie was pulling her out of the water, trying to wrap her up with towels and her robe.

"Damn it, Charlie, I was vibing, what are you doing?" It was then that Alia noticed she was freezing. The lighting in the room seemed off, too, like it was much later in the day than it should have been.

"Shit Alia you're about half frozen. How long have you been in there? Why didn't you get out before the water went cold."

Sitting up, she pushed his hands away, a bit irritated at him. "What are you talking about, Charlie? I just got in not a few minutes ago." Except when she looked into the tub, she saw that the bubbles were all gone. Putting her hand in, Alia felt the water was frigid.

Getting another towel, Charlie wrapped it around her head. "I tried calling you to say I was running late, but you never answered. What is up with you? You had to have been in there for hours."

"No, it's not possible. Charlie, I'm telling you I just got in there. I must have fallen asleep, but I didn't even feel that tired."

Charlie helped her into the bedroom, sitting her down on the edge of the bed. He dried her off and got some nice warm sweat pants and socks. "Alia, you were wide awake. When I came into the bathroom, you were sitting up in the tub, eyes wide open. But it was like you were in a trance or something." he looked up at her, concern etched on his face. "Do you remember anything else?"

"No, Charlie, I came home and got in the bath, it was so nice and warm, and then suddenly you're pulling me out, and I'm freezing," she said, shivering.

Charlie took off the wet towels and robe, and he gave her one of his sweatshirts she always loved to put on. After pulling down the comforter on the bed, he picked her up and put her there under the covers. "I'll go make you some hot tea. Just stay there and try to warm up." In the kitchen, Charlie put on the kettle for the tea. While he waited for the water to boil, he called Deputy Cole and asked about what had happened with Alia that day. After the call, he went from worried to very worried. Something was wrong, and he didn't think it was a lack of sleep or a stressful week. With the tea done, Charlie took it into her and had Alia sit up to drink. He observed her as she sipped the tea, looking for anything that might indicate what was going on with her. "How are you feeling?" he asked after a while.

"Warmer, thank you. Oh, and starving." She looked over at the clock. She had left the Sheriff's department around four and was in the tub by no later than five. Now it was almost nine. No wonder she was so hungry. "How the hell was I in the tub that long? I had to have fallen asleep. Maybe you coming in woke me up."

"Maybe," said Charlie, but he doubted it. He had called for her several times, and after he found her shivering in the tub, he kept calling her name and even shook her a bit, but she kept just staring off into nothing. It scared the hell out of him. "How about I order us some delivery, and we just stay in the rest of the night?"

"Sounds great," she said with a smile. They ordered food then he went to take a shower. Only first, he made a call to his father.

"Dad, I'm worried about Alia," he said when his father answered. He told Harper what had happened when he got home.

"How is she doing now?"

"Resting in bed. She seems fine other than a little cold and hungry."

"Just a second, let me tell your mother." Charlie waited while Harper told Ellen what had happened at the apartment and today at work. "She seems to agree with me. It could be a seizure, maybe."

"Three in one day? Isn't that a bad sign?"

"Look, son, there is nothing we can do tonight as long as she is fine now. Your mother will make a few calls in the morning and, if she can, get her in to be seen. Meanwhile, just keep an eye on her. And I don't want her at work or to drive tomorrow. Drop her off at the house with Ellen before you go to work."

"Will do. See you in the morning."

"And Charlie, don't worry too much. It really could be nothing."

Or it could be something. Charlie thought as he ended the call. After a quick shower, Charlie looked in on Alia, and she was sitting up in bed reading as though nothing had happened. Later they ate dinner, read some more, and fell asleep, her in his arms. Charlie lay there holding her for hours before he allowed himself to sleep, expecting her to seize up on him at any moment.

The following day Ellen drove Alia to a specialty care clinic a friend ran. It was usually a non-patient day for him so they could catch up on paperwork. Still, under the circumstances, the least of all her being a cop and future daughter-in-law of Ellen's, he made an exception.

Before the tests, Alia described what had happened the day before as best she could. He agreed that it was odd. However, when the results from the scans came back, they were clear. No anomalies of any kind. The same could be said for her blood work as well.

"I believe you may have experienced an intense period of micro-sleep. My concern is that this condition doesn't usually last as long as you described. I will send the CT results out and have another specialist look at them. For now, my suggestion is to make sure you're getting enough sleep."

Later she and Ellen had lunch at the Cafe in town. It was strange being here with Ellen after being here with Trish the day before.

"So honestly, how are you feeling?"

"I feel fine. Yesterday I was dragging a bit, but then I think most of us were. It was a hectic holiday."

"Yes, it was emotionally draining too, I would say. Between the kids and the animals."

Alia agreed.

"I wonder if it was the weekend and what you have been dealing with these past few weeks. How is that going?"

Alia knew Ellen didn't want to so much as utter Trish's name. She and Harper both were very adamant about their position of her changing. She had fooled them once before they were not about to allow it to happen again.

"I don't know. It's all still so strange to me. I would have thought she'd have cracked by now. I'm practically going out of my way to be rude or indifferent to her, and she hasn't flinched. I had planned on calling it off by now, but now I'm curious to see where she is taking this."

"So you don't trust her?" asked Ellen.

"Hell no. Even if this all turns out to be real, and I don't think it will, I still don't care. She admitted to doing the things she did and saying what she did about Charlie on purpose. I thought she had a mental disorder all this time, and it turns out she's just a raving bitch."

"Well, let's still not discount the mental issues. I believe she has problems, but we still shouldn't let our guard down."

The rest of the week, Alia was fine. No more weird moments, her mood got better, and she was back to being the silly, adventurous young woman Charlie knew. The CT scan came back clean twice now, and they all chalked it up to lack of sleep and stress.

Alia had such a good week that when she caught up with Trish at the Cafe at their usual time on Monday, she found it hard to stay focused on anything Trish was saying. She was eager to get back to work and see her man in his uniform because it drove her wild. Trish didn't seem to mind as she kept up her end of the conversation and more.

When Alia got back to work at the station, she felt rather randy and had difficulty keeping her hands off of Charlie. It was at the point that the other officers started to take notice that he took her to the side.

"What has gotten into you today?" They were alone in one of the smaller supply rooms.

Alia practically threw herself at him, reaching for his belt with one hand and trying to take off his shirt with another. Charlie put his back against the door and hoped no one would try to come in. He didn't stop her but tried to talk some sense into her.

"Alia, what are you doing, sweetheart? You know we can't do this here. If Harper finds out, we will be working opposite shifts for months. Come on, this isn't like you, talk to me."

"I can't help it. I'm so horny right now I feel like I'm going to explode. Just a real fast one…please, Charlie, I need this." She kissed him all over, rubbing one leg between his and driving him crazy.

Charlie kissed her back while she worked on getting her pants off. The unique connection they had was working on him too. He could feel her need and desire like never before. All thoughts of how wrong this was given away to reckless abandon. Charlie dropped his pants to his ankles, picked her up, turned her back on the door, and gave her what she wanted, what they both now needed. It was the first time their lovemaking was more akin to ravenous sex. And as much as he loved every moment of it, there was a nagging voice of worry in the back of his mind.

When they were done and getting their clothes back on, Charlie looked over at Alia. "So what was that all about?" he asked with a sheepish grin. "Not that I'm complaining, of course."

Alia barely looked up at him, her face red.

"You're blushing. Alia?"

"Can we just forget that happened," she said shyly

"That's going to be pretty hard to forget."

"I'm sorry. I promise it won't happen again." *What the hell was I thinking? Harper would have my head, and I don't even want to think about what he would do to Charlie.*

Charlie knelt down before her. Alia sat on a box, buttoning her shirt back up. "Hey, what are you apologizing for? As much as I admit we shouldn't do that here, you have nothing to be sorry for."

"I know it's just, I really don't know what came over me." she looked at him hesitantly. "And you have to stop."

"Stop with what?"

"With that shit-ass eating grin of yours." she laughed. "You go out there looking like that, and everyone will know. Well, they are going to know we did something."

"Point taken. Are you sure you're okay? It's not because things are getting boring, is it, you know, in that area."

Now she looked up at him. "No, Charlie, not at all…I don't know…chalk it up to hormones. You are the one talking about having kids; my ovaries must agree with you, " she grinned.

"Okay, but next time you're in a mood like that, let's meet up at the apartment. I have no problems with a midday quickie."

"Agreed," she said, giving him a quick kiss. "Now I'm going to go get a car and patrol or something before we end up going for round two." And with that, she was up and out the door.

Charlie waited a bit before going out, thinking of sad things but finding himself grinning just the same.

The following Wednesday, two days after another visit with Trish, Alia had a lunch date at the same place with the family. The Harper's had a charity event to go to, so family dinner night was now family lunch.

When Toby came to take their order, he told Alia he was glad she was feeling better today.

"I'm sorry, what do you mean?"

The young man looked a little flustered like he regretted mentioning anything. "Well, you were here with that other woman."

"My mother," Alia said rather curtly to all their surprise. "That woman is my mother," she repeated.

"Yes, well, it's just that you seemed a little out of sorts. You acted like you barely even saw me when I brought you your wine."

"Wine…I don't drink wine, you know that. I always get the raspberry tea when I come here."

"I know I brought you one of those as well when that woman, your mother, first came. Then she insisted you needed a glass, that you were having a rough day. But you look much better now. Your color is back."

"Well, thank you, yes, I feel fine," said Alia, perplexed.

When Toby walked away, they all looked at her with concern.

"Okay, I know what you all are thinking, and you can stop right there, I'm fine."

"So why were you drinking, on the job and in uniform out in public?" asked Harper with a scowl on his face.

"Harper, not now, that's not what this is about. Are you sure you're okay, Alia? It's not happening again, is it?"

"Look, I don't know what Toby is even talking about. I don't remember drinking any wine. I don't remember any wine at all. Maybe she drank some, and I just didn't notice. I'm fine, all of you, stop looking at me like I'm a bug. Tell them, Charlie, I haven't had any more episodes, and the CT came back fine."

"She's right," said Charlie. But even he had his doubts. The thing about calling Trish her mother bugged

513

him. She hadn't referred to that woman as her mother since she started to call his mother, Mom. Still, he backed her up in her assertions that she was okay. That was until after he talked more later with his parents on the subject.

On Thursday, Charlie got off work before she did. Alia was about to go home to their apartment when Charlie texted her to come to the Harper's house instead. She entered as usual from the side door, leaving her gun and holster in the case with the others and joining them in the living room. As soon as she did, she felt something was wrong.

Charlie and Mom were sitting on the couch while Harper sat on the coffee table in front of a recliner chair he asked her to sit in. Alia sat looking at them, feeling worried.

"We have been talking, Alia." Said Harper, "And we have decided that when it comes to this thing with Trish, enough is enough."

"What is that supposed to mean?" Alia asked, feeling her blood pressure start to rise. It may have just been the fact that Harper said it, but she found herself surprisingly annoyed.

"It means." said Charlie. "that we don't think you should see her anymore."

"Well, why the hell not." she shot back at them defensively.

"Because dear, you have been acting increasingly off after your visits with her for several weeks now," said Ellen.

Alia sat there stunned, not believing what she was hearing. "I have a few off days, and the three of you conspire behind my back about it?"

"It's not like that," said Charlie. "But you have to admit you've been acting kind of strange the last few weeks."

"And let me guess you're worried about me," she said snidely.

"Yes, we are," said Ellen.

"Well then, just stop, for the sake of Pete, just stop already." Alia looked around wildly at all three of them. "I'm not some little kid anymore. I can take care of myself. This thing with my mother is my business, and frankly, it's really none of yours. Not any of yours." she emphasized as she looked at Charlie. "She's certainly not making me act any different."

"Oh no," said Harper, getting up and starting to pace. "Since when do you call her your mother? Because you haven't done that in years. And right now, you're not acting like yourself, Alia. Something is going on here. I don't know what it is, but until we figure it out, we just think it's a good idea you don't see her for a while."

Alia couldn't believe what she was hearing. Harper and Ellen were some of the most non-judgmental people she knew, yet they were attacking her mother for no good reason. "This is stupid. I know you hate her, but the three of you have lost your minds over nothing. I had a vogue state because I was exhausted, and some waiter said I was off one day. I was out of character two times maybe, not exactly enough of a reason for a witch hunt against my mother and me."

"This isn't anything against you." Charlie moved over to the coffee table so he could be right in front of her. "And it wasn't just those two times, and you know it. What happened last week was out of character for you as well." he tried taking her hand, and for the first time ever, she snatched it away like he repulsed her.

"Oh, so now wanting to fuck my fiance in a broom closet is my mother's fault. Will you people listen to yourselves?"

"Us," said Harper with a roar. "How about you, Alia? You're starting to sound…."

"Harper, your temper, aren't we supposed to be trying to help," said Ellen.

"You're starting to sound like Trish." he roared.

"You mean like trash, don't you. Because that is what all of you think of her as, right?" Alia sat there trembling with tears in her eyes. "So what am I trash now too?"

Alia looked at the three of them then got up. "She's trying to become a better person, and here all you can do is hold on to your hate of her instead of giving her a chance."

"Alia honey, just last week, you said you didn't trust her."

"I said no such thing." Alia snapped.

Ellen looked back at her, stunned. When she tried to speak again, Alia held up her hand.

"You know I would have expected much better out of all of you. You gave me so many chances, but you won't give her one."

"This isn't about her, it's about you, Alia," said Charlie. "Please, can we all just sit down and calm down and talk about this rationally. Alia, sweetheart, please, you're getting upset, we're all upset, and this whole thing is going off the rails. This wasn't how this was supposed to go."

"Then how was it supposed to go, Charles? You just tell me what to do, and I do it?" Alia looked down at Charlie, and part of her screamed out to him. Some part of her knew he was right and something was wrong, but for some reason, all she could do was be angry with him. To be mad at them all. And hurt. "I can't do this," she said, tears spilling over. "I'll see you at home Charles." she barely could get out his name. Without a second look back, Alia half-ran to the kitchen.

Charlie tried to go after her, but Harper stopped him. "Let her go, son."

"But dad, can't you see she's hurting?"

"Yes, dear." Said Ellen. "But she's mad right now too. We're not going to get through to her when she's like that."

"So what do we do now," he said as he heard her leave the driveway in her jeep.

"Be damned if I know," said Harper. "Did you hear her? She's not herself. That woman is infecting her somehow, I just know it. I really thought she would have gotten over it all by now."

"It's not that simple, Harper. That woman has had eighteen years of mentally and physically torturing a growing human being. There's no telling what kind of lasting effects that could have had on her. We talked about this before. When you wanted her to join the academy, we worried about her mental state."

"No, Ellen, even with everything, that kid was always strong. And she passed all the psychological exams. She has a temper. I'll give her that, but she came by that honestly."

"Maybe she was always strong before because she had to be," said Charlie. "She was alone before. Now she has us. Maybe this is her way of calling out for help. Before she left, I felt like she was silently screaming for me to help her."

"Which is why we did this," said Harper

"Maybe ganging up on her was the wrong way to go about it," said Ellen. "And Harper, I told you not to lose your temper. The two of you always butt heads, and being angry never helps. Charlie, give her a little bit, then go home to her. Don't talk about any of this unless she wants to. Tell her we're sorry, but that's it. And that we love her. Please make sure she knows that. Just be there for her. But I think after this, we need to keep a closer eye on Alia."

Charlie nodded and hugged his mother. "I know it bothers you to hear her call Trish mom again, and I'm sorry."

"Oh Charlie, I just want her to be okay. My heart can take a few cracks in it." tears fell from her eyes. "Just as long as we don't lose her again, we can't lose her again, Charlie, not to that vile woman."

Harper came over and took his wife into his arms as she sobbed.

Charlie left for home, his heart hurting and his mind in turmoil. He hadn't thought about losing her until his mother said it. On the drive home, he wondered just how possible that was. Charlie sat for a while in the parking lot of their complex when he first arrived, just looking up into the apartment they shared. He saw her shadow pass the window, and his heart skipped a beat. He longed to hold her but was afraid of who may be waiting for him inside. He tried connecting with her, and it only made his heart ache more with her pain. Charlie looked at the tattoo on the inside of his right wrist, then collecting himself, he went up to her.

In their bedroom, Charlie couldn't find her at first. Then he heard her sobs. In the closet, she had shoved herself all the way in the back, where they had extra blankets stacked on the floor. Alia was sitting with her knees up to her chest, the lullaby bear held tightly in her arms, crying big heavy sobs. She thankfully didn't fight him when he sat next to her and pulled her into his arms. His silent tears joined hers as he sat there holding her.

"I'm losing them, Charlie." she sobbed after a while. "I'm losing them both."

"No, sweet girl, you're not losing any of us. You never will. They both send their love."

"Then why would they do that? Why would they attack me like that."

Her choice of words was a mystery to him. The last thing he would have called what happened that evening was an attack. Sure his father did get upset, but that was Harper being his usual gruff self. Something she had stood up to several times. He wasn't about to tell her that, though.

"I'm sorry sweet girl. I'm so sorry. You know we love you. We will always love you no matter what." he cradled her in his arms till her sobs faded away. Later as she lay in bed sleeping, he sat in a chair next to her just to watch her for a few hours. Her sleep was anything but restful. She murmured in her sleep, flinched a lot, and kept telling someone to stop. When she woke a few hours later, late in the evening hungry, she didn't remember any of her dreams. They ate delivery in bed, talking about their day but avoiding the mess at the house. And just like that, it was as if he had his girl back. They even made love that night, although she seemed more timid than before.

Friday seemed to go off without a hitch. Alia made a point of avoiding Harper though she didn't understand why. That evening when they got off, Charlie suggested they go to the cabin for the weekend since they both had a rare one off. She was overjoyed at the idea.

The whole weekend Alia acted like the girl he had fallen in love with. No snide remarks, no leftover hostility, no vogue moments, just two days of the two of them enjoying each other.

It came as a shock to him Monday morning when getting ready for work at home she seemed to get excited at the prospect of seeing Trish later for lunch.

"I can't wait to see how her progress is coming along. You know Charlie, the three of us should have dinner one night. Yes, I know what you're going to say, we said we wouldn't do that, but I feel like she has earned it."

"What are you talking about?" *And who are you?* Charlie thought to himself.

"Well, I mean, she has been doing so well with her therapy and everything. I think if we give a little, maybe the show of support will do her some good."

"Okay, well, we are riding together today. Why don't I join you two for lunch."

Out of the corner of his eye, Charlie saw Alia stop mid tucking in her blouse. She was still as a statue, just looking off at nothing. It was the first time since the night at his parents he noticed anything strange. Just as he was about to say something, she came back to life like she never paused at all.

"No, better not impose on her with no notice. Besides, lunches are our special thing. I'll talk to her about it today, see when she can get back to town." They finished getting ready for work with no more incidents then drove into town together.

Charlie had Alia gas up his patrol car while he went in to talk to Harper. He told him how everything had been great the entire weekend, then suddenly this morning, something odd happened. "It's like a switch was thrown for a few seconds. If I didn't know better, I would think she was thinking about what to say next. It was eerie."

"Well, your mother and I talked about this at length this weekend and made a decision. If Alia won't or can't for whatever reason back off, maybe we can get Trish to." From out of his desk Harper pulled a piece of paper and handed it to Charlie. "She leaves the cafe by the same route every time, taking the alley shortcut to the parking garage. Confront her in the alley if she's alone and give that to her. Tell her it's hers if she never comes back again."

Charlie looked at the paper check his father had given him. The amount was enough to set Trish up with a nice little place and live off of for a long while if she was careful with it. He didn't even want to think about what they had to do to get access to that much money.

"Dad, this is insane. This is the kind of shit they do in movies all the time, and it never works. And even if it does, I'm sorry I can't let you do this, this is too much money. This has got to be all your retirement and then some."

"Small price to pay for saving our girl, don't you think?"

"But dad, this is yours and mom's future. I'm sorry, but I don't know if I am convinced that something bad enough is going on to justify this. I think you're jumping the gun a little here. It's one thing to ask Alia not to see Trish anymore, but I can't let you do this. If Alia found out about this, she would have a real fit. She wouldn't want you to give all this up for her."

"It's our choice, Charlie. We all know Trish is working some kind of angle. Even Alia knows deep down. I don't know what she is doing or how but Ellen agrees that there is something not right going on. Trish may not be smart, but she is a master manipulator, and she knows Alia like the back of her hand. Once Trish is gone, if Alia is still acting strange, maybe we can get her some help. This will at least give your mother some peace of mind until then. She's worried about losing her again, Charlie. She's frantic about that. We can't let that happen."

"No, we can't. And what do I do if she rips it up in my face ?"

"She won't. I'm telling you this woman has an angle. It may or may not have anything to do with the way Alia is acting, but at least with her gone, we will know one less thing that it is."

That afternoon Charlie hid in a location nearby while Alia had her lunch with Trish. He could see them with his binoculars from his vantage point. Nothing seemed out of the ordinary other than the hug Alia gave the woman when she had arrived. Trish had already been there, with an order of drinks on the table.

He watched as the two of them mostly talked. At no time did Charlie notice Alia go into any vague state, but the scene before him still set him on edge. He saw that Alia didn't eat either. She just kept drinking her ice tea a little at a time and laughing at whatever Trish said. At one point, it did look like they were planning something they didn't want anyone else around them to hear. The two leaned in on each other and bowed their heads together. But that was it. He had really been hoping to see something that would explain why Alia was acting so strange.

So he wouldn't miss Trish walking back to her car Charlie left before Alia did, hoping he wouldn't miss anything. In the alley, he waited for Trish, who was startled when she came around the corner and saw him. Again, a look came over her, only this time it was her face. She seemed to sneer for a second seeing him, then broke out into a grin.

"Well, if it isn't my future son-in-law. Alia and I were just talking about you. She said something about us catching dinner some time. That would be so ...."

"Cut the shit Trish." he harshly interrupted her. "Your act may be working on your daughter, but the rest of us are not so easily convinced."

"I don't know what you mean, Charlie," Trish said.

"You know damn well what I'm talking about. And it's going to stop. You're not to see her anymore. You're not to even come to Union county anymore." Charlie thrust the check at her. "Here. My father will probably have to forget about retirement, but this should be more than enough to set you up somewhere far away from here."

Trish looked at the check, shook her head, then handed it back to him. "I don't want this. You can't put a price on my relationship with my child Charlie."

"Sure we can. We know damn well this is all some kind of con of yours. Even Alia knows that." Looking her in the eyes, Charlie saw that flash again. Still, the smile on her face never wavered.

"Oh really. Well, you just may not know your future wife as well as you think you do. If she didn't trust me, then why did she invite me to the wedding?"

"You're lying. We don't even have a firm date set yet."

"Just what she said today. But she still wants me to be there whenever it is. You know I'm still hoping the two of us can work out our problems, for Alia's sake. I would be well within my right to go to her with that check right now. But that would hurt her too much, and I'm not going to do that to her. Now, if the three of you can't get over all of this mess of the past and see that I have changed and only want to be a part of my daughter's life, then you're the ones that are going to hurt her, not me. Don't mess up the good thing you have with her just to spite me, Charlie." Trish walked past him back down the alley.

"We're on to you, Trish. We know you're doing something to her. We don't know what it is, but you're doing something at those lunches."

Trish stopped and turned back around. She was no longer smiling, but the look on her face was not the Trish he knew of before. Trish looked concerned and even upset, but the hostility he came to expect from her just wasn't there. "For heaven's sake, Charlie, listen to yourself. You sound paranoid. You know what, fine, if that's what's bothering you, then join us next week. Hell, have your mother come too if it makes her feel any better. If there is something wrong with my daughter, I'm not the cause of it." Trish walked away for good, this time shaking her head as she went.

I just might take you up on that.

Back at the station, Charlie threw the now crumbled-up check onto his father's desk. "Well, at least now you can retire, I guess." He told Harper about everything, including watching her at lunch. "Maybe we're wrong about all of this.

Maybe she doesn't directly have anything to do with the way Alia is acting."

Harper sighed heavily. "You know, if that's the case, then she could be in bigger trouble than we thought. I still think getting rid of Trish would help, but we may just be covering up the symptoms of a bigger issue by doing so."

"Yeah, I can tell you have been talking to mom." Ellen had studied to be a therapist and special needs educator in college. The psychological side of her studies had fascinated her. Had it not been for having Charlie, she may have pursued a psychology degree.

"Yes, well, she's apprehensive, Charlie. And I am too. You know this goes beyond those big moments she's been having. I don't even want to know what broom closet she was talking about if that was a real thing. It's her attitude and the things she's been saying. It's not like her, like the old her maybe but not the girl we have known for the past few years."

"I know. And I know that if the cat scan and blood work are fine, then that means it could be psychological. Which means even if Trish did leave her alone, we have a battle on our hands. I'm taking Trish up on the lunch thing. Maybe if I'm right there and see how they interact, I can better understand where Alia's head is."

"You do that. Meanwhile, let's just act like everything is normal until it's not. Wednesday is family dinner night if she'll still come, of course."

"She will, Dad. She's just as much upset by all this as we are." Charlie spent the rest of the day with her as they cruised around handing out speeding tickets, dealing with a minor accident, and playing basketball in the park with a group of kids. Through it all, Alia seemed like her own self.

Wednesday night's family dinner was full of laughter and talked like the week before never happened. Their favorite night of the week was back as their favorite once again. It was going so well that Charlie doubted again that Trish was the cause after all. He still wasn't buying her act, though. They made love that night, and later, he held her all night, her sleep restful and calm.

The next day at work, when Alia volunteered to run the speed trap out on the highway, he and Harper couldn't see a reason to say no. All the other guys loved her for it since the job was more tedious than even handing out parking fines.

Alia settled in behind the usual billboard, set up her radar, and kicked back. Before her alarm went off at two, she gave out three tickets and a warning to a young kid she felt like giving a break.

On the other side of the woods line from where she was watching traffic was a little-known wayside park. It wasn't anything special, just a small plot in the woods with picnic tables and cast iron grills.

When her alarm went off at two, Alia turned off her radar, drove half a mile down the road, and turned back on the minor road leading to the park. If anyone was watching her on the GPS back at the station, it would look like she was pretty much still in the same spot.

When she arrived, Trish was already there at one of the picnic areas. In the shade of a sizable drivable camper, she had a couple of lounge chairs set up with a cooler in between the two full of ice and cold teas. Trish sat back in one of the lounges and gave Alia a drink opening the bottle up for her.

"Take a load off, kid. It's hot today. I thought we would just relax here in the shade. You sure no one is going to know you're here?"

"Not with the patrol car parked so far over there," she said, pointing at the car. "Just have to listen in for the radio." Alia plunked down on the lounge letting out a big breath of air. "This was a good idea. Nice to get a break away from prying eyes."

"My thoughts exactly. How's the tea? I know it's nowhere near as good as the stuff they serve at the cafe."

"No, but it's not bad. You found my favorite flavor too."

"I know the distributor. He made some raspberry special just for me."

Alia laid back, and for the next hour, she and her mother talked about random stuff and life in general. When they were done, Alia returned to her car and her spot on the highway. She gave out a few more tickets then returned to the station to clock out for the day. She was doing just that in the locker room when one of the other officers popped their head in and told her Sheriff Harper wanted to see her.

In her street clothes, Alia went in and shut the door when he indicated her to. Harper pointed to a chair, and she sat down, noticing right away that he wasn't in a good mood.

"I just got off the phone with a woman I had to talk down from filing a complaint about you after an incident with her today," Harper said, looking at her with his brow creased. "She said you gave her a speeding ticket."

"I gave a few people a speeding ticket today. Pretty sure that's how the speed traps are supposed to work," Alia said with a grin.

There was something about that grin Harper didn't like. She looked smug. "You might want to cut out the smart ass routine for today. In case you haven't noticed, I'm not in the mood."

"Yes, sir, sorry," she said, feeling a slight flush.

"This particular ticket was to a woman driving a red Tesla. In fact, to say she was driving may be a stretch since it was on autopilot."

"That would explain why it took her some time to pull over, I guess."

"It doesn't explain why you felt the need to berate her for going only four miles over the limit."

Alia sat up the smug look back. "Harper, she was speeding. Then she liked to take forever to pull over when I gave pursuit. Check my dashcam. She started in on me as soon as I got up to her window."

"She was only going four miles over Alia. Since when do we give tickets out to anyone going less than six over on the highway?"

Alia cocked her head, "I'm sorry, perhaps I misunderstood the term speed limit. As in, the speed limit was only fifty-five in that zone." she retorted. "So some entitled white Karen had a bitch fit because she got caught. It's not like she can't afford it."

"First of all, you need to calm your tone down. Second, I don't care if she's a millionaire, we don't give out tickets like that, and you know it. And apparently, you called her this Karen name, which she took offense to for some reason."

At that, Alia laughed.

Looking at her, Harper wondered who this kid was. They had a row or two over the years since she started to work for him, but in the end, she had been in the right and only standing up for herself. Now she wasn't, and this attitude wasn't like her. "Oh, so you think it's funny?"

"That some entitled white chick is bent out of shape over a meme? Uh yeah."

"Okay, what the hell is up with you today? This is completely out of character for you, Alia. You were trained better than this."

Alia shook her head. "Oh, here we go again with this bullshit. I do my job, and suddenly I'm acting out again because I've been seeing my mother, is that it? Only I didn't see her today, did I? Because it's not Monday. I saw her then and didn't have an issue all week. Maybe I'm just fed up with these entitled rich shits thinking they can get away with crap all the time." Alia got up from the chair. "You know what, I don't have to put up with this. I'm clocked out for the day. I'm on my time now. If you want to chew me out some more over doing my damn job, then you're going to have to wait till Friday morning."

Harper jumped up out of his chair as she rounded her own and headed for the door. "Deputy Miller, get your ass back in that chair. Don't you dare walk out that door." But too late, she walked out and slammed it behind her.

The officers at the desks out in the common area looked over at her with shock and surprise.

"Fuck off," she said to them and stormed down the hall and out the back door.

Still fuming from her confrontation with Harper, Alia was halfway home walking down the sidewalk in town when Charlie pulled up in his patrol car.

"Come on, Alia, get in the car."

"No, thank you, I feel like walking," she said with arms crossed and a scowl on her face. The evening was hot and muggy, storm clouds off to the west promised a wet relief, but even those clouds were too far away to stop the relentless sun. Sweat was pouring off of her, her shirt clinging to her back. No one would choose to walk on a day like today.

"Get in the damn car Alia," he said on the verge of losing patience. Without Alia to bark at, Harper had taken his anger out of Charlie, who arrived just moments after Alia had stormed out.

"Why so you can shit on me for doing my job too?" she asked, still very much angry.

Trying to remain calm, Charlie tried again. "No, so I can take you home, and we can both get out of this heat. It's been a miserable day. Let's go home and cool off. Then we can talk if you want to."

"And If I don't want to." she stopped with her arms still crossed, her eyes like angry storm clouds.

"Then I guess we won't. Just get in the car Alia."

Shaking her head, Alia did as he said but sat with her arms crossed, not looking at or speaking to him the whole way home. At the apartment, he let her go take a shower first, hoping her mood would be better when she came out. It wasn't. Instead, she grabbed a book, sat in the little window nook he had made for her, and watched as the storm clouds came closer. She didn't even bother to open the book, which let him know she was still pissed off without even having to feel it from her.

Watching her from the bedroom chair where he took off his uniform, not having time to do so at work, Charlie felt her anger. He wanted to approach her to ask her what was wrong, but the feeling coming from her was definitely one that said she wanted to be left alone. Usually, she wanted him to comfort her when she was mad or upset, but not today. Before he went in to shower, Charlie asked her if she was mad at him.

"No, Charlie. I'm mad at myself. And that stupid Karen acting bitch, and Harper. I'm just mad."

"Okay," he said and dared to give her a kiss on her head, at which she flinched like he had tried to hit her instead. His heart cracked a bit at her reaction, and he stood there looking at her at a loss of what to do or say.

Looking out the window, Alia told him he better get his shower before the storm arrived. No anger in what she said, just a statement. Still, he could feel her pain, knowing she had hurt him as well.

After his shower, while the storm raged outside, Charlie cooked some dinner while she sat in the nook looking off at the storm. As it raged on, her anger subsided. Storms always had a way of calming her. They usually would watch them together, feeding off its energy then making love while the thunder lingered in the mountains.

Tonight though, he was happy just to get her to eat with him in their little kitchen. There wasn't any of the usual flirtatious laughter and talking that was typical for their meals. He did, however, get a smile or two out of her.

Still, when they went to bed that night, Alia faced away from him on the farthest side of her bed she could get without falling off. She didn't know why, but she didn't want his comfort and reassurance. "Harper is going to have my ass in the morning, isn't he," she asked as Charlie climbed into bed.

He looked at his phone, which his father had been blowing up most of the evening with text after text. "Yeah, I'm afraid so. I'm sorry."

Alia just shook her head. "All my own fault."

When Charlie tried to reach out and put his hand on her shoulder, she flinched again, and he pulled back as though his very touch had hurt her. He knew then she was crying. Worse, she hid it from him, which she hadn't done for a very long time. Wanting to comfort her but not daring to, Charlie lay in the darkness of the room looking at her back, feeling her shudder. The gulf between them seemed miles long though it was less than a foot.

Sometime in the night, Charlie was awoken by Alia trying to wiggle into his arms. He pulled her into him, taking note that she still looked asleep but figuring something in her must-have finally needed to seek out his comfort. For this, he was glad. He needed to have her in his arms as much as she needed to be in them. Because to be honest with himself, Charlie felt her slowly slipping away.

The next day, Alia, before Harper in uniform, took her chewing out with her head held high. She didn't even complain when he saddled her with desk duty the whole day or when he added an extra shift Sunday evening to her punishment. Alia spent the rest of the day withdrawn, even angry at her fellow officers. Of course, it didn't help that they snickered behind her back like they would anyone that got reamed by the boss. Still, it agitated her like it never had before, putting her into a funk the rest of the day.

That evening was another quiet one at home. Charlie was really missing her laughter and smile. Again when they went to bed, the gulf was between them, but she found her way into his arms in the early morning hours before dawn, and he thought that at least that was something.

The following day Charlie woke up with a great idea. Slipping out of bed so Alia could sleep in, he took her cell into the other room and out on their little patio. It was still a bit early for a Saturday, but he called anyway to get a hold of people before they made plans for the day. His first call was to Crystal.

Chrystal wasn't even awake yet, but when she heard the call was Charlie and not Alia, she sat up expecting the worst. She had been aware of Alia's problems since Trish returned. Charlie first filled her in at the latest. He then proposed his idea for the day, and she agreed it was a great one. They usually would do this kind of thing at the Harper's home, but he wanted this to be a friend-only event, so they would use the little picnic area by the pool in their complex. Besides, the last thing he felt Alia needed was to spend the day with Harper glaring at her.

"I just really think a little get-together with her friends is what she needs to get her out of this funk, even if just for a little while."

"I think we are dealing with more than just a funk Charlie. It's almost like a spell has been put on her. Oh, I know I'll bring my crystals and stuff, do a little cleansing of her aura. I can make a special vial for her to carry around too. I should have thought of that earlier."

Charlie had to chuckle a little. "Well, you do that. She loves that kind of stuff from you. I'm going to make more calls and see who else I can get to come."

"Let me do that, you worry about the food and drink thing, and I'll call you in a bit and let you know how many to expect."

"That works for me. And I'll remember to get you some of those plant burgers you love so much."

"See, Charlie, I always knew you were a smart guy. I'll call you in a bit."

Feeling in a great mood now, Charlie went to the kitchen and started making a list of things they would need from the store. Done with that, he made a nice breakfast of eggs, bacon, and fruit, put it on a tray, and took it into her. Alia was still asleep (something else he marked as unusual. Alia was an early riser and not prone to sleep in much), so he got back into bed and coaxed her awake with kisses hoping she was receptive to it.

Alia's eyes opened to see Charlie kissing her fingers and hand. He looked up at her, his green eyes shining, and her heart swelled. Just knowing he still loved her despite all the mess of the past few days thrilled her. "Someone is in a good mood this morning."

"Yes, I am. How are you feeling?"

"Pretty good, better. Hungry." she smiled, knowing he had cooked for her.

While she ate, Charlie told her about his idea of having some of her friends over for the day and having a cookout by the pool.

She agreed it was a great idea and a much-needed break from what they had been going through. Not to mention a distraction from the fact that she had to work in the morning.

Since she actually mentioned it, Charlie thought it safe to ask her about it. "What do you think is going on? I mean, is there something bothering you? Have I done something wrong?"

Putting aside the food tray Alia had Charlie sit next to her. With a heavy sigh, she took one of his hands in hers. "Charlie, no matter what I say or do later, I need you to believe what I'm saying right now." Alia looked him in his eyes and saw nothing but love. "This isn't you, Charlie. You haven't done anything wrong. Even if I act like you have, you haven't."

"Alia, you're not making any sense."

"I know. I don't feel like myself all the time, Charlie. I'm angry for no reason. I'm hurt and sad. Hell, I'm even over the top happy sometimes. I see these things, I hear what I'm saying, and I'm appalled, yet I can't stop. The anger just takes over. I know you have been trying to comfort me, but sometimes just your touch sets me off." She lowered her eyes as tears formed in them. "I don't know what is going on, but I know that I love you. Please don't give up on me. I'll work my way through this, I promise."

Taking her into his arms, Charlie kissed her lips, jaw, and neck. "I won't ever give up on you, sweet girl. We will work this out together no matter what is going on."

Smiling, Alia kissed him then whispered in his ear. "I need you, Charlie...I need you right now before it starts again." In the back of her mind, she could feel an itching, burning feeling start to grow. Alia was convinced that if he didn't make love to her right, then the anger would come back and consume her. Having slipped out of her pajama shorts while Charlie kissed her, Alia reached out for him bringing him into her.

Charlie worried only for a moment about not having any protection, but her desire was so strong it engulfed him. His only concern was that this was all her and needed only to look into her eyes to know it was. The two of them spent the rest of the morning making love, with Alia holding on to him like she was afraid she would drift away from him if she didn't.

The get-together was set for late that afternoon and evening when it would be a bit cooler. Along with Crystal came Alia's friends Raya, Lara, and Carina. Ethan was the only one that had to back out, and George came because he hadn't seen Charlie in a while.

While the guys cooked the food (Charlie cooked, George watched and drank beer), the girls went for a swim. Charlie watched as Alia laughed and joked with her friends, confident that this was what she really needed. The whole evening everyone had a great time. After dark, George and Crystal were the only ones left. They helped clean up then Crystal told Alia that it was time for her cleansing.

Alia wasn't a huge believer in all the crystal stuff, but she did think the idea was fun and tried to keep an open mind. And after the cleansing, Alia had to admit she did feel better, even though she believed that it was only a placebo effect.

When Crystal and George were gone, and Charlie was taking a shower, Alia slipped in there with him feeling like she hadn't seen his body in ages despite having just made love that morning. After a day, she knew was all about her, she took great pleasure in making that night all about him. When they slept, there was no gulf between them. Which made it all the stranger when Charlie woke up in the morning and Alia was gone.

Chapter 27
From bad to Worse

Charlie didn't panic at first when he woke and found Alia wasn't in bed. He checked all the usual spots around their small apartment, which didn't take long. Then he checked the closet, and when he didn't find her in there, he started to worry. Out in the living room, Charlie noticed her key was missing from the bowl by the door. He looked out over their balcony and saw that her jeep was gone. Still not too alarmed as it wasn't unusual for her to run out to the stores early if they ran out of something. When he called her, the phone rang from inside the apartment. That's when Charlie really started to worry.

In the bedroom, he found her phone on the floor under the bed, not unusual. Her leaving without it was highly unusual. Rechecking the closet, he saw that the day bag she used when not working was still hung up on the back of the door. In her nightstand drawer was her wallet. Now he was panicking.

Charlie searched the apartment again, feeling like a mad man, but he knew she wasn't there. Stopping to take a few deep breaths, he tried to reach out to her. The thing was, even after all these years, he wasn't sure how this whole connection thing worked. It just did. When they were kids, and she came to town to see her father, he just knew. It came to him as a casual thought, oh, by the way, Alia's at her dad's.

Even when he would find her because she was in trouble, it wasn't something that he did; he just seemed to be drawn in the right direction. So all he managed to do by standing in only his boxers in the middle of their living room was feel foolish. What broke his heart was that he couldn't feel her at all. He always felt her ever since that first night they had made love. The only time he didn't was when she was out of the county in the Academy. Even when she was off in the woods looking for the kids, he at least felt cold like she had been. Now nothing.

Throwing on a pair of jeans and a t-shirt, Charlie called his Father while putting on his socks.

"Dad Alia is missing."

"What do you mean missing?" Harper was barely awake and wasn't sure he even heard Charlie right.

"She's gone dad, she took her jeep, but her cell and wallet are still here in the apartment. I searched everywhere, and she's not here."

Harper sat up in bed, and so did Ellen beside him. "Now, just hold on, son. I know you're starting to panic, but maybe she's just out on a run or something. Have you checked the complex yet?"

Having a bad feeling, Ellen sprang out of bed and dressed.

"No, Dad, you don't understand, she's gone. I don't feel her at all. Nothing. What if, shit, what if something happened? What if she's hurt, if we can't find her?" *What if it's too late to find her?* Was what he was trying not to say.

"Charlie, you need to calm down." Harper was now out of bed, trying with one hand to put on the clothes Ellen had thrown at him. "Did anything happen yesterday, anything that may have made her mad?"

"No, dad, we had a great time." Charlie felt himself on the verge of sheer panic and knew he had to get himself under control. After taking a few deep breaths, he told his father what they had done the day before. "She was happy, dad. Happier than I have seen her for a few days."

"Then we shouldn't panic just yet. Maybe she went out for a drive. I don't know what to tell you, son, but look around the complex first. Make sure she didn't move her jeep. Meanwhile, I'll call the station and put a BOLO out for the jeep. But Charlie, more importantly, you need to calm down."

"I can't fucking calm down." he practically yelled. "Not after how she's been acting lately."

On the other end, even Ellen heard her son. "He's right, Harper. I have a bad feeling about this." She also got on her phone and called her contacts at the hospital.

"Charlie, listen to me. Go look outside, make double sure the jeep is gone, check to see if she's at the pool or anywhere else. We are coming over, don't go anywhere until we get there. Promise me you won't drive right now, Charlie."

"Just hurry. If I feel like I can get a bead on her, I'm leaving to follow it." He ended the call and raced out of the apartment, checking the pool, the entire complex, and even the playground.

At the Harper's, Ellen got off the phone and said she hadn't shown up at the hospital, so there was always that at least.

Harper called in the BOLO to the station, informing them that it was Deputy Miller's Jeep they were looking for and to not approach her if they found her. Leaving the house, they took his patrol car to listen in on the radio. They arrived to find Charlie sitting on the stairs to their building, his hair a mess, his eyes red, and his hands shaking.

Ellen was the first to get to him, taking him into her arms as much as possible with her petite frame.

"I can't feel her mom. Why can't I feel her?" he cried in her arms like he was a little boy again. "What if she's hurt? What if it's bad, and we never find her?"

"We'll find her, Charlie, don't you worry," Ellen said.

But hours later, as morning turned to noon and they had driven all over town several times. Still, they had no idea where she was, just many ideas where she wasn't. They all had taken turns making phone calls asking if anyone saw her or heard from her, and no one had.

Charlie couldn't help but see the similarities to when Billy disappeared. Like he was just zapped out of existence, no trace, no witnesses. The only difference was that Alia had her jeep, which would be pretty hard to hide. Unfortunately, it also made it where she, or whoever drove it, could get her very far away.

At noon they took a break and went to the station. Officially they couldn't start a missing person's case on an adult until they were missing for twenty-four hours. Officially Harper didn't give a damn. He called in extra officers and had them all meet him at the station. Once they were all there and he and Charlie had put on spare uniforms, Harper filled them in on what was going on.

"Normally protocol for missing persons, of course, is to wait longer. But Deputy Miller is one of ours. She's family. She may be hurt somewhere or even held against her will. If you do see her, be very cautious in approaching her. I will not say this more than once. She is a victim here, not a suspect. She is to be brought in unharmed. If you can't get her to come in or if she is acting out of character, you are to call Sergeant Harper or me and wait for us. Do I make myself perfectly clear?"

They all agreed then left to continue the search. Harper made some calls to the departments in the surrounding counties and the substations in their own county. Confident everyone knew the situation, he and Charlie took Ellen back home and went back on the search.

Hours later, around dinner, Ellen called Harper on his cell. "She's here. Tell Charlie she's here. Come home quick, Harper. You have to see her." Harper practically threw the phone on the car's seat and made an illegal u-turn to head back towards the house.

"She's at the house," he told Charlie.

"What? How is she? Where has she been?" Charlie wanted to be happy, but the look on his father's face concerned him. "What's wrong with her?"

"I don't know. Your mother just said to get there to see her."

A few minutes later, they pulled up the drive. In the house, they didn't bother to lock up their guns they just ran in. Harper was the first to see them on the back porch, but Charlie beat him there.

Alia was sitting on a chair on the back porch, staring off into space, smiling and humming softly to herself. She wore jeans and one of Charlie's t-shirts that she swam in, it was so large. She and the clothes were covered in mud, leaves, dirt, and blood. Not a lot of blood but enough to make the macabre scene before them even worse.

Charlie fell on his knees before her, looking all over for the source of the blood. Here and there, she had cuts and nicks, no significant damage he could see other than a knot of swollen flesh over one eye. Alia just sat there the whole time, not looking at anything and humming. Charlie cupped her face in his hands, forcing her to look at him.

Meanwhile, Harper, not taking his eyes off her, asked Ellen where she had come from.

"From down at the lake. Like she used to when she would come over here. I was sitting out here thinking about whether I should bother with cooking dinner when I looked up, and she was slowly walking up the hill. I got her to sit down, but she's been like that the whole time, just smiling and humming. I tried talking to her, but she wouldn't respond."

And now Charlie was trying as well. Her face still cupped in his large, long-fingered hands, he tried to force her eyes on him. "Alia, hey sweet girl, look at me, come back to me."

With a blink of her eyes, Alia's pupils focused. She looked at him and smiled. "Hi Charlie," she said.

"Hi there, sweet girl." he smiled as the tears fell. He wiped at the mud and blood on her face but only seemed to make it worse. "Where have you been?"

Alia looked around, still smiling, but it was fading a bit. "How'd I get here, Charlie?" She looked down at her mess of clothes and frowned. "Why am I such a mess?"

"That's what we'd like to know," said Harper, coming to sit down on a stool to the side of her. Over his shoulder, he told Ellen to call an ambulance. He wanted to have her checked out right away. As she did, Harper turned his attention back to the mess of a girl in front of him.

Alia had her hand on Charlie's face telling him not to cry, she was fine. Very hungry and tired but okay.

Charlie fussed over every little mark and cut he found on her. When his mother was done on the phone, he asked her to get a wet rag so they could clean her up and see how bad she was hurt.

"I'm fine, Charlie." Alia insisted, but they both noticed she seemed to still be in an almost dreamlike state.

"You're not fine, Alia. You've been gone all day. Where have you been?" asked Harper.

Alia looked over at him and smiled. "I have no idea," she said.

To Harper, she looked like she was stoned. "Did you take something, Alia? Maybe before you left the apartment this morning."

"Uhm, I don't think so," she said in a very sing-songy kind of way.

"We don't have anything stronger than ibuprofen at the apartment," said Charlie, his relief of seeing her alive turning into worry again. "She would have had to take the whole bottle and still wouldn't be like this. Alia, did someone give you something to eat or drink? Did you see anyone?"

"I see you, Charlie," she said with a giggle. "My sweet Charlie boy. I'm kinda tired. Can I go lay down?"

"No, not just yet. We need to have someone come take a look at you." Said Harper.

Ellen returned with a few damp rags, and after Harper took a few photos with his phone, she helped Charlie clean Alia up. They got the mud and dirt off her arms and face before the paramedics arrived. All over her, under the mud, they found cuts and scrapes. Some looked like they were from thorns, the scrapes they weren't sure about. She had either fallen or brushed up against something hard. That could have been anything out in the woods.

The paramedics came around back, and Charlie let them work on her while still staying at her side. They checked out her blood pressure, pulse, heart, and lungs, declaring them all fine. However, they were concerned with the large knot above her eye and her general state of behavior.

"I think she may have a concussion. I'd like to run her in, let the docs get a good look at her." Said Tony, the paramedic.

At that, she pouted and reached out for Charlie. "No hospital, Charlie, I just want to eat and go to bed."

"I tell you what. You go to the hospital, and I'll have mom bring over some of her key lime pie you like so much."

Alia smiled and let them put her on a stretcher. Before Charlie joined her in the back, his father pulled him aside.

"Do what you can to not leave her side until we get there. I want them to run a tox screen and a full workup. I'm going to see if we can track down her jeep. I may know where it's at."

When Harper sent an officer to Harkening Hill park around the corner from the house, her jeep was still there with the keys in it. Harper met the officer over at the park and, using gloves, looked over the jeep for signs of drugs or other people. Not finding anything but a mess of mud and leaves, he told the officer to rope the area off until the forensics people from the city could come have it towed and checked.

Harper called off the BOLO on Alia and her jeep, sending the extra officers home. However, when he and Ellen arrived at the hospital, a few of them were there and wanted to see how she was doing. They offered to donate blood or anything else they could do to help. Harper wasn't just talking when he said she was family. However, he told them to go home, and he would fill everyone in, in the morning.

By the time they got there, Alia had been admitted into the hospital for the night. They had collected blood and urine for the tox screen and even ran her through the cat scan again. When they came in, Alia seemed more lucid and begged Ellen to help her take a shower to get all the mud off. While they were busy doing that, the boys talked.

Harper told Charlie about finding the jeep at the park, and that was having forensics come to haul it in.

"So we are treating this as a crime now?" asked Charlie

"Until proven otherwise, I am. I don't care how she has been acting. I don't think Alia did this to herself. I mean, it's possible, I guess, but I'm not convinced."

"Neither am I. I tried getting her to tell me where she was, but she still doesn't know. Whatever she's on, it seems to be wearing off, though."

With Alia done with her shower, they got her back in the bed and fed her the promised key lime pie. She also got a food tray for dinner but turned her nose up at most of it. After eating Ellen's cooking, nothing else quite matched up.

Harper wanted to talk to her, and for what seemed like the hundredth time, she told him that she felt fine. No, she didn't know where she was. No, she didn't remember leaving the apartment, and no, she didn't take anything. He tried questioning her some more, but she was falling asleep.

"Give her a break and let her sleep, Harper." Said Ellen. Results of the blood work and cat scan came back negative again. They would have to wait till the next day to get the tox results, so Ellen and Harper went home.

Charlie stayed behind, staying awake as long as he could until he drifted to sleep in a chair next to her. He woke hours later to Alia screaming hysterically and pulling the IV she had for hydration out of her arm.

Charlie grabbed her arms, trying to stop her, but she slapped at him.

"No, No, he poisoned me, stay away from me, don't hurt me!" she screamed. Alia scratched at the port in her arm where the IV had been in, digging into it and cutting it open. "Get it out of me, get it out of me." When she looked up for a second and saw Charlie, she screamed for him to help her.

Charlie went back to her to try and help when the door burst open, and a couple of nurses ran in.

Alia became more hysterical, screaming for them to get away. Before Charlie could stop her, she jumped out of bed and started to grab and throw everything within reach at the nurses screaming at them the whole time. Charlie tried to stop her, but she was freaky fast and ran into a corner of the room, grabbing and throwing things as she went. The nurses left, and he had her backed into a corner. Alia was no longer screaming, but her eyes were wild, and she was breathing like she had been running.

"Alia, please tell me what's wrong, what happened."

"They poisoned me," she said.

"Who did Alia, who poisoned you?"

"It was a nurse. A male nurse came in, and he put something in the IV." As if she had just remembered again, she started to dig at the hole in her arm that was now bleeding pretty bad.

Lunging forward, Charlie grabbed her arms and was able to get her to stop, but the blood was flowing, getting all over her, him, and the floor. "Alia, stop, just stop, I'll help you, but you've got to stop this."

Alia looked down as if she was unaware of what she had been doing and saw the blood. "Oh Charlie, help me, please help me. I can feel it. I can feel something inside of me."

Letting her go long enough to look in the drawers in the room, he found some gauze and started what he knew was a shitty job of wrapping up her arm, but his hands shook so bad it was the best he could do.

Before he was done, one of the nurses and a few male nurses burst back into the room. The nurse had a needle, and Charlie knew what they wanted to do.

Alia saw them too and let out a piercing scream. Pulling away from him, she curled up the best she could into a ball on the floor, crying and screaming uncontrollably.

Charlie put his back to her and spread out his long arms protectively. "Back off, just back the fuck off. No one is touching her but me."

"Be reasonable, Sergeant. She needs to be sedated. She's hysterical and bleeding all over the place." said the nurse with the needle. The three of them moved forward, and Alia must have sensed it somehow because she let out another piercing screech.

"No, no, no no, just stop, stop! Can't you see she's terrified? She said someone came in and put something in her IV. A male nurse. So until I know what the hell is going on, these two need to get the fuck out of here." When they wouldn't move, Charlie took out his taser. "I mean it, get the fuck out of here."

"You can only tase one of us. That leaves one to restrain her." said the bigger of the two.

"No, that leaves one to get his ass kicked by me and both your asses locked up for assaulting an officer. Now, last time, back the fuck off. She will get the sedative but not until the two of you leave."

The door opened again. This time, three men from security pushed their way in.

"I'm Sergeant Harper," said Charlie. "This Deputy has been assaulted. I order you to take these two men out of this room and hold them in custody till I can question them."

Seeing the young women on the ground still curled up in a ball and bleeding, they didn't hesitate. Despite the objections of the male nurses, they were removed from the room.

"Okay," Charlie talked to the last nurse. "Now, very slowly give me the needle, and I will give it to her."

"Sir, I can't let you...."

"The hell you can't. You can see she's still bleeding. You're not going to be able to get near her with that while she's like this. All you're going to do is get hurt. Now give me the damn needle."

Shaking her head, the nurse handed Charlie the needle.

"Where?" he demanded.

"In her buttocks, or as close as you can get, the whole thing too."

Turning back to Alia, Charlie whispered in her ear, trying to soothe her. He could have just jammed it in since she was exposed in her position curled up like that, but he didn't want to do it without her knowing. Telling her it would be okay, he asked if he could do it, and she nodded thankfully, still trusting him. Carefully Charlie inserted the needle into her exposed ass cheek and pushed the plunger all the way in. Taking it back out, he tossed it aside and pulled her into his lap. Slowly her tense muscles relaxed. Soon after, she was asleep.

"Okay, please stop the bleeding," he begged the nurse.

She got fresh supplies and tentatively took Alia's arm with no resistance. Alia had dug a rather large hole into the crook of her arm, and even with the bandage Charlie had put on, it was bleeding freely. As she bandaged up the arm the best she could, Charlie apologized repeatedly. He explained she said she had been attacked as an excuse for her hysteria. In his arms, she slept, all the fury run out of her.

"I'll check the roster, but we don't have any male nurses on this floor tonight. I had to call those two in from other areas."

"Is there another room we can have? My father is going to want this room to stay the way it is until we can investigate what happened tonight" *If anything did actually happen,*

"Sure, we can move her right next door."

"I want security at that door until we can get one of our own here. And no one, I mean no one, comes into this room. Anyone who comes in will be arrested for obstructing an investigation."

"Understood, Sergeant. Can you lift her? We should really get her in a bed. She's going to need blood and a few stitches."

Being mindful of the blood on the floor, Charlie got up with Alia in his arms. Cradling her, he walked to the room next door and placed her on a clean bed. He watched while the nurse and a few others tended to her. They put an IV for blood into her other arm and one for fluids into her hand. When they strapped her arms down, he started to protest, but they told him it was for her own protection. The other arm they cleaned up some more, put in a few stitches, and tied a board to it to keep her from moving it too much.

When they were done, and she was still sleeping, Charlie walked out to the hall. As requested, one of the security guards was at the door. "I've got to call this in," he said to the guard. "No one is to go into either room till I get back. I want those two male nurses held till the Sheriff gets here. I've got to get some fresh air."

The guard pointed to a door that led out onto a deck once used for smokers when hospitals allowed such things. Now patients use it to get some sun and staff for lunch or seeking a smoke themselves.

Charlie went out into the warm night, still hours till dawn, leaned on the railing with both his hands and stood there shaking uncontrollably for a few minutes. He was exhausted both physically and mentally, and his uniform was covered in blood. Charlie would have to get his father to bring him a change of clothes. He needed to call Harper but still felt his hands shaking too much. What he really wanted was to take Alia away from here. Somewhere far away, just the two of them where no one knew who they were and whoever was doing this to her couldn't find them.

What really scared him was that no one was doing anything. That after years of the kind of abuse she suffered, her mind had just had enough. She always played off what happened to her like it was nothing compared to the horrors other kids suffered. But the mind doesn't care if someone else gets worse. It only cares what happens to it. Some minds are more fragile than others. Charlie always thought of Alia as brave and strong, but maybe she wasn't as strong as he thought she was. After a few deep breaths, Charlie called his father.

Chapter 28
Shit to Deal With

"No one goes into the room or out." Said Harper the next morning. They checked all the cameras in the hall, and at no time did anyone enter the room until she became hysterical. The two male nurses were questioned, had people verify their whereabouts, and let go. "It had to have been a nightmare she had, Charlie. We still don't know what happened to her while she was gone yesterday. It's possible she remembered enough, and it scared her."

"So now what?"

"We wait. Still waiting on the tox screen, waiting on forensics. We can't do much until we know more. In the meantime, I think it would be good if the two of you got away for a few days. Take her up to the cabin. She loves it up there. Go do some fishing, sleep all day, hell, I don't care. Just get her out of town for a while. Both of you have personal days and vacation time saved up. Use some of it."

"We have something we need to do first, you and I. We need to grab some lunch today at the cafe."

"Good idea. Your mother can stay here with Alia. But we need to do this unofficially, no uniforms, no guns. I don't want her to come back later and accuse the department of intimidating her. We wait till she shows up, tell her Alia won't make it, and it's over. We offer to buy her lunch, and we leave."

But if only it went that smoothly.

Harper and Charlie parked half a block away in Harper's truck, where they could see the cafe. When Trish arrived, they crossed the road and walked up. The waiter had just walked away when they arrived.

Trish looked surprised to see them and even more surprised when they sat down across from her. Her eyes went right to Charlie. "Charlie, I'm sorry, but you look terrible. What happened? Where's Alia?"

"She's not coming." Said Harper trying to take her attention off his son. He could feel Charlie tense up before they even sat down. He was looking at Trish like he wanted nothing more than to beat the hell out of her. "She's in the hospital."

Trish looked alarmed. "Why, what happened? What room is she in? I want to go see her."

Charlie shook his head. "Absolutely not, no. Not going to happen."

"She's my daughter Charlie. I have every right to go see her."

"You gave up that right when you threw a fucking ashtray at her face." he seethed. "Or do you conveniently not remember doing that?"

"Charlie, son, stop. This is not how we said we were going to do this."

Charlie shook his head but kept his mouth shut.

"Not going to do what? What is this all about, Harper? Got another check in your pocket to try and bribe me to go away? Well, it's not going to work. Seems to me things are not going as great as Alia makes it out to be. She's been acting odd ever since I came back. I can't help but wonder if she's not crying out for help because something is wrong in her life. Now you tell me she's in the hospital and I can't even see her. What happened, Charlie? Did the two of you get into a fight or something? Did you hurt her? If you need help, I can...."

"You fucking bitch how fucking dare you.." Charlie said, getting up out of his chair.

Harper got up as well and grabbed Charlie by the back of his collar. "Excuse us a minute," he said to Trish, then hauled Charlie, still cursing Trish, halfway down the sidewalk. When he let go, Charlie jerked his shoulders and started pacing back and forth in front of his father. "I should have known it was a mistake bringing you here. Dammit, Charlie, I wanted this to go smoothly, for Alia's sake."

Charlie wiped his hand over his face, then wagged his finger in her direction as he paced back and forth. "That fucking bitch is going to sit there and look us right in the face and act like she's ever given a damn about Alia. Then to fucking accuse me...me of hurting her. She's got the fucking nerve." *I should have dealt with her a long time ago when I had the chance.*

"Well, you're blowing this. Get your ass back in the truck. I'll deal with her." Harper forced his truck keys into Charlie's hands. "Go sit in the truck and do whatever it is you need to do to calm the fuck down. Go."

Glaring over at Trish one last time, Charlie ran his hands through his hair in frustration and stormed off.

Back at the table, Harper sat down. "Sorry about that." a small part of him died having to apologize to her. "You're right. Alia has been going through something lately. Yesterday she came up missing for most of the day. You wouldn't happen to know anything about that, would you?"

"How would I? I spent most of the day Sunday in church."

"Trish, I'm going, to be honest here. I don't like you. I know you are playing some kind of con on Alia. Whether you're responsible for her behavior or not, I don't trust you or this act of yours. If you genuinely care about her, you will back the fuck off for a while and let us deal with it."

"It doesn't seem like you're dealing with it very well. Why is she in the hospital."

"Because when she came back, she looked like she was drugged and had been dragged around the woods." Harper thought he saw something in her eyes, a hint of fear maybe. "Now, are you sure you know nothing about that or anything else that's been going on with her?"

Trish shook her head but kept calm, very much unlike herself. "How would I, Harper? I see her once a week for not even an hour."

"Personally, I find it interesting that she didn't start acting like this until soon after you arrived."

"So Harper explain to me just what it is that I am doing in the little bit of time I have with her? Did you ever think that maybe she wasn't ready for all of this? You all pushed her into becoming a cop right out of high school, now she's barely in her twenties, and you're pushing her into marriage."

Harper was finding it hard to keep his temper to himself. "No one pushed Alia into doing anything. She came to me about wanting to be a cop. You just can't stand the fact that you lost control over the only person you had any over. And I'm warning you right now, Trish. We are waiting on tox screens to come back and forensics from her Jeep. If I find out you had anything to do with what is going on with her, I will personally make sure you stay locked up in prison for the rest of your miserable life." Again he saw it, a flinch of her eye. It was small, but it was there. Getting up, Harper tossed a ten on the table to tip the waiter. "Have a nice lunch on us, it's your last one here. You're not to see her anymore. I don't want to so much as see you in my county. It's done, Trish. Whatever game you're playing, it's over. You stay the hell away from my daughter." He noticed that one pissed her off, and she didn't even try to hide it.

"You can't keep me from her, Harper," Trish said to his back as he walked away.

Harper stopped long enough to scowl at her. "Yes, I most certainly can." And he walked away before his own temper got the best of him.

"I am her mother, and I have every right to see her." Trish was at the hospital and managed to make it up to Alia's floor, where she was stopped by security. They took her to the nurse's desk, and a young nurse told her that she was not on the list of approved visitors.

"I'm sorry, ma'am, but there was an incident on the floor last night, and it's all on lockdown until the situation is handled. I can direct you to the officer in charge."

"Let me guess, Sheriff Harper is the one in charge."

"Yes, ma'am, he is. Oh, in fact, here he comes now."

Trish turned to see Harper walking down the hallway, his uniform shirt on this time, and of course, so was his gun. He scowled at her when he saw she was the one who he had been alerted was trying to get to the patients' rooms. Of course, she was.

"It's okay, Sharon. I've got this." Harper took Trish by her elbow and gently escorted her down the hallway. "I told you, you couldn't see her, and I meant it."

"Why is the floor on lockdown, Harper? What happened in here last night?"

"Nothing happened. It turned out to be a false alarm."

"So the floor isn't on lockdown?, so I can see Alia?"

"Yes and no. The floor is no longer on lockdown. No, you can not see her."

"Then I demand to see her. My church group has a lawyer."

"I bet it does." he scoffed. "But he's not going to do you any good. Alia isn't here anymore. She was discharged while we were talking at the cafe, and my wife took her home. And don't even be stupid enough to go there. Ellen is not one of your biggest fans, and I wouldn't be surprised if she shot you for trespassing."

Trish whirled around on him. "Is that a threat, Sheriff?"

That's it, Trish, lose your shit here in front of everyone, do me a favor. "No, not at all, just a friendly warning. Besides, she won't be there anymore either. She and Charlie are going to take a few days' vacation away from town. Unwind a little while we wait on the results of our investigation. I have a feeling you may want to be well out of town before that's done."

Trish looked like she was about to get very angry, but then grasped her cross and took a deep breath. "I have nothing to do with what is wrong with Alia. I love my daughter. I'll admit I was a horrible parent to her, and if she's having a mental break, I'm just as much to blame for it as you for pushing her too hard. But I have not done anything to hurt her since I have gotten back. I've just been trying to make up for lost time and atone for my mistakes."

Harper leaned closer to her so no one could hear. "Whoever is coaching you is doing a spectacular job. Unfortunately for you both, my years of work in law enforcement have made me able to spot well-rehearsed bullshit like yours from a mile away."

Trish flinched again.

"Get out of my county, Trish, before I lose my patience with you and find a reason to lock you up." Harper pushed the elevator button and motioned her inside when the doors opened.

Trish went in looking a mixture of mad and scared. "This isn't over," she said as the doors closed.

I count on it. He thought.

At the cabin, Charlie tried bringing Alia out of her shell, but all she would do was sit in a chair by the window and watch as a summer rain fell. She was upset to learn that no one had been in her room that night other than Charlie. She insisted she saw a man in nurse's scrubs put something in her IV.

Sitting there watching the rain, Alia felt so many emotions it was hard to keep track of them all. She was angry no one believed her, she was sad Because she could feel the pain Charlie felt every time he looked at her, she felt lonely, and worst of all, she felt scared. Alia had always prided herself on coming through her childhood with her sanity intact. Now she felt even that slipping away.

Knowing the pain she was putting Charlie through broke her heart. He had always been so good to her. He didn't deserve to be saddled with such a crazy bitch. As much as she longed for his comfort, his pity cut like a knife. Alia had hoped if she just sat there for a while and meditated on the rain, then maybe she would remember what happened on Sunday. If she did, then perhaps he could go after whoever was responsible. Possibly that would be enough to make him stop looking at her like she was fragile glass. To his credit, Charlie was trying to give her space. However, even when he was outside, their connection to one another was so strong it was as if he was standing right next to her. In a way, she figured he was.

With the rain falling in buckets, Charlie had no choice but to be in the cabin. He tried to occupy himself in another room, but his thoughts were always on her. The connection between them was back, had been since he saw her at the house. That connection made it hard for him to actually give her any real space. The fact that he kept walking by the bedroom door, compelled to check in on her with his own eyes, didn't help either.

Around dinner time, Charlie went in to see if she was up to eating anything. Sitting on the ottoman in front of her chair, he took her hands in his. Not for the first time, he marveled over how small her hands and fingers were compared to his long ones. He could almost take both of her hands in one of his. The back of one had a bruise on it where they had put an IV there. He kissed it gently, and as he did, she brushed his cheek with one of her fingers. It was enough to give his heart hope.

"What if I'm crazy?" she asked, barely above a whisper.

"I've always known you were crazy, Alia. It's part of what I love about you." he joked, hoping for a smile from her.

"I'm serious, Charlie. My mother is crazy. Her mother wasn't exactly stable either. What if I'm sick?"

"Then we will do everything we can to make you better. Whatever it takes, Alia, I'll be right there with you."

"What if I don't…what if I can't get better."

"You will. For once, Alia, please stop overthinking about things. Dad and I are still convinced your mother has something to do with all of this. That she is somehow doing something to you."

"And I tried to tell both of you she's not. I know her tricks. I would know if she was manipulating me. The only thing that makes sense is that I've lost my mind. After all this time it's, it's just I'm getting tired again, Charlie. I've been there before. You know I have."

Looking at her with tears in her eyes liked to shatter his heart. "And what did I say I would do if you got tired again, huh? I said I would carry you, and I meant it." tears fell from his eyes. "And I will carry you through hell itself if I have to. I'm not letting go of you, Alia, no matter what. I couldn't if I wanted to. We were connected before we ever even met, and a connection like that can never be broken."

Alia allowed herself to be pulled into his arms. He picked her up and sat in the chair, putting her back down on his lap. Together they sat and watched the rain.

Chapter 29

Falling Apart

Alia wanted to go home for family dinner night, so she and Charli returned to town on Wednesday evening.

Ellen greeted them at the door, happy to see both her kids. They were looking much better. Alia's color was back, and so was Charlie's smile. The little family ate dinner, laughing and talking about anything that was not about the bad way Alia had been. After eating, they lingered at the table for a while, having a few drinks and catching up. If they had known that family dinner could be their last, they might have never left the table.

Before leaving, Harper pulled Charlie to the side. "You can tell her this on your own time if you want. But the tox screen came back on Alia, and they found nothing."

Charlie felt like his heart dropped on the floor. He thought for sure there would have been something in her system. "What about forensics? Have you heard from them?"

"They are waiting for some lab results, but they have found nothing so far. No sign anyone else was in the car or attempted to get rid of the evidence. Unfortunately, that leaves only one thing."

"It's psychological, yes I know. But that still doesn't rule out Trish. You saw her tonight, Dad. She's still a bit tired and still having trouble sleeping a little, but she's been great."

"She's been great before too, Charlie. We need to think rationally about this. Her mother is bipolar. She may be too."

"Okay, yes, maybe, but she was fine till Trish. I think now that she's gone, Alia will be fine again. I really do."

"Well, we'll have to see, won't we? If not, then you know we will have to look into getting her some help. Even at the cost of her job."

Charlie agreed but had his heart set on things being better now. He took Alia back to their apartment, made love to her, and held her in his arms all night. In the morning, she was there. All there.

Eager to get things back to normal, Charlie worked for a few hours that day. He left her at home to clean the apartment and wash a mound of clothes. He joked on the way out how he didn't know who had the worst job. She smiled, her eyes sparkling. He would come to miss that smile of hers.

When Charlie got home that afternoon, he found Alia curled up in a chair, absorbed in a book. The house was clean and the laundry done, so he let her have some time to herself while he cooked them dinner. Had he bothered to pay closer attention, he would have noticed the dream-like state she was in. Or the fact that despite reading, she never changed the page. He noticed later that her smile seemed slightly off, but she yawned and complained of being tired from cleaning all day, so he let it go.

The next day when he showed up after work with her jeep, Alia didn't have the reaction that he thought she would. She just said okay and went back to reading. Charlie couldn't say that this was very unusual for her because Alia had a way of falling into a world when she had a good book. So he shrugged it off. He only grew a little concerned when she spent most of the weekend on the patio reading. More like a little jealous, perhaps. He suggested they spend Sunday reading in bed like they liked to do when it was too hot or cold to enjoy the outdoors, and Alia agreed.

When she shooed away his caresses as a precursor for lovemaking in the middle of the day, he remarked that the book must be really good. She said it was, and he left it at that. It was odd for her to be so distant. Then looking at the book cover, Charlie realized it was one she had ordered a while ago and was eager to start it. A bit of jealousy flared up in him again, and he laughed it off. In a few days, she would be done with the book, and he would hear for weeks about how good it was and how much she loved certain parts and hated certain characters. Things were not exactly back to normal, but given what they had been dealing with, he wasn't complaining. The only thing that bugged him was her smile. When she did offer him one, it seemed forced.

Monday morning, Charlie awoke to Alia bouncing around the apartment in a maniacal glee about going to work that day. He hadn't even gotten out of bed, and she was dressed and ready to go. After she practically dragged him out of bed, telling him to hurry so they could get to work early, he asked her if she had drank all the coffee in the house.

"Oh silly, you know I don't touch that stuff. I'm just happy to get our lives back, aren't you?" She smiled at him but wouldn't meet his eyes. And her smile was odd as well. Still, her energy was infectious, so he just enjoyed her being happy despite himself.

At work, she insisted that she was fine and wanted to get back out on the road. Harper allowed it, happy to see her enthusiasm but insisted she go with Charlie for the day.

Grabbing the keys to his patrol car, she told Charlie she would gas it up and meet him out back.

They both watched as she practically skipped down the hallway. Charlie thought she was just being funny, but Harper was more cautious.

"Keep a close eye on her today. I hate to be so negative when she's in such a good mood, but."

"People with bipolar can have highs just like they do lows. I know I was thinking that too. Or rather, I was trying not to."

"But what are you feeling, you know from her?"

"All good, she's just happy. Maybe we are making too much of this. Maybe she's finally feeling like herself. You know, once she got out from under her and Trish left town, she was always pretty happy. Silly at times, even. I think the storm has passed dad, I really do."

By that afternoon, they would have learned it had not. The worst was yet to come.

The morning seemed to go along fine. Sure they may have given out more tickets than usual, but Alia did it all with a smile on her face, if not her eyes. Not that she would let him look into them. Whenever he would try, she would look away like she was seeing something interesting. While they were working, he let it go, but when he got home, Charlie planned on pinning her down if he had to.

That afternoon Alia was driving and getting antsy when a big one came over the radio. Someone had just knocked over a convenience store outside of town, shots fired, and all units respond.

"Hot damn," said Alia. "Finally, something worth being a cop for. In the August heat, they hadn't had their vests on, so Charlie had her pull over so they could get them out of the back. Alia called him a party pooper, then he reminded her she had already gotten shot once. That was enough for one lifetime. She got hers on just barely and jumped back in the driver's seat. When he protested, she reminded him that she did better on her driving course at the academy than he did.

As they raced towards the store, lights flashing and siren blaring, Alia was practically bouncing in her seat. Being silly during downtime was one thing. Her adolescent behavior was starting to make him angry. Not to mention it was highly unusual for her to act like this. When it came to work, Alia was always professional and serious. Charlie wondered if it had been a mistake to have her come back to work, let alone drive.

"Alright, you had your fun. This is serious, Alia. You need to calm the hell down and focus on the job."

She shook her head but calmed down. Her face was set, but he felt like she was pouting.

Over the radio, more information on the call came in. There were three victims of gunshot wounds at the store. One critical two minor. The suspect got away in a green Ford pickup truck. No number on the plates just yet.

"Fucking murderous prick," Alia said, hitting the gas harder. They were going around a curve when out of nowhere, a green pickup roared past them. Alia did a u-turn maneuver in the middle of the street that Charlie had to admit he would have rolled the SUV trying to do. As she gave chase, he called it in.

The pickup truck was an older model piece of crap on its last leg. Despite how fast it was going, the newer patrol car had no trouble catching up. Instead of pulling over, the driver stuck his hand out the window and flipped them off.

With a smile on her face, Alia flipped him off right back and laughed like they were friends goofing around and not some suspect that just shot three people.

"Get your head in the game Miller, don't let him goad you into a pissing contest," Charlie called it in that they were on his tail.

A minute later, dispatch came on and told him to break pursuit. State boys up ahead had a roadblock. They were to back off and give the staties some room.

"Fuck that. Why should the state boys get all the fun?"

"Miller, back off. I said back the fuck off." Never had she defied direct orders like that. Alia was a stickler for the rules when it came to the job, much like his father.

"We got him, Charlie, we got this piece of shit. It's not the state boy's people he shot, it's ours."

"You know that's not our call and not procedure, now back off."

"Fuck procedure, this is our bust. I just have to pit him."

"You try that at this speed, and you're going to put us off the road with him."

"I got this. I know what I'm doing," Alia insisted.

"That's it, Miller. I order you to stand down. Stop the pursuit immediately." Charlie had never yelled at her like this, not on the job or at home. He hated doing it, but once again, she wasn't acting like herself, and under the circumstances, it scared the hell out of him.

Alia turned to look at him, taking her eyes off the road for a frighteningly long time. But that's not what worried him. When she looked him in his eyes, it wasn't Alia staring back at him. He didn't know who it was, but her eyes were the dark blue of angry storm clouds, and the sweet girl he loved was nowhere in sight.

Looking back at the road, Charlie watched in horror as she slid to the middle of the road and sped up for the pit move. As soon as she hit the back of the pickup, he knew it was a mistake. Faster than his mind or eyes could process it, the pickup spun around, hitting the driver's side of the SUV. They then flipped over onto the passenger side, skidding across the road and into the soft dirt ditch on the side of it. If it hadn't been for the airbags deploying, he might have seen the pickup roll over and over past them, off the road and far into the field on the same side they landed on. But all he could see was the white of the airbag in front of him and a bright flash of white in his head as his head hit something hard.

When everything except the siren stopped, and the bag deflated, Charlie's first instinct was to reach out for Alia. His hands touched nothing but air, and when he looked, her seat was already empty. Looking around frantically, he finally heard her outside of the patrol car yelling.

In his panic, it took Charlie several minutes to get the seat belt undone. Someone that sounded strangely like his father was yelling over the radio. Still, he couldn't make out anything over someone yelling inside of him. When he finally got the seat belt off and twisted himself around, Charlie scrambled up and out of the now broken driver-side window. His brain barely noted how the driver-side door was smashed in before his eyes started combing the area for Alia. He heard her before he saw her. She stood in the field next to the half-demolished pickup truck, her gun drawn, screaming orders.

He had no idea how she was able to get out or even walk right then. Jumping down, Charlie wobbled for a minute, then got his long legs under him to work again. Pulling his gun, he ran out into the field, keeping his eye on both her and the truck in an action that made him feel dizzy and sick to his stomach. Getting closer to her, he could hear what Alia was screaming.

"Run, you son of a bitch! Get up and fucking run! Go on, I dare you, give me a reason to plug a hole in your ass." There was blood running down the side of her head, and she seemed to favor her left arm while still thrusting the gun out in front of her. Alia swayed back and forth on her feet as well.

Rounding the side of the truck, Charlie saw the driver trying in vain to crawl out across the field where he and the truck had rolled to a stop.

The man saw Charlie and started to holler himself. "Call her off, man, call her off! For Christ's sake, she's gonna shoot me." Looking down at the man, Charlie could see he wasn't going to go anywhere. Lowering his gun, Charlie told her he would check the man for weapons to lower her firearm.

"He's going to run. He's gonna run, and I'm gonna blow his fucking head off," she yelled.

"He's not running anywhere, Alia. His legs are broken. Lower your weapon so I can clear him, Damn it, Miller, do what I say."

Alia lowered her gun enough to not put Charlie in danger but still up enough to cover him while he went in and cleared the suspect.

Charlie pulled one gun off the man as he begged and pleaded for his life. "You shot three people back there, so kindly shut the fuck up," he said as he cuffed the guy. In the distance, he could hear more sirens as the others caught up with them. Charlie thankfully still had his radio attached to his shoulder. He called it in that the suspect was down and ambulances were needed. Walking back over to Alia on shaky legs, Charlie forced her to sit down before she fell down. Still, she wouldn't lower her gun until other officers arrived with their own drawn on the suspect.

With the gun down, Alia sat there shaking. All the adrenaline that got her out of the crashed police car, seeping out of her.

Charlie sat next to her, suddenly exhausted. Behind their officers, the state boys showed up. One of them, he assumed the one in charge, was hollering at them and anyone else that would listen but neither one of them heard much as adrenaline gave way to shock. The paramedics arrived, and while one set worked on the suspect, two more came over and started to work on them.

Alia tried to get them to stop, but she had very little energy left to fight them off. They both allowed their vests to be removed, Alia wincing in pain the whole time. Charlie remembered that her side of the car had been smashed in and told the paramedic that worked on her. He reached over and cupped the side of her face with one hand and carefully turned her head to look at him. Her eyes were clear, the dark storm gone, and his girl looked back at him.

"What a rush, huh," she said, laughing a little but stopping because of the pain in her side. The paramedic said she may have a few cracked ribs, but it would have been much worse without the vest. Her arm was hurt badly, and he wasn't ruling out that she could have a fracture.

Charlie's hand came back wet with blood as that side of her head had a bad cut just above the ear. He was amazed she was alive. He was about to access his own injuries when he saw Harper coming out into the field towards them.

"Oh, shit, dad's here. We're in trouble now." Alia fell back laughing, much to the dismay of the paramedic still trying to work on her. She stopped when she looked up and saw Harper staring back at her. She expected him to be angry, hell for some reason, she didn't know, wanted him to be angry. *He's supposed to hate me.* A strange thought occurred to her before it flew away.

Harper got her to sit up so the paramedic could finish wrapping her arm to the side of her body for transport. He then checked on Charlie, who said he was fine, it was Alia's side of the car that got hit. She was checked for a concussion, but the side of her head was more of a gash than a bump.

The paramedics loaded her up on a stretcher while Harper helped his son to his feet. When he did, Charlie turned a pasty shade of white and babbled like he was trying to apologize. Then he bent over at his waist, threw up on the ground, and collapsed into his father's arms, losing consciousness.

Alarmed, Alia tried reaching out for him, but they had her strapped in pretty good. She struggled, but she didn't have much fight left in her.

Harper frantically placed his son down on another stretcher and stepped back to let the medics work on him. After a few minutes, Charlie regained consciousness again, but they didn't like his vitals. The medics raced off with both of them while Harper stood there trying to figure out the best way to tell Ellen that both the kids were on their way to the hospital. And that it may be all Alia's fault.

That evening in the hospital again, only this time it was Charlie's bed they sat and stood around. Both of them had been put in the same room, but as soon as her x-rays were done, Alia got out of bed, despite the protests of both Ellen and Harper. She insisted on sitting on a chair next to Charlie. He had a concussion from when the patrol car went over and suffered from shock but thankfully was otherwise okay. He was resting peacefully, having been given a sedative for the pain. Alia held his hand and laid her head on his leg, much as he had done for her. The position hurt her side terribly, but she didn't care.

When the doctor had talked to them, he said in his opinion it was Charlie jumping out of the car so soon after the accident that sent him into shock. Why Alia hadn't, he didn't know. She had a shock, too, just not as bad as he did. Considering her side got hit, she was very fortunate not to be hurt a lot worse than a badly bruised arm, bruised ribs, and a laceration to the head. He felt confident that Charlie would be fine in the morning, he just needed some rest. They both did.

Alia sat there holding Charlie's hand. The lights were set low to allow him to sleep. Her high earlier in the day was nothing compared to the low she was feeling now. She could feel Harper with his eyes on her back as she sat there. The fact that he said nothing and only seemed concerned about her made her feel worse than if he gave her the chewing out she deserved. She knew it would come in time, that right now, he was playing the father role, not the Sheriff role. But she wished that he would. Not to get it over with, but because she was afraid that later would be too late. Alia wanted him to do it now while it would hurt the most, and maybe just maybe, whatever it was that came over her today would stop for good this time.

He wouldn't, and she knew he wouldn't. When he came up behind her and put his big meaty hand on her small shoulder, Alia sobbed, hiding her face in Charlie's bed. The idea that she could have killed him could have killed them both permeated her mind. And she didn't know why she did it. As soon as the adrenaline wore off, she knew she had messed up bad and felt horrible even before Charlie collapsed. That was the other thing that kept playing in her mind like a skipped record. Over and over again, she saw him fall into his father's arms. As tall as Charlie was, he folded right over like he was made of fragile twigs and not strong bones.

Harper left her, and Ellen went over and put her head on Alia's back, hugging her from behind as she cried. "Ssh now, he's going to be fine, Alia. You heard what the doctor said. He'll be ready to get out of here and go home by morning."

But if it wasn't for me, he'd be home right now. Probably cooking dinner so I could read. Or doing something to make me laugh and smile. She thought. Because for Charlie, it was always about her. He was the least selfish person she knew, unlike her, who had once again made her own problems his. This time she could have killed him.

Ellen and Harper stayed the whole night. Not out of concern for Charlie as much as to console Alia. But no matter what they tried or what they said, it didn't stop her heart-wrenching sobs born of guilt. Sometime in the night, she did manage to fall asleep, but they didn't have the heart to separate them. Harper tucked a blanket around her as best he could and sat there watching them both.

"You can't be too hard on her, Harper. In the state she's in, your liable to break her."

Harper nodded, but his worry was that it was already too late.

"I knew it. Nothing I do is ever fucking good enough." Two days after the accident, Alia and Charlie were in Harper's office at the station. Charlie had been fine the following day, just as the doctor said, aside from some aches and pains and a mad ass headache. Alia had her arm in a sling, the cut on her head bandaged, and sore all over as well, but she managed to take care of Charlie all day, not letting him do much more than go to the bathroom.

Alia had been sad. Sadder than she had been in a very long time. She was prone to bouts of crying and crushed by guilt the whole day. She spent most of the day apologizing for everything, including her own existence. Charlie had tried to comfort her, but she wouldn't let him, saying she deserved to feel like shit. She wanted to be miserable and never forget what her stupidity had almost lost her.

But now, in Harper's office, that sadness had turned to anger. Even as part of her knew she deserved nothing less than to have her ass handed to her when it came time for it, she resented Harper for doing it. Alia had planned on handling it all differently. Still, as soon as she got into the office light a switch, she was uncontrollably angry.

"It's always something, I'm too happy or too angry. I do my job, hell I stop a murderer, and you shit on me." While still at the hospital, they had learned that the elderly store clerk died of his wounds.

"It wasn't your job to stop him, Miller. You were told to back off. Your Sergeant told you to back down. I told you to back down. You were given a direct order. It was reckless and stupid. The two of you could have been killed pulling that stunt. I have a trashed patrol car and the state police on my ass. I have half a mind to tell you to turn in your badge." Harper barked at her.

Alia jumped out of her chair despite the flash of pain. "And I have half a mind to shove it up your ass," she said, unsure where all the anger was coming from.

Charlie jumped in between them as Harper rounded his desk.

"Okay, the two of you need to just stop right now. This is getting out of hand." he turned to Alia. "You know what you did was wrong." he turned back to his father. "And you know Alia isn't acting like herself right now."

"No, she's acting like the angry little punk she was when I had to haul her ass in here as a kid."

That, of course, just made her madder. "My mother was right, Harper. You're just some fucking pig."

"That's it, young lady, you're suspended! Effective immediately," Harper roared.

The words hit Alia harder than the truck did. She wanted to apologize. Wanted to beg both of them for forgiveness. But there was that itching in the back of her head. It squirmed around inside her, whispering things to her. "Fine." Alia wasted no time taking off her badge and slamming it on the desk. Then she fought to get her gun belt off.

"Come on, Dad, she doesn't need this right now. She needs our help," pled Charlie.

"I'm not Dad here, Sergeant. I'm Sheriff. And as Sheriff, I have a job to protect my officers, even from themselves.

Behind them, Alia managed to get her gun belt off and slammed it on his desk next to her badge knocking things everywhere. Before they could stop her, she stormed out the door.

"Shit, I've got to go stop her…Just stay here, please, let me deal with this you're too angry right now." Charlie ran out the door and caught up with Alia in the locker room.

Alia had ripped her uniform shirt half off, and when the locker wouldn't open, she began punching it with the fist of her good arm. She was mad and crying at the same time.

Charlie grabbed her fist, forcing her with all his strength to stop. "Stop, Alia, please just stop. You're hurting yourself."

"I don't care….I don't fucking care….just go away, Charlie, please. Please just go away. I don't want to hurt you anymore," she sobbed. Once she had left Harper's office, Alia's anger had turned inward. Once again, she saw what she was doing and saying but was in no control over it. Her mind kept going back to the thought that they had to hate her, that they all had to hate her. And the fact that she was succeeding, at least with Harper, was unbearably painful.

"Then stop," begged Charlie. "If you don't want to hurt me, you'll stop hurting yourself."

Alia stopped fighting him and leaned her head onto his chest, sobbing. "Help me, Charlie...I feel like I'm losing my mind. It's like I'm not in control of anything anymore. I'm so scared...why is this happening to me?"

"I don't know, but I promise you we will figure this out, sweet girl. And as much as you're mad at him right now, dad is right. You don't need to be working until we do."

"It's not fair, Charlie," she said, the anger building up again. "I worked hard to get here, and now it's all slipping through my hands."

He took her head in his hands and told her again that they would fix this. "For now, I'm going to take you home. Here let me help you with the shirt." He took her uniform shirt off, being careful of her hurt arm and inspecting its damage. "I'll send this to Mom later so she can sew the buttons back on. We will have it looking like new when you're ready to come back to work." He offered her a smile, but his heart and eyes weren't in it, and she could see that. Before they left, Charlie wrapped a small bandage around her fist that bled a little from punching the locker. He was going to make a joke about having seen more blood in the past week than he cared to but decided that would just make her feel worse.

Charlie had her go wait out in his truck while he went back and told Harper he would run her home then come back so they could talk about what they were going to do.

"Sergeant...Charlie, son." the wind had gone out of his sails, and now he too was feeling guilty. "I think I went too far with her today. Considering this isn't really her fault. I just don't know what to do. I don't know how to help her."

Charlie nodded. If his father was looking for sympathy, he just didn't have it for him right now.

"Tell her I'm sorry. I didn't mean for it to go so bad."

"I can't do it. Only you can, Sheriff." Charlie left Harper standing there feeling bad, and he was okay with that. He would get over it. Right now, getting help for Alia was his priority, not protecting his father's feelings. Charlie left the man there, holding Alia's badge in his hands with a look of desperation on his face.

Charlie took Alia home in unusual silence. At the apartment, he asked her if she needed anything, and she just shook her head. She sat in the nook of the window, so he handed her the book she had been reading. "At least you'll have some time to finish this." he tried.

Alia just clutched the book to her chest while staring out the window, not meeting his eyes.

"If I don't come back before then, I'll be home by six and get us some dinner. Are you going to be okay here alone?"

Alia nodded.

"I love you, sweet girl." he kissed her on top of her head and headed out the door.

"Some sweet girl I am. I almost got you killed, Charlie. Harper had every right to say what he did. I'm just a fuck up. Always have been always will be," she said before he made it out the bedroom door.

Charlie turned back and knelt before her. "You're not a fuck up, Alia. You're one of the best cops I know and one of the kindest people I have ever met. This isn't you. My sweet girl is still in there somewhere. I know she is. I am going to do everything in my power to get her back, too, don't worry about that." Charlie kissed her forehead then forced himself to leave.

From the window, Alia watched as he walked to his truck. Before he got in, Charlie looked up at her. She gave him a little wave, and with a smile, he waved back. It both thrilled her heart and hurt it. When he drove off, she wept.

On his way back to the station, Charlie called his mother and asked her to check up on Alia if she could. He told her what happened that morning, not that she was surprised.

"Those two always butt heads when they're angry, and I think they always will. I should have come in with him this morning to help keep him calm."

"I don't think it would have mattered, mom. As soon as she walked into his office, she seemed to want a fight. And she knew he would give her one."

"Still, he knows something isn't right with her. What are we going to do about our girl Charlie?"

"Going to talk to dad about that right now. I think it's time we get her some help. Maybe something like what I got when she was in the Academy."

"That's a good idea. Let me know what your father says. I'm going to get us some lunch at the cafe and pay her a visit."

"She'll like that, thanks, Mom. And try to see if she will talk to you. She said some things after the fight with Dad. Alia doesn't feel like she is in control of herself. Maybe you can help, I don't know."

"I'll see what I can do, Charlie."

Charlie and Harper agreed that the time had come for some outside help. Alia hadn't seen her mother that week, and still, she acted out of character. When Charlie told him what she had said in the locker room, Harper was convinced this was something beyond their ability to help her with. He said he would talk to Ellen that night and see if the guy that helped Charlie with his anger would work or if they needed someone else.

A little after noon, Ellen surprised Alia with some of her favorites from the cafe, including the raspberry tea. She gulped the tea down but only picked at her food and was quiet most of the time. It broke Ellen's heart to see her like that. She stayed for a while, trying to engage Alia while puttering around the apartment, feeding the cat, watering plants, and bringing in the mail when it arrived. Alia barely acknowledged anything that was said to her. Ellen had needed to go to the store before going home to cook for family dinner night, so she told Alia she would see her that night and went to leave.

"I'm sorry," Alia said as Ellen was about to open the door. She was sitting on the couch with her legs pulled up to her chest. "I'm sorry I hurt Charlie."

Ellen came over and sat on the couch next to her. "Alia, honey, it's not your fault. We all know that."

"It feels like my fault. I kept telling myself to stop; I swear I did. It was like I was two different people the whole time. Charlie is your whole world, your miracle baby, and I almost took that away from you." Alia cried, then seemed to get angry at herself for crying.

Ellen brushed back her hair and smiled with tears in her eyes as well. "Baby girl, you're my whole world too, not just Charlie. He's not the only one that fell in love with you the first time he saw you. I saw you sitting there red-faced and screaming, and I knew I wanted you to be mine. We love you so much, Alia. Don't you ever forget that. No matter what happens, no matter how hard things get, please remember you are loved."

But you're not supposed to. The thought once again flicked through Alia's mind. *You're supposed to hate me. All of you are.* This she was sure of, but once again, she didn't know why.

Ellen sat there with her a little while longer, both shedding tears. When Alia laid back on the couch, her eyes closed, Ellen covered her with a blanket and left so she could rest.

Charlie was out patrolling, almost done for the day, when he got a call on his cell. Pulling over, he saw that it was the Wayside bar just on the outskirts of town. He thought it was a little early in the evening for trouble, especially during the week. So he hoped whatever it would be an easy fix so he could get Alia and go to a much-needed family dinner. It wasn't.

"I believe I've got one of yours here," said Pat, the bartender. "I already had to pull her off of one guy who thought he would put his hands on her. She hasn't drank much, but she sure is tanked."

"What now?" he asked, having trouble processing what he heard for some reason.

"I have one of your officers in here drunker than shit and looking for a fight. She only had a six-pack worth of ponies and two shots of whiskey because, and I quote, 'what bitch can't shoot whiskey, but she's about floored. I figure I call you instead of the Sheriff; maybe she doesn't get in so much trouble. You know on account of her being a hero saving them kids and all."

Charlie couldn't believe what he was hearing. Alia was at a bar and drunk. He could barely get her to drink wine with dinner once in a while. She hated bars after spending significant portions of her childhood in them while her mother drank. She hated drinking.

"You have Alia there at your bar. My Alia, my fiance?"

"Yea, that's right, I forgot you two were a thing. But yes, that's her, alright. Come in about an hour ago. Like I said, some out-of-towner that didn't know she was a deputy tried to cop a feel. He won't be making that mistake for about six to eight weeks. Pretty sure she broke his hand. Wiry little one, she is feisty too. You better get here fast, though. I had a couple of loudmouth bikers come in, and she's been staring them down like a rabid dog."

"I'm on my way, don't serve her anymore, and try to keep her away from those guys if you can."

"I'll try, but I'm not laying a hand on her after what she did to that other guy. I need my fingers."

Clocking out from his patrol car Charlie hit the lights and raced silently to the bar. When he pulled up to the bar, he knew he was too late. A few patrons were standing at the open door, looking in. Charlie ran past them and into a chaotic scene.

One of the bikers, a big burly guy three times her size, had Alia backed up into a corner. He grinned like he had the upper hand, but Charlie could have told him he'd made a big mistake.

Another biker sat on the floor among the remains of a shattered beer mug, his head bleeding. He looked a little dazed and confused as he watched his partner try to handle the little woman that had taken his ass out.

Alia, in the corner, had a pool stick in her hand, whirling it between her fingers, egging the guy on. Her lip bled, and she still favored the arm, but she didn't look like herself. Her eyes were wild and shining like they were on fire. He hadn't seen her like that in years. Where before, he got a kick out of seeing her get riled up. Now he was only afraid for her.

Before he had a chance to announce police presence, the biker lunged at Alia, which he realized too late was a mistake. She managed to slip right under and around him then proceeded to break the pool stick on the biker's exposed back. When he reared back, she hit him with the broken piece she had left upside his head. Dropping the piece, she went in for the attack while he was now on all fours, only Charlie grabbed her shoulder from behind to stop her. Before he could duck, she whirled around astoundingly fast and slammed one of her small fists surprisingly hard right into his jaw. He made a grab for her again, her attention already back to the biker still on all fours on the floor. This time he wrapped his arms around her waist and hoisted her up off the floor like she was made of nothing more than air. He realized when he did that she had lost a good deal of weight in the past few weeks. Charlie was almost afraid he would hurt her because she fought him like a wild cat.

"Alia, stop, dammit, it's me…it's Charlie…just stop."

"Charlie," she said, seeming to snap out of her rage.

"Yes, it's me, Alia; now cool your shit down." When she stopped trying to wiggle away from him, he loosened his grip and put her back down on her feet. Only when he let go, she wobbled on shaky legs, and he had to catch her by her arm before she fell.

"Charlie!." she said in drunken excitement. "Hey everybody, Charlie is here." she waved her whole good arm at him like she was introducing him. However, no one was

there other than the bartender and two bikers on the floor.
"Hey ... .hey...where'd where'd everybody go?"

"The same place you're going. Home," said Charlie.

"Whoo-hoo everybody, party at my house." she declared, forgetting no one was there.

"No, no party, Alia. I'm taking you home before Harper finds out and kicks both our asses."

"Oh poo...I ...I can kick his ass...ain't that right fellas...little bitches"

Charlie tried to pull her by her arm, but she slithered out of his grip.

"Wait, Charlie, jus wait..the fat one owes me forty bucks." Alia went over to the guy still on all fours. "Hey, fat ass...where's...where's my money...was a matter you hurt? Here I'll help you up." Before Charlie could stop her, Alia kicked the guy on the ground in the ribs twice. He fell on his stomach in a whoosh of air.

Charlie grabbed her around the waist and picked her up off her feet again. As he carried her out that way, the bartender asked if she was going to be okay.

"Her? What about them two?" he asked, nodding to the two men on the ground.

"To hell with them, she beat them at pool, and they tried to stiff her. Granted, she did get a bit carried away. Little hellcat, you got there."

Alia giggled, then meowed like a cat and laughed like it was the funniest thing she had ever heard.

"I'll come back later and pay for the damages."

"Nah, all she broke was a pool stick and some balls...and those weren't my balls." Pat chuckled.

"Ha!" Alia laughed out loud, still in Charlie's grip...barely. "That's some funny shit right there. Love you, man...hey, Charlie, pay the tab. Do a man right."

"On the house, Alia, hero's special," declared Pat.

Alia gave him two thumbs up, wincing at using her bad arm. "You rock, man. This bar is fucking awesome."

Charlie dragged Alia out of the bar, passed the two people at the door, and to his patrol car. He held her as best he could with one arm as she swayed on her feet. With the other, he opened the car door.

"Get in, Alia," he said gruffer than he intended. Charlie was once again finding himself losing his patients with her. People were coming into the bar's parking lot and had stopped to watch. He wanted to get her out of there before they realized who she was.

"Am I under arrest Occifer?" Alia leaned in on him, trying to get on her tiptoes to whisper in his ear. She got about as far as his chin and really wasn't whispering. "If you want to put me in cuffs and do some kinky shit, I promise I won't tell," she giggled again.

Sure to be careful of her head, Charlie lifted her and sat her down in the car. He then had to push her over so she wouldn't fall out before he closed the door. He got in the driver's side and put her seatbelt on despite her trying to slide off the seat. The whole time he had to tell himself that this wasn't her. That she couldn't help acting this way, and he loved her too much to hurt her. When he had her strapped in good enough, he drove off.

"Lights and siren, Charlie," Alia begged.

"No lights and siren, Alia," Charlie said gruffly and realized he sounded like his father.

"Aw, come on. Why are you mad at me?"

Charlie gave her a look of frustration, then reminded himself again she was not herself. "I'm not mad, Alia, I love you, but you're out of control right now."

"No, I'm drunk right now. Had to, had to drink away the crazy."

"What is that supposed to mean?"

"Oh, Charlie. Poor, poor Charlie, you love a crazy woman."

"No, I know that," he said with a bit of a smile. "Why did you think drinking would help?"

Alia leaned over as far as the seatbelt would allow and put a finger to her lips. "Ssh. To stop the voices," she whispered.

"Voices? Then why whisper?"

"They listen too," she said matter of factly. She even almost sounded sober for a second. Then she sat back up and started to cackle.

"Alia...Alia, stop. Who is listening?"

"I told you...the voices. The voices Charlie. They don't like you. They don't like anyone I know, but they really don't like you."

Seeing a dirt road, Charlie pulled into it and parked the car. Turning in his seat, he asked her again who the voices were.

"Oh, Charlie. Do you remember, remember Charlie, how we used to make love in the back seat." she looked in the back and smiled. "Let's do that again, Charlie...I want to go back and start over, don't you? I wonder if the condoms are still stashed under the seat." she giggled.

"No, because you wrecked that patrol car, remember." Not that the condemns had been in there since those days.

Alia looked back up at him with a frown on her face and sadness in her eyes. "No...no, now be fair, Charlie...they made me do it. I'm a good cop...they don't want me to be one, but I am."

Taking off his seat belt, he got as close to her as the center console would allow. Charlie brushed her wild hair back from her face."

"Yes, you are, Alia. You're a great cop. That's why you're going to tell me who did this to you."

She looked confused for a minute, then shook her head. "I got me drunk. The ponies were OK...but the whiskey? Shit, I know why Harper drinks that shit ....woo."

"No, Alia, the voices...who are the voices."

Once again, she put her finger to her lips. "It's a secret."

"Come on, Alia, we don't have secrets, not us. You can tell me."

"No, Charlie...I won't...I have secrets. Like how I'm scared you're going to leave me, and I'll die. I'll die, Charlie, I will."

The look on her face was one of complete honesty, and it broke his heart. "I'm never going to leave you, Alia. But you have to tell me who is hurting you." Charlie saw tears welling up in her eyes.

"Take me home, Charlie. Just forget about this and take me home. I know It's family night lets go have dinner with Mom and Harper. I'll do anything. Just don't make me tell you."

"It's okay, Alia. I want to help you. You can tell me."

"I can't, Charlie," she shouted and slapped away his hand.

"Why not," he said, feeling his anger rise.

"Because they'll kill you." she sobbed. "And everyone will hate me, and I'll be alone again. I can't lose you, Charlie...I just can't."

Charlie had given her a blanket from the back, and the rest of the ride home, they both were quiet. Alia curled up the best she could on the passenger seat, a tear falling down her wet cheeks from time to time. She had completely shut down on him and wouldn't say a thing. The only good part was that without her drunk ramblings, he could think clearer.

Once again, Charlie was confident someone was doing something to her. He just couldn't figure out how. She hadn't seen her mother in over a week and had barely been out of anyone's sight for long. Course, she had enough time to drive her jeep to the bar. Was it possible that she was meeting up with someone and they were threatening to hurt him if she said anything? The thing was, he had his doubts about that. The incident at the bar was proof that even drunk, she could take care of herself. He didn't think she would put up with anyone making threats towards him. That only left one thing, and that was that they were somehow keeping her from remembering what they were doing to her. *So why was the tox screen negative? It could also be that she's going crazy.* He brushed that thought away, refusing to believe that.

At the apartment, Charlie got her upstairs and into bed and took her shoes off. "How does some hot tea sound?"

Alia nodded but refused to meet his eyes.

He kissed her forehead and went to the living room, shutting the door. While her tea water boiled, Charlie contemplated what to do next. He needed to tell Harper what she said. Still, he didn't want to tell Harper she was at a bar getting drunk, least of all into a fight (even if part of him would have gotten a kick out of her taking on two big ass men on her own). The problem with keeping that to himself was that several people saw him leave with her. The county was big, but their town was small and filled with people that had little to do but talk about each other. Deciding it was best Harper found out from him, Charlie called. He told Harper everything. Most notably, what she said on the way home.

"How much of this do you think she believes and how much is just drunken rambling?"

"She was looking terrified, Dad. Now she won't even talk or look at me. She may be afraid she said too much. This whole, they are listening thing freaks me out."

"What's bothering me is that Trish is not smart enough to come up with all of this. That means she either has someone else pulling the strings, or it's someone else altogether...or worse."

As they had talked, Charlie made Alia's tea. "I agree. What about this Jacob guy? The one that runs the church group she is part of?"

"I'll have one of the boys at the station do a record search on him, see what they can come up with."

"I can do that," offered Charlie.

"No, I want you to focus on Alia right now. Beer and whisky are no combination. She is going to feel like hell soon."

"I should go then. I made her some tea."

"I'll let you know if we find out anything. And son...thanks for being honest with me...I know that wasn't easy."

"I just, I just want my girl back. Tell Mom I'm sorry, but we won't make family dinner tonight."

"Don't worry about that, son. Just take care of Alia."

Charlie ended the call feeling a little guilty. When he went into the bedroom, Alia was gone. Putting the tea on her nightstand, he heard her in the bathroom. Her bad night had begun.

Charlie went in to find her praying to the porcelain god. He got one of her hair scrunchies and put her hair back up out of her way. She wretched again as he wet a cloth and put it on the back of her neck, then he got another one ready for when she was done. Charlie knelt next to her, rubbing her back telling her not to fight it, it was easier that way. He wasn't much of a drinker either, but he had gotten wasted on his twenty-first like most American kids did and ended up just where she was now.

Charlie handed her the other rag to wipe her face and mouth off when she was sure she was done. She sat on the floor, her back against the wall, looking pasty and pale.

"Feel better now?"

"I don't think I'll ever feel better again." she moaned.

"Sure you will. Tomorrow will be hell, but after that, you'll be fine. I promise."

"Will I?" she asked, looking at him knowingly.

"If I have anything to do with it, yes. Do you want to talk now about what you said in the car?"

Alia looked at him, puzzled.

"About the voices?"

Still the puzzled look. "What voices? I don't remember saying anything in the car. Come to think of it, I don't remember getting here from the bar."

"Alia, that wasn't even an hour ago. How can you not remember?"

"Duh, I'm drunk. Did you make the tea?"

"Yeah, you think you can brush first without, you know?"

"Hurling again?" she laughed a little.

Her smile still wasn't the one he had been missing, but it seemed he had her back again. Charlie wondered how long he would get to have her this time.

Charlie had work the next day, so Ellen came over early to stay with Alia. After the bar incident, they didn't want to leave her alone. Not that it looked like she was going to get out of bed anytime soon. When the early morning sunshine came into the bedroom, as usual, Alia moaned and hid under the covers. Charlie was able to get her to drink some hot tea but had to first lower all the blinds and put spare blankets over the windows. Their bedside lamps worked on a dimmer switch that he set to low. When he asked if she wanted some food, she turned a little green and hid back under the covers. At least one positive thing would come out of her adventure, she wouldn't try drinking again any time soon. When Ellen arrived, he peeled back her covers enough to kiss her on the head. She groaned at that as well.

Around noon that day, Ellen was out getting the mail when she saw Alia coming down the apartment stairs. When she asked what Alia was doing up, the girl didn't acknowledge her at all and just kept walking. What bothered her was the blank look on Alia's face. At the bottom of the stairs, Ellen stood right in Alia's path, and without looking like she had seen her, Alia walked around her. When Ellen Stopped in front of her again, she grabbed Alia's arms. Once more, she tried to just go around, then her brow furrowed, and the blank look was replaced with one of recognition.

"Hey, Mom," she said strangely causally.

"Where are you going, Alia?"

"It's as s…," she started, then stopped. The blank look returned but only for the smallest of seconds. "Checking the mail," she said at last.

"I have the mail, dear." Ellen showed it to her.

"Oh," she said. She then looked over Ellen's shoulder towards the parking lot. "Where's my Jeep?" she seemed to ask more to herself than to Ellen.

"You left it at the bar last night. The boys will pick it up later today."

"Oh," she said, then with a barely perceptible shake, she seemed to come fully alive. "Boy, it's hot today, isn't it." Alia looked down at the sweat clothes she had gone to bed in inside the nice air-conditioned apartment. "We should go inside. It's nice of you to come and visit. Are you here for lunch?"

Ellen wasn't sure what had just happened. She needed to piece it all together In her head. But first, she needed to get Alia back inside. "Yes, baby girl, I am, but I think you need a shower first. You're about drenched in those clothes."

"Yeah, I don't know what I was thinking."

I don't think you were thinking at all.

While Alia took a shower, Ellen called Harper and told him what had happened. "It was like she was in a trance. I have gone over it in my head a few times, and I know she was trying to go somewhere. She snapped out of it as soon as she realized her jeep was gone. Harper, I'll be damned if I don't feel like I'm in the middle of a bad soap opera. This all just keeps getting weirder."

"Is it possible she was just trying to go back to the bar?" he asked.

"No, Harper, this wasn't like yesterday. Charlie said she was dressed to go out. This time she got up out of bed and didn't bother to so much as change her clothes. Her hair was a mess as well. I'm telling you she was trying to go somewhere. Or more like she was being lured somewhere."

"I need to talk to Charlie about this, see if she has tried to wander off before. For now, we shouldn't leave her alone, not even for a little bit."

"I don't plan on it. I will order us some food and try to keep her occupied."

Later at the station, Harper and Charlie talked about what had happened at the apartment. Other than going to the bar, and the day she went missing, he hadn't known Alia to go anywhere without telling him first. However, there was something that did bother him. It had to do with the timing of how she started acting odd. It made sense to him that she acted this way after seeing Trish on Mondays. But now that they had stopped, she still had days that she seemed fine, only to go back to being odd again. She had been doing really good the last week, then when he got home from work, she seemed very distant.

"At the time, I didn't think I wanted to see it. She was reading, which we all know is very normal for her. But she still seemed like she was away. And for her to read so much, she didn't get very far in the book. Still, I wouldn't have thought anything weird about it if it hadn't been for the way she woke up Monday morning."

"In a manic high."

"Yes. Now I know she didn't go anywhere all weekend, but what if she slipped out sometime on Thursday."

"You think maybe she snuck off to go see Trish? They had to have met somewhere no one would see them. I doubt they just met up at the cafe."

"Exactly, which got me thinking about the last time she started acting odd again. Didn't you say you had a complaint about her giving some women a hard time over a speeding ticket?"

Harper nodded

"I went back to look over the GPS records on the patrol car she used that day. There was nothing out of the ordinary until around two. The car moved about a half a mile down the road then returned. There was no record of her in pursuit of a speeder or anything. Then no movement for over an hour, then the car drove a half a mile down the road again, doubled back again but this time came back over a mile. She then went back to where she had been stopped behind the billboard. Once again, no record of a pursuit."

"There is a little wayside park right across from where the speed trap is. I would have said that she went there to use the bathroom but not for an hour," said Harper.

"I think it's possible she met someone there, like her mother. Or maybe even someone else. Right after that, she gave that woman a ticket."

"Didn't you say she was doing great the rest of the time?"

"Yes, but then she went missing. What if, now stay with me here because it's bizarre, but what if whatever they did to her the day she was at the speed trap didn't work, right? So then they get her again, only something goes wrong, and she escapes from them. That would explain why she came back in such a mess. So after that, other than the issue at the hospital, which could have just been a nightmare, she's fine again. That is until I leave her at home to go to work."

"How's that?"

"When I went to work, she said she was going to stay home and clean all day. And the apartment was fine when I got there but didn't smell clean, you know. But she was so absorbed in her new book I just didn't make it an issue. She was like that all weekend, very distant. And as fast as Alia reads, she should have finished that book. Yet when I handed it to her today, she wasn't even half done."

"So you think whoever is doing this did it again? But how, Charlie? There were no drugs in her system."

"Plenty of drugs out there that can fool a tox screen. My point is someone is getting to her. Or she is going to them. I think we need to give her some breathing room and see where she goes."

"Running kind of risk. What if they see us and call it off. Or she sees us?"

"I can hack her GPS anti-theft tracking on her Jeep."

"And if she doesn't take the Jeep?"

"Then at least we know when she comes back that she's not going to be herself. We have to do something. We have to get to the bottom of this mess because even when Alia is lucid, she feels like she's losing her mind."

Chapter 30
Let Her Go

The following day Charlie got ready for work like usual. Alia's hangover was gone, so she felt better but looked sad as she watched him get ready for work. Noticing Charlie went over to talk to her. She was nestled in her nook again, only looking in this time. "Talk to me." He said, brushing a few strands of hair away from her face.

"When do you think Harper will let me come back to work?"

Charlie sighed heavily. "Honestly, Alia, even if you hadn't said the thing about shoving your badge up his ass, he wouldn't let you go back to work yet. Do you really think you should? I mean, don't you think we should wait to see what's really going on?"

"I worked so hard..." she began.

"I know. And you'll be there again. For now, we need to get you in to see someone. The important thing is to get to the bottom of what is going on, so we know how to fix it."

"You're right. I know you are. The last thing I want to do is hurt you again." Alia reached up and touched the small cut on his head from the accident.

Charlie took her hand away and kissed the back of it. "I've got to go. Mom is busy this morning, so she might not be able to check up on you till lunch. I'm leaving the keys to the Jeep because I want to be able to trust you. But I would rather you not go anywhere, not by yourself."

"I won't, I promise. Love you, Charlie."

But as he knew she would, she did. Harper and Charlie waited in their patrol car down the road from the apartment. Other officers were sitting in their cars around town waiting for a signal. Sure enough, after about an hour of waiting the GPS signal on the app, Charlie had for the Jeep started to move. As much as he knew they needed to see where she was going, he was still disappointed. *She had promised me. I cain't thrust anything she says right now.*

With Harper driving, the two of them hung back to give her plenty of space, then followed as she drove out of town. Calling in three of the other vehicles they had, the four of them followed the signal from a couple of miles behind. It led out to a park on the edge of Union county. Like the one by the speed trap, it was relatively small and not used by many people.

Watching as the car on the app pulled into the park and stopped, Charlie felt vindicated. This was proof, at least enough for him, that someone was doing this to her. And he had an idea just who was going to be at the park when they got there.

The four squad cars parked along the side of the road about half a mile from the park. They wanted to give her enough time to start whatever they were doing to catch them in the act and make sure she didn't move again.

This was the part Charlie hated. He wanted to swoop in there right away and get her far away from whoever was doing this to her before they could damage her more than they had. But Harper insisted they needed evidence that something was going on other than Alia just sneaking off to see Trish.

While they were waiting, Charlie suddenly sat up in the patrol car with his hand on his chest. He had felt like someone had cut a cord going from him to Alia. One minute he could feel her, she was surprisingly calm, and the next minute she was gone. He had a sinking feeling in his chest like his heart fell to his feet.

"Charlie, what's wrong?"

"It's Alia. I just feel disconnected from her. It happened the other day when she went missing, only this time I actually felt it happen. Whatever they are doing to her, it may be happening now."

"Then it's about time we get moving then." Harper used his cell to let the others know they were about to pull out. He didn't know if they were being listened to on the radio and didn't want to chance giving them a warning. As the patrol cars pulled out, they didn't turn on any lights and sirens either.

Harper and Charlie were in the lead car with Charlie in the passenger seat, poised to get out as soon as he saw Alia. When they drove into the park, they first saw a large older model camper. It wasn't until they pulled up into the parking area that he saw her, or rather them. Alia lay on a lounge chair with a cooler next to her and Trish on another lounger next to that. When they pulled up, Trish bolted upright from where she was lying. Charlie noticed that Alia didn't move a muscle, sending his heart racing in fear that they were already too late.

With the car barely stopped, Charlie jumped out and pulled his sidearm. "Stop right there, Trish, don't you fucking move." He ran over to Alia with his father and several other officers not far behind them. Keeping his eye on Trish, Charlie looked down at Alia, who still hadn't noticed them arriving.

Two officers went over to grab Trish despite her shouts of protest. Another two went into the camper and pulled out a tall white, older male with long hair, wire-rimmed glasses, and a gray-haired streaked beard.

Charlie didn't notice much of this at all. His attention was all on Alia. Her eyes were not closed like he expected. Instead, she lay there with her eyes open and a slight smile on her face, humming softly to herself, much like the day she had gone missing. Holstering his gun, Charlie knelt down beside the lounge, taking one of her limp hands in his. "Alia, sweetheart, can you hear me?"

She didn't so much as bat an eyelash.

Charlie looked over at Trish, now standing in cuffs, and sneered. "What the hell did you do to her?" Charlie gripped Alia's hand with no response back from her. As was the case, anytime his girl was in trouble, he could feel the burning hot fury build up within him.

"She's just resting. With all that you people have been putting her through, the child needs her rest." Said the man from the camper they knew was Jacob.

"You shut the hell up! I didn't fucking ask you. If you have hurt her."

"She's fine," said Trish, pulling at the officers that held her. "It's a meditation technique Jacob teaches. Just talk to her, Charlie, and she'll snap out of it. Alia, honey, it's okay, snap out of it, dear."

Charlie looked into Alia's eyes and saw a flicker of something. "Alia, come on, Alia, come on, sweet girl, come back to me." Slowly some light came into her eyes, and they locked on his.

"Hey, Charlie." She said dreamily. "Your home."

Harper came over and knelt down next to her as well. "Alia, do you know where you are?"

Alia gave her head a slight shake, and her eyes cleared a little more, but when she spoke, she sounded like she was still in a dream. "Why am I not home? I promised Charlie I would stay home." She looked over, saw her mother, and cringed, reaching out for Charlie. "Charlie, where am I...why is she...what's going on?" She asked, sounding a lot more present at last but desperate, even terrified.

"You're fine, Alia, honey. It's just going to take a few minutes for things to clear," said Trish.

Harper noticed she was keeping up the good act, which infuriated him. "Not another word out of either of you." Barked Harper. He had the officers search both of them then told them to put the two into separate squad cars.

"Are we under arrest? On what charges? We haven't done anything wrong." Protested Jacob.

Charlie got up from Alia and approached the man. "Nothing wrong? Just look at her. We have been going through hell for weeks because of you, because of whatever the hell you are doing to her."

Struggling with the officers, Jacob stood his ground. "You have been the one that has put this poor child through the misery she's been having. I've been only trying to help her get through the trauma you have caused her."

Jacob's matter-of-fact tone got the best of Charlie, and he rushed the man. Several officers intercepted Charlie before he could get to Jacob. "You've been drugging her for weeks. She almost killed us in a car wreck. Don't you dare stand there and act like we are the ones that did this to her. She doesn't even know she's here."

"She's just not completely out of it yet. That girl came here of her own free will. She's been begging us to help."

Behind him, Alia tried getting up from the lounge, but her legs wobbled under her.
Charlie yanked his arms out of the officer's hands and sprinted back to Alia just in time to keep her from going to her knees.

Clinging to Charlie, she whispered in his ear. "It's all a lie, Charlie, please believe me. I don't remember coming here. I don't even know where here is."

"I know, it's okay, I believe you. Come on, I'm getting you out of here." Wrapping his arms around her, Charlie took her to her jeep. On the way, he stopped and told Harper what she said.

Harper turned to Jacob. "Jacob Fuller, I'm placing you under arrest for the kidnapping of Deputy Alia Miller."

"Sheriff, be reasonable. Her Jeep is right there. She drove here herself."

"He's right, Harper, we didn't do anything to her. Alia honey, tell them, tell Harper we haven't laid a hand on you."

Charlie was still holding on to Alia by her jeep when she went still at her mother's words. Very still and looked off at nothing. Half a beat later, she moved again. "They didn't..." she started but then looked into Charlie's eyes. When she did, he at first saw a thin cloud there, then in an instant, it cleared and was replaced with fear. "I want to go home, Charlie. I don't feel right. I can't keep my thoughts in my head." She hid her face in Charlie's chest, not wanting to see Trish or Jacob.

Charlie wrapped his arms around her protectively and glared back at Trish.
"What did the two of you do to her, you bitch?"

"Charlie, just take her home. I'll meet up with you there." Harper turned to Trish and told her she was under arrest as well. Both she and Jacob protested, claiming their innocence.

As a last-ditch effort, Jacob called out to Alia, "Just remember Alia, not all birds fly south for the winter."

In his arms, Alia went stiff for a second then once again pleaded with Charlie to take her home.

While the officers struggled to get Jacob and Trish, still protesting, into patrol cars, Charlie put Alia in the passenger side of her jeep. He then got behind the wheel, the keys already in the ignition, and drove them out of there as fast as he could.

As he drove, Alia sat with her feet on the seat, her knees drawn up to her chest, her hands over her ears.

Glancing over at her, Charlie couldn't help but think she looked like a scared little kid. He had once gone to a domestic dispute case where the two parents were shouting at each other. When he went to go check on the kid, he found a boy of about ten years in the corner of his room looking much like Alia did now with hands over his ears, his eyes shut tight, and his knees drawn up, rocking back and forth. The kid had been absolutely terrified listening to his parents' fight. Seeing his girl looking like that poor kid tore at Charlie's heart. As they pulled out onto the highway and headed back to town, Charlie pulled her one hand away from her ears.

"It's okay, Alia, we're gone now."

She shook her head. "No, it's not okay. How the hell did I get there, Charlie...and how did you know to come to find me?"

"We activated the GPS tracker for your Jeep. I knew the code you used on your app, so I just got the app for my phone. We had a feeling you may try to leave again."

"Again?"

Charlie told her about trying to leave the house the day before, and his mother stopped her.

Alia listened, growing more frightened. "I don't remember going there at all. How is that? If I was in some kind of trance, what kept me from running off the road, or worse, running over some kids? Charlie, we have to put an end to this. I could have hurt someone. Who's to say I haven't."

"Hey, you are the only one I'm worried about right now. We need to find out what they did, and frankly, I'm at a loss as to how to do that. I'm not even sure what they did. Do you remember anything about when you got here? Did they give you a shot or a pill.."

Shaking her head again, she said. "We did a tox screen, and there was nothing. I've looked all over for needle marks and saw nothing."

"They had to have done something. It was like you were in a trance when we showed up, and I don't believe that meditation bullshit story Jacob was trying to sell. Mom said you were acting the same way yesterday."

Alia thought for a bit. "I have my doubts it would cause me to do these things I have been doing, but maybe they hypnotized me? It seems pretty far-fetched, but I don't know what else to think. Well, that's not true. There's still one other thing."

"You're not crazy, Alia."

"How can you be so sure? When the hell am I going to see that doctor of yours anyway?"

"That's not until next week. But I'm telling you, Alia, you're not crazy. They did something to you. Why else would you be here and not know how you got here."

"I don't know, maybe because I'm fucking crazy!" She shouted and instantly regretted yelling at him. "You just don't want me to be crazy because that will mess up this stupid perfect image you have of me. Well, I'm not perfect, Charlie, and I've tried really hard to be everything you want me to be, but I feel like I'm falling apart." Turning her head from him, the tears rolled down her face.

Charlie pulled the patrol car off to the side of the highway and parked. Not looking at her, he gave himself a moment to breathe. He didn't want her to hear the anger he was feeling and think it was directed towards her in any way. "I don't want to think you're crazy because the thought of you being hurt and in pain like that, " he paused. "To think I'm not enough…." Charlie stared out the windshield, still not daring to look at her. His chest hurt like his heart was breaking. He gripped the steering wheel so tight his knuckles were starting to hurt. He wanted to punch something, someone, hurt them for putting her through this. And if she was crazy, who would he take it out on then? His worst fear was that this was somehow all his fault. "I don't want to think that I'm not good enough to make you happy, Alia. Because why would you be in so much pain if you were happy?"

Alia looked up and over at Charlie. He still sat staring straight ahead, and she could tell he was trying his best to be strong for her but was losing the battle. Getting out of her seatbelt Alia climbed over the center console and slipped into his lap. Thanks to his legs being so long, she had plenty of room to get into the space between him and the steering wheel. She wrapped her arms around him the best she could, and after a few seconds, he wrapped his around hers.

"Oh Charlie, you have no idea, my silly sweet boy. You have made me happier than I ever dreamed of being. This isn't your fault. I was broken long before we ever met. If I'm crazy, it's despite you, not because of you. You're not only enough for me, you are the only thing holding me together at all." They held each other for several minutes. Sitting back a little, Alia cupped his face like he had done hers so many times and looked him in the eyes. His beautiful green eyes were usually full of so much love and laughter. "Maybe you're right. Okay. Because I was happy, Charlie, I promise you. I was so very happy before Trish came back here. I was mad at first when she showed up, and I knew I should have stopped seeing her."

"Then why didn't you?"

"I don't know. Whenever I would go to the cafe, I would say to myself, today is the day I tell her to fuck off. Then I don't know, I told her we would meet the next week. So maybe you're right, Charlie. I don't know how she could have done it, but maybe with Jacob's help, she did."

"And we fix it how?"

"I think maybe Crystal could help us with that. She's into all that weird shit. She's got to know someone that knows about hypnosis. She goes to those witch fairs all the time, she's dragged me to a few, and I know I have seen them there. Never believed in that stuff much, but, then again, I never would have thought I'd take on two bikers in a bar on my own either."

Smiling, Charlie kissed her. "That's my girl. Please don't give up. We will get to the bottom of this."

"I won't as long as you don't."

Charlie held her close to him again. "Never, my sweet girl. I won't ever give up on you, I promise." Alia returned to her seat as Charlie drove them the rest of the way home. Every time she looked over at him, her heart broke a little. She was afraid of what would happen to him once he realized that she was losing her mind.

Chapter 31
Help

At the apartment, Charlie called Crystal at work and told her what had happened and Alia's idea that she may have been hypnotized.

Chrystal did indeed know a hypnotist. He was a psychologist as well. Later she called Charlie back to tell him they would be there that evening.

With that done, Charlie called Harper and told him what they planned on doing. He was skeptical as well but figured at this point it couldn't hurt.

Unfortunately, he was wrong. Unknown to them all, an irreversible process was already put into place. One that would make all they had been through seem to pale in comparison.

That evening, Crystal brought over her friend Lawson, a psychologist and practicing hypnotist. Lawson stood just under six feet with a stocky frame, receding hairline, and soft kind eyes. He grew up in Australia and had a soothing Aussie accent.

Shortly after they showed up, Harper and Ellen arrived, wanting to lend any support they could. When they arrived, Harper took Charlie aside. "Jacob and Trish made bail, and the district attorney has been up my ass all afternoon. Can't say I didn't think it was going to happen. It's not like we have much in the way of evidence. We may have to drop all charges."

"Can't you get him on something? They had to find whatever drug they are using on Alia in that camper."

Harper shook his head. "Much like Jacob himself, it was clean. We searched the entire camper, and there wasn't anything more than a first aid kit and some tea bottles in the fridge. I have been on the phone all afternoon when I wasn't getting my ass chewed. That man Jacob is a very well-respected member of his community. He gets people off the street, cleans them up, and sets them on the straight and narrow. The members of his compound do community work as well. Guy hasn't had so much as a speeding record since his youth."

"What about before that?"

"Small town mischief, according to the Sheriff up there. He couldn't give me details, of course, but he said Jacob never had anything to do with hurting or kidnapping anyone. He seemed quite pissed off at the very suggestion."

Charlie ran his hand through his hair and down his face in frustration. "So now what?"

"First, we see what happens here tonight. At the morning briefing, we will give every officer a description of the two of them and that camper. If it so much as belches gray vapor, I want it pulled over. When I told them I wanted them out of the county, Trish said she wasn't going anywhere without Alia."

"Now she wants her. She spent years telling Alia how much of a burden she was and threatening to kill her, and now she wants her." Charlie shook his head in anger.

"Relax, son, we are not going to let that happen."

Ready to start, Lawson, Alia, and Charlie went alone into the bedroom. They had Alia sit comfortably in a chair. Charlie sat on the ottoman next to her, holding one of her hands as instructed.

"You are going to keep her grounded here." Started Lawson. "If someone is trying to manipulate her, they could use the hypnotic state to call to her in a way. That we don't want."

"What happens if they call to me?"

"They may be able to control you where I can't. They could try to use you to hurt me or even yourself to stop me from interfering."

"I'm sorry, no disrespect, but that sounds like a lot of Hollywood bullshit. I mean, this stuff isn't genuine, is it?" asked Charlie

"Yes and no. The thing is, the human brain is very complex, and we know very little about it. We do know it's easy to manipulate. Take, for example, placebo effects. If a person is given something and told it will make them feel better, sometimes they do actually feel better. We don't know why exactly. Hypnosis is kind of the same thing. No one can be hypnotized to do anything they really don't want to do. However, if people don't know that, they may allow themselves to be coerced into doing what they are told."

"But I do know that, so how in the hell are they getting me to act like this? How would they make me hurt you if I don't want to?" Alia squeezed Charlie's hand. "I change my mind. I don't want to do this."

"Alia, this may be the only way we can find out what is going on," said Charlie. "And maybe stop this shit."

"I don't want to hurt anybody. I don't want to hurt you again."

"More reasons why we need to do this. You've been disappearing, getting into bar fights, taking risks on the job. Not to mention Trish is hellbent on getting you back. I'm not going to let her hurt you anymore. Please let's just try this at least."

"And I'm going to give you a trigger word as I put you under so that if you do try and get violent, it'll wake you up."

"And stop me?"

"That's the idea." Lawson nodded.

"But will it work?"

"I've never had to use it. I've read about it. It's very rare. I doubt we will even have an issue. And a little thing like you, I'm sure two grown men of at almost six feet each can handle you if need be."

Charlie thought back to the bar and had doubts.

"And Charlie is going to be right here to keep you grounded. Crystal tells me the two of you have a special kind of connection, a profound and strong one. It's that connection we will use to keep you with us. And don't think of it in terms of anything you have seen in the movies. It's not like these people are out there somewhere ready and waiting to tap into your brain, hoping we put you under so they can do something dodgy. It's more likely they have something planted already, a kind of fail-safe in case someone tries to get you to tell them too much."

Charlie thought back to what Alia said the night she went to the bar, about the voices listening in. "He's right, Alia, you said it yourself. I know you don't remember, but you said they were listening in."

Alia shook her head. "I keep telling you I don't remember any of that."

"That may be because they made you forget it," said Lawson. "Commanding someone to do something isn't easy, making them forget, well that isn't very hard. Your brain still has the information stored away. It's just blocked from you accessing it."

"I still don't know if this is a good idea. You have to assure me I won't hurt anyone or even go running off out of here."

"As I said, Charlie here is going to keep you grounded. As long as you can feel him, you should feel like you're still here and safe."

Charlie was having doubts Because the connection didn't work when she had gone missing, and today it was like the cord between them had been cut. Again he was worried that he wasn't enough for her. Or at least not strong enough.

Lawson set himself up on a stool right in front of Alia. From his pocket, he took out a watch on a chain. "I reckon I like to do things the old-fashioned way," he explained. "Pretty much anything can be used to put people in a relaxed state. In fact, it's imperative that you listen to my voice more than following the watch. Okay, now I want you to relax. You have to be compliant for this to work, so no mucking around. If you try and fight me, I'll never get you under. Are you ready?"

Alia nodded. With one final squeeze of Charlie's hand, she sat back and tried to relax.

Charlie got up long enough to kiss the side of her head and tell her he loved her.

Alia smiled back at him with worried eyes.

Lawson began by rocking the watch back and forth in front of her telling her to concentrate on it and his voice as it swung. He sent her deeper and deeper into a relaxed state as he talked.

Charlie saw her eyes begin to blink then slowly start to close. The hand in his loosened its grip as she sunk further and further under.

"Before we start, I'm going to give you a trigger word, Alia. When I.." Lawson looked over at Charlie for a moment. "When Charlie or I say this word, you are to slam the door on whatever is going on. Tell it to piss off and come back to us fully awake. Do you understand?"

Alia slowly nodded.

"Good, the word is mischievous. The next time you hear this word, Alia, you will return to us."

She nodded again.

"Let's begin then," Lawson asked Alia random questions about herself that Charlie could confirm as accurate. Then he started asking her about the park. "Alia, why did you leave the house today?"

She scrunched her face up like she was confused by the question. "I had to go."

"Why did you have to go?"

"I'm not supposed to tell. It's a secret."

"Alia Charlie is here. Can you feel him holding your hand?"

Charlie felt her give his hand a little squeeze.

"Yes, Charlie, my sweet boy." she smiled.

"That's right. Can you tell Charlie why you left the apartment today?"

Again with the face as she shook her head.

"Why not Alia?"

"They don't like him," she whispered.

Lawson looked over at Charlie then back to Alia. "Who doesn't like him?"

Alia didn't answer. Instead, her breathing increased, and she shook her head slightly from side to side.

"It's okay, Alia, we know where you went. We know you were at Settler's park this morning. Can you tell us why you went there?"

She shook her head again. The crease above her nose deepened as she did.

"Alia, I need to know who told you to go to Settler's park. Who is it that doesn't like Charlie?"

Suddenly Alia gripped Charlie's hand tightly, so much so that even Lawson noticed.

"It's alright, Alia, you're safe here. You can tell us why you went to Settler's park. No one here is going to hurt you."

Tighter on the hand as she shook her head back and forth. When she stopped, they could see tears slip from her closed eyes. Charlie reached out to comfort her, but Lawson waved him back.

"How important is it to get this information from her?"

"Very important. We have no evidence at all. We need to know what they are doing to her."

Lawson nodded. "Then this might get a little dodgy. Just hold her hand, don't try to touch her otherwise." He turned back to her. "Alia, I need you to go back there, but I want you to keep holding on to Charlie. He's right here with you. Go back to Settler's park, back to arriving there in your Jeep. Is Trish there waiting for you?"

She hesitated a bit, then nodded.

"Is Jacob there?"

Another hesitation, then she shook her head.

"Where is he, Alia? Where is Jacob?"

She scrunched her face up again, more tears falling as she struggled to speak. "He's pre...pre...preparing," she said with a stutter.

"Preparing for what, Alia? What do you reckon he's going to do?"

Crying, she shook her head violently.

"Alia, what is Jacob preparing to do?"

Sitting before him, Alia starts to shake. "No...no...please don't."

Beside her, Charlie gripped her hand in both of his. He could feel her pain and fear, almost as if it was his own. He was afraid to hear what she would say, afraid they may have hurt her more than just mentally.

"Alia, you're safe here. Trish can't hurt you. Jacob can't hurt you. Charlie has you, he is right here with you. You can tell us. Did he hurt you? Did Jacob do something to hurt you?"

"Stop....please stop..." she cried out.

"Alia, is Jacob hurting you?"

"No.." she cried. "Not Jacob...he's not...it's...." Breathing fast and shaking all over, Alia looked to be struggling with what to say.

"Then who is it? Is it your mother?"

"No!"

"Who is Hurting you, Alia? What are they doing?"

"No!"

"Alia, I demand that you tell me. Charlie wants you to tell him who is hurting you."

Reaching up with her hand not held by Charlie, Alia grabbed the side of her head, gripping her hair tightly.

Both Lawson and Charlie could see that she was having some kind of battle within herself. She started to pound the side of her head, and Charlie went to stop her, but Lawson pushed him back down and stood over her.

"Who is hurting you, Alia? What are they doing to you?"

Charlie watched and not only saw her pain and struggle but felt it as well. He felt her struggle hard one last time, then it was as if he could feel her collapse under some tremendous pressure.

"It's Charlie!!" She shouts. However, as soon as she did, she shook her head violently and hit herself as she struggled again. "No, no damn it no, I won't tell them that no!" she practically screamed.

"Tell us what, Alia? Who is making you say this? Who is trying to control you?" begged Lawson.

Alia continued to struggle, shaking her head, pounding it with her fist, then suddenly she went limp, and her head fell forward with her chin to her chest.

The sudden quiet was unnerving after all the shouting from her and Lawson. Her hand in Charlie's was limp and damp. He looked over at Lawson, who looked as confused as he was.

"Alia, are you still with us?" asked Lawson as he towers over her.

In an instant, Alia's head snapped up, and the look on her face was alien to them both. "Fuck off," she screamed in a voice, not like her own. She brought up both her legs and kicked out at Lawson, sending him flying across the room, striking the wall.

Laying on the floor, Lawson struggled to get air into his lungs as he waved helplessly at Charlie.

Alia released Charlie's grip and stood up, headed right for Lawson when Charlie grabbed her from behind.

"Mischievous," he shouted. Whatever Charlie had been expecting her reaction to be at the trigger word, it was nothing like what he saw. When she first turned to him, Alia's face was contorted into one filled with rage. That only lasted for a second or two before her face fell utterly flat, her eyes rolled up into the back of her head, and she collapsed into Charlie's arms. Down on his knees, he held her limp sweat-soaked body close to his, calling out her name repeatedly.

Hearing the noise from the other room, Harper barged in to see Charlie and Alia on the floor. Charlie with his arms around her and Alia unconscious. Lawson was on the floor in front of the wall across from them, coughing and gasping for air. Behind Harper, Crystal and Ellen look in as well.

Harper ran over to the kids on the ground, helping Charlie pick up Alia and put her on the bed.

"Alia, wake up, come on, sweet girl, wake up for me," Begged Charlie.

"She's breathing." said Harper, "I think she just passed out, Charlie.

Charlie got into the bed with her and pulled Alia into his lap, wiping her sweaty brow. "Come on, Alia, wake up for me, please wake up."

Harper went over to help Lawson up, who could finally breathe, albeit painfully. "What the hell happened here?"

Lawson went over to check on Alia, but Charlie pulled her back protectively. "It's okay, Charlie. Let me check her out."

Charlie relented but still held her as Lawson checked her pupils and pulse.

"I think she will be fine. We could probably wake her up if we had some smelling salts."

"I have some in the first aid kit under the bathroom sink," said Charlie.

"I'll get them." Said Ellen.

"Why won't she wake up?" asked Charlie. "You said she was supposed to wake up at the trigger word."

"She should have, but that was very exhausting for her. She was fighting something. In fact, I have never seen anyone fight so hard under hypnosis like that. It was as if she was afraid to tell us the answer. Charlie, why did she say you were the one hurting her?"

He shook his head. "I would never, I have never. This is her mother doing this. They forced her to say that."

"My son has never laid a hand on her in that way. Not even with all this going on," said Harper. "There's no way anyone could convince me he did."

"Or me," Ellen said, returning with the smelling salts. Sitting on the edge of the bed, she snapped one and held it a few inches from Alia's nose.

A few seconds later, Alia gave a jerk and opened her eyes.

"Hi there, baby girl. How are you feeling?" Ellen smiled down at her.

"What happened? Charlie, I didn't hurt you again, did I?"

"No, you gave Lawson a kick he won't soon forget about, though."

Alia looked over at the man that stood beside the bed, rubbing his chest.

"Do you remember anything?" asked Charlie.

Alia shook her head. "Just Lawson telling me to follow the watch. I'm sorry, Lawson, I don't remember any of it. Are you okay?"

"I'll be fine, don't worry about me, just get some rest. We need to talk," said Lawson to Harper. "And not here, not in front of her. Charlie, I want you to join us."

"Mom, will you stay with her?"

"Of course. Crystal honey, get us a wet rag, the poor girl is about drenched." Ellen lifted Alia's upper body and put her in her lap. "Go on, Charlie. I want to know what went on in here."

The men went out to the living room, shutting the door behind them.

"Are you alright?" Charlie asked Lawson

"Yeah, I'm going to be sore for a day or so. Your girl has a strong kick. Felt like I was bucked by a mule."

"She kicked you?" asked Harper.

"Well, no, I'm not sure that was her. At least not all of her. The hypnotist in me wants to tell you that someone, someone really good, has gotten to her. The thing is, with how she was fighting it, I've never heard of any kind of hypnosis that strong. Basically, a person can not be hypnotized into doing something they don't want to do or is against what they believe in. That's why it doesn't always work on everyone. I had my doubts about this from the start with everything you all said she has done."

"Then why did you put her through that?" said Charlie, angry.

"I needed to see how weak she was, how easily swayed she could be. She's not. That girl of yours is strong. She was definitely fighting."

"Fighting what?" asked Harper.

"Look, no one can have this strong of a hold on someone through hypnotism alone. If it is hypnotism, then there has to be something else involved here, some kind of drug or something."

"The Tox screen on her came back negative, more than once. And she has no needle marks anywhere I've looked," said Charlie.

"Well, that doesn't mean we rule anything out. Some drugs can go undetected to an average tox screen. And she could have ingested it somehow. It wouldn't have to necessarily be via a needle. I don't know of any off-hand that could do this. I'd have to do some research. The thing is, and something you need to prepare yourselves for, it's possible that there's another reason for her acting like this, a strong possibility."

"That she's crazy," said Charlie frowning.

"Well, we don't like to use that term professionally. But yes, it's possible she's had some kind of psychological break. The good news is if it is that, as I said, she's strong. She's trying to fight it."

"Which would maybe explain her more lucid moments where she seems fine?" asked Harper.

"Yes, exactly. Crystal gave me a little run down of Alia's childhood traumas and this thing with her mother. It's possible. Now I'm just making a guess here. I really need to have several sessions with her before I can know for sure. Still, it's possible the return of her mother triggered something. Maybe she felt she was free from this woman, then she returned, bringing it all up again."

"So why in the hell would she want to go have lunch with that bitch for almost two months."

"Charlie, son, calm down."

"No, dammit. They are doing something to her. She's not crazy….she can't be…." Charlie walked off then came back. "I would fucking know if she was…I would know. She's hurting. I can feel it, and she's scared. She was terrified in there. She kept saying someone was hurting her."

"Yes, and the only one she named was you," said Lawson accusingly.

Charlie got right up in Lawson's face. "I would never hurt her, dammit, never!"

Harper pulled Charlie by his shirt off of the man. "Just back off and cool down for a minute," he told him.

Charlie walked off again, his arms crossed, brushing his hand through his hair to the back of his neck.

"I'm not saying you would, or even did. Not intentionally anyway. We hurt people sometimes without even realizing it, in small ways. But I'm not even convinced it's that."

"Then what is it?" asked Harper. Because right now, it looks like we are back to square one. We don't know anything more than we did before."

"Oh, that's not true," said Lawson with a smile. "We know whatever it is, she's fighting it and fighting hard. That's why she is lying in there, exhausted and drenched. Charlie, you saw it, you saw how hard she was fighting."

"It's true," he nodded. "I swear it was like she was trying to tell us something, but something stopped her."

"I want to see her," said Lawson. " I know you have another doctor lined up, but I want to see her. Starting tomorrow if she's up for it. Tonight I pushed her to try and break this or give you some answers. I'd like to take my time with her, work with her, see if we can get her past this."

"No hypnosis," said Charlie. "I won't make her go through that again."

"Of course not, no, we don't want a repeat of that," he said, rubbing his sore chest. In the meantime, she can't be left alone. Whether they are doing something to her or not, she is compelled to go to them. Now hypnosis and any toxins they may have been able to slip her will wear off over time. But if she is given a chance to go back to them, she just might, making it harder for us to eliminate them."

"If you think they may be doing this, why have sessions with her?" asked Charlie. "No offense, but a cop being seen by a psychiatrist isn't usually viewed very well by the general public."

"Of course not, and I understand. We will be as discreet as we possibly can. But she's going to have trauma from all of this. Hell, she's already had a lifetime full of trauma if half of what Crystal told me is true. If she ever wants to be a cop again, she will have to work this all out one way or another."

"I want to know." said Harper, "Just what side are you leaning on in this? Honestly?"

"Honestly, I don't know. Right now, it's about fifty-fifty. For her sake, though, I hope they have done something, and it'll wear off soon. A mental break takes a lot longer to get over…and some never do."

When everyone left that night, Charlie helped Alia take a nice hot relaxing bath. She looked exhausted and as if she had aged years in just one day. She was also unusually quiet. She didn't cry, but once in a while, a tear would slip from her eye breaking his heart every time it did. He told her Lawson wanted to see her in the morning, and she agreed to go. After getting her into bed, he set the alarms and took a quick shower, afraid to leave her alone for long.

When he joined her, Alia went right into his open arms, laying her head on his chest. Usually, when she did that, she liked to play with the dark line of hair that went from his navel down to under his pajama pants. Tonight though, she just wrapped her arms around his chest like she was afraid of letting go.

He told her that Trish and Jacob had made bail and how her mother swore she wouldn't leave without her. It pained him to tell her, but they were not in the habit of keeping things from each other. When he did, she hugged him tighter, and he felt the wetness of a tear on his chest.

Charlie told her how much he loved her. How he loved her more and more with every passing day, this one being no exception. He promised her again that they would fix this one way or another.

Alia remained quiet, too afraid to even say she loved him, knowing if she uttered so much as one word, she would break down crying again. She didn't want him to see her constantly in tears. She wanted him to believe that she was strong like she heard Lawson say she was. But the truth was she had never felt weaker in her life.

She could feel it. Something inside her crawled around in her head like a bug whispering bad things to her. Telling her Charlie was going to hurt her, telling her no one was going to love her anymore, telling her she was still that lonely, scared little girl no matter how hard she tried to grow up. It filled her head up with lies, telling her she was no good, ugly, useless, stupid, and worst of all, unloved.

She knew the voice. It was one that she had heard her entire life. One she had hoped to have banished and replaced with all the good and beautiful things her sweet boy said to her every day. But she hadn't. It had burrowed back into her brain like the bug it was, reclaiming its old residence, making itself at home. And it was driving her insane.

When Charlie woke to a sound in the bedroom, it was still dark and the other side of the bed empty. "Shit." coming fully awake and tossing his blankets aside, he got up out of bed.

"Ssh." hissed Alia. "Get down, Charlie," she whispered intensely.

Instinctively Charlie ducked down. Alia was at their bedroom window that overlooked the parking lot. She was standing to the side of it peeking through the blinds, her own personal gun in her hand.

"What the hell are you doing," he whispered back.

"They're outside Charlie…out in the parking lot. I saw them looking through the window."

Charlie thought that had to have been some trick since they lived on the second floor. Slowly he approached the window and peered through the blinds. He scanned the parking lot but saw nothing. "Where I don't see anything?"

"Behind the cars, they're hiding behind, just come over here you can see better from this angle. But be careful. They saw me, and they know I'm watching."

Charlie dropped to all fours, crawled past the window, and stood next to Alia. He could feel her shaking slightly as waves of fear rippled out from her. "Show me."

"See there the car next to the white pickup truck."

"Yeah, the light blue Honda? Are they inside? I'm still not seeing anything."

"No, No, Charlie, look at the back bumper, just under it, there is a shadow."

He did, and sure enough, there was a rounded shadow just under the Honda's bumper. He watched it for several minutes, but the shadow never moved or wavered. He was beginning to have his doubts.

"What makes you think that it's someone out there?"

"I saw them, Charlie. I woke up, and there was this face in the window. I could just barely make it out through the blinds. I wasn't even sure until it moved and when it did, I ran to the window and saw him run behind the car. There was another one as well, but I didn't see where he got off too."

Charlie looked at the car again, and still no movement. No matter how still a person tries to be, they can never stay perfectly still. Someone crouched behind a vehicle would have to shift positions to remain that way. He looked down from the window, but there was no ladder, and unless it was Spider-man or the guy levitated, there's no way someone was looking in. Stepping back from the window, Charlie was once again aware of the gun she had in her hands. She was doing the right thing and pointing it down, but he saw with alarm that the safety was off.

"Hey, I'm up now. How about you give me the gun."

"What if they start shooting?" she asked, not taking her eyes off the parking lot.

"I'll have the gun."

"But I'm a better shot than you." she insisted.

He would typically smile at the little jab seeing how she always liked to bring that up. It was part of their usual back and forth banter he loved so much. But tonight, she wasn't joking.

"Alia, sweetheart, you're tired, you're shaking. Let me take over watch for a while. Give me the gun."

With a sigh and clicking on the safety, she handed it to him.

Taking it, Charlie unloaded the firearm and cleared the chamber.

"What are you doing? Charlie, they're going to kill us. You said you would stand watch."

"And I will, but I'm not going to stand here in a complex full of people in the middle of the night with a loaded gun. Not until I know for sure who is out there." *And you wouldn't do it either if you were in the right frame of mind.*

"But I saw them, Charlie, I saw the man at the window, and I saw them run off."

"Who, Alia? Who did you see."

She looked unsure. "I, I don't know, some man."

"Was it Jacob?"

"I don't' know Charlie, it was dark. The light was behind him," she said, growing frustrated.

"Okay, so let's say someone could peer in through our window on the second floor."

She started to protest, and he cut her off.

"Let's just say it is possible. If you didn't get a good look at them, then it could be anyone, right?"

She nodded.

"It could just be some perv or even some kid."

Alia looked more alarmed at that.

"And did you see a gun? Did they have a gun, Alia?"

"Well, no. I mean, I don't know. I didn't see. Charlie, why don't you believe me? I saw some guy at our window. You said she wouldn't stop Charlie. You said she said that." Alia was getting very upset. "What if she sent them here…what…what if they tried to hurt you to get me."

Charlie put the gun down on the nearby dresser and took Alia into his arms. "No one is going to hurt me. And no one is ever going to take you away from me." He let go and cupped her face in his hands. "I think you had a nightmare, and when you woke up, you thought you saw something. But no one is there, Alia. Come look out the window." He pulled up the blind, and she grabbed him back from the window.

"Charlie, no!"

"It's okay, come look, see the car. The shadow is still there."

She looked, and yes, it was still there and still perfectly still.

"Now look down, see how high up we are? There's no way anyone could have gotten up here to look in the window. They would have needed a ladder, a nice size one at that. Did they have a ladder when they ran off?"

Alia shook her head no, confused. Her head pounded, and she felt like she hadn't slept in days.

"It was a nightmare, Alia. The alarms are on, we are perfectly safe up here."

"But I know what I saw, Charlie…I know…" Looking out the window, she had doubts of her own now. Alia looked over at the gun on the dresser and was suddenly afraid. *What if she had shot someone…what if she had shot Charlie.* With that thought, Alia ran into the bathroom and vomited into the toilet so hard she thought her stomach was going to rip.

Charlie went to get a wet rag to clean her up and held back her hair.
When she was done, she shook all over and had trouble standing up.

Charlie picked her up for the second time that night and carried her to bed, sitting her down on the edge.
Looking over at the clock on his side of the bed, he saw that it was just past four in the morning. There was no way either of them was going back to sleep tonight. Charlie wrapped a blanket around her shoulders and told her he would be right back. At the window, he closed the blinds again. Then he got the gun off the dresser and put it in the open safe in the closet. He then returned to Alia at a loss for what to do. He sat next to her, taking her hand in his.

"It was just a nightmare. You used to have them all the time, remember?"

She did. When she and Charlie first started to spend nights together, she often woke up from them in the night. It wasn't very unusual for her to even before then. She'd often had terrible dreams, ones in which she was hurt or killed by her mother, others where she killed her mother. Most were just a nighttime continuation of the abuse she suffered during the day. Alia had grown used to them. After she and Charlie reunited, a lot of them were about him. The most terrifying ones involved him dying or just getting sick of her shit and leaving. But she hadn't had any real bad ones in a long time. After the academy, they faded away and seemed to go away entirely once Trish was out of their lives.

Wish she had just stayed out. Alia thought, then yelped in pain as a stabbing white light flashed across her vision.

"You okay? What's wrong."

"I don't know, I was thinking about Trish, and then I had this stabbing pain. It's gone now, but dammit, that hurt." Alia looked at Charlie pleadingly. "What's happening to me, Charlie? Why is this happening? We, we were so happy. Weren't we happy?"

Charlie left the bed and knelt down before her. "Yes, we were, and I still am."

But looking into his green eyes, she knew that wasn't true. "Not like you were. You're sad now, Charlie, I can see it in your eyes. And it's all my fault. Even your smile it's not the same anymore."

"What's happening to you isn't your fault. If anything, it's mine. It's my job to protect you, I promised you I would, but I let you go see her anyway. I was just trying to support you, but I should have made you stop." Charlie was startled to see her eyes suddenly become hard and cold.

"You should have made me?" she asked with contempt. "Charles, just who the hell do you think you are?"

Her sudden anger took him by surprise. "Alia, I just meant...."

"To hell with what you just meant, Charles. You don't own me, you don't control me, you have no right to keep me from seeing my mother." she pushed him away.

Charlie shot up to his feet, looking down at her bewildered. This wasn't like her. She never spoke to him like this. Hell, he couldn't even remember the last time she was ever really upset with him. They could read each other better than any book. But now, he couldn't understand where this anger at him was coming from when she seemed so afraid for him just a moment ago.

"What the hell, Alia?" he asked, spreading his arms. He knew this was not all her, but he fed off her anger and had difficulty keeping from being angry himself.

"That's your whole problem, Charlie," she said, standing up now too. "You think you have the right to control me just because you rescued me from my sad, pathetic life, but you don't. Maybe I went to my mother because I needed something from her you couldn't give me," she shouted.

Feeding off her energy more, Charlie struck back with more anger. "What's that, huh? A slap in the face? An ashtray thrown at your head? Or maybe you want me to fill your head with all that bullshit about how ugly and stupid you are like she did."

Tears filled Alia's eyes, but she stood her ground before him. "At least that would be the truth. At least she was honest with me. Sometimes you have to be told like it is, Charles."

It was what she said that snapped him out of his anger. "What did you just say?"

"I said she tells it like it is. Not the bullshit lies about loving me as you and your family does."

That wasn't it, not exactly, but it was close enough. At that moment, Charlie was convinced that she was being manipulated by her mother. That telling it like it is crap was one of Trish's favorite sayings. Alia wouldn't even utter the same thing. She had hated Trish's mother-isms as she called them and refused to repeat them.

She's been programmed to say this. The trigger was talking about keeping her from seeing her mother. Now he wondered what she was thinking before the pain in her head.

Charlie backed up, needing to think for a minute what to do next because he was positive this whole scene was somehow being orchestrated. Trish wanted them to fight, she knew they fed off each other's energy, and a fight between them would only get uglier as it went on. It was like with her calling Trish her mother, Alia hadn't done that in years, not until Trish came back. Charlie took a few deep breaths knowing he was the only one that was able to de-escalate this situation.

"You're right," he said. "I don't have any right to try to control you or keep you from seeing…your mother." he saw her visibly flinch, and some of the anger went out of her eyes. "I love you, Alia. I'm not here to hurt you. I'm sorry." The apology was crucial because Trish never did that, not even when she was wrong. He projected as much love towards her as he possibly could. It was easy now that he calmed because the actual truth, the one that he was sure Trish was afraid of, was that he loved her more than life itself. Always had. No longer in a defensive posture, he reached his hand out for hers. "I love you, sweet girl. Come back to me, please."

And like that, the anger melted from her eyes and face. She reached out her smaller hand and let him take it into his. He then pulled her into his arms. "I love you more," she said in tears.

"More and more all the time," he said back, hugging her like their lives depended on it, and it just may have.

Charlie made them some breakfast that morning, of which she ate very little of. When it was time, they went to Lawson's house, where he dropped Alia off. Lawson wanted to see her alone for at least the first few sessions. Charlie didn't like leaving her there and wasn't even sure if he trusted Lawson yet. However, there were a few things he wanted to do while she was occupied, so he agreed to come back in a few hours.

Lawson worked out of his home, which he had worked on the plans of himself. The bottom floor was for his practice. Along with an office and reception area, there were several rooms he had explicitly designed to be of warmth and comfort to his patients. There was a small library with a fireplace and large windows looking out on the back yard and acres of trees. That room was best used by his clients in the winter when a roaring fire was going, and the yard was filled with snow.

A more traditional therapy room was complete with a couch for his more practical patients. He had a colorful room full of toys and fun gadgets for his younger patients. One room was full of bean bag chairs, buddha statues, incense, and plants everywhere for those who wanted to relax during their sessions. The last was a sunroom.

The home's second floor was Lawson's own private rooms, including kitchen and living areas. The stairs to that area were concealed behind locked doors that blended so well into the surrounding hall most people didn't notice it.

For their first session, Lawson allowed Alia to explore the bottom floor and pick a room she wanted to talk to him in. He found this to be very revealing of a person's character even before talking to them.

Alia chose the sunroom even after seeing the library. With all the books she had on the shelves in her apartment, Lawson was surprised that she passed that room up. Alia chose the sunroom with its floor-to-ceiling windows overlooking the large backyard with the mountains as a backdrop, simply because she could see outside and if anyone was lurking about. She, of course, didn't tell Lawson that at the risk of sounding paranoid.

Alia settled in the room on a large sofa with warm fuzzy blankets folded on the back and pillows on each end. Lawson spent some time getting background information on Alia. Mostly about her home life with her mother and her father's death. At first, she didn't want to say much and didn't want to talk about her mother at all. When talking about her father, Alia became more animated. He could tell that she had loved him very much, and his death was a huge pivotal point in her life. The only good thing that came of it was moving back to Union county and nearer the town of Bedford. Nearer to Charlie.

When Lawson insisted they talk about her mother, Alia became distant and moody. "Alia, if we are going with the assumption that Trish is behind what has been going on with you lately, then it would be helpful to me if I could better understand your relationship with her."

"There's nothing to understand. She wasn't the best mom in the world, but she tried." Alia said, hearing the words but their meaning not really registering to her.

"It's my understanding that it was worse than that, that she was very abusive. Crystal said your mother was also very controlling."

Alia started to say something, then put her hand to her head and groaned.

"You alright?"

"Crystal…she…she doesn't get it. My mom had to be tough. I was…she wasn't going to let me rule the roost. She had to keep me in line." If Charlie had been there, he would have recognized another of the mom-isms she hated so much. "Look, can we not do this right now?" Her head pounded, and something about what she was saying didn't

609

sound right to her, but the more Alia tried to think about it, the more her head hurt.

"Do what, Alia? The whole point of you coming here was to find out why your mother would have such a hold on you that no matter what exactly is going on, she is the cause of it."

"The point of coming here was to prove that I'm not crazy. Because Charlie can't face the idea that I may not be happy in the perfect little life he forced me into," she said with a hint of icy contempt.

"Forced you into?"

"Not just him, all of them. They pushed me into walking out on my mother when she needed me the most. And now she is back, and she wants me, and they are not happy about that." *no, that's wrong,* she thought and was rewarded with yet another sharp stab of pain in her head.

Lawson sat back, watching her, and thought for a moment. Leaning forward again, he continued. "Alia, I want to know why you're lying to me. And don't look so surprised I'm a psychologist, after all. It's part of the job."

Just then, her facial expression changed. A darkness came into her eyes, turning the blue into that of approaching dark storm clouds. "Don't call me a liar." she said with a sneer."

"Then stop lying and mucking around, and I won't have to. Remember, I'm here to help. I reckon you want help, Alia. I know you're fighting whatever is happening to you. Now I insist you tell me the truth about your mother." For a moment, the stormy color of her eyes lightened. Lawson took that opportunity to push further. "Tell me about the incident with the ashtray, you know, before you graduated."

Alia sat back, put one leg over the other at the knee, and bounced her foot up and down. Once again, her face became cold and hard.

Lawson hadn't known Trish, so he didn't recognize this position of irritation she often got into.

"There was no incident, I tossed it to the stupid girl, and she missed catching it." Alia held her right hand up, almost like she was holding something in it.

To Lawson, it looked as though she held on to a ciggy though nothing was there. That wasn't near as unnerving as what she had said. "What did you just say?"

Alia visibly twitched, then put her hand down and stopped bouncing her foot. "I said my mother tossed the ashtray at me, and I missed it. It hit my eye and caused a little bruise."

The transformation Alia went through before him was both fascinating and frightening. Wanting to see what would happen, Lawson switched tactics. "Tell me about the night in the motel with Charlie." What he saw was yet another amazing transformation. Alia's face softened, her eyes now shining bright sparkling blue had almost a dreamy quality to them. Best of all, she smiled radiantly for the first time during the session.

"We didn't do much, just talked. It was the first time we ever had time to just sit and talk. It was when I realized.." she flushed a little. "That I was in love with him. Then when the tornado came, he held me so tight, I have never been so scared and felt so safe at the same time before."

"Did anything happen that night between the two of you?"

Flushing some more, she looked away. Alia had pulled her legs up and sat with them crossed in front of her. The impression she gave was of a younger girl. "No, Charlie was a complete gentleman. I was kind of disappointed about that. I thought maybe he didn't like me like I did him. Then later, when I had a nightmare, oh it was horrible, but he held me the rest of the night."

Lawson had wanted her to leave here on a good note, but the session was almost over, and he wanted to see if he could get her to change again. It was apparent the trigger was her mother, more accurately perhaps defending her mother's character. He thought back to the conversation he had with Crystal to develop a way to lead her back quickly. Or maybe even elicit another reaction.

"Tell me," he said. "If Charlie is such a good guy, why does Trish say such horrible things about him?"

"Because she's a jealous bit...." Before she could finish, Alia screamed in pain, grabbing her head and falling to the floor."

Lawson got up to go to her, but before he could, the door to the sunroom burst open, and Charlie ran in. Lawson's assistant must have let him in to pick her up, and he heard her holler out in pain.

At her side, Charlie looked up at him accusingly. "What did you do to her?"

"Nothing, I tried to trigger a response, but I never thought she would react like this."

"Alia, are you alright? Come on, can you sit up?" He could get her to sit up, but she still held onto her head tightly. "What's wrong, Alia? What happened?"

"I don't know....my head hurts like mad. Take me home, Charlie. I think I've had enough for today."

Charlie looked up at Lawson, and he nodded. He helped her out to his patrol car out front then turned to Lawson, who had followed them out. "What the hell went on in there?"

Lawson pulled Charlie by the arm away from the squad car. "I'm not altogether sure. If I didn't know better, I would say she had some kind of split personality disorder, but I think it's more complicated than that. And I have other news as well. Last night, I researched drugs that can help a person become more susceptible to a hypnotic state and found something alarming. A few drugs can do what I'm suggesting, but one stands out in particular for its potency. And it wouldn't show up on a tox screen."

"So what, we wait a few days and let it get out of her system, and she's fine."

"No, unfortunately, if that is the drug they are using on her and she's been given it long enough, she could still be dodgy for some time. I reckon this kind of thing builds up in the system over time. When first used, it lasts only a few hours, at most a day or so. As it's used, it lasts longer and longer. Even then, its effects depend on the person's taking its suggestibility. Which, and I know I'm starting to sound like a broken record, but it would explain her fighting so hard. Part of her knows what she is saying and doing is wrong but whoever is planting these seeds in her head has one big damn green thumb."

"So how would they have gotten this stuff, and how did they give it to her."

"Well, its main component is natural, a root that grows freely in the desert. Its synthetic component can be found in a lot of over-the-counter medicines. Because of the case studies' side effects, it's not legally marketed, but it can be found on the black market and instructions on how to make it on the dark web."

"Wait, what kind of side effects are we talking about?"

"In the studies, those subjects it was tested on became increasingly violent and paranoid."

Charlie ran a hand over his mouth and through his hair. "So you're telling me this could get worse?"

"No, not necessarily. It all depends on how much she got for how long. This drug is dissolvable and virtually tasteless in certain things that are acidic like orange juice, coffee or tea, for example."

Charlie stopped and stared at the man, alarmed. "Tea? Could it have just been added in or what…"

"It's broken down into liquid form and can be added very easily."

"Shit, Trish, she would meet Alia in town once a week at a cafe she likes. Alia always orders the raspberry tea there." Charlie started to pace, aggravated. "They were meeting there for weeks. She's been drugging Alia for weeks. When we found her the other day, there was a cooler, and on top of it was a bottle of tea. I didn't think anything of it at the time. And when they searched Jacob's camper, they found some in the fridge as well. Damn it. We had them…we had the evidence right there."

"Most likely wouldn't have done any good. The way the natural components break down, it goes virtually undetected, and the synthetic stuff is nothing stronger than what you would find in cough and cold medicines."

"So, what do we do?"

"It's a waiting game, I'm afraid. We have no way of knowing how much has built up in her system. Or if she was ever drugged at all, though I reckon she was. Alia could be fine in a few days…or it could take months."

"Months? We don't have months. I woke up this morning to her with her gun in her hand, loaded and the safety off, saying someone was looking in on us, on the second floor."

"That would be paranoia. Now I still want to see her. There are techniques I can use that may help her channel this thing better. Make her less of a danger to others and herself?"

"Herself?"

"Yes, several of the test subjects either tried or managed to kill themselves. Now don't freak out, they were apes. No human trials were ever done. The human mind is much more complex and resilient. It can survive things better than weaker-minded species."

Charlie looked at this man and shook his head. "What about people whose minds are already well damaged? Alia is strong because she has had to be, but she's been hurt badly for a very long time. I know none of that has left her. She's gotten better, sure, but she still has that voice in the back of her mind that won't let her forget about her past."

"That's why you must keep bringing her here. And that no matter what, you stand by her and support her through this. She's fighting, that's the good thing, but she's exhausted, and I honestly don't know how much more fight she has in her."

"I need to get her home. I need to think about all of this."

"Understandable. Bring her back on Monday, same time. I'd like to get to her when she's still fresh into the day."

Charlie started to walk off to the patrol car.

"Oh and Charlie, whatever you do, don't bring up her mother. If she brings her up, fine, but don't say anything bad about her whatever you do. And don't call her a liar. She doesn't seem to like that."

"That's her mother's hang-up. I remember that from when we were kids."

"Yeah, well, her mother is a big trigger. And get rid of the guns."

Charlie nodded and left.

Lawson watched them go and wondered if letting them leave was a mistake.

Chapter 32
Agitated

Alia was quiet the whole way home, only speaking to complain of a headache. At the apartment, Charlie gave her some acetaminophen and told her to go lay down. When she asked for some tea, he lied and said they didn't have any. Feeling paranoid himself, Charlie went through their cabinets and got rid of every bag of tea they had. Then he called his father and told him everything Lawson said. Ellen wanted to come over and sit with Alia that afternoon while Charlie went back to work, but he told her Crystal was coming over anyway. Charlie didn't admit that he was worried about her being there alone with Alia.

When Charlie went to check in on her, she had fallen asleep. Charlie removed their guns from their safe as quietly as he could be. He then took them downstairs to put in the lockbox of his patrol car along with his service weapon. While he was down there, Charlie went over to the blue Honda to see what made the rounded shape they saw from the window. There was nothing. In the light of the sun, the shade spot was gone.

Back inside, he kicked off his boots and slipped into bed behind her, wrapping an arm over her and holding her hand. She murmured in her sleep, but he couldn't understand what she was saying. Shortly before his lunch break was over, Charlie slipped back off the bed and went to the living room, closing the bedroom door. A few minutes later, he saw Crystal arrive, still driving that old Buick.

Once she was inside, he explained the latest to her, giving Crystal the same warnings as Lawson gave him. "And feel free to leave the apartment but don't let her go anywhere alone. We have no idea how long this stuff will stay in her system or just what they may have tried to get her to do."

"So you really think this is all being done to her? That she's being controlled somehow?"

Charlie sighed, "Yes, and as horrible as it sounds, it's still better than the alternative."

"Well, I don't think for a minute that she's crazy. I mean, not like really crazy. Alia's always had anxiety and issues coping with things in her life. Since I have known her anyway, we all do in a way. And these past few years since the two of you have gotten together, she's been much better. It's like she liked living, really liked living for the first time." Crystal went to Charlie and laid a hand on his chest. "And you, Charlie, are the main reason for that. You have meant the world to her."

Charlie shook his head a little. "Yet I feel like I'm failing her."

Just then, Alia opened the bedroom door and stood in the doorway.

Charlie went over and kissed her on the cheek. "Feeling better?"

Alia nodded but frowned. "What's she doing here?"

She said it low, but he had a feeling Crystal still heard her. "Well, she's your best friend Alia, she came to spend some time with you. I've got to get back to work." he looked at her, and her eyes begged him to stay. "I've got to go in, I'm sorry. The other guys have been pulling extra shifts to cover both mine and yours."

"And you need a break from me," she said, casting her eyes down from his.

"Stop that. You know that's not true."

"I don't need a babysitter. Least of all her," said Alia sounding strangely contemptuous.

The look on her face when she said that startled him. "It's just for a few hours. And you know you shouldn't be left alone."

"You're afraid I'll run off again? Go see her?"

"Yes, I am. Lawson thinks you were drugged, that she may have drugged your tea when the two of you would meet up. The drug he suspects can make you more prone to suggestions, and it may be how they lured you out of the house and back to them before. So I'm sorry, but we can't take any chances."

"Oh, come on, Charlie, I'm a cop. I think I would notice someone spiking my drink. And Lawson is a hack. She found him at one of her witch festivals, for Pete's sake."

"Which was exactly what you suggested we do. Look, we can talk about this tonight when I get home. For now, be nice, she's your friend, and she's worried about you. Don't take this out on her." Charlie kissed her again, said goodbye to them both, and left.

Crystal, who had heard most of the conversation, tried to approach her friend for their usual hug, but Alia backed off.

"Sorry, I'm not in the mood right now. I'm not a child. I don't need to be coddled."

"Well, of course, you don't. I am just here to hang out like we usually do. So what do you want to do?"

Sitting down on the couch, they discussed several options, all of which Alia snubbed her nose at. She just didn't feel like doing much of anything. Well, that wasn't true. She wanted to go to work, needed to. She was already getting sick and tired of being sick and tired. Alia let Crystal talk her into watching Harry Potter because that was one thing they both had loved mutually. They even took tests before to see what house they were in. Alia was a Gryffindor, no surprise to Crystal, and Crystal was a Hufflepuff. Both had a collection of wands and figures from their favorite characters. Binge-watching all the movies was a favorite pastime of theirs.

However, the more the movie went on, the more annoyed Alia got. The friendship between the three kids that reminded her of her Crystal and Ethan set her on edge. What made it worse was Crystal's usual childlike delight in virtually all aspects of the movie. As usual, she pointed out her favorite parts, spoke most of the lines and shared whatever trivia information she knew of the film. And usually, Alia loved all of that, even doing her part saying different lines as well. However, that day was different. About halfway through, Alia had about enough.

"Alright, that's it. I can't take this shit anymore." grabbing the remote, she turned off the TV, got up, and headed for the kitchen.

"What's wrong? You love this part."

In the kitchen, Alia looked through cabinet after cabinet. "I don't love this part, you love this part. Hell, you love all the parts. Why do we have to see this damn movie all the time?" she said, still searching cabinets.

Crystal joined her in the kitchen. "What are you looking for? I'll help."

"Coffee. Charlie usually keeps a jar of instant coffee somewhere. Ah, bingo." She cracked open the jar and took a big whiff.

"Since when do you do the bean?" asked Crystal.

Laughing, Alia shook her head. "You know Crystal, some people grow up and change. Not everyone is stuck in their childhood." She got a mug out of the cabinet, filled it with water, and set it in the microwave to heat up.

"What's that supposed to mean?" Crystal asked, looking hurt.

"It means what it means, Alia." she slipped but didn't notice.

Crystal not only noticed the slip but recognized the mom-ism as well.

"You need to get out of this fantasy world you insist on living in. The spells, and charms, and believing you are a witch. Face it, Crystal. There is no magic, fairy tales are bullshit, and your letter from Hogwarts is never going to come." Alia made her coffee, heavy on the cream and way more sugar than Crystal had ever seen her use. "You need to grow the hell up." she sat snidely, leaving the kitchen.

"Why are you doing this?" asked Crystal, almost in tears. It was hard for her to remember that Alia may not be in control of herself, mostly because she seemed so aware of what she was saying. "Charlie said the session went bad today, but it's not my fault."

"Oh really?" she snorted. "Uh, I do believe you're the one that brought that flake Lawson here. And I find it funny how he seemed to know so much about me. What goes on in the home stays in the home, you know that."

Crystal recognized yet another mom-ism. Charlie tried to warn her that her behavior was all over the place but seeing it was different. As with most good friendships, Crystal and Alia had their bad times. Usually impatience on Alia's side or lack of communication on Crystals. But never had Alia spoken to her with such venom in her voice before.

"And the fucking crystals and cleansing, that's a joke. They didn't work now, did they, Crystal. I nearly fucking killed Charlie after you did your stupid shit," Alia spat.

"Okay, Alia, I know you're not feeling like yourself, but you need to stop. You don't mean what you're saying; I know you don't. So maybe you should just, I don't know, go take another nap or something."

The two stood in the living room, Alia sipping on her coffee and Crystal trying to keep calm. "You would like that, wouldn't you? So you could snoop around and tell more lies about me. Why don't you just go home, Crystal? Go back to the perfect little fantasy world in that shitty hole of a house you live in and leave me the fuck alone."

"Because I can't," said Crystal, exasperated.

"Why, because you're afraid I might wander off again. I am free, white, and well over twenty-one. I can take care of myself."

There it was again. The fact that Alia wasn't even twenty-one yet was something anyone could have picked up on. It was like she was channeling Trish. And Trish hated

Crystal almost as much as Charlie. If this was the way she was going to be right now, Crystal had a feeling there was nothing she could do to stop her. She walked to the glass door to the patio, opened it then stopped.

"I can't leave because I love you, Alia. But I won't let you do this to me either. I'll be out here until you're more like yourself and ready to apologize." Crystal went out on the porch, where she spent the rest of her time until Charlie came home. She watched videos on her phone and looked at pictures of her and Alia together during happier times. She was doing her best to remember that this wasn't Alia, not her Alia, but it only made her sadder. At the same time, she kept an eye on the living room, making sure Alia didn't try to leave.

After looking out at Crystal for a few minutes, Alia had gone off to her room, slamming the door.

When Charlie arrived, Crystal practically knocked him over, passing him in the doorway.

Charlie looked after her, calling for her to stop. He looked inside to see Alia standing in the bedroom doorway with a strange look on her face. "Just, just give me a second," he told her, then shutting the door, he raced after Crystal.

Upstairs, Alia watched through the patio door. Crystal, visibly upset but not crying, said something to Charlie. They talked for a little while, glancing up at the apartment a few times as they did. Charlie nodded, then hugged Crystal. Watching this, a fire burned inside of Alia. She returned to the bedroom and was there when Charlie came back in.

He didn't say anything, just looked at her, his brow furrowed.

Alia stood before him, arms crossed one up, her hand like she was holding something. It reminded him of when he had seen Trish mad with a cigarette in her hand. "So how long, Charles? How long have you been fucking her behind my back."

Charlie was so floored by what she said he almost laughed. "You're kidding me, right?"

"I saw you out there, Charles, so don't lie to me. I saw the way you hugged her."

Charlie shook his head, having a hard time believing she was actually accusing him of cheating on her. "She was upset. She told me what you said to her today. That's your best friend out there. She's having a little bit of trouble dealing with what's going on with you."

"So you fucked her?"

"Damn it, Alia, no, I hugged her, you saw that. It's not like I've never done it before. You know Crystal is like a little sister to me. She was long before I introduced the two of you. Look, you're not thinking clearly. I told you they drugged you. They're making you behave like this. They're making you think things that are not real."

"Or maybe I'm seeing things the right way for a change. Maybe it's you that have been drugging me. You and your parents because they were determined to take away what was never theirs. Is that why the tea is all gone? Is that how you've been doing it? Huh, well is it?" she demanded.

Charlie wasn't angry. He couldn't be, not at her. He was upset and hurt even though he knew in his heart this wasn't her. He wanted to go to her, to hold her until this was all over, but he knew in her current state, she wouldn't have him. "You know I would never hurt you. Especially not like that." he looked up at her, but the furry in her eyes was still there, and he couldn't bear to look at them. "I'm going to take a shower." he left her standing there looking after him with a fire he could feel. In the shower, the hot water scalding his skin, he cried out his frustration.

In the bedroom, the fury that had so engulfed her all day was slowly replaced with a feeling of painful deep sorrow. Alia looked at the cup of coffee in her hands with disgust and went to the kitchen, where she tossed the mess. Back in the bedroom, she hung at the bathroom door, feeling Charlie's pain as it also became hers. She wanted to go to him but was afraid he wouldn't have her and that rejection would crush her.

Instead, she got on her phone and ordered some of his favorite Chinese delivery for dinner. In the kitchen, she got out a bottle of wine and two glasses. Alia didn't care much for wine or alcohol at all, and the thought of drinking it after the other night made her feel ill. But Charlie, a romantic like her, loved candlelight dinners and sipping on glasses of wine. So she set their little kitchen table up and lowered the lights, then sat and waited for him to come out, wiping a tear from her cheeks from time to time.

When he got out of the bathroom, having put on sweats and a t-shirt, Charlie became alarmed at first not seeing her in the bedroom. After the start, he realized she was still close and found her in the kitchen, table set, candles burning, and wine waiting for him. Looking at it, he wished for a moment it was a nice shot of whiskey instead.

"Come on, sit down, Charlie, I promise I won't bite," she begged him with eyes he knew of as her own.

Charlie sat down and took her hand when she extended it across the table.

"How are you still here? Why are you putting up with all of this?"

Charlie leaned forward onto his elbows. "You know why."

"What I said was awful.."

"Was not you." he interrupted her.

"Still, I hurt you. You know I can tell."

"It'll heal. And no, you didn't. I'm hurting for you, Alia, not because of you."

"That's not entirely true, and you know it. You may believe the words are not from me, but I know hearing it from me hurts you."

"It does hurt. But I know my sweet girl is still there, and when this is all over, I'll have you back again. That's all that matters. Everybody goes through struggles in their lives. We will get through this."

"I'm tired of struggling. Haven't I been through enough already," she asked, then mentally kicked herself for sounding like she was whining.

"Maybe this isn't your struggle. Maybe this is mine. You've said it before I've had a pretty easy life. I've never had to work very hard to get what I wanted. Maybe this is what I have to go through, so I'll never doubt how much you mean to me and how much I love you. And if carrying you through hell is what it's going to take for me to be with you forever, I would do it a hundred times over again no matter how much it hurts." Charlie reached across the table and kissed her gently on the lips.

As he went to sit back down, she grabbed the back of his neck, keeping his lips close to hers. "Don't give up on me, Charlie."

He cupped her face in his free hand. "I never will," he said, kissing her gently. They spent the evening picking at their food, trying to talk and capture the thing that flowed so easily between them both. Then they went to be early exhausted from the day. Alia allowed Charlie to hold her, which he felt he needed to do so desperately. He was reminded once again of their night in the motel, where he promised he would never let her go. Holding her tight, he promised again as the both of them fell into a restless night's sleep.

Chapter 33
Bring Her Home

In the very early hours of the morning, Charlie was awakened to Alia straddling over him with one hand over his mouth and the finger of her other hand over her lips. Slowly she removed the hand on his mouth. "There's someone in the living room," she whispered.

Charlie sat up with a start, and she shushed him again. He looked over at the bedroom door, which was ajar, and tried to see or hear anything. It occurred to him that he couldn't remember if they set the alarms before going to bed. Charlie was about to get up when he heard a noise coming from the other room. Pausing, he tried to listen, and sure enough, there was a shuffling sound.

Alia got out of his way so he could get up and followed him to the door, where Charlie peeped through the crack. "Where are our guns? I checked the safe, and they're gone."

Mentally kicking himself in the ass, Charlie told her they were in the safe at Dad's house.

Alia smacked him on the arm. "Damn it, Charlie, I know you were worried about me, but now we're defenseless."

Pulling her over to the bed, Charlie gave her his phone. "I'm going out there. If anything goes wrong, I want you to call Dad."

"No, Charlie, you're not going out there without a weapon. What if the guy is armed? This is stupid. Just call the Sheriff's office and tell dispatch to get their asses out here."

"Not yet, and I have a weapon." Charlie went to the closet and got out a baseball bat he used for the Sheriff's department's charity games.

"No." she tried telling him but watched in horror as Charlie went out through the door anyway. A minute later, that seemed to be forever, he called from the living room.

"It's okay. I found the intruder."

Alia got up from where she had sat on the other side of the bed.

Charlie walked in with their cat in his arms. "Somebody is in a playful mood this morning," he smiled, petting the cat. He tried giving the cat to her, but Alia flinched away from it. "What's wrong? It's just Bella."

"No, no, no, no, Charlie, I saw someone out there. I saw them pass the door, and it wasn't any damn cat."

"Okay, come on, I'll show you." Charlie put the cat down on the bed and took Alia by the hand. She tried to pull back, but he held on to her tighter. "You need to see that there's no one out there, Alia. Come on, I wouldn't let anyone hurt you, you know that."

Alia let herself be led into the other room. There was just enough light from the lampposts outside that they could make out the living room rather well. He showed her the front closet, the kitchen, and the laundry room. No one was there, of course. Then he showed her that the alarm had indeed been set.

"There's no one here."

"They left then. They heard us get up and left."

"The alarm would have gone off."

"Then it's malfunctioning."

Charlie went over to the front door and opened it. The alarm announced the front door opened and started to beep. Before the real and deafening alarm kicked in, he put in the code to reset it.

Turning back to her, Charlie said, "See, there's no way anyone was in here."

"I know what I saw, Charles," she said with a touch of anger in her voice.

"And I know you believe that. Just like you did the other night. But no one is here."

"You're making fun of me," she said, putting her hands on her hips.

"Alia, no, I'm not. I'm trying to assure you that we are safe. That's it. Now come back to bed, let's get some more sleep."

"What about the patio? They could have gone out there. They could be in the storage closet." she insisted.

"Let's see then." Charlie opened the blinds to nothing on the porch but their two chairs, a table, and covered electric grill. He even went out and checked the storage closet. Not that with the freezer and bikes in there, there was enough room for a person. When he came back, Alia shook her head in confusion, and he pulled her into his arms.

"I know what I saw, Charlie."

"It's the drug, Alia. Lawson warned me that things might worsen before it starts to wear off. And that includes hallucinations."

"So nothing I see can be trusted?" She pulled back from him a little. "Then how do I know this is real? How do I know any of this is real? What if it's all wrong? What if it's all a lie?" she asked, sounding on the verge of hysterics.

Charlie took her face in his hands. "Hey, now hey, it's going to be alright. This is real. I am real. Look into my eyes and tell me what you think."

"I think I'm scared, Charlie. I feel like I'm losing it. And it's not just seeing things. I hear things, too, like whispers in my head. I don't even know what they are saying most of the time, but they scare the hell out of me."

Charlie looked back into her eyes and saw how afraid she was. She hadn't even looked this scared when she had gotten shot. Charlie took Alia into his arms with a heavy sigh as if that alone was all he needed to do to protect her. "I know you're scared, sweet girl, but I promise you I will not let anyone hurt you. And I won't let you hurt anyone else either. It's why I took the guns to Dad's until we can work this whole thing out. Until this mess is out of your system, we just need to be patient and vigilant. And we can do that, right?"

Alia nodded even though she had never been very patient.

Still, he couldn't get her to go back to bed, so Charlie made breakfast instead while she sat on the couch with the baseball bat and looked out the patio door. He tried getting her to eat, but all she would do was pick at her toast and jump at every least little sound the neighbors around them made as they woke up and went about their everyday lives.

"Why don't we go somewhere? How about a hike in the woods? That always makes you feel better," he suggested.

"Leave the apartment?" she asked, looking suddenly terrified. "No, no, that's, that's not a good idea. We need our guns back, that's what we need, Charlie. We need to be able to defend ourselves when they come back."

He put his fork down and sighed heavily. "Who comes back? We already established there was no one here."

Alia scrunched her forehead and looked confused. "This morning, Charlie remember, there was someone here this morning."

"No, that was the cat. That was Bella in here playing around."

Alia looked off into the air like she was thinking. "Oh yeah, okay." she looked at him and offered a weary smile. "Maybe we should have some lunch, I'm hungry. Lunch would make me think more clearly."

Charlie pointed down at her plate. "We're still having breakfast. You haven't touched a thing on your plate."

Alia looked down at her plate and smiled. "Oh, that was fast. Thanks, Charlie." she smiled. Still, she only poked her fork around her already mashed-up eggs.

Charlie watched with growing concern replaying the odd scene over in his head. Alia had her one hand on the table, and she flinched back when he tried to reach for it.

"Don't touch me," she said, sounding more scared than angry. "Just…just please don't touch me…I…please don't." she shuddered. Alia then put her hands up by her head and her feet up on the chair, making herself as small as possible.

"Okay, hey, it's okay, Alia. I won't touch you." Charlie held up his own hand to show her he was backing off.

"Shouldn't you be going to work?" she asked, putting her hands down but not her feet.

"It's Sunday. I'm not working today. Do you want me to leave?"

Her eyes went wide, and she sat up. "No…no…don't leave me…you said you wouldn't leave me…they'll get me if you leave Charlie….they'll come back. The people from this morning will come back and hurt me if you leave." she stammered hysterically with fresh tears in her eyes.

Charlie got up to go to her, then hesitated, not wanting to touch her and scare her more than she already was. Instead, he went to his knees in front of her. "Alia, no one is coming here to hurt you. I won't ever let anyone hurt you," he said, not thinking he could ever be wrong about that.

Alia looked down at Charlie with a puzzled expression, then around her like she didn't know where she was. "What are you doing here, Charlie? If my mom comes home and sees you here, she'll kill us both."

Charlie's heart sank, and for the first time, he wondered if he was going to be able to deal with this on his own.

Someone in one of the other apartments slammed a door, startling Alia so much she flew up out of the chair. "She's here…she's here…She's going to kill me," she said, backing up and staring off into nothing. Alia was so terrified that she shook, and Charlie had to fight the fear that was now invading him.

Getting up, he went to her, forcing her to look into his eyes. "Alia, look at me…there's no one here," he said, trying to talk as calmly as possible.

Alia looked into those amazing green eyes and melted into his arms. "Charlie, what the hell is happening to me? Make it stop, Charlie. I don't feel like I'm in control anymore. I can't keep my thoughts in order…I'm scared…I'm so very scared."

"I know, I know, sweet girl. I am too." Picking her up, he sat with her on the couch, kissing and caressing her hair. Alia sobbed for a while, then blessedly fell asleep in his arms. Charlie laid her down on the couch, not wanting to risk waking her by taking her to bed. He pulled a blanket off of the back, draped it over her, then sat there on the floor next to her, working through his own pain. At a loss of what else to do, he called his parents. Talking to them in the bedroom so Alia would sleep, he told them about this morning.

"I'm afraid for her, Mom. And I don't know what to do. I don't think I can do this alone anymore. I feel her pain and fear too much. I'm afraid she's going to drag me down with her, and I won't be there to protect her." Admitting this hurt his heart, but it was the truth. Her emotional roller coaster was draining him, and the last thing he wanted was to fail her when she needed him the most.

"Your father and I have been talking about just that," said Ellen. "And we both agree you should bring her here. This is her home, Charlie. The first real home she ever had. She's always felt better being here. We have your room cleaned out and put the guest room mattress in there. Bring her home Charlie, bring my baby girl home."

While Alia still slept, Charlie packed up their things, put the cat in its carrier, and put everything except Bella out into his truck. Back inside, he woke her up, kissing her forehead and stroking her hair. She was alarmed at first when he said he was taking her home, then calmed when he said his parents' house. She seemed to like the idea though she wasn't thrilled about going outside to get to the truck. The whole way down the stairs and the sidewalk, she clung to him, terrified. Charlie hated seeing his usually brave and beautiful girl acting like that. He put the cat carrier in the middle of the seat then helped her get in. He noticed once again that she had been losing a lot of weight. Good thing they were going to the home of the best cook ever. Mom would fatten her up again.

The whole drive over to the house, Alia peered out through the hoodie she insisted on wearing, jumping at every least little thing. Those that recognized them enough to smile and wave were met instead with scorn and suspicion by her. When they pulled into the drive only a few minutes later, she let out an audible sigh of relief. There was a bit of a smile on her face, and it took some of the weight off Charlie's heart.

Ellen met them at the door, and Alia ran into her arms, crying, laughing, and smiling all at the same time.

Watching them, Charlie was confident this had been a good choice. The apartment was okay, but this was a house of love. And in it were the people that took in a tiny baby that no one else wanted and loved her like their own.

Seeing Charlie watching them with tears in his own eyes, Ellen waved him over and pulled him into their hug.

"This was the right thing, Charlie. This is where she belongs. We'll get her through this. All of us will."

"There's my girl." Said Harper in his booming voice as he came to the door.

Alia let go of Ellen and went willingly into his big meaty arms. "I'm so sorry for what I said to you," she cried.

Harper wrapped his arms around her until she begged for air. "Come on in, you two, Ellen, go take her up, and I'll help Charlie with bags." When the two women left, Harper turned to Charlie with a look of concern on his face. "She looks tired, Charlie, and she's lost a lot of weight."

"I know, I can't get her to eat much. She sleeps but tosses and turns most of the night. Lawson said she's fighting this, and I can see that, but it's wearing her down."

"She's not the only one." Said Harper taking note of the fact that Charlie looked worn out as well. "We should have done this earlier. Give you more of a chance to take a break from time to time. But you're here now, and I'm sure Ellen will do her best to put some weight on both of you kids. Hopefully, this whole detox process won't take too long."

"What's going on with Trish and Jacob, any word on them."

"Yes, actually, Eddy Grayber called me last night. Said he rented that cabin, the one the lost kids stayed at. He rented it to some guy Saturday. Description of him and the camper matches Jacob's. He didn't think anything about it at first until he saw Trish."

"Think we should tell him to run them off?"

"Not yet. I don't like having them in our county, but I do like knowing where they are. Got Eddy keeping an eye on them. Something else he told me too. She's rented from him before. Or rather, she and Billy did. Just a weekend getaway type thing, long before he disappeared. I don't know why but something about that has my hackles up. For now, let's keep that between ourselves. I don't want Alia to know where they are or that they are even still in Union county."

"No, neither do I. In fact, Lawson warned that we shouldn't mention Trish at all. It may be some sort of trigger for her. I do know that ever since he mentioned her, it has set Alia off in a weird way."

"Yes, it hurt Ellen hearing Alia call that bitch her mother. She's not referred to her in that way since she started calling Ellen Mom again. I remember once back then when Trish was over here to see Alia. She was about two at the time. Alia slipped and called Ellen Mommy right in front of Trish. Ellen had her back turned, you didn't see anything, and Trish didn't see me. But I saw the look on her face. Should have known then, but hell, she was young, it made sense that would tick her off."

"Yeah, I remember that too. You got me to tell her not to say that again, not in front of Trish."

"She always listened to you better. Our girl always had a bit of a wild streak in her. Little spitfire. Never thought I would miss that, but I do. Her rage now…it's something different…something not her own."

"We'll get her back. And when we do, you're gonna regret you ever said you missed it." he laughed, and so did Harper.

After getting the kids settled in upstairs, Harper and Ellen left them alone. Ellen went running off to the store to get stuff to make Alia's favorite dinner of fried chicken, coleslaw, and her own homemade rolls. Harper made sure the safes were locked and the alarm systems were working. Even with all three of them there, he didn't want to take any chances.

In his old bedroom, Charlie sat in a chair and marveled over Alia's change in mood as she puttered around the room, putting away their things. She smiled and hummed to herself a song he recognized as one of her favorites. When she walked past him, he grabbed her and pulled her down into his lap. She let out a little laugh sounding more like his angel again. Charlie snuggled her hair, taking in every breath of her he could get. Kissing her, he thought that everything may just turn out to be okay after all.

Before dinner, Alia had wanted another nap. This drew some concern from Charlie, but he figured after all she was going through, if she needed to rest, he should let her. When he came up two hours later to get her for dinner, he found the bed empty. Before panicking, he checked his bathroom, but she wasn't there either. He was about to check the spare bedroom that had been hers once upon a time when he heard a whimper in the closet.

Charlie opened the door only to hear a shriek and have a golf club fly past his head. Charlie had ducked just in time, then looked in to see Alia as far back into the closet as she could go, brandishing another golf club. Her eyes were wild and fearful, but oddly she looked as though she didn't really see him there.

"Get away from me, don't come near me…go away…go away," she screamed, still not really looking at him. Alia swung the club around wildly, managing only to knock down the remnants of his old clothes his mother didn't have the heart to give away. The clothes falling around her made her panic and swing more.

Charlie tried to approach her telling her it was him and it was okay, but she wouldn't look at him, instead just screamed and swung.

Behind him, Charlie's parents came into the room, Harper trying to keep Ellen out of the room, but she slipped past him.

"What the hell is she doing, Charlie?" he yelled to be heard over her screams.

Charlie could feel her fear, but it was far away, like she wasn't there in the room with him. And if she wasn't there, then where the hell was she and who was trying to hurt her. "I think she's having a nightmare," Charlie said.

"Alia, honey, it's okay, we are here with you, sweetheart it's okay," yelled Ellen.

But Alia continued to scream.

"Charlie, you have to stop her. She's going to rip her throat to shreds screaming like that," said Ellen.

Going into the closet, Charlie tried to time her swings but miscalculated and got whacked on the side of his head by his old nine iron. He fell back out of the closet, his head bleeding. Ellen ran to him while Harper ran into the closet hunched over so that when Alia hit him, she only got his back and shoulder. Once he was in too close for her to swing again, he wrestled the club from her. Now she was more hysterical than ever, screaming louder than he thought possible with a look in her eyes that told him she was somewhere other than with them.

Harper tried shaking her awake, or back to them, to no avail. Looking back at his son on the ground, the side of his face covered in blood, Harper turned back to Alia and did something that he regretted the rest of his days. Trying one last time to reach her with no effect, he slapped her sharply across the face.

Alia came out of the nightmare of being chased by the thing in the caves, with the side of her face burning hot. She saw Charlie on the floor bloodied and Ellen trying to hold him back.

Yelling at Harper to get away from her, Charlie broke his mother's hold and ran into the closet, pushing his father hard out of the way. Falling to the floor, he grabbed Alia and pulled her protectively into his arms.

Harper picked himself up from where Charlie had shoved him into the wall and looked down at the two of them. Charlie was cradling Alia in his arms, kissing the side of her face where Harper could see his handprint, large and red on her small cheek. He reached out to offer help only to be rebuffed by Charlie.

"No…No, don't you fucking touch her."

Feeling horrible, looking at Alia just sitting there in his son's arms in a daze, Harper went to try again, but this time Ellen stopped him.

"No, Harper, leave them be. Go get an ice pack. She's going to need it."

He hesitated, but she insisted that he go. At the closet door, Harper looked back. "Charlie, son, I'm sorry, I didn't know what else to do."

"Go away, just go away," Charlie yelled as he tried to console Alia. In his arms, she trembled.

Harper went off to get the ice pack and a shot of whiskey or two for himself.

"What happened, Charlie? Why am I in here?" Alia asked. She reached up to him, wiping some of the blood from his face as well as a tear or two. She then touched the side of her own face with one hand and flinched at the pain.

"Don't touch it, dear." Said Ellen, having gotten down on her knees in front of them. "It's okayCharlie, she's going to be alright."

But she wasn't. He knew she wasn't. Bringing her here hadn't worked. Nothing he was doing was helping. Now his own father had hit the one person in the world he would kill for. Charlie felt the old familiar rage he worked so hard to control mixed with the remnants of Alia's fear that had come with her out of the nightmare.

Ellen put a gentle hand on the bloodless side of his face. "Charlie, come on, you need to breathe, don't let the anger control you; you control it."

Charlie closed his eyes and did as she told him, shuddering with each deep breath. In his arms, Alia placed a hand on the other side of his head, and together she and Ellen soothed him until his breathing became more even. Opening his eyes again, he looked down at his angel, the hand mark taking up most of her face and looking angry and red.

Harper came back into the room, handing Ellen the ice-pack in a towel and smelling of whiskey. She gave him a scolding look, but he just shook his head. Ellen shooed him back out, but he planted himself on the edge of the bed.

Turning back to them, Ellen gave the ice-pack to Charlie and told him to be gentle, not that she needed to.

When Charlie put the pack on her face, Alia winced but then held his hand in place with hers when he tried to take it off. The coldness made her face feel a little better as it felt like the heat was going to burn her.

Charlie had himself under control now, but his eyes brimmed with tears.

"I'm okay, Charlie. It only hurts a little."

He smiled down at her through the tears knowing she was only saying that to make him feel better. "He shouldn't have done it. He should have never hit you. I'll never forgive him for that, Alia, never."

Out in the bedroom, Harper heard what his son said, and his heart sank.

Alia reached up to Charlie, touching the cut above his eye gently. "If you can forgive me, you can forgive him. It was just a slap, Charlie, I've had worse." she strained to tell him with a voice sounding broken. Bringing his face down to hers, Alia kissed him, then slowly got to her feet and brought him up with her.

Charlie let her lead him to the bedroom, where Harper was sitting on the bed.

Alia went over and wrapped her arms around Harper's neck, hugging him tightly. "Thank you for saving me, Harper. That thing was going to kill me," she said in a barely audible voice.

"Charlie and I won't ever let that happen. We won't let Trish hurt you, I promise." Said Harper, barely able to look at her, only seeing his handmark on her face when he did.

"It wasn't Trish trying to kill me."

"Then who was it, dear?" asked Ellen.

Alia turned to face Ellen. "It was me," she said and went back into Charlie's arms.

The three of them just looked at each other, unsure what to think about that.

Sitting on the bed drinking a cup of tea with almost more honey in it than water, Alia explained the nightmare the best she could. She was in the caves again, being chased around. Every corner she turned, there was another dead body. Crystal, Ethan, George, Ellen, Harper, and the worst was Charlie. When she saw him, she had fallen to her knees, ready to face whoever it was that had killed all of them, when out from the shadows of the cave came herself. It had been terrifying realizing that she had been the one to kill them. "All I could do was scream," she said hoarsely with fresh tears in her eyes.

Ellen took the empty mug of tea from her and took Alia into the bathroom. "I'll help her get a shower. Harper help Charlie to get cleaned up. And Charlie, don't be a stubborn ass. Forgive your father." She left the two boys alone.

Charlie followed Harper into the main bathroom and sat on the toilet seat while Harper cleaned and bandaged the cut above Charlie's eye. After a while, Charlie relented. "I'm sorry for what I said. I do forgive you. I'm still a little angry, but I understand why you did it."

Harper knelt down before his son. Earlier, he thought Charlie had looked older, the kind of aging only stress can do. But now sitting here, his hair wet, his eyes red, he looked like a little boy again. "Charlie, you know the last thing I would ever want to do is hurt either one of you. I've never so much as swatted your bottom as a kid. She would have been coughing up blood if I hadn't stopped her. I hate that I did it, but I really had no choice."

Charlie nodded, "We have to do something. I don't think she can take much more. I don't know if I can..." he hung his head feeling ashamed. "I don't know if I can be there for her like she needs me to."

Harper put a hand on Charlie's shoulder. "That's why you're here, Charlie. You shouldn't have to go through this alone. We won't let you." They both stood up, and Charlie hugged his father. When he did, Harper winced.

"She got me good with that nine iron," he said.

Charlie lifted his father's shirt at the back and saw an ugly bruise line taking shape along his shoulder.

"Don't say anything to her about it, okay?" said Harper. "She doesn't need to know."

After her shower and back into bed, Charlie tried getting Alia to eat. She took a few bites to make him happy then begged to go back to sleep. This time he stayed with her, laying with her head on his chest and his arm around her. She jerked and moaned in her sleep but managed to make it through the night.

Once again, when he woke in the morning, Charlie found Alia gone from the bed. Both the bathroom and closet were empty as well. Throwing on a shirt, he ran downstairs and heard voices and laughter coming from the kitchen. Charlie went in to see a site that put a smile on his face. His two favorite girls in the world were sitting at the kitchen island talking, both with smiles on their faces. When Alia saw him, her face lit up.

"Hey Charlie," she said.

Her smile both thrilled him and broke his heart just a little. He loved seeing her happy but couldn't help but wonder when she would be gone again. Charlie went to her, kissed her on her good cheek, and then checked the other. It was still a bit red and swollen, but the handprint could no longer be seen.

"I'm fine, Charlie. How's your head?" she asked with a raspy voice.

He didn't answer but instead took the mug in her hand, peered inside, and looked at his mother. "Is this tea? Mom, she really shouldn't.."

"It's a fresh new box, Charlie. I made it myself. She needs something for her throat."

He nodded, handing the mug back to Alia and wiping a hand over his weary face.

"Sorry I didn't wake you. I wanted you to get as much sleep as possible," said Alia.

"And I wanted to spend some alone time with my girl," said Ellen.

"It's okay," he told her, kissing her good cheek again.

Alia laid her head on Charlie's chest and hugged him with one arm. He returned the hug with both of his careful not to slosh her tea.

"I'm going to go get ready for work. I hear dad pounding around up there already. Don't forget you have a session with Lawson today. I'll come back to take you."

"No, you won't. Today is girls' day. I'll take her to her session. Don't frown at me, Charlie. The two of us already talked about it this morning, it'll be fine."

"She's right, Charlie. I'm having a good day. Besides, you could use a break from your crazy girlfriend for a while."

Charlie scolded her with a look. "My fiance is not crazy. Well, no more than usual." he ribbed. "What if your day turns not so good?"

"Then we will call you," said Ellen. "Now go get ready. I'll start breakfast."

Charlie looked at his mother, and she nodded at him. Giving Alia another kiss, he went to get ready for the day.

When the boys were ready for work, they all sat and ate together. Well, most did. Alia still picked at her food, and Charlie didn't do much better. With breakfast done, Charlie and Harper got their guns from the safe.

They were about to leave when Alia pulled Charlie aside. She had one of their Kevlar vests in her hand.

"I want you to wear this today…please."

He looked down at her searching her eyes for some hint of mood change or any sign that it wasn't really her talking.

"Alia, you know we only use those when we have to. Bedford is still a relatively safe town."

"I know, but I also know that there are two people out there that are not happy with us right now. This isn't the paranoia talking Charlie. It's me, a future wife of a cop. Please do this for me. You know it's not always about just protecting me. I would die without you."

Charlie looked into eyes that looked sane, even glistening with unspent tears. Taking off his gun belt and shirt, he did as she asked.

"And don't be a smart ass and take it off when you get to the station." she smiled at him.

"I won't," he promised, then kissed her goodbye.

As she watched him leave, Alia searched the driveway, yard, and road as best she could from the doorway without Ellen noticing. They were out there, she could tell. Somewhere, hiding, waiting for a chance to leap out at them. Well, she wasn't about to let them do that. If her family wouldn't let her protect them, then she would have to do what she needed to do despite them.

Chapter 34
The Hidden Ones

Trying to be cooperative, Alia went to her session with Lawson despite not seeing the point of it all. Once again, they had the session in the sunroom, where Alia did her best not to look as paranoid as she felt.

Lawson asked how the weekend went, and she was honest with him yet aloof. Although she remained pleasant, he found her easily distracted and prone to staring out the windows, like with her mind on something else.

"What are you thinking about Alia, because it's certainly not on this session."

"I'm sorry. I'm just worried about Charlie. Trish and Jacob are still out there somewhere."

"Charlie is a strong young man. I have a feeling he is more than capable of taking care of himself."

"Yes, I know you're right. It's just," she shook her head.

"You're letting the paranoia get to you."

"Isn't that out of my control?" she sighed.

"Not entirely. Once again, no one can be made to do anything they don't want to do via hypnosis."

"Are you telling me I want to do all these things? That somewhere deep down, I want to hurt the people that I love? That I wanted to go after Charlie with a nine iron?" she asked, getting angry. "Besides, Charlie said there was a drug as well."

"No, that's not what I'm saying at all. The drug, if indeed they did use one, is different. That is capable of making you do these things, or rather put you in a heightened sense of alert that you are prone to lash out. But that doesn't mean you can't keep fighting and fight harder."

Alia sighed heavily. She felt like she was fighting, yet she was getting nowhere except exhausted.

"Actually, making an effort to fight back the thoughts will go even further to helping get through this better. It can be as simple as just questioning how you feel. For example, if you get a feeling that Charlie is in danger, just ask yourself if there is really any cause for concern. The mere act of breaking up that thought process can go a long way to alleviate the paranoia."

Alia thought this over then shook her head. "This is all really just speculation on your part, right? I mean, we don't even know for sure there is a drug."

"Still, doesn't make me wrong about you giving these bad thoughts a good shove back. Your more lucid moments, your regret, your pain over what you have done, that is all proof you're not too far gone no matter what is causing this." Lawson saw her ponder all of this and hoped he was getting through to her. According to what she had described about the weekend, her bad moments were escalating. Striking out at others, hurting them, in the throes of a nightmare or not, was not a good sign. If she continued to hurt people, he would have no choice but to commit her involuntarily. And that was the last thing he wanted to put this poor girl and her family through.

Not wanting a repeat of their last session, Lawson tried ending it on a good note, talking to her about the things she enjoyed doing and how she could incorporate those things into getting through the rough moments. Unfortunately, he could tell that her mind was back off the session again as she continued to peer out the windows.

On the car ride home, Alia was very quiet. Ellen glanced at her now and then, concerned, but she merely seemed to be watching the scenery and thinking.
Only Alia was doing more than that. She was taking in everything. People walking the streets. Kids at the park. Drivers going past them. She scrutinized everyone she saw, wondering which ones were the ones hiding from her.

Lawson is a fool. You're only paranoid if no one is out to get you.

Alia knew someone was out to get her. They always have been. The problem was finding the ones who hid themselves.

Back at the house, Alia begged off of lunch, claiming she needed to take a nap that the session had worn her out. Ellen relented despite worrying over how thin the poor girl was getting.

Upstairs, Alia prepared the bed, making it look the best she could like she was sleeping under the covers. Ellen was the type to check up on her from time to time, so it was better to fool her for as long as possible.

An interesting feature of the house was the built-in fire ladders each bedroom had. Under one of the windows was a little door with a rolled-up bar ladder inside. Charlie had shown it to her one of their first nights she slept there.

Careful not to make any noise, Alia took the one out from under Charlie's window and lowered it out down the side of the house. Not able to take the ladder off or close the window all the way once she got down, Alia instead covered it with a chair and some clothes the best she could and closed the window as much as possible before descending. If Ellen paid close enough attention, she would see the window was still cracked and the ladder deployed, but that was a chance she would have to take.

On the ground, Alia was able to get to the backyard unseen and down to the lake. There she took a hoodie, baseball cap, and glasses out of the backpack she had and put them on. Not only did she not want to be recognized by anyone in town, but it was most important that she not be noticed by those that intended to harm her and Charlie.

Again telling herself it wasn't paranoia if someone was after you, Alia went through the path in the woods and came out at Harkening Hill park. Careful not to attract too much attention, she walked several blocks, dodging patrol cars and town people until she arrived at her destination. Looking around to make sure she wasn't seen, Alia entered Harvey's Gun shop. She took off the hat and glasses as she went in because this was the one place she wanted to be recognized.

Harvey himself stood behind the counter of a thankfully empty store and smiled when he saw her. In his fifties, with the start of gray hair in his beard and more in his hair than he cared for, Harvey had the look of the ex-marine that he was. Despite the start of a decent beer belly, he was still relatively fit. That and his demeanor let most people know he wasn't a man to be messed with. "Well, look what the cat dragged in, welcome Deputy Miller…or is it Harper yet, and I wasn't invited to the wedding?" he said with a fake child-like pout.

Smiling, Alia showed him the ring on her finger. "Nope, I'm still just engaged. It's only been a few months. And don't worry, we wouldn't think of not inviting you."

"Yeah, I know, but you kids these days are always in a hurry. Besides, half the town has been shipping you two for, well, two years at least now."

"And the other half?' she asked.

"Fuck them." he roared with laughter. "So what are you in here for, looking for a wedding gift or wanting to upgrade that little pea shooter Charlie talked you into buying?"

Alia smiled. She had wanted a nice large gun with some real stopping power when they had come in here a few years earlier. However, Charlie insisted that she didn't need something quite so big for home protection.

"We don't need you to punch holes through walls, just take down someone stupid enough to mess with you." he had said.

"Yes, I think it's time for an upgrade. I figure if I spend a few days with it at the range before telling Charlie, I'll be able to show him I can handle it."

"Oh, I don't have any doubts you can handle something a bit bigger. I've seen you at the range. Put grown men like myself to shame." Still, Harvey didn't fail to notice that the girl before him was not entirely like the one he knew. This version of her was paler, her cheeks shallower, and even with the hoodie on, she looked too thin. He didn't want to say anything, though, seeing how from his three divorces, he had learned that women were sensitive about that kind of shit. And speaking of shit, she looked like a warmed-over plate of it. Looking at her, he started to doubt that she could handle the firepower of a larger caliber handgun. "So Charlie boy not with you today?"

"No, he's working. As I said, I want to prove to him I can handle it before he knows I got it."

"Hoo boy, don't you be telling him you told me that. He'll have my ass for selling you something you don't need."

"But you're still going to sell it to me, right?" she asked with a knowing smile.

"Well, of course, I am." he boomed. "Having three exes isn't cheap, you know." Harvey laughed. For the next twenty minutes, he showed her a few things. They discussed what she was looking to do, and she finally settled on a Sig Sauer P220 with a bit more firepower than her P320 service pistol and a lot more than the .22 she had at home. She took a box of 45 ACP Cartridges to go along with it to 'practice at the range' and a new shoulder holster.

With the sale final, Harvey got the nerve to ask her if she was feeling alright.

"Yeah, I guess I'm just worried about the argument Charlie and I will have once he finds out about this," she said with a bit of laugh.

"Give him hell, girl." he laughed again as she walked out the shop with her hat and glasses back on. "Good cop there…but a horrible liar," he said to himself. Taking his phone out of his pocket Harvey made a call. Usually, he wrote this kind of thing off as none of his damn business, but there was an itching in the back of his brain he didn't much care for. Best to scratch it and see what relief it brings.

Alone in the alley behind the gun store, Alia unzipped the hoodie, put the shoulder holster on, loaded the gun, put it in the holster, and put the hoodie back on. The hoodie belonged to Charlie, so it was big enough, especially on her now, to lose the bulk of the gun in its folds. She then shoved all of the packaging into an old tire, reminding herself to come back and get it later. For now, she needed to track down the hiding ones and flush them out. It was time to end this shit.

Charlie was patrolling just outside of town when the call from Harvey came in. Pulling over, he listened to what Harvey had to say with growing alarm.

"I hope I'm not stirring up any domestic shit between the two of you, but that girl, she didn't look right, and it's not just the bags under her eyes either."

"No, Harvey, you did the right thing." *Though it would have been better to call before selling her something that could take someone's head off.* Charlie hung up with him and called his mother, not that he doubted Harvey, but before calling out the cavalry, he had to be sure.

"Hi Charlie, how's the day going, dear?"

"Where's Alia?"

"She's upstairs taking a nap. That session rung her out, I think."

"Please go check on her mom."

"I did just a few minutes ago. She's out of it and all wrapped up in the blankets."

"Check again, make sure she's actually in bed. Wake her up if you have to."

"Why, Charlie, what's going on?"

"Harvey just called and said she was in his shop buying a gun."

"Charlie, I'm telling you she hasn't left the house."

He could hear her going up the stairs at the house over the phone.

"I'll check, of course. Just give me a second. I don't want to wake her unless I have to."

He held on to the line, in the meantime scanning the area he was in like she might walk up at any minute despite him being miles away from the gun shop. Over the phone, he heard his mother curse then she was back on the line.

"She's gone, Charlie. She had the covers and pillows made up to look like she was in bed. Damn Charlie, I'm so sorry, but how the hell did she get out. Wait a minute. The fire ladder. Charlie, she went out on the fire ladder. I'm so so sorry I was supposed to watch her. I never gave that ladder a moment's thought."

"It's not your fault, mom. I didn't think of it either. Call dad tell him I'm headed out to the cabin from the search and rescue. Trish and Jacob are renting a place out there. I don't know how she would know, but, hell, I can't think of anywhere else to look."

"No, Charlie, don't you go out there by yourself. You wait for your father or call for backup. The last thing we need right now is you hurt or in jail. I'll go out and start looking for her in town starting at the gun shop, just you wait for your father."

"Mom stay at the house in case she tries to get back in. Dad will put an APB out on her. We'll have plenty of eyes out looking, but I've got to get out to that cabin before she's the one hurt or in jail." No time for her to protest more. He ended the call with her, hit his lights and sirens, and sped off towards the cabin.

Alia was headed back towardsHarkening Hill park when she heard sirens and saw Sheriff Harper speeding down the road in front of the two buildings she was sneaking out from behind. She jumped back, sure he didn't see her, then peeked and saw that he was indeed driving away. Not thinking this had anything to do with her, she tucked her head down and crossed the road, still heading back for the park.

Near the woods, away from the baseball fields and tennis courts, was an area with a small older picnic table. It had once been part of a larger group of wooden tables, but this one was all that was left. The new picnic area was set up closer to the fields so people could watch games while having a cookout. It was here that she sat, took off the sunglasses, and surveyed the park.

Alia knew they were here. She could feel them. Lurking in the bushes, hiding behind a bench, and maybe openly walking one of the many paths. From her vantage point, she could make out most of the park down below her. To her back was the woods where it would be hard, if not plain impossible, for someone to sneak up on her.

Since it was a weekday, there weren't many people in the park, but she didn't let that fool her. A man was walking an Australian Shepherd up by the tennis courts. Alia recognized both of them, which assured her they were not the hidden ones. In the courts was a woman and what could be none other than her daughter playing tennis rather badly and ribbing each other. Two mothers were sitting on a bench by the playground while three children played on the set. Thankfully the playground was far from where she was because she didn't want any children hurt if things went wrong.

To Alia's left in the direction of the Harper's home, she could make out something stirring in the bushes. This something had to be large. Certainly, no bunny or squirrel would make everything move around so much. Trying not to focus her attention on any one spot and be caught off guard, Alia kept that end of the park at the edge of her vision.

Another advantage to where she was, up here on the little hill overlooking the park, was that she was visible. Before, she wanted to remain hidden. Now, she wanted to be seen. She wanted the hidden things to come out, to be forced out of hiding into the open for her and others to see. She wanted to make herself a target they couldn't resist. If they were determined to kill someone, she was determined to be sure that they would come after her and not Charlie. Alia felt reasonably safe with him working since he was armed and often with other officers or in his car and not an easy target. However, airing on the side of caution, she had insisted he wear his vest.

He better not have taken the damn vest off.

Now thinking about it, she should have grabbed one as well, though that may have given her away too much. It would be nothing for one of them to snipe her where she sat. But she had a feeling that when they were ready, they would want to make their presence known. So she sat and watched and waited, feeling their eyes on her, just not able to pinpoint where it was they watched her from. And when they did come out to play, she would have a pleasant little surprise waiting for them.

Charlie was racing down a single-lane back road headed for the Cabin when he heard sirens behind him. Thinking it was backup coming to help, he slowed down just slightly. It was enough for the driver to not only catch up but pass as well. Then the car stopped in the road diagonally, blocking it. Charlie slammed on the brakes. Stopped in the middle of the road, he saw Harper staring back at him.

Charlie got out of his patrol car in a fury. "What the hell are you doing? We have to get out to the cabin before Alia does."

"She's not there, Charlie," said Harper, getting out and approaching his son.

"How do you know?"

"Because another officer just spotted her back in town at Harkening Hill park. She's sitting on that old picnic table on the hill out in the open."

"No," he said, not believing. "No, she's going out to the cabin, that's why she got the gun, she's going to kill Trish, she's going…."

Harper grabbed Charlie by the shoulders. "Calm down for a minute. Feel for her, Charlie…you have always been able to find her…where is she? What direction would you go in if you wanted to find her."

"But I do want to find her," he insisted.

"Yes, but you're letting your anger cloud your thinking, and maybe the connection you have with her as well. Think Charlie, concentrate. Can you feel her where she is?"

Charlie backed up from his father, his head baking from the august heat and blood pounding in its veins. He started to walk in circles, being pulled one way then another. Instinct told him north to the cabin. Something else drew him back towards town. He took a deep breath and tried to clear his mind and thought only of her. When he opened them back up, he found himself walking back towards town and knew his father was right.

"She's in town," he said, turning to his father.

"Then let's go get her son."

To Alia's, right where all the tennis courts and baseball fields were, the ground was mostly flat with a few trees. To her left, towards the parking areas for hiking down to the lake, the land was not as flat and had many trees and bushes. More and more, her eyes were drawn to that area which made perfect sense to her. That way was also the house, hidden behind a small forest of trees. She knew they had been there earlier in the day and the night before, watching the house, waiting for the perfect moment to come out and shatter their lives.

Alia was scanning the area once more when she saw something duck behind a tree. A minute later, she saw it again, off to the other side. This time she knew it was a person and an adult person at that. The area she looked in also housed the start of the Frisbee golf course, so she had to be careful that it wasn't someone playing the game. Trying to pretend like she didn't notice, Alia looked off but kept the wooded area in her peripheral vision. Again she saw it. The trees overhead created a shadowy space underneath them. However, she still caught a dark figure going from one tree to another. And more importantly, she could feel their eyes on her.

Still, she sat for a bit more, giving no hint that she noticed. After waiting ten minutes, Alia faked checking her phone. It was actually turned off so she couldn't be tracked by Charlie and Harper. She gave a long stretch, yawned, and casually got up, walking towards the more wooded area of the park.

Along the way, Alia made a show of taking her time. Kicking pine cones on the ground, stopping to look up into the trees, pretending to take pictures, all in the hopes that she looked like a regular park visitor. All the time, still keeping her eyes on the area she last saw movement. She was about halfway there and so preoccupied with her task that she never noticed the four Sheriff's cars pull up in the parking lot.

With another flash out of the corner of her eye, Alia focused more in that direction, pretending to be looking at the trees, even talking to the little bugs crawling up trunks. Anything to throw off those she was pursuing. Zipping down her hoodie, she reached inside to assure herself the gun was still there and snapped off the clip that held it in.

Once again, in front of her and off to the right, someone ducked behind a tree. Alia halted and, dropping the charade, called out to the hidden ones she knew were stalking her. "Why don't we just stop this game? Come out and show yourself." she slid her hand into the hoodie gripping the gun. "Whoever you are, the jig is up. Come out with your hands where I can see them, and maybe we can end this thing peacefully." She was about to move forward some more when she heard a voice behind her.

"Alia, who are you talking to?"

Whipping around, hand still on the gun inside the hoodie, Alia saw Charlie and, not far behind him, Harper. Four other officers stood at the edge of the wooded area. In the parking lot, Alia could see a few people watching what was going on as two of the officers moved them back. Her heart sank seeing Charlie there, and she immediately regretted taunting the hidden ones. She had fallen into their trap despite how clever she thought she was.

"Charlie, no…no, you can't be here. Get out of here, Charlie." Just on the edge of her vision, Alia saw the hidden one on the move again.

"Okay, Alia, I'll leave, but I want you to come with me, alright? You should be home resting. Let's get you back there. Mom is worried about you." Charlie pleaded with her.

"No, Charlie, they are here. The ones from the apartment followed us to the house, and they are here. I won't let them hurt you. I won't let them take you away from me. Go on, get the hell out of here I can handle this. Harper, I'm begging you get Charlie out of here." Behind her, Alia could hear footsteps in the leaves and dry grass as the hidden ones moved again. Pulling the gun, Alia spun around back in the direction she had been pursuing. Still, she didn't catch them before they made it to cover again. Then from all around her, she both heard and felt it. Eyes, blazing on her, footfalls in the leaves, quick flashes of movement from one tree to another. Alia spun around from point to point, her hand out with the p220 thrust in front of her. There were several of them, and they had her surrounded.

"Alia...Alia put the gun down." she heard Charlie beg.

"Go home, Charlie, get out of here before they hurt you, please." Alia turned her head partially towards him while still training the gun on the last spot she saw movement. "Damn it, Charlie, get out of here. They have me surrounded. It was a trap, go, please go." She spun again as another noise came from behind her.

Charlie tried to move closer, his hands out palms forward. "Alia, there's no one here. It's just us. Now put the gun down."

She only shook her head with a pained look on her face and kept training her gun on the things that were not there.

"Deputy Miller put the damn gun down." Called out Harper, hoping a voice of authority would reach her.

"Get Charlie out of here, Harper. They're going to kill him. You have to get him out of here." she hollered in the grips of sheer panic.

Out in the parking lot, more officers arrived, as did civilians witnessing what appeared to them as one of their deputies drawing down on their Sergeant and Sheriff. Charlie tried to circle around more towards where Alia was first pointing at in an attempt to draw her attention to him. "Alia, honey, please look at me."

"No," she screamed at him now in tears. "They'll kill you, the hidden ones, please Charlie, please leave. I don't care if they kill me, just leave." she spun again, pointing the gun for a second at Harper, trying to come up behind her, then she turned again to her right.

"Alia, damn it, now put the gun down. There is no one out here," yelled Charlie, his own panic starting to get to him.

"That's bullshit. They are here. Don't you see them? Don't you see? They are all around us." Alia whirled around again, catching glimpses of something darting from tree to tree. Sweat poured off of her trying to drip into her eyes and making the shapes before her all fuzzy. Behind her, they moved again. Only when she spun around, she started to become dizzy and disoriented. The next sound she heard was the running of feet right behind Harper. She turned fast and fired off a shot wildly. Alia saw a flash of red as the bullet hit just the very edge of Harper's arm ripping his shirt as well as his flesh.

Again running feet from behind her, and when she turned, she saw a massive mountain of a man brandishing an ax going right for Charlie.

Before Charlie could even react to her shooting Harper, she had spun around and aimed the gun right at him this time.

"Charlie get down," she screamed.

Charlie instinctively flinched, bending at the knees just enough that the four shots she fired went well over him. But instead of going into the ax-wielding man, they went into a tree, and the man was gone.

Alia spun wildly around, looking for signs of the hidden ones. Looking for the giant man. But they had vanished. The eyes she had felt watching her were gone as well. Confused and terrified they would jump out when she least expected it, she still spun around in circles with the gun thrust before her trying to fight panic and dizziness. All around her, Harper, Charlie, and other officers ordered her to put her gun down. But she barely heard them as she frantically looked for the hidden ones.

"Where are they…where did they go…no…no I had him…I had…" Alia turned to Charlie, her eyes pleading with him only to see him pointing a gun at her. In her agitated state, she didn't realize it was only a taser, and the hurt in her eyes could be seen by him as clearly as he felt. It. "Charlie….no…I..no please don't."

"Put the gun down, Alia…it's over; just put the gun down." Charlie's hands shook because even just pointing a taser at the woman he loved was terrifying. Almost as much as her behavior.

Alia looked at him, confused suddenly, unsure where she was. She looked down and noticed the gun in her hands, now pointed at Charlie, and she flinched, almost dropping it. Immediately she lowered it, still looking at it like it was some kind of strange thing she had never seen before.

"Alia, look at me," called Charlie.

She looked up at him, almost afraid to meet his eyes. She could smell gunpowder, could tell she had fired the gun in her hand and was horrified at the thought she may have shot someone as a vision of blood danced in the corners of her mind.

"Just put the gun down," Charlie begged as he slowly approached her.

Looking at Charlie, Alia shook her head, not understanding what exactly was going on but knowing it was bad. "I want to go home, Charlie."

"Then put the gun down, and we will." he lied.

Alia knew he had lied but still went down to her knees sobbing as a faint realization of what was going on dawned on her. Shaking, she put the gun on the ground, then without being told to, clasped her hands together over the back of her head.

"Please, Charlie." she begged and shook. "don't shoot...I'm so sorry...I don't know..," Alia cried.

"I'm not going to hurt you, just be still okay? I'm going for the gun, just don't move, stay like you are, and everything will be fine." But it wouldn't, really. Charlie knew they were well beyond the point of anything being fine.

Behind her, Harper and four other officers had their tasers drawn as well and pointed at her while Charlie slowly walked towards her and picked up the gun. He handed it to one of the officers who cleared it, then he put away his taser and fell to his knees in front of her, taking her into his arms as she sobbed.

Harper came up behind Alia lowered her arms, fastening them loosely with a pair of cuffs.

Charlie looked up at him accusingly.

"It's for her own good," he said. "We have a shit ton of witnesses to deal with as well."

Which Charlie knew meant no chance of sweeping this under the rug. Not that he would ask his father to do such a thing.

"You know what we need to do, don't you, son?" Looking at the two of them, Harper's heart ached more than his arm hurt.

Charlie nodded, tears in his own eyes as he held her tighter, knowing it would be a while before he did so again.

An ambulance arrived, and medics tended to Harper's arm. The bullet had only grazed him, so other than burning like hell and bleeding like a bitch he was fine. Alia, however, had fallen into an almost catatonic state by the time they got there. She just laid in Charlie's arms, not speaking, barely moving, tears still streaming from her eyes as she silently cried. They removed the cuffs long enough to put her on a stretcher then cuffed her to it. Charlie went with her in the ambulance to the hospital while Harper lagged behind, ensuring the scene was correctly processed. They didn't want any investigation done by internal affairs to show they tried to hide or cover up anything.

Before heading to the hospital to join Charley in the arduous task of what he had no choice but to do, Harper went to the house to let Ellen know what had happened. He got there to find her frantic. She had heard the shots Alia fired at the park and bits and pieces that were allowed out over the scanner. When her husband came through the door, she ran into his arms, asking about the kids, asking about his arm, pleading with him to tell her everything would be okay.

Sitting her down, Harper did his best to tell her what had happened. "It was the scariest thing, Ellen. She was convinced someone was there. I saw her eyes; she was absolutely terrified."

As the story spun out, Ellen felt her heart breaking. "Oh, my poor baby girl. Harper, what are we going to do?"

"Charlie's at the hospital now already doing it."

She knew what he meant just by the look in his eyes. "No, Harper, please no…there has to be another way. There has to be something else we can do."

"You know there isn't. It's beyond us now, Ellen. She's a danger to herself and others. She shot me. I don't believe for one minute she meant to hurt me, but she could have killed one of us or someone else. It's only for a few days…or more if they really think she needs it. But we have no choice, Ellen. We really don't."

"You can't make him do this by himself, Harper. We need to go…we need to go be with Charlie. We need to say goodbye…My poor baby girl, this is all my fault. I promised Charlie I would take care of her." she burst into tears.

Harper took her and held her tight. "It's not your fault Ellen. Alia was determined to leave. There's nothing you could have done. And of course, we won't let Charlie do this on his own."

A while later, Ellen still leaking at the eyes but containing herself, and Harper joined Charlie at the hospital. Considering who she was, they put Alia into a private room until the admission process and paperwork could be done. When they walked in, Alia was in a bed. They had swapped her clothes for a gown and given her a mild sedative but still had one of her wrists handcuffed to the rail. Charlie stood at her side, holding her free hand, but Alia had her head turned away from him and stared at the wall. Joining their son, they hugged him as much as he would allow, but he wouldn't take his eyes off of her. His body shuddered, his chin quivered, but the tears in his eyes didn't fall. That was until two large male nurses arrived to take her away.

"Just give us a few minutes, please…just to say goodbye," said Harper.

The two men nodded and hung at the door, giving them what little privacy they could.

Ellen leaned over, giving Alia a kiss on her cheek. "You be the strong, brave woman I know you are, Alia. We'll come to see you, I promise. I love you, my baby girl."

Tears streamed from Alia's eyes, but she didn't say a word and wouldn't look at Ellen.

Harper gave her a kiss as well. "No hard feelings about the arm. We'll just call it even." He tried for a smile, but she wouldn't look at or acknowledge him either.

Charlie, at first, just stood there looking down at her. Harper put his hand on his son's back. "It's time, son, you have to let her go."

Charlie shook his head, his tears now turning to sobs his body shook with.

"You need to be strong for her, Charlie come one, don't you see what you're doing to her," Harper whispered in his ear. "It's only for a few days, we'll come to see her, we won't leave her here all alone, I promise. But you have to let her go."

Taking a deep breath and wiping a hand over his face, Charlie knelt down and kissed her forehead. "I'm so sorry sweet girl...please forgive me." he gave her hand a squeeze, and when she didn't do it back, a crack that he would feel for years to come opened in his heart. "I love you, and I always will." he kissed her one last time then allowed Harper to pull him away so the nurses could wheel her from the room. As they did, a large part of Charlie broke, and he swore he was going to kill whoever did this to them.

Once all paperwork was done, and Alia was secured for the night in the hospital's psychiatric ward, the Harpers, their hearts heavy and their ranks down by one, drove home.

When they arrived, Charlie couldn't bear to go in. Once again, his happy family home was missing the one thing that made him complete. He felt like the sad little boy he once was all those years ago when he lost her the first time. Reluctantly he let himself be led inside. He went through the motions of removing his gun belt placing it in the safe next to Alia's with a pang to his heart. He sat on the couch in the living room, not wanting to go upstairs to the bed they had shared, knowing he would smell her on its sheets.

Harper came over with a bottle of whiskey and two shot glasses. Charlie wasn't much of a drinker outside of a few beers occasionally and wine at dinner. Still, he took the drink when offered, relishing the burning pain of it because it was better than the pain he was feeling.

"You had no other choice, son. Don't beat yourself up about it," Harper said as Charlie took his third shot. "She'll be safe where she is, and it will give us some time to try and figure out just what is going on with her. It's for the best." He said, trying to relieve some of the guilt he knew Charlie was feeling. But the truth was that Harper himself had doubts that they were all going to survive this one.

Her fists full of tissues, Ellen sat next to her son, her fists full of tissues, trying to comfort him as tears fell from her own eyes.

Looking up at his father and feeling a little lightheaded from the whiskey, Charlie spoke for the first time since leaving the hospital. "You should have let me go to the cabin," he said, his head nodding a little drunkenly.

"The only thing you would have done there was something stupid, Charlie."

"Exactly. But it would be over. She would really be safe."

"You listen to me right now. That's the last thing we need. I know you're grieving and feel guilty, but you need to get your head out of your ass. This isn't over yet."

"Harper, please not right now. Let him be."

"Ellen…"

"Let the boy be. He's a good man. He won't do anything foolish. And you won't either." she said to Charlie sternly. "Right now, as much as I know you hate to admit it, you did the right thing. The best possible thing we could do for her right now. We'll get her back again, Charlie. And this time, we won't wait for years to do it."

"But will she want us back, Mom? Will she want me back after betraying her like that?"

"Yes, she will. Because when this is all over, she will realize you did it to protect her as well as others. You know the last thing she would want is to hurt someone."

"This still feels so wrong. I promised I would be there for her, that I would carry her when she got tired. No wonder she wouldn't even look at me. I failed her mom, and the worst part is that bitch is still out there."

"We will deal with Trish, don't you worry about that," said Harper. "But we will do it in the right way. We don't want to get Alia back in a few days just to lose you." Harper put his meaty hand on the side of his son's face. "Look at me, Charlie."

Charlie did, his head swimming a bit.

"We will put an end to this, I promise you. Just bear with us, Charlie. We deal with Alia first, then one way or another, we get to the bottom of what is going on, and we do it the right way.

Charlie nodded, but in his heart, he knew that given a chance, he wouldn't hesitate to end Trish's life.

Chapter 35
A Little Help

Charlie woke the following day, still on the couch in his uniform, feeling a little hungover and a lot lost. The lack of noise told him his parents were still asleep. Very much in need of a shower, he trudged upstairs to his room. Walking in, his heart broke seeing the empty bed and Alia's things scattered around the room. Sitting down on the bed, Charlie relived again showing up at the park, watching Alia look like she was hunting something amongst the trees. Again, he felt the panic he experienced when she had pulled the gun out from inside her jacket and had wielded it so dangerously. Not in any way like she'd handled a gun before. The sickening feeling he had when he had to pull the taser, praying he wouldn't have to resort to using it, came back to him as well. At the hospital, signing the papers to have her admitted was the hardest thing he ever did in his life. That was until he had to say goodbye. Alia wouldn't so much as look at him, and he couldn't blame her.

Looking on the inside of his right wrist, Charlie saw her name tattooed there. Often when he was at work and away from her, he would look at that tattoo and smile. Now looking at it wrenched his heart. And it was there in his heart that he could still feel connected to her. Charlie felt her loneliness, sadness, and guilt for what she had done as if they were an extension of his own feelings.

As he went to take off his pants, Charlie reached in the pockets to empty them out and found her engagement ring. At the hospital, one of the nurses had given it to him for safekeeping, and he had thrust it into his pocket, not even wanting to look at it. Now that he did, he was reminded that they had been happy just a few months ago. A few months ago, he had put the ring on the finger of the woman he loved making him the happiest man alive. And now, here it was in his trembling hand. Staring at the ring, he let the tears fall from his eyes. Picking up her pillow, smelling her scent but not being able to touch her, he cried some more. He couldn't help but wonder if they would ever get it all back. The love, the trust, and the joy they shared so easily with one another, or was this the beginning of the end?

At the hospital, Alia woke in a small room with soft padded walls, a single one-piece bed with a mattress, and a window up high, letting in a bit of morning sunlight. The night before, they gave her something to sleep. Now awake, she felt groggy. Worse, she felt more alone than she ever had in life. She reached out for Charlie for that special connection of theirs and got nothing but a splitting headache for her efforts. Sitting up, Alia pulled her knees up to her chest, in which lay a heart that felt like it was crushed.

She heard what people said around her last night, she knew this was all just temporary, but the pain. The pain was something she didn't think she would ever get over. She wasn't mad at Charlie. She was hurt. She knew they didn't have much of a choice. She hadn't given them much of an option, but that did little to comfort her. Right then, the only thing she wanted was to go home and wake up in Charlie's arms, this whole thing just being one big nightmare. Instead, the cold hard reality was right in her face as she looked around the tiny room. Hiding her head in her knees, Alia cried. She was almost half asleep again, in that same position when there was a rattle at her door. Fear washed over her, and she tried to melt into the wall. The door opened, and in walked a familiar round smiling face.

"How are you doing this morning, kid," asked Lawson, his voice as warm and soothing as ever.

Alia couldn't bring herself to talk but offered him a weary smile."

"That good, huh?" he said, sitting down on the edge of the hard little bed. "I'm sorry this happened, Alia. Worse than that, I'm sorry for the way it happened. You don't belong here. You're not crazy."

"Are you sure about that? I was chasing invisible men in the park. I could have killed someone. I hate that I'm here, but maybe it's where I belong. Maybe you're wrong about the whole drug thing."

"Let me ask you something. Do you understand that what you did was wrong?"

"Of course."

"Do you feel remorseful, especially for shooting your future father-in-law?"

Alia nodded, trying to hold back the tears.
"Then you're not insane. At least not any more than most people. Let's say we rule out the drug and hypnosis. All you're left with is a lifetime of abuse and trauma that will test even the most solid of people. When someone has had the kind of childhood you did, we don't expect them to enter adulthood completely intact. The only problem I see is maybe you rushed into this whole adult thing a little fast. If I had known you before, I would have recommended taking a year away from the abuse. To have counseling and learn to live without Trish before diving into the deep end of the pool. And I'm not blaming the Harper's. Charlie became a cop at eighteen as well, and so do many others, or they join the military or become parents. Some people like Charlie thrive from it. But then some people don't grow up living with the kind of abuse you did."

"So now what? I can't change what has already happened."

"No, but you can begin to fix it." Lawson got up. "Step one, cooperate with the doctors here. They will insist this is all you, so don't be mad if they don't believe the whole drug and hypnosis theory. My area of psychology could be cataloged under the definition of pseudoscience. I tend to think outside of the ...well box." he said, motioning to her surroundings. "And I know right now you want to wallow in your pain or even lash out. That kind of behavior can turn a three-day hold into a fourteen-day hold. Take their tests, answer their questions honestly and above all." he knelt down before her. "Keep fighting, Because it still may not be over yet. If you wake up not feeling like yourself, tell them. If you're paranoid, tell them. The worst they will do is prescribe something that, for all I know, may help calm things down for you some. You understand what I'm saying?"

"I think so." she nodded.

"Step two, you get through these three days, and you get the hell out of here and never look back. Don't even worry about coming back because that is a sure-fire way to end up right back. Step three, this is the best part, you come to see me. Even if you get out and everything looks like sunshine and roses again, you come to see me. Because no matter if someone is manipulating you or not, there is a lot of trauma stuck inside you that needs to be worked out. If there wasn't, I don't believe all of this would have worked so well."

Lawson got up again and headed for the door. "I know your sad, Alia. I know you miss your old life and your family, and that sadness hurts but don't shut down. Let yourself feel the pain. Pain lets us know we're still alive and kicking."

"Can I ask a favor?"

"Sure. No guarantees I can do it, of course."

"I want you to see Charlie." Mentioning his name brought tears to her eyes. "He's going through a lot of trauma right now too, and I don't want it to mess up his future. Our future if there is one."

"You know the biggest reason why I know you're not crazy? It's the empathy you have for others. I'll see him if he'll have me. It would be my pleasure." with that, he tapped on the door and was let out.

Alia let her tears fall.

After breakfast, which she refused to eat, Alia spent the whole morning taking tests of one shape or form. There was blood work, urine work, another cat scan, MRI, a long list of questions she had to answer, and then just before lunch, she finally met who would be her Doctor.

Dr. Solomon was a kind-faced older, rather portly, brown-skinned woman. She had spent the morning going over Alia's test results as they came in but needed further study to get an accurate first assessment. The Doctor asked Alia a few basic starter questions and explanations to some of the questions she had been asked. Then for an hour, they talked about what had been going on since the arrival of Trish back into her life.

When they were done, Alia, having it all laid out like that, thought that this woman would never let her out of this place. So she was surprised by what the Dr said.

"Good news, I don't think you're severely mentally unstable. And no, I don't believe the whole drug hypnotism thing Lawson came up with. He means well, but that is all rather far-fetched. Something fit for a movie or daytime soap opera but not real life. No, what I think is, seeing your mother again, more importantly, seeing how she fixed her life after you but not before you, caused a small mental break. The issue here is that you went through a lot in your childhood and should have been in counseling in one form or another long before now. I think you're angry, very angry. Would it be fair to say when you first saw Tish, you were angry at her for doing so well?"

"I was angry with her for showing back up at all. But yes, coming back like that, it pissed me off."

"Did you want her to come back to you hurting and begging for help?"

"I didn't want her to come back. I don't care about how she treated me, but the things, the horrible things she said about Charlie." she cracked, saying his name as her heart hurt. "That was too much, he didn't deserve that. Neither did Ellen and Harper."

"Charlie is pretty special to you. I know he's your fiance, of course, but why do I get the feeling it's beyond that?"

"He is," She said, eyes brimming with tears. "Very much so."

"Then why don't you want to see him? Earlier, you were asked who you would allow to come to see you. Yet his name wasn't mentioned. Why is that?"

"Because it's Charlie That boy, he has a heart so big you could fill the whole world into it and still have the room it seems like. And for whatever reason, I am the one he has set his heart on. I can't let him see me in here like this. It'll haunt him forever. I can't hurt him like that."

"Even though he's the one that put you here?"

Alia looked away as the tears fell, nodding her head.

"And you don't resent him?"

"No, it hurts, but I could never hate him. He's saved my life in more ways than I could ever explain. And all I've brought him is pain and grief. He's not the one I resent. He's not the one I hate right now."

"So who do you hate then?"

"Myself," Alia said matter of factly.

All three of the Harpers showed up at the hospital together shortly after noon. That morning at their house had been a solemn one. Ellen cooked, but neither one of her boys ate. Charlie moped around, sitting outside for a while and coming back in with his eyes all red. Harper made some calls, asking for favors and making promises to give him and Charlie the day off unless there was an emergency.

Ellen tried to cheer Charlie up, helping him get ready to go see Alia. She fixed his tie and told him how happy Alia would be to see him. It had worked a little, which made it all the harder when the nurse told them only Harper was allowed in.

"What do you mean I'm the only one?" Harper demanded, his bark frightening the nurse. "This young man is her fiance, for crying out loud. Let me talk to her Doctor. Maybe he misunderstood something. These two kids are crazy about each other. It'll crush them to go three days without a visit."

"Dr. Solomon has nothing to do with it," she said timidly but standing firm. "She has cleared Alia to see whoever she wants. I'm sorry." said the nurse, directing that last thing at Charlie.

That hit him like a sack of cement right in the chest. Charlie stumbled back a few steps so fast that Ellen had to shore him up.

"Now, just relax. I'm sure there's some explanation Charlie." Ellen soothed.

"Yes, there is; she doesn't want to see me." *She's mad at me, angry that I locked her away in this awful place. She's never going to forgive me. I'm losing her. I know it. I know I'm losing my sweet girl.*

"Not necessarily," said Harper. "She may just be upset after what she did. Or maybe she thinks you are mad at her. Let me go talk to her, Charlie. I'm sure once she hears you're not upset with her, she'll want to see you. "

Charlie nodded, looking hurt. With his mother guiding his way, he walked back to the waiting area, sat, and hung his head. Ellen sat down with him taking one of his hands into hers, trying to comfort him.

After the morning assessment, they changed Alia to more permanent quarters, one more like a hospital room than the box she woke up in. Still, it was sparse, with cameras in the corners and safety measures to prevent suicides, like fake mirrors and bars on the windows. She was given gray sweatpants and a plain white t-shirt as well instead of just a hospital gown and warm slip-proof socks.

When Harper came in, Alia sat in a chair by a mesh-covered window, looking and not looking outside. Next to her was a food tray with no bites taken and only the apple juice empty. Grabbing a chair and pulling it up to where she was, Harper sat down. She wouldn't look at him for several minutes, so he sat in silence, waiting her out.

Fighting her fear, Alia turned to him at last. Looking at him, she could see Charlie, just a little, even though he favored his mother. It brought pain to her heart. She knew he was here, could feel him at last. Could feel his grief.

"You look tired," he said. "Rough night?"

"Don't think so. Pretty sure they had me drugged up." She whispered, finding it hard to look him in the eyes. Instead, she looked at his arm and the bandage that covered the wound where she had shot him.

"Don't you even worry yourself about that. It's nothing more than a scratch, I promise you."

Alia nodded.

"You know Charlie is here. He wants to see you. He's not mad at you, Alia. None of us are. We know what happened wasn't you."

Alia nodded again and had to look away, with fresh tears in her eyes.

"Can I ask why you don't want to see him?"

"I do." she wiped a tear from her face. "But I can't. I don't want him to see me like this." *I don't want him to see his girl so broken.*

"Why not?" he asked, keeping a softness in his voice he rarely used outside of his home.

"Because I can't bear to have him look at me the way you are right now. Like I'm some fragile half-broken thing you're afraid to admit you're scared of. I can't hurt him like that."

"But you're OK with hurting me?" he said lightheartedly.

"You're pretty tough. I'm sure you can take it." she smiled at him. "You barely flinched when I shot you."

"You mean when you grazed me. Still stings like a bitch, though."

"I'm never going to be able to forgive myself for all of this. I've hurt the three of you so much."

"Sure you will, it'll take time, but eventually you will. It's not your fault."

"But what if it is? What if Lawson is wrong, and I'm just broken?

"What if I can never be the woman Charlie needs me to be."

"Sweetheart, you already are. You always have been. Even at your lowest when you were hanging out with all the wrong people, Charlie never stopped loving you. Ellen and I didn't either. Though I will admit you and I had our moments."

"No, you don't understand. He wants children. Charlie wants a family. He wants to be a great parent like you and Mom. What kind of mother am I ever going to be? Will I even be able to love them, or will I hate them like my mother hated me? And Ellen, she wants grandchildren so bad. I can't have kids and do the same things to them my mother did to me."

"Hey now, slow down a little. You're talking about things years from now. Don't worry about tomorrow or the maybes. The only thing we need to focus on is the now. Getting you out of here, getting you well, and getting the two of you back to that sappy happy life the two of you had that made even Ellen and I look like hacks. One step at a time."

"I want that so bad," she said with a quivering chin.

"So does Charlie. And you'll get it. When you reconnected with him and realized how much you loved him, I bet it seemed like the two of you would never make it all work out. But you did. This is going to be the same thing. It's all dark now, but the dark doesn't ever last forever."

"You sure he still wants that? I mean with me?"

"I know he does. No matter the reason you're sick, Alia, and we will be there with you every step of the way and make you well again. We wouldn't leave you or stop loving you anymore now than if you had cancer, or a drug problem, or any other sickness. I know your real family bailed on you time and time again, but we are your family now, and we don't do that shit." Now Harper could feel the sting of tears in his eyes despite his promise to himself to be strong.

Getting out of her chair Alia wrapped her arms around his neck, hugging as tight as she could. In the end, Harper couldn't convince her to let Charlie in. The same went for Ellen. She said to tell them that she loved them both but that her heart just couldn't take it. Harper could see his son's heart shatter as he told him.

"Can I give her a note? Can I do that much?"

"Sure, son, just be careful what you say, Charlie. She's very hurt and vulnerable right now. We want her back in a few days, not a few weeks."

A nurse gave Charlie some paper and a pen. He jotted down a quick note, then from a bag he had brought from home, he pulled out the music box bear that had once been his.

Ellen gasped when she saw it and had to turn away so he wouldn't see her tears.

Charlie taped the note to the bear and gave it to the nurse, who assured him as long as the Doctor approved, she would give it to her. With a heavy heart, Charlie let his parents take him home. He went right to his room, lay on the bed they had shared and urged time to march a little faster.

That evening when the nurse came in with the bear, Alia couldn't believe what she was seeing. Taped to its chest was a small note. "The handsome young man in the waiting room wanted me to give you this. Sorry it took so long, Dr. Solomon had to approve, and she was busy."

Alia read the note, her heart shining and hurting simultaneously. She smelled the bear and noticed Charlie had sprayed it with his cologne that she loved the most. Laying down in the bed, she hugged the bear and read the four simple words he wrote over and over.

I love you more.

In this day and age, not many doctors are willing to make house calls. Lawson was not one of those kinds of doctors. As a psychologist, he thought seeing someone's home was a significant part of the process. Most of his sessions were conducted at his home office. Still, in some exceptional cases, he felt he needed to get a feel for the environment a person lived in. Alia and Charlie's was one such case.

This is why when he called Charlie about seeing him as Alia wanted him to, he asked to meet at the Harper's home. True, that wasn't where the two lived the most, but he had already seen the apartment. When Lawson arrived, he asked them not to say a word and just let him explore the home.

Lawson's first impression was of a very warm and inviting home. It was very tidy but also had a very lived-in feel that only comes with a place that a family has been in for a long time. The walls of the home were adorned with family photos, most of which were of Charlie in different stages of childhood. A few, however, were of a baby girl up to the age of three and recent ones of Alia. It was no doubt the little girl was her. One such photo was a very large one of the little girl in a white dress sitting in a rocking chair. It held a place of honor over the fireplace right next to one of Charlie about the same age.

When he was done, Lawson asked to be left alone with Charlie outside so they could talk. Out on the back porch, they sat at a little iron table and chair set across from each other.

"Alia wanted me to come to talk to you, did you know that?"

Just the sound of her name made Charlie's heart skip a beat. "No, I didn't know that. When did you see her?"

"Yesterday morning when she woke. Wish I could say she was looking good, but I don't believe in lying for the sake of lying. Hard to ask my clients to be honest if I won't be." Charlie nodded. He appreciated Lawson being honest despite not liking that his girl wasn't doing so good.

"She's worried about you. Even with everything she is going through, it's your mental health she's worried about."

"But yet she won't see me. At least she wouldn't yesterday. I'm going to try again today."

"Yes, I heard, and that's part of it. She knows what you did was hard on you. She's trying to make things easier."

Charlie's chin quivered as he tried to keep his tears to himself. *How could she possibly think me not seeing her would make things better?*

"I know it must be hard for you to imagine, but she's not wrong. People that see their loved ones in dodgy places like that often come away feeling haunted. I reckon she doesn't want the person she is right now to be the image of her in your mind. Least not until she can walk out of there feeling better."

"She's not mad at me?"

"You would have to ask her about that, but no, I don't believe she is. As I said, she wanted me to see you to help you through this, not punish you. She's worried about you. And seeing you, I'm worried about you myself. When's the last time you slept a full night? Or ate a decent meal?"

Charlie shook his head. "I can't. I just can't. Even before I sent her away, I didn't sleep well knowing what she was going through. Now, now I barely...I close my eyes and I see her...pointing that gun at me."

"And that makes you angry? I know you love her, of course, but surely you're angry at her for what she did?"

Charlie shook his head again. "No, no far from it. The look on her face, in her eyes. She was terrified. And worse, when she realized what she had done...." Charlie stopped, unable to continue as tears fell.

Lawson gave the boy a few minutes to recover, handing him a box of tissues.

"I'm not angry with her. I don't think I ever really could be. I know how she felt that day. I know because I could feel it. It was all I could do to keep from falling down the rabbit hole with her."

"Because of this connection the two of you had since you met?"

Charlie shook his head. "It was before that. That night, before my parents ever brought her home. Before my mother left to go get her, I could feel her pain. I woke up to the sounds of her crying, only it was in my head. I know it sounds insane. Whenever Alia isn't too far away, I can sense her. Since we have become closer, it's even more than that. We pick up on each other's emotions even when we are not around each other."

"What about now? Do you sense her now?"

"Yes, I do. I was afraid it would stop while she was in there, but it hasn't. I can feel her, and she's scared. She's tired too, I mean exhausted, and she's lonely. She's hurting so bad, and I did that to her."

"No, Charlie, you can't blame yourself for this."

"You don't understand. I blame myself for letting it get this far. I blame myself for not being here with her, so it didn't go the way it did. It's my fault she's hurting now. If it turns out that we have been right this whole time and Trish is behind this, then the way Alia feels right now is all on me. It was my job to protect her. I said I would, and I failed."

"Which I assume is why she wanted me to talk with you. Think about it, Charlie. If you know how she feels, then she also knows how you feel. She knows you're hurting. Any guesses as to who she blames for hurting you?"

Charlie looked up at Lawson. "I'm guessing not Trish."

"You would guess right. The two of you blame yourselves for each other's pain, and if you don't do something about that and learn to heal, this could break the both of you."

Charlie nodded tears in his eyes. "Then let's start healing."

"How are you feeling today?"

Alia looked up at Dr. Solomon and sighed. "I'm angry."

"And who are you angry with?"

"Everyone, myself, I'm angry with myself."

"Good, glad to see you're being honest with me. Now tell me why?"

"I feel like I'm not doing enough to end this mess. I feel like I'm whining and acting like a spoiled child looking for attention instead of snapping out of it and being who I need to be for Charlie."

You always were a spoiled little shit.

The all too familiar voice wasn't as loud as it used to be. Alia figured the medications they had her on had something to do with that. Still, it was there, and without the distraction of Charlie or work, it wasn't shutting up either.

"And are you? Acting like a spoiled child?"

Yes. Boo hoo, poor little Alia.

"I don't know, am I? I mean, I know what is causing this, so shouldn't I just be able to snap out of it, pick myself up, and move on?"

"If it was that easy, I would be out of a job." Dr. Lawson smiled. "I think what you're trying to ask is are you sabotaging things."

"Well, am I ?"

You always were a pain in the ass. Nothing but a whiny little shit. Always trouble, always in the way.

Alia had hoped the medications they insisted she be on would get rid of Trish's nagging voice, yet they hadn't. She supposed she should tell them about it but was afraid they would keep her here longer if she did.

"To what purpose?"

"I don't know. Push people away before I can be pushed away by them. Been doing that my whole life. Why should this be any different?"

"Do you want to push them away?"

Alia thought about that and shook her head no, afraid to speak.

"And?"

Alia shook her head again, not understanding.

"I think there is more than just anger there."

Alia sighed, "I'm scared." she confessed, wiping away a tear.

Aww, poor little Alia is scared. I'll give you something to be scared about.

"What are you scared of?"

"I'm afraid that the past two years were nothing more than a wonderful dream, and now the nightmare is back."

That's right, you're not getting rid of me.

"Are you talking about being abused? Are you afraid of someone close to you hurting you?"

"No...no, not like that."

"So enlighten me."

"I'm afraid of not being loved ever again. That's my nightmare. A life surrounded by people but desperately alone and unloved."

Nobody loves an ugly little brat like you. Your own mother doesn't love you, how can anyone else?

"You know he came again today. Even knowing you wouldn't see him. They both did."

Alia nodded, fighting back the tears. Harper had told her.

"Seems to me there's still a lot of love there. So why so afraid?"

Liar Liar Liar Liar! Screamed the voice, and Alia felt herself flinch involuntarily.

"I feel like it's all slipping through my hands. I don't deserve it. I don't know. I just want to go back."

You don't deserve anything for leaving your poor mother. Ungrateful little bitch.

"And do what?"

"Tell her to fuck off like I should have." She said angrily.

Always with the nasty mouth.

"Do you always resort to anger when you're afraid?"

Alia shrugged her shoulders.

"Anger is a perfectly reasonable emotion, under certain conditions. It's also a defense mechanism. Often used by those like yourself that are sad and afraid. But anger can also be dangerous."

"That's what I'm afraid of. I'm afraid of hurting someone. I mean more than I already have."

You shot the boy's father. He only wants to see you to tell you he's done with your shit.

"Physically or mentally."

"Both. But mentally more."

"How so?"

"Physical pain goes away. Wounds heal. But mental pain lingers, sometimes for a very long time. Sometimes no matter how good things are, there's always a cloud, a dark, nasty cloud threatening to burst at any moment. And you laugh and love and pretend to ignore it, but it's always there. The worst part is no one else can see it. They may look in your eyes and see a shadow there, but they can never have an idea just how big what causes that shadow is. I don't want to be the reason for someone else's cloud."

Poor baby, poor Alia, always the victim. I'll show you a cloud.

"Your mother is the reason for your cloud?"

"Trish is the reason. And her family to a certain extent."

Oh, here we go again. It's always everyone's fault but Alia's. If only she had any idea what a pain in the ass you always were.

"And you hate her for it, hate them?"

"Oh yes, very much so. I know I'm not supposed to, but I do."

Yeah, well, I hate you too. No one really loves you. You will see, even Charlie will get sick of your shit.

"Why are you not supposed to?"

"Because they're family."

"What makes them family?"

Alia shrugged again. "Blood, I guess."

"When you think of family, and I don't mean your own just in general, what do you associate that word with? Other than blood, what is family?"

"Love, support, acceptance, and guidance."

Dr. Solomon pulled out her phone, typed something in, and handed it to Alia. "Read over that."

On the phone was the definition of family. Alia read it all then looked up questioningly.

"Anywhere there, do you see love mentioned?"

Alia shook her head and handed back the phone.

The Doctor typed something else in and handed it back to her.

The word defined this time was Love.

"Is the word family used to define the word love anywhere there?"

Alia shook her head and thought she was beginning to understand.

"You had it right the first time. Biological family is blood simply that. It would be nice if we loved them and they, us, but we are under no obligation to. You don't need to feel like you have to love your family simply because biology made them related to you. You certainly don't have to feel like you owe someone something they won't give back to you. Just like love has nothing to do with family. Love is a feeling we have for people we care about simply because we care about them, not because they share the same blood we do. You don't need to love or be loved by your blood family. You have people that love you unconditionally because they chose to and because you chose to love them. Hate is every bit as valid an emotion as love when it is earned. And if they have earned your hate, then there's nothing wrong with that. Just don't let that hate make that cloud any bigger because people like that are not worth the pain. The people that do love you can make that cloud go away. It may take some time and help, but they can. You just have to let them and trust them."

Alia nodded and looked down at the musical bear on her lap.

After getting back home from another day not seeing Alia, Charlie pulled the note his father had given him from her out of his front jeans pocket and read it.

More and more every day, my sweet boy.

Smiling, Charlie read it over and over.

Chapter 36
Going Home

"How are you feeling today?" asked Dr. Solomon.

"That depends."

"On what?"

"On if I get out of here today," Alia said, feeling scared but hopeful.

Dr. Solomon smiled. "Well, that all depends on you now, doesn't it? Do you want to stay? Feel like you need more time?"

Alia shook her head no.

"I know you discussed working with Dr. Lawson. Do you still plan on doing that?"

She nodded.

"Good, I may disagree with his processes, but like I said the first day, you're not clinically insane. You do, however, need someone to talk to and work things out with. All of you do. If you are comfortable with Lawson, I have no problems with that."

"I like him. I think he means well."

"It's the accent," she said with a smile. "All the girls are crazy over his accent."

Alia laughed.

"Oh my, she is capable of something other than a frown. I was afraid you would leave here without me seeing you smile, a real smile, of course."

"Does that mean I can go home?"

"How do you feel compared to the day of the incident?"

"Astonishingly myself for the first time in a long time. Honestly." And she did. Even the nasty feeling in the back of her head was gone.

"Then I don't see why not. However, I'm not yet ready to clear you for active duty just yet. We need to make sure these spells, whatever they are, won't happen again before I'm going to set you loose on the streets armed."

"Perfectly understandable. I doubt Harper would be in a big hurry either."

" And don't you think you have me fooled. I know you've been forcing yourself to eat just so I will release you."

Lowering her eyes, Alia smiled again, blushing a little. The nurse who brought her the bear warned her that they wouldn't let her leave if she didn't start eating. So she had been, as the doctor said, forcing herself to eat. The worst part was just how horrible the food here was after Mom taught her how to cook.

"But I'll at least give you credit for keeping it down. So you're going home. How do you feel about that?"

Alia thought for a bit and was surprised Trish's angry voice had been silent most of the day. "Scared, nervous, a little nauseous."

"Not angry at anyone you're going home to?"

Alia shook her head, wiping at another tear.

"Not afraid of anyone?"

She shook her head again.

"What about yourself? Are you afraid of yourself?"

She nodded, afraid to speak.

"You haven't had any issues since you have been here. No bouts of anger, no paranoia, no reckless behavior, no manic episodes of any kind. In fact, if, well, half the town wasn't talking about what happened at the park, I would think your admit was an overreaction."

Alia looked away from the doctor and bit at her lower lip, trying not to cry more than she already was. She hadn't thought about how what she did had been seen by others. The town that once claimed her as a hero probably now saw her as a complete nut job.

"Are you afraid it will start back up again?"

Alia nodded again.

"What did we say about positive thinking?"

"It's half the battle." she sniffed.

"Exactly. We will be giving you the medications we have been giving you here to take home. Keep taking them, talk to Dr. Lawson and be honest with your loved ones like you have with me. I know you're still upset about Charlie putting you here, so tell him."

"I can't. It's not his fault."

"Fault or not, your feelings are valid. And holding it in only makes that cloud bigger. If you're worried, you need to tell them. If you're mad, you need to tell them. Hell, if you want a cheeseburger, you need to tell them. You may be surprised what you get in return when you do. Now, are you ready to go home?"

Alia nodded.

"Good because I have a feeling they are more than ready to get you back."

I sure hope so.

A couple of hours later, Dr. Solomon sat in her office with Harper, Ellen, and Charlie. The poor boy looked like a wreck. He was dressed in a nice button-down shirt and jeans, his dark hair combed with a few very stubborn locks falling over his forehead. But his eyes were red with bags under them, his cheeks sunken, and his paler pail. He fidgeted as he sat, running his hand through his hair and over his jawline. She could tell he was both anxious and nervous. But most of all, he looked worried. So the first thing she did was to assure them that Alia was coming home.

"She's getting a shower and dressing right now, but I've cleared her to go home."
Ellen wept, clinging to her husband's arms, and relief washed over Charlie's face.

"Now I know you three tend to like Dr. Lawson's theory in all of this. The only problem with that is that it ignores the obvious issues here, and that is Alia suffered a very traumatic childhood. Between the abuse from her mother, the death of her father, and I would say even her separation from all of you at a young age, she's been through a lot. One thing we talked about, and she needs to work on, is this assertion that what she went through was no big deal simply because others have been through worse. So no more letting her compare traumas to justify not working on her own. Also, I believe her mother coming back into this almost perfect little life she had was just too much of a reminder of where she came from for her to manage. She's angry, sad, worried, anxious, and hurt, but she's not crazy, at least not in the clinical sense. But she will need help to get through all of these emotions and use them more constructively. And I don't just mean her sessions with Dr. Lawson or medication. The three of you must be an integral part of her recovery as well."

"We will." Said Harper. "Our days of standing by and watching her suffer are over." he took Charlie's hand. "I promise you, son, we won't give up on her."

"Of course, we won't," said Ellen, drying her tears. "She's family always has been."

"Understand that also means not giving in to any delusions of mind control and drugs. As long as her problems are blamed on someone else, she won't fully start to recover. Okay then. My advice for now is to just take things slowly. Don't push her to recover at any rate other than her own. I know she loves her job and is eager to get back to it, but the job will always be there. And she will be better at it once she is well. Oh, and I have given her permission to speak her mind more freely, so don't be surprised what she may have to say. Just listen."

The three of them looked at each other and smiled.

Alia stood in front of a break-less mirror, looking at herself and sighing heavily. The clothes Ellen brought for her hung off her thinning frame.

I guess I'm not such a fat ass anymore.

And it wasn't just the weight that was a problem. She had bags under her eyes, and her hair was limp from the cheap hospital shampoo. Alia had never felt she was beautiful, but now she looked tired and older than her young years. She had tried her best to look nice, wanted Charlie to see her happy and looking good, but she only had so much to work with. When the nurse came in to walk her down to a private room set aside for reuniting loved ones, she offered to do Alia's makeup, but she declined. Grabbing her few belongings, Alia followed the nurse, feeling nervous and a little shaky on her feet.

At the door of the room, Alia paused, taking in a few good deep breaths. When she opened the door, there was Charlie, a pink carnation in his hands and in his beautiful green eyes the look of such love that it made her heart soar. She ran into his arms, crying. He picked her up, hugging her more petite, thinner frame against his tall, lanky one.

"I missed you so much, sweet girl," he whispered into her ear. "I'm so sorry, I'm so very sorry."

Alia so much wanted to tell him it was okay, that it was all her fault, that she never for a moment hated him, but the words failed her. Instead, she clung to him as Ellen and Harper wrapped their arms around them both. When she finally loosened her grip, he set her back down.

Charlie gave her the half-crushed carnation. He, too, had things he needed to say, but the words choked in his throat. Instead, he reached into the pocket of his pants, pulling out her engagement ring. Hands shaking, he put the ring back on her finger then kissed her cheek gently.

Alia looked down at the ring and knew in her heart the two of them were going to be alright. The fact that he still wanted her to have the ring said more than any words either of them could have managed would have.

Taking a deep breath, Alia forced herself to speak. "I want to go home, Charlie. Please take me home."

"Of course, sweet girl, anything you want." After another hug, the four of them left the hospital and drove back to the Harper's. No one had to ask Alia where she meant by home. They all knew her heart called her back there.

Home for the first time in three days, Alia went upstairs with Charlie while Harper and Ellen ordered food for the night. She walked into the bedroom, put down the one bag she had, and smiled with a sigh.

"What is it?" asked Charlie.
"I expected it to feel different."
"What?"

"Here, less warm, less inviting, less like home, more like I was intruding."

"Why would it be different?"

"Because after what I did, I expected to feel unwelcome and unwanted." Alia sat on the bed and asked Charlie to sit next to her. "I have something to say, Charlie, something that's hard to say, but If I don't, it will be between us until I do, and I can't have that." She thought of the enormous cloud over her head and was determined not to allow it to become larger than it already was, no matter how hard it would be.

"Alia, you know you can tell me anything."

"I usually do, but I'm not so sure now. I have the feeling you want to pretend like this whole thing didn't happen, and you want me to do the same. But we can't. It's not healthy."

Charlie nodded his head. "Alia, you don't have to say it. I know you're hurting, and I know I'm the cause of that pain. And yes, I would like to pretend this was all just some fucked up nightmare, but I know you need to do this, so have at it." He took her hand in both of his.

"I am hurt." Alia looked off into the room, afraid that she wouldn't say it if she looked at him, and it would eat at her. "You said you would always be by my side, but in there, in there, I was alone, again."

"I know." Charlie wrapped his one arm around her and pressed his forehead to the side of her head. "Believe me, Alia, please, I love you more than life itself. I didn't want to do it. The last thing I wanted was to send you away."

"Then why did you?" She knew damn well he didn't have a choice. That still did little to quench the hurt she felt.

Charlie moved and knelt down in front of her forcing her to face him. His beautiful green eyes were rimmed in tears, and the sadness in them like to break her heart a million times over.

"I did it because you were scaring the crap out of me, Alia, and you didn't give us much choice after the park."

"So you're afraid of me?"

"No, sweet girl, no, I was afraid for you. Alia, I know you, you have such a big heart, and you feel so hard. I know if you would have hurt someone, you would never forgive yourself. It would break a part of you, a very special part. Dad and I had talked about it, and we both agreed that if things got out of hand, if you got violent or hurt someone, what we would have to do. It broke my heart to send you away, but I didn't know what else to do. I'm sorry, I won't do it ever again. I promise no matter what, I won't send you away again. Look at me, three days without you, and I'm a wreck."

Alia put her hands on his face and forced herself to look into his eyes. "No, you're my beautiful Charlie." she cried. "My wonderful man with the most beautiful and loving eyes. I know you're hurting too, I can see it, and I can feel it." She wiped her tears and looked at him more seriously. "Charles Nathaniel Harper, you listen to me. If you have to, you will do it again. Don't let me hurt you. Don't let me hurt Mom and Dad. Promise me no matter how much it hurts, you will send me away again if I try to hurt any of you. I know why you had to do it, Charlie, and as much as it hurt and still hurts, I forgive you because I love you so much." She kissed him for what seemed like the first time in a very long time.

Laying her down on the bed, Charlie kissed her back. Her lips tasted of strawberry gloss, and he felt himself become instantly aroused. He backed off to give himself time to relax a bit, not wanting to push her into doing anything despite how much he longed for it.

Reaching up for him, Alia pulled Charlie back down on top of her. "Make love to me, Charlie, please. I need to feel you right now. I need us to reconnect."

He looked into her eyes, making sure it was really her, and could tell it was, and he could feel her desire matching his own. Charlie made love to her slow and gentle, not ever wanting to stop, not ever wanting to leave now that he was inside her again. When they were done, he pulled her onto him, wrapping his arms around her and covering them both with a blanket. There they lay in each other's arms, enjoying the much needed skin-to-skin contact, and waited for dinner to arrive.

After Helping his mother clean up from dinner, Charlie went upstairs to find Alia and his father working on his closet door in the bedroom.

"That should do it," said Harper.

Charlie watched, confused, as his father left with his old closet door knob in his hands. In place of it was a new handle with a lock on the outside.

"What's all this about?"

Alia sighed. "It was one of the conditions of me coming back here."

"What? My father wants to lock you up in the closet?" As was the case with Alia, Charle felt his anger start to boil up.

"No, Charlie, this was my idea. I'll stay, but you have to lock me in at night…at least until we know for sure this is over."

"No, no, absolutely not, no Alia, I'm not locking you up at night," he said.

"If you don't want me to have to go back or go away, you will. Charlie, I never know who I will be when I wake up. I'm afraid of what I might do." she looked at him pleadingly.

"You said it was over. You said you were feeling like yourself for the first time in months. You would never hurt me."

Reaching out with her hand, Alia touched the side of his eye where a cut was still healing from hitting him with the nine iron.

"That wasn't you." He stopped her hand before she could reach for the scar above his other eye he got in the accident. "And that was an accident."

"They are both good reasons to lock me up at night. Not to mention shooting Harper and shooting over your head. I could have killed you. And I know what I said. And you left out the part where I said, I think. My biggest fear is that I will come to one day with blood all over my hands, and you hurt or dead. We will still be together. I'll just be on the other side of the door. It's this, or I go back right now, tonight until I'm sure this is over and you're safe." She laid her head on his chest and wrapped her arms around him.

Charlie looked in the closet and saw that she had a small bed of an air mattress made up. Everything else in the closet had been removed. "It might get warm in there. I'll get a box fan from the basement. If that's okay."

"That sounds like a great idea Charlie." letting him go, she looked up at him. "Do you remember what you said to me when we first started seeing each other, and we had to sneak around? You said this wasn't going to be forever. Well, neither will this Charlie, I promise."

Charlie nodded. "I know, and I still don't like it. But I won't have you go back there. If this is what it takes for you to feel safe, then it's what we will do." Taking her into his arms, Charlie held her.

That night when Alia came out of the bathroom from brushing her teeth, Charlie was making a bed of his own right in front of the closet door. "What are you doing, sweet boy?" she asked with a laugh.

"I just thought. I just want to be as close as I can to you, that's all."

Smiling, she walked up to him and gave him a big kiss.

He looked at her blue eyes and noticed they were sparkling just a little. "You seem to be feeling better since you got home."

"Well, since we, you know, anyway." she grinned and flushed. "And I do. I feel like we needed to reconnect. I was feeling lost without you."

"Maybe we don't need to do this, after all. Maybe we should try reconnecting some more." smiling, he got closer to her and brushed her lips with his, but she put a hand on his chest and gently pushed him away.

"Nice try there, stud, but sorry. I'll sleep better if we do this. So will you."

"I doubt that, but okay. Do I at least get one more kiss?" he asked, moving up to her again until their faces almost touched.

"Just keep your hands to yourself." she giggled.

"No promises," he said and kissed her, running his hand through her hair before she could protest.

When he closed and locked the door on her that night, Charlie told himself to be grateful that she was there and thinking clearly for a change. He turned off the lights and lay with his head right next to the door. "Goodnight, sweet girl."

"Goodnight, my sweet boy."

Before he closed his eyes, he heard a light tap on the door, then in the light from the moons' glow in through the window, he saw Alia's hand come out from under the closet door. The space between the door and floor was large enough that most of her hand came through. He put his long fingers on her smaller ones and gave a little squeeze.

Alia gave one back, and that is how they fell asleep.

Friday morning arrived, and when Charlie let Alia out of the closet, her smile and eyes said she was once more feeling like herself. When asked, she concurred. His heart leapt with such great joy that he actually swung her around when he picked her up.

"Don't get too carried away there," she said when he put her down. "We've been down this road before. I don't want us to celebrate too early, okay?"

"Of course. But I'm telling you, Alia, I see it in your eyes. You look better than you have in weeks, And there is no way you have seen Trish or Jacob. Now we just need to fatten you back up again." he joked.

"Oh, you're one to talk, Mr. no ass having a long boy." her old familiar ribbing brought a smile to his face and a light in his eyes she hadn't seen for a long time.

"What is it with you and your obsession with my ass?"

"What ass?"

"That's it, you're getting tickled." The two ran around the room laughing and screaming like a couple of kids. Charlie poked and tickled her until she squealed. He got her cornered by the bed and tossed her down on it, tickling her most sensitive spots until she begged for mercy. Charlie was kissing her when Harper barged into the room.

"What the hell?" he roared. Seeing them on the bed, both flushed but laughing and smiling, he shook his head. "Just keep it down to a low roar, you two, some of us are trying to sleep in."

From behind him, they heard Ellen.

"Oh, leave them alone, Harper." she fussed at him with a laugh. "It's about time we had some laughter back in this house. Breakfast will be on in a bit. We have a session with Lawson in a few hours." They heard her as she walked down the stairs.

"Now see what you have done." crouched Harper. "So much for sleeping in." he left, shutting the door, and the two of them laughed.

"Dad's mad, we best behave." giggled Alia.

"Hell no, I can take on my old man." Charlie laughingly boasted, then commenced tickling her until she screamed again.

Downstairs with his wife in the kitchen, Harper waited impatiently for the coffee to finish brewing, his eyes darting up with every thump and squeal of laughter. "Well, those two sure are in a much better mood this morning," he grumbled but with a smile.

"Yes, they are, and we should be as well. Maybe this is over."

"It's not, not really. You heard what the doctor said. Bringing her back, all the way back will take time."

"Then time is what we will give it. Right now, I'm enjoying hearing her laugh again."

From upstairs came a considerable thump that rattled the dishes in the cabinets. "Shit, sorry." They heard Charlie yell from above them, followed by Alia's laughter.

"We don't have much time if they keep trying to tear the house down," fussed Harper

"Oh, hush, you old fart. You and I have rattled the dishes in this house a time or two ourselves."

"I'll rattle you, lady," Harper said, grabbing Ellen at the waist and kissing her neck.

After breakfast, they climbed into one car and went to Lawson's. Driving through town was the one thing Alia was worried about. She kind of expected to see people lined up in the streets pointing and talking in hushed whispers. Or worse. The paranoia that had been almost a constant companion in the past few weeks to come back. But other than a few waves from neighbors, no one seemed to notice, and she didn't see anyone out of the ordinary. Only that was a problem as well. Had she felt even a tad bit paranoid, she may have paid closer attention. She may have noticed an unfamiliar face here and there that seemed very interested in the car as it drove by.

At Lawson's, the family waited in the front room, set up as a reception area with chairs and sofas. This would be a family session, but first, he wanted to talk to Alia alone. Today she chose to go into the library. There wouldn't be a fire on such a warm summer day, but Alia found that being surrounded by all the books comforted her.

"You're looking much better," Lawson said as they sat. "I would like to see you put on some more weight and get better sleep, but the smile is a big improvement. The real question, though, is how do you feel?"

"A lot better. Dr. Solomon's meds make me feel a little sleepy, but no more than my allergy medicines do. And that nagging little ticking I had in the back of my brain is gone. Actually, I didn't even know I had it until it wasn't there anymore."

"Tickling?"

"Maybe not the best word, more like a foggy kind of pain. But centered in one area of my head. I don't know why I couldn't feel it before."

"Well, that lends more credence to the theory that you were drugged. How about the paranoia?"

"Nothing. And I feel pretty much fully connected to Charlie again too. It's been great. And I know it's only been less than a day, but still. I went home thinking I would feel like a stranger in a familiar place, but it just felt like home, I mean home, home."

The two of them talked for a while longer than Lawson let in the family. The rest of the session mainly was Lawson asking about their opinion on how Alia was and giving them a layout of what he was planning to accomplish over the next several months. For the first few weeks, Alia would have a session three days a week, so they made plans to bring her back on Wednesday and called it a day.

After the session and lunch back at the house, Charlie begged off, saying he needed to check on things at the apartment and run some errands that they had been neglecting. He was cautious to ensure that no one saw him take his personal revolver out of the safe. In his truck, he put the firearm in the glove box. Charlie didn't think he would need it, but he also didn't want to not have it if he did. Driving out of town, he went down the same old country back road his father had stopped him on earlier in the week.

Pulling up into the drive of the cabin from the case of the missing kids' Charlie scanned for any signs of Jacob or Trish. The camper was parked in the driveway with no other vehicle in sight. Inside the cabin, the lights were off. He walked up the steps and pounded on the door anyway. When there was no answer, he did the same to the camper. Still not getting an answer, he tried the handle and was surprised to find it was unlocked.

Inside the camper was a pretty typical layout. Cockpit in the front with windows covered, small living room area with pullout side set to make the room larger. Small kitchen, bath, and large bedroom in the back. Everything was neat as a pin. On the walls and doors were crosses and pictures of religious figures and religious quotes. Charlie and his family didn't have a thing against people's religions; they just didn't have a belief, choosing instead to lean on the side of science and facts. Still, the images and quotes set him on edge. The whole camper set him on edge. It gave an appearance of stage dressing. A little too perfect to be real.

When he first started to root through the many cubbies in the camper, Charlie expected to find not just some form of whatever drug they gave Alia but other incriminating evidence as well. When the first search didn't turn up anything, Charlie searched harder, this time looking for false bottoms and such and ransacking the place.

The only thing he found that made him think of Alia was in the fridge. There was very little food. However, there were several bottles of cold tea. Raspberry flavored, to be exact, which just happened to be the flavor she drank at the cafe. Thinking back, Charlie remembered the day they found her with Trish. There had been a cooler between the two lounge chairs, and on Alia's side was an almost empty bottle of tea, this tea, sitting on top of the cooler. Looking closer at the bottles, he realized these were not bottled by one of the big brand name companies. Looked to him more like a small private business kind of thing. Taking one of the bottles, Charlie looked around at the mess he had made when he heard a car come down the drive. Tucking the bottle in the back of his pants, Charlie walked out of the camper as Jacob stopped and parked the small ford he was driving. In the passenger seat was Trish looking shocked to see him there.

Jacob motioned for her to stay put, got out, and approached Charlie. "Well, hello Sergeant Harper, what can we do for you today? If you're looking for Alia, I'm sorry to tell you she's not here."

"I'm not Sergeant anything today. And I know she isn't, so let me ask you, what the hell are you doing here?"

"I'll assume you don't mean at the cabin and cut to the chase."

"I would appreciate that," Charlie said with a stern tone.

"I'm here helping Trish. She's concerned that her daughter may be in danger and doesn't want to leave Union county without her."

"Well, let me assure you that she's not. Now pack your shit and get the fuck out of my county."

"Interesting you should say that. Did she not just spend time in the hospital on a seventy-two-hour psych hold? That is after discharging her gun in a public park."

Charlie's jaw clenched as he bore his eyes into that of the man in front of him.

"Now I'm no psychologist, but it seems to me like the girl is screaming out for help. Like maybe the perfect little life of hers is anything but."

"Cut the shit, Jacob. You and I both know this is your doing, and I'm here to tell you it's over. Whatever it was you were doing has worn off, and there's no way I'm letting you or that bitch get anywhere near her ever again. So heed my warning and get the hell out of here while I still have a bit of my humor intact."

"Is that a threat, Sergeant? Because I'm pretty sure your Daddy the Sheriff would frown on such things. Doesn't he pride himself on running a clean and fair department during these trying times?"

"I'm not here as a cop today. I'm here as Alia's fiance. As her family."

"Well, we'll see about that, won't we?" Jacob said with a smirk.

Charlie rushed up to the man getting right in his face. Jacob didn't back down, but he did cringe a little. "What's that supposed to mean, you fucking piece of shit?"

"It just means that Trish is working with my lawyers to file a false imprisonment charge against you and your family if that's what it comes down to."

Charlie laughed. "Now I know you're a joke. Not only is Alia an adult, but she's free to come and go as she wants."

"Oh really? Then why did you try to bribe Trish to stay away? Why is it when she came to us of her free will, you all rushed in like we were the bad guys and whisked her away? One would wonder why you wouldn't want her to see her mother. Is it because you're afraid she may tell the truth?"

"And what truth would that be, Jacob?" Charlie was finding it hard to keep his temper in check with this man. Jacob was calm and smooth, no hint that he was intimidated by anything about Charlie other than maybe his size.

"About how you and your father brainwashed an impressionable young girl. How at barely eighteen, you, a man of the law, took her to her prom then disappeared for the rest of the weekend. How the two of you had been secretly meeting, even having sex in the back of your patrol car. Yes, yes, we know about that too. This is a small-town Sergeant. It's hard to hide things for very long. And now it seems that these past few years are starting to catch up with her. And let me guess. She's at your parents' home, and she's not left alone or allowed to leave alone, is she?"

"I don't have to be a cop to know that these unsubstantiated claims won't hold up in any court."

Jacob smiled. "I wouldn't call them that exactly. Not since we have several video recordings of Alia admitting to being both mentally and sexually abused by you."

"Bull shit." spat Charlie.

Jacob pulled out his cell phone from his coat pocket, tapped around on it, and showed it to Charlie. On it was a video, and in the video was Alia. Jacob pushed play, and Charlie watched with growing horror.

Jacob's voice off-camera: I know it's hard, Alia, but if you could just tell us again what you said about Charlie. Your fiance Charlie.

Alia looked at the phone glassy-eyed: he won't let me come see my mother. Says she's manipulating me. He should know all about that. He's been doing it for years.

Jacob: Just what is it he has done, Alia

Alia: Do I have to say it?

Trish off-camera: we can't help you unless you do.

Alia: he...he...forces me to have sex with him, has for years. He threatens to hurt me If I don't do what he says. (tears fall down her face).

Seeing her lie and crying about things he would never, could never do enraged Charlie. He grabbed the cell phone and smashed it into the nearest tree. Then before he could run, Charlie picked Jacob up by the collar and slammed him down on the car's hood, getting up in his face.

"You made her say that. You made her say those things, you son of a bitch, and you know it."

"Doesn't matter if we did or not, now does it, son?" smiled Jacob trying his best to keep his composure. "That video is going to be awfully hard to refute. And it's not the only one. Oh, she goes into great detail once she gets started. Now, if you would just allow Trish to see her daughter…maybe it gets lost, and we can all work out our differences."

Pulling his arm back, Charlie punched the man hard in the face slamming the back of his head on the car hood.

"You listen to me, you piece of shit. Neither one of you is going to see her again. Do I make myself clear? Because the next time I see either of you with her, I'm putting a bullet in your brains." he heard a door slam as Trish got out of the car.

"You get off of him, Charlie, or I swear to you I'll see to it that video ends up on the local news, and you will be ruined."

Charlie slammed Jacob on the car one last time, making a point, then turned his attention to Trish getting right up into her face hovering over her.

"Try me bitch."

Trish shrunk down from him. The look in his eyes scared her.

"Pack your shit and get the hell out of my county and never ever come back here again."

"There's more Charlie, more than just that video." Trish laughed. "Oh, the things we were able to get her to say. So easy too. You've got to wonder why."

"Trish shut up." choked Jacob.

"No, Jacob let her talk. It's okay because I've known from the start that this born-again Christian bullshit was an act. You just can't stand that she's happy. You've got to have somebody you can step on and beat under. It's over, Trish. I won't ever allow you to hurt her again. Right now, Alia is the only thing keeping you alive. I won't have her taken away from me again, or me from her." brushing past her, Charlie walked off to his truck.

"I'll have her, Charlie, one way or another, I'll have her. She's mine, do you hear me? She's mine. You'll regret that you ever fucked with me, little boy."

Without looking, Charlie flipped her off.

"I'll get her back, Charlie. If I have to destroy you and your family to do it, I will. If I have to destroy everything she loves, I will have her back."

"Over my dead body," he said, getting in the truck and driving off.

"That's the plan exactly," Trish said with a grin.

When Charlie arrived back home, he was met at the side door by his father, looking angry and with his arms crossed over his chest. "What the hell did you do, boy?" Even at his age, and although the man never laid a hand on him, Charlie feared his father's anger.

"Dad, let me...."

"Basement now." Harper roared, his face red.

As Charlie followed his father to the basement door in the kitchen, he glanced out the window to the back porch and saw his mother and Alia. Alia waved to him with a smile that about melted him. He was about to wave back when Harper yanked him down the stairs by his shirt collar.

Down in the unfinished basement, Harper glared at his son. "Why is it that just when it looks like we are getting things back on track, you've got to run off and fuck it all up?"

"So I made a mess in their camper? The real issue here is that Trish showed her true colors. It has all been a con job like we thought."

"Oh, of course, it has Charlie, that was never up for debate in the first place. But I'm not talking about a mess, and you know it. I had to talk Jacob out of pressing assault charges against you. In uniform or not, you know your actions represent the department, and I won't have any of my officers going off half-cocked. Not even you."

Charlie became alarmed. "Talk him out of how?" he asked, fearing his father may have done something stupid.

Harper didn't answer, just hung his head.

"No, you didn't. Damn it, dad tell me you didn't make some kind of deal with them?"

"I had to give them something. The visit will be in a public place with us present. She won't go near them alone."

"Fuck that." Charlie spun away from his father and punched a box of decorations sending fourth of July banners and ribbons flying. "That is absolute bullshit, and I won't make her do it."

"This is your fault, Charlie. You should have just left well enough alone."

"You don't understand."

"I understand you punched him and slammed him on his car twice, then threatened to kill them both. A shit lawyer could have your badge for that, a decent one, your balls."

"They have a recording of Alia saying I raped her." Charlie blurted out.

Harper took two steps back, stunned. "They have what now?"

"I saw it myself. And apparently more than that. If they're not using that to demand to see her, then that means they are saving that up to get something more out of us later or to keep us from going after them. They are playing you, dad. I bet they want to see how far you're willing to go to give them what they want."

"Once again, who's fault is that, Charlie?"

"Fuck them, dad. Fuck my job. Let them try and get me fired. I'm not letting them near her. Here." From out of the back of his pants, Charlie pulled the bottle of tea.

"What the hell is that?'

"I think it's what they have been using to drug her. I looked up the bottling company. It's Jacob's. There was an almost empty bottle of this beside her that day we found her with them. And the day I tried bribing Trish, I noticed that she had Alia's tea drink ready and waiting for her. I have the evidence we need to at least get them to leave us the hell alone. Or at least I did. I talked to Lawson on the way back. The drug used on Alia wouldn't be detected in her blood because the body breaks it down. But if it's mixed with something, it can be. I was going to swap it for the video, or at the very least threaten them with it."

"Why don't they just release the video regardless."

"Because, as I said, they are holding that for something bigger. Trish told me she would get Alia back, one way or another. She said she would destroy all of us, everyone Alia loved if that's what it would take."

"She tried that before, Charlie, but that tactic didn't work."

"No, it did. Saving those kids is what turned the tide of opinion on her, and you know that as well as I do. Now, unless you plan on staging another rescue, we could be screwed." Charlie stepped up to his father. "This is where you decide if you're going to do what you promised today or not. When it comes to my career or my reputation, I don't care. I'd give it all up to save her. Are you willing to do the same?"

Harper stood up tall facing his son. "Yes, Charlie, I am. You're right. She's what's most important. If we have to do more, we will. We can't lose her again. Your mother, she can't go through that again."

"No…No No No." Said Alia appearing on the stairs behind them. She and Ellen had heard the yelling from outside and came in to see what was going on. Ellen was on the steps behind her looking pale. "I will not let the two of you throw away your careers and everything this family worked hard for just over a visit. I'm not weak, Charlie. I can handle seeing her."

Charlie went up to Alia, looking her deep in her eyes.

"Yes, Charlie, it's all me. I don't want to see her, but I can handle it. Unless, of course, you think I am crazy, and I'll crack again at the sight of her."

"Alia, honey, you know I don't believe that. She is determined to get you back. She is up to something. I don't want you in the same county as her, let alone a meet-up. I don't care if we are there or not."

"It's not your choice to make Charlie. We go there, meet with her, and show her you have that bottle, and if they release that video or anything like it, we will have that tested and prove what they have been doing." Alia placed her hands on his face and looked into his eyes. "Let me do this for you, Charlie. You've done so much for me. You rescued me from her. Let me do this for you. For all of you, please,"

Charlie looked over at his dad.

"We can make it safe for her. They won't get near her, I promise."

"We do this my way," he said, looking at Alia. "If I don't like something, I stop it no matter what. And you never leave my side. No hugs, no touching, nothing, no matter how much she insists."

"Of course, Charlie. You're not going to lose me again, not to her, I promise." she went into his arms, and he held her tight.

Wanting to have an end to all of it sooner rather than later, Harper called Trish and set the meet-up for that evening at Harkening Hill park. He also told her to come ready to leave the county. She just laughed then hung upon him.

A few hours later, when they were getting ready to leave, Charlie pulled out one of the Kevlar vests and handed it to Alia. "I am begging you to wear this. Just in case."

"Do you really think she would just shoot me out in the open like that?"

"Honestly, I don't know what to think about her at this point. She's up to something. She has us by the balls. Well, she thinks she does anyway."

"Charlie, the video you saw, I don't ever remember saying those things. I swear I don't."

Charlie smiled at her and brushed her hair out of her face. "I know, I could tell you looked out of it, glassy-eyed. Don't get your hopes up though it wasn't obvious enough to be noticed by someone that doesn't know you."

With a heavy sigh, Alia put on the vest. The four of them got to the park early. With the help of some of the Sheriff's department officers, they blocked off one section of the parking lot, leaving enough room for the camper and wouldn't let anyone else in. Harper had two officers posted at the start of the parking lot, two more in the parking lot itself with them and two in a patrol car outside the park entrance. If Trish and Jacob tried pulling anything, they would not get very far.

They had taken Charlies' truck and put the back down so Alia could sit on the tailgate. They had cones set up in front of the tailgate to keep Trish at the distance they wanted her to be. Charlie and Harper remained in their street clothes, but both were armed with their own personal handguns.

Waiting for Trish and Jacob to arrive, Alia looked around. It was strange being back in the park. Not to mention the same parking area where she had fired her weapon. Not that she remembered much about that whole day. Most of what she did was like she had come out of a strange sleep, her gun in her hand and the smell of fresh gunpowder in the air. And Charlie. Charlie was standing before her, pointing not his service weapon but his taser at her. That in itself was enough to chill her and something she knew she would never be able to get out of her mind. Alia doubted the image of her wielding her gun around like she had would ever escape his mind, either. She looked off at the grouping of trees when Charlie's voice came to her, sounding far off.

"Alia, hey, are you alright?."

Turning away from the scene of the nightmare, she turned to Charlie and offered him a smile. "I'm fine." not entirely true.

"No, you were a million miles away. Or should I say several feet and days away? I don't know what dad was thinking about setting the meet-up here. You're not seeing them again, are you?"

"It's fine, Charlie," she said, offering him a more genuine smile. "It's not like it's something any of us are ever going to forget about anyway. Avoiding it is just silly."

"Still, it's a little soon, yet. Personally, I feel a little weird being back here so soon after."

Alia looked up at him and could see a haunted look in his eyes and wondered if he saw the same in hers.

Without her having to say anything, he leaned down, kissing her on her forehead. "Yes," he said, looking at her knowingly. "But they are still beautiful."

Alia was about to ask him if he had read her mind, but just then, the RV arrived, pulling the ford behind it. The officers let them in then directed them where to park. With it barely stopped, Trish got out of the RV and slapped her hands on her thighs, a sign of her frustration.

"Don't you think this is a bit much, Harper? We are not here for a shootout. I just want to talk to Alia and make sure she is alright."

Charlie standing next to Alia in front of the tailgate bristled at that and stood up straight. Of all things she could have said, he knew she chose a shootout on purpose.

Harper came out from the front of the truck and gave Charlie a warning glare, then turned his attention to Trish. "Not too much at all, considering you kidnapped, drugged, and coerced an officer of the law. The fact that you seem so insistent on getting your daughter back when you spoke to Charlie earlier makes us feel like we can't take enough precautions."

"The little shit threatened to kill us, not the other way around. He…"

"Stop it now, Trish…." Jacob came from around the side of the RV.

"But."

"I said stop," he said sternly.

To Alia's surprise, Trish backed down, and something about that didn't sit well with her.

"You'll have to forgive her, Sheriff. She's a tad bit agitated. What with her daughter shooting up the place and having to be institutionalized. Certainly, you as a father can understand how she may be unsettled." Jacob stood before them, looking as smarmy and self-righteous as ever despite the bruising on his cheek where Charlie punched him.

"And I'm sure you'll forgive us for taking added precautions under the circumstances," said Harper. Standing tall, he let his large frame be the imposing force he needed it to be.

"Do what you feel you need to, Sheriff. I personally welcome the protection after what your son did today." he motioned to his cheek with a finger ever so slightly. "It's nice to have all these extra armed witnesses if he gets out of line again. We are simply here to talk to the girl. I'm confident that once she hears what we have to say, the **three** of us will leave peacefully."

Charlie took a few steps closer but no more than arm's length from Alia. "If you think you're leaving here with her, then you've wasted your time. Our boys will show you out of town now," said Charlie.

"Now, now Sergeant, let's not be so hasty. I believe she can speak for herself. Alia dear, I hope you remember that not all birds fly south for the winter."

Alia sat still and looked at the man with a strange expression on her face. "What the hell is that supposed to mean?" she said at last.

"Yeah, what the Fuck is that supposed to mean?" asked Harper.

Jacob looked over at Trish and her at him. Both looked perplexed, perhaps even worried. "Well, try it again." she hissed.

Jacob started to speak, but before he could, Charlie rushed him, putting a hand over his mouth and slamming the man against the RV.

"That's what he said to her last time. It's a trigger phrase. The son of a bitch is trying to do it to her again." Pulling Jacob back a little, Charlie slammed him against the RV again hard enough to rock it a little. "Isn't that what you're trying to do, you piece of shit? I've got news for you, it's not going to work this time." Charlie put his mouth close to the man's ear. Also, you may want to know I have one of your tea bottles from your RV."

Jacobs' eyes widened.

"That's right, preacher boy. I wonder just what kind of crap the FBI will find floating around in the damn thing."

"Alia. Alia, listen. Not all birds fly south for the winter. Not all birds fly south for the winter." Trish yelled.

Harper pulled his gun on her, shutting her mouth with one final yelp. "Not another word, Trish."

Ellen ran around the side of the truck to Alia. "Alia, baby girl, are you alright?"

"I'm fine." Alia reached up and pulled two earplugs out of her ears and tossed them on the ground in front of Trish with a smirk. "Did you really think we were that stupid?"

The angry look on Trish's face was enough of an answer.

"Come on, we're getting in the truck. Let the boys deal with this." The two of them sat in the truck's cabin, where Ellen turned to her again. "Are you sure you're okay?"

"Yeah, fine, I mean, I don't feel any different."

"You're shaking."

"She was really going to do it, wasn't she? She really was going to take me away from him, from all of you?" tears brimmed in her eyes. "Why, why does she hate me so much? Why can't she just leave me alone and let me be happy."

Ellen pulled the sobbing girl into her arms. "She's a sad, pathetic person, Alia. She's sick. She needs someone to control to feel better. But we are not going to let that happen. We will not let her take you away from us, I promise you."

Meanwhile, Charlie still had Jacob pinned to the camper. Harper holstered his gun and went up to Charlie, putting a hand on his shoulder. "Let him go, son."

"Let him go? Are you kidding me? You saw what they tried to do."

"Yes, I did. And I think they realize it didn't work. Let go of him."

Pounding the man on the camper one last time for good measure, Charlie let Jacob go and allowed his father to pull him back over to the truck.

Harper turned to Jacob and Trish. "The video, the one of Alia saying Charlie did things to her…that will never see the light of day. Or the bottle of tea we have as well as witness testimony." he pointed to the officers. "Will be handed over to the FBI. I certainly hope I make myself clear."

"And I'm just supposed to take your word for it that he has a bottle."

Charlie pulled out a bag from the truck's toolbox and showed him the bottle of tea.

Jacobs' face turned sour.

"Also, you will be escorted out of the county, and you will not return."

"Wait...Dad, we can't let them leave."

Harper pulled his son aside.

"You can't let them leave. What if there are other people, other girls like Alia. Now that we know for sure that they have been drugging her, we can't just let them go.."

"I know what you're saying, Charlie. But right now, my responsibility is to you and Alia. We will see what we can do later, but right now, I want these people out of our lives. I want to give Alia time to heal and get strong again. She may need that strength later." Harper went back over to Jacob. "So as I was saying, the two of you are to leave and not return again, or the bottle gets handed over to the FBI."

"Fuck you, Harper. This isn't over. I will have her. I will have my daughter back."

"Shut up, Trish," said Jacob, exasperated.

"No, I won't. You said we would get her back, you promised."

"I said shut up, women, know your place, or I will show it to you," he growled. "Get in the camper...now...go."

Trish glared at Charlie. "Enjoy her while you have her." she sneered.

"Get in the damn camper now, Trish," said Jacob, clearly losing his patience with her.

Trish got into the camper, practically stamping her feet like a child, slamming the door.

"Now, I don't know what you think happened here," started Jacob.

"I know exactly what happened, you piece of shit." Charlie advanced again, fists clenched, but Harper stopped him.

"No, I don't think you do. I was just trying to help a woman recover from the loss of her child."

"You say that like Alia's dead," seethed Charlie.

"Well, in a way, she is. Alia left without notice and refused to see her mother again or even talk to her. It's all the same kind of grief."

"Grief my ass. Did Trish tell you how she used to beat the crap out of Alia when we were kids? Would embarrass her in front of her friends screaming and cursing at her? How she would say the ugliest and horrible things to her until she not only believed them but still does. No matter how often I tell her how beautiful she is, she still hears her mother telling her she's ugly. Did she tell you about that?"

"No," Jacob smirked. She told me a story of a little boy with a sick infatuation with a baby girl that almost grew up alongside him as his sister. A little boy that touched the baby in ways no little girl should ever be touched."

That time when Charlie advanced on Jacob, he got the front of the man's shirt in his fists before Harper was able to pull him off with the help of the two officers there with them.

"You son of a bitch I never..never. She's the one that used to pinch and poke at Alia till she cried. I never…never in my life…." Charlie spat, his anger in danger of getting out of control.

"Never, son? So you're telling me you've never lain with the girl? You've never had sex with her in the back of your patrol car when she was still in high school? Now I find that very hard to believe. Such a pretty young girl that you're living with, in sin, and you've never touched her."

"I'll fucking kill you, you and her both," Charlie growled, still being held back by the two officers.

"And see there you go folks, you fine officers heard that, right? You heard him threaten me?"

Deputy Tackard and Deputy Johnson looked at each other, then Tackard looked at Jacob. "We didn't hear a thing, isn't that right, Johnson?"

"That's right, not a damn thing." Letting go of Charlie, he looked at him seriously. "Not any of it, Sergeant. And neither will anyone else." Then he patted Charlie on the back, and the two officers stepped back together but stayed close enough in case Charlie lunged at Jacob again.

Jacob looked at them incredulously. "Fucking cowards. Never mind water under the bridge. So I guess it's a stalemate, gentlemen. I have something on you, you have something on me. This means we do as you say and leave town all nice and peaceful like, and you two, don't ever come after me. That includes my bottling business, which is about to overgo a major makeover. A rebranding, if you will," Jacob winked.

"That's the deal, Jacob, and I mean it for the both of you. Never come back." Said Harper

"Well, you know, women…I'll do my best. As for you, young man, do we have a deal?"

"No," said Charlie, giving him the look of death.

"No? I don't think you appreciate the position you're in, son. I could destroy you with that video. Sure she'll deny it. But it's a small town. People talk. All one needs is to plant a seed of doubt. Some will put two and two together. The kids from the prom will talk. Yeah, I bet they have some interesting things to say. They will run you out on a rail boy. And even if they don't, you can kiss, following in your father's footsteps, goodbye. Damn shame, Sheriff is an elected position. And the two of you plan on marrying? A scandal like that could put a lot of stress and strain on a young marriage. Next thing you know, it will be an argument here, a fight there. You'll turn to drinking, she'll resent you for it. Till one day, it all goes too far. You hit her. You cheat on her, whatever. I've seen it happen over and over, Charlie. You have seen it too, you know I'm right. Mess with me, boy, and you will lose her one day, sooner or later."

"That would never happen." Alia walked out from behind Charlie and Harper and stood her ground before

them. "Charlie and I have something special, something all your little tricks, videos, or whatever bullshit you have been trying to pull to break us up will never beat. So try it, Jacob, be stupid and try and do something and it won't be him you have to worry about coming after you." she said, "Because I'm the better shot."
Jacob laughed, but his eyes spoke of the fear he felt. "We'll see, little girl, we will see."

Looking behind Jacob, Alia flipped off Trish, who looked out at them through the camper's window. "And that goes double for you bitch." she turned, went into Charlie's arms, and the two of them walked back to the front of the truck.

Harper watched as Jacob went back into the camper on the driver's side and started it up. Harper told the officers he was on his way and stood there as they escorted him out of the park and out of town.

Later that night, after dinner and a few drinks (even Alia had a shot of whiskey), Alia and Charlie were up in the bedroom getting ready for bed. Charlie was disappointed to find that she was setting her bed up in the closet again.

Leaning in the doorway, he frowned. "You still think this is necessary?"

"Just erring on the side of caution. Especially after today."

"But the trigger word didn't work. You said you didn't hear anything."

"How do you know for sure? How do you know me telling you that isn't all a part of it?"

"Because last time you went all stiff in my arms and spacey."

"You mean spacier than usual." she joked.

"Alia, I'm serious."

Without even looking at him, she could tell that he was. Getting up, she went to him and gave him a kiss. "I am too. We don't know if this thing can have some kind of delayed effect, and I'm not taking the chance of hurting you again. Besides, a few things he said has me freaked out a little."

"Like what?"

"Well, there's the prom thing, but I told her about prom. Making out in the back of your patrol car, I did not. I mean, at least I don't think I did. I don't remember saying those things you said I did either. I'm just still creeped out by this whole thing. A few more nights isn't going to kill us."

"I know, and you're right. It's just I sleep better at night curled up next to you. And I sleep much much better at night after…." Charlie smiled a sheepish grin.

"Well, that we can do something about." Pulling him into the closet, she shut the door, then turned off the light.

Chapter 37
Getting Back to Normal

Alia spent a few more nights in the closet, then at last, on Tuesday night, Charlie convinced her it was safe for her to sleep in the bed. She was nervous and had trouble falling asleep, so they lay awake till late talking. Then they made love and fell asleep in each other's arms once again. Alia's sleep was a fitful one where she jerked and moaned, but Charlie would just give her a kiss or caress her hair till she relaxed again.

That weekend was Labor day weekend, which meant the boys were gone for long hours Friday through Monday. Then they came home exhausted with stories of car accidents, bar-b-Que brawls, and traffic everywhere.

When Alia lamented how much she had missed working, Harper didn't say anything. He just gave her his usual grouchy look and shook his head.

So instead, she started to work out again. First, just walking in the park with Ellen and some weights with Charlie's old set in the basement. When she became bored with that, Ellen would sit and watch while she ran around the track marveling over how fast she was recovering and happy her girl was eating again.

Labor day, she and Ellen had a small backyard bar-b-Que with some Alia's friends she hadn't seen. Having mended fences with Crystal, the two of them were like sisters once again.

In the second week in September, Alia had the last of her three times a week sessions. She had been doing so well Lawson dropped it down to two with a promise to make it one if she kept up the good work. Meantime she continued to put on weight mostly in lean muscle, looking and feeling better.

By week three, She and Charlie broke the news to Mom and Harper that they felt it was time for them to go back to their own place.

Ellen cried, but it was a mixture of sadness and happy tears, she said. Harper pretended like it was about time, but when he hugged them before they left, he almost wouldn't let go.

Alia loved being back in her own place but admitted to Charlie she felt a little anxious about being there by herself most of the day. So she ended up running through town a few days a week and popping in at the Sheriff's office as well. The guys all loved seeing her and begged Harper to let her come back to work, but the choice wasn't his. That they left up to Lawson. He cautioned them that it had only been a few weeks, and the last thing they wanted to do was to rush her back into work.

One day, bored, Alia found herself at the library. After a long talk with Mrs. Stackhouse, Alia got a temporary job as library assistant back. Her favorite part was storytime for the little kids twice a week.

Charlie made a habit of sneaking in just so he could watch her. She had such a great rapport with the little ones, and they loved her. Watching her with them made him long for their own.

One night in the second week of October, after watching her flit around the apartment all day decorating for her favorite holiday, he asked her about starting a family.

Tears welled in her eyes right away, and she kissed him but told him to ask her again after the first of the year. Alia wanted to be the best mother she could and felt she still had some things to work on. He promised he would and then made love to her.

As a Halloween gift to her for all the excellent work she had done, Lawson asked Alia if she was ready to go back to work. Her response was to jump on the couch in the library room and hug him, almost choking him. He did a mental health evaluation which she passed with flying colors, and he let Harper know she was cleared for active duty.

In a press briefing shortly after that, Harper let it be known she was rejoining the force. It would help alleviate a staff shortage they had after one senior officer retired and another had moved. She would return the second week of November, starting off with desk duty for a while then moving back into her regular duties after the first of the year. Only when the news hit the streets the response wasn't what they expected.

That first week of November, the Sheriff's office was flooded with calls by concerned citizens that she would be allowed back to active duty. The only thing that seemed odd to Harper was that no one was willing to leave their names or identify who they were. They just voiced their concerns. One morning there was a story in the paper right on the front page.

Deputy Headed Back to Active Duty After Firing Gun in Crowded Park.

Deputy Miller has been on leave since the incident in which she fired several rounds in a crowded park in what was described as a manic episode. The deputy was then put on a seventy-two-hour psych hold at the local hospital and later released to her fiance Sergeant Harper and his family.

Since then, she's been recovering from what can only be described as post-traumatic stress disorder though stemming from what we don't know. Mrs. Miller can currently be seen working at the local library, a job she once had in high school. Although most citizens seem to not have a problem with her working there, many raise concerns about her being fit for duty. We interviewed a few, and they had this to say...

She's a nice enough girl, and the kids love her at storytime, but I'm not sure if I'm comfortable with her being back out on the streets with a gun again. She could have killed somebody. Maybe it's best that she just stays working at the library and the Sheriff fixes his shortage issue some other way.

I heard what she did, and I'll be damned if I want some nutty women running the streets of our town waving a gun around.

I don't understand why she isn't in jail. She shot the Sheriff and unloaded a whole clip, almost hitting her own fiance. Sheriff Harper claims to run an honest corrupt-free department, then he goes and pulls this mess. I'll remember that come election time.

She was a hero once, but I'm not happy with her being back out on the streets. We have children to worry about.

A small group in town plans on protesting in front of the Sheriff's department this week, demanding Deputy Miller has her badge taken away for good. They claim she is a danger to the town if she were to return on active duty.

The paper said more on the inside, but Alia never got that far. She read what the people said about her repeatedly, feeling a mixture of anger, grief, and pity flooding over her. After all the abuse and bullying she suffered as a child, you would think this didn't even phase her. On the contrary, it hurt like hell. She had come to love her town and the people in it. Charlie had been dressing up for work in their bedroom when he came in and saw her silently crying.

"Hey, sweet girl, what's wrong?"

She threw the paper on the table, pointed at it, then ran for the bedroom, slamming the door.

Picking up the paper, Charlie read the article and felt an old familiar fury rise in him. More than that, he felt her pain. He found her at her reading nook in the bedroom by the window, only she had the shade drawn, her knees up to her chest and sobbing.

Sitting down in the nook with her, he pulled her onto his lap. In his pocket, his phone buzzed, but he didn't have to check it to know it was his father. He let it ring as he cradled her in his arms. "Alia, sweetheart, it's going to be OK. Dad will fix this."

"He can't fix this, Charlie. He can't make people change their minds. They're scared. And I don't blame them. I would be too. I just never thought the people of this town would say things like that about me. Not anymore anyway."

"They're only scared because they don't know the truth. If they did, they would know it wasn't your fault."

"And we can't tell them. Not without risking Jacob releasing those videos, and there is no way in hell I am doing that to you. Face it, Charlie…it's over. It worked. That bitch got what she wanted. They all hate me."

"No, Alia, they don't hate you." the phone buzzed again in his pocket. "Look, we suck it up, and you go back to work anyway. When they see you're doing your job, they'll be glad your back."

Alia jumped up out of his arms. "Damn it, Charlie, stop. Just stop. They will never trust me. This town will always undermine everything I do. I won't be taken seriously. I'll put anyone that works with me in danger. That is if any of the guys even want to work with me."

"You know the guys at the station are crazy about you."

"And I love them too, which is why I can't put them in danger. Or you. Call Harper tell him to tell the press I declined the work offer." She headed to the bathroom.

"What are you doing, Alia?"

"Getting ready for my job at the library," she said, slamming the door.

In his pocket, the phone rang again. This time he picked it up.

"How is she taking it?" Harper asked.

"How do you think? She's upset. She said that she declines the job, that she won't do it."

"This is that fucking bitch Trish's fault. No, Ellen, I won't calm down. Look, Charlie, just tell her to give me some time. I'll see what I can do to fix this. First, I have a reporter I want to throttle. And I want to know why no one in this town has the balls to say who they are when leaving comments like that. Didn't know we were surrounded by so many gutless cowards. I know Ellen, but right now, I'm mad."

"The only thing that will fix this is exposing Jacob. If we can prove she wasn't responsible, they would have no legitimate reason to be afraid of her."

"You know we can't do that, son. As long as he has that tape of her saying you raped her, we would just be trading one bad situation for another. Let me deal with this. Tell her to just go on doing what she's been doing, and I'll see what I can do."

When Charlie and Harper arrived at the station that morning, there was already a group of about twenty people gathered out front picketing Deputy miller's reinstatement. Harper called the local paper to find out who had written the article. The editor said it was a freelance job done by someone new in town. Harper chewed him out for running with the article without checking with him first or at least warning him.

The editor reminded him of a little thing called the constitution. If Harper had anything to add in her defense, he would write the article himself. "Look, I like the kid. I interviewed her when she rescued those two kids and almost died keeping them warm. She's done some great work, but some people have legit concerns about her mental health."

"She's seeing someone. She's been cleared."

"You mean that quack, Lawson? Sorry, but he's not exactly the most credible doctor out there. I wouldn't be surprised if he gave her a crystal and claimed she was healed. Get someone legit to do an evaluation on her, and if she passes, I'll post it. Until then, the story stays."

When Harper went to find Charlie to fill him in, he found him in the station lobby looking at the group out front.

"Who are these people?" Charlie asked.

"What do you mean?"

"Other than one or two, I don't recognize any of them."

"Well, it's a big county, son, and people are moving in and out all the time."

"I know that, but still. Even the two I recognize aren't exactly in line for citizens of the year themselves. And that reporter. I've never seen his name in the paper before."

"The Editor said he was some freelance guy. Don't get yourself too wrapped up in these people, Charlie. We need to find a way to solve this mess. Time to see if we can get her in to see Dr. Solomon."

Charlie knew his father was right. He also knew Alia would not be thrilled about seeing Dr. Solomon again.

Wednesday, Charlie was walking to the library from the station with a hot coffee in one hand and texting on his phone with the other. He wanted to go see Alia do her storytime, hoping an hour with the kids would get her out of the low mood she'd been in since reading the article.

He was almost there when some guy bumped into him hard enough to knock his phone out of his hand and spill the coffee on his uniform shirt. They both made their apologies, both agreeing they were not looking. The guy even held Charlie's phone while he tried to clean up his shirt. It was no use though the mess was too bad. Charlie was closer to the apartments than the station, so he just went there to change.

When he went inside, he found Alia sitting on the couch with a crumpled-up paper at her feet. "Hey, sweet girl, what are you doing at home? Shouldn't you be reading to the kids? I was just on my way over."

"I can't do it, Charlie. I doubt many of their parents would let them come and have the town's crazy lady read to them anyway," she said in a huff.

"Damn it, Alia, we've been through this already. You're not crazy." He wasn't angry with her, just frustrated that she still had a habit of talking down about herself despite all the therapy.

"Yeah, tell that to a couple of dozen people protesting down at the station. Or the reporter that keeps bringing it up." she pointed to the paper on the floor.

Charlie picked up the crumpled paper and tossed it in the recycling bin. While in the kitchen, he took his uniform and t-shirt off to throw in the washing machine. "You go to see Dr. Solomon in the morning. I'm sure her assessment will go great, and we can have the paper print a retraction."

"The damage is done, Charlie. Nothing is going to change that."

He sat on the couch with her. " Listen to me, this is a big county, and only about two dozen people are protesting. Maybe another more being interviewed or hell, maybe the same ones. This whole campaign to keep you out of your job isn't gaining much steam. I don't think things are as bad as they look."

Alia was about to protest when she realized Charlie was sitting in front of her shirtless. "Um, why?" she asked, pointing at his bare chest.

"Spilled my coffee. That's why I came home, so I could change before going to see you."

Her eyes turned sad.

"What is it?"

"I don't think I'm going to go back to the library. I don't know. I haven't decided yet."

"Well then, don't. Decide yet that is. Why don't we wait to see what Dr. Solomon says first? Meanwhile, you love that place, and what else are you going to do?"

"I don't know. Maybe we should reconsider starting that family. That is if you still want the crazy lady's babies." she said as she rubbed her hand on his chest.

"I have always wanted the crazy lady's babies." he teased, getting a bit of a smile out of her. Charlie began kissing her when her phone on the table started to ring.

When she picked it up, she told him it was the station. A second after saying hello, she handed the phone to him. "It's for you."

Charlie took it, wondering why they didn't call him when it dawned on him. He never got his cell back from the guy. Fortunately, it was locked, and the guy had been decent enough to run it down to the Sheriff's department, where it was waiting for him at the front desk.

"Shit," he said, hanging up. "Got to go. I ran into some guy, and he had my phone while I tried cleaning my shirt, and I forgot to get it from him. It's at the station, and Rusty has it. Better get it before the old man finds out," he told her as he ran into the bedroom and put on his clean shirts. Coming back in, he kissed her on the forehead. "Raincheck on the...well what we were about to get into, I promise." he smiled. See you tonight."

Only by the time he got home that night after dealing with a nasty car wreck out on the highway leading out of the county, it was late. Charlie was tired, smelled of smoke, and feeling grief-stricken. A baby in a car seat in a minivan that caught fire never stood a chance. They pulled his charred remains out of the van as well as the body of his mother once the fire was put out. Everyone there was heartbroken.

After his shower, Charlie allowed himself to be comforted by Alia for a change though she too felt his pain as her own. His night was plagued with nightmares in which it had been Alia and their baby pulled from the van. Each time he awoke with a start, his sweet girl was right there to soothe him back to sleep again.

In the morning, they both were quiet. Charlie was still reeling over the accident and lack of good sleep. Alia was worried about her evaluation. Before leaving for work, Charlie sat Alia down.

"Please don't bail on the evaluation today."

She looked away from him, feeling guilty. Once again, it was as if he was reading her mind, and it unnerved her a little.

"I know you were thinking about it. And go back to work, please. I want our lives to get back to normal and stay there as much as possible. I don't even care what that definition of normal is as long as you're happy. If you want to stay home and have a family, I'll support you. If you want to work at the library, hell, Mrs. Stackhouse will have to retire eventually, then I'll support you on that too. If being a cop is what you want, then I will fight right alongside you until you get your job back. I love you, and as long as you're happy, I will be too." he kissed her long and hard.

"I love you too, Charlie."

"I love you more," he said with a smile

"More than yesterday?" she asked, playing along.

"More and more all the time," he smiled, his eyes sparkling.

When they parted, they both felt a little better. But their lives would not be getting back to normal.

Ellen went with Alia for the evaluation because the thought of going to that part of the hospital alone freaked her out. She spent the whole morning talking to Dr. Soloman and taking tests. Dr. Solomon was impressed with Alia's recovery, even if current events had shadowed the smile on her face just a little. After all the tests, they met up in the doctor's office. Ellen held Alia's hand because she was shaking a little.

"Well, this is just a preliminary report. I have to go over the results better. However, I see no reason why you are not fit to return to active duty."

Alia let out a massive sigh of relief.

"More importantly, I am willing to put my reputation as a doctor at this hospital on the line. I encourage you to continue to see Lawson. No matter what some may think of him, he has done good work. In fact, after what I heard about the accident last night, it would do Charlie and the other officers involved some good to talk to someone. We need to get over the stigma associated with officers seeking therapy. Getting help is nothing to be ashamed of. Needing help and not getting it is. On a lighter note, it's nice to see such a big smile on your face. Let's try to keep it there awhile." Before they left, Dr. Solomon gave both Alia and Ellen a hug.

Ellen wanted to celebrate, so they drove to the cafe. It was a fantastic day. The sun was out, the air had a bit of a chill to it but not so much that they couldn't eat outside. They got their usual table, and when the waiter Toby saw them, he was all smiles.

"Well, if it isn't my two favorite ladies. What will it be, the usual raspberry teas?"

Ellen and Alia both looked at each other and laughed.

"No, I think I'm going off tea for a while," said Alia. "I'll tell you what, I'm celebrating. Bring me a cup of your thickest richest hot chocolate with enough whipped cream to fill a boat. Oh, and some chocolate drizzle."

"Same for me," said Ellen with a laugh.

"Yes, my ladies on the wild side today. I'll bring them right out."

When he was gone, Ellen smiled at Alia. "I see you're feeling better. I don't think I have seen you have anything that decedent in a while."

"Yeah, I'll regret it when I step on the scale in the morning, I'm sure."

"Stop now. You've gotten yourself looking great. All the weight back but lean and muscular. Charlie has too."

"Yes, he has." she grinned.

The waiter came back with the drinks and took their orders.

"So how is Charlie, after last night?"

"Upset understandably. He tossed and turned most of the night, having nightmares. What about Harper?"

"About the same." When he awoke that morning, he told her that in his nightmares, it was Alia and Charlie's baby burning in the van. He wouldn't have been too surprised to know he and Charlie shared that nightmare.

"So did you notice the protesters on the way here?" asked Alia.

"Yes, I was hoping you didn't."

"The crowd is bigger than it was. Not by much, but still."

"Nothing we need to worry about. Harper will get the paper to print a retraction. Time will take care of the rest. Trish, did this before, remember? When she couldn't ruin Charlie, she went after you, and it ended up backfiring. Besides, I see something funny about that crowd."

"How's that?"

"I don't recognize anyone in it. At first, I did, you know, the first few days it went on. But when we just passed, not one face looked familiar. Harper just says it's a big county, and we don't know everyone, but he's wrong. With all the work we do with the community, a face or two should be at least a little familiar to me. But they're not. Not to Harper or Charlie either. And it's as if it's different people each time I go by as well."

"Well, people do have jobs, lives to attend to. I know some group is spearheading the protest. Maybe they are cycling people in and out. Too many, and they stand to get a nuisance charge. Too little, and they're not getting their point out there."

"And just what group is that? I'm going to have to look into this whole thing. It stinks of a personal vendetta."

"Do you think it may be Trish's friends that started this? She was told not to come back to town, but she still has friends here. She's done things like that before. She used to get the neighbors to make sure I wasn't out running the streets while she worked."

"Only thing is the people Trish hung out with were not exactly the type to do something like this. Most of them go out of their way to avoid the police. Besides, even what friends she did have know how she is. If we were talking about gun restriction, then maybe. But they have no stake in this and no real loyalty to that woman. And once again, they would be people we know. No, I think this is something else." Ellen retreated a little, seeing the growing look of concern on Alia's face. "But don't you worry about it. You worry about Charlie and getting your job back. I'll look into this group and see who is behind all of this."

After lunch, Alia had Ellen drop her off at the library to work that afternoon. Mrs. Stackhouse was happy to see her back and happy to see she would be getting her job back even though she was sad at losing her again. She also told her that the kids and parents had missed her at storytime.

"I tell you what, If I get my job back, why don't I see if Harper will let me come and do storytime still. If they'll come, that is."

"Why wouldn't they?"

"I have a feeling some people in this town are content to let me live my life as long as it's without a gun in my hand."

"Well, tough shit on them. You're one of our best deputies. As much as I hate to lose you here, I, for one, feel perfectly safe with you out there."

That evening as she was about to get off of work, Alia got a text message from Charlie.

It's been crazy lately, we need to reconnect. Maybe rewind things a little. Meet me at our old spot?

Alia grinned, knowing just what he meant. After sending a text back, she decided not to go home and get her Jeep but instead take the bus there like she used to. Getting on the bus, she started to get the feeling of butterflies in her stomach, and her heartbeat sped it.

This is fun. She thought. *Charlie always has a way of knowing what I need even when I don't always.*

Getting off at the usual stop across from the little strip mall Alia walked the three blocks to the front of the apartment complex in the dark. They still hadn't installed any street lights on the road, even with the school at the end of it. When she arrived at the head of the apartment complex she used to live in, red and blue lights flashed up by the school. Her heart soared as she tried her best not to run the last couple of blocks. Off in a dark part of the school's parking lot, Alia could just barely make out a patrol car. When she was several feet away, the headlights came on, blinding her.

"Come on, Charlie cut that out. I can't see shit." The lights went out, and she was plunged into darkness again. Only now she had spots dancing in front of her eyes and couldn't see but the faint image of Charlie getting out of the car. It was then that something felt off. Maybe it was just her eyes adjusting, but Charlie looked shorter and thicker. Most alarming was realizing that even though she felt him, he didn't feel close to her. Alia stopped, but the shadowy figure that got out of the car kept approaching.

Charlie had gone to his parents' house that morning so he and his father could ride in together and talk things over about the night before. It was the usual thing they did, starting with the first time Charlie had to work a death. They did the same thing for Alia. Sometimes the ones you need to talk to, the only ones you feel you can talk to, are those that went through the same thing. Sometimes the shoulder you cry on is crying as well.

When they got off for the night, they both went back to the house for Charlie to pick up his truck. Then he drove to the apartment and noticed the lights were off even though Alia should have been home from the library already. Her Jeep was still there, so he went up thinking maybe she was lying down and hoped it wasn't more bad news. But the apartment was empty. Charlie tried not to panic, but his heart started to race, and his mind was already screaming at him. Telling himself that she was either stuck at the library or with Crystal, he called her phone. It went straight to voicemail.

    Charlie called the library next, but at nine at night, it was closed. Next, he tried Crystal, but she hadn't seen Alia either. Now he was panicking. It wasn't until then that Charlie realized he no longer felt connected with her.

    No, please, no, this can't be happening again. Not wasting any more time, he called Harper.

    "Hello, Charlie, did you forget something?"

    "Dad…It's happening again."

Chapter 38
Gone

    The first thing Alia noticed was that she was lying on something cold, hard, and damp. The light sweater and jeans she wore to work did nothing to fight off the chill that seeped into her. Her head felt groggy, like thick soup. When she opened her eyes, she looked up into a long dark tunnel. Blinking a few times, she was able to see the tunnel was instead a shaft lined with ivy, leaves, and brush that had fallen in from the surface. Giving her head a shake, Alia looked again and realized with horror where she was.

    "The cave." she barely whispered. Alia was lying under the bottom of the deep shaft that ran into the cave she had found the little kids in two years earlier. She was convinced it was the very same cave she dreamt about finding Charlie dead at the bottom of a shaft.

    Alia tried to sit up, but her arms were out to her sides, bound by rope to something. Her legs duct taped together at the ankles were also bound in rope and tied off somewhere out of sight. She struggled at the ties, but it only made them tighter.

    "Oh, by all means, struggle, my child. Give it all you got, one last good heave-ho."

Recognizing the voice, Alia snapped her head to her right, and there in the cave with her was Jacob. Right behind him was Trish with a lecherous grin on her face. Terror gripping her, Alia struggled more, calling on the strength of the weeks of working out to break her bonds. Realizing it was of no use, she stopped, feeling blood trickling down from her torn wrists and ankles.

"What the hell is going on? What did you do to me, you bastard?"

"Nothing yet, just a little chloroform to get you here without making too much of a fuss," Jacob said, walking to the stone platform she was tied down on and looking down at her.

"Yeah, we had to be sure to keep your big damn mouth shut." her mother piped in. "That's always been your biggest problem, Alia, running your damn mouth all the time. That and acting like you're some kind of big badass." Trish walked over and slapped Alia in the face hard. "How big of a badass do you feel like now, Alia, huh? Being the better shot is not doing you much good now, is it?"

"You fucking bitch let me go. You're making a big mistake…let me the fuck go."

"Oh, no, little chickie, the party is just starting. Pretty soon, your little diddling fagot boyfriend is going to realize you're gone. But we need to make sure you're unable to be found while Jacob works his magic on you."

Hearing that and fearing the worst, she instinctively struggled again. "Get the fuck away from me, you sick bastard, don't you dare touch me."

"Touch you…you? No, no, my dear, I wouldn't so much as soil my pinky touching you, you sinful bitch. No, my dear, what we have planned for you is much more fun." grinned Jacob with evil delight.

"And by the time we are done, you'll have no one Alia, no one that is but me." Her mother said, looking down at her with a maniacal grin.

Closing her eyes, Alia reached out to Charlie. She tried so hard to call for him in her mind her head screamed at her in anger. She couldn't feel a thing. It was like with the radio. The rocks around her kept them from connecting, perhaps. However, Alia suspected it was more than that. That it was more than chloroform, they had used on her.

"Let me go. Charlie is going to come find me, and he'll kill you for this."

"Oh, he will come to find you alright but not until we get you ready for him first." leered Jacob.

"What the hell are you talking about?"

"You were right all along, Alia, we were drugging you." cackled Trish. "Only the drug itself doesn't do much more than make a person paranoid and very suggestible. The human brain is a pretty complex thing. At least that's what Jacob says."

Jacob looked at Trish shaking his head because, as usual, she butchered his words. "That's not exactly what I said, but her point is close. The mind can also be easily manipulated, molded like clay if you will. You know that yourself, Alia. Didn't your mother mold you as a child? Didn't she make you this angry, scared, little sad thing that thought she was ugly and stupid? I bet you still hear her, don't you? In the back of your mind, like a whisper from the bottom of a well. I bet that no matter how often Charlie tells you how pretty you are or how nice you look, you still hear that voice. I bet it tells you that he's lying, that he's using you, toying with you. Because deep down, you know you really are that ugly, sad, pathetic little girl that no one wants. Whose own father would rather walk into a burning building and die than spend his last few months on earth with her, don't you?"

Despite knowing it was useless, Alia struggled again, tearing at the flesh of her wrists and ankles. "Shut up…you shut the fuck up about my father," she screamed, tears running down her face because damn it, it was all true. Not a day went by that she didn't ask herself what Charlie saw in her. Every day everything from which clothes to wear to how she walked to pleasing him in bed, she constantly second-guessed. With each choice she made, each word she said, even his every response, she still found herself overthinking. It was easier when he was around. When he left, and she was alone, the old her, the old Alia, wanted to come sit and talk. Every time she made a mistake, Trish's voice was there to tell her she was a mistake from the start. That she never did anything right. That she was a burden on everyone. Charlie had done a lot to quiet that voice inside her, but he hadn't been able to get rid of it entirely, and she was afraid he never would.

"So your going to torture me, is that it?" Alia was hoping she could keep them talking, stalling them as much as possible to give Charlie and Harper time to find her. She had no idea how long she had been gone or even what time it was other than it was still dark as no light came down through the shaft. "You going to tell me how sad and lost I am then send me broken back to him to ruin our lives? You're a fucking joke, Jacob. That's not going to work on him. You may convince others, but Charlie is possibly more hard-headed than even I am. If he hasn't given up after I've attacked him, pulled a gun on him, and shot his father, he never will."

Jacob and Trish both laughed, "Which is precisely why we are not going to do that. You see, that was our plan at first. We figured if we made you seem unhinged enough, the boy and his family would tire of you and be more than happy to toss you back into your mother's arms. I have to say I underestimated them and their propensity for putting up with your bullshit. If I didn't know better, I would think Charlie actually had feelings for you and didn't just like you for your two big holes." he spat.

Alia struggled again as more blood dripped from her wrists.

"What we have planned this time will be much more fun."

"No, Jacob, I want to tell her. She's mine."

"The fuck I am, you bitch. Ellen is my mom. She always has been. Your just the cunt my father fucked." That earned her another hard slap across the face, this one hard enough to bring tears to her eyes.

"You know I hate that word. You always did have a filthy mouth on you, Alia."

"Learned it from the best." she glared up at Trish, daring her to slap her again, anything to make more time, anything to make more emotion that maybe Charlie would feel.

"Oh, this is going to be so much more fun now. You're going to regret ever messing with me, little girl. You see, once Jacob is done with you, we are going to get Charlie to come here for you. Then watch as you kill him."

"I won't, I won't. There's nothing you can do that would make me hurt him," she screamed and struggled again, ripping her wrists and more, fresh blood was now tripping off of all four of them.

Jacob laughed. "But you already have Alia. I saw the scars, the one above his eye, the one to his temple, kinda like the one you have. Only unlike you, he wasn't clumsy. His scars were caused by you. And I can get you to do worse, much worse. I just need a little time."

"Clumsy? Is that what she told you, Jacob? That I was a clumsy kid? I guess I fell into her fists because I was clumsy. After the first time I ran into her cigarette, you would think I would have learned not to do it another several dozen or so times. You bought her bullshit hook line and sinker, and now you're going to commit murder for her?"

"Me murder? No, I wouldn't want to get my hands dirty. I'm just a facilitator. I like to push a few buttons in people's brains and then set them loose and see how much fun they have. Kind of like those people in town. The ones protesting the return of your badge and gun. Not to mention all the ones that have been keeping a very close eye on you and your loved ones. They would be all mine. People like your mother. Drunks, druggies, thieves, the homeless, and the heartbroken. People with nowhere to turn and no one to give much of a rat's ass about them. I take them off the streets, feed them, clean them up, give them their lives back. But they are all under my control. In fact, they are still there right now, watching and waiting to let me know when Charlie comes to look for you."

Alia's eyes went wide with understanding. Ellen had been right. She hadn't recognized any of those people at the protests because none of them were from Union county at all.

"Yes, my dear, that was all my handy work. Had to remind the small brains in this shit hole that you are not the hero they want you to be. Of course, we knew that wouldn't last very long, so we had to quickly come up with something else. The irony is you will fall in the same place you rose up as a hero in."

"When you kill their boy, that's going to be it, Alia. No one is going to want you anymore. His parents will hate you for taking away their precious miracle baby. The whole town is going to hate you. You'll have no choice but to come away with me then. We will be the only ones that can hide and protect you."

Alia laughed hysterically. "Come away with you? Even if I did kill Charlie, there's no fucking way I'd go anywhere with you. I'd rather kill myself first."

This time Trish was the one whose eyes widened. "You can't do that." She turned to Jacob. "She can't do that. It'll ruin all of it. She's mine. I have to have her. They have to know she is still alive. They have to pay for what they did. They have to pay for taking my baby away from me, for turning her against me. Charlie has to be taken from them by her, that's what I said, and she has to be alive."

"Alright, alright, Trish, I know. Damn women. Once it is all over, I will see what I can do," he said, sounding exasperated.

Turning away from Alia, Trish started poking her finger at Jacob. "No, you will not see, you will do it. I know too much about you, Jacob don't fuck this up, or I will make sure you get exposed."

Jacob stopped what he had been fiddling with and confronted Trish. "And I know things about you too, Trish. Like that thing that's hiding in these very caves. That little thing would put you away for a very long time, so don't fuck with me. I'll keep her from killing herself one way or another just back the fuck off."

"Don't trust her, Jacob. Once she has what she wants, she will turn you in, sure as shit. You have no stake in this. This is all her mess, let me go, and I'll tell them it was all her, that you had nothing to do with any of it."

"Oh my dear child, no one is going to believe this stupid bitch came up with all this on her own." laughed Jacob.

"Fuck you, Jacob," said Trish.

Jacob ignored her. "Besides, I do have a stake in this. I have been working with this formula for, let's say, guiding people for years. But even with taking hopeless cases like your mother off the streets, I have had to be careful. I have had to make sure I didn't get too carried away with my little lab rats. But you, my dear, oh you have been my special little lab rat. When your mother told me what she wanted, she gave me the perfect opportunity to test out a few things out in the field, so to speak. And it was working too."

"Didn't work too damn well, or you wouldn't have had to trick me to get me here and change your plans."

"Yes, that goes back to what you were saying before. Charlie proved to be more stubborn than I expected. Someone," he paused to look at Trish. "Said the boy would be easy, that he was just some pervert using you as a toy. Well, he must really like his toys then because he kept an annoyingly close eye on you. When the trigger word didn't work at the meeting in the park, I knew it was too late. He knew what we were up to. The formula we used on you before wasn't powerful. This new batch, though, this new batch will have you doing my bidding with a smile on your face." Jacob reached into a box and pulled something out she couldn't see at the angle she was lying down in. "Now, my dear, I hope you're thirsty because it's time for some tea. It's your favorite. Raspberry." He said as though speaking to a child.

"No thanks, I've sworn off the tea," she said sarcastically.

"Yes, I heard. Hot chocolate and an ass-ton of whip topping, and here I thought you were trying to stay nice and trim for your boy. Oh well, once he's dead, you can get as fat as you want. Now open wide." Jacob lifted the thing he had in his hands. It was a beer bong funnel like the ones the frat boys use in movies all the time. This one was modified with a face and mouthpiece to keep the funnel in place. When Alia refused to open her mouth, he motioned for Trish to help.

Trish held Alia's nose until she couldn't hold it any longer and gasped for air.

Then Jacob shoved the short part of the hose in her mouth and duct-taped it to her face. "Now for what we are going to do, you're going to have to be a good girl and drink a few of these, so bottoms up," said Jacob jiggling a bottle of tea over her.

Alia struggled with all her might, but it was no use. Jacob poured the first bottle in the funnel, and it came rushing down the tube into her mouth and throat. At first, she choked a little but then swallowed with a substantial throat-burning gulp. When the first one was done, he poured in another. Alia thought she would drown, thought it may even be a good idea if she did. She had the feeling that if she did, though, they would just bring her back and do it again. As the third one came down to her, she had a moment of panic where she thought she would throw up mid-swallow. Trying to breathe through her nose, she snorted out some of the tea, but most of it managed to make it down. Once all three drinks were gone, the tube and tape were painfully removed.

Already Alia's head felt spinney and full of fog. As she looked up into the shaft, she sent out one last thought for Charlie to come to find her, but she could almost see the words come crashing back down on her. Then Jacob was right there standing over her.

"Let's begin, shall we?"

Alia tried to scream, but it was no use.

"Where is she, Charlie? Where is Alia? Come on, Charlie, tell me you feel her at least, tell us something." sobbed Ellen.

Charlie, Harper, and Ellen stood in the yard behind their house. When Charlie arrived, they were both on their phones talking to anyone that may have seen her. As far as they knew, the last person to see her was Mrs. Stackhouse when Alia left the library, which had been hours ago.

Charlie wandered the yard trying to get a sense of her but felt nothing. His mother was distraught, and that wasn't helping at all either.

"I can't, I just can't. I have no clue where she is. Mom, please just calm down. We'll find her."

"This doesn't make any sense," she continued. "It's been weeks, Charlie. She's been fine this whole time. Something else is going on. They can't have gotten to her." Charlie took his mother into his arms as she sobbed and shook.

Harper got on the line to dispatch and called in all available officers to meet him at his house. As soon as they heard it was about Alia, officers from all over the county, not just those in town, called in, offering assistance. To them, she wasn't just a hero, wasn't just a cop, she was family. Harper put an APB out on the camper, the ford, and Jacob and Trish.

Once all the local officers arrived, Harper had them gather in the backyard. He gave them all sections of town and the surrounding county to check out, including all parks, abandoned buildings, and farms. For now, they were not going to do a door-to-door just in case she showed up on her own as she had done once before.

"At this point, I know it's going to be hard to keep this under wraps, but we need to try as much as possible. We have checked with Harvey she's not shown up at the gun store, and all of her own guns are locked up or back at the Sheriff's office. If you see her, call it in and wait for us to arrive unless you think she is a harm to herself or others. Now let's go and find our girl."

Charlie had enough sense when he had called Crystal to tell her to come and stay with his mother. She was almost in hysterics, convinced that Alia was in danger.

"They have my baby girl. I know they do. Charlie, if they have gotten out of town with her, we may never see her again. We have to get her back."

"I know, mom, we will. I'm going with dad. I need you to stay here with Crystal in case she shows up. Okay?" He hugged her tightly, her small frame reminding him of Alia's. "I won't stop until I find her mom. I'll bring your little girl home," he whispered to her.

Hours later, after checking yet another wayside park, Charlie still wasn't feeling anything other than grief, anger, and weariness.

I should have killed them both when I had the chance be damned the consequences.

The only thing was one of those consequences was sitting right next to him, sick with grief as well. And then there was his mother. She would still love him, but her disappointment would have been enough to destroy him. Worst of all, he would have been taken away from Alia. But now, she was taken away from him. He felt like he just couldn't win.

"We'll find her, Charlie, we did before."

"This is different. I feel it. I'm sick with it. I don't understand what happened. She was good. The trigger didn't work, she was, we were talking about..." he couldn't finish.

"About what, Charlie?"

Charlie didn't answer, just looked at his father.

Harper didn't have to have Charlie and Alia's unique connection to know his son was talking about them having children. "Really, Charlie?"

"She said to ask again after the first of the year. I know we're not even married yet, and I know we said we'd have a long engagement, but...."

"No need to explain. You weren't exactly conceived, well without sin."

"This whole thing is driving me insane. Alia may be small, but she's built too. If someone tried to pick her up on the street, she'd fight them off. There would be something. Someone would have heard or seen something."

"Alright, so let's go to the library, park the car and walk the way she would have gone home. Maybe we will see something."

But they didn't. Alia had vanished off the streets of their town without a trace or witnesses. In the morning, they all gathered again, only this time at the Sheriff's station. Some officers were sent home to sleep in shifts until she was found. Others were sent door to door in town looking for any witnesses.

In his office, Harper called the Sheriff's departments of the surrounding counties and the state police. He called the local press and said there would be a news briefing that evening had she not been found by then.

"Go home, Charlie, get some food and rest. I'll stay here and handle the phones till you get back."

Charlie shook his head, getting up from where he had been sitting. "No, I'm going to take one of the cars and go back out. Retrace her steps again. There's something. We had to have missed something."

"Son, I'm not asking, I'm telling you to go home. You're a wreck. You'll be no good to her if you run your car off the road because you fell asleep. Now go."

Charlie shook his head again, stopping midway because it made him feel dizzy. "Sorry, I'm not doing it. I'll take my own truck if I have to, but I'm going to get an energy drink or two and keep looking."

"Charlie." Harper pleaded.

"If they find her and I'm napping it up at home, and it's too late, I'll never forgive myself. I'll be fine. I went longer on no sleep when she was in the hospital. If I get too tired, I'll, I don't know, I'll do something."

Harper watched as his son walked out the door, head hanging low.

At five that evening, there was still no news of Alia's whereabouts. No one heard anything along the route she took. All parks were checked repeatedly, and the RV and car hadn't been seen anywhere. She was just gone. Harper, going on only a two-hour nap he took on the couch in his office, stood out in front of the Sheriff's office for the news conference. One thing he noticed right away was that the picketers were gone. They, too, had vanished much as she did. That reminded him that he needed to check out who was behind the campaign to keep Alia from getting her job back. Charlie was next to him, looking grieved and about falling on his feet. He had been out all day scouring the parks over and over again.

The briefing was short. Harper told them her last whereabouts, that she had walked home, and that they thought she might be in the custody of Trish Miller and Jacob Fuller due to issues in the recent past. When asked if she might have wandered off on her own, he refuted it, saying she had passed yet another mental health exam and was looking forward to getting back to work.

About an hour later, Harper was in his office watching Charlie nod off in a chair when one of the officers came in.

"Good news, we have a witness," said Deputy Hawks.

Charlie perked right up and bolted out of the chair.

"Where…do they know where she is."

"No, but he thinks he may have seen her last. He's out in the lobby."

Charlie rushed out to the lobby, where a smallish older gentleman stood waiting for them. He told them he was a bus driver running the late shift last night when Alia got on his bus.

"I remember her from a few years ago. She used to ride my route all the time."

"Where did you take her?"

"Same stop as always. She used to live in that one apartment complex out by the farm where they built the new elementary school. I know because when it would rain really hard, I'd take her to the entrance instead of the stop, so she wouldn't have to walk as much."

"Was she alone? Did anyone else get off with her?" Charlie asked.

"Yes, she was alone. And no, no one else got off with her. In fact, she was my only passenger. She was in a really good mood too. I mean, she was always a nice kid, but she seemed really happy about something." said the driver.

Happy? Thought Charlie *Like maybe happy because she would see Trish for the first time in weeks? Is it possible the drug was still in her system, that the trigger word did work, and they were merely biding their time?*

Charlie shook his head because that didn't seem plausible, not even with how insane the whole thing was in the first place. No, something else was going on here, but why she would go back to her old apartment, he had no clue.

Could this be an actual breakdown? Has she somehow forgotten who she is, when she is and thought she was going home?

Again he shook his head more because his thoughts made him feel like he was going mad.

The station became a flurry as officers who had been dead on their feet were now wide awake and scrambling to get their gear and to their patrol cars.

Charlie and Harper were the first ones out and the first to arrive at the small strip mall where the bus stop was. Harper had already called for canine that morning, and the nearest unit that had been going over the parks were on their way. Meanwhile, the other officers blocked all traffic on the road as the two of them walked down it looking for clues.

"Charlie, why do you suppose she came out here? Does she still have friends here?"

"Not that I know of. There was Paul, the boy that lived downstairs from her. But he and his family moved back to Ohio after graduation. I only remember Because we get a Christmas card from them each year. They were crazy about her too."

"What about Paul?"

"They were good friends, but that's it. She wasn't his type."

"Why not?"

Charlie stopped for a moment and looked at his father. "Because Alia is a girl."

"Oh." he nodded understandingly, "So no one else she would visit?"

"She knew a few kids in the trailer park, next door. Lacy, her mom, and her sister moved. The other kids she was never really close enough to. Besides, the driver said he saw her walk down this way. There's one thing, but that doesn't make any sense either." he said with a yawn.

"Let's hear it anyway."

Charlie stopped and once again looked at his father. "You know, I used to meet her out here some nights. When I was working, and she'd be getting off the bus from working at the library. We would meet up at the school like you, and I did that one night when we brought her some food from Mom. We would hang out in my patrol car for a while before I had to get back on the road."

Harper knew by the look on his son's face just what he had meant by hanging out. But now was not the time to scold him for improper use of his work time. "Did anyone see you? Someone walking a dog, maybe?"

"I never saw anyone." Of course, he had been a bit distracted. "The school wasn't even finished then yet."

They continued walking, noting a few things along the way, but most of it was just trash, and Alia wasn't one to throw garbage on the ground. One side of the road had a few houses on it and a sidewalk for her to walk on. The other side where the farm was didn't have any side, so they stuck to the one she usually traveled on.

"You know the farm has been sold, right? Going to build townhouses on it, well, part of it anyway. The town is growing." said Harper. The two moved out of the way as a car coming from the complex was given a police escort down the road.

"I hated that she had to walk down this road alone. There were no lights, not even at the school back then. There's one at the start of the complex, but no more until you get well off the road. Makes a good place to snatch someone." Charlie remarked.

"Even under these conditions, I think it would be something more complicated than a snatching to catch Alia off guard. She always looked like she was on alert as it was, but since all of this, she's had her head on a swivel more than usual," said Harper.

A call came on their radios that the canine had shown up. They looked back to see the hound dog and its trainer a few blocks back the way they came. Harper told them to give the dog the shirt they had gotten from the house and let him go. All traffic was stopped despite a few protests on both ends.

They watched as the dog sniffed the shirt, sniffed on the ground, howled, then let off-leash and came running right at them. With another howl as he went past them, the dog sprinted down the road towards the entrance to the complex, where two more officers waited. The trainer had hopped in a patrol car and was following. Charlie gave chase after the dog. Harper waited to catch a ride in the cruiser. They all reached the entrance to the complex at the same time, but the dog kept going further down the dead-end road and into the parking lot of the school. Charlie jumped on the hood of the car, and they followed. In the parking lot, the dog had stopped in a spot very close to the place Charlie used to park before there was even any pavement. With a final howl, he sniffed the ground then sat down.

Charlie jumped off the car before it stopped and looked around on the ground with his penlight as he approached the dog. They would never have found the tiny silver earring had it not been for the dog.

Harper went over to where Charlie knelt down with his hands shaking. When he saw what his son was looking at, his heart sank. "It's hers, isn't it?"

"She left the apartment wearing those yesterday when I dropped her off at home."

The dog trainer fetched the dog taking him off to the side for a good boy reward play.

Someone Charlie didn't even notice who brought him over a pair of gloves and an evidence bag. Before picking up the earring, he took a few snaps with his phone, his hands still shaking.

Giving the boy some air Harper started ordering officers to corner off the whole area. He called in more as well and started those that were there searching the nearby woods and farm. When more officers arrived, he would send them into the school, the custodians would still be there to let them in.

When Harper got back to Charlie, he found him staring glassy-eyed, hands shaking at the earring in the evidence bag. For the first time in a long time, his six-foot-tall son looked small to him. Charlie handed the bag over to Harper then looked some more, but there was nothing.

"She was here, that's something," said Harper.

"But why? Why the hell would she come out here late and in the dark."

"She didn't send you a text or anything saying she…no sorry, of course, she didn't you would have said something."

"Wait, what was that?"

"What was what?"

"You asked if she sent me a text. The thing is, she didn't."

"I realize that."

"No, I mean, she didn't send me one at all. Alia always lets me know when she's leaving somewhere or has arrived somewhere. Shit, how in the hell am I just now thinking about that?"

"You're tired, Charlie. You haven't gotten any sleep since you woke up yesterday morning. I told you, you needed some rest."

Charlie waved his father off and pulled out his phone to check his texts. "Nothing. In fact, I haven't gotten a text in two days. Or even a call for that matter."

Harper pulled out his phone and texted Charlie. They waited a few minutes and nothing. He tried calling, but nothing again on Charlie's end, and on his end, it went right to voicemail. "Are you sure your service is working?"

Charlie called his father, and the line rang right away.

"How is that possible?" asked Harper.

"The phone could be cloned," said the dog trainer. The hound dog was back on a leash, waiting to be used again if need be.

"What?" asked Harper.

The canine officer explained how the phone could have been cloned, which may be why he could make calls but not get them. "The only thing is someone would need access to your phone, even for just a little while. A good hacker can have a phone cloned and back to you in minutes."

Charlie suddenly felt the world around him spin, and he had to reach out for Harper to stay up on his feet.

"My phone. That bastard the other day, the one that ran into me when I was going to see Alia. He held my phone while I cleaned my shirt, and I was in such a hurry I didn't get it back. He returned it to the station."

"Who did he return it to, who was on duty that day."

"Um…it was Rusty, Deputy Cole. "

Talking into his radio Harper called for Deputy Cole to meet them at the school. As they waited, Charlie started pacing. This had been his fault. They got his phone and cloned it to call her and lure her out here. "They have her dad. I told you they have her."

They have her, and I have no idea where the hell she is because I can't feel anything. She could be miles away from here by now. All my fault; I should have picked her up from work. I should have never left her alone.

"I'm calling judge Fergusen. He owes me a favor for not telling his wife about him kissing that waitress when he got drunk. I'll see if he can talk to the judge in Jacobs county about a search warrant. We are going to get their asses, Charlie. We are going to nail them good for this."

Charlie nodded, but he had his doubts.

It's all my fault. Everything she has gone through, all of it has been my fault.

Hours later, the scene had been processed, the woods and school searched, and every door in the apartment complex knocked on. They were no closer to finding Alia than when they got there. The hound dog found no more traces, and Charlie and Harper both were on their last legs.

With a heavy heart, Harper sent most of his officers home. State police and Sheriff's departments from three other counties were looking. The news of an officer missing spread and another news conference had been done at the school. With nothing more they could do, Harper put a reluctant Charlie into his car and drove them home.

Arriving at home, Charlie's mother waited for him at the door and took him into her arms. "I'm going to find her mom. I won't stop until I do," he said again, but his eyes were already practically closed, and he swayed precariously on his long legs.

"I know, Charlie, but you need to get some sleep. The both of you do."

Charlie shook his head. "I just need to rest for a little bit…then head back out…check some more places," he said, slurring his speech.

"Not tonight, Charlie, please." his mother begged him. "Here, let me get this." She took off his holster and handed it to Harper to put into the safe.

"She should be back by now." Charlie slurred, his eyes trying to close on their own against his wishes

"Crystal dear, walk him to the couch before he falls over."

"Come on, Charlie, I've got you." Crystal led him to the living room, where he plopped down on the couch. Charlie was asleep in seconds. She pushed him over to his side and covered him with a blanket from the back of the sofa. In the kitchen, she returned to hear the last of what they found that evening.

"You're sure it's them, aren't you, Harper?"

"Nothing else makes any sense. They used the cloned phone to lure her out there, pretending to be Charlie. Had to be what happened. Why else would she have gone? They must have gotten the jump on her before she realized it wasn't him. We have people working on getting a warrant for Jacob's compound. We'll know something more in the morning."

"There's even more to it than that," said Ellen. "Crystal helped me do some searching online today. The group that was trying to keep Alia from getting her job back, they have ties to Jacobs compound."

"What? How?"

"We just had to follow the links," said Crystal. "It took us a while, but eventually, several of the links led to a site about Jacobs compound, The Restitution. Apparently, his program claims to restore lost souls to those that have fallen along the way. The Restitution made a healthy monetary contribution to the protest movement about Alia."

"Can you have everything you found printed up?"

"Already done," said Ellen."Right now, the two of you need a shower and bed. You'll need to be fresh in the morning in case you need to drive out there to bring her home."

"Charlie's already out on the couch," said Crystal.

"Not surprised, that boy was asleep on his feet half the day. We have to keep a close eye on him, Ellen. He'll practically kill himself looking for her if we let him," said Harper.

So it came to no real surprise to any of them when they woke in the morning, he too was gone.

Alia woke up. Or at least she thought she did. The night around her was pitch black. Her back was sore, and ice cold from laying on the stone platform, and her arms and legs were still bound. She tried to think, but her head pounded and swam with dizziness. Above her, she could feel a faint breeze as the air came down the natural shaft. Trying to move, she opened up the scabbed wounds on her ankles and wrists, making them bleed once more. Every ounce of her hurt like she had never hurt before.

"Charlie...Charlie, where are you..." she coughed in a hoarse whisper. Her throat felt as though she had been screaming for hours. "Please, Charlie, come find me." she sobbed. "I need you, Charlie...help me." The only response she heard to her cries was an all too familiar laugh.

Charlie woke up with a start. "Alia?" he cried out. He sat up on the couch in the house, the room lit only by the glow of a light in the kitchen. Checking his watch, he noticed he was only out for a couple of hours. Sitting still for a minute, he tried to process the feeling he woke up with.

Charlie didn't know if it had been a dream or if he had actually felt her. His back felt ice-cold, and his arms were numb from sleeping on the couch. Whatever it had been, he felt nothing now. Charlie got up and retrieved his gun belt from the safe, the patrol car keys from the shelf, and quietly left the house. He spent hours that morning patrolling around and around in circles, checking in with the few officers that stayed on for the night. Just before sunrise, he got a call over the radio.

"Charlie, you there." boomed his father's voice over the radio.

"Charlie here."

"Dammit, boy, don't do that again. You just about gave your mother a heart attack." Harper barked.

"Sorry, sir, tell her I'm sorry."

"Just meet me at the station."

About an hour later, they sat in Harper's office staring at the phone on his desk. When it finally rang, they both jumped. Harper listened for a bit, then turned to his son and shook his head.

Charlie slumped back down into the chair.

"Thank you for letting us know so soon. Yes, and keep us up with what's going on over there." Harper hung up the phone and sighed. "She wasn't there, but then neither was Trish or Jacob. In fact, no one has seen them for weeks. Or at least they wouldn't admit to it anyway. The RV is missing as well. However, they believe they have found at least half a dozen other missing people. Not to mention some of the people they found there were acting odd."

"Odd how?"

"He wouldn't elaborate, not just yet."

"So now what?"

"Now, except for here in our town, it's pretty much out of our hands. They're bringing in the FBI, and the bottling plant will be the next to be hit. I'm sorry, son...I don't know what more we can do. We've looked everywhere."

"Then we keep looking," he said, getting up.

"Charlie, be reasonable."

"Me? You sat in the hospital and said that the days of you just sitting back was over. You promised to take care of her. We don't stop looking until we find her."

"Charlie...son."

"No, no excuses, we don't stop." Charlie shook with rage. "I don't care if it takes days, weeks, months, or even years." his voice cracked, his eyes brimming with tears. "We don't stop looking for her, not ever. Not us."

"Okay, Charlie. We won't just promise me something for your mother's sake. Promise me we won't lose you too in the process."

"Sorry, I can't. Without her, there is no me." grabbing his coat, Charlie stormed out of the office, heading out for another long day of searching.

Late that afternoon, Charlie was back in his father's office. Harper had gone home to eat and rest a little. Charlie lied and said he already ate and sat in the office waiting for any word to come in. As he waited, he watched the news.

Alia's disappearance made the national news. As did the raid on both the compound and the bottling company. The FBI reported they had found some curious things at both sites but refused to give out details until a more thorough investigation could be done. Each time they mentioned Alia, they showed a picture of her, and his heart ached.

This is serious this time. She isn't just going to walk back up to the house from the lake. She's gone.

Charlie was on the verge of drifting off at the desk when the phone rang.

"Sheriff's office, Sergeant Harper, speaking." he half-slurred.

"Sergeant? Where's your father, son?"

"He's at home. What you need, Eddie." Eddie Grayber was the man who owned the rental cabin (and many others) the missing kids had been staying at.

"It's not me, it's you. Aren't you all looking for that camper, the one that Jacob feller drove?"

Charlie sat up straight. "Yes…yes, we are."

"Well, I'm down at the cabin. No guests here, so I came to do some repairs. I saw something off in the woods at the end of the drive, and I'll be damned if it wasn't that camper. I don't know how they plan to get the damn thing out. She looks wedge in there pretty good. I know they are saying on the news to call the FBI but fuck them. Alia's one of ours. I thought you and the Sheriff would want to know first."

"Did you see anyone…is anyone around?"

"No, I took a peek in the camper too, just a fast one. Don't look like anyone has been there in a few days. The power is out. Stuff in the fridge has gone warm."

"Elmer, get out of there. Go wait for me at the store up the road but get out of there."

"I got my shotgun, son. I'm not afraid of no insane preacher man."

"I know Elmer, but that man may be the only person that knows where Alia is. Just go wait for me at the store. Sorry, no disrespect, but I don't need you blasting a hole in this guy before I get to talk to him."

"None taken, my old ass can't see half worth a shit anyway. I'll see you at the store in a bit."

Hanging up the phone, Charlie walked out of the office. He told the guys out front he was running out for a bite to man the phones. Before leaving, Charlie grabbed his goodie bag. Not wanting to be interrupted in what he may have to do, Charlie took his truck instead of a patrol car with built-in tracking. Feeling half-mad from worry, lack of sleep, and food, Charlie raced out to the cabin to end this once and for all.

Charlie met up with Elmer at the store and gave him some bullshit story about finding Jacob's car somewhere else and evidence that Alia had been with them in that. He was there to secure the scene and then head back to wait for more news. Charlie sent Elmer back home with the promise he wouldn't come back until they cleared the camper and called him.

Down at the cabin, Charlie followed the tracks at the end of the drive that led to the camper. It indeed was wedged into the woods so far there is no way they planned on getting it out. He looked inside for any clues as to where they might be, but there was nothing. He noticed there were no longer any personal items left in the camper and none of the teas in the fridge. Another sign it had been abandoned for good.

Outside Charlie sat on a stump, ran his hands through his hair, and tried to think. They likely put Alia in the car and were several states away by now. But for some reason, his gut told him they didn't do that. He had a nagging feeling they were not done yet.

For Trish, it was all about revenge. He felt this whole thing went beyond just getting Alia back. Had it been, they could have talked her through the drugs and hypnosis to just walk off with them anytime they wanted. But having her daughter back wasn't the only thing she wanted. She wanted Alia broken. And he was sure she wanted Charlie and his family to pay for taking her away not once but twice.

They are still in Union county. I know it, he thought.

Then suddenly, like a flash, it came to him. When he woke up earlier, he had heard Alia. Somehow he had, and not only that, his back was ice cold and stiff like he had been laying on something hard and cold, not a warm couch. Very cold, like he felt when Alia had gone missing looking for the kids.

Charlie jumped to his feet and looked up the drive towards the path that led to the caves. "No...No," he said to himself. In the fading light of day, Charlie half ran up the drive. The path was half-covered in the first leaves of fall, but he saw what looked like dragging marks a few feet in. A few feet more, there were more marks and further even more.

Charlie stopped in the middle of the path, looked off into the woods, then down at the tattoo on his wrist. "I'm coming, sweet girl."

Chapter 39
Hell

Alia woke, and once again, all was pitch black around her. However, she lay on her side this time, her arms and legs no longer bound. Her head felt stuffed, and there was a nagging and oddly familiar pain there as well. Alia ached all over, and when she tried to move, she let out a scream scarring herself. Slowly she moved again, trying to pull her legs up under her. She managed to make it to a sitting position before she had to rest, sucking in great swallows of air as her heart raced.

Around Alia's neck was a string with something long hanging from it. When she grabbed for it, her sore wrists cried out in pain, and blood oozed from the cuts there. The thing hanging from her neck felt familiar. Carefully removing the string from around her neck, she examined the object with her hands. Having an idea of what it was, she tested the theory by bending the long thing in the middle. That caused another scream of pain and more blood to ooze from both her wrists, but she was rewarded with a snap and green light emanating from it.

"A chem light." said in a voice so hoarse she barely recognized it. Shaking it, the light grew brighter, hurting her tender eyes. She trained the light over her wrists, and what she saw there was ghastly. They were bloody and raw, with no resemblance to the strong but delicate wrists she knew. And to her dismay, the tennis bracelet Charlie had given her years ago was gone.

Raising the light up, Alia tried to make out where she was and, to her horror, discovered she wasn't alone.

"Charley," she yelled, but when she reached out for it, her hand sunk into a mess of wet clothes, decayed matter, and bone. With a scream, she pulled her hand back, heart pounding in her chest. Calming a little, Alia crawled over closer and shined the light on the corpse. To her relief, it wasn't Charlie. At first, she didn't realize it, but when she looked over it from top to bottom, she couldn't deny who her macabre roommate was.

"Billy?" Horrified, she backed up again, leaning against the damp cave wall. Sitting there looking at the body of Trish's ex-boyfriend Billy, she remembered that when she found the kids, there had been a foul decaying odor. This had to be what Jacob had been talking about with Trish. She had killed Billy and dumped his body down here.

"I'm so sorry, billy. I wouldn't have left you here had I known." Wearing only jeans and a thin fall sweater, Alia shivered both cold and damp. She sat there for a good while wincing in pain, just trying to clear her head enough so that she could think. Using the chem-light, she looked around. Alia could see she was in a small low ceiling chamber somewhere deep within the caves. Next to where she woke up was a burlap sack bag. Pulling it over to her, she emptied its contents on the ground. Out fell a small flashlight and a rather large and very sharp knife. She looked inside, but that was all there was. The flashlight worked, even had a strap for around the wrist. She put it on even though it caused much pain and bleeding again. The blade looked sharp and felt good in her hand.

Alia looked around the cavern and wondered what she should do next. Should she stay put and hope rescue would come, or should she play the game Trish and Jacob brought her here to play? Closing her eyes, Alia desperately reached out for Charlie. She was instantly blinded by a bright white light that lit her up inside. She shrieked in pain, grabbed the sides of her head, and fell over head first in the dirt of the cave floor. The light slowly faded, but the pain lingered strongly in her head. Alia felt much like she had the morning after her little adventure at the bar. While she was down on the ground, face in the dirt, that she heard a low guttural growl.

Still laying on the ground, Alia looked off into the darkness of the chamber. There was a slight shift in the dark as one part of it slipped to her left and with it another growl.

It's the killer…run! Her voice screamed in her head, and despite the pain, Alia got up like a shot, aimed the flashlight, and ran out the only exit ducking the whole way so as not to hit her head.

Behind her, the thing pursued her relentlessly. Alia ran stumbling down corridors, through chambers, around outcroppings running into walls, scraping herself, always running because the thing, the man, the killer behind her, wasn't stopping.

Alia turned left down one shaft that was so low she was forced to crawl. She was going along slowly on her hands and knees when something blocked her path. Shining the light ahead of her, Alia came face to face with the bloodied, hollowed-out remains of her best friend Crystal. "No!! She screamed, scrambling on her knees, tearing her jeans and ripping her flesh raw. The ground before her was covered in blood, the soft dirt sucking at her hands like quicksand.

To her horror, on the other side of the body was the man that had been right behind her. She could see his cold eyes reflect back at her in the light of the flashlight as he growled and lunged. Screaming, Alia managed to crawl to a place where she could get up and run again. Still, the man-thing was right behind her. She found herself slowing, begging for air, but it was no use. He would taunt her by slowing just enough to let her get a gulp or two and then push her own again with another guttural growl.

Alia ran, turning left and right, having no clue where she was going, feeling as though she were running for hours. She scraped against the cave walls, cutting into her skin on the hard limestone repeatedly. The walls around her felt like they were closing in on her. The light in her hand shown around her like a disco ball. She was dizzy, disorientated, running low on oxygen and energy.

At one point, too exhausted to run, Alia found a hole in the cave wall that she crawled into, heedless of any bugs or other critters taking up residence in there. Trying to keep as quiet as possible, she sat in the hole, shivering from both cold and fear. Hearing the man run back and forth, Alia cowered in the hole.

Please just go away, please just go away. She begged silently.

Then suddenly, it was quiet. From outside of the hole, she didn't hear the killer stalking her anymore. All Alia heard was the sound of water dripping somewhere very close to her, not even aware that it was dripping right on her. Shaking, she was about to look out the hole when from behind her she heard the growl.

That's impossible…he can't be…I'm surrounded by a wall he can't be.

Even with the solid cave wall behind her, Alia could feel a faint warm breath on her neck. Terrified, Alia slowly turned her head to look at what should have been a solid limestone wall. Instead, she looked into a pair of familiar green eyes, only they were so soulless and cold her brain fought against what it was seeing. "No…no…no…no please no," she whispered as she could now feel the thing's breath on her lips. Could smell the putrid warm decay coming from its mouth. The thing grinned, only it was not the soft kind smile of the man she loved but rather the grin of a madman.

"Boo." The Charlie thing said, turning Alia's very blood icy cold. Before she realized she had even left the hole, not sure how she got out in the first place, she was running again as the Charlie thing chased behind her.

"No," she screamed. "No, please, Charlie, don't…please don't do this to me." She ran down another shaft, and once again, her way was blocked. This time Harper lay before her bloodied and half dismembered. Shaking her head, she started to back up when she saw one of his eyes blink. Alia ran and fell on her knees before him, but Harper pushed her away with the one remaining arm he had attached.

"Run Alia...run...Charlie...he's coming...he's coming run!!"

"No!" she screamed, her throat raw. She grabbed his hand, begging for him to get up, pleading for him to be okay.

This can't be real, this can't be...no, no, not Charlie, not my sweet boy.

"Run, Alia." Harper groaned, but she refused to let go of him. As she pulled at Harper's arm, bloodied disembodied hands came out of the darkness, grabbed Harper's head, and with a snap silenced the man forever.

Alia scrambled back on all fours, and the Charlie thing lunged for her. Again, she ran, stumbling down dark passages, tripping and ripping her hands to shreds, cutting her knees, and bouncing off walls. Only to run down yet another route. All the while, the Charlie thing was relentless. Always behind her. Always just on the verge of catching her, playing so skillfully at this game of cat and mouse.

Shaking from exhaustion, Alia stumbled upon another low ceiling chamber, one that forced her once again to crawl on her bloodied hands and knees. Just when she thought she was getting away, the sounds of her pursuer fading, her hand found yet another body. Alia pulled herself up to the corpse. Ellen's battered and bruised face stared at her sightlessly. Alia felt as her heart shattered into a million pieces and blew away like dust in the wind.

"Mom, no!" she screamed as images flashed into her mind. Images of her looking up into the kind and gentle face of the woman she considered mommy more than her biological mother. Ellen extending a hand out to her as she learned to walk. Green eyes so much like her son's filled with tears and pain as she said goodbye to the little baby girl she had fallen in love with. Images and memories Alia never before remembered of the kindest, gentlest woman she had ever met.

Alia fell on top of Ellen's body, holding it close to her, sobbing. She was no longer able to go on, not wanting to. She knew the Charlie thing was crawling up behind her and didn't care.

I can't do it...I can't go on anymore...why...why...how could he...how could Charlie ever do this? She lay there hugging the corpse of her only true mother, shaking, crying, and screaming when a voice whispered in her ear.

"Run, baby girl, run!"

Charlie found the immense cavern of the cave without much trouble. Shaking from exhaustion from running most of the way there, after the past couple of days he had, Charlie stopped trying to catch his breath. It was then that he saw the ropes tied to rebar buried deep in the ground next to the natural stone platform. He examined the ropes and saw they were crusted in dried blood, and there was even more blood on the ground. Giving off a few faint sparkles in the light, Charlie found the tennis bracelet he had given to Alia, broken and encrusted with blood. Also, on the ground, he found several bottles of the tea he saw in the refrigerator in Jacobs RV, all empty, along with a drinking funnel and duct tape.

What the hell?

Charlie looked to see what else he could find when he heard a faint but distinct sound from somewhere off in the caves. Listening closer, he heard it again, a scream.
"Alia!" he yelled, his heart threatening to beat its way out of his chest. He was trying to hear which direction he should go in when he realized that all but one passage, other than the one he came in, from the main chamber was cut off.

It's a trap, but then, of course, it is.

That was what this whole thing had been about, and now he was here. Hearing her scream again, Charlie had no choice. He rushed forward and plunged further into the depths of the cave.

Running, running again, always running, never stopping for more than a few gulps worth of air, the Charlie thing always behind her. She didn't remember leaving

Ellen's corpse, just remembered the pervasive feeling of hopelessness that engulfed her. She had been running and screaming for ages, lighting her way with the piddly little excuse for a flashlight, when suddenly she remembered she had the knife too. Switching hands, so the knife was in her more dominant right, she still ran but with the knife now thrust before her.

    Charlie twisted and turned through chambers, shafts, and corridors, Alia's screams getting closer, then falling off, then getting closer again. Some passages were blocked off with tree limbs and other debris, and he knew they were being led to a trap like rats. But with each scream, he ran faster, scraping his arms and legs open on the sharp limestone walls, not caring about the pain or the blood.
    "Alia. He screamed over and over, and although she had to hear him by now, she didn't answer back. "Alia…Alia, please answer me." He went backtracking, dodging outcroppings that seemed to want to take his head off. He had entered another passage when he saw a flash of movement at the end of it and caught the last of her long hair as she ran.
    "Alia…Alia stop it's me…it's Charlie" he ran after her, glimpsing her again and again. Still, she was smaller than him, faster, able to navigate the narrow passages better than his tall six-foot frame could. Running past one passage, Charlie saw her with her back against a wall.
    Stopping, he called out to her, begging for her to stop. Despite having to have been able to see him and know who he was, she screamed and bolted to her left into a chamber he couldn't see from where he stood.
    "Alia…Alia, wait, it's me, Alia, it's Charlie." She had to have heard, but he knew they had gotten to her again, and for whatever reason, she couldn't see him. Knowing this was the way he would die…Charlie plunged on anyway.

    He almost had her cornered. Her back was against a wall, and he had stopped. A monster of a man, he filled the entire passage. She couldn't rectify with her mind Charlie being so big before, so she imagined he had grown when he turned into this mad murdering thing that stalked her. She screamed again and bolted through a hole in the wall to her right, heedless of where she was going. Dodging here and there, she burst out of the tight passage into the large stone chamber and fell to her knees.

Alia looked around frantically, but all the offshoots were closed off except for the one she just came through. The one where she could hear the Charlie thing growling and getting closer. This was it, she had no choice but to stand her ground. Placing her back as flat against the cave wall as she could, Alia waited at the passage entrance for him to run in past her.

Somewhere a part of her mind screamed and begged her not to. It tried to tell her that this thing, or not, this was Charlie...her Charlie. Then images of the bodies she had stumbled upon flashed through her mind. Their horribly mutilated corpses, he had done that. She watched as he snapped the neck of his own father. And he hunted her, playing with her, toying with her out of the sheer pleasure of her terror. Trish had been right. Her mother had been right from the start. Charlie was a monster, and she was the only one left. She had to kill him, or he would kill her too. With her back against the wall, Alia was terrified and shaking, but mostly she was angry. Angry at him for what he did, angry at him for making her do this. So much blind and red hot rage.

Charlie almost fell coming out of the passage so fast, finding himself to his surprise back in the large central chamber. Alia was nowhere to be seen. Then out of the corner of his eye, he saw movement and turned to see her just as she plunged the knife into him. With a painful gasp, Charlie grabbed her hand, holding it tight, to keep her from pulling out the knife to stab him again. The pain was white-hot and searing, blood already running down his shirt and soaking into his pants. Still, he kept a grip on her wrist and looked into her terrified eyes.

She's not seeing me. He thought...she sees something, but it's not me.

With his other hand shaking, Charlie cupped the side of her face. She flinched at his touch and let out a small screech.

"Alia...sweet girl...my sweet girl please...look at me...look at me, see me, Alia. It's Charlie...Alia...it's your Charlie. You have to stop Alia, please."

He saw her head give a little shake..her eyes seemed to clear, then go muddy, then clear again.

"Alia come on...see me...see me, Alia...feel me." Charlie kissed her forehead, then put his on hers and left it there for the briefest of seconds.

Alia flinched back and looked into the eyes in front of her. The striking green eyes and her memory of those eyes flashed in her mind, a million images a second, always those same green eyes.

Little Charlie in a blue romper, her hand in his, smiling. "That's it, take a step...like me...do it like this, Alia." And a step she did take and another toward the boy with the smiling green eyes.

Little Charlie again, fishing pole in hand, laughing as she pulled in with all her might a little fish on her own pole. "Look, Alia, your first fishy...Mommy, Daddy, she did it. Alia caught a fishy." Such sweet laughter from the boy.

Charlie, a little older, blowing on her knee she had scrapped, falling off her first two-wheeler. "It's okay, Alia. It'll only hurt for a little while." She could feel his tender touch.

Charlie, with a small group of other kids watching with sadness and tears in his eyes as Trish screamed profanities at the poor girl and dragged her away by her arm. A look back rewarded her with a wave from the green-eyed boy.

Charlie older still, calming and reassuring her as he pulled a large piece of glass out of her foot as gently as he could, then taking off his shirt to wrap her bleeding foot in it. Her boy, so gentle, so brave.

Charlie holding her hand, cradling her as pain tore through her stomach, his tears falling as they took her away from him.

Charlie wiping mud off her neck as she laughed, asking if she was okay.

Charlie, his hand reaching out for her's, much older now, a smile on his face as he led her out of the copse of trees she had been hiding in.

Charlie reaching down to kiss her for the first time as they stood at the back of an old Buick.

Charlie dancing with her at the prom as he sang to her, with so much love in his beautiful green eyes.

Charlie, down on one knee, looking up at her and begging her with all his heart.

A smile here, a laugh there, sadness, grief, pain,...love. Love... so much love. The eyes that looked at her with such love that she could never doubt it, not even now.

"Charlie?"

He saw the look of clarity in her eyes. "Yes, sweet girl, it's your Charlie. I'm here. I finally found you."

"My sweet boy," she said, barely a whisper. At that moment, Alia realized that it was his love for her that had kept her from falling off the deep end all this time. And it was that love that was shattering whatever hold Jacob had put on her. Alia looked down and saw her hand holding the knife that went into his flesh and bled. "No...no no-no-no. What have I done?" she screamed, letting go of the blade and backing off in horror. "No Charlie...please no... I'm so sorry, I'm so sorry."

With a pained grimace, Charlie pulled the knife from his side and dropped it to the ground. It hurt like hell, but he could tell that it had barely gone very deep into his side, and despite the flood of blood, it wasn't as bad as it looked. "It's okay...Alia, it's going to be okay" he went to her only to lose his footing, all the running, lack of food, and rest making his legs feel weak and rubbery.

Alia went to him using what little strength she had left herself to try and prop him up.

Still, Charlie went down to his knees, grasping at her for support.

"Charlie...no-no, my poor Charlie, what have I done."

Pulling her down to him, Charlie put an arm around her while holding his side with the other.

"It's okay," he insisted. "Calm down, Alia...I'm going to be fine...just a little tired is all. Just need a few minutes to catch my breath." Charlie pulled her into him holding her tight.

"Oh, for God's sake must I do everything myself." boomed Jacob from inside the chamber.

They looked up to see Jacob, Trish behind him, pointing a gun at them.

"You know you two make me sick. I am so over the two of you at this point. You and your connection and love. I spent two days, two days planting the perfect scenario in her head, and it was working. Then you just waltz in here, kiss her on the forehead and ruin it. You know what, fuck you both." Jacob aimed the gun at them, but before he could pull the trigger, Trish knocked it out of his hand.

"No..no, no, we are not doing it this way...she has to kill him. She has to be the one to do it. I have to break her. Break her and those sons of bitches that stole her from me. Now fix this, Jacob."

"This is beyond fixing, you dumb bitch. The boy is mine now. I'm going to take great satisfaction in ripping him to shreds with my bare hands." Too fast for Charlie or Alia to react, Jacob advanced on them, grabbed Charlie by his belt, tossed him across the ground, and kicked him repeatedly in the stomach.

Alia grabbed Jacob's leg, but she didn't have much strength left in her after the terrifying run through the caves. She instead only managed to cover Charlie and spare him Jacob's foot while he turned his attention to her kicking her in the stomach then in the head, leaving her crawling on the sandy ground of the cave.

Charlie, his rage at an all-time high, used that to give him strength. He then charged the man knocking Jacob off his feet but went down with him as he did.

Jacob was able to get the upper hand and jumped on Charlie's back, punching the boy in the back of the head repeatedly.

Screaming, Trish jumped on Jacob's back, hitting him upside the head with a flashlight. He brushed her off of him with a shake then turned to her. "I'm tired of your shit too. Good thing I came up with a little backup plan. The leaves don't fall in the springtime," he said with a laugh and a sneer. "Now go get your daughter, you bitch."
Jacob turned back to Charlie, picking him up to his feet. "Come on, boy, at least go out fighting, give me a little bit of fun on this shit night."

Charlie tried to fight back, but his swing went wild, and Jacob jabbed him twice fast, right where Alia stabbed him.

Preoccupied with Jacob, Charlie didn't notice the glassy-eyed look that came over Trish when Jacob spoke the trigger words to her.

She picked up the discarded knife with a snarl and hurled herself at Alia.

It was Alia's screams of pain and anguish that got his attention. Looking around for her, Charlie took a cheap shot to the jaw, spun, and landed on the cave floor. Where he lay, he had a direct view of Trish taking the knife and plunging it again and again into Alia's torso.

"NO!" Charlie screamed with a guttural growl and within him grew a strength built of a rage even he never thought he was capable of. When Jacob kicked at him, this time Charlie grabbed his foot, twisted it, breaking his ankle, and brought the man to the ground where he then drove his elbow into the man's leg, breaking it as well. Charlie then, without any hesitation, pulled his gun and shot the man twice in the head.

In the corner, Trish was stabbing away at Alia, who was splayed on the ground, blood pouring from her. Their eyes locked, and through the pain, she reached out for him.

"I love you, Charlie," Alia said in a spray of spit and blood.

" I love you more." Not taking his eyes off of hers, Charlie unloaded every round in his gun into Trish, finally doing what he had wanted to for years. Dropping the gun, Charlie ran to Alia and scooped her up in his arms. He rushed her over to the platform, ripping off his shirt, tossing aside his radio, breaking it, and pushing down on her wounds as hard as he dared. Looking around frantically, he saw the roll of duct tape discarded on the ground. He dared to leave her for only a moment to grab it. Doing the best he could, Charlie wrapped the tape around her over and over as she gasped in pain.

"Stay with me, Alia, stay…please don't leave me…don't close your eyes, stay here." he cried, he begged, but there was so much blood. Looking into her eyes, he could see her light growing dim.

"I'm so tired, Charlie…so tired." she choked, looking up at him. She looked into those amazing green eyes of his. They were the last things she wanted to see before fading away from this world.

"That's why I'm here. To carry you just like I promised. But you have to hold on for me, Alia. You have to fight just one more time, just a little longer." Charlie lifted her up off the stone and carried her out of the cave all the time, begging her not to leave him. When he got outside, he realized no one knew where they were, and it was all his fault. In his haste to give her aid, he broke his radio. They were out in the middle of nowhere, with no cell reception, they were alone, and she lay bleeding to death in his arms.

Her eyes were still open, but at this point, he wasn't sure if she was seeing him anymore. "Come on, Alia…stay with me…don't leave me…please don't leave me." Alia looked up at him, her eyes focusing just a little. She tried to speak, but he hushed her.

"Save your strength. I need you to hold on. Just keep holding on, sweet girl." He kissed her forehead, then, standing back up, headed down to the river with a last bit of hope that someone would be hiking or camping along its banks. As he walked, her blood dripped down his arms.

Charlie slipped and slid down the steep hill hoping he wouldn't trip and fall, knowing he wouldn't have the strength to get back up if he did. When he approached the river, Charlie thought in his grief and pain that the water sure sounded loud today. Like it had just rained, and the water gushed over the rocks. When a light hit him from above, he realized that a helicopter was hovering low in the sky.

Then suddenly, all around him, the forest seemed to come alive. Voices called out, shouting his and Alia's names. Branches snapped, leaves crunched as hundreds of pairs of feet walked through the woods, calling out for him and Alia.

Charlie stopped and turned, then fell to his knees as before him dozens upon dozens of people emerged from the woods. There was Harvey from the gun shop, Eddie the cabin owner, Pat the bartender, Crystal, George, kids from school, people from town, deputies, firemen, scores, and scores of familiar faces. Charlie thought for sure this was a dream. That they both must be lying on the floor of the cave dying.

"We got them." someone shouted. And now, the sound of running footsteps was like thunder.

Someone tried taking Alia from his arms, but Charlie fought them, holding her tighter to him.

"Let her go, son...let her go. We've got her now." Charlie looked up into the eyes of his father.

"Don't let her die," Charlie said, sobbing.

"Don't plan on it. Let us have her, Charlie. The helicopter is landing. We need to get her there."

Charlie relented, letting her go into the arms of another officer while two people picked him up off the ground as well. Across the river was a field just big enough to put the chopper down. Running across the river, up the embankment, and out to the field, they got Charlie and Alia inside. Harper jumped in with them, and up and away, they flew. Alia was placed on a stretcher, and two paramedics frantically worked on her, getting IVs for blood, shots for pain, and staunching the flow of blood.

Harper tended to his son's stab wound as Charlie looked and saw the woods alight with what looked like hundreds of lights, all flashlights twinkling amongst the trees.

"Eddie told us you went to the cabin. He said there was something about you that was off that he didn't care for. So instead of doing what you said, he called me. When word got around you and Alia may be in danger, hundreds of volunteers from town showed up to help search. We couldn't have kept them away if we tried." his father yelled over the roar of the chopper.

Charlie looked down at Alia. She had an oxygen mask on, and they were pumping blood into her as fast as they could squeeze it. "Did you hear that, my sweet girl? Practically the whole town came out here looking for you. I told you, you'd be surprised how they really felt about you." Charlie kissed her on her bloody forehead, tears falling as she looked up at him and smiled.

Chapter 40
Charlie

Alia slowly opened her eyes, blinked several times to focus, and looked into the green eyes and smiling face of the most wonderful man in the world, her Charlie. He had found her just like he always promised he would. She could feel his hand in hers, gave it a little squeeze, and he gave hers one back.

"You're going to be okay now, Alia. I'm right here with you and always will be." he smiled at her, lighting up her heart.

Alia felt a large hand on her other arm and looked over to see Harper on the other side with Ellen standing behind him. There were more people, one a nurse, but the others were in the dark shadows of the room, only lit by one light over the hospital bed.

"Alia...honey do you see Charlie?" asked Harper.

"I sure do. He found me again just like I knew he would. Isn't that right, Charlie?" she asked, looking back at her sweet boy.

"That's right, my sweet girl."

Harper looked over at Ellen, and so did Alia.

The woman put her hand over her mouth, looking visibly upset. "Oh, Harper, you have to tell her." she cried.

"Tell me what?" Alia asked. "Am I hurt really bad? I don't feel like I'm in much pain. It must not have been as bad as I thought.

Harper sat gently on the edge of her hospital bed and took her small hand in his large meaty one. "No, Alia, your not hurt. We found you in a cave, the same..." Harper took a deep breath working up his courage. "The same cave we found Charlie's body in years ago."

Alia looked up at Harper feeling confused. "What body...what are you talking about?" she squeezed Charlie's hand harder. "Charlie, what is he talking about, what body?"

"I'm right here. I'll never let you go," said Charlie.

Pulling her attention back to him, Harper continued, "You have to remember Alia. We told you all about him. We told you all about our boy Charlie."

Alia's head felt fuzzy, the words Harper was saying not making any sense.

It must be the drug. I'm not understanding him right because of the drugs Jacob forced me to drink.

"I know all about Charlie." she agreed with a smile.

"Yes, you really do. Ellen and I told you all about him...."

"My sweet boy, my sweet man." Alia interrupted. "He loves me like no one else ever has. Isn't that right, Charlie?" she asked, turning back to his smiling face once more.

Charlie will understand. He will work this all out.

"I love you more." Charlie grinned at her.

"More and more every day," she said back, glad her brain wasn't so foggy that she didn't remember their familiar game.

I'll be fine, once the drugs wear off, I'll be just fine, Charlie and I both.

Harper reached over and turned Allia's face back to him gently. "Yes, sweetheart, he did. He loved you from the moment we brought you home. You were his little angel. He loved you so much that when we gave you back to your mother, well, he was never the same again after that. Remember Alia, remember we told you just last month, at dinner, all about Charlie. It was right after you took your SATs in Alexandria. Please try to remember."

"I remember," she said. "We were all together, like a family. You, me, Mom, and Charlie. It was wonderful."

"No, Honey, that's a lie. One you have been telling yourself for a while now. We told you the truth. We told you what happened. We took him out to our cabin in the woods because the two of you loved playing there so much. We thought it would make him feel better. He was just so sad, so heartbroken. But he wandered off. We think he went looking for you. He got lost and fell down a long shaft into a cave. We found his body..we found him a week later." Harper said through tears. "Alia Charlie's gone…he's gone baby, he's been gone for a very long time."

Alia suddenly felt alarmed.

Why, why is he telling me this. Why is Harper telling me this awful lie?

"No, Charlie's not gone, Harper, he's right here. He's right here, and he swore he'd never leave me." she gripped Charlie's hand tighter, but his grip back seemed less and less. "Tell them, Charlie," she begged. "Make them stop. This isn't funny."

Charlie just looked at her with those sad, soulful green eyes of his and smiled.

"No, Alia, he's gone," Harper said, getting firmer with her. "You've had some kind of mental break, but we can help you. You've just got to let us help you."

"No…no." she cried. "You're wrong. You're lying. Charlie took me to Alexandria for my SATs, he drove all night, so I wouldn't be late."

"No, Alia, I drove you there. You were so worried about doing bad and disappointing all of us that you had spent days studying, barely eating or sleeping. There was no way we were going to let you drive all the way up there like that. Your mother had to work, so I took you."

"You're lying. Charlie took me there. We had to stay in a motel because of the storms. We talked all night, and then he held me in bed all night when I had a nightmare."

"The only storms are the ones going on inside you, Alia. That's our fault. We should have seen you were hurting after we told you about him. You always said you felt like a piece of you was missing. That no matter how happy you were, there was always something not right. We had hoped telling you about Charlie, about how much our boy loved you, it would fill in that hole in her heart. But it just made things worse for you."

"You're wrong…Charlie told me he loved me…he took me to the prom…we made love that night for the first time…at the cabin…the one in the mountains we used to go to," Alia sobbed close to hysterics.

Harper looked over at Ellen, tears rolling down her face. "Alia honey, that cabin of ours…the one by the river, it's barely even standing anymore. After what happened to Charlie, we couldn't bear to go back out there anymore…it's in ruins."

"No, I was there. I was there with Charlie. It was beautiful." she turned back to Charlie. "Charlie, tell them, please Charlie, tell them to stop. I'm sorry for what I did. I'm sorry I hurt you, but you have to make them stop. This isn't funny, Charlie, please."

Charlie only looked at her and held her hand loosely. Before her, he seemed to shimmer and fade.

"No, Charlie, please…" she begged and turned back to them. "Charlie loves me. He's been there for me for years. He's always been around. He's always been there for me when I needed him. We're connected…." Only to her growing alarm Alia realized that she couldn't feel him despite Charlie being right there. "He introduced me to Crystal...my best friend Crystal, she'll tell you." she sobbed.

"Crystal...who's Crystal?" Harper asked, looking off into the shadows of the room.

"That was her imaginary friend." said a familiar voice that sounded oddly soft. "Not long after we lost her father, she started talking about Crystal and her brother George. Eventually, I realized they were not real." Out of the shadows stepped a woman that reassembled Trish. Only she was kinder looking, less old, and haggard. Almost how Alia often imagined her mother could have been had it not been for all the drugs and drinking. "It got so bad that I had to sort of banish her from the house. I thought she would get over it once she worked through the grief."

Cold fear washed over Alia as she stared at Trish. Images of the woman in a cave stabbing her over and over flashed through her mind. Flashes of Charlie yelling but on the ground bleeding. "What the hell is she doing here? Get her, Harper ... .arrest her...she took me...she's the one that took me, Harper...Harper, keep her away from me...Charlie help me. She stabbed me. Trish tried to kill me."

Alia watched as the thing posing as her mother started to cry then ran into Ellen's open arms, where they both sobbed. Horror struck, and in fear for Ellen, Alia began to scream.

"No, Harper, stop this, get that bitch away from my mother. Trish tried to kill me, Harper. She tried to kill me in the cave."

"Okay, that's it, Alia...that's it now...I know you're in pain. I know how hard this must be for you, but what you're doing to your mother, the things you are saying, it's just not right. Your mother would never try to hurt you, and you know it. You have to stop this, damn it. You have to stop living in this delusion."

"What I'm doing to her? Harper, you know, you know what she's done to me. The years of abuse, all the time making me feel ugly and stupid. She, she pretended to be Charlie...she lured me to her to kill me because she was jealous that Charlie loved me. She tried killing me, Harper, I'm telling you she did, her and Jacob both."

"I was wondering when I was going to be included in on her tirade this time." said another eerily familiar voice from the darkness of the room. As he stepped into the light, Jacob crossed his arms over his chest, looking at them all. "I do always seem to be her favorite punching bag."

Alia felt as though the bed under her was gone, and her body hurled into a dark abyss. "No…No, get him away from me…Charlie kill him…kill him, Charlie. Harper, please, you have got to believe me. They tried to kill us, the both of them tried to kill Charlie and me."

"Oh, and now I'm a murderer. Young lady, I know the two of us haven't gotten along very well, but I don't think I'm the only one that feels you are taking all this a bit far. I've told you I'm not here to replace your father. Sheriff, really, she listens to you talk some sense into her. Because I'm not going away, Alia, no matter what you try to do, you're not breaking your mother and me up."

"Give it a rest Jacob. There's more to all of this than just you dating her mother."

"Is there sheriff, is there really? Her insane delusions only got really bad after I proposed to Trish."

"Damit Jacob, I told you to let me deal with this. You're only making matters worse."

Alia lay there listening to all of this with growing horror.

This can't be real. This can't be. Something is wrong, I'm still in the caves…or I'm dying or…or…I don't know, but this can't be real.

"He has a point, Harper," said Trish trying to contain herself. "This all started with Charlie, but Jacob is part of it too. Alia, honey, please listen to Harper. He's only trying to help you. We all are. I know I have been busy spending time with Jacob and didn't realize how much the story about Charlie was hurting you, but I never thought you would run off as you did. I know how painful it must be, Alia, but you have to remember, you have to believe Charlie is gone. If you don't, they're going to take you away from us, from all of us."

"But Charlie...he's right here." She raised her hand a little, but it was empty. Looking around frantically, she saw that Charlie was gone. "No...No...you bitch...what did you do...what did you do to my Charlie?" Alia tried to get up but realized for the first time that she couldn't. Her wrist of the hand Charlie had been holding was handcuffed to the bed rail. Her legs and feet were strapped down tight to the gurney as well as her waist. There was no pain, no stab wounds, nothing from her time in the cave. She struggled against the restraints, but it was no use.

"Harper, I'm so sorry to put you two through this. I swear I never thought it would get this far. I would have gotten her the care she needed a long time ago if I had known. Help her, Harper, please...help my little girl." Cried Trish, still in Ellen's arms.

"Alia, look at me, stop struggling, look at me, and really listen. You know I would never lie to you. Your father was like a brother to me, and I swore to him when he died I would take care of you like you were my own. I'm sorry, baby girl, I know you're in pain right now. I know you're confused but sweetheart....Charlie is gone...he's dead. He died when he was six years old at the bottom of a cave shaft."

"No...No..he's...he's not dead, he can't be dead please stop." Alia looked at Harper with tears in her eyes, begging him to stop. She continued to fight the restraints but got nowhere.

"No, I won't stop, Alia. You have to remember the truth. You have to accept it no matter how hard it is and how much it hurts. Charlie is gone. You have to let him go for the sake of your own sanity, if nothing else. You have to stop pretending like Charlie is still here. You have to stop talking to him, or they will take you away. Please don't make them do that to us. We have already lost our son. We don't want to lose you too. He's gone, baby girl...you have to accept that, he's gone, and he's never coming back."

"No…no …no…," she cried, "My Charlie…I need my Charlie…my heart..no." she sobbed. "Charlie, no, don't leave me..please you promised…please Charlie!!!!"

"Come back to us, Alia, please, we all love you, we all need you," begged Harper, tears rolling down his face.

The women cried in each other's arms. At the foot of her bed, Jacob looked concerned and shook his head. The nurse ran to get help, and Harper tried calming her down. Still, she fought the restraints reaching out her hand and screaming for the lost boy dead for so many years.

Alia's heart couldn't take it. She didn't want to live in a world without Charlie. She didn't want to live in a world that didn't know his smile, his beautiful green eyes, his humor, and his love. If this was what it was like to be alive, to be in constant pain, to feel such unbearable loss, then she would just rather not. She couldn't live in a world where the man she loved, that was so loved by his parents, perished at such a young age. So she fought, and she reached out both body and mind to once again find that which connected them.

"No…No, let me go…I want to be with him…I want to be with Charlie…Charlie, please come back. You promised Charlie you promised you would never let go of me." fighting the cuffs, Alia reached out her hand. "Save me, Charlie, save me one last time…Charlie!!"

Chapter 41
Alia

On the hospital's surgical floor in the family waiting room sat the family. Ellen sniffed into her tissues. Harper had his arm around his wife, trying to calm her fears. Crystal with her charms in her hands. Several officers from the sheriff's department were drinking coffee. In a wheelchair, his stab wound stitched and bandaged, was Charlie. They had wanted him to stay downstairs in his own room to rest, but he refused, even tried to walk out and fight them. So they put him in the wheelchair and brought him up to be closer to her.

Charlie was sitting there, still trembling from the events in the cave. Seeing over and over Alia being stabbed by Trish…him shooting and killing her. The killing brought him none of the pleasure he thought it would. It just made him sick, and he supposed that was for the better. After all, they had gone through, the last thing he wanted was to turn into something cold and hard. Someone Alia would have a hard time loving. That is if she made it through all of this.

No one in the waiting room talked. Some prayed silently. Others shuffled in and out, getting more and more cups of coffee. All of the officers, including the several more waiting in another room downstairs, had bandages on their arms from donating blood. Even those that were not Alia's blood type. Scores of people from town having returned from the search party also donated. Many of them were outside the hospital, still holding a vigil of sorts, waiting to hear news. Some left, going home to hug their family members a little closer. All, even those that went home, waited anxiously for word about their girl.

Charlie felt himself dozing in the wheelchair when suddenly he heard something. Despite the pain it gave him, he stood bolt upright out of the chair. Many of the others in the room were startled, but Charlie didn't notice.

"Did anyone hear that?" he asked them all while straining to hear what he thought he heard again.

Harper got up and went to Charlie. "Hear what, son?"

"It's her," he said, still hearing the echo of his name in his head. "She's calling for me."

"That's not possible, son; she's in surgery. Even if she was awake, you wouldn't hear her all the way out here."

"But I can. And she is in trouble."

"Come on, son, you're looking pale. You need to rest. You shouldn't be standing up right now."

Looking at him, others in the room nodded in agreement, including his mother.

"No...I heard her...I still hear her." Looking at his father, Charlie's eyes grew wide with fear. "She needs me."

And before Harper could react, the boy had slipped his hand and ran out the door. Behind him, people shouted, pleading for him to come back. His mother cried, but he kept going right through the double doors of the surgery department. Nurses shouted for him to stop as well as security, but it all fell on deaf ears. There was only one voice Charlie could hear, and that was hers, and it was getting fainter and fainter. Charlie knew...he knew in his heart he was losing her. His sweet girl was slipping away.

Frantic, Charlie burst into the surgery room, looking like a madman. The scene he came into was of chaos. Doctors and nurses surrounded Alia's lifeless-looking body while others were attending to machines that were hooked up to her. Alia's naked and splayed body was covered in blood, as was the operating table and the floor. A nurse with a blood bag in his hand squeezed it as hard as he could, yet still, it dripped out of her. Most of the stab wounds had been sewn, but one was wide open and had the surgeon's hands deep within it.

Machines beeped, oxygen forced its way into her lungs, while a nurse shouted her pressure was dropping, yet another one shouted for more blood. The surgeon seeing Charlie shouted as well.

"Get that man out of here!"

Charlie stood there horrified at what he was seeing...the blood, so much of it.

She's so small, yet there's so much blood.

A nurse came up to him, trying to push Charlie out the door.

"I'm sorry, Sergeant, but you'll have to leave. You can't be in here."

"You don't understand she needs me...she called for me.." he said, not able to take his eyes off of her.

"Where the hell is security...get that man out of here before we lose her," the surgeon shouted again.

"She needs me." he insisted. Breaking the hold, the sight before him had he reached out for her hand tied to a board stretched out from her body.

Just as he did, security came in, grabbing Charlie by his arms and shoulders and pulling him back. "Sorry, Sergeant, you can't be in here. Let's go back to the waiting room. Let them do their job."

Still hearing her call for him but just barely, Charlie fought them. He pushed the one guard off into the arms of his father, that had followed them through the door, and the other he punched in the jaw. He didn't even notice when a few of his stitches popped, dripping his own blood on the ground. When he was treated, they had taken Charlie's utility belt off, but no one thought to frisk him, nor had reason to. He pulled out his spare revolver from the ankle holster that he put on before searching for Alia at the caves. He had come armed, planning on ending the lives of Trish and Jacob no matter what. Now they were gone, but he still had to fight for her, and he knew he would take on anyone to do so.

"Stop...just Stop...I don't want to hurt anyone, but she needs me...she needs me, and I promised. I won't let her die alone...just back the fuck off."

Harper stood in front of the guards and nurses at the door so that now the only one Charlie had a gun on was him. In his current state, he couldn't be sure, but he hoped Charlie wouldn't shoot him.

"It's OK, Charlie..no one is going to stop you...but put the gun down, son, just put the gun down for us."

Behind him, the doctors and nurses were still frantically trying to save Alia's life.

"Pressures still dropping, doctor...we're losing her."

"I know, damn it. I'm literally holding her together with my hands."

All of this was but a whisper to Charlie. For a moment, he was back in the motel, back in the tub, his arms around Alia while above them the storm raged, threatening to take the roof off and them with it. He was holding on to her and promising to never let her go.

"I made a promise," he said to his father. With one hand, he reached behind him and grabbed hers. Then daring to turn his back to them, he bent his tall frame despite the pain so that his mouth was right at her ear. "I'm here, my sweet girl...I'm here, and I'm never letting go. Don't leave me...please stay...just stay with me."

"Whatever you're doing, doctor, keep it up. Her pressure is coming up...vitals are starting to stabilize."

At the door, Harper pushed back the guards, trying to get in at Charlie again. "Just let him be for a minute," he growled at them.

"I'm here,...sitting right next to you on an old mossy log. The sun is sparkling through the trees. The birds are singing. The air smells clean and fresh, and I am there with you. Sitting next to you, holding your hand. Stay here, Alia...stay with me. Please don't go. I would die without you." In his hand, Charlie felt hers squeeze. He looked up, and to his amazement, her eyes were open, sparkling like ocean waters in the sun. Even with the bagger still working, pumping oxygen into her, Charlie could see a slight smile.

"Vitals are stable, heart and BP back to normal, she's awake, she shouldn't be, but she is...you did it, Doctor, you got her back you did it."

No, thought Alia, despite her brain still feeling foggy, *Charlie did...Charlie brought me back to him, back to where I belong, back to my family.*

Around them, the doctors and nurses worked to get her last wound sewn up. The bagger stopped and removed the mask. Charlie put the gun on the ground, where Harper was quick to retrieve it and put his hand on her forehead.

"There you are, Charlie." she barely whispered. "There's my sweet boy."

"Of course, my sweet girl," he said, shedding tears. "I told you I'd never let go."

Chapter 42

Only time will tell

It hadn't been easy, but Charlie watched as the women he loved worked hard to get stronger again day after day. Not only did she have the surgery to recover from but the drugs in her system as well. Jacob wasn't joking when he said his new formula was more potent. Alia spent weeks in and out of vague moments and suffering from hallucinations. Most of which involved Charlie having died at a devastatingly young age. Trish and Jacob materialized out of the very walls to attack her in others. Often those staying with her through the night were awoken to her screaming. Charlie suffered with her through the bad days and laughed with her through the good ones. Before long, she was out running him, out gunning him again and making love to him like every time was their last.

Part of that healing included more sessions with Lawson once again. First, he came to her in the hospital during the weeks she was there recovering. Then it was the Harper's home where Ellen had insisted she stay till Alia was up on her feet better. Some of the sessions were just the two of them, but many of them involved not only her and Charlie but Harper and Ellen as well. They healed as a family the same way they did everything…together.

Several sessions Lawson and Alia focused on what happened to her when she was being operated on. Alia's biggest complaint was how the event felt so real to her. After talking about it several times, the consensus between them was that it was a leftover product of the drugging and hypnosis done by Jacob. Lawson hypothesized that the suggestion of such an event might have been planted to leave Alia in a state of constant confusion if their initial plan did not work. Or even just to break her into giving up entirely. Despite the weeks and months of therapy sessions and constant reassurance of those around her, it took Alia a very long time to get over the feeling that the nightmare scenario was real. She was afraid that she was locked in a padded room somewhere lost in the happier delusion everyone insisted was real life.

The FBI investigation into Jacob Fuller revealed him for the monster he truly was. For years, he experimented with a mind-controlling drug, taking the used and desperate people of the streets as his lab rats. Using the drug alongside hypnosis, Jacob would get them cleaned off of any substances they were using (as they tended to interfere with the drug's full potential). He then put them to work in various ways to help with his work. One of those ways was having several of his people go to Union county to protest Alia going back to work and keep an eye on her and the family.

And Charlie had been right. There were others like Alia. Lost children Jacob had taken into his fold to use and manipulate. Many of them came from broken homes but most had at least one loved one looking for them. Jacob may have gotten away with it for many more years had he not gotten too cocky and chosen a lab rat he underestimated. Several journals had been found laying out the story Trish had told him how she was the perfect subject to test the next level of his "drug therapy," as he called it. What he hadn't counted on was Trish's ability to embellish details. Essential details that made Alia out to be a better test subject than she was. He certainly never counted on the connection between Alia and Charlie to be real, let alone so strong.

The body of Billy Wise, Trish's ex-boyfriend, was recovered after an exhaustive search of the caves. Evidence left on the body in the cave proved he had been killed by Trish, having been struck in the head repeatedly by a hammer she had left with the corpse. Meridith Wise was devastated by the news, having hoped her son would return one day. She went to the hospital several times to visit Alia. Still, a few weeks after burying her only son, she passed away in her sleep.

Alia's best, however a bit belated, birthday gift that next year in February came in the form of her badge and service revolver back. She was stuck on desk duty and reduced hours for some time, but she didn't mind at all. She was just happy to have that part of her life back. Charlie was delighted to have her closer to him again during the day, but more so that she would be safe at the office. When Harper gave them back to her, She went to him, giving him the biggest hug she could manage, and they both cried.

"Welcome back, Deputy Miller."

Only she didn't Stay Deputy Miller for long. Giving up on the idea of a long engagement, She and Charlie instead married on their anniversary that year. An event they had planned years earlier to be a small family affair was very large because half the town wanted to show up for it. Alia's old study partner and roommate from her academy days was a maid of honor right along with Crystal. Even after all the well wishes, cards, gifts, visitors, and countless outpourings of love while she had been in the hospital, Alia had no idea the number of people in the county whose lives the two of them had touched. As large as the Harper's backyard was, it was still crammed shoulder to shoulder with people the day of the wedding.

When Alia walked down the aisle to Charlie, who awaited her, the sun setting on the lake behind him, there was not a dry eye to be found. No one had any doubts that the two kids were madly in love.

Charlie thought his heart would burst when he first saw her, the white of the dress making her honey tanned skin gleam. Tears streamed from his eyes, but he didn't care.

When Alia saw Charlie in his tux waiting for her with George at his side, she did the same, and Harper had to practically hold her back from running to him. As a wedding gift to Charlie, Alia got his name tattooed on the inside of her wrist just like he had hers. When he took her hands at the altar, he saw it for the first time, still wrapped in plastic. He kissed it gingerly and whispered to her that she would never have to worry about exing it out. They both shook so much, saying their vowels they had written, they barely got through them. Charlie got lost in Alia's eyes halfway through his until George whispered in his ear.

"Dude, you got this."

He and Alia both laughed and Charlie finished not taking his eyes off of hers. When they kissed, it was like the first time. Her lips tasted of strawberry. He kissed them softly at first, then more passionately.

Their honeymoon was at the family cabin in the mountains because no other place, no matter how amazing and exotic, could make them happier than they were there. It was a wonderful week all to their own where they made love under the stars at night and stayed in each other's arms all day.

That next year they got a new year's present in the form of twins. One boy, and one girl, two weeks into January. The boy had green eyes like his father and the girl blue eyes like his mother. Any worries Alia had about being a good mother vanished the moment the two of them were put into her arms.

"You two are going to be loved so much." she cried as she and Charlie both looked down on their tiny faces.

And time moved on. Life was good when it was good. And because of their bond, not so hard when it was hard. There was plenty of love and laughter throughout the days. The girl who grew up feeling unloved and unwanted never again doubted just how much she was cared for. She had her little family; she had the love of her friends, fellow officers, and a community that refused to give up on her and let her go when she became lost. Because as you can see, this is indeed a love story…it's just not that kind of love story.

THE END?

Made in the USA
Columbia, SC
09 April 2022